BONDS OF TRUTHS

BONDS OF
TRUTHS

Davis Ashura

Printed in the United States of America

Trade Paperback ISBN: 978-1-960031-00-6

Hardcover ISBN: 978-1-960031-01-3

First Printing: 2023

DuSum Publishing, LLC

Books by Davis Ashura

The Castes and the OutCastes:

A Warrior's Path

A Warrior's Knowledge

A Warrior's Penance

Omnibus Edition (only available on Kindle)

Stories for Arisa (short-story collection)

The Chronicles of William Wilde:

William Wilde and the Necrosed

William Wilde and the Stolen Life

William Wilde and the Unusual Suspects

William Wilde and the Sons of Deceit

William Wilde and the Lord of Mourning

Instrument of Omens

A Testament of Steel

Memories of Prophecies

A Necessary Heresy

Bonds of Truths

The Eternal Ephemera

Blood of a Novice

To Jim and Karol. The best in-laws a son-in-law could have.

Contents

Acknowledgements

To the usual suspects, such as my wonderful alpha and beta readers. They know who they are, but I'll mention them again: James Clausi, Bruce Ewing, Jay Jenkins, and Stephen Kutz; all of whom helped me keep the story straight. And also to my editors Christopher Xander and Anthony Holabird. I really don't mean to write so many typos.

And I can't forget Tom Burkhalter and the rest of the crew at CVAKWG.

I truly owe a debt of gratitude to all y'all.

Author's Note

The best thing I did in writing *Bonds of Truths* was not writing it straight after finishing *A Necessary Heresy*. Instead, I wrote *Blood of a Novice*, book one of a new series, *The Eternal Ephemera*. Writing that novel was just flat-out fun. Yes, yes. I know. The characters in *Blood of a Novice* carry psychological wounds, they struggle with their dumb decisions, and Rukh and Jessira don't play a big role. But still, I love those characters. I love their story, and I can't wait to get back to seeing what they're doing.

But just as importantly for this book—to *Bonds of Truths*—writing *Blood of a Novice* gave me the distance and clarity I needed after the trials and challenges of *A Necessary Heresy*. I was able to approach *Bonds of Truths* rejuvenated and with a fresh frame of mind; ready to rumble and excited to the point that I even wrote during DragonCon. Gasp! I know. Writing on vacation? What was I thinking?

I was thinking I had a story that I was absolutely enthusiastic to tell. And the final result? Well, that's easy. I love this book! I love how it turned out. I love everything about it, especially how Cinder and Anya figure out their…

Whoops! Don't want to spoil what happens before y'all even start the book.

Anyway, that's all I have for this author's note except to thank everyone who has taken this journey with me so far. It means everything. There really is no other way to describe it.

And with that: drumroll please…

Happy reading!

Davis Ashura

Calendar

1. Jevasth
2. Arasth
3. Indrunasth
4. Kev
5. Vahasth
6. Devasth
7. Agniasth
8. Brulasth
9. Karnasth
10. Winasth

*OF NOTE: there are ten days in a week

The Trials So Far

Cinder Shade, a young man from the remote village of Swallow, survives an attack by Brilliance, a deadly snowtiger, but in the process, he loses all knowledge of himself and his family. An orphan, he is sent to the city of Swift Sword where he befriends the siblings, Riner and Coral Strain. He also comes to the attention of Lerid File, the martial master of *Steel-Graced Adepts*. Cinder quickly shows proficiency as a warrior, doing well enough to gain admittance into the Third Directorate, the prestigious military academy in the elven empire of Yaksha.

At his new school, Cinder makes enormous strides as a warrior, forms deep friendships with his fellow students, and bonds with Fastness, one of the fabled Yavana horses. However, it is his meeting with Anya Aruyen, princess of Yaksha Sithe, that catalyzes the greatest changes within him. The two form an unexpected friendship.

By the end of his first year at the Directorate, Cinder proves his worth, placing first amongst all the students in his class. However, the Unitary Trial, a challenging scouting mission within a deadly stretch of the Dagger Mountains, proves a disaster. A nest of spiderkin attack, and many of Cinder's brother Firsters are slaughtered and the rest barely survive.

Later, upon their return to the Third Directorate, Anya offers to sponsor Cinder for his Secondary Trial. Cinder accepts, but first, he has to master more than just his martial abilities. He learns more about the link between *lorethasra* and *Jivatma*—magic that humans were thought to have lost. He also forges better bonds with the elves in his class, including Riyne, his one-time nemesis at the Directorate.

His training continues, including the Autumn Trial: another scouting mission and another battle against the dreaded spiderkin. As before, the elven commanders are inept at simple tactics—possibly a racial flaw—and the unit takes heavy losses. However, thanks to Cinder's swift intervention, disaster is averted and they manage to defeat the spiderkin.

Months later, the dreams of a past life—which have haunted Cinder since his time in Swift Sword—persist, and he starts to believe they might indicate real memories. Anya has similar visions, and strangely, so does Fastness.

With those troubling thoughts, the three of them leave for the Secondary Trial, stopping first at Revelant, Yaksha's capital. There, Cinder and Anya discuss their dreams and come to believe they might be the reborn mythical heroes Shokan and Sira. They also meet Quelchon Ginala, the elderly and powerful imperial advisor, who relates a terrifying prophecy about Cinder.

Before more can be made of the matter, they leave Revelant and journey into the Dagger Mountains where they are set upon by wraiths. Surviving through the timely intervention of Sepia, a yakshin, as well as Brilliance, Cinder is grievously wounded, and the only place he can be healed is Shalla Valley, home of the yakshins.

Anya accompanies him, and after Cinder is healed, they meet Aranya—Mahamatha—the oldest of the sentient Ashoka trees. She tasks Cinder and Anya with journeying into the heart of the Dagger Mountains, and following that, to the ancient city of Mahadev.

They do so, and during the trek, Fastness changes. Rather than playful, he becomes hard-edged. Brilliance joins their small group, and together, they reach Mount Kirindor. There, they witness a dragon, a creature not seen in millennia; Serena, a woman Cinder and Anya both recognize despite having never met her; and Shet, the dark god, who is now reborn.

Cinder and Anya flee, intent on carrying word of their discoveries to the world. But at Fort Carnate, Cinder is arrested on orders of the empress. It is a short-lived imprisonment, and Cinder manages to escape, boarding a ship bound for Swift Sword with Anya and the dwarves: Sriovey, Derius, and Jozep. Cinder and Anya share their feelings for one another as well as their first kiss.

Upon reaching Swift Sword, they are beset by fresh challenges.

Cinder is attacked by *hashains*, legendary assassins sent by Genka Devesth, while Anya has to deal with warriors sent by her mother. Both are successful in defeating their foes, and the surviving *hashains* 'leash' themselves to Cinder, who they believe is the Grimyogi—their name for Shokan. The assassins are then tasked with finding a better way to live their lives.

Afterward, Cinder and Anya depart Swift Sword, traveling with Fastness and Jozep toward Mahadev. First, though, they reach Titan's Reach, a strange village whose inhabitants worship Shet, hate woven—such as dwarves and elves—and have the ability to conduct *Jivatma*.

Cinder has to fight his way free of Titan's Reach, and from there, he and the others eventually arrive at Mahadev where they encounter Rabisu, the Rakshasa of Dissolution, who immediately attacks and tries to kill them. Cinder, Anya, Jozep, and Fastness along with Salt Tangent, a woman of Titan's Reach, escape the demon by entering Ardevesh, the temple at the heart of the city.

Within its grounds, they meet Manifold Fulsom, a Mythaspuri, who has survived for three millennia. They also learn that Fastness is the reincarnation of Sapient Dormant, another ancient Mythaspuri.

Manifold informs them of a foe greater than Shet. It is Zahhack, the Son of Emptiness. He also tells them of Heremisth—a duchess from the Realms of the Rakshasas with whom he shares Ardevesh. The two of them exist in an uneasy truce, seeking safety from Rabisu. In addition, Heremisth is the one who maintains the anchor line connecting Seminal with Zahhack's forbidding home, and she is also sister to Sheoboth—the mother of the spiderkin—and Ginala.

By then, the remaining members of Cinder's class at the Third Directorate have returned to the academy. They, too, believe Cinder likely to be Shokan and that Anya might be Sira, a conviction shared by the *Lamarin Hosh*, a secret elven society devoted to the Blessed Ones.

Sriovey and Derius, meanwhile, return to their home of Surent Crèche and discover a dire situation. The Baptisers, a military force led by Stipe, Sriovey's father, have gained power over the wisdoms, the traditional leaders of their nation. The peaceful, matriarchal society of

Surent leans on the edge of collapse.

Worse, by then, Shet and his Titans are fully restored. They have gathered, rebuilt the god's ancient palace of Naraka, and are intent on conquest.

Zahhack hasn't been idle either. He sends a herd of wraiths, which nearly destroys Genka Devesth's empire of Shang Mendi. The wraiths are only defeated when one of them inexplicably attacks and kills the commander of the herd.

During these events, Cinder and Anya spend months within the Lucid Foe and learn that they are, indeed, Shokan and Sira, but that their true names are actually Rukh and Jessira Shektan. And they also learn that they must first gather the Orbs of Peace and see them destroyed.

However, Shet—who is the only one able to destroy the Orbs and thereafter close the anchor line leading to Zahhack—is also Rukh and Jessira's greatest enemy. He will kill them without hesitation, and the best solution would be for the so-called god to never recognize them. It will require Rabisu's help. He is to place a weave that won't allow Rukh and Jessira to know their full past but will also prevent both friend and foe from recognizing them.

This, Rabisu does in exchange for his freedom. But he betrays his promise, and in the ensuing battle, he appears to die while Rukh and Jessira once again believe themselves to be Cinder Shade and Anya Aruyen. Worse, they believe that their love was a lie.

They seem to dislike one another, but for the sake of the world, they set aside their grievances and continue their mission. They first journey to Naraka and seek Shet's aid, which he grants, essentially having Liline, one of his Titans, serve their needs.

Prior to all this, though, Jozep and Salt have left Cinder and Anya's side. They travel alone to Surent where Jozep seeks to restore his people to their original peaceful nature. Fastness has also departed, stating he has his own Trial to complete. He meets with Brilliance and Kela, an *aether*-cursed dog, and they trek to the far north where the three of them encounter a handful of wraiths who have survived the battle in

Shang Mendi. Fastness wants to help them.

Eventually, Cinder and Anya reach Surent Crèche themselves and steal the Orb of Eretria. And following the destruction of the Orb of Eretria, they then set out for Flatiron Death and obtain the Orb of Flames. They nearly die in the process, but the months of traveling together have calmed their anger. Their friendship is rekindled.

But the entire time, the weaves Rabisu placed on their memories continuously seek to strip away their affection.

The Wraith Lands

The Sunset Kingdoms

Shakaran Ocean

Toil

Fare

Crown

Hinane

Bolia

Flail

Shimala

Whip

Elasmara

Purge

Sun

Prune

1

Time is not the arbiter of what is, what was, and what will be. It is Memory. Without it, falsehoods are believed and truths are discarded. Or so it is thought…

Cinder grunted in aggravation as he worked on the confusion of kindling. All he wanted was to get a fire started, which should have been easy. Would have been in most circumstances, but currently wasn't since he was attempting to do so by sourcing *lorethasra* and forming a weave of Fire. Even then, given the memories, skills, and Talents granted to him by Shokan, this shouldn't have been such a problem.

But it was, and Cinder knew why.

It was the fragging blue-and-green lightning woven throughout his *lorethasra*. The pain from it was worse than usual, which wasn't a surprise since he had barely sourced his *lorethasra* or conducted *Jivatma* since escaping from Flatiron Death two weeks ago. Two weeks since he and Anya had nearly died. Two weeks of rest and recovery, one at an oasis south of that scorching desert and another in the mountainous wilds west of Naraka.

But he wasn't fully rested, and he wasn't fully recovered. Which was a large part of why lighting a simple fire was so hard.

Cinder sighed, rolling his shoulders. He'd been crouched over the kindling for a while, and he needed a break. A stretch of his neck, and he glanced about.

Snow-covered peaks soared all about the shallow ravine in which he and Anya were camped. While the western slopes blocked much of the gusting wind, Cinder could still hear it moaning. A small strand of evergreen trees leaned over a stream that was teeth-numbingly cold but free of ice since spring's thaw had finally arrived. The neighing of horses drew Cinder's attention to where Anya was caring for their mounts: Barton, Painter, Cigarello, and the pack mules.

"Still having trouble with the fire?" Anya asked, wandering over.

"It's the lightning," Cinder explained.

Anya nodded understanding, lips pursed in sympathy. "I don't have your limitations, but I know what you mean. Ever since Flatiron, I feel empty inside; weaker. All my skills and Talents are lessened."

"We almost died in there," Cinder replied, figuring that had to be part of the reason for both of their regressions.

"Maybe we have to train harder if we want to reclaim what we lost?"

"Accept the pain and embrace the grind." Cinder was familiar with the concept since most of his life, it seemed like that's all he had ever known—pain and the need to grow.

But Devesh, he was tired of it.

Anya squatted next to him and rested a hand on his shoulder, squeezing it gently. "We both have to work harder."

Cinder nodded, appreciating her support.

It was strange. Their time prior to Flatiron Death had too often been riddled with an eruption of irrational rage but now… Now it seemed like their anger toward each other had burned out during their trek through Flatiron's sweltering heat. If nothing else came from that excursion, Cinder would have counted his improved relationship with Anya as worth the hazards they'd endured.

But there was another issue raised at Flatiron as well, one they rarely spoke about: *what if our memories aren't trustworthy?*

The question had been asked in the oasis after surviving the burning desert, and once voiced, it had burrowed into Cinder's thinking like a mind-worm. He couldn't help but regularly ponder the possibility, especially since his recollection of the Third Directorate was vastly different from Anya's, and when deliberating over the matter in the clean light of rationality, it was obvious that her version made more sense.

"Let me start the fire?" Anya offered.

Cinder turned to her, unsurprised when their faces were inches apart and she failed to withdraw. She had always pressed into his personal space, from nearly the first time they'd met, and it hadn't bothered him then—would have bothered him a month ago—and no longer bothered him now. He smiled. "Like I said. At some point, I'm going to have to accept the pain."

"I'll leave you to it then," she said, rising to her feet.

"Where are you going?"

Anya grinned. "Off to scrounge some food. We've been camped here for most of the past week, and the stupider prey are all gone." She tapped the side of her head. "I'll have to be more cunning if we want to eat more than dried meat tonight."

Cinder grunted. "Better to go hungry here than have a full belly in Naraka."

"You won't get a disagreement from me."

As soon as Cinder and Anya had delivered the Orb of Flames to Shet, they had departed Naraka, not wanting to spend even a single night in that brutal black palace. Both had wanted to fully recover from Flatiron's challenges somewhere—anywhere, including this rugged, isolated place—rather than the home of their great enemy.

And it didn't matter that they were working with Shet; they had to—for comically complicated reasons—but that didn't mean they'd ever trust the so-called god or any of his Titans.

Anya peered off in the distance. "Maybe there are some rabbits or squirrels deeper in the ravine."

"I'm surprised the spiderkin or the zahhacks haven't hunted this place bare."

"Just be glad for the truce between them. If it weren't for that, we would have had to stay in Naraka."

She made to head off then, and Cinder could have left her to it. But something in him didn't want her to leave. "Wait. Let me get the fire started, and I'll go with you."

Anya tilted her head in silent scrutiny. She shrugged, but Cinder could see a pleased smile barely detected at the corner of her lips. "We shouldn't leave the fire unattended," she said. "And I'll be back soon enough." She walked to the copse of pine, easing gracefully through their reaching limbs and needles.

Cinder watched as she disappeared from sight, staring after her for a moment before his eyes went back to the kindling. *Time to light that fire.* He focused on *lorethasra*. The familiar blue-and-green lightning—thicker now—was wrapped within and throughout the silver stream, which he studied.

There was a time when he thought he was the only one who could see his *lorethasra*, but it had turned out to be his *Jivatma* that he was visualizing. And later on, he'd learned that while elves and other woven could also visualize the silver stream, they didn't consider it to be *lorethasra*.

"A stream has a source, and that source is lorethasra, *not the stream itself. The stream is simply* lorethasra's *immanence. Nothing more."* So had Master Molni once stated, although to Cinder, the explanation had sounded like sophistry.

"You're delaying," Anya chided.

Cinder started, doing a double take. He hadn't heard her return. And what was she doing back so soon anyway?

The answer came when she displayed a dead rabbit. "We got lucky. One of the traps snared us supper."

"Then I better get the fire started," Cinder replied. He reached again for *lorethasra*, prepared to accept the burning pain of a thousand fiery needles.

It was worse than ever, the lightning feeling like armor, as if Cinder needed to punch through chain mail. But he never backed away. *Embrace the grind.* He'd never had a problem doing so in the past, and he refused to have a problem now. That was the only way to grow and become who the world needed.

With a shudder that left him feeling like he was about to topple forward, Cinder finally managed to wrench his way through the lightning and source his *lorethasra*. With an exhalation of relief, he quickly cycled it through his body, and at the same time, he tried to open *Muladhara*, his root Chakra. More pain—and again it was worse than before—had him grinding his teeth, but he endured. Until finally, *Muladhara* blossomed, and into it, Cinder poured his *lorethasra*, watching it exit as golden *prana* before it suffused his *nadis*.

Power and abilities filled him, and a simple weave of Fire sparked to life. Cinder sent it into the kindling, and a slow burn built. The flames flickered, setting the smaller pieces of wood alight and licking at the larger logs until they, too, caught fire.

Finally.

Cinder smiled at his success, facing Anya with a triumphant grin. His smile faded and fled when he noticed her waving a hand in front of her face. His *lorethasra* smelled like bloody iron. "It's not that bad," he said, knowing he sounded petulant.

"Yes, it is," Anya said in clear disgust. She finally gave off the hand-waving and offered a tight-lipped expression of sympathy. "I'm sorry. You shouldn't feel bad about the smell. It isn't like you chose it."

Cinder grunted. No, he hadn't chosen such a foul aroma for his *lorethasra*.

"There's something strange, though," Anya said. "You were able to use your *lorethasra* from the very moment Mother Ashoka allowed you access to Shokan's Talents, but at the time, you were actually conducting *Jivatma* through *Muladhara*. And then later on, you couldn't. What happened?" She lifted her brows in silent query.

Cinder squirmed, not wanting to admit an embarrassing truth.

Anya noticed. "What is it?"

"I lied. I didn't send *Jivatma* through *Muladhara*. I was just concentrating on keeping the Chakra open, and I happened to be conducting *Jivatma* at the same time. When it all worked out—my Talent manifesting—I thought that was how it was supposed to be."

Anya's eyes boggled, and a moment later, she threw her head back, laughing in delight. "My poor, silly Cinder."

The next morning, a clapping of wings distracted Cinder while he was making breakfast. His eyes went to the sky where a hawk ascended, chased by a quarrel of sparrows. He could appreciate the hawk's dilemma. No matter where an Orb of Peace might be found, he and Anya would be chased by those seeking to get it back.

His wonderings next took him to the Sunset Kingdoms. Cinder still felt the emotions and ties from the *hashains* leashed to him: *Jeet Condune and Stren Coldire*. He hadn't asked for the subservience of the assassins, but they had granted it to him anyway, and through it, Cinder could sense their emotions and locations. He even had a rough approximation of their thoughts. Right now, Jeet and Stren were far away to the west, likely back home, full of passion and certainty, a driving desire to bring awareness of a truth they had learned.

It was easy to reckon on the latter. *The Grimyogi*. It had been the name given to him by Jeet, the leader of the *hashains*, and was yet another fateful title for Shokan.

Cinder scowled. Just how many prophecies and portents did one person need? And worse—or maybe best, depending on how he considered the situation—he wasn't any of those things. He wasn't the Grimyogi, the *Zuthrum lon Varshin*—the Reaper of the Whirlwind—or the Fated Foe. He was just a man fortuitous enough to have received the last memories and knowledge of the great hero Shokan. His eyes went to Anya, who stood in the morning sunshine braiding her hair. Her back was slightly arched, and Cinder traced her curves…

He cut off his observations. Anya didn't need—or want—him lusting after her. That part of their relationship was dead and buried. As for the *hashains*, while Cinder couldn't do anything about their plans on announcing him as the Grimyogi—it was a fool's mission—he still hoped the best for them.

Speaking of missions… Cinder's eyes went again to Anya, trying his best not to appreciate her loveliness. He cleared his throat. "I think we've been here long enough." He felt rested and refreshed, and an abrupt need to travel washed over him like a spring fever.

Anya smiled. "Off to Revelant then?"

Cinder could understand why she would think that would be their destination. Revelant was Anya's home, and she had to miss her family, not having seen them in over two years. It was also where they would find the next Orb of Peace.

But that wasn't where Cinder intended on traveling. "Let's stop by Shalla Valley," he suggested.

Anya frowned. "Why Shalla?"

Going to Shalla felt right, but until Cinder had stated his intentions, he couldn't say for sure why. Nevertheless, a longing drew him in that direction. He didn't know what it meant, but he'd learned to trust his instincts. As a result, he paused before responding, piecing together his answer.

"I want to talk to Sadana about our plans," he said after a few moments of deliberation. "I want someone else's advice on how to approach our future."

"Our future?"

Had there been a hitch in Anya's voice? Cinder shot her a glance, but her expression appeared untroubled. "Our future on how best to obtain the Orbs," he confirmed.

"I think we already have a good plan for the Orb of Moss, the one in Revelant," Anya said.

"I agree, but there might be a simpler solution we don't know about. The same with the Orb of Undying Light in Bharat."

Anya stared at him. "There's something else, isn't there?"

Until she'd voiced the question, Cinder hadn't realized it was the case. "I think Fastness is somewhere close to the valley. It feels like it."

Anya frowned. "You're that closely connected?"

Cinder nodded. "I think he's near that eastern entrance we used near the Bloody Snake. I want to see him."

"You miss him." She pursed her lips in sympathy. "Then Shalla Valley it is." A moment later, she grinned, clapping her hands in excitement. "Do you think we'll get to speak to Mahamatha again?"

Cinder smiled at her. Usually Anya was so serious and reserved, but other times, she could be utterly sweet. "I'm sure we'll *simply* have to ask."

Anya's grin transformed into a throaty chuckle. "Ah. I see we've resumed your usual joke."

Cinder laughed. Naming her 'Simply Anya' *was* an old joke, but it hadn't felt right to say it to her ever since they'd discovered their truths about Shokan and Sira. But in this moment, it did feel right, and even better, it felt right to laugh with Anya.

"This is nice," Cinder said after a few seconds. He meant it. It had been a long time since he and Anya had shared humor. They needed more of these moments.

"You realize I wasn't laughing at your joke, right?" Anya asked.

Cinder frowned. "What do you mean?"

"I mean I wasn't laughing at you calling me 'Simply Anya.' I was laughing at how pleased you were with yourself. It was charming… in a childish way."

"So you're saying I'm charming?"

Anya sighed. "Yes, but in a childish way. Now help me break down the camp so we can get moving."

A surge of rage flashed across Cinder's mind at having her order him about. But rather than say something he'd regret, he kept his mouth closed, eyes too, breathing deep—in and out—calming himself. Only when the fury was gone did he open his eyes, finding Anya staring at him in concern.

"The anger?" she asked.

"The anger."

"It can't be natural," Anya mused, and she would know just as well as he since she experienced the same nonsensical rage. For months after leaving Mahadev, their days had been filled with meaningless arguments, spurred by a fury that in hindsight had always felt foreign.

"I know," Cinder said, and although he agreed with her, he also didn't want to talk about it right now. They had more important tasks to complete. "Let's get packed."

Anya nodded, not pressing the matter.

By then, a thin sliver of the sun had crested the horizon, casting the sky in orange and rose. The night was banished, and as if that was their signal, small birds began flitting about, trilling. The clean smell of pine filled the air, carried on a calm breeze that had replaced yesterday's gusting wind. Cinder inhaled deep, enjoying the fresh aroma and appreciating the ravine's serenity as well as the day's promise of warmth.

It didn't take them long to break camp, and they were soon on the road, heading southwest toward Shalla Valley.

The entire way, they remained alert. Shet had forged a temporary truce with the spiderkin and emptied this part of the Daggers of both their forces, but it didn't mean there was no danger. In addition to normal animals, such as bears coming out of hibernation, snowtigers out on the hunt to feed young cubs, or wolves hungry after a long winter, there were other terrors. *Wraiths.* They were known to haunt the Dagger Mountains, and who knew if any lurked close at hand.

As they journeyed, Cinder maintained a slight hold on both *Jivatma* and *lorethasra*. Just enough to reach through the lightning—thinning it in the process—and enhance his focus. He cast his eyes about for movement, ears honed for unnatural sounds. Even his nose, seeking the fetid stink of a wraith.

Anya kept the same outward attention, and they eventually stopped for a cold lunch before continuing onward.

Day's end saw them reach a wide valley where they camped in a small cluster of cedars. The ground was wet, and a blanket of snow had yet to melt, but the stand was nestled out of the way from the rest of the valley.

"I'll start the fire," Cinder said.

"You sure?"

"I'm sure. I need to keep sourcing my *lorethasra* and conducting *Jivatma*."

"Then I'll see to the horses and pack mules."

As she worked, Cinder gathered whatever kindling and logs he could find. It didn't matter if the wood was wet. With fire from *lorethasra*, even if the logs were soaked, he could get them to light. When he returned from his collecting, he spied Anya brushing Barton, crooning softly to him. A soft cinnamon scent perfumed the air.

He inhaled automatically. The cinnamon aroma came from Anya, her natural scent, and he hadn't smelled it in a long time.

"Do you plan on just standing there?" Anya asked, not bothering to turn around.

Cinder entered the stand of cedar. "I noticed your cinnamon scent."

Anya quirked a brow. "Really? I didn't think you'd ever notice it again. Even my family rarely smells it."

"But it's not your *lorethasra*?"

Anya twisted about, facing him over her shoulder. "No. Mine is a mountain stream, remember? And didn't you used to say you could see which Element of *lorethasra* a woven was using based on the color of their eyes?"

"The sclerae," Cinder confirmed. "Blue means Water, yellow is Fire, green is Earth, and white is Air."

"Let me see," Anya said.

"See what?"

"Let me see you source *lorethasra* and connect to an Element. I want to see if your sclerae change color."

Cinder smiled at her demanding tone. "You can watch when I start the fire."

"Make sure to look at me when you do," Anya ordered.

"Of course, Isha," Cinder said, still smiling.

"That's kind of you *bishan*," Anya replied. "You remember what *bishan* means, don't you?"

"A wonderful person everyone should emulate?"

"I was thinking of 'an incompetent person who has potential.'"

"Is that what Isha means?" Cinder asked, pretending surprise. "I thought it meant 'old crone.'"

Anya rolled her eyes. "Just for that, you get to do the dishes, too."

"How is that any different than normal?"

"We should also train," Anya said, overlooking his comment. "It's been weeks since we last sparred."

"We can't afford to lose our sharp edge."

Anya nodded agreement. "We'll need our sharpest edge in Revelant."

"I don't think our memories are reliable," Anya stated.

Cinder didn't reply at once. The two of them sat atop a low rocky rise, looking down on a deep valley forested in hardwoods. The trees were only now showing their buds with a few pale green leaves scattered amongst their limbs. A lone bird, an eagle maybe, swept in slow circles above the woods, wings tilted as it hunted. The sun crested the mountains behind them, warming Cinder's back, and a warm spring breeze stirred the air, carrying the scent of the flowers blooming in the mountain meadow where they had camped for the night.

Cinder forced his gaze away from the view and considered her statement. This was a conversation long in the making, and he still wasn't sure he was ready to discuss it. Their recollections about their pasts were too different, and in the few times when they'd spoken about those oddities, one or both of them usually became unreasonably angry.

In Anya's remembrances, Cinder's time in the Third Directorate had been one of fraternity and friendship, and his life prior: that of an anonymous son of an anonymous farmer in an anonymous village in Rakesh.

His own memories, however, had been vastly different. Yes, he had been the anonymous son of an anonymous farmer, but in his recollections, he had also been tested by the elves of Yaksha Sithe on his thirteenth birthday and demonstrated a rare ability to bond with metal and master the sword.

It was a testing all children of Rakesh—the human nation ruled by elves—had to undergo, but for Cinder, despite his talent, the elves had set him aside. They had no need for a cripple, and instead, they had cast a braid of forgetting on him, making it impossible for him to recall his gifts or what the elves had done. Later, his encounter with Brilliance, the *aether*-cursed snowtiger had set forth changes that somehow healed Cinder and allowed him entrance into the Third Directorate.

But was any of it true?

Time and experience had taught him that it likely wasn't the case. There was a lie within his remembrances. Something small or large. And while he didn't fear what that might mean—on considering his life, he feared nothing—nevertheless, the idea that his memories might be false had him uneasy. And his mild reaction to what should be greatly troubling was itself concerning. Shouldn't he be more worried?

"Cinder," Anya prodded.

He stirred, not wanting to answer but eventually doing so. "You're right." The confession was like the opening of a flood-gate. "Prophecies can be corrupted, so why not our memories? And if our memories aren't true, then who are we really? How can we know the truth? Who are we to one another?" Sweat broke on his brow, his heart felt like it was ready to race out of his chest, and a sense of doom settled like a bruise-colored cloud on his mind.

As if it was the most natural motion, Anya drew him into her arms. "We'll figure it out," she whispered, her lips against his ear.

The strange sensation of doom lifted enough for Cinder to shudder. Tears pricked his eyes, and he pulled away from Anya, wiping his face. What was happening to him?

"I'm afraid," Anya said. "Just like you."

Her words caused Cinder to tilt his head in consideration. Is that what he was feeling? Fear? But he never feared anything. Why now?

What had really happened in Mahadev? What had been done to him? To both of them?

Anya, in that strange way they still had of knowing the other's thoughts, spoke what was on his mind. "Rabisu." She said the name like it was a curse. "He did more than make us less recognizable to others. I don't think Manifold's braid protected us as well as it was supposed to. Rabisu ruined us."

Ruined us? It wasn't what Cinder had expected her to say. A moment later, his surprise faded as greater understanding of what she meant took hold. "He altered our memories. Or maybe he did that and even more? Like stole some of them?"

They fell silent, each of them staring out into the distance as the sun rose higher.

They continued to stare, and Cinder found himself reaching for Anya. She met him in the middle, and they held hands, squeezing softly. It no longer bothered him to touch her. In fact, he doubted he could stop himself even if he wanted to.

His need to touch her overwhelmed his recollections of how she had stood aside while he'd been brutalized in the Third Directorate; of her merely watching but not helping him or any of the other humans. Especially because he didn't believe it.

How could he have fallen in love with someone who had enslaved him? He wouldn't have, and although he'd once been certain of her callousness, it wasn't the case any longer. Anya would never have behaved like that. It wasn't in her to stand aside and allow evil to flourish.

She…

A moment later, he frowned as a lassitude settled over his mind, a fog encouraging him to let go of his concerns. What had he been thinking about? The recollection wouldn't come, and it had seemed important.

"Let it go. It was nothing," a voice seemed to whisper.

But Cinder wouldn't give up. This had happened before, and he wouldn't just lie down and accept it. He fought against the stupor, and slowly, like he was pulling a ship to shore, his mind fired and a memory flared.

Anya…

What about her? She had stood aside while he'd been tormented at the Third Directorate.

No. That wasn't true. She didn't do that. He couldn't have loved someone so casually cruel or cowardly. And more importantly, that wasn't who she was. He knew it.

Like a burst soap bubble, Cinder remembered the entirety of his brief conversation with Anya, and the abrupt awareness caused him to lurch forward. He quickly caught his balance, Anya bracing him.

"It happened again?" she asked.

This loss of memory in the midst of conversation was something they had both experienced, and by now, it wasn't new; not to him or Anya. However, this was the first time Cinder could recall either of them fighting through whatever influence lay low their minds and lied to them. He had reclaimed some brief bit of what was lost, and he was determined to reclaim it all.

"It happened," Cinder said. "But this time I was able to remember."

Anya smiled, and the sun might have dawned, Seminal's moons might have shed an ethereal light on a secret glade, and stars might have twinkled with joy. Again, as if it was the most natural thing, she drew him into a hug. "Then we can figure it out."

"We'll find an answer and a solution," Cinder agreed. A notion occurred to him, and he pulled back from Anya. "And you should know that I don't consider you a *pandmendi chon*."

Anya's brow wrinkled in confusion. "A what?"

"It's *Shevasra*. It means—"

"I know what it means." Anya's brow remained furrowed. "It's a reference to a rotten fruit."

"It also refers to a beautiful woman who is full of deception, or evil hidden within beauty."

Anya tilted her head, still clearly confused. "Is that what you thought I was? A *pandmendi chon*?"

Cinder reddened. He hadn't truly considered what his confession might mean, for either him or Anya. And for the second time that morning, his heart raced and sweat broke out on his forehead. "At least I called you beautiful."

"Deceitful, too."

"Not anymore. Not ever."

Anya seemed to study him a moment before breaking once more into a smile. "Then you don't have to worry because I thought you were a *pandi*."

"You thought I was rotten?"

"The absolute worst."

2

Anya recognized this part of the Daggers. The cliff rearing to their right, red and with the appearance of a chipped tooth, told the tale. It was the Bloody Snake, the landmark that indicated the deadly place where she and Cinder had once been chased by wraiths. Who was to say this wasn't a common hunting ground for the creatures? They might still be lurking, and while she felt confident that she and Cinder could handle them this time, there was no reason to take unnecessary risks.

Although, when considering the matter, traveling here *had* been a risk since this snow-and-ice-covered valley led to their destination, one of Shalla Valley's three entrances. And shortly their journey might become interesting. Hopefully, though, Cinder's sense that Fastness might be lurking close at hand would prove to be true as well.

The sun hung high, burning bright through a cloudless vault, and a golden eagle soared on the thermals of a warm spring afternoon. Patches of grass poked through the clinging snow, and Anya reckoned that in the next few weeks, winter's grasp would finally leave the valley. It was a pleasant scene, but she wasn't fooled by the serenity. Danger could lurk at any point.

"I smell something," Cinder said. He was frowning, focused on a bluff close at hand.

"What is it?" Anya asked, peering in the same direction. She searched for any movement, sound, or even smell.

Seconds later, Cinder shook his head. "It's gone. I can't smell it anymore."

"It's not gone," Anya said. "We're being watched."

Cinder gazed about before giving a slow nod of agreement. "Let's pick up the pace."

Minutes later, just as they reached a steep incline leading out of the valley, Cinder drew Cigarello short. "Ahead of us." He gestured with his chin. "*Aether*-cursed and maybe a wraith."

"Behind us, too," Anya said. Her gaze went to a ridge from which she sensed someone staring down at them.

An instant later, Cinder barked laughter. "It's that idiot cat."

It took a few seconds for Anya to understand who he was talking about. For a moment, the image of a huge tawny feline entered her mind. A blink, and the image was gone, replaced by whom Cinder meant. "Brilliance."

"She's up there, likely planning on trying to scare us again."

"And she's with a wraith?"

Cinder tilted his head. "Maybe." A moment later, he frowned. "I'm not sure. What about behind us?"

"Someone is watching, but that's all I can tell." The strange part was that whoever or whatever was observing them didn't seem malicious, no evil emanations like when they had encountered zahhacks. "What do you think?"

"I think we ride forward, Shielded and ready to burn whomever we encounter." His words spoken, Cinder heeled Cigarello forward. "Unless it's just the stupid cat," he called over his shoulder.

Anya privately agreed, but nonetheless, she scowled. Cinder was riding ahead when he should be letting her take the lead. It's how they always did things. Even her long-dead husband, Rukh, had done so.

She set aside her irritation and followed after Cinder, senses alert as they filed through a narrow passage. It was shadowed with the walls closing in tight. Anya could reach both sides with outstretched hands. Just as she pulled up next to Cinder upon exiting, a yowling roar echoed from directly ahead. A massive snowtiger as large as Cigarello leapt off a large boulder, teeth bared, and barring their way. With her was a dog of almost equal size, gnarly toothed, bat-eared like a goblin, and growling softly. Both had the glowing white eyes of an *aether*-cursed.

Anya knew both these creatures. *Brilliance and Kela.*

Cinder leaped off Cigarello, landing in a crouch. The green webbing of a *Jivatma*-powered Shield encompassed him, and he held a Fireball. He stared at the snowtiger while the dog whimpered, slinking to the ground, tail between his legs. "You sure you want to dance like this?" Cinder asked the snowtiger.

"*No. But I'm a hunter, and hunters don't beg for their lives,*" Brilliance stated.

"You're an idiot, is what you are," Cinder said, letting go of the Fireball.

"*No, I'm not.*"

"Yes, you are. What were you thinking, trying to ambush us like that?"

The cat's ears drooped in apparent dejection. "*I thought it would be funny.*"

Cinder folded his arms. "You mean like the last time? Was it funny then?"

"*I didn't think it would be funny,*" the dog interjected. "*I told her what a stupid idea it was.*"

"*Lickspittle,*" Brilliance growled.

"*Dipstickspittle,*" Kela countered.

"*That's not even a word, stupid.*"

Anya had heard enough. "Children!" Her shout earned silence as both of the *aether*-cursed cut off their arguing. "Why are you here?"

"*They are here because of me.*" From behind them came the slow clip-clop hoofbeats of a horse Anya feared she would never again see.

He looked the same as ever. Powerful, muscled, and white as bone.

She smiled, broad and happy. "Fastness."

"It is good to see you both." The white stallion greeted Cinder first, the horse nuzzling his shoulder while being drawn into a hug. The two of them had always been close, rider and Yavana, close enough for Cinder to have sensed the white's presence at such a far distance. Next, Fastness came to Anya, shoving gently into her chest. *"Where have you been, and why is Cinder riding that poor old gelding?"*

Cinder chuckled. "We have a lot to discuss."

"Can we discuss them over apples?"

"And you say we act like children," Brilliance complained.

Fastness whickered. *"Hush. Your elders are busy."*

Anya's humor at the interplay cut off when a wraith stepped out from behind a large boulder. He was shorter than she, blue-eyed, lean, and with a tuft of blond hair. She hissed, conducting *Jivatma* even as she drew her sword. Cinder did the same.

Fastness placed himself between her and the wraith. *"He's not who you think."*

The wraith stood at stiff attention, appearing unalarmed. "Might I interest the two of you in a spot of tea while we get to know each other?"

It was the last thing Anya would have expected from the wraith, and she shared a wondering look with Cinder. What was going on? And why didn't the wraith have the same putrid stink as the rest of his kind?

"Like I said, he's not what you think."

"What is he then?" Cinder asked, staring hard at the wraith, who of all things, appeared fussy. And his eyes… they didn't glow entirely white. Instead, there was an unremarkable blue hue underneath.

Cinder frowned, confused by the situation.

"He was once human like you," the fussy-seeming wraith said. "But

because of soul-tearing pain, he became what you see. A wraith." He inclined his head to Fastness. "And then through the teaching of this horse who is unlike any other, he is now becoming something else. Something better and good."

"You will become human once again," Fastness promised the man.

Still unsure what to make of him, Cinder stared at the not-wraith. If Fastness truly had found a way to redeem wraiths, then he had accomplished a miracle. But was the man's transformation real? Could he be trusted? Cinder glanced to Anya, who shook her head minutely. She didn't have any good idea on what was happening either.

Cinder mentally shrugged. In the end, he'd have to trust Fastness. After all, his proper name was Sapient Dormant, one of the great Mythaspuris who had saved Seminal from Shet's tyranny three millennia ago. If the stallion believed the wraiths could be saved and he knew how, then Cinder would have to have faith in his friend.

"What about that tea?" the wraith asked.

Cinder had a question of his own. "What's your name?"

"Selin Heron," the wraith replied.

Cinder introduced himself, and so did Anya. "It's good to meet you," Cinder said. "Are there any others of your kind?"

"Wraiths who are recovering?" Selin said. "Six others. They wait by the campsite. I'm the least intimidating of our company, and they thought you'd be less likely to fear someone like me." He flashed a nervous smile. "Please don't kill me."

Anya chuckled. "If Fastness says we can trust you, then you have nothing to fear from us. The stallion might be a pest—"

"He's actually a brat," Cinder corrected. "Lord Brat."

Fastness rustled, while Selin drew himself upright, surprised and clearly outraged. The not-wraith looked to the stallion in question. "They speak so disrespectfully to you."

Fastness laughed. *"I never told you the story of how I met Cinder, did I? When you learn, you'll understand why he doesn't hold me in the same esteem as you and the others."*

Cinder smiled. "You didn't always use such fancy words, Lord Brat."

"*I've learned fancy words,*" Brilliance said, butting in—literally—as she pressed her massive head in between Cinder and Fastness. "*One of the wraiths—*"

"We're not wraiths any longer," Selin cut in.

"*Yes, yes. Of course,*" Brilliance said with a breezy dismissal. "*Anyway, one of the wraiths is a teacher. She's taught me all sorts of words. I like her.*"

"*I like Residar,*" Kela declared. "*He's mine.*"

"*You're a dog. That means you belong to him. Not the other way around,*" Brilliance corrected. "*And you only like him because he treats you like a puppy.*"

Cinder could see another argument brewing, and it reminded him of an old phrase about cats and dogs. "Maybe we can talk about it later," he suggested before addressing Fastness. "It looks like you have a story to tell."

They spent the next hour learning what Fastness, Brilliance, and Kela had been doing over the months since Cinder and Anya had last seen them. The trio had headed north, delving deep into the Savage Kingdoms and discovering what Fastness had been hoping to find: a small group of wraiths. The white had gone there in order to teach the fell creatures how to accept the evil they'd done and through that acceptance, find a path to forgiveness.

The work wasn't complete, not even close, but through months of work, of prayer and meditation, the wraiths had come far.

Fastness snorted when Cinder praised him. "*I only knew what to say because of what Sachi taught me in the Realms of the Rakshasas. She helped me accept Devesh's healing love.*"

"And so have we," Selin chimed in. "Accepted Devesh's feeling love, I mean."

"You did well, old son," Cinder said, rubbing the stallion's forehead.

Fastness whuffled, leaning into the rub. "*You used to call me lad.*"

Cinder laughed. "I think you're a bit long in the tooth to be called lad. You're what? Thousands of years old?"

The stallion stomped a hoof like a petulant child. "*I'm not that old.*"

Brilliance's ears perked. *"I wouldn't doubt it, as grumpy as he is. Or maybe it's because his sire was a jacka—"*

Fastness whickered warning. *"Don't say it."*

Brilliance silently laughed.

"We taught the wraiths, too," Kela said, tail wagging hesitantly. *"We taught them to give us food and not shout at each other."* He nudged his nose into Anya's palm and stared longingly at her.

She laughed, rubbing the dog's head. "That's because you're a good boy, aren't you," she said, sounding like she was talking to a baby while she petted Kela.

Cinder did a double take. He had never seen—or expected to see—Anya speak like that or be so sweet.

"I can be sweet," Anya said, picking up on his unspoken thoughts.

"As sweet as a grapefruit," Cinder muttered.

"What was that?"

"Nothing," Cinder quickly replied.

"It's good to see the two of you getting along better," Fastness said with a chuckle.

Cinder grunted, not wanting to discuss his relationship with Anya. They *were* getting along better, and though there was something odd about their memories, he didn't want to talk about it with Fastness. There were other matters the stallion needed to know.

"We should tell you what we've been doing," Cinder said, going on to speak about the Orbs of Peace.

Silence settled over the small group as he spoke.

"And after the Orb of Flames was destroyed, we left Naraka," Anya stated.

"We couldn't stand the notion of spending another minute there," Cinder added. "Weakened in front of our enemy."

"And now you're off to Revelant?" Fastness asked.

"It's where the next Orb can be found," Anya said. "The Orb of Moss." She indicated the small group with Fastness. "What about you? I know you're teaching the wraiths, and Brilliance wants to help other *aether*-cursed, but why are you here? Why so close to Shalla Valley?"

Selin was the one who answered. "Because one day, we'll be pure enough to enter the holy vale, but until that day comes, we'll protect this entrance. If Shet allies more fully with the spiderkin, he might be powerful enough to breach the valley's defenses and destroy it. We will make sure it never comes to pass."

It was a good notion as far as Cinder was concerned. In spite of their skill, the holders were few in number, and the yakshins, despite their deadliness, never struck him as being violent enough to do what was needed against Shet.

"There is another reason," Fastness said. *"The valley has a Gate. We can't allow Shet to gain control of it. Right now, he has to forge anchor lines to wherever he wishes to send his forces, and even then, it can only be somewhere he's already visited. A Gate erases some of those limits."*

Cinder had known of Shalla Valley's Gate, but he hadn't fully contemplated what it might mean. He did now and shared a considering expression with Anya.

"We can use the Gate to go to the Third Directorate," she said, thinking along his lines.

"It'll save us months of travel."

"But we'd be better off leaving the island by way of the sea," Anya continued. "We don't want my mother's attention to ever go to the Directorate. They don't deserve that kind of scrutiny, especially Ginala's."

"No one does," Cinder agreed. He addressed Fastness. "Since you're teaching wraiths, do you mind teaching humans?"

"Who do you have in mind?"

"My brothers."

Brilliance stood on a ledge, watching as her human and his mate rode away. They hadn't stayed long, claiming they had important work to do. Even if true, there was something different about the two of them, and she couldn't put a paw on what it meant.

Fastness might know, but he wouldn't tell her. With the stallion, everything was about meditation and learning on her own.

Brilliance grimaced. She was a snowtiger, and snowtigers didn't sit and stare at the back of their eyelids.

Still, seeing Cinder like that—distant to his mate—it bothered her. He wasn't happy, and she wanted to see him happy. After killing his parents, she at least owed him that much.

Whimpering slightly, Kela sat next to her.

Brilliance sighed to herself, knowing what was bothering the dog. *"I shouldn't have called you lickspittle. I'm sorry."*

"And I shouldn't have called you dipstickspittle. Friends?"

Brilliance nudged Kela's shoulder, rubbing the side of her head against the top of his. As she did so, she made a note to groom him later. His fur needed cleaning. *"Friends."*

They fell silent then, watching Cinder and Anya ascend.

"I was once a man-killer, did I ever tell you that?" Brilliance asked.

Kela thumped his tail.

"I liked it," Brilliance admitted. *"It was the hunt. It's still the hunt that I enjoy above all else."*

"You thought I was a man-killer," Kela reminded her.

Brilliance blinked, ears flicking with recognition. *"The two-legs believe all our kind are man-killers."*

"Are we?"

Brilliance didn't know, but she reckoned it was likely correct. *"I think we are. Or we used to be. We needed* aether. *I did. It's why I killed Cinder's parents."* She admitted what she'd done as a statement of fact. While Fastness seemed to think she should feel guilty over the matter, Brilliance didn't see it that way. Her actions hadn't been done out of malice. Rather, they had simply been behavior that was true to herself. Brilliance was a hunter, a predator, and predators killed their prey.

At least, Kela understood. The gnarly-toothed dog, who all humans, holders, and wraiths loved, had once felt that same hunger, and he simply gazed at her without judgment.

It was part of why Brilliance could tolerate him. She grunted on reconsideration. She did more than tolerate him. She actually liked Kela, and in truth, the ugly little fellow was a good sort. She just didn't like saying so.

"*But that hunger left once I had enough* aether." Brilliance continued her explanation, her ears lifting as she smiled in recollection. "*I didn't realize how much I'd changed. Didn't realize I didn't need* aether *in the same way.*"

"*It happened for me when I killed those zahhacks.*"

Brilliance nodded, recalling their first meeting. "*It's a good thing not every animal who drinks* aether *becomes* aether-cursed. *Just imagine how many two-legs would have to die.*"

"*It's not* aether," Kela said. "*It's called* lorasra."

"*I know what it's called,*" Brilliance snapped. She hated when Kela corrected her. "*Anyway, since I didn't know how much I'd changed, it's also why I hunted Cinder afterward.*"

"*You hunted* him?" Amazement laced Kela. "*Were you mad? He'd have killed you.*"

Brilliance growled warning. Weakness was something she could never admit. Kela should know better than to test her like that. "*Cinder is strong, but I could take him.*"

Kela eyed her in disbelief. "*No, you couldn't, liar.*"

Brilliance hissed. "*I'm not lying!*"

Kela laughed, and Brilliance turned away with a huff.

The dog continued to laugh, and Brilliance growled again, facing him. "*Fine. Cinder would have killed me if I ever caught him.*" Her tail lashed. "*Just promise not to tell him. He already thinks of me as his… I don't know what, but I don't like it. He belongs to me. Not the other way around.*"

Kela's mouth opened in a grin, and his tail wagged. "*You shouldn't think of it like that. If you were like me, you'd get all sorts of treats and people would be nicer. They pet me all the time. It feels good.*"

Brilliance scoffed. "*Be like you? You mean how people coo over you all the time?*"

"*Exactly. Watch.*" He demonstrated by rolling on his side and offering his belly for a rub.

Kela was shameless, and Brilliance had to laugh. *"It is not my way. I own. I am not owned."*

"I'm not owned," Kela disagreed. *"I'm a partner. There's a difference."*

Brilliance contemplated his words.

"What are you two talking about?" It was Residar. With him was Selin. The two wraiths ascended the slope, both of them rubbing the dog's head in obvious fondness before sitting.

Brilliance studied the wraiths. When she'd first met them, their eyes had held the same white glow as hers and Kela's. At first, she thought it meant wraiths were *aether*-cursed as well. But over the past few months, Residar's and Selin's eyes didn't glow so much. In fact, a normal color filled the center of their eyes. They smelled different, too.

Brilliance lifted her nose, inhaling. *"You don't stink anymore."* She grinned when, as expected, Selin sniffed himself. He was so easy to tease. She distractedly wondered what game she'd later on have him play to keep her amused.

"What did we smell like?" Residar asked, unimpressed by her claim.

Brilliance stared at him. Residar was a difficult one. He honored Kela, petting the dog and making admiring noises, and it made her jealous. More importantly, it also made her consider how she could get him to do the same for her… so long as she didn't have to beg for attention like Kela.

"Well?" Residar prompted.

"You stank of rotting meat."

Again, Selin sniffed himself. "My goodness. How ghastly. Thankfully, we're well past that stage in our growth."

"The Hungering Heart still reaches for us," Residar said, his eyes glowing a bit and growing distant. "I can still feel Him here." He touched his chest, directly over his heart.

They fell silent as Residar's words cast a pall on their gathering.

"Yakshins smell like bark, dark soil, and leaves," Kela said.

Brilliance shot him a glance. What was that about?

Before she could ask, Fastness arrived. *"Who died? You four look like you've seen your own funeral."*

Residar scowled. "We were talking about the Hungering Heart. About how He still reaches for us."

"Deny Him," Fastness immediately said. *"Accept Devesh's yoke. It is gentle."*

"I accept no one's yoke," Residar growled, and Brilliance silently agreed with him.

"And yet you have," Fastness replied. *"You accepted His forgiveness, and before that, the yoke of love. To your family. To Brissianna. Even to us. It is no different with Devesh. Accept His love, that is the yoke of which I speak."*

His words didn't seem to appease Residar, and the wraith's scowl deepened. "It's easy for you. You want to be yoked. You're a horse."

"Correct. I am currently a horse," Fastness said. *"But I was once a holder. Then I became a necrosed. And it was only because of Indrun Agni and Sachi Mithara that I then became a Mythaspuri. And finally, after all that, I was reborn as a horse, a Yavana colt named Sunbane who killed an* aether-*cursed wolf. I have been many things, had many names, and—"*

"Lord Brat," Brilliance piped in, recalling the name Cinder had given the white stallion.

Fastness stomped the ground. *"Only Cinder gets to call me that,"* he said, glaring at her.

Brilliance wilted. No matter how brave she tried to be, the horse terrified her. Once again, she rallied, and it was thinking about her boy, about Cinder, that granted her courage. *"When do you think we'll see them again?"* She hoped it wasn't long, not like this last time where it had been many seasons.

"Soon enough, I hope," Fastness answered before addressing Residar and Selin. *"In the meantime, I need the two of you."*

"For what?" Residar asked.

"There's an apple tree in bloom, and there's an apple I want. Fetch it for me."

Residar sighed, levering himself to his feet. "Yes, Lord Brat."

Fastness whinnied. *"Only Cinder gets to call me that!"*

"Of course." Residar helped Selin rise. "Come. We wouldn't want Lord Brat to get fussy."

The three of them departed, still arguing, but Brilliance could hear the amusement in their voices. She rose to her feet as well. *"We have our own work,"* she said to Kela. *"And it's time we saw to it."*

The dog sighed. *"Finding aether-cursed beasts to save is hard work."*

"Which is why we're helping Fastness save the wraiths. Go see him." She nudged Kela. *"He'll have something for you to do, something other than fetching apples,"* she added with a chuckle.

"What about you?"

Brilliance's gaze went to Cinder. *"I want to tell my human something."*

3

Overlooking a deep bay of tropical colors loomed an isolated island that reared like a stony sentinel out of the aquamarine waters. Lichen-covered boulders the size of cabins littered the base of a cliff where wave-washed kelp ebbed back and forth before settling in crags and gaps. And all the while, the sea smashed, cascading rainbows high up the bluff. But the colors didn't reach to the heights of the hollow cave near the cliff's crest. Black and empty, the opening appeared to stare at the mainland like a dark eye sighting a vast desert of brown and red escarpments.

No one living seemed to exist in this lonesome stretch of shore and island, but that wasn't actually the case. From within the cavern, Aia, the Calico dragon, took a set of halting steps toward the exit. It had been millennia since she'd felt the sun's warmth, and she wanted to once more know that comforting embrace. She edged outward, feet unsteady. Prior to her recent awakening, she had slept for uncounted centuries, and while she had regained some of her strength, much of it was still missing. Nosing out of the cave, her eyes slitted in pleasure, and she smiled as the sun's glory lit upon her.

Something about it felt good and right, better even than Rukh's fingers scratching her chin. The great dragon edged farther out of her cave, onto a broad platform, her wings outspread to catch as much sunlight as possible. She stood there for hours, enjoying the healing warmth. True, the sunshine wouldn't take the place of actual food, but for now it was nourishing enough.

With it, Aia could fly, possibly even far enough to visit Wren—Aranya, as she called herself now. It had been too long since Aia had seen her adopted daughter. Their last conversation had taken place during the *NusraelShev*, shortly after Wren had forced her way into Seminal, determined to save her parents.

Aia smiled again at the name Wren had chosen. *Aranya*. Chosen due to the foresight of a quelchon, but still, somewhat silly—*Ar*, which in *Shevasra* meant 'or.' Her smile faded. But such a journey would have to wait. Aia needed to hunt and eat, and even then, it would be months longer before her full health was restored.

A heavy inhalation, and Aia stared into the cavern where a small orb—glowing with blue-and-green lightning—sat upon a shelf. For a human, it would be the size of a fist, and as heavy as a similarly sized stone. But its purpose was far weightier. This was the Orb of the Wings, an Orb of Peace, and it was Aia's duty to see it protected until Rukh came to claim it. She sensed that would be soon.

Aia growled inwardly. It had better be. She was growing impatient with him.

And that said nothing about her brother. Where was that silly kitten? Several years ago, she had felt his coming into Seminal—it had certainly taken him long enough to finally arrive—but ever since that brief flash there had been nothing.

Aia worried over the matter. What had become of Shon? Surely, he hadn't died. It couldn't be. Indrun had vowed Shon would come to this world—been utterly certain of it, both him and Sachi—and Antalagore had confirmed their promises. So where was he? And where was Rukh?

The wind whipped, whistling past the lonesome island, drawing Aia out of her longings. She lifted her nose, but the gusts brought no interesting scents. Just brine and the dust of the Coalescent Desert from across the bay where no useful food would be found, not for miles inland, and she didn't have the energy to hunt so deep.

Her gaze shifted south. Prune was in that direction along with its massive oasis. She could hunt there, although she'd have to be careful. She didn't want anyone knowing of her awakening. Not yet. While Rukh had taught her to Blend, right now she lacked the energy to do so. Which meant she would have to hunt with her physical limitations.

Aia mentally grimaced. She hated limitations, and she hated having to be careful. But it was necessary. Just as she'd noticed Shon's and Rukh's emergence into Seminal, she had also felt Shet's power rising again. He couldn't know of her presence, not when she was so weak. She'd be an easy kill for the false god and his Titans.

But when she was fully restored? When Rukh flew upon her, or better yet, *next* to her—she grinned at a memory—then she would fear no one.

Her sight went to the sea. Rather than flying south to Prune, perhaps she should eat a shark. She pondered the matter, trying to imagine the taste of such a creature. She'd never actually eaten one before. Did it taste like chicken? Rukh used to say every kind of meat tasted like chicken, but Aia didn't think he was right. She liked fish, and fish didn't taste like chicken. And since both sharks and fishes lived in the sea, shouldn't a shark taste like a fish?

She hoped so, and without any further hesitation, Aia leapt off the platform, wings unfurled, including those tapered along her tail, catching the thermals, letting the wind do the work. She drifted and circled, searching downward until she saw what she was looking for. With a roar, she tucked her wings and streaked down at her prey.

The air streamed past her, but her vision remained unimpaired. As the sea's surface loomed, Aia winged backward. Her claws punched through the water, grasping her prey and her meal. A shark, ten feet in length, wrenched about in her grasp. Strong wing strokes lifted her back into the air.

She panted as she gained altitude. This wasn't easy. In fact, it was hard, and Aia struggled to gain height. She wasn't sure she could do this. Fear poured through her. This might have been a terrible decision. She needed more height. Otherwise, she could easily die, unable to stay aloft before plummeting to the sea where she'd drown.

No. Rukh wouldn't give up. He'd fight regardless of the odds.

More strong wingbeats caused Aia to surge upward, high enough to catch the thermals. At last, she could rest. Her wings swept out, filled by the wind, and she simply glided a moment, resting. Her wings tilted now and then to keep her balanced, and a twist of them had her aimed back to her cave. She continued to glide, and the cavern slowly filled her vision. Aia automatically back-winged to kill the last of her speed. She had done this a thousand times, but on this occasion, she lacked the strength.

Rather than land gracefully, Aia plowed into the platform, nearly sliding off. She lay there a moment, shocked and appalled by the entire hunt. It could have been an utter disaster. Groaning, she leveraged herself upright, wings out for balance. She viewed the shark, which had been squished by her rough landing.

At least it wasn't squirming any longer.

Jeet Condune stepped out of a rickety wooden cottage and onto a porch overlooking the streets of Querel. His breath plumed from a late autumn chill, and he paused just past the doorway's lip, gazing at the village in distaste. Meeting his sight was the first, faint hints of dawn shining down on a hamlet that was still largely asleep. But there were some signs of life—lights flooding from the cracks in shuttered windows, roosters crowing, and a few men shuffling along with whatever tasks peasants did this early in the morning.

Sighing, Jeet prayed for the strength to endure this unwholesome place. How had he been laid so low as to have to live in this impoverished village? Querel was a collection of poorly built cottages and hovels that squatted along rutted dirt roads. And the people themselves largely fit their destitute homes. Loud and brash, clothed in rags, and unaware of the finer matters in life, such as discipline and authority.

Yet this was the only place Jeet imagined he might be safe. After the infidels at Chapterhouse had proclaimed him an apostate, this was where he and Stren had journeyed following their escape. It was where Jeet's sister, Brena, had gone following proof that she was unable to conceive a *hashain*. She and her untalented children lived here, farmers wallowing in the dirt.

Another scowl.

And Jeet's loss of status—his wretched humbling—was all due to those vultures at Chapterhouse, the Council of Sabala, who had guided Jeet's brothers into sacrilege. The Grimyogi was come. The man who was beyond man. The killer beyond killers. The greatest of warriors strode Seminal once again, and what did the Council of Sabala do? Did they celebrate his wondrous return?

Of course not. The jackals had circled to protect their own status—which would have declined in the face of the Grimyogi's glory—and declared Jeet and Stren to be liars and apostates.

Untrue. All of it, and the brothers should have known. Although they had some of a troll's ability to sense the truth, Jeet's fellow *hashains* had refused to do so.

Another headshake. How had it come to this?

"So. Another day in this glorious village at the back end of nowhere," a voice spoke from behind Jeet, the tone laced in sarcasm. An instant later, Stren Coldire, the only brother to have kept faith in the Grimyogi—whether he had wanted to or not—moved to stand alongside Jeet.

"So it is," Jeet agreed. The two of them stood silently, scrutinizing Querel.

"Is this to be our lives then?" Stren asked. "I had imagined heralding the Grimyogi would bring us acclaim." He indicated the village, mouth curling into a sneer. "Not this pathetic crotch-rot."

While Stren's statements echoed Jeet's own thinking, it wouldn't do for him to agree. The younger *hashain* needed hope and optimism.

They both did if they were to accomplish what was required.

But hope and optimism were in short supply in Querel, which meant that their success would be all the sweeter for the current bitterness. And who knew? Maybe it would also mean that as the unwavering heralds of the Grimyogi, Jeet and Stren would be accounted as holy figures themselves. It was possible.

Either that, or they would die as martyrs, but for someone trained since birth to never fear death, such an outcome would also be an acceptable ending to this life. A good ending. A worthy one. And perhaps the next time the wheel spun Jeet out again, it would be as a figure even grander than a *hashain*. Maybe next time, he would be reborn as an *asrasin*.

Jeet smiled inwardly at the possibility.

"You're pleased," Stren noted. "Why?"

Jeet was about to answer, but just then Brena, his harpy of a sister, exited her bedroom. A widow, the years hadn't been kind to her. Grayhaired, wrinkled like a raisin, and with wiry limbs, she appeared old enough to be Jeet's mother although she was younger by half a decade. Unfortunately, she had a mouth and demeanor equal to her coarse appearance.

"Who cares why he's pleased," Brena said. "When will the two of you start earning your keep? My food was meant to feed me through the winter. Not both of you. And if you insist on playing with your swords all day instead of helping gather the last of the harvest, that food won't last."

Jeet closed his eyes, praying for patience. He wanted to do nothing other than silence this venomous cretin in the form of a crone, but it was not to be. The Grimyogi's leash wouldn't allow it.

The leash—a bonding to the holy one that Jeet had willingly offered, and through it, also Stren—kept the two *hashains* limited in their actions. The Grimyogi disapproved of killing unless absolutely necessary, such as in the defense of themselves, the innocent, or against those seeking to do evil. Unfortunately, Brena, despite her appearance and temperament, did not fall into the latter category.

Jeet's gaze went to his sister, and by an act of heroic will, he managed not to jeer at her. *Disgusting filth.* She should be bowing and scraping before him and Stren, not offering insults. If she had dared slight them at Chapterhouse, she would have been bound to a post and lashed until her back was a bloody mess. Jeet would have happily administered the punishment, but not because of some desire to inflict pain. No. It was because people needed a shepherd's firm hand to instruct them, and Jeet considered himself a teacher.

"You know why we are here, Sister," Jeet said.

"The Grimyogi," Brena spat. "Will he grind the grain? Milk the goats? Feed the chickens?"

Jeet clenched his jaw. From where did she get her courage? This pathetic drudge who dared mock a *hashain*. If Brena wasn't so infuriating, Jeet would have found her audacity impressive. "No," he allowed. "But he will free you to do so and grow. Yours can be more than a peasant's life."

Brena looked ready to scoff, but her eyes widened in shock, and Jeet turned to where she was staring. A massive creature marched into view. Jeet blinked. He'd never before seen such a being. He blinked again, trying to clear away what seemed like an impossibility. The creature, whatever it was, marched in their direction, gigantic and overtopping him by at least two feet.

Without conscious thought, Jeet stepped off the porch, studying the approaching beast. His eyes narrowed. What was it?

He noted Stren moving alongside him. Both of them were armed and armored, ready for what was coming, and Jeet's mind finally identified what he was seeing. *A troll.* Despite the autumn cold, the woven creature wore only a loincloth and was otherwise garbed in short fur the color of bark. Dark braided hair was gathered in a ponytail, and ram's horns flared off his temples. A prominent brow overtopped dark, deep-set eyes and heavy features, including a lantern jaw. A thick staff set a steady rhythm as the troll walked with purpose, a pace that reminded Jeet of unyielding stone or a moving mountain. And where the creature passed, silence echoed outward in a wave as everyone in

Querel ceased their activities.

With the troll were a pair of men. They walked like warriors and seemed to know how to use the swords at their waists. Holders then, reputedly the equal of a brother, possibly even better. Jeet's eyes narrowed in further assessment. How good were the holders really? He'd like to know.

"Come no farther," Jeet commanded once the troll was within a half-dozen yards. Even with its reach, he felt confident the creature couldn't touch him with its staff. "State your purpose."

The holders never stopped glancing about, searching for whatever might be out of place.

Jeet silently applauded their skill.

"I am Maize," the troll said. "And I have been looking for the two of you, Jeet Condune and Stren Coldire. Tell me what you know of the Grimyogi."

4

Cinder wished they could have visited longer with Fastness, Brilliance, and Kela. The meeting had been bittersweet but welcome, and in some ways, everything he needed—seeing the stallion again, knowing that the white was thriving and had a worthy purpose. Even reconnecting with Brilliance, who remained her normal cat-like self, which was to say maddening and yet somehow endearing. Sometimes Cinder wanted to kiss the snowtiger on the forehead and other times, he wanted to bop her on the nose. And it didn't matter that he occasionally caught her staring his way like she wanted to take a bite out of him. Brilliance was a lovely pain.

But the pressing of time urged him and Anya on. They had spent long enough recovering from Flatiron and couldn't afford to waste any more days or even hours while Shet rebuilt his strength.

But Brilliance's question had resonated in Cinder's mind.

"Why are you so angry at your mate?" The snowtiger had asked that of him shortly prior to his departure, and the words resonated in his mind, even after they had entered Shalla Valley and made the long journey to Shriven Grove.

Cinder pondered the answer as he and Anya rode through a glorious savanna, fragrant with musky scents from a warm wind billowing the grass. Lions lounged in the distance, and a herd of wildebeests munched contentedly next to the massive lake centered within Shalla Vale. An elephant trumpeted, and a silver-headed eagle screeched from high above as the sun lowered toward setting.

"What's wrong?" Anya asked. "You've been distracted ever since we talked to Fastness." She hadn't commented on his behavior until now, although he could tell the question had been on her mind.

"It was something Brilliance said." He repeated the snowtiger's question.

"She thinks we're mates?" Anya snorted in amusement. "We must have been insufferable."

"What do you mean?"

"Think about it. If a snowtiger could tell we loved one another, imagine how sickeningly sweet it must have been for everyone else." Anya smiled. "All 'darling' this and 'dearling' that."

"We weren't that bad." He hoped not, anyway.

"I think we were. I mean, Brilliance isn't exactly the most empathetic of creatures, and even she noticed."

Cinder pursed his mouth, contemplating Anya's explanation and ultimately finding himself forced to agree. Still, he struggled imagining that the two of them had really behaved in such a treacly manner.

Whatever other considerations he might have had ended when a yakshin confronted them on the path leading to the Shriven Grove.

Cinder smiled on seeing her. *Sadana.* She was the leader of the tree maidens, the tallest and oldest of them, with thin, mossy hair and crevasses in her bark-like skin that were infiltrated by white mold. Cinder's smile faded when he noticed that Sadana's long, pitted face held a frown rather than a welcoming expression. He might have worried, but he recalled her playing a similar prank the last time he and Anya had traveled to Shalla Valley.

"Mother Ashoka said friends were coming," Sadana said, "but nut and root if I know the two of you."

Cinder drew Painter to a halt, frowning. "You don't know us?"

"Rabisu's weave," Anya reminded him.

Cinder's frown became a glower. He'd forgotten. In order to protect themselves from Shet, they had bargained with the Rakshasa of Dissolution to create a weave to make him and Anya difficult to recognize by the false god. The braid worked, but it also made it difficult for friends and possibly even family to identify them. But then how had Fastness and Brilliance managed it?

Anya eased Barton forward. "I am Anya Aruyen," she announced. "Princess of Yaksha Sithe. Do you remember me?"

Sadana tilted her head. "Anya Aruyen." Bewilderment was evident on her face, but after a few seconds of study, awareness took its place. "I can see it." The yakshin's eyes shifted. "And you are Cinder Shade."

"It's good to see you again," Cinder said, relieved by the yakshin's recognition.

"You have a story to tell, yes?" Sadana said. "It would be best if it was done with all my sisters present. Come. I will lead you." She knelt, pressing a palm to the soft grass. A green glow slowly built in her arm, the color of fresh growth and spring. It enveloped the yakshin, and a sound, rustling like ivy, whispered from her—a braid of Earth, then. The glow brightened, forming root-like threads all around Sadana before emptying out of her in a rush. The color fled into the ground, spreading outward, raising the sturdy turf before flashing beyond Cinder's vision.

"There," Sadana said. "Those yakshins not at the grove and all the holders know of you now. You will not be accosted." She stood then, and without another word, strode off, clearly expecting them to follow.

Cinder shared an uncertain look with Anya. Although Sadana's distrust was gone, her doubt remained. It made him worry over the holders. How would they react? Cinder continued to stare after the tree maiden before eventually shaking off his concerns. They'd find out what they faced once they reached the grove.

He and Anya paced after Sadana, and the three of them headed north, away from the lake and toward a set of low-lying hills. Hours later, their path eventually wound its way toward a copse of Ashoka trees, the size of which became clearer the closer they approached.

Cinder idly wondered at the name, its odd familiarity, even as he studied the Grove. *Ashoka trees.* Each one was massive, hundreds of feet in height and of similar breadth, and an acre of land lay shaded beneath their broad limbs. However, it was the one in the center that stole his breath. She was half again as tall and wide as the others, and her names were many: Mahamatha, Mother Ashoka, and Aranya. From her arose a calm watchfulness, a tranquility that set aside some of Cinder's burdens.

He breathed easier, knowing that whatever was to happen would happen, and he would be fine with it. He trusted the mother of the Ashokas like he did no one else except Anya.

Cinder and Anya arrived at the Grove, where they were greeted by a circle of yakshins who stood near Mahamatha. But where were the holders? They should have been here to protect their wards. Cinder glanced about, searching for them.

"It is good to see you again," said Sepia, one of the yakshins.

She was the tree maiden who had saved Cinder during his Secondary Trial, and although his memories from that time were hazy, he recalled her. Sepia was taller than most of her sisters but otherwise shared similar features with the rest of them. Her eyes had the appearance of hazelnuts and her skin, the texture of bark. However, in Sepia's case, she also had a circlet consisting of a living vine that extended from her forehead and wrapped about to keep her mossy-gray hair off her face.

"It is good to see you as well," Cinder said, dismounting from Painter. "It's even better that you know us."

"Of course I know you. Sadana mentioned your presence." Sepia leaned down to view him more closely. "You don't require another Aushadha fruit, do you?"

Cinder smiled. "I don't think so, but if you're offering…"

Sepia chuckled in response.

"Maynalor," said another yakshin.

Cinder faced her, recognizing Turquoise, the tree maiden who had labeled him Maynalor—someone of interest with a secret. Or at least that was the translation from old *Shevasra*, the language spoken by Shokan and Sira. Turquoise had given him the name just prior to the start of his training at *Steel-Graced Adepts*, during a time when Cinder had been wandering the streets of Swift Sword and encountered the yakshin.

It seemed a lifetime ago, well before the passed-along memories from Shokan, but not so distant when measured in years. And while at the time he hadn't known what secret she had meant—neither had she—he did now.

"Turquoise," Cinder said, smiling as he addressed the yakshin. "How have you been?"

"Better than you, it seems," Turquoise said. "When Sadana mentioned she hardly recognized you, I thought she was exaggerating." Her eyes fell on Anya. "But it seems she wasn't. I hardly recognize either of you."

Anya cleared her throat. "We've had an interesting couple of years since we last saw you."

"And on that note," Sadana cut in. "It's time you tell us just what those interesting years entailed."

Cinder ordered his thoughts before speaking. There was so much to summarize. After a moment of deliberation, he spoke about what they had done and seen. He described the journey to Mahadev, the truths he and Anya had discovered—that they *weren't* legendary heroes reborn.

"We both really thought the memories were ours," Anya said. "Not just those given to us by Shokan and Sira."

"Is that so?" Sadana asked.

Cinder nodded. "Shokan and Sira gave us more than just their memories. They also gave us their skills and Talents." He spoke on, telling about Manifold Fulsom, Heremisth, Rabisu, and Zahhack.

Sadana hissed. "The Son of Emptiness seeks entrance into Seminal?"

"You know Him?" Cinder asked, his tone sharp. No one else had ever heard of Zahhack. They only knew that the word referenced Shet's minions.

"We know *of* Him," Sadana said. "Mahamatha taught us about Him once. She taught us to fear Him."

Anya picked up the explanation, describing the weave Rabisu had placed upon her and Cinder, and the task they had chosen to undertake: the destruction of the Orbs of Peace. When she finished, the yakshins were silent and troubled.

"You bring grave news," Sadana said.

"But they also bring hope," Sepia countered. "We wondered why those seven wraiths weren't moving off from the entrance to Shalla Valley. Now we know, and even better, they have a chance at redemption." She breathed out as if in delight. "What greater hope and holiness can there be than the redemption of the fallen?"

She was right. Fastness' task *was* holy, and Cinder wished he could do more to help or at least do something similar. Something akin to creation rather than destruction.

But Cinder had a different duty—at least for now. His was focused on defending those who couldn't defend themselves, people such as the yakshins, which made the absence of the holders more disturbing. Where were they? "I would have expected the holders to be guarding against the wraiths," Cinder said. His last time here, the holders had never left their charges alone like this.

"We will speak on it later," Sadana said. "You have come to us on a day of sorrow." She gestured to a bundle lying at her feet. It was wrapped in a binding of what might have been hardened soil.

"A seeding," Anya said. "What happened?"

"Holifer, one of our sisters, died a week ago," Sadana said. "Her shraddha is tonight."

Cinder stared at the seeding in fascination. Sepia had housed him in something similar when he'd been injured by the wraiths. "Isn't the ceremony supposed to be for loved ones only?" Again, he thought of the holders.

"Family alone is meant for the shraddha," Sepia answered.

"We aren't family," Anya said, echoing Cinder's thoughts.

"Your presence is a direct request from Mahamatha," Sadana told them.

Why would Mother Ashoka want them present? Cinder shared a perplexed expression with Anya, but she seemed to know just as little as him. "Did she say why she wanted us here?" he asked.

Sadana shook her head. "No. But after the ceremony, I will tell you what you need to know."

"And this is?" Anya asked.

"You will learn," Sadana said. "For now, let us lay our sister to rest." She and the rest of the tree maidens formed an arc around Holifer's seeding, leaving an opening in their line through which the distant lake could be spied. The ceremony began, and it was one that was oddly familiar to Cinder.

"Twilight," Sadana intoned. "It is the most auspicious time to send forth our beloved Holifer to Devesh's loving embrace. May Shokan, Sira, and Mahamatha guide her steps."

The yakshins began singing, low and melodic, and while Shokan's memories told Cinder the words of the song, he didn't know what all of them meant. Nevertheless, they felt right, honoring the legacy of a loved one and the life they had lived.

Cinder began to sing, and so did Anya, her voice fitting in with his, or maybe it was the other way around.

The song ended, and the tree maidens now hummed, and starting with Sadana, each one slowly approached their fallen sister. They walked a full circle around Holifer before depositing a handful of soil on her. Once each yakshin had made their offering, Sadana gestured for Cinder and Anya to do so as well.

Together, they bent, gathering soil and doing the same as the yakshins. Afterward, they stepped back and waited for what was to come.

"Holifer!" Sadana shouted. "Never forgotten! Forever ascending!"

"Holifer!" the yakshins cried out, Cinder and Anya a beat behind.

"Never forgotten! Forever ascending!" The shouts echoed across the plains of the savanna, fading away to a silence that ended when the yakshins dispersed in a murmuring of conversation.

Cinder watched them leave, still unsure why he and Anya had been included in the ceremony.

"Let me show you what you need to know," Sadana said. She indicated for them to follow her as she strode off into the farther depths of the Shriven Grove.

Sadana led them deeper through the grove, past Mahamatha's towering bulk. For a moment, Cinder wanted to touch the great tree's rough bark and commune with her. He'd only spoken to Mother Ashoka once, but that one meeting had left an impression. Her tranquility and peace had left a longing in his heart, and he wished there might come a time when he could fully embrace such a life.

It seemed unlikely, at least in this world, given the task set in front of him and Anya.

"You already knew about the wraiths," Anya said to Sadana.

The yakshin glanced back. "Yes. All of us did, but having you confirm what Mahamatha told us was a balm."

"You doubted her?" Anya asked, sounding as surprised as Cinder felt.

"No, but it is always good to hear confirmation from those we trust."

Cinder stared at the tree maiden, confused again. Since when had he and Anya become so trustworthy to the yakshins?

He didn't bother asking, knowing he'd likely not get a definitive answer, and their conversation fell off. They exited the Shriven Grove, and Cinder drifted back to walk next to Anya. He wanted to discuss everything they'd heard and encountered since meeting Sadana, but it would have to wait until they were alone.

Instead, they paced after Sadana, leading their mounts as they marched into the savanna, headed east to a line of forested hills. The sun settled beyond the horizon, washing the sky in deep oranges and reds. Night slowly crept across the heavens, revealing Dormant and Manifold, each moon emanating a lovely, soft light onto the savanna. Near at hand, insects droned, but farther away, a clan of hyenas cackled. A warm breeze swirled now and then, rippling across the grasslands and setting trees to rustling in a gentle whispering of sound.

Hours they journeyed, well past sunset, their path illuminated by the *diptha* lantern Sadana held aloft. Under the lamp's yards-wide golden glow, they marched toward the tree-shrouded hills beyond the grove, eventually reaching a game trail where they entered a world of gloom as the forest canopy hid the light of the moons. The breeze died there, too, and the air became heavy and unmoving, thick with the smell of loam. Small animals chittered in counterpoint to the croaking of bullfrogs from a nearby pond.

Their journey finally ended when they reached a wildflower meadow where Dormant and Manifold lit the clearing in soft loveliness. But there was no sound. It was as if the world had gone mute. A floral scent filled the air while an erratic breeze bent the tall grasses and low-lying flowers.

But Cinder's eyes were locked on the large doorway in the shape of a tree nut of some kind. It stood centered within the meadow, and upon seeing it, excitement filled him. Fastness had mentioned Twilight Gate—this one—and it would vastly shorten their journey to Revelant.

He continued studying the Gate, which might have been made of a dark granite or bark, but Cinder knew neither was the case. It was made of something else with symbols or runes carved into its surface. He inwardly frowned. He could almost read them…

"This is what I brought you to see," Sadana said, interrupting Cinder's thoughts. "You can reach Revelant from here if you know how to utilize Twilight Gate."

"We know how to use it," Anya said.

"Excellent," Sadana said. "And what of Verity Foe? Do you know how to activate it?"

"If it's like the other Foes, then yes," Cinder replied.

Sadana nodded. "Good. Then know that Verity Foe's name is eponymous. Enter it if you so choose, but for now, I will be leaving you."

"Wait!" Cinder called out. "Can you take care of Cigarello? He's earned a rest."

Sadana glanced at the old gelding, smiling slightly. "Of course." She gathered Cigarello's reins. "Come along, young man," she said to the gelding, and without another word, she departed the clearing.

Cinder watched as the yakshin disappeared into the forest. Once she was no longer visible, he faced Anya. "We have a lot to discuss."

"Yes, we do," Anya agreed. "My biggest question is why they included us in that shraddha ceremony? Amongst elves, only family are supposed to be present. They didn't even invite the holders."

Cinder didn't know what to say, and in fact, he'd been hoping Anya might have some inkling of what was going on. "Maybe the yakshins do things differently?" he suggested. "But what's got me more puzzled is that Mother Ashoka already told them about the wraiths, but they needed our word of confirmation?"

A line furrowed Anya's brow. "It doesn't make any sense."

They fell quiet until Cinder sighed. "I wish we could have spoken to her again."

"Mahamatha? So do I."

"And then there's the Foe. Should we even bother with it? Can it teach us anything useful?"

"I don't know," Anya replied with a shrug. "Right now, I want to take care of the Orb of Moss in Revelant. We can worry about Verity Foe after."

"We'll want to contact Master Absin," Cinder said. He figured if there was anyone at the Directorate they could trust, it would be his old arms master. Either him or Master Molni.

"Why not General Arwan?" Anya asked. "I doubt he'd turn us over to my mother."

Cinder didn't know the Directorate's commandant, a high-ranking officer in the Imperial Army. "You're that certain? That he won't send word to your mother?"

"I'm that certain. He trained me. We're close. He won't turn us in."

Cinder wished he could feel so sure, but in the end, he had to trust Anya's judgment. "The fewer people who know about us, the better."

"Agreed," Anya said. "You ready to go?"

"Now?" It was already well into the depths of the night.

Anya quirked a challenging eyebrow. "When did you think we should go? During the day when everyone can see us?"

Cinder chuckled ruefully, indicating for her to go first. "After you."

Anya stared at him in surprise.

"What?" he asked.

She shook her head. "You just have this way about you. Of living in the moment and accepting the future. No reservations."

Cinder smiled wryly. "I have plenty of reservations."

"Not like me. I worry."

Cinder squeezed her hand. "You worry for both of us. We work well together because of that. Go ahead and activate the gate."

Anya stared at him an instant longer, gave him a small smile, squeezing his hand in return before pacing forward to activate Twilight Gate.

5

Anya paused for a moment, staring at Twilight Gate. In just a few seconds, she'd be back home, back at the Third Directorate, the military academy that had defined her as a person. Without the instructors and her self-imposed pressure to live up to the school's motto, *mastha par iti krathe lomon pa*—to cultivate perfection and vanquish foes—she wouldn't have become the woman she was today. She was a warrior because of what she'd learned at the academy; a defender of her people through the skills gained at the Directorate, and the person she'd always seen herself to be.

Why then did it sometimes feel like she'd spent so much of her time chasing a ghost? Like she'd needed to become an uncompromising warrior in order to live up to a memory of someone even better?

Her glance fell on Cinder, who patiently waited by the horses.

Maybe the memories endowed to her by Sira had something to do with it. In those recollections, the Lady of Fire had fought alongside Shokan, defending him whenever he so often charged the enemy. In order to protect her husband, Sira had been forced to forge out all weaknesses, and Anya had unwittingly done the same.

The price, though… Anya wasn't a proper elven maiden. She was too tall, too powerfully built, and she'd never taken a lover. Again, her glance fell on Cinder. *Not true.* Nonetheless, amongst her people, that last alone would have named her an oddity, but add in her status as a warrior, and she was all-but an Outcaste. Some might even label her a *ghrina* or a *naaja*.

She paused her deliberations, frowning. No, she wasn't an Outcaste to her people, and she certainly wasn't a *ghrina* or a *naaja*. She was a princess of Yaksha Sithe, respected—and feared—in spite of her oddities.

From where had those bizarre notions arisen? Anya continued to frown, trying to tease out the source.

"Anya."

She started, flushing in mild embarrassment as Cinder broke into her thoughts. "I know."

Pausing only a moment longer, Anya recalled the set of sequences, of pressed runes and *lorethasra*, that would connect Twilight Gate to the one at the Directorate, Misery Gate. She prepared herself, distantly perceiving Cinder keeping their mounts calm, soothing Painter and Barton.

A breath to steady her nerves, and she sourced her *lorethasra*, letting the silver stream flow, reaching for it, starting with a single thread of Earth. A rustling sound like ivy swept across the clearing, and what appeared to be glowing roots spread across Twilight's bark-like surface, bleeding into the Gate's interior. The growths solidified, flashing green before disintegrating, flaking away like ash and exposing an aqua-reflective surface. In connecting Twilight to Misery, she had created a type of anchor line.

Moving to stand next to her, Cinder viewed the aqua material, examining it. "It's different than Misery and Salutation."

"So it is," Anya agreed. But the difference didn't strike her as important. "Ready?"

Cinder's eyes remained locked on the Gate's surface, and in the end, he nodded, leading the line of horses and pack mules forward. He passed Barton off to Anya before stepping without hesitation toward Twilight Gate, clearly meaning to go first.

Anya wrinkled her nose in distaste. Cinder had sourced his *lorethasra* and conducted *Jivatma*, and it was the former that caused her antipathy. How could such a graceful, handsome man have a *lorethasra* with such a disgusting scent?

She set the question aside. Now wasn't the time to ponder life's peculiarities. "Expecting trouble?" she asked Cinder.

He shrugged. "We have no idea what we'll be facing at the Third Directorate. It's an important part of Yaksha Sithe. Who knows if the empress has decided to have Misery guarded against what we're attempting?"

Anya grunted. It was a good point. "In that case, let me go first. I'm still a princess. I can scout the situation and let you know if it's safe."

Based on the scowl on his face, Cinder clearly didn't like that idea, but he nodded agreement anyway.

"Wish me luck," Anya said, flashing a wavering smile. An unexpected mix of fearful longing and nervousness fluttered inside her stomach like a flock of butterflies.

"You don't need luck," Cinder replied. "You're Anya Aruyen. You make your own luck."

She stared at him, surprised by his words. He wasn't sweet, but sometimes he said the sweetest things. A moment longer she gazed at him before offering a shallow nod of thanks and entering Twilight Gate.

A single, slow step with Barton trailing after her, and immediately a feeling of movement encompassed her, a sensation of twisting and turning. The roar of an avalanche filled her ears, and freezing cold nearly stole the life from her marrow. She exited, stumbling, nausea cramping her stomach. She needed a moment to gain her bearings before she could scan for danger.

Anya stood in a familiar basement, one tucked beneath Firemirror Hall. It was a dirt-covered room, rough-hewn and rectangular, yards across and even more in length. Dimly lit *diptha* lamps provided bare illumination, and behind her rose a circular doorway made of black stone. *Misery Gate.* It was currently filled with what might have been quicksilver or glistening water, and Anya knew that branching behind it was a small, unlit room, little more than an undecorated alcove.

For her needs, though, the empty basement was all that mattered. It was perfect.

She stepped back through Misery Gate, to where Cinder stood waiting. Once again came the freezing cold, and upon her exit, there was the nausea.

"It's empty?" Cinder asked.

Anya managed a stiff nod, even as she hunched over at the knees, seeking to steady her roiling stomach.

"Stay here until you're ready to go back," Cinder said. "Barton's alone. I don't want him neighing or letting anyone know he's there."

Anya could only watch as Cinder led Painter and the rest of their animals through Twilight Gate, and it was only after the last of them had disappeared that she felt well enough to follow. She faced the glowing aqua material filling Twilight Gate and inhaled deeply. A steadying breath, and she stepped forward.

It was her third time traveling through the Gate in the past few minutes, and Anya wished familiarity would breed resistance to the journey's difficulties. Sadly, such wasn't the case. She exited into Firemirror Hall, every bit as miserable as the first instance through.

"How are you feeling?" Cinder asked. He'd already closed the Gate, and he kneeled next to her, peering in concern.

Anya remained hunched over, collecting herself, and while doing so, she wondered about her relationship with Cinder, all the twists and turns it had taken. It had changed again. This time it was a tenuous, slowly deepening friendship built amidst the scattered untruths left by Rabisu. What might it become by the time the last of the Orbs was destroyed?

She looked forward to finding out.

A final shuddering breath, and Anya straightened. A vagrant thought had her smiling. "At least this time you didn't go first."

Cinder's brow creased in confusion. "What do you mean? Why wouldn't I go first?"

"Because whenever we're facing danger, you either place yourself in front of me or you face it first."

"Is that a problem?" He still seemed confused.

Anya hadn't started out irritated, but Cinder's lack of understanding had her annoyed. "It's like when we faced the dromas. You tried to protect me when I didn't need it. I can help us do what's needed."

"I never thought you couldn't," Cinder said. He might have wanted to say more, but in the end, he kept silent.

Nevertheless, in that strange way they still had, Anya sensed what Cinder was feeling. No matter what she had just said, Cinder wouldn't step aside and let Anya face any danger first. It wasn't because he didn't think her capable but because…

Anya shied away from where her guesses seemed to be taking her. In that direction lay unnecessary torment.

A silence settled over the basement under Firemirror Hall, and Cinder recognized the underlying reason. It was because of what he had left unspoken. Anya had noticed and understood, and oddly enough, he noticed and understood as well.

"We should leave the mounts and find Master Absin," Cinder said, breaking the quiet. "I know you trust General Arwan, but I want to see Master Absin first. If anyone can sneak us out of the Directorate, it would be him." He stared toward the ceiling, recalling all the time spent in the places above, of how it reminded him of the fellowship of his brother cadets. He missed them terribly.

"Are you afraid?" Anya asked, mistaking his quiet for a different emotion.

Cinder offered her a faint smile. "The wise warrior controls his emotions. His passions are bound to his needs."

"Shokan said that. And you didn't answer my question."

This time, it was Cinder who grew aggravated. Why couldn't Anya just let a matter lie? Why did she have to question everything? The angry words were on the tip of his tongue, but Cinder didn't let them escape. Instead, he took a cleansing breath. Another. Only after the annoyance was gone did he feel comfortable in answering. "I'm not afraid. I was just thinking about the other cadets. I miss them."

Anya's lips pursed into a tight-lipped expression of sympathy. "I know." She reached out, briefly clasping his hand in support. "I'm sorry."

Cinder clasped back, glad for Anya's caring, and the last of his annoyance fled. Somewhere during their months of journeying, the two of them had achieved a fragile friendship.

Most likely it was because Cinder simply liked Anya. He liked her nearly as much as he did before Mahadev. And while elven women weren't supposed to allow the touch of any men other than of their own kind, Anya continually broke that commandment. The two of them regularly touched one another, nothing beyond holding hands, but even that should have been anathema to her.

It wasn't, and Cinder doubted Anya much cared.

"Cinder."

He realized he was still staring at her, and they were still holding hands. "Let's go see Master Absin."

Anya, smiling slightly, tugged him back. "Let me go first."

Cinder chuckled, gesturing for her to lead them.

Minutes later, after seeing to the horses and pack mules, they departed Firemirror Hall's basement.

"We'll want to Blend as deeply as possible," Anya advised. "None of the elves at Fort Carnate noticed your Blend."

Cinder nodded in agreement. "We'll still want to be careful."

She flicked him another smile. "Of course."

A moment for them to Blend and Link, and Anya led them out of the basement, ascending a set of stairs with Cinder trailing a few paces behind. He left her enough room to fight or flee if needed, all the while smiling to himself. Yaksha's empress also required that anyone accompanying her in a formal setting was to maintain a distance of two paces back. He and Anya had once joked about it, and here he was doing exactly that.

His vagrant ruminations cut off when they reached the top of the stairs. Anya edged open the door, peering both ways. Apparently satisfied, she eased into a darkened hallway, pausing as she held up a hand, halting Cinder.

He waited until she signaled for him to join her. Once she gave the motion, he edged out, quietly closing the basement door and following. She led them creeping along dimly lit hallways with *diptha* lamps turned down for the night. No one else was about, and the soft silence of night's rest held sway. They ascended more stairs, and the musty smell of the lower levels gave way to that of the fresh-cut flowers in large vases, the lingering aroma from the evening's supper, and the warmth of wood-burning fires in someone's hearth.

The latter was something Cinder could appreciate. It was rarely cold in Yaksha proper, but there was a comfort to a crackling fire.

On they went, maintaining silence, moving into the more residential portions of Firemirror Hall, where the flooring transitioned to long rugs that softened the dark wood and further quieted their footsteps. Paneling replaced bare stone and brick, and paintings and murals decorated the walls.

They passed by a broad window, and through their gauzy reflections, a familiar view could be seen. The Cauldron—where low-lying rings of stacked stones were set amidst close-cropped grass that marked out sparring circles. This was the place where Cinder had been tempered and forged into a finer warrior than he could have ever imagined.

There was no time to reminisce, though, and Anya led them on. Thus far, they'd encountered no one, which was a minor miracle. However, at a crossway, Anya paused, peeking around a corner. She pulled back, holding up a hand, indicating the presence of someone else. Despite their Blends, neither of them wanted to take the chance of being noticed. Again, Anya peeked around the corner, darting over to the other side.

Cinder checked both directions before hustling after her. He recognized this part of Firemirror Hall. They were nearing their destination: Master Absin's quarters.

As they stole along the last few yards, he wondered if he might see anyone else at the Third Directorate. Despite his terrible memories of his time here, he recalled Master Molni, the librarian, whom he counted as a friend.

Cinder nearly halted then, frowning. How could he have been friends with Master Molni when his memories—vague though they were—insisted he'd been brutalized in this school? The same could be asked about his relationship with Master Absin or even the earlier warmth and fellowship he'd felt when thinking about his fellow cadets.

He found Anya eyeing him in concern.

"Later," he whispered. But ringing in his thoughts was the statement Anya had made a few days back: *"I don't think our memories are reliable."*

So did he. Constantly.

Moments later, they reached Master Absin's office and quarters, discovering a light bleeding out from under the doorway. *Excellent.* The swordmaster was still awake. Anya knocked, a single rap. A muffled voice ordered them to enter, and they did so. Both of them flitted into the room and swiftly shut the door. They dropped their Blends.

Cinder glanced about.

Master Absin's office was unchanged from the few other times Cinder had been here. A simple desk and a pair of bookshelves filled out the square space. A low-lit *diptha* lamp provided illumination, and the only decoration was a painting on a wall of Empress Sala. A familiar switch, one that Master Absin regularly rapped against his thigh when giving out instructions, rested in a corner.

All of this Cinder noted, but the majority of his attention was centered on the man himself. *Master Absin Morewe.* He was several centuries old, and it showed in his weathered appearance and white hair. However, in spite of his age, he remained a surpassingly skilled warrior, one of a dozen or so living Yaksha elves who bore the title of *"Sai,"* an ancient honorific from Shokan's time.

Currently Master Absin had his feet propped on his desk, reading a book. He glanced up, eyes narrowing and brow furrowed. The old elf wore the puzzled expression of a person who had come upon someone familiar but couldn't recognize them. But recognition or not, Master Absin wasn't one to take any chances. His feet left the desk, and he stood. The scent of wet stone, his *lorethasra*, became evident. "Can I help you?"

"I hope so," Anya said. Blended or not, she had cowled her face during the short trek through Firemirror Hall. But she dropped the hood now. "Do you recognize me?"

Master Absin's face retained its expression of uncertainty. His hand went to the sword on his desk, distrust obvious. "No." His eyes flicked to Cinder, who had also dropped his cowl. "Neither of you, which isn't to your benefit. Who are you?"

Anya sighed, a mix of relief and irritation, and Cinder recognized why. Master Absin couldn't immediately recognize them, which was good news since it also meant that her family likely wouldn't either. However, they also needed Master Absin's help, and that same lack of recognition was currently working against them.

"I am Anya Aruyen. Can you see it?"

Master Absin's *lorethasra* never faded, and his hand never left the hilt of his sword. But at least he hadn't drawn it. Instead, he stared at Anya, head tilted in that same expression of uncertain recognition. An instant later, his eyes widened in shocked awareness. "Anya," he breathed. "How are you here? Where have you been?"

Cinder knew dozens of questions were likely to flood out from Master Absin, but they didn't have time to answer them. It was better if they did so in one sitting, in the company of all the others whose help they might need here. "What about me?" he asked Master Absin. "Do you know who I am?"

Master Absin's gaze went to him, the mistrust gone, but the puzzlement still present. "I feel like I should."

"Cinder Shade."

Again, it took a few moments for recognition to cross Master Absin's face, and when it did, a warm smile bloomed. The smell of his *lorethasra* faded, and he stepped around his desk. "Cinder. My boy, it is good to see you."

There was an undeniable warmth and joy to his voice, and Cinder found himself being embraced by his old master. For a moment, shock kept Cinder's arms limp by his side, but once his mind started working again, he returned the hug from his old master. In addition, he realized that if he had ever needed any further proof that his memories about the Directorate were false, this was it—Master Absin's warm and heartfelt greeting. If he'd been the monster Cinder's recollections indicated, it would never have been the case.

Master Absin pulled back, addressing Cinder. "I expect you have much to tell."

Cinder glanced at Anya, who shrugged minutely, letting him explain. "We do, and we also need your help."

"And you will have it," Master Absin replied, no hesitation in his voice.

Absin listened in burgeoning astonishment at what Cinder and Anya needed: the Orb of Moss, one of Yaksha's most prized possessions. Why? What for? And why the strained formality between the two of them, especially on Anya's part? The last time he had seen Anya and Cinder, their genuine warmth for one another had been obvious. Now, they stood like friends too long apart, uncertain of one another.

He cut off his meandering thoughts, holding up a hand to halt Cinder's explanation. "I think you'll need more than just my help," he said. "Let me get some others, and we can decide together on how best to handle what you need."

"Whom else do you intend to bring?" Anya asked.

Absin eyed the princess. There was no doubting the challenge in her voice. He also didn't miss Cinder edging toward the door, sealing off his exit.

"Those of the *Lamarin Hosh*," Absin said in answer to Anya's question. He was taking a risk here. The society to which he had long been pledged had survived the past three millennia through strict secrecy. Exposing them to Cinder and Anya—even if they were whom he and the rest of the *Lamarin Hosh* hoped they might be—could be a mistake. But he also knew these two. He'd trained them, and if he and the *Lamarin Hosh* couldn't trust Cinder and Anya, then the world was probably doomed anyway.

"The *Lamarin Hosh*?" Anya's lips were pursed. "Meaning the Saviors of Hope in old *Shevasra*. Who or what is that?"

"They are friends," Absin said, going on to tell them about the nature of the society. "Your brother is a member."

Anya's brows raised in surprise. "Estin?"

"Estin," Absin confirmed. "A few months ago, we actually got word that the two of you had survived Mahadev, and he wanted to go straight to Rakesh to find you." He grinned. "Thankfully, he's not so stupid as to do something like that anymore."

Anya chuckled, but Cinder seemed irritated, angry even.

Absin sighed to himself. He had hoped Cinder's antipathy toward Estin would have resolved by now. They'd seemingly gotten along better towards the end of their second year at the Directorate. In fact, at the end of their Secondary Trials, it had been Estin who had helped free Cinder from his imprisonment at Fort Carnate. By doing so, the prince had gone against the express will of his mother, although only Absin knew that particular detail.

Nevertheless, to learn that Cinder still harbored resentment toward Estin, even after the prince's attempt at reconciliation… well, to say it was disappointing was an understatement. It was behavior unworthy of the person Absin believed Cinder to be.

"The *Lamarin Hosh*," Anya said, drawing Absin's attention back to the conversation at hand. "They are your friends, but are they ours?"

Absin smiled. "They can be your friends as well. You can trust them."

Cinder grunted, the displeasure on his face receding some. "How quickly can you gather whomever you need?" he asked, stepping away from the door.

"A half hour at the most," Absin replied.

"Meet us at Misery Gate," Cinder ordered. "We left our animals in the basement." He quirked a grin. "Wouldn't do for them to grow restless and make their presence known."

Absin nodded, not missing the way Cinder automatically expected to be obeyed. He'd changed. There was a time when the boy—no, he was a man now—would have never dared speak to him in such a fashion.

"I'll be quick," Absin promised.

"Thank you for this," Anya said.

Frowning, Absin gazed at her. Why would a princess of the sithe need to thank him for anything? He mentally shrugged. "I'll meet you at Misery Gate." He left his office then, striding down the hall and planning on whom to bring to the meeting. He only hoped Cinder and Anya wouldn't have any trouble getting back to Firemirror's basement.

6

Seconds after Master Absin's departure, Cinder was trailing Anya—both of them Blended and Linked as they quickly made their way back toward Misery Gate. While striding through the classroom section of Firemirror Hall, Cinder glanced through a window and slowed when he caught sight of Krathe House, his home at the Directorate.

He halted as remembrances spilled across his mind in a warm rush. To say he had been intimidated upon arriving at the school would have been an understatement. There had been a third year to show him and the other Firsters around. Cor Garwing had been his name, and at the time, he'd seemed so composed and strong.

Still, Cinder had taken courage from the third year, vowing to become like him during his time at the academy. And then there were his brother cadets. Cinder blinked, recollecting sharing laughter with them: Nathaz, who could always make him smile; Sriovey, who hated those fucking romantic songs; Bones, cocky as a rooster and able to back it up; Depth, who was soft-spoken but tough as nails; and Ishmay, who hated to study almost as much as he hated losing. Cinder smiled in reminiscence. He missed them. Even missed playing music with Riyne, who was skilled on the fiddle, or teaching Mohal the finer points of euchre, which his fellow cadet never could quite grasp.

Cinder's smile went faint, thinking about how unlikely their bonding should have been. Especially friendship with an elf. And yet it had happened, and it had been real, no matter what aspects of his memories tried to claim. Almost against his volition, he whispered the academy's motto. "*Mastha par iti krathe lomon pa.*"

Anya tugged him along, getting them going again even as she translated the phrase from *Shevasra.* "To cultivate perfection and vanquish foes," she said, a smile tugging at the corner of her lips. "I also like Yaksha's maxim: *Porash nazah loni, telemarr rul.*"

"If you want peace, prepare for war." It was a wise aphorism.

They fell silent after that and continued on to Firemirror Hall, encountering a few early risers. However, with their Blends in place, no one actually noticed their presence, and they reached their destination without any difficulty. In the welcome darkness of the basement, the horses and pack mules whickered softly when they dropped their Blends.

Then it was just a matter of waiting for the others.

The first to arrive was Master Molni, the head librarian. Even older than Master Absin, he had a stooped posture, skin with the wrinkled-thin aspect of fine paper, and shock-white hair. He shuffled down the stairs, viewing Cinder and Anya in unsurety. But once he recognized them, a welcoming smile creased his seamed face.

"I assume I won't find any books slipped down your trousers," he said to Cinder.

It was an old joke, and Cinder laughed, moving forward to embrace Master Molni. "It's good to see you."

"You as well, my boy," Master Molni said, going on to greet Anya. He bowed low. "Your Highness."

"None of that," Anya said, drawing the librarian to stand straight.

They spoke then about the Third Directorate and their shared experiences. Minutes later, their conversation was interrupted when Master Absin returned. Accompanying him were General Arwan, the commandant of the Third Directorate, and Lieutenant Capshin, the commander's aide-de-camp. The general was in his late three hundreds, older for an elf but not ancient, and his blond hair was merely streaked. As for Lieutenant Capshin, he was still relatively young, black-haired and fighting-fit. All three officers wore the uniform of the Third Directorate: a gray shirt with a pin depicting a silver eagle clutching a sword—the Directorate's symbol—attached to their left chests and dark blue slacks slipped over black boots.

Cinder stirred in discomfort on seeing everyone present. "There sure seems to be a lot of people for what should be a secret meeting."

"You need to know some things first," General Arwan said.

"And everyone here already knows it?" Anya asked, the very question on Cinder's mind.

"They do," General Arwan confirmed.

"We should be quick," said Lieutenant Capshin. "If anyone saw us coming here, they're bound to gossip. And gossip might lead back to Ruom Shale and Master Nuhlin."

Cinder recalled the men. Ruom Shale was a slim elf with red hair and a prim and proper way of speaking and even moving. He had also served as a guide, bringing Cinder, Bones, Depth, and Wark to the Third Directorate when they'd been rising Firsters. As for Master Nuhlin, he was of middle years with black hair and a distracted manner. He was also a genius with a fund of knowledge in many fields, including art, music, poetry, history, theology, and war. Cinder was disappointed at having to avoid him. He liked Master Nuhlin.

"They're loyal to the empress?" Anya asked.

"Intensely so," Master Absin answered. "They'll almost certainly let the empress know you were here." He jutted his chin to Cinder. "Especially him."

"And to whom are you loyal?" Anya asked the room at large.

"Yaksha first, and the world, second," Master Molni answered. "Everything else comes third."

"We all feel that way," General Arwan confirmed.

Someone was missing, and only now did Cinder realize it. "Where's

Estin?" He tried not to growl out the name. His dislike toward Anya's brother had diminished over the years, but it hadn't entirely faded. He also wondered if some of what he felt might be connected to the irrational anger he and Anya often experienced.

"He's readying the horses you'll need," Master Absin said. "He'll be joining you."

Cinder viewed the men gathered here through narrowed eyes. There was something else going on, and it likely had to do with this *Lamarin Hosh* that Master Absin had briefly mentioned. He and Anya needed to know more about it. He addressed the question to Master Absin.

"We are devoted to Shokan and Sira," Master Absin said, going on to describe in greater detail this secret society of elven followers of the Blessed Ones. Apparently, the *Lamarin Hosh* had been around since just after the *NusraelShev*, spawned by a reciting from Quelchon Sarienne Cervine, the ancient forebear of the current duchess of Certitude, Marielle Cervine.

"And she's a member of the *Lamarin Hosh*, too?" Anya asked in surprise. "Same with Duchess Simone?"

General Arwan nodded. "Marielle is the one who recruited me."

"And you're all members?" Cinder needed their confirmation.

As one, they nodded.

Cinder exhaled heavily. Master Absin and Master Molni were friends, and he respected the other two elves. And all of them would be disappointed by what he had to tell them.

However, it was Anya who revealed the hard truth. "We aren't Sira and Shokan."

The announcement landed like a bucket of rocks. No one said a word. Instead, the four men of the *Lamarin Hosh* viewed one another in stunned disbelief.

"You aren't Shokan and Sira?" Master Absin asked, the first to recover from his shock.

"We have much to tell you," Cinder said, going on to describe what he and Anya had experienced since leaving the Third Directorate for his Secondary Trial. The explanation took a long time, and Anya filled in some of the details. But in the end, he told them nearly everything, only hedging when discussing Rabisu and the weaves the rakshasa had placed upon them.

When he was done, the room hushed until General Arwan cleared his throat. "That is quite a story," he said. "The Orbs of Peace. Shet. Surviving the Flatiron Desert." He sighed. "But even if you're not Shokan and Sira and only hold their memories, we'll help you. It seems you're our only hope." He addressed Lieutenant Capshin. "See to their horses. They'll need fresh mounts."

Anya disagreed. "We need a way to leave as quickly and quietly as possible. No one can see us. Not even for fresh mounts."

"Go through the library, then," Master Molni suggested. "It's empty and only a few hallways over from the basement. There's also a back-door exit."

It was an unexpected offer. Cinder knew how much Master Molni loved the books and scrolls stored in the library. That he was willing to allow horses and pack mules to walk amongst his treasures... Cinder viewed the librarian in surprise. "You know horses make messes, right?"

Master Molni grimaced. "Don't remind me."

"We still need to make sure Ruom and Nuhlin don't learn about us," Anya said.

Cinder had a notion on how to make that happen. He spoke to General Arwan. "Have Ruom, Nuhlin, and anyone else loyal to the empress meet you somewhere far away from the Directorate's exit. Gather everyone, actually. Have them in a place where they'll never even know we were here."

"They'll still be suspicious," Master Absin said.

Anya smiled. "But they won't know why they should be." She faced Cinder. "A sneaky plan." She nudged him with a shoulder. "I like it."

He nudged her back. "I'm smarter than you think."

"But not smarter than you look."

Cinder made a noise, inhaling sharply as if he'd been mortally wounded by her words, earning him a laugh.

General Arwan cleared his throat again. "I'll see it done. We'll pass the word to Estin, too. Let him know to saddle up and meet you on Whileaway Path."

"Is there anything else you need?" Lieutenant Capshin asked.

Cinder nodded. "How good are you at forgery?"

"We need diplomatic papers for Bharat." Anya explained what they had in mind.

"It's not easy, but I can see it done," General Arwan said. "Down to the imperial seal and proper signature. We'll send the papers by pigeon to Revelant. They should be there before you arrive. Estin will know who to contact to retrieve them."

Cinder led Painter and the line of pack mules out of the library's rear entrance while directly ahead of them, Anya was already seated atop Barton.

"We need to be quick," she said as soon as he was mounted and had reached her side. Her words spoken, Anya urged Barton to a canter, and Cinder heeled Painter to follow.

Just a few hundred yards, and they would be gone with no one the wiser. Cinder had his cowl raised to hide his non-elven features, but he doubted anyone would be able to overlook his build. He had the brawn of a human rather than the slim elegance of an elf. Maybe they'd mistake his bulk for the leather armor he wore.

Better yet if no one actually paid him any attention or even saw him, which was why he was Blended as deep as possible. Plus, even now, the early morning assemblage called by General Arwan was gathering on the other side of Firemirror Hall. Hopefully, they'd stay there long enough for Cinder and Anya to exit the Directorate completely unnoticed.

The two of them skirted the edges of the academy, their way lit by *diptha* lanterns on tall posts. Soon they'd no longer need the illumination since dawn's first breath already graced the sky. Light spread across the heavens, brightening the world and banishing the night.

The front gates loomed ahead, and Cinder and Anya slowed their mounts to a walk, dropping their Blends. It was too difficult to hide themselves, their mounts, *and* the pack mules. On reaching the guards at the gate, Anya nodded to them, and they simply flicked their gazes over her, paying her no special mind. As bundled as she was in her cloak and robes, they likely overlooked her feminine lines and mistook her for a student or a warrior-in-training. They certainly didn't glance her way and see their missing princess. Even Cinder didn't warrant a second look.

Once they were through the gates, he breathed out in relief, sharing a triumphant smile with Anya. This was the easiest part of their Trial, but that didn't mean it had been easy.

"To Whileaway Path," Anya said.

Cinder nodded, glancing back at the Third Directorate, taking in the setting for what he realized might be the last time. The academy had been built at the base of a mountain pass, seemingly taking inspiration from its obdurate surroundings. Rugged buildings appeared to give no quarter to the soaring mountains, and the setting itself struck Cinder as a powerful place to train warriors worthy of the name.

"Where's Estin?" Anya asked, studying the area ahead of them.

Cinder turned away from the Directorate and examined the way ahead. He had expected her brother to be close at hand as well, but no one else was on the road with them. "General Arwan said he'd be waiting for us on Whileaway Path, but he didn't say where."

"True enough," Anya said. "So long as we don't have to look for him in Certitude. I want to take the long way around the city."

Cinder grunted agreement. Anya knew her home island and people better than he did. Let her lead.

They continued along Whileaway, and a mile later, they finally came across Estin. He sat astride Byerley, his black Yavana, and trailing after him were a couple of packhorses. When they came abreast of him, he tilted his head, curious but clearly not recognizing them. More proof that Rabisu's weave should work when they reached Revelant.

Anya dismounted, and Cinder did the same.

"It's me," she said, smiling broadly.

Estin's confusion cleared, and a broad grin took its place. He dismounted with a whoop, reaching for Anya and pulling her into a crushing hug. Cinder stood aside while they got reacquainted, doing his best to push down his dislike of the prince. There was too much bad blood for him to ever forgive Estin for all he'd done to him during his years at the Directorate.

Then again, how much of that was real? He already knew most of his bad memories—many of which at this point weren't actual memories but mere feelings—weren't true. What about his relationship with Estin? Might it have been warmer than his emotions were trying to tell him? While he wrestled with his thoughts, he realized it was unlikely the case. He had seen Masters Absin and Molni and felt nothing but friendship. Same with Mohal and Riyne, who evoked feelings of brotherhood.

But not Estin. With the prince there was no sense of warmth or kind thoughts, only irritation.

Finally, Anya and Estin finished their greetings and turned to him. Cinder took a calming breath, wanting to remain civil for Anya's sake. This was her brother, after all. However, he drew himself short when he noted the prince's sickly expression. Estin appeared nervous. Why?

"Blessed One," Estin began.

Cinder closed his eyes, sighing. So that was the reason for Estin's nervousness. The prince was a member of the *Lamarin Hosh*, all of whom were apparently devoted to Shokan and Sira. Estin was no different, although why he would feel such dedication to a pair of humans—a race toward which the prince's contempt knew no bounds—was beyond Cinder.

"I should never have treated you as I did," Estin was saying.

Cinder opened his eyes, finding the prince looking as if he was ready to kneel before him. "Stop," Cinder said before Estin could say another word. "We'll discuss this on the road. But first we need distance from the Directorate."

Estin bowed. "As you say, Blessed One."

His statement drew another disappointed sigh from Cinder. He didn't like being worshiped or whatever it was Estin was doing to him.

They mounted, and Anya drew Barton next to Painter. "I didn't have a chance to tell him yet," she whispered. "He's going to be so disappointed."

"He needs to know," Cinder growled.

"Know what?" Estin asked. Apparently, his habit of gossipmongering overwhelmed his devotion to Shokan and Sira.

"The truth," Cinder said, going on to explain what Anya was obviously uncomfortable in stating.

"You're not Shokan and Sira?" Estin asked, his tone flat. "You only have their memories and abilities?"

Cinder nodded.

Estin's response took him aback. He appeared relieved rather than crestfallen. "Thank Devesh. I thought I'd be forever cursed given how I used to treat you."

"Well, that is a relief," Cinder said, not bothering to hide his sarcasm. "Only those humans who are legendary heroes deserve to be treated with kindness and respect."

Estin flushed, surprising Cinder by not responding in anger. "I deserved that," he said. "But I've also grown." He went on to speak of those who had left the Directorate and formed a scouting unit they named the Shokans, including Mohal and Riyne.

When Cinder learned their purpose—to find him and Anya—it was his turn to flush. "We didn't mean for everyone to worry."

Estin shrugged. "My mother and father were certain Anya was dead. They were relieved when the Shokans confirmed that she was still alive."

"We aren't going to Revelant for a reunion," Anya said, breaking into their conversation.

"What?" Estin barked. "Why not?"

"There's more you need to know," Cinder said.

Estin listened as they told him about Zahhack and the Orbs of Peace, about needing Shet's help to destroy them. Thankfully, the prince didn't interrupt much, and once they were done explaining, he simply nodded his head.

"And the memories from Shokan and Sira confirm this?" Estin asked.

"They do," Anya answered.

"Then I'll help," the prince replied.

Cinder studied Estin. This wasn't the arrogant prince he had known, who may or may not have tortured him. This was someone risen in wisdom. An unexpected, if welcome, change. "Why do you trust us?" he asked. "I'm not actually Shokan."

"But you're the closest thing to Shokan," Estin replied.

It wasn't much of an answer. "You never even liked me, though."

Estin shrugged. "I still don't."

"The feeling is mutual."

"Boys," Anya chided.

"I only hope you have a plan on how to get into Taj Wada," Estin said. "Stealing the Orb won't be easy. It's in Mother's personal throne hall, the one where she receives visitors privately."

"As a matter of fact, we do," Anya said. "You'll bring us into the palace, and we'll be Blended, and if anyone notices us, we'll pretend to be your servants."

"How about the Blend itself?" Estin asked. "If anyone notices, it'll be a problem. No one's supposed to hold a Blend at Taj Wada."

"We'll say we're practicing our abilities," Anya said. "I was caught a few times doing exactly the same thing."

"And if that happens, I tell them you're my servants?" An anticipatory gleam lit Estin's eyes as he faced Cinder. "That sounds like a wonderful plan."

Cinder scowled. "She only said we'll *pretend* to be your servants. We won't actually be your servants."

Cinder reined Painter to a halt beside Anya, and together, they stared down at Revelant from a quiet lane overlooking the city. They had already passed through the eastern gate, and from there, she had led them on a roundabout fashion to this empty area. No other travelers were about.

"It's beautiful," Cinder whispered, feeling like he needed to speak in a hush in the face of such beauty. This was his first time seeing Revelant in all its glory. Always before, his view had been cut short or he'd been traveling in a carriage with blackened windows to prevent human eyes from witnessing elven beauty. It should have been a ridiculous conceit, but upon seeing Revelant, Cinder could understand the arrogance of the Yaksha elves.

He, Anya, and Estin had arrived just prior to sunset, and Revelant stood bathed in the light of the golden hour, a magnificent place where tall, stony hills embraced the glistening waters of the Sentient Sea like a protective hand. And upon those rocky prominences stood various houses and buildings, high-peaked and tiled in terra cotta or bright silver as they nestled amongst large thickets of conifers and tall shrubs.

Cinder eyed paths carved by wide boulevards of cobbled stone and bricks as they swept around natural barriers and circled Revelant. The view guided him farther inward to where he spied Taj Wada, which was composed of a plethora of structures set upon a cluster of lumpy hills. The buildings were massive, but they retained a grace, all of them bowing before the imperial palace, which gleamed white and reminded Cinder of Ardevesh and its many domes. And of course, the compound's spires and battlements all flew Yaksha's standard: a fiery crown on a field of red.

"Do you remember a lovelier city?" Anya asked, sounding wistful, as if she actually did remember such a place.

Cinder eyed her askance, not sure what she meant. This was her home. Surely, she couldn't believe there was any city lovelier than Revelant. He certainly couldn't imagine one.

Anya faced him from where she sat astride Barton, offering a wan smile. "Sira's memories. She lived in a city next to the sea, like Revelant but even more beautiful. It was built upon nine forested hills like a jewel in an emerald crown."

Her words sparked a faint recognition, but one Cinder couldn't fully capture. In the dim recesses of Shokan's memories, the Blessed One might have recalled a city amidst nine hills. But it wasn't as important as what Anya's words revealed. There was something to them—not a lie, but an omission—and Cinder wondered what had her so troubled that she didn't feel comfortable speaking to him about it.

Anya's wan smile firmed. "It's not important. We should go on before Estin starts wondering what we're getting up to." She heeled Barton forward, and Cinder watched her depart, still picking over her words.

A moment later, he shook off his ruminations. If Anya wanted to tell him what was really on her mind, she would. In the meantime, she was right. Estin had already drawn Byerley to a halt and was staring back at them, an appraising expression on his face.

Cinder didn't have to guess as to what the prince was pondering. Thus far in their days of shared travel, Estin had been nothing if not well-mannered and polite, but there had always been an air of judging curiosity about him, and that judgment was present now.

Cinder understood what it meant. The prince wanted to know about Cinder's relationship with Anya. Were they more than just friends? Had they ever been?

"What were you talking about?" Estin asked when they reached him.

"Revelant," Anya answered. There again was the omission. "Cinder has never seen it before."

"What do you think?" Estin asked.

Cinder had no hesitation in answering. "It's beautiful. I can understand why the elves love it so much."

Estin nodded, a smug expression taking hold. "It's worth loving."

Cinder responded with a distracted nod. He didn't want to talk about beautiful architecture any longer. His conversation with Anya still bothered him. Why couldn't he remember the city that sounded like it was important to her? He delved Shokan's memories, searching, but in the end, he couldn't pull forth any true image of the city of nine hills. It might have been there, but if so, it was also frustratingly out of reach.

With an irritated grunt, Cinder shifted the conversation. "Tell me about Yaksha's governmental structure. I want to know about the Directorates. I already know about the Third, but what about the First and the Second?"

"We've reviewed this before," Anya chided.

"Humor me."

Anya sighed. "Fine. You know about the Third Directorate. You trained there. The First Directorate was founded by Koran Yaksha, the first empress. It is an organization of spies, nominally commanded by Shamira Quill."

Cinder didn't miss the emphasized word. "Nominally?"

Anya nodded. "Nominally. I suspect it is actually Ginala who rules the First Directorate."

"Her offices are within their building," Estin supplied.

"And these spies answer to Shamira?" Cinder asked. "But they could also just as easily answer to Ginala?"

"They almost certainly answer to her," Anya replied. "Think it through. With command of her own network of spies—"

"And assassins," Estin chimed.

Anya dipped her head in acknowledgment. "And assassins. With them, Ginala would have access to many secrets. Secrets that a humble quelchon shouldn't know."

Cinder wanted to agree with Anya, but her obvious dislike of the quelchon could also be shading her opinion. "And you think Ginala rules the First Directorate because…"

"Because of exactly what I just said. She knows too much. It isn't just her recitations. It's her skill. No quelchon could be that good."

"Then how did she come to be in charge of the First Directorate?" Cinder asked. "How did she accrue so much power?"

"Ginala was already old when our mother was young," Anya answered. "And Mother was essentially raised by the quelchon. Is it a surprise that she defers to Ginala in so many matters?"

It made sense. An impressionable young girl guided by a revered figure, and that guidance continuing even after the girl became a woman.

Too bad the revered figure wasn't worth revering. "What about the Second Directorate?" he asked.

"It no longer exists," Anya said. "It used to be a priestly order, men and women who held sway on imperial decision making. A prior empress thought they had too much sway and had them killed."

Cinder blinked, not expecting such a brutal ending.

"And before you ask," she added, "there are no other Directorates. Just those two."

"The First Directorate and the Third," Cinder mused. "One to train warriors. The other for spies. And if anyone might have learned about the Orbs, it would be the First, meaning probably Ginala."

"Not necessarily," Anya said. "Any word about what happened in Surent Crèche could certainly have reached Yaksha by now, but I doubt the dwarves will want it known that the Orb of Eretria was stolen. I would bet Sriovey's father will do his best to keep it quiet. And as for Flatiron, how would anyone learn about that?"

A good point. "If that's the case, then hopefully your mother hasn't ordered increased security around the Orb of Moss."

Anya grimaced. "If she has, making off with it will be a challenge."

"Even *without* those increased measures, I don't see how you'll make off with it," Estin said. "The Orb is kept in Mother's private throne hall. There are four members of the Sun Guard stationed outside of it at all hours, and it's locked in a box to which only Mother has the key."

"But the key is a *nomasra*, correct?" Cinder said, sharing an amused smile with Anya. They had already discussed this.

"Yes," Estin allowed, hesitant.

"Then leave the Orb to us," Anya ordered, addressing her brother. "Just get us those diplomatic papers and passage out of Revelant. We'll be long gone by the time our theft is discovered."

"But the key," Estin argued.

"*Nomasras* can be replicated," Cinder replied.

"Not anymore," Estin argued. "Only the most skilled practitioners of *lorethasra*—Oh."

7

Cinder paced alongside Anya, both of them Blended but also cowled as they followed Estin through the hallways of the imperial palace. So far, they'd made it into the residential areas, and only a few people had bothered halting the prince's progress. In nearly every case, it was a sycophant wishing to speak to him with the only exception being Redwinth, Enma's husband, who somehow noticed their Blends.

They dropped it, and Estin offered the explanation they'd settled on, about how they were practicing their skills. Redwinth had accepted the answer with a shrug, apparently not recognizing Anya through Rabisu's weave. He spoke to Estin a few moments longer, and afterward, they departed, Blended again and marching at a quick clip.

"We're almost there," Anya whispered when they took a left-hand turn.

This corridor was lined in shiplap and decorated with exquisite murals and paintings along with priceless vases. Expensive rugs of royal purple and rich reds culled their footsteps, but otherwise the hallway was quiet. The smell of fragrant flowers and burning incense perfumed the air, the smoke merging with the day's late-afternoon light as it beamed through the western-facing windows.

Thus far, their plan had worked to perfection, and—

Cinder nearly stumbled when an obvious problem manifested.

Anya noticed. "What is it?"

"Barton. They'll recognize him." He cursed. "We'll have to steal the Orb tonight. There's no other choice." Cinder continued to curse.

Estin glared at him. "Shut up. You want someone noticing your Blend?"

Cinder scowled. The prince was right, which Cinder hated admitting.

Thankfully, just a final turn later and they reached the prince's quarters and hustled inside. Estin's rooms were just what Cinder had expected: large, lush, and exuding wealth. The amount of money spent on the furnishings alone could likely purchase all of Swallow, the village from which Cinder hailed.

"What were you two so angry about?" Estin asked, interrupting Cinder's inspection.

Anya explained. "We need the Orb tonight as well as that ship."

Estin chuckled. "So it's just like when I helped Cinder escape from Fort Carnate. This is starting to become a habit."

"Not a good one," Cinder muttered, still upset with himself. How could he have overlooked such an obvious problem?

"We can still do this," Anya said. She gestured to the balcony. "Several floors down is where we need to be anyway. It's a balcony that opens into Mother's private throne hall."

Cinder already knew this, but there was still Barton. Getting out of Taj Wada would be impossible if he were found and reported.

"You don't have to worry about Barton," Estin said. "We housed him in my private stables, not Mother's. They'll figure him to be one of my own."

Cinder wished he could be as optimistic, and Anya apparently agreed with him.

"It's still risky," she noted.

"Everything you're doing is risky," Estin countered. "And are you sure you can replicate the *nomasra* as easily as you seem to think you can?" He wore a smirk, clearly not forgetting Cinder's earlier claim.

"Stop being an ass," Anya said. "And I agree with Cinder. We should board a ship as soon as we have the Orb." Her lips tightened briefly. "I just wish I could see our family. I miss them."

Cinder's annoyance eased in the face of Anya's despondence.

"So do I," Estin said. "I can tell you some of what's been going on."

Soon, he and Anya were chatting about their home life here: their family, friends, and shared upbringing. It didn't matter that Anya was decades older than the prince. They had many commonalities, just like she did with Lisandre, Riyne's older brother, who was everything a warrior should be. Beyond being skilled, Lisandre was also forthright and honest as well as respectful of others, even humans. It was too bad Anya had never seemed to fully appreciate his good qualities. Lisandre would have made a good husband for her.

Cinder smirked inwardly. Was he trying to play matchmaker for Anya? He doubted she would appreciate his help. Besides which, a thick rope of jealousy told him how little he'd like to see her love someone else. It didn't matter that the two of them weren't Shokan and Sira. Cinder had loved Anya, and he wasn't yet ready to see her with another man.

As if she recognized the direction of his deliberations, Anya glanced back at him, a questioning expression on her face.

Cinder schooled his features to stillness, offering a mere nod of his head. He hoped she didn't realize what he'd been thinking.

Anya wasn't sure what might have been on Cinder's mind, but his unexpressive features told her he didn't want to talk about it right now. She mentally shrugged. He'd tell her if he thought it was important.

Instead, she faced Estin. Given their shortened timeline, they had to update their plan on escaping from Taj Wada. "You'll have to see the family soon," she said. "They'll be expecting you. But first we need those diplomatic papers and passage off the island."

"I'll send Mother a message," Estin said. "I'll say I'm out buying her a present. It should earn me a few hours."

It was a good enough plan, and it should even work, which in its own way was impressive. Two years ago, Estin wouldn't have been able to come up with something like that. Anya viewed her brother in consideration. He'd grown, become more studious and patient, more willing to listen—a better person overall. Was that the only reason why he was helping them, though? Anya continued to stare at her brother. He'd joined the *Lamarin Hosh*. Had they ordered him to follow after her and Cinder? Was that his purpose here?

A moment later, she threw off her musings. It didn't matter. Right now, she and Cinder needed him. They needed everyone if they were to defeat Shet.

"Go," Anya said to her brother. "Do what you need. But let us know which ship you found and its berth. We'll wait here."

Estin gave a brief bob of his head before exiting his quarters.

Upon his leaving, the room fell silent. Cinder paced, clearly still angry with himself for not considering Barton's presence. Anya didn't feel like speaking either, and they waited a while in private islands of quiet.

"Should we practice how to create the *nomasra*?" Cinder finally asked.

They had already done so on many occasions. In the wilderness after departing Naraka, but one more practice run wouldn't hurt.

Cinder made to join her, but he hesitated. Wearing a frown, he peered at a corner, miming for Anya to remain quiet. He approached the area that had his attention, the iron-rich smell of his *lorethasra* filling the room. He gave a sharp intake but an instant later, wore a satisfied smile. "I sensed a weave," he said. "It was made for eavesdropping and would let someone listen to anything said in this room."

Anya frowned, having an immediate suspicion on who might have created such a braid. "That's something that would come in handy for a spy."

"Ginala."

"Ginala," Anya agreed. Her frown deepened. But how had the old quelchon known of the braid? It was from the ancient *asrasins* of Shokan and Sira's time, too complex for today's woven. She voiced her question.

"That's assuming it was Ginala."

"You thought it was."

Cinder shrugged. "If it is or it isn't, I dulled the weave so it will only hear silence. I'm more concerned about the smell of my *lorethasra*. Will it be noticed?"

"It's gone now," Anya said. "And it likely didn't penetrate past the door. Besides, no one actually knows your scent."

"And there's no risk to your sourcing *lorethasra*? Someone recognizing it?"

Anya shook her head. "Highly unlikely. Let's get started. I'll create the *nomasra* while you infuse it with *Jivatma*."

That was what they'd always done, and it only made sense. Anya was the one who had seen and observed the key that could unlock the box housing the Orb of Moss. Her mother had even let her use the *nomasra* a few times, study it, too. All in order to prove to a younger Anya that no one could ever hope to replicate the key and steal the Orb.

However, that version of herself hadn't yet gained Sira's memories and skills, and with those abilities, Anya felt sure she could replicate the *nomasra*. It was nothing more than a simple iron spike, smooth and straight and with the color of fresh-turned earth mixed with golden speckles. *Lorethasra* had clearly gone into its manufacture, but Sira's recollections told her how common such a key actually was.

Anya withdrew a thin rod of iron, one of a dozen they'd had fashioned at Naraka prior to departing Shet's palace. It was the size and shape Anya remembered, and she had already practiced the weave on many occasions. By now, it was fairly simple and straightforward.

The only question was whether Cinder could infuse the *nomasra* with *Jivatma*. That was the secret, one that her younger self hadn't realized until much later. Her mother's *nomasra* had a weave of Earth *and* an infusion of *Jivatma*. In this, it was almost as if the key was alive. And while the iron rod Anya held could contain the braid of Earth, neither she nor Cinder could permanently infuse it with *Jivatma*. They lacked the correct materials and would have to make do with what they had.

Anya seated herself on the ground, legs folded underneath. The Orb's housing rested on a low, granite pedestal, and this would be the position in which she would have to create the *nomasra*. She focused inward, seeking the peace of *lorethasra*. In her mind's eye, she imagined a flowing silver stream, and from it, she quickly wove the necessary braid, pouring it into the spike.

The iron slowly brightened, taking on a brown sheen.

Cinder settled himself behind her, arms around her waist, reaching up to rest his hands upon hers. Together, they held the spike. Anya exhaled softly. It was a position that many elves would have considered compromising, but it was also the only way this could work. She would create the *nomasra*, and if he didn't immediately pass his *Jivatma* through her body and into the spike, they would fail. They had practiced many times until settling on this position.

Anya wished, however, that the instinct urging her to lean back against Cinder's comforting form would cease. It was whipsawing. Right after Mahadev, she had detested his touch, and now she had to fight the longing to feel him hold her—

Not now. She focused on the iron, silencing her recollections and maintaining the weave. The spike formed, brightening to the proper shade of dull brown, and Cinder sent *Jivatma* through her and into the iron, infusing the *nomasra*. Whenever he did, Anya felt him more keenly, to his very depths. It frightened her, and she wasn't sure why.

Thankfully, their linkage was short-lived since within moments the spike had attained the rich golden-speckled earthy color that Anya recalled. Of course, the *nomasra* wouldn't last long. Within less than a minute, it would disintegrate to dust.

"Fastest yet," Cinder said. "Should we try again?"

Anya chuckled. "I think you just like holding me." She knew the words were a mistake even as they left her lips.

Cinder abruptly stood. "I think we've practiced enough."

Anya cursed herself. She shouldn't have said that. Cinder moved away to a different part of the room, and an uncomfortable stillness fell over them. Anya glanced at Cinder, trying to figure out what to say to make it right. If it wasn't an apology he wanted, then what?

She didn't know, but the hours passed and the quiet remained even as night fell. Then the chance to sort out what to say to Cinder was lost when Estin returned.

"Sorry I took so long," her brother said after shutting the door. "I managed to find us passage. The ship is even going to Swift Sword." He went on to name the vessel and its berth along with his evening so far, which included having dinner with the family. "Unfortunately, Redwinth mentioned you. Mother wasn't all that curious—Enma was—but I'd rather none of them knew about you at all."

"It won't matter," Cinder said. "We'll be long gone by the time her curiosity is roused."

"We'd better be," Estin said. "Mother wants to discuss something else tonight. Family only in the private throne hall. Rumors about the dwarves and the Orb of Eretria."

Anya cursed softly.

It was the middle of the night, and patrolling guards secured Taj Wada's grounds. Their muffled voices were audible, but otherwise, beyond the occasional droning of crickets, all was quiet. The *diptha* lanterns on their tall posts provided circles of illumination, including the balcony on which Anya and Cinder crouched. But the light didn't extend to where they hid in the shadows.

From the ground, they would be nearly invisible, especially with their darkened faces. In addition, both of them had their cowls raised, hiding the shine of Anya's hair. They had no weapons, however, having to leave them with the packs they'd stored in Estin's part of the stables. Anya would have felt more comfortable with a sword at her hip, although she couldn't see any situation where she would raise a blade against one of her own.

Her mind flashed back to Orinin Silvesthin, the oily elf who had planned on kidnapping her and using her for his own foul purposes. That had been different, though. Orinin had planned on doing her and Cinder harm, whereas any elf here would be part of her community, only doing their duty in protecting the empress.

Which made it even more imperative that she and Cinder steal the Orb and escape Taj Wada without raising an alarm.

Anya peered into the throne hall, cursing under her breath. What was her family doing there? Usually meetings of this sort took place in her mother's study.

Speaking of her mother, she was seated on the throne, discussing some matter or another and showing no signs of leaving.

Anya studied the empress, searching for changes.

There were none.

Her mother was several centuries old—middle years for an elf—and her hair had the same white-blonde shade as Enma's, Anya's older sister. Otherwise, she was unremarkable. But her forceful gaze told a different tale. In this regard, she was very much remarkable. When the dark eyes of the empress lit on a person, her dominating presence became manifest, and there was no doubting that she was a woman of power.

The rest of the family was gathered as well, Estin included, although he kept shifting about like he had to go to the bathroom. In truth, he was likely just nervous, and Anya wished he'd sit still before someone noticed.

Then there was her father, speaking now to the empress, and longing filled Anya's heart. She respected her mother, loved her, too, but not like she did her father, who had always been a parent to her first and the consort to the Empress of Yaksha Sithe second. With her mother, it had always been the opposite: empress first and mother second.

In the two years since Anya had last seen her father, he'd aged. His dark hair showed streaks of white, barely discernible but present. Sighting it caused a guilty lump in her throat. Her disappearance would have broken her father's heart and caused many of his new frown lines. Certainly, there were other reasons—with Shet's rise, he would have been given greater authority in the management of the sithe—but her absence would still be the most prominent source of his unhappiness.

Enma was also present, beautiful as a spring morning with blonde hair that was nearly white and certainly more attractive than Anya's honey-gold locks. Enma also had the tall, sharply pointed ears of their noble class, which was yet another sign of her sister's beauty. Anya's hands automatically went to her unfortunately rounder ears. She could never match up to her sister—not in beauty, grace, or all the other gentle qualities of a proper elven woman.

However, Anya had her own gifts—those of a warrior, of someone willing to give unto others and to listen. She counted them as better gifts than Enma's beauty. Because right now, all of her sister's loveliness meant nothing. Right now, Enma wore a bored expression, which was unfortunately all-too typical. While she was certainly intelligent, Enma found politics tiresome, and it was something she couldn't afford. She was the heir to the throne, and whatever their mother was telling the family, Enma needed to pay attention.

Anya tilted her head in consideration. Or was this all an act? It was certainly possible. Enma's eyes had recently gone to their brother in apparent scrutiny, her lips pursed and a frown briefly creasing her regal brow. And Enma's curiosity when Redwinth had mentioned them? Did she know who they were just based on that brief description?

Seeing Enma's lackadaisical attitude return, Anya realized it was, in fact, possible. She whispered her concern to Cinder, who nodded.

"I saw her reaction, too," he murmured in agreement. "We'll have to be careful around her."

"She might come back when we're in the middle of the theft."

"She won't be alone, though. Redwinth will be with her. He saw us. He'll tell her."

This time it was Anya who nodded, and her attention went to Redwinth Wheat, Enma's husband. According to Estin, the wedding had taken place several months ago, and Anya recalled what she knew of the man: nephew to the empress of Apsara Sithe and a ranger at one time, although as the consort to the heir, those duties had undoubtedly been curtailed. Not that Redwinth would have complained. His interests lay in music, art, and economics.

The final person in the room caused Anya to glower: Quelchon Ginala. She was an ancient crone, older than Master Molni by at least a century with hair the color of chalk and a wizened face as wrinkled as crumpled parchment. But like the empress, it was her eyes which marked her as being different. In Ginala's case, they were the constantly shifting colors of a rainbow, marking her as a quelchon, someone who could recite a person.

Cinder shifted at Anya's side, and she gazed his way. Ginala had recited him the last time they'd been through Revelant, and the words had sparked her mother's fear about him. It didn't matter that the quelchon's words had been meaningless babble. *"A nameless curse threatens. An ancient shadow looms. The world's hour is late. Death and destruction come for Seminal. The Elonic Festh, the World-Killer comes. And this man wields a white blade."*

Utter nonsense as far as Anya reckoned.

Her attention on the throne heightened when her mother stood. She finally appeared ready to end the meeting. *Thank Devesh.* Anya's mother rose to her feet, gesturing to the far doors. As one, the rest of the family stood, and they followed after her, two paces behind.

The far doors opened momentarily, just long enough for Anya to see four members of the Sun Guard, those warriors trusted with the protection of the imperial family, gathered outside. Anya breathed out relief. The guard hadn't been increased, which meant her mother didn't suspect someone might abscond with the Orb of Moss.

"Your mother doesn't believe the rumors about the dwarves," Cinder said, coming to the same conclusion.

Anya gave a slow nod of agreement. "We'll still give it a half hour. If nothing changes, then we go in."

"And make sure there aren't any eavesdropping braids planted in the room."

Enma had left her quarters minutes after arriving. Something was going on, and she needed to be on hand to decide what to do about it. But it was a decision best made in private. Thus, upon exiting her chambers, she had dismissed the Sun Guard, telling them she and Redwinth simply planned on strolling around the palace. But mostly she just didn't want them around for what she suspected might happen tonight.

"You truly believe your sister is here?" Redwinth asked, striding at her side as they approached the empress' private throne hall. "Why?"

Enma flicked him a glance. Although she had developed an appreciation for Redwinth's qualities, what she didn't appreciate was his need to question. He liked to think matters through, while she often operated on instinct. She made decisions that felt right, sometimes without any rational reason. And that meant she didn't always have easy answers for him.

Her mother had learned that the Orb of Eretria might have been stolen from Surent Crèche by Anya and Cinder and that they might be planning on gathering them all for Shet to destroy and free humanity. There was even some fool story about a dark god even more powerful than Shet. Zahhack was what He was called, and Enma had scoffed upon hearing it. It was the same name as that given to Shet's grotesque warriors. What kind of dark god would allow such an insult?

More likely, it was a fable that the dwarves were using to explain their incompetence.

Regardless, the reason was immaterial. Of greater importance was that during tonight's meeting, Enma had sensed a regard. Someone had been studying her, and she had a notion who it might be. Estin was the key. The boy couldn't hide anything. His story to Redwinth about his pair of servants—a husband and wife—bound for Agnisahar had been patently absurd.

Enma had asked Redwinth about them and learned enough to worry they might be Anya and Cinder. And the chestnut Yavana gelding currently housed in Estin's portion of the stables certainly sounded like Barton. But why hadn't Redwinth recognized Anya? They had met on many occasions when her sister had visited Apsara Sithe. Was it because she had changed that much?

Enma figured she'd find out soon enough.

She reached the throne hall, and while the guards were alert, they relaxed upon seeing her, letting her and Redwinth pass inside without issue.

"It took you long enough," a voice proclaimed as soon as the doors were shut.

Estin. Enma viewed him deadpan. She'd expected him to be here but had yet to learn what he wanted.

"You noticed my nervousness?" Estin asked.

"A senseless person would have noticed it," Enma said. "Why are you here?"

Estin smirked. "Our parents didn't notice. Neither did Ginala. Only you. Then again, you know me better than they do, and I figured you'd pick up on my nervousness. I wanted you to."

Although her brother wasn't the cunning sort, Anya was. Which meant she was close at hand. Nonetheless, Enma wished for Estin to explain himself further. She feigned a scowl. "You have a reason for this charade?"

Estin nodded. "I do. It's so he'd be present." He pointed to Redwinth.

"Redwinth?" Enma's brows lifted in surprise. "What does he have to do with this?"

"He knows."

Enma stared at Redwinth, and his frown gave away the truth. He did know. But what?

"And I'm also sure he told you about my servants, and you guessed their identities," Estin said.

From the shadows emerged two people—a woman and a man. They hadn't been Blended, but rather had simply darkened their faces and wore clothing that melded with the shadows. Still, it took Enma many seconds to piece their features together and recognize her sister... which meant the other one was Cinder Shade.

Enma wanted to dart forward and embrace Anya. The two of them had never gotten along well, but they were still family, and she would always love her.

Striding forward and hugging her, Anya took the matter out of her hand. "I'm so happy to see you."

Enma tightened their embrace. She'd missed her little sister. Although, she didn't seem so little any longer. It wasn't just that Anya was taller and stronger but also because she seemed so much older. She had always had a certain gravitas, but now there was an even greater weight to her presence along with a wisdom Enma hadn't noticed before.

When Anya stepped back, Enma studied her companion—Cinder Shade. He was certainly handsome. There was no denying that simple fact. But more significantly, compared to him, even the most elegant of elven warriors moved like clumsy oafs. And he, too, possessed Anya's weightiness... enough that for a moment Enma wondered about the stories of *thoraythons*—people of fate. Did such folk really exist?

Enma's thoughts scattered, and she swallowed heavily when she felt Cinder's regard.

"Enma," Anya said, "I wish we had more hours to spend, but our time is limited, and we have much to discuss."

Her sister's statement twisted Enma's gaze away from the human, but it was difficult. It was like he was a lodestone, and she was iron. She wanted to stare at him, study him.

Enma's unsettling reaction toward him had her blurting out the first thing that crossed her mind. "Mother also heard about Estin's servants. She doesn't realize who you are, but she still wants to eventually meet you in the main throne hall. She expects you to crawl on your hands and knees. It's an old tradition that she revived." Enma flushed at the inanity of what she had just spoken.

"Interesting." Cinder's deadpan tone expressed his lack of concern for such a possibility.

His reaction also caused Enma's flush to deepen. For some reason, this human, whom she had so easily dismissed during their first encounter, now had a charisma that made her feel small.

Cinder smiled, and Enma's pulse quickened. What was this? Why was she reacting to him in such a fashion? "It's good to see you again, Enma."

Her mouth went dry upon hearing her name on his lips.

"We'll tell you what we can, but we don't have much time," Anya said.

Enma's attention was dragged away from Cinder, and she made herself meet her sister's gaze. "Why do you need the Orbs?"

8

Redwinth listened as Anya and Cinder spoke about their past and what they intended to do in the future. Their explanation was short and to the point, but when it was over, there were a thousand questions raised by their responses. Redwinth could have spoken to them for hours.

"They say that they don't believe themselves to be Shokan and Sira," Estin added. "They only think they have their memories."

Redwinth's gaze darted to Estin. There had been an odd emphasis to his phrasing. Stated in that way, it was also a confirmation of the recitation from Duchess Sarienne Cervine, the founder of the *Lamarin Hosh*, who had stated that the Blessed Ones wouldn't know themselves. But wasn't it supposed to be their memories that they lacked? Cinder claimed to have a clear recollection of Shokan's past, and Anya said the same about Sira. Didn't that mean they *did* know themselves?

"Yaksha endured, and she endures," Enma was saying to Anya. "We possess an unbroken lineage that continues to this day with our mother. We are but twelve generations removed from our founding. Do you understand why I'm telling you this?"

Anya did appear to know. "Because of what Ginala said about me."

"The quelchon said you would betray the sithe. And if you steal the Orb of Moss, you'll have proven her correct."

"She said I would betray the empress. I would never betray the sithe. What Ginala said was this: '*your daughter's spirit is changed, and she is no longer entirely yours. She will betray you.*' She said nothing about the sithe."

"Our mother is the sithe." The words weren't spoken with conviction but rather as a didactic challenge, like Enma wanted to hear Anya's thoughts on the matter.

Regardless, Redwinth disagreed with his wife. Every sithe was comprised of millions of elves. The empress was simply the most important member. However, in Yaksha Sithe, as merely the husband to the heir, offering such an opinion would be considered speaking out of turn.

Anya, thankfully, seemed to feel the same way as Redwinth. She shook her head at Enma and said about the same as what he had been thinking.

Cinder had moved off from where he'd been examining the steel casing that housed the Orb of Moss. Redwinth's eyes widened in astonishment. He'd seen many warriors in his time but none like Cinder Shade. The man moved with an uncanny economy of purpose and restrained power. There was no wasted motion in his gait, and he made even the act of walking appear fluid.

"Time's wasting," Cinder said, his voice as deep and resonant as what Redwinth would have expected for someone of his status. "We need an answer."

Enma's eyes flashed to him. "Be silent. Your betters are speaking."

Redwinth gaped. No matter who or what Cinder Shade believed of himself, there was still a chance he was Shokan. And if he truly wasn't, he still had the memories of the Blessed One. That alone warranted respect.

Enma must have realized her mistake because she flushed. "My apologies," she muttered, staring at the ground and apparently unable to meet Cinder's gaze. "I spoke without thinking."

Cinder seemed to consider Enma, causing her to shift about on her feet, embarrassment obvious. Redwinth eyed his wife in concern. He'd never known her to be so discomfited.

"Apology accepted," Cinder said.

Enma dipped her head, and Redwinth viewed her in fresh shock. He had also never known her to defer to anyone except her mother and rarely, her father. Not even to Ginala did she offer such respect.

"He's right, though," Anya said. "We need an answer. Mother will see what I'm doing as a betrayal, but it's necessary."

That got Enma's attention. She glared at Anya. "But why does it have to be you? Why do you have to be the one to risk your reputation, your future, your life? Why can't Cinder do this? You can stay at Taj Wada. Shelter our people against the storm to come. Shet isn't the puffed-up pretender Mother claims. We need you. You are a princess of Yaksha Sithe. Your place is here." Enma was breathing heavily at the end, her words heavy with passion.

And had she ever spoken to Redwinth in such a way, he would have done anything she asked.

But Anya was made of sterner stuff. "I cannot," she said. "I've already told you why. I hold Sira's memories. And they tell me that I have to work with Cinder. Only together can we do what's required. I need to protect the entire world from the storm to come. And that storm isn't just Shet."

"Zahhack," Estin said, silent until then.

"The Son of Emptiness," Cinder said. "We witnessed His power, just His finger clawing out of a dark pit that led to a realm of despair. It's where He resides, where He wants to drag Seminal." Cinder grimaced. "Better to be dead than to exist in such a place."

Redwinth stared at Cinder, recalling all this man had endured and overcome. He was already a legend amongst the warriors of Yaksha, although no one would dare express such admiration in front of the empress. Nevertheless, what could make a man like Cinder grimace like that? Redwinth feared to learn.

Meanwhile, Enma had her attention frozen on Anya. "Evil needs to be contained if it can't be changed. Killed if it can't be contained. Is that what you're saying?"

Anya smiled. "I said that to you at some point. I'm surprised you remembered."

"It was memorable," Enma said with an answering smile. An instant later, her humor evaporated, and she gestured to Redwinth, drawing his attention. "What do you think?"

Redwinth glanced at his wife, happy to provide his opinion. In the time since he'd joined Yaksha's royal family, he and Enma had found a way to bond. They weren't yet partners, but they were moving in that direction. And in this instance, the answer to Enma's question was obvious. "I think we should let them get on with it."

"Why?" Enma asked.

"Because they've accomplished too much," Redwinth said. "Cinder, especially. You've read the after-action reports about him. He fights too well to be a mere human. He has *lorethasra*, something we've always thought impossible for humans. And now there are more impossibilities. He survived Mahadev. He has Shokan's memories. He met Manifold Fulsom, *the* Manifold Fulsom, a Mythaspuri. Why not one other impossibility? A dark god more dangerous than Shet, and the only way to stop Him begins by destroying the Orbs of Peace."

Enma exhaled heavily, not replying at once. "You're right." She addressed Cinder and Anya. "Then be quick about it. Estin might be right that only I recognized his nervousness, but he may also be wrong. You don't want to test the likelihood that Mother or Ginala are on their way to question him even now."

"We'll be gone within an hour," Anya said. "But be careful what you say about tonight and where you say it. There was a braid in Estin's room. It's meant to allow a spy to listen in to whatever you're saying."

"My room?" Estin's face had gone pasty, while Redwinth hissed in shock.

"That's impossible," Redwinth said. "No one living has the skill to create something like that."

"Then someone living has relearned the skill," Anya said. "Just be careful what you say and where you say it. But you can also find the weave if you look. You'll see a shimmer in the air when you're sourcing *lorethasra* and using a braid of Air to bring distant objects closer."

As Enma stared at Anya, her head tilted as if she was just seeing her sister for the first time. "You're certain of this?"

"I am." Anya vacillated. "And thank you for listening."

Redwinth viewed Anya in sorrow. If she was actually Sira, they should all be on their knees before her. She shouldn't be thanking her older sister like a peasant. It was wrong. He bowed low before Anya. "As you will, Your Highness."

"We should go," Enma ordered.

"Enma." Anya rushed to hug her sister again. "Be safe."

Enma's arms tightened around Anya. "Take your own advice." Her eyes might have flicked to Cinder. "Especially with your heart."

Her words spoken, Enma released her sister, and with a gesture, she gathered Redwinth to her side. Together, they left the throne hall, but as they were about to depart, he glanced back, noticing Cinder seated behind Anya, arms wrapped around her as they faced the steel lock-box where the Orb was secured. It was an intimate position no elven woman would allow unless that elven woman was Sira and the man was Shokan.

Cinder exhaled in relief. Enma wasn't going to turn them in, and they could finally get on with it.

The room was quiet, and the *diptha* lamps and chandeliers were turned down, leaving the outskirts of the throne hall robed in shadow. A lovely floral scent, no doubt arising from the fresh roses and gardenia arrangements, filled the air with freshness and hope. And pacing in the middle of the room was Estin, chewing on a fingernail, nervous and wanting to get gone.

Cinder shared his desire, but first there was this one vital task to complete.

He sat behind Anya, thighs on either side of her own as they faced a low stone pedestal that was fashioned of white-and-gray-veined granite. Intricate carvings of vines and roses swirled to meet a broad platform upon which rested a similarly fanciful large steel case. Decorated with precious gems and inlaid with gold, there was a single needle-thin slot for the *nomasra*. In addition, the box itself was directly attached to the pedestal, which was similarly affixed to the black floor tiling. Even if he and Anya had wanted to, there was no way to simply make off with the box itself.

They had to unlock it. Focused on this one duty, Cinder set his mind to what was needed since time might be slipping away. His instincts warned him that either the empress or Ginala would be back soon. He wasn't sure which one it would be, and he didn't care to find out, especially with him and Anya in such a compromising position, like they were lovers.

The mountain-fresh scent of Anya's *lorethasra* banished the floral aroma, and Cinder inhaled automatically, savoring the familiar smell as it mixed with her usual earthy cinnamon fragrance. There was something comforting about it, and had this been any other moment and any other place, he might have wanted to tighten his arms around Anya and have her lay her head on his chest.

But now wasn't the time, and it might be best if it never was.

"Be ready," Anya said, alerting him as she quickly formed a *nomasra*.

It was Cinder's turn. He conducted *Jivatma*, punching through the blue-and-green lightning housing the mirror-bright pond that might be his soul. The pain had him wincing, and he involuntarily tightened his arms around Anya.

"Easy," she admonished.

"Sorry." Cinder reached deeper into his *Jivatma*, and the world heightened. The room's shadows were banished, and he could pick out the rustling of the guards outside the throne hall; Estin's strides sounded like claps of a drum; and Anya's cinnamon fragrance became richer.

But Cinder didn't let any of it distract him. He concentrated on his hands, which rested on Anya's, and together they held the iron spike that she had transformed into a *nomasra*, needle-thin just like the key she remembered. He sent the infusion of *Jivatma* then, a thin line, based on a memory from Shokan. In actuality, it wasn't truly his *Jivatma*, but rather a means by which he could further transform the *nomasra*.

Anya allowed it to course through her, and they were linked, her emotions open to him.

Cinder could have remained in that state for hours. There was an undeniable beauty to how Anya's mind worked, an openness and accepting nature. Was this why she had been willing to see him as something other than an undeserving human?

However, there was also a darkness that stirred in Anya's depths. Cinder didn't know what it meant, but it was there. Possibly the weave Rabisu had created to hide their identity. Was it also the cause of her bouts of anger? And did he have something similar inside of himself?

Seconds into the process, the spike brightened, growing richer in color until it held the fresh-turned color of dirt that Anya mentioned about her mother's key.

"Let's see if it fits," she said.

Cinder scrambled to his feet, Estin hurrying over to their sides. Anya inserted the *nomasra*. It slid in smoothly, but Cinder wasn't yet ready to celebrate. The first step was done. Again came the mountain-fresh scent of Anya's *lorethasra* as she formed a twining braid of Earth and Air, attaching it to the key. This was the critical moment. Would the *nomasra* actually work?

Time was ticking, but this part of the plan couldn't be rushed. If they tried to open the box and were unsuccessful, an alarm would sound, alerting the guards outside the throne hall. They'd be inside in seconds, and Cinder and Anya would be lucky to escape with the clothes on their backs. Worse, their failure might see the Orb of Moss forever beyond their reach. The empress would no doubt have it secreted in some unknown vault.

Anya licked her lips. "Here we go."

Cinder held his breath as she twisted the key. It moved easily, rotating without slowing. Then came a click, and the box unlatched, opening a fraction. Cinder let out a relieved chuckle, sharing a broad smile with Anya.

"It worked," Estin said, sounding stunned.

"I told you we could create a *nomasra*," Cinder said, unable to resist a dig at his longtime rival.

Anya opened the box, and from within, a glow emanated. Nestled upon a velvet cushion was a globe, the source of the light. It was the size of a skull, and inside the strange structure was a frozen lance of blue-and-green lightning.

"The Orb of Moss," Anya breathed. She reached forward, drawing out the globe. Cinder knew from memory that it would have an un-expected weight, light as a feather one moment and heavier than a bucket of steel shavings the next. Anya stared at the Orb for a second longer before placing it in her cloak's *null pocket*. "All safe now," she said, patting her cloak. It was no longer visible even as a round shape from within the *null pocket*.

But they still couldn't celebrate. "We're not free yet," Cinder re-minded them. "We still have to escape the palace, elude any guards, and hope our ship is still in the harbor."

"We've faced worse odds," Anya said. "Remember how hard we had it in the Flatiron?"

Cinder pulled an expression of distaste. "Don't remind me."

Estin gave a darting glance from one of them to the other. "Can we go now? Mother is going to be furious if she finds me down here helping you."

"Then let's go," Anya said. "We wouldn't want your mother to be mad at you."

9

Minutes later, they neared the stables and crouched low amongst cattails and tall grass. The reeds bobbed and rustled in the wake of a moist wind that heralded a rain to come. To their right spread a wildflower field, their long stems bending before that same breeze, while to their left reared a grove of oak, maple, and elm—almost a small forest. And directly behind them, closer at hand, there lapped a broad pond with a stone-and-wooden bridge, elegant with carvings, that arched across the water. It ended at a lovely gazebo that was lit by small *diptha* lamps shedding soft illumination.

Cinder reckoned it might be a romantic place to take a stroll.

Of their own volition, his eyes went to Anya, before—with a wrench—he forced himself to face forward once again. *The stables.* He needed to case it. It rose in front of them, large but otherwise unremarkable. Crickets chirped and frogs crooned while Fulsom's light, especially subtle and delicate tonight, bathed the entire area in an ethereal gold.

The setting appeared peaceful, but when Estin made ready to leave the reeds, Cinder held him back. "Wait."

The prince did as he was bid but cast a questioning look.

Anya did the same, and Cinder shrugged her way. There wasn't anything alarming about the barn, but they were so close to getting free of Revelant. There was no need to take any unnecessary risks. A few seconds of scrutiny might be the difference between spotting an ambush and walking straight into it. Anya seemed to recognize the wisdom of his prudence, and she settled next to Cinder, viewing the scene the same as he.

There was nothing but silence and stillness up ahead, but Cinder didn't trust what he was seeing. There were no warning signs telling him he shouldn't, but by now, with everything he and Anya had experienced, he would rather be cautious now than deal with the consequences of careless haste.

He conducted *Jivatma* and let his senses expand as he examined the stables. The structure loomed fifty yards distant, a long building cloaked in darkness, except for where regularly spaced *diptha* lamps along its length yielded a warm glow.

A few seconds of scrutiny showed nothing out of the ordinary, and Cinder grunted. "Let's go."

The three of them ran in a hunched posture, keeping to the darkest part of the night. They entered the barn. A few horses nickered in question and shuffled, but otherwise the stables were quiet and dark. Empty, too. No one was about.

Moving quickly, they gathered their mounts and soon were off with pack animals trailing after them.

Cinder patted Painter in affection. "Just a short ride, girl." He smiled when she whickered at him.

Afterward came the main gate leading out of the palace and getting through them proved easy. While he and Anya remained cowled and cloaked, Estin rode like the prince he was—posture erect and features set in an arrogant sneer. He ordered the gate guards to let them out through the wicket.

Seconds later, they were free of the palace, and Revelant was spread before them. Still, Cinder remained tense. Only when they reached

Swift Sword would he relax.

Estin, though, was grinning wide. "That was so simp—"

Cinder desperately reached for the idiot, but Anya got to him first. She slapped a hand over her brother's mouth. "Don't say it."

Estin might have mumbled something, but Anya didn't remove her hand until he nodded.

"Never tempt karma," Anya warned. "Celebrate when we've arrived at Swift Sword, and even then, don't celebrate too much."

Cinder scowled at Estin. The prince should have known better.

A half-hour ride saw them through Revelant's broad boulevards where only a few elves were still out. Otherwise, the large city was quiet and sedate, so unlike Swift Sword, which remained boisterous and loud at nearly all hours. A final left turn, and they reached a wharf, and from it, a number of piers jutted out into the water. Ships of all sorts were docked but most appeared to be merchant vessels. Some lay low in the water, their holds clearly full.

Estin led them unerringly to one such ship, narrower of beam than many of the others, with a stance and rigging that marked it as having a chance at speed. Quickness was always appreciated, but Cinder wouldn't have cared if the vessel had the speed and grace of a lumbering elephant if it got them free of Revelant and to where they needed to be.

The captain of the ship, a broad-shouldered elf not much taller than a dwarf, met them at the gangplank. "Good thing you got here when you did," he said. "We were readying to set sail before the next bell. The tide rolled in higher and quicker than expected."

"You'd have waited," Estin said in a tone of absolute certainty.

"Of course I would, Your Highness," the captain said. "But we wouldn't have been pleased at the delay."

"I understand," Estin said, reaching into his coat-pocket and withdrawing a handful of coins. "Will this cover your inconvenience?"

The captain snatched the coins as quickly as an illusionist hiding cards. "Most definitely, Your Highness." His eyes went to Cinder and Anya. "And these two? The servants you mentioned?" He bent, trying to peer past their shadowed cowls. "What are your names?"

Cinder kept quiet, knowing his accent would give him away as being from some place other than Yaksha. Anya didn't answer either.

"Their names are unimportant," Estin said with a lofty air. "They are my servants. That is all you need to know. Now come. Let us make haste. The tide won't wait on your curiosity."

"As you say, my lord," the captain said, shooting Cinder and Anya a wary glance.

Afterward, it was only a matter of sorting out their horses and pack animals before they were ready to catch the tide. Estin would have his own room, while Cinder and Anya, pretending to be married servants looking for a fresh start in Agnisahar, had one for themselves.

Before they separated for their quarters, Estin cornered Cinder. "She is my sister, and a princess of Yaksha," he hissed. "The fact that you held her as you did this evening is corruption enough. Do not corrupt her further."

Cinder inwardly smirked, unimpressed by Estin's attempt at a brother's chivalry. Nevertheless, he held back from mocking the prince. "Good night, Your Highness."

Anya was waiting inside. "What was that about?"

"What do you think?" Cinder asked with a sour grimace.

Anya broke into a chuckle. "I see. It was Estin trying to assert a brother's prerogative?"

"By prerogative, do you mean warning me away from taking advantage of you?"

"Or maybe I'll be the one taking advantage of you."

Cinder rocked back on his feet, shocked. Had Anya just said that? He replayed the words in his head. Yes, she had said that. He viewed her, not sure how to respond, noting that Anya wore a similar expression on her face.

A tense silence held the room.

"I'm sorry," Anya said at last. "I don't know why I'd say such a thing. After everything we've been through. Shokan's and Sira's memories making us feel—"

"They didn't make us feel anything," Cinder said. "Whatever our emotions, they were ours." He mentally gaped when he finished speaking. Now it was he who had spoken words he shouldn't have. And yet the words sounded exactly like what was in his heart.

Anya eyed him in calm appraisal. "What are you saying?"

"I'm not sure," Cinder replied, unprepared to examine what his words might mean, and he doubted Anya was either, no matter how cool and collected she appeared.

She studied him a moment longer. "Let's get some sleep. It's been a long day."

Cinder gazed ahead, looking forward to the journey's end. Their vessel had made good time, only three days from Revelant to Swift Sword, and they were pulling in a few hours after noon. The day was sweltering, and the smell of brine and dead fish mingled in a distasteful tang. A din arose from the wharf: merchants barking for their wares, food vendors hawking spiced meat and street food, and workers shouting at their tasks. The worst noises, however, came from the seagulls cawing moronically.

Anya moved to stand next to him. "Don't you just love those birds?"

Cinder offered an amused smile. "I was trying not to notice."

"At least you're home."

Cinder's scowl transitioned to a smile. That's right. He was home. *Swift Sword.* At least he was if there was any place on this world that he could consider home.

He eyed Anya askance. What did she consider home? Was it Taj Wada? The Third Directorate? Or some other place, like the winding road, wherever it might lead? He could see it being the latter. Anya was a ranger, and rangers traveled to wherever they were needed, rarely settling in one place.

"I miss the mountains," Anya began. "The cool wind in summer. Autumn's rain, and even the snow. It's where I'm most at home."

She had answered his unvoiced wonderings, and Cinder was left trying to understand the many mysteries between them. When would they ever talk about it? Both of them seemed to shy away from such a discussion. Even during the three-day journey to Swift Sword, they hadn't done so. Instead, they spent their time reading, meditating, or just thinking. And it wasn't because they were angry with one another. More, it was because they had a lot to consider.

"There you are." Cinder glanced back to where Estin had joined them on deck. The prince had his packs with him, while Cinder and Anya had theirs gathered at their feet. Included were their swords, bows, and quivers of arrows. On boarding their ship, they had pretended all the weapons belonged to Estin, but with their imminent disembarkment, neither of them saw the need to continue the deception.

Estin neared them, and he lowered his voice. "I've spoken to the captain. There have been interesting rumors afoot in Swift Sword for the past few months. Rumors about Shokan." His eyes went to Cinder. "They also involve you."

Cinder sighed inwardly. He had a suspicion what those rumors might entail, but nonetheless, he needed to know for certain. "What kind of rumors?"

Estin didn't answer him directly. "It's best if both of you remain cowled while we're in Swift Sword. We can't let anyone recognize you. Either of you."

"What kind of rumors?" Cinder repeated.

"Rumors that you are Shokan," Estin said. "There are many who believe it. The Errows for certain."

Cinder could reckon on the reason why. Some of their warriors had seen him battle the *hashains* and heard Jeet Condune name him the Grimyogi. No doubt they had revealed what they'd seen and heard, and it wouldn't take much for their stories to grow into a caricature of what had actually happened.

He hadn't thought of the *hashains* who had leashed themselves to him in days, and he stretched out his senses, reaching for them. The assassins appeared focused and dedicated—which was their typical state—but they also seemed strangely content. For months, Jeet and Stren had often been miserable, and Cinder wondered at the change.

"It's understandable," Anya said. "All people need a source of hope. Someone who might shield them from Shet. They need their hero. They need Shokan."

"And I am not he," Cinder reminded her.

"They also speak of Sira," Estin said. He looked to Anya. "They speak of you when they speak of her."

"Of course they do," Anya said, arms folded. "They think I'm her because I travel with Cinder, who they are certain is Shokan. And the woman who travels with Shokan must be Sira. They think we're lovers."

Estin mutely nodded. "Whether or not it's true, that's what people are saying."

Anya sighed heavily. "It doesn't matter. They can say what they want. So long as they continue preparing for what's to come."

Estin brightened. "At least you don't have to worry about that. The Errow Council and the *Lamarin Hosh* have been working together. We've placed a number of elven warriors in the High Army, and their Ramoni unit continues to graduate competent officers. They'll eventually take command of the rest of their forces."

Cinder nodded in distraction. The prince had explained all this to them aboard ship on the journey from Revelant. "I won't get to stop by *Steel-Graced Adepts* or see Riner. The same with Dorr and Coral." He sighed, unhappy. From Estin, Cinder had learned that Dorr and Coral had a daughter, and he had hoped to meet her. He shook off his disappointment. "It's probably for the best. But it also means Anya and I will have to leave Swift Sword today." He addressed Estin. "Stay here and get us a boat that leaves tonight."

Estin grimaced. "I thought I'd get to come with you."

"And do what? See Shet?" Anya asked in a voice of disbelief. "What did you think that would accomplish?"

Estin shrugged. "Nothing good, but I'm tired of being left behind. The rest of our brothers are in the Shokans. They're off fighting zah-hacks while I've been stuck at the Directorate. I just want to take part in something more than teaching and training."

Cinder could understand Estin's frustration. "Well, here's your chance. Send word to the Shokans. I want them to meet us at Char."

Estin frowned. "You're going to Apsara Sithe? Why?"

"Because Char is the elven city closest to Bharat," Anya answered. "It's where we're going next."

Estin blanched. "Come to think of it, maybe teaching and training isn't so bad."

"Too late now," Cinder said with a laugh, clapping Estin on the shoulder and feeling an odd fondness for him.

"I'll go see to the rest of my things," Estin said, dipping his head as he left them.

"It would have been nice to meet with the Errow Council, too," Cinder said after Estin departed.

"We can't delay. We need to get the Orb to Shet."

Cinder nodded. "More importantly, the council probably won't be able to keep our visit secret. Once people learn about the meeting—and they will—who knows what we'll face when trying to leave Swift Sword. There might be crowds of people just wanting to catch a glimpse of us."

"Or even throngs."

Cinder noticed a gleam in her eye. "What's so funny?"

She broke into laughter. "Nothing. It's just you're so serious sometimes. Laugh a little."

Cinder chuckled darkly. "I'll laugh plenty when this is done."

Anya had no response, but a momentary shadow ghosted across her face. Her jaw tightened in what might have been a flash of fury, but seconds later, she was relaxed.

Cinder eyed her in momentary concern, but her features remained smooth and unruffled. He discarded his concern, and together, they watched as their ship finished docking.

10

Genka Devesth stood upon a wooden tower that overlooked a large field. From it, he observed the happenings down below. The sun stood at its zenith, weak and without warmth as it beamed down through a pale, cloudless sky. His breath frosted in the autumn chill. The smell of wood burning from the nearby campfires lingered in the air. All of it meant that winter's icy promise was likely to come early this year. Maybe only a few more weeks before the first snow.

But none of that mattered.

All that counted was what was happening to Genka's newly constituted army. Exhortations, shouts, and curses filled the air as fresh recruits were put through their paces.

Genka studied them from atop his platform, which rose some twenty feet above the ground. The tower offered him an expansive view of what was taking place, and he was heartened to see improvement. Three weeks into their training, and the recruits were finally starting to demonstrate unit cohesion. Their spears were mostly held at the proper angle, and their overlapping shields offered defense, not just for themselves but also the warriors to their right and left. The seniors, those officers of his army who had survived the battle against the wraiths from nearly two years ago, were the ones giving the young men their instruction.

All of it was going well enough, but in truth Genka wished it didn't have to occur at all. Saving the Sunset Kingdoms from the herd of wraiths had required the sacrifice of a generation of young men.

And those poor fools down below, who should have been working on their farms and in their small towns, were instead here, learning to make war while their families were forced to bear the burden of their absence. Those back in the villages would still have to plant the crops and bring them to harvest, and they'd have to do so without the help of their sons, who were off training to become soldiers.

The farmers would struggle, and Genka wished it could be otherwise. But in this one regard, his wishes counted for as little as any peasant's. Even Mede's Heir, the *Garnala lon Anarin*—the Reaper of the Whirlwind—bowed before reality's inevitability because in truth, Genka needed these men, not just to rebuild his army but to maintain his restored empire of Shang Mendi. Without these men and without his army, the Sunsets would devolve into chaos, scattering into the fragmented city-states that had existed since Mede last strode Seminal some two thousand years ago.

Genka wouldn't allow it. The world needed his firm hand to provide guidance or chaos would ensue. Shet was risen, and while Genka reckoned the supposed god nothing more than a puffed-up Immortal, his armies could not be so easily disregarded. Naraka had been rebuilt, and already legions of zahhacks marched to occupy its black ramparts: necrosed, goblins, vampires, ghouls, and all manner of foul fiends.

But they wouldn't be content to remain there. They would eventually come storming out of Naraka and savage the world.

And Genka would meet that black tide. He would stop the zahhacks. In Seminal's darkest hour, he would stride forth and restore freedom and order to the world. Genka straightened, imagining how it would play out. It would be because of his work, his prowess and planning in battle that would prevent monsters from dragging Seminal into the depths.

But only if Shima Sithe and Aurelian Crèche were willing to listen to reason. Surely, they saw the danger posed by the wraiths. If the Sunsets were mangled further, how would their realms fare when Shet came west in force? Genka needed the success of his diplomats sent south. He needed more warriors to properly garrison the Sunsets and end the wraith threat once and for all. After that, he could turn that seasoned army against whatever zahhacks Shet might send west.

"They are coming along," said Vel Parnesth, ending Genka's meanderings. His oldest, most-trusted advisor stood next to him, bundled in heavy clothing. He was round-bellied, thin of limb, and pale, and his age showed in the tremble in his hands. It had started a year ago, and every week it seemed to be worse. Sometimes Vel couldn't even hold a spoon and needed to be fed.

But his mind remained crisp and sharp.

"It is a tragedy that we require them at all," Vel added with a disconsolate sigh.

"We all bow before necessity," Genka replied. He didn't speak about Shet and what he knew to be his destiny. Even Vel might consider it hubris. "The wraiths are still there. They might yet come at us again."

"So they might, my *Garnala lon Anarin*," Vel agreed. "But even then, these untrained wretches won't stop them. Not if your prior army, well-trained, blooded, and backed by Immortals and *hashains* alike, proved unable." He sighed. "We have to hope Shima Sithe and Aurelian Crèche act in their best interests rather than in their bitter pleasure."

Genka had already made the same grim calculation, but there was nothing else to be done. These recruits would have to learn, and then he'd have to bring in those even younger, possibly women, too. None could be spared if the Sunsets were to have a hope of surviving a second herd of wraiths.

But survive they would. Genka was the *Garnala lon Anarin*. It had to mean something. Shang Mendi couldn't simply be destroyed with him helpless to prevent it. His life had to have a greater purpose than that of a mere witness to catastrophe.

So yes, he would defeat the wraiths once and for all, and afterward would come the defense against Shet. Those were the two tasks that would see him protect all the free peoples of Seminal. Those were the two tasks that would see Genka's name rise to rival and eclipse Mede's legend and Shokan's myth.

"I'm cold," Vel stated. "Do you still need me?"

Genka did, but the conversation didn't have to take place here. "Follow me."

He made his way down the steep staircase leading to the ground where his guards formed around him, giving him and Vel distance for a private discussion.

However, rather than speak, Genka and Vel shared nothing but a companionable silence as they marched back toward *Rud jin Darab*—the Bastion of the Fist—his fortress and home. The structure reared like a loathsome growth in the near distance while miles beyond, the graceful pink and gold spires of *Rone Orn Sion*—the Palace of Beautiful Leaves—stood unfinished. Genka feared it would always be the case. With all these looming threats, when would he find the time to oversee its completion?

He spoke of one of those very threats. "What news of Jeet and Stren?"

The wraiths threatened Shang Mendi from without, but those two erstwhile *hashains* threatened his empire from within. Rumors abounded regarding them—their pronouncement of the Grimyogi—and despite Genka's best efforts, the rumors were spreading. He feared they might catch fire and become a conflagration.

"We've heard nothing about them," Vel said. "The only report of interest is the sighting of a troll in the village of Querel."

Genka's gaze lit on his old advisor. What would a troll be doing in the Sunsets? "How reliable is your source?"

"Very," Vel said. "I've also verified it from two other directions."

Which was the same as saying the information was unimpeachable. "And do your sources indicate why the troll is in Shang Mendi?"

Vel shook his head. "We are still trying to place a source in the village itself, but they've encountered difficulties."

It couldn't be a coincidence. "Someone is killing them?"

"That would be my guess," Vel confirmed.

"Is there anything of note about this village?" Genka asked.

"Not that I have been able to learn," Vel said.

A notion occurred to Genka, and he came to an abrupt halt. Could it be? His gaze latched on Vel. "Ask Chapterhouse. Find out if the *ha-shains* have any information about Querel."

"Chapterhouse?" Vel appeared startled for a moment, but an instant later, he understood. "You're wondering if Jeet or Stren might have family there."

Genka nodded, pleased to finally have some potentially good news. "And if they do, then we finally know from whence this cult of the Grimyogi is arising."

Vel shared his enthusiasm. "I'll send out inquiries immediately."

Dyrk Paterash puffed on a pipe while the rest of the Errow Council argued. He generally watched and listened to the discussions for a while before taking part. And while they were going on, there was nothing like his pipe to keep him focused. The distraction of inhaling and puffing set his mind at ease and allowed him to concentrate.

And right now, that concentration was telling him a problem: the Errow Council was divided and showed no signs of coming to a decision.

Dyrk grimaced. The prophets of their people needed to do better if they were to lead the Errows, especially since the rest of Rakesh, and by extension Gandharva and maybe even Yaksha Sithe and Surent Crèche, would need their guidance as well.

Shet had risen, and the human nations were the only ones who could stop him. But they needed Shokan and Sira. Where were they? That was at the heart of the council's troubles.

Dyrk listened as he gazed about the room, still puffing on his pipe.

The prophets were meeting in their usual location, a room in the House of the Pious. Mahogany paneling; crafted, leaded windows; a fine-oak table; and a gleaming crystal chandelier were among the decorations that lent the space an air of taste and wealth, but it was the paintings that had always struck Dyrk with a sense of optimism, humility, and prayerful longing.

It began with images of their greatest prophets.

First in glory and the founder of their faith was Lavian the Pious. Next was Juliya the Wise, who had discovered redemption for the True Tribe—the Errows—and led them from Gandharva to Rakesh. Then there was Chima the Virtuous, the woman who had uncovered the lies obscured in the *Medeian Scryings*. The only significant truth in that nest of fabrications was regarding Mede's Orb, which had been instrumental in the creation of the Immortals. And finally, there was Chima's wife, Soujourn the Truthteller, whose teachings on the *Lor Agni*, the Secret Fire, had sent the Errows on their long trek out of the miserable Sunset Kingdoms. A trek Dyrk was grateful his ancestors had undertaken. Living in a place where they were demeaned and expected to do the worst work possible: preparing the dead, cleaning latrines, and butchering animals... he couldn't imagine bending his pride like that.

However, the painting that captured Dyrk's attention and heart was the image of Shokan and Sira as massive granite statues that stood on the opposite banks of a river, hands clasped well above the waters.

Dyrk's eyes automatically went to the two empty chairs in the room. Around the table was a total of seven seats, five belonging to the prophets and the other two waiting for the Blessed Ones. But would they be filled soon? In essence, that was the chief question the prophets had been asking, ever since they'd learned of Cinder Shade.

"We cannot be certain of this dwarven tale," said Prophet Karia Orso, middle-aged and stern. As was generally the case, she had her arms folded across her chest and wore a scowl. "Stealing the Orb of Eretria and delivering it to Shet... how could the Blessed Ones take part in such heresy?"

"Unless it was a necessary heresy," said Prophet Shara Lakato, their oldest and most senior member. Despite her wizened features, her blues eyes had once twinkled with a childish delight, but these days, they rarely did so.

"I don't think they did any such thing," said Prophet Arima Terrel, the youngest member of the council and easily the most beautiful. "For Cinder and Anya to deliver an Orb to Shet would be just as much a heresy for them to claim *not* to be the Blessed Ones. Or in love."

Karia grimaced. "Heresies be damned. That is what is being reported from Surent Crèche. That they aren't the Blessed Ones. I won't comment on their feelings for one another."

Bryce Dayweaver, the only other male on the council and the flightiest, leaned forward, passionate as always. "And those reports also come from the same fuckers in Surent who say that Cinder and Anya stole the Orb of Eretria and gave it to Shet."

Dyrk smiled at Bryce's language. The man didn't care for the pomp and circumstance of a prophet. He spoke what was on his mind and without much of a filter.

"What about Anya?" Karia asked. "Is she Sira?"

"She is," Shara said, her pronouncement momentarily stifling the budding argument.

Karia rallied, though. "Even if Anya herself states otherwise? Even if Anya is only an elf?"

Bryce rapped the table. "If she isn't Sira, then who is?" He faced Karia. "Especially since that same report from Surent says that Anya has Sira's memories."

"The Blessed Ones don't know themselves." Dyrk spoke up for the first time. He reminded the others then of what they had recently learned from their allies, the *Lamarin Hosh*, and the recitation of their ancient founder. "It's the only thing that makes sense."

The room fell silent as the others processed Dyrk's reasoning.

"He may be right," Bryce eventually allowed, stroking his chin.

"Indeed," Shara said. "Remember, it isn't just our prophecies which can guide us. We should look elsewhere as well. To the portents written in the holy works of other nations."

"I still don't see how this is possible," Karia said. "For the *Cipre Elonicon*, the Destroyer of Falsehood, to himself claim a falsehood. Wouldn't that go against his very nature?"

Dyrk smirked to himself, drawing a drag on his pipe. Karia, like she always did, was arguing for argument's sake. *Fine.* He'd have fun poking the bear. "If we're going to make an assertion and base it on Shokan's titles, then don't forget he is also labeled the *Zuthrum lon Varshin*, the Reaper of the Whirlwind. Literally, he should be some kind of ruler of storms."

As predicted, Karia scowled at him. "That's not what I meant, and you know it."

Bryce ignored her anger, speaking to Dyrk. "What are you trying to say?"

Dyrk shrugged. "I'm not *trying* to say anything, except that we shouldn't worry so much about impressive-sounding titles." He rapped the table, just like Bryce had done. "Besides which, Shara is right. We need to examine the other holy works. The *Lor Agni* served Soujourn. It can serve us. Or are we too proud to learn what other nations believe about the Blessed Ones?"

"Some people in Rakesh believe in the *Lor Agni*," Arima reminded them all. "The book states that during humanity's greatest test, Shokan and Sira will arise once more, ascending like phoenixes to reclaim their lost glory." She emphasized the last. "Their lost glory. What if Cinder and Anya are lost to their glory? What if that's why they believe that they *aren't* Shokan and Sira?"

Bryce frowned. "You're talking about the final set of quatrains in *the Lor Agni, the Denthera*—the Time of the Great Wielder."

"*The Denthera* also mentions the coming of the Hydra of the Realms," Shara noted. "Could that be Shet?"

Dyrk didn't think so. "It sounds like this other being. The one Cinder and Anya warned the dwarves about. The Son of Emptiness."

The room went quiet. Ever since learning of Shet's reemergence, the Errow Council had done all they could to prepare their nation. They had gained political power; founded and funded the Ramoni, the brigade at the heart of the High Army; allied with Gandharva and the *Lamarin Hosh*. They'd even recruited Yaksha's elves, and because of all these changes, the High Army had become far deadlier.

But that was all to defend against Shet's zahhacks, not this grave new evil.

Dyrk hid a shiver. He hated thinking that there might be some power out there even worse than Shet.

Coral collected her skirt, making sure her ankles weren't visible before settling herself next to Dorr and Riner.

Only then did she glance around the Lonely Donkey, the alehouse where she had once busked for coin. Coral hadn't been here in years, but the tavern was the same. Familiar faces were seated in their usual places—at the long bar or at stained, round tables—and some of them looked like they might not have moved from when Coral had last been here.

She could empathize. The life of a worker wasn't generally easy, and for these laborers and craftsmen, the Lonely Donkey was where everyone knew their names and where they went to forget about their troubles. They drank their beers, slowly or quickly, talking in soft or loud tones while the waitresses rushed about filling orders.

Coral glanced about again. The alehouse was boisterous tonight, which wasn't a surprise. The world was changing and becoming more dangerous. Shet was risen and rumors abounded regarding his zahhacks. In the face of all that bad news, folks wanted to celebrate some, especially this evening, which was the last of the Days of Deliverance, the festival heralding the end of the *NusraelShev*.

Thank Devesh for the festival. Since learning of Shet's revival, times had been grim. Folks had been harsh with one another, unnecessarily cruel, but right now at least, everyone was in a good mood.

Coral only wished she could share in that good cheer, but the Lonely Donkey no longer felt familiar. She had been away too long, and although she had always meant to come back sooner, there had always been some reason why she shouldn't.

For instance, Dorr. She hadn't wanted their relationship to be tarnished by reminders of the man she had once loved. *Cinder Shade.* Memories of him and this tavern were inextricably intertwined, and Coral didn't want what she had built with Dorr to be ruined by comparisons to her first love.

Later on, coming here had seemed pointless. There were far greater issues commanding her attention, such as discovering exactly who Cinder truly was. She'd learned of it after being kidnapped by the *hashains* and seeing him in the arms of the elven princess, the two of them so clearly meant for each other. That image—of Cinder kissing Anya Aruyen—had finally doused any last, lingering emotions Coral might have felt for him.

That was a lie.

She'd always love Cinder, or Shokan as he was more rightly called, but it was a helpless kind of love, of knowing he was never meant to be hers.

And so she'd done her best to set aside her feelings for him, throwing herself fully into her relationship with Dorr. Not holding back, and their lives were the fuller for it. They'd married and had their first child—little Chima, who was an utter rascal. Coral smiled fondly on thinking of her.

Of course, there was also Dorr's work with the Ramoni, helping build out the unit and train a new generation of officers and soldiers. Coral had been similarly productive, but in her case, it had been from her employment as a maid and later on, working with the Errows.

She still flushed whenever she considered how poorly she had once thought of their entire tribe, especially calling them by that name, which only they were allowed to use. It shamed her. Shamed her in how she had spoken to the first Errows she'd ever known.

But then again, she also wished those boys hadn't been such poor examples of their tribe. Fortunately, Jarde and Stard had become much better people since their time at *Our Lady of Fire.* They were now members of the Ramoni, good soldiers and solid citizens.

"Coral!" A large, bearded man shouted. It was Trip Badger, the owner of the Lonely Donkey. He ambled over to their table, smiling broadly and in genuine pleasure.

Coral rose to embrace him, and after reintroducing him to Dorr and Riner, she caught Trip up on her life and also learned what he'd been doing. He left them shortly thereafter, and Coral seated herself again.

"He missed you," Dorr said.

Coral laughed. "I earned him a lot of money with my busking. More than anything, that's probably what he missed."

"Don't sell yourself short," Riner said, disagreeing with her, which she silently applauded. Her brother had always been unsure of himself, but seeing him grow into a fine young man, strong of mind and body, was everything she could have hoped for him.

Dorr cleared his throat. "I'm glad we have this night," he said. "Starting next week, I'll be busier than ever. The shrewds are wanting more recruits."

Coral frowned, deliberating and as she did so, her eyes lighted on her husband. He stared back at her, calm. She smiled to herself. In the past, Dorr used to stiffen whenever she did so, claiming there was a 'scary intensity' to her gaze when she looked at him like that. He no longer flinched, but it still amused her at how a fine warrior like her husband could have ever found her intimidating.

"Where will they get the money for the new recruits?" Coral asked. The higher taxes needed to bolster the army and upgrade Rakesh's defenses against Shet already had many people stirring in discontent. Some of them whined that it was unnecessary since the Yaksha elves didn't seem afraid of the so-called god.

But those people were fools. Didn't they see how many elves disagreed with their empress? How many had joined the High Army? That should have told them the truth of the wind's direction.

"The money will come from letting go of soldiers who can't or won't measure up to what we need."

Coral nodded in relief. *Good.* Then no new taxes.

"I had a meeting today with Bryce Dayweaver," Riner said.

"The prophet?" Dorr asked.

Riner nodded. "He wants a report on any mentions of Shokan in holy texts other than the Errow version of the *Medeian Scryings.*"

An unusual request, and Coral's gaze centered on her brother. "Did he say why?"

He might have recoiled in response to her 'scary intensity' but rallied an instant later. "He didn't, but I think it's because of what the dwarves said about Cinder and Anya."

Dorr growled. "Let's keep that quiet."

The Errow Council had done magnificent work in getting Rakesh on a war footing, but in one way, they had blundered badly. They had lost control of the information about Cinder. Someone present when he'd destroyed an entire sect of *hashains* had spoken out of turn, spilling secrets that the Errow Council had wanted kept quiet. Within days, the city had been aflame with wild stories about Cinder Shade.

People remembered how a willowy youth, only a year into his training, had bested most every warrior in the Maker's Tournament and earned a place at the Third Directorate. Other stories abounded of how Cinder had defeated spiderkin, elves, necrosed, and dwarves with surpassing ease, and in the process, earned the title of Prime of his class. More tales included abilities and Talents that no human had possessed since the ending of the *NusraelShev*: Fireballs, Blending, Shielding, and the Wildness.

From there, it hadn't taken long to see Cinder labeled as the *Cipre Elonicon* from Gandharva's *Lor Agni* and the dwarven *Crèche Prani* or the Grimyogi, a name many Errows recognized from the Sunset Kingdoms. There were other stories, too, but those were about Anya. They were about a princess of Yaksha Sithe who traveled with Cinder, the two of them devoted to one another and in love.

Riner leaned forward, speaking to Dorr. "Do you believe the dwarves? What they said about Cinder and Anya?"

Dorr leaned back in his chair. "I don't know, and I also don't think it matters. Shokan and Sira will show or they won't. But in either case, we have to face Shet, and we better be prepared because he's coming."

Coral agreed with her husband, and she allowed the fear she rarely let anyone see course through her. She reached out then, needing Dorr's steadying presence, and based on his expression and how he gripped her hand, it looked like he needed hers as well.

11

Cinder hadn't wanted to spend much time in Swift Sword. Even just the potential of having to deal with people who believed he might be Shokan was an aggravation he could do without, and had it been his choice, he and Anya would have already left the city.

But there were still a few items to which he first had to attend.

Most importantly, he needed to finish writing to his friends. His last time through Swift Sword had been nearly three years ago, when he and Anya had planned their journey to Mahadev, and no one had received direct word from the two of them since. It didn't matter that his friends had already learned of his survival from the Shokans.

In the end, Cinder needed to personally let them know that he was alive and healthy. He'd penned most of the letters he had to send on the voyage to Swift Sword, but he'd somehow overlooked Master Choff at *Our Lady of Fire* and Masters Jine and Fain from *Steel-Graced Adepts*. There was also an extra one to Riner, speaking of their shared love of history and of Mahadev's architecture, and another to Master Lerid on some training exercises he might find useful.

While he scribbled away, he sat with Anya at Rozero's Place, a nice-enough restaurant. The last time Cinder had eaten here, it had been with Coral, and he still recalled the meal and how he'd had to save his money for many weeks beforehand. Rozero's wasn't a fine-dining establishment—stiff attendants and servers on hand—but for an orphan short of funds, it had felt like one. The prices back then had certainly made Cinder's eyes widen in amazement.

Nevertheless, he'd wanted to impress a woman, and sometimes men did stupid things when faced with that challenge.

Speaking of stupid things…

Cinder surveyed the space. Rozero's dining room was mostly empty, yet to fill with the evening guests, but of those present, he hoped no one was watching him and Anya too closely: a human man seated next to a beautiful elven woman. If anyone was, he also hoped they wouldn't put the obvious answer together and guess their identities. Cinder just wanted a quiet dinner before he and Anya had to leave Swift Sword.

"You're going to wear out your hand, writing so much," Anya said.

Cinder glanced her way, and she stared back at him from over the lip of her tumbler, a half-smile on her face as she took a sip of hot chai.

"You could help me write the letters," Cinder replied.

"Oh, no. I'm Simply Anya, remember?" she said in an uneducated accent. "I don't know my letters too good."

Cinder laughed. "You're right. We wouldn't want to tax your womanly mind."

Anya arched an elegant eyebrow. "Womanly? Now you're insulting all of womankind?"

Cinder answered with a shameless grin, taking a sip of his own drink, enjoying the soothing blend of chai spiced with cinnamon sticks, cardamom pods, and ginger. He'd developed a taste for the drink from Master Lerid, who had a cup of it every evening. His grin grew wistful.

"Whom are you thinking about?"

"Master Lerid," Cinder replied. "And there's something about him that I was always meaning to ask you. When did you have time to send a letter to Ald Prince?"

Anya frowned in puzzlement. "Who?"

"The promotor who purchased *Steel-Graced Adepts*. I found out about it before my Secondary Trial, and you said you were going to send him a letter. But by the time we came back to Swift Sword from Fort Carnate, the issue with him had already been settled."

Anya's face cleared. "Oh, him. I sent the letter to him at Fort Carmine when we were leaving Swift Sword. I never told you?"

Cinder shook his head. "You didn't, and I've never thanked you for it either."

Anya waved aside his words. "It wasn't much. I just wrote him a letter and leaned on my status as a princess of Yaksha Sithe."

"It still meant a lot to me."

Anya's frown returned, softer and quizzical this time. "Cinder Shade, when did you learn such politeness?"

Cinder sniffed. "I've always been polite. You must have forgotten. Being so old and all. Over a hundred, right?"

Anya sighed. "Then you ruin it."

Cinder chuckled, but an instant later, he cut off his humor when an elf walked through the front door. It was Lisandre Coushinre, Riyne's more-accomplished, older brother. He was here because Cinder and Anya had asked Estin to find the man. There were some issues they wanted to discuss with him.

Lisandre approached their table, handsome like all elves, tall and dark-haired. At his waist was an *insufi* blade, given only to the finest of Yaksha's warriors. Anya had one as well—fashioned by her father, in fact—but what she didn't have was Lisandre's title of *Sai*—masterful warrior—but Cinder figured it was only a formality.

"It's good to see the two of you," Lisandre said with a genuine smile, taking a seat at their table. "Estin…" He shook his head in seeming disbelief. "I still can't believe he finally made it out of the Directorate. The empress won't be happy."

"There's a lot she won't like," Anya agreed, going on to give a truncated account of Shet, Zahhack, and the Orbs of Peace.

"We have to see the Orbs destroyed," Cinder urged. "It's the only way to close the anchor line leading to the Son of Emptiness."

During their explanation, Lisandre had leaned back in his chair. "That's a lot to take in. A lot you're asking me to take on faith. But disregarding all of that, what do you need from me? And why should I do it?"

Cinder answered the last question first. "You'll do it because it's the only way to survive what's coming. For any of us. As for what we need, get the Shokans assigned to Char. We need them to help us at Bharat."

"We've already discussed it with Estin." Anya said. "He'll be with us."

Lisandre's gaze sharpened. "You plan on shipping from Char to Bharat? How? The rishis will never let that many warriors onto their island. You know how they are about privacy."

"They will for a diplomatic mission," Cinder said. He went on to explain their plan. "Can you do it?" he asked. "*Will* you do it?" He stared intently at Lisandre, never breaking eye contact.

Lisandre stared back at him, not responding at first until he finally gave a slow nod. "I'll have the Shokans reassigned." An instant later, he gave a small bark of laughter. "And to think, before this afternoon, I thought Shet was the most dangerous foe we would have to face." He sobered. "I better get to work."

He rose, and Cinder did so as well, shaking Lisandre's hand. "Thank you," he said, infusing his words with all the gratitude he was feeling.

"Thank me by succeeding." He indicated Anya. "You'll have two members of the royal family on another mad venture. See them home safely."

With that, Lisandre took his leave, and Cinder settled back in his seat, exhaling heavily in relieved satisfaction.

Anya smiled. "It worked. Did you have any doubts?"

"I doubted everything," Cinder said with a chuckle. He still couldn't believe that in a couple of months or so, he'd get to see his brothers again.

"What are you smiling about now?" Anya asked.

He told her.

"You really think of them as brothers, don't you? Even Mohal and

Riyne?"

Cinder nodded. "Of course."

"Then that's how you know your memories from the Directorate must be false."

It was something he'd already come to accept.

Cinder grunted when a warrior rammed a shoulder against his. They had been passing by one another on a narrow straightaway, and while there had been plenty of room for the other man to slip past, he hadn't done so. Instead, he'd slammed an armored shoulder into Cinder's seemingly unprotected one. If not for the clothing Manifold had given him—which acted as armor even though it looked and felt like simple clothing—the blow could have hurt.

As it was, it merely served to irritate Cinder, and he glared at the other man who was surrounded by a group of his friends. Six warriors in total, and given the odds, a glare was all Cinder intended. Nothing more. He didn't want to get caught up in an alley brawl.

After Lisandre had left Rozero's Place, Estin had met them there and passed on the diplomatic papers General Arwan had promised. It had been their last task before departing Swift Sword, and their ship was heading out within the next couple of hours. If he and Anya wanted to make it on board, they needed to hustle.

So after shooting his glare, Cinder made to move on.

But someone spun him around.

"You got a problem?" It was the man who'd smacked his shoulder into Cinder's. A long scar set the left side of his face in a permanent sneer, and he glowered in promised violence. His friends shifted to encircle Cinder and Anya.

Not a good sign.

Cinder faced up with the man, studying him and his friends more closely. Mercenaries, and he recognized their unit insignia. *The Red Flags.* He'd fought against others of their kind back when he'd been a student at *Steel-Graced Adepts*. And just as then, he was unimpressed now. Their demeanor of barely restrained ferocity didn't frighten him in the slightest.

Kesarins don't run from sheep.

But if this dance went the way Cinder didn't want, he needed to be ready. He punched past the pain of the blue-and-green lightning and conducted *Jivatma*.

The dimly lit street, little more than an alley, lifted to noon brightness. The harsh breaths of the mercenaries came clear. Even Scarface's heartbeat, which sounded slow and steady in spite of the man's obvious anger. A slow drip of water plinked from a nearby roof. The smell of garlic and onions from what the Red Flags had recently eaten.

"We don't want any trouble," Anya said. The fresh scent of a mountain stream became evident as she sourced *lorethasra*. She, too, was ready for a fight even while she tried to talk their way out of it. "Just let us—"

"Weren't talking to you," Scarface snapped, eyes locked on Cinder. "You're an elf, but you ain't immortal. Move on."

"But she's right," Cinder said. "This was just a misunderstanding on my part. We'll be going our way now. Leave us be, and we'll do the same."

Scarface smirked. "Fuck you." He hauled back to land a punch.

Jaide Fallet didn't know why he wanted to throw down with the well-dressed noble. Maybe it had something to do with the beautiful elf the man had at his side, walking like they was a proper couple. Fucking nobles had all the good things in the world already. And now they were having their way with the elves, too?

Elves. A race of stuck-up fuckers who wouldn't bother pissing on a real man if he was on fire. And here came this arrogant bastard, with a fine piece of tail on his arm, likely getting the kind of fun Jaide couldn't even dream of having.

It wasn't right. Not when the Red Flags fought and bled all over Devesh's creation. They died for folks like this noble, a coward who'd likely never even drawn the sword at his hip. And what was their reward? Some coin, sure, but when they returned to the lands of men, how were the Flags greeted? Was it with wine and willing women?

No. It was with scowls from tight-fisted merchants, hard stares from panty-waisted guards, and arrogant lip from whores, no matter how much they were paid.

So, yes, Jaide had already been feeling peckish when he caught sight of the noble and his elven woman. And so what if he'd shoulder-checked the soft-handed chicken heart. If the man had been smart, he'd have taken it, seen the odds against him, and shut his piehole.

But he hadn't. He'd glared at Jaide. And worse, his woman had talked down to them. Then the man had done the same damn thing.

Fuckers.

Shooting a glare at Jaide might have only earned the noble a punch to face, but add in the words, and he was sure to get a beating. And a beating was exactly what Jaide was fixing to start when he hauled back. He shot a fist forward, fully expecting to bash the little bitch's nose through the back of his head.

Jaide stumbled, though, when he connected with nothing but air. Kelly, to his left, crumpled, laid out cold. Kaper, right next to his brother, Kelly, fell, his nose spurting blood. Another shot and Tondo was down.

Jaide gaped, backing off. What the fuck? What in the actual fuck! He hadn't even seen the blows coming, much less landing.

The answer came to him: *elves.* The woman must have Blended or had others with her who were Blended. They were the ones taking down the Flags.

Fucking cheating bastards!

Jaide roared, swinging wildly. "Come on, you fuckers! Show yourselves."

Warren collapsed like a puppet with his strings cut. This time Jaide had seen his attacker. It had been the noble, and the way he moved. No man could move like that. Faster than any elf. It was impossible.

Jaide's vision blurred. His head ached, his ears rang, and his eyes wouldn't see right. What the fucking—

He was suddenly off the ground, no time to even squawk before being slammed into the alley wall. The noble was holding him there, arm extended, like it was no trouble at all, like Jaide weighed no more than a bouquet of flowers. He gaped, head aching, and unable to make sense of any of it. No one was that strong. No one was that fast. No one…

The blood drained from Jaide's face. Ever since coming ashore to Swift Sword, he'd heard stories about someone who could do all that and more. A man who traveled with a beautiful elf woman. "Shokan," he whispered.

"You did not see me," the man ordered. "Forget what happened here, and I'll leave you in peace."

"But the world needs to know—"

"The alternative is far worse," the elf woman said, stepping close and wearing an expression cold enough to cause Death himself to piss a stream. "We leave you in pieces."

Princess Anya. It had to be her. "Sira," Jaide breathed. He wasn't a religious man but coming face-to-face with the Blessed Ones made a man reconsider certain things.

"Keep what happened to yourself," the woman commanded, more regal than an empress. "Are we understood?"

Jaide nodded his head as fast as he could. "I'll tell no one. Except maybe myself, but even then, I won't believe it." He offered a sickly grin. "I'm a liar. Everyone says so. You can count on me to stay quiet." The fuck was he babbling so much for?

"Very good," the noble said. "See that you do."

Jaide was dropped, and he collapsed to the ground, falling over on his side. He lay there for a few seconds before scrambling to his feet, spinning about.

There was no one else with him in the alley. No one except his friends.

In spite of Jaide's promise to Shokan and Sira, he knew he'd tell of what happened before the night was over, probably as soon as he and his boys reached their first pub. It was too juicy a story to keep to themselves anyway. He and the boys wouldn't have to pay for drinks the whole night and then some.

Jaide drew himself proud. Imagine that. He'd just gotten his ass kicked by Shokan. He grinned in excitement, eager to tell someone about it.

"You realize he's probably going to start talking as soon as he hits a pub, right?" Anya asked.

She didn't sound accusatory, but she didn't have to. Cinder had messed up. "He was supposed to go down when I punched him in the head."

"You pulled it?"

A single nod. If he hadn't, he'd likely have caved in Scarface's head. Unfortunately, Cinder had misjudged how much he needed to pull his punch. He sighed. No use worrying about it now; what was done was done. "Let's get the horses."

A moment later, Anya chuckled. "I thought he'd wet himself when I made that comment about leaving him in pieces."

Cinder smiled. "It's a pretty stupid phrase, but you're also wrong. I think it was your face that scared him."

Anya touched her cheek, appearing hurt. "What's wrong with my face?"

Cinder hadn't meant anything by his comment, but upon seeing her stricken expression, he broke into laughter. "You're a beautiful woman, Anya, but you can be very scary when you want to be."

Anya stared at him a moment before turning away with a satisfied smirk. "And don't you forget it."

12

Cinder glanced about when he and Anya disembarked at a small village a week west of Swift Sword. It was in an isolated region of Gandharva, far from Rakesh's capital and cloaked in rugged terrain. In sum, a terrible place for Shet to forge an anchor line and gather his forces and attack Swift Sword. But even then, it was still too close to Cinder's home for his comfort.

Which was why he and Anya didn't stop in the small village. Instead, they continued their journey, traveling northeast for three more weeks before finally halting when they reached a barren stretch of badlands in the foothills west of the Daggers. It was a place where hardly any water, greenery, or animals could be found, an awful area for an army to find food or sustenance as well as distant from any villages or towns. In short, it was the perfect place for contacting Liline.

Early on the morning after their arrival to the desolate area, Anya did so, using the *divasvapna*.

Seconds later a black line split the world, rotating on its axis to reveal a doorway filled with rainbow colors. A bridge formed from the chaos, and Liline Salt, the Water Death, stepped forth. She was one of

Shet's original seven Titans, and Cinder recollected them all.

Or rather Shokan did. The Blessed One's memories had many involving the Titans, including the last time he had battled their commander, Sture Mael. In it, Shokan had left a scar on the man's face, one running from his mouth to his collarbone. He remembered the brothers Tomag and Tormak Jury as well. Big men with competent minds for strategy. And then there was Drak Renter, the youngest Titan and thankfully, incompetent in many ways. But handsome Garad Lull was anything but incompetent. He had a viper's way of finding weaknesses and exploiting them. And finally, Rence Darim, the Illwind; full of bitterness and rage, she sought vengeance for any perceived slight and was also one of the only two women who were Titans.

The other, of course, being Liline, who towered over them, almost twice their height, even when they were seated on their mounts. Liline was as beautiful as the sunset, and she wore silver armor forged to fit her form, emphasize her curves, and match the color of her calm eyes.

Cinder recalled Liline as well, all the malice she'd visited on the innocent. He forced down the glare he wanted to send her way, viewing her instead with an emotionless gaze.

"You're learning," Liline said in amusement. "Hide your emotions equally well before Lord Shet. He is far less forgiving than I." Her smile fled. "You have it?"

Anya answered by withdrawing the Orb of Moss from her *null pocket*.

Liline's smile returned. "Well done." She glanced around. "Should I ask how you managed to travel so swiftly from Naraka to Revelant and then this place? Where are we, by the way?"

Cinder shrugged, unwilling to divulge even the tiniest morsel of information. "You have your secrets. We have ours."

Liline laughed. "Say that to Lord Shet, little human, and see how far that gets you."

"I imagine he's waiting for us," Cinder said, not rising to her bait.

"Yes, he is. Come." Liline gestured to the anchor line.

Cinder sourced *lorethasra*, working through the cursed

blue-and-green lightning laced throughout it. From there he tethered to the anchor line, making sure he was halting in the creation of the braid. Anya did the same, and in an instant, they traveled.

Cinder's ears rang with a screaming sound, and his body stretched, feeling like he was about to be torn in two. He stumbled on exiting the anchor line, exiting into a familiar alcove off one of Naraka's court-yards, fighting down abrupt nausea but refusing to show weakness be-fore Liline.

In less than a second, he had his gorge under control, and he exam-ined their location.

It was early afternoon in this part of the world, and although early summer held sway in the lowlands of Yaksha, Rakesh, and Gandharva, here in the heights of Mount Kirindor, winter never truly let go of its hold. An icy wind moaned amongst the mountains and across the flat plateau where Shet had constructed an outdoor courtyard and throne hall, and beyond it rose the god's rebuilt black palace of Naraka, which lofted to the sky like a gangrenous growth, all hard lines, brutal ar-chitecture, and square towers. There was no subtlety to the building, which was meant to inspire fear and awe.

Same with the god himself who currently waited for Cinder. He sat upon his black throne, which rested atop a large dais, twenty feet above the rest of the plateau and surmounted by a red canopy. The same tawny-furred dragon slumbered at the foot of the throne, and Cinder wondered anew how the god had tamed such a powerful beast.

His attention went back to Shet. The god sat still, wearing a mock-ing smile, one that crossed the midline, including the white mask that perfectly mimicked the features on the right side of his face. And in his hands, Shet held a red-runed, black spear topped by a leaf blade. Cinder hadn't before seen the weapon, which seemed to soak in the light but gave off no reflection.

He didn't like the spear—had never liked spear wielders—and he vowed to do more than burn the god when next they clashed.

"Careful," Anya warned.

Cinder realized he was a few shades from glowering, and he quickly smoothed his features to a neutral expression.

"Better," Anya said, passing him the Orb of Moss.

"I will leave you to our lord," Liline said, making ready to depart. "And you didn't ask, but the camels you brought with you from Flatiron are doing well."

Cinder shot her retreating form a look of surprise. She'd promised to see to the camels they'd used in Flatiron, but he hadn't expected her to actually keep her vow.

"Come and deliver your news."

It was a command from Shet, and Cinder started forward. As before, the plateau had a plethora of zahhacks, arranged in ranks of importance. In the outer rings were the scourskin, vermin who feasted on filth. Then came the tattered-garbed gray ghouls and insect-like goblins. None of the poorly formed creatures were able to contend with their more powerful brethren, such as the unformed shapeshifters or the vampires in their elegant attire. And even those two races gave way to the necrosed, who stood closest to Shet.

But regardless of stature, all the zahhacks glared, hissed, and threatened as Cinder marched through their lines. He paid them no mind until reaching the necrosed. There, he startled. Seven of their number were familiar. They should have been dead. He'd killed four of them when he and Anya had first met Shet—a fifth he'd burned to ash with a Fireball—and the other three during their first journey to Mount Kirindor—a short battle at night in a winter-cold valley.

Cinder stared at the necrosed, focused as he closed with them. They jeered, made crude comments and threats, every last one of them, including the ones who should by all rights be deceased. Apparently, the legends of how a necrosed could only be killed by burning their dismantled parts or through the Wildness were true. He made a note to do so the next time he faced any of the creatures. He'd not give them another chance to reconstitute.

There was no more time for planning because Cinder had reached his destination, and at the prescribed twenty feet, he crashed to a halt, bowing low before the so-called god.

"Pass it over," Shet said without preamble, holding out a waiting hand.

Cinder straightened and did so, extending his arm as he offered the Orb.

The gardenia-fresh fragrance of Shet's *lorethasra* filled the air as the Orb was guided to him. A smile creased Shet's face then, followed by a flexing of his forearm. The sound of tinkling bells rang forth as the Orb shattered into powdered fragments that drifted away to nothingness in a rainbow of light.

Cinder exhaled, feeling a weight he hadn't before noticed lift from his chest. Shet must have felt the same relief since he breathed out in obvious satisfaction. Which proved that no matter how much Shet proclaimed himself a deity, it was untrue. He was merely a human drunk on power and hubris.

And Cinder would choke him on that pride. It was a vow he had made to himself, and each destruction of an Orb would bring that promise one step closer to reality. Even now, Cinder sensed that the blue-and-green lightning shrouding his *Jivatma* was thinner, but it would still hinder his abilities to a significant extent.

It seemed that every Orb built on the next, limiting him, not just in how much he could conduct or source but also in how skillfully he could use his *Jivatma* and weave his *lorethasra*. In addition, while the destruction of an Orb allowed him greater control of his skills and Talents, the improvement was proving incremental. Cinder reckoned that it likely wouldn't be until the final Orb was destroyed that he would regain the full panoply of his abilities.

Nevertheless, even now his Talents and skills were already enhanced, of greater dexterity and power, but he'd have to make sure to train to use them properly. He remembered how long it had taken him to properly use his Talents once Mahamatha had unlocked them.

"Where will you go next?" Shet asked.

"Char," Cinder said in the deadpan tone with which he'd always addressed Shet. "It is the closest city to Bharat."

"I assume you have a plan?"

Cinder nodded. "I do, my lord."

Shet grunted. "You are lucky. We have a location a week's ride from the elven city. You won't have to waste too much time riding there."

Cinder couldn't prevent his eyes from widening in shock. He hadn't expected Shet to have made such deep inroads into Apsara Sithe. How else would the god have knowledge of a place so close to one of that nation's most important cities?

Shet laughed. "You have your secrets, and I have mine." His smile became mocking. "Is that not what you said to Liline?"

Another surprise. Cinder had never seen Liline communicate with Shet, which meant… He hid a frown. What exactly? Did the Titans have a way of speaking mind-to-mind, like Fastness? Or did she merely throw her voice using a braid? He threw off his reflections. He'd discuss it later with Anya.

"No offense was intended, my lord," Cinder said in eventual reply to Shet's statement.

The god answered with a desultory wave of his hand. "Find Liline. Gather what you need and go."

Anya broke away from reading *Shet's Council*, the so-called god's so-called holy book. She and Cinder had decided to read his writings, learn all they could from them, and hopefully glean some insight into their foe. Anya turned the book over, staring at the black cover, considering. Thus far, the book was nothing but an utter bore, a collection of stupid aphorisms posing as wisdom. And this was what inspired Shet's people?

She shook her head, giving a disconsolate sigh. How sad. Nevertheless, she'd keep at it, studying *Shet's Council*, even though she found the material contemptible.

Prior to resuming her reading, though, she turned her attention to Cinder, watching as he worked on his Chakras. He had five of them open already, but with the destruction of the Orb of Moss, he could solidify those gains.

Eyes closed, he was currently working on doing just that, here in these rolling hills east of Char. A gentle wind fingered his short hair, sparking the flames in their fire pit, swirling the aroma of tonight's stew, and mixing it with that of smoke. Painter and Barton shifted about while from a wooded area to the north came the yipping of foxes playing.

Anya smiled at the sound. Playing sounded like a great idea, and she wished she could. *Maybe sometime. Hopefully, someday soon.*

Her gaze went back to Cinder.

"You're staring," he said, not opening his eyes.

She put aside *Shet's Council*, unsurprised by his awareness. Much of the time, Cinder knew what she was thinking, so why not also know when she was looking at him? They should have lost that profound sense of the other after Mahadev, but for some inexplicable reason, they hadn't.

Mahadev.

So many changes had happened there, including to Manifold. The Mythaspuri had been healed after the battle with Rabisu, but his task remained challenging. It was Manifold who had to prevent Heremisth from widening the anchor line leading to her true master, Zahhack. He was likely managing well enough since the world hadn't ended, but they couldn't afford to leave the work too long on his shoulders. He'd suffered enough.

Cinder grunted, opening his eyes. "I've done what I can."

He rose to his feet and arched his back, stretching, and Anya stifled an appreciative inhalation. In this pose—or any—Cinder was as handsome as the night sky.

"Can you see your *lorethasra*?" he asked.

It was an unexpected question—one to which he should already know the answer. Nonetheless, she took a moment to collect her thoughts, pushing off the ground and joining Cinder in gazing west toward Char. "No one can. It's how you realized you weren't actually seeing *lorethasra*, but *Jivatma*."

"But you can see *Jivatma*?"

"I can now." Anya peered at Cinder's shadowed features, unable to read his expression. "What's this about?"

"When I first was trying to use *lorethasra*, everyone told me they couldn't see it. But then when I actually did start using it, I could see it."

Anya already knew all this. "And?"

"And it was what everyone told me to look for," Cinder said, sounding frustrated. "Everyone told me to look for a silver stream, which I found. Except mine has the blue-and-green lightning wrapped throughout it."

Anya still wasn't following, but rather than press him on the matter, she waited for him to finish what was on his mind.

"So if everyone can see the silver stream, why did all the elves and dwarves say they *can't* see *lorethasra*?"

That was what this was about? Anya would have thought Cinder could have figured out the explanation on his own. Then again, she hadn't. When she'd first learned to source her *lorethasra*, she had also assumed that the silver stream was *lorethasra*. However, every teacher, wise person, and instructor she had asked had insisted it wasn't the case.

And having no reason to argue with her elders, Anya had considered the matter settled. She still did. "It's because the stream isn't *lorethasra*."

"Because all streams have sources, and the source is *lorethasra*?" Cinder snorted. "That's what Master Molni said, but it still sounds pedantic. It's basically explaining a distinction that doesn't exist."

Anya shrugged. Maybe Cinder was right. "I don't know, but it's what I was taught."

Cinder still gazed off into the distance, arms folded. "I think you were taught wrong. I worry about that."

Anya's brows lifted in disbelief. "You think thousands of years of elven instruction is wrong? Thousands of years of dwarven teaching, too?"

"Shokan's memories say that the stream is *lorethasra*. That's what he believed." Cinder turned his gaze on her. "What do Sira's memories say?"

"I don't know." Anya had never considered the matter, but she did so then and realized Cinder was right. Sira had thought the same way: the silver stream *was lorethasra*. Still, what difference did it make? She asked.

"Just another brick in the wall."

"Another brick in the wall?" A unique phrase.

Cinder grinned. "Back before Mahadev, I used to imagine myself creating a wall between my mind and my feelings for you."

Anya's eyes widened in shock. "Really?"

He nodded.

She laughed. "So did I. I even thought of it in the same way."

"Adding a brick to the wall?"

"But this time, we're pulling it down."

"That's how I see it," Cinder agreed. "Tear down our surety. Don't believe everything we think, like the teachings about the silver stream *not* being *lorethasra*."

Anya chuckled. "You're never going to let that go, are you?"

"I might," Cinder said with a slight smile.

They faced outward again, falling into a companionable quiet.

"I wonder what we'll find on the other side," Anya said after a few minutes of silence.

"Of the wall?"

She nodded.

"Maybe the truth?"

Anya pursed her lips, hoping he was right. Also, maybe there was a way to speed the process along. "The Gate of Saints in Bharat. That's how we'll escape their island. To Twilight Gate, which has Verity Foe."

Cinder inhaled deeply, not responding at first, but Anya could sense his excitement build. "And verity means truth. It's what Sadana mentioned. You think we can learn the truth there?" Another moment, and his excitement ebbed, transforming to sorrow. "Whatever we learn, it won't change us. We are who we are."

There was a finality to his tone, and Anya frowned. What was he talking about? That wasn't what Cinder had said on the other occasions when they had discussed their memories.

An odd change to his expression heralded confusion. "What were we talking about?"

"You don't remember?"

Cinder shook his head.

It was just like the other times for both of them then, and Anya explained what they had been discussing.

"Really?" Cinder sounded stunned. Seconds later, his amazement became a glower. "Entering Verity Foe can't come soon enough."

Anya offered a wan smile, empathizing with his frustration. "Just a few more weeks, and we'll be there."

Cinder's glower transformed into a grimace. "I hate waiting."

"You are not a man meant to hate." The statement slipped out automatically, but it was one that Anya had said to Cinder on prior occasions. And it still felt right.

Cinder was smiling wryly, though. "Tell that to our enemies, *priya*."

Anya laughed. "I'm sure they'll be terrified."

Priya. The word awoke Anya in the middle of the night, and her eyes went to Cinder. He had the watch and was pacing beyond the firelight. She viewed him, considering their relationship.

Why had he called her that? And did she want to know? *Of course I do.*

She shifted her gaze, staring upward at the moon, Dormant, which shined ghostly across the hills. The earlier wind had died down, and only the occasional crackle of their campfire disturbed the night. There was no more playing of foxes.

The world was at peace, and Anya clutched her knees, still lost in contemplation. Cinder hadn't recognized the word and at the time, neither had she. But she did now. The word was from *Shevasra*, and it was what Shokan and Sira called each other. *Beloved.* Why would he—

She blinked. What had she been thinking? Something about—

Another blink. *No.* She must have been having a nightmare. That's why she had woken. A soothing sensation spread out from within her, urging her to close her eyes and rest. There was nothing to worry about.

But what about—

Rest, the sensation encouraged.

Anya fought to stay awake. There had been other episodes of her mind frozen out of whatever she had been thinking, and—

No, the sensation insisted. *Close your eyes. Sleep.*

Anya lay down, and her eyes drifted shut, but just as she settled, a grinding noise drifted through her mind, and she imagined the scent of acrid smoke.

She could barely breathe. The battle was all-but won, but it had taken her all. And she only lived because he'd absorbed a blow meant for her. Even now he clutched his side, stomach leaking blood. Temple as well. His face was a mask of red. He limped, an ankle likely twisted or worse.

Glancing at the other two left on the bridge, she drew back at the fury on the other woman's face. What was the cause of her rage?

Understanding bloomed. It was the man. Rukh, the husband who had betrayed her.

No. *That wasn't right. He loved her—*

A recognition deep within cut through her confusion, and she recognized this place and this time and what she had to do.

Anya woke again, gasping, terrified. The dream… She recalled a similar one but from a different perspective, and even as she sought to retain the images and feelings, they melted through her fingers like snowflakes.

There had been a time when dreams that she couldn't remember upon awakening had convinced her that she was Sira. Was this the same, then? Had she just experienced another memory from the Blessed One? And if so, why? Didn't she already have all of Sira's memories?

"What's wrong?"

It was Cinder. He crouched close at hand, and of course, he'd recognized her troubled mind.

"Just a dream," Anya replied. She threw an arm over her eyes, not wanting to see the concern on his face. The dream, whatever it had been, would have likely involved him—they always did—and she wasn't in the mood to discuss it right now.

"Some dream," Cinder noted. "You were thrashing."

Rage coursed through her like fire. Why couldn't he shut his stupid mouth? Why did he always have to challenge her? She was about to scream at him to leave her be, but he surprised her into silence.

"I'm sorry."

The apology snipped Anya's anger like a cut thread.

"I'm sorry you have to have these troubles and dreams," Cinder said, standing. "Sometimes it feels like I'm the reason. That's why I'm sorry."

She sat up in her bedrolls. He was being ridiculous. How could any of this be his fault? But upon thinking about it, she could understand why he might believe it so. After all, she felt the same guilt toward him.

Again came the grinding of metal and stench of smoke. A fleeting sensation that was gone, but she recognized it this time.

"Rabisu," she whispered.

"What about him?" Cinder asked.

"Is he truly dead?" After recalling the sensations of metal and smoke, she worried, the rakshasa might have found a way to bury his way into her mind. How was that even possible?

"He has to be. Manifold killed him."

He sounded so certain, but Anya wondered.

She shivered, rising to her feet and moving to stand next to Cinder, to where he stared across the line of marching hills. Not thinking, she rested her head on his shoulder, arm going around his waist. She was once again breaking the prohibition of an elven woman touching a man not of their kind. Besides, what of it? She'd done this and worse on so many other instances. What was one more time?

As if he recognized her need, Cinder pulled her into a hug, and Anya stood within the circle of his embrace, comforted as she placed her cheek next to his. "You don't need to be sorry," she said, adding a silent *priya* at the end.

"*Sleep. Rest. Forget,*" he ordered, curling deeper into Sira's mind. She had almost found him out, and that was something that could never occur. Not yet. Not when he was so close. Only a few more months…

13

An hour after entering Char, Cinder and Anya were still making their way toward the home where they were supposed to meet Estin and the Shokans. The streets this late in the day—an hour before sunset—had grown steadily emptier, occupied by fewer and fewer people, especially in this neighborhood, a wealthy district of fine homes. However, just like in Revelant and the other elven cities Cinder had visited, there was no poverty to be found in Char. Everyone was well-fed, well-clothed, and content as they walked along clean streets or ambled through the plentiful green spaces.

Why couldn't the human cities be so lovely? Certainly, portions of them were, but there were also areas where poverty and misery ruled. Drow was one such place, where the wealthy saw no obligation to help those with less. Cinder couldn't forget the children in that sad city, their bones protruding and a hopeless lethargy on their faces. They'd seen too much, experienced too much, and even when young, they seemed to have given up on finding a better life for themselves.

Anya had noticed the same thing, which is why she supported a number of charities and educational endeavors in Swift Sword. It was all to make a better future for those who needed a helping hand.

Cinder glanced at Anya. How could he have overlooked her generous heart? She was a princess of Yaksha Sithe, and she used that station in a way that was worthy. Anya served, and it was with a startled recognition that Cinder realized that it was also how he had always thought of himself.

"What is it?" Anya asked, apparently noticing his regard.

Cinder explained.

Anya offered a wistful smile. "Maybe when all this is over, we'll become servants. Rather than fight for the needs of the worlds, we'll serve the needs of individuals."

The way she had said the word—servant—she wasn't joking. Cinder's eyes narrowed. Was that what she wanted with her life? And by saying *we*, did she think they would share this new purpose of discovering their truths? And if so, why not? It made sense for them to go on together. He wanted to.

But before any of that could happen, there were these tasks and battles ahead of them.

"We're really putting the cart before the horse, aren't we?" Anya said with a laugh, picking up on his unspoken thoughts like she always could. "Figuring on what we'll do when all this is done? When there is so much to get done?"

"It does seem a bit much," Cinder murmured, not willing to admit that he wanted what she'd earlier mentioned.

"I know," she said with a breezy confidence.

Their conversation faded, and they traveled on. As they did so, Cinder recognized a difference between Char and most other elven cities. Char was a fortress, similar to Fort Carnate, with narrower roads and buildings pressed closer, especially compared to Yaksha's capital or even Agnisahar. In addition, Char's blocky buildings lacked Revelant's elegance and easy grace. Even the elves here had a sterner demeanor. Many were armed, and their gazes swept about, hard and evaluating as if searching for lurking enemies.

"Keep your hood up," Anya warned when one particularly nosy elf seemed to study them for a few seconds too long.

Cinder wasn't a child. He didn't need the reminder, and he wanted to roll his eyes at her unhelpful advice. Instead, he settled for sarcasm. "Yes, Mother."

He smiled to himself when Anya scowled his way. In the months after Mahadev, Cinder had forgotten how much fun it was to gently irritate her. He had no idea why it was so, but aggravating Anya was entertaining, especially since she rarely stayed upset with him for long. Usually, she'd laugh at whatever he did and claim she had no notion as to why she let him get away with such nonsense. It was an old game, one they used to play before Mahadev, but never in the immediate months afterward.

It seemed they were falling into the habit again, and Cinder was glad for it.

"Be serious," Anya chided in response to his comment. "We're still in an elven sithe. You know what that means."

Cinder tilted his head as if in thought. "Why, no, I don't think I do know what that means. Why don't you tell me?"

"Are you being obstinate on purpose?"

"Is that what it's called?"

Anya huffed, an expression of feigned incredulity on her face. "Idiot. Why do I put up with you?" She muttered the words but made it loud enough so he could hear.

"Because I'm charming and witty," Cinder said with a smile.

"You're something," Anya agreed. "But I think you left out the simple part."

Cinder's smile became an anticipatory grin. It was the perfect opening.

Anya recognized it. "Don't say it."

"You mean like Simply—"

"I said don't say it."

Cinder chuckled.

He caught Anya rolling her eyes. "Why are you so pleased with yourself whenever you do that?"

"It's because—"

"It doesn't matter why you're pleased!" Anya barked.

Cinder's mouth dropped, and his reaction caused Anya to break out in laughter. She only stifled her humor when she noticed people glancing their way. Cinder could still see her shoulders shaking, though.

After a moment, he had to laugh with her. He nudged Painter toward Barton, nudging her leg. "Well played."

Anya made to reply, but they had just entered a side street and she cut herself off, gazing about in study, a frown furrowing her brow. A moment later, her features clarified into a satisfied expression. "We're here." She shot a glance at Cinder. "Try not to embarrass me."

Cinder smirked. "No promises."

They approached the home where they were supposed to meet the Shokans, a house owned by Duchess Cervine of Certitude. Constructed of pale stone, it was a two-story manor where a set of wide stairs led to a broad porch that granted entry through large, double doors. Numerous windows, framed with dark shutters and crowns, peered out at a brick-paved street, and the neighborhood itself was quiet with no one else about. Birds sang, soaring along the limbs of tall trees—pin oaks, magnolias, and crepe myrtles—while butterflies flitted amongst flowering shrubs, whose aroma perfumed the air.

It would be a good place to rest and recover.

Anya led them through the open wrought-iron gates and into a brick-lined courtyard out back. Close at hand, a pergola, canopied by wisteria and jasmine, provided shade while farther in the rear rose a small set of stables. It already held a number of fine horses, including Byerley. Cinder grinned. The Shokans were here, and he couldn't wait to see them.

Cinder dismounted Painter, taking care of her first, although he wanted to do nothing more than to hurry into the manor. He longed to see his brothers.

Cinder didn't know if any servants might be present, but they'd surely question why he was barging into Duchess Cervine's home. As a result, although impatience crackled through him like lightning, he waited on Anya to lead the way inside.

They exited the stables, and Cinder found himself walking close behind her, trying to hustle her along. He nudged so close that he almost stepped on her heels, earning him an arched expression.

Anya's eyes dipped toward his hands. "Cinder Shade, if you walk any closer, you'll have your hands where they aren't meant to be."

Cinder glanced down and realized that only a couple of inches farther and his hands would be pressed against Anya's backside. He made to step away from her, but she handled it on her own by hip-checking him.

He might have pushed past her then, in spite of what he'd earlier been worrying about as far as servants were concerned, but Anya put a hand on his chest, holding him in place. "Don't worry. You'll see them soon enough."

They stepped onto a large, covered porch before entering an empty kitchen. A sink was filled with soaking pots and pans, while freshly washed plates and mugs rested on a drying rack. The smell of something deliciously spicy lingered in the air, and Cinder's stomach growled. He and Anya hadn't stopped for supper, but he ignored his hunger. Familiar voices were raised from just beyond an open doorway on the other end of the kitchen.

Anya didn't try to hold him back any longer. Instead, she stepped aside and gestured him forward. "Go on. It sounds like Estin gave the servants the night off."

Cinder reckoned the same, and he swept by Anya, slowing only long enough to softly clap her on the shoulder before stepping through the doorway...

And he was swept back into a time when life had been full of fellowship. Nearly everyone was here.

Sash, Riyne, Wark, and Mirk were playing euchre while Ishmay, Gorant, Depth, and Mohal were throwing darts. Estin stood off to the side, commenting with Bones. It was a scene that could have been lifted from back at Krathe House when they'd all been cadets at the Directorate.

There were some obvious changes, though. The Shokans had been fighting zahhacks for the past several years, and it showed. They were fitter, harder, but more haggard. Tired. Some of them had fresh lines of worry etched in wrinkles at the corners of their eyes.

But they were still Cinder's brothers, and he was overjoyed to see them. Devesh, he only wished the dwarves could be here. They'd have loved it.

In the meantime, since no one had seen him yet, he simply observed.

Mirk slammed a card on the table. "Fuck me, I'm euchred." He gestured to Riyne. "Pointy-eared bastard was holding back the left."

Riyne laughed at Mirk. "Should have counted the trumps, dumbass."

Cinder smiled. If nothing else, Sriovey would have appreciated the cursing.

It was then that Ishmay glanced over and saw him. His eyes widened in confusion, like Cinder was someone familiar maybe.

Rabisu's weave.

"Hello, Sash," Cinder said.

The words were a trigger, and sheer joy replaced Sash's uncertainty. "Hotgate!"

The floodgates opened, and Cinder found himself enveloped by his brothers, all of them reaching out to embrace him. It took a while to hug everyone, laughing as they rubbed his head and asked where he'd been. He smiled at the shouted questions and did his best to answer them.

"You remember the last time we were together?" Bones asked. "It was at Fort… What was the name again?"

"Fort Carnate," Estin supplied.

Bones snapped his fingers. "That's right. That's when we finally figured out Estin wasn't a complete asshole. Seeing as how he broke Hotgate out of prison and all."

"Yes. He's only a partial asshole," Ishmay said.

"Don't you mean jackhole?" Wark asked.

"I don't want to hear those fucking made-up curse words," Riyne growled in his best imitation of Sriovey.

"In that case," Cinder said with a grin, "it should be fragging made-up curse words."

"Fragging is the worst of those fucking words," Mirk declared.

Everyone laughed, and Cinder received a few more hearty slaps to his back. It was only then that the others noticed Anya leaning against the doorway, watching them in amusement.

"Don't stop on my account." She gestured for them to continue.

"Don't you dare continue," Estin said to the room at large. "I don't want my sister's ears polluted by your rude cursing."

"I think your sister's ears have been polluted by far worse than our cursing," Bones said. "Remember, she had to listen to Cinder play his mandolin and all those love songs."

"Not another fucking romantic song," Riyne said, imitating Sriovey once more.

They shared another laugh, this one of bittersweet reminiscence.

Cinder stared about, looking for something with which to offer a toast, but there was nothing available. "What's a man have to do to get a drink around here?"

"Who says you're a man?" Bones asked with a laugh.

"Your sister," Cinder replied.

Hoots met his words.

"Hotgate coming in strong with a sister joke," Ishmay said.

"Sisters are off limits," Bones complained.

"Not yours," Estin said, shocking everyone by joining in the joking. He'd always been stiff and formal back at the Directorate.

"What about that drink?" Cinder asked. An ale was quickly thrust into his hands, and he raised his mug, calling for everyone else to do so as well. "To those brothers who aren't here but will never be forgotten. To Sriovey, Derius, and Jozep!"

"To the iron idiots!" Ishmay stated.

Cinder still had no idea what that insult meant, but with a glad smile, he joined everyone in drinking to their missing brothers.

"Have you eaten anything?" Gorant asked after the toast. It wasn't surprising that he'd been the one to ask since Gorant was more polite than the others. It didn't mean he wasn't deadly with a blade and willing to kill, but he was also the type of person who first saw to the needs of his friends.

Soon enough, Cinder had a plate of prawn pakoras and a fish masala stew served over lemon rice. Anya sat across the table from him while the Shokans peppered them with questions. Cinder had answered many of them on multiple occasions, but he didn't want to do so tonight. Tonight was about reunion and celebration, not worrying about the future. He made his feelings plain, and the questions died down.

But then fresh ones started up, such as what happened to Fastness and whether he'd really gone to Mahadev.

"Let him eat," Anya chided. "You can pester him about gossip afterward."

Bones nudged Ishmay. "I told you not to bother him."

"Oh, shut up," Ishmay said with a scowl. "You want to know the answers just as much as I do."

Bones nodded. "But I'm not stupid enough to irritate Hotgate when he's trying to eat."

Ishmay, for a wonder, seemed taken aback and even quieted—a miracle as far as Cinder was concerned. From what he remembered about Ishmay, the man was never one to let an argument die.

"How's the food?" Mirk asked.

Cinder glanced at him. "You asking means you probably did the cooking, right?"

"I'll answer your question when you answer mine."

Cinder smiled. "It's delicious. Best of all, the fish doesn't taste like fish. Nothing is as bad as fish that takes like fish."

"Jozep used to say things like that," Anya said with a rueful chuckle.

"The little runt was always saying funny things like that," Mohal agreed. "I didn't figure out what he meant until I ate unseasoned chicken one time." He pulled a face. "Disgusting."

"Speaking of funny sayings," Anya said, wiping her lips with a napkin. "Cinder had one that was memorable." She went on to tell the story of Drow and the four bandits that had followed them out of the city, of how she, Cinder, and Jozep had ambushed the men.

Cinder made a point not to add anything in Anya's telling. Instead, he bent his head over his masala stew, pretending he wasn't listening. He knew where Anya's story was leading.

Sure enough, when she neared the end of the story and Cinder glanced her way, she was grinning, ready to deliver the embarrassment.

"And then Cinder says, *I'll put an arrow in between your frugly eyes.*"

Quiet met her words, ruined by Riyne, who stared at Cinder in disappointment. "Please tell me you didn't actually say that?"

Bones just looked puzzled. "What does frugly mean?"

"I think it means fragging ugly," Mohal explained.

"Oh, Cinder." This time it was Gorant.

"It wasn't that bad," Cinder protested.

"Yes, it was," Bones declared. He broke into laughter, raising his glass in a toast. "Here's to Cinder Shade. Our leader who should never be allowed to make threats."

The Shokans clinked their mugs, agreeing with the toasting and laughing again.

The whole while, Cinder kept his face down, pretending to grimace in embarrassment, but inside he was smiling.

He had missed his brothers.

That evening, Cinder and Anya fully explained what the two of them had experienced over the past nearly three years, and the mood grew somber by the time they finished.

Estin could see it in the eyes of the Shokans—the awareness of *exactly* what they faced. It was intimidating. But that sense of pressure and worry was largely gone the next morning, forgotten due to the banter between Cinder and the Shokans.

Watching them together lent Estin a fresh perspective.

The weeks spent with his brothers before Cinder's arrival, after they had eventually reconnected in Swift Sword and along with the voyage to Char, had left the prince glum. Where had the energy of his brothers gone? Their ribbing and jokes? It had been almost two years since Estin had last seen most of them, and it saddened him to realize how much they'd experienced without him. And how hard those experiences seemed to have made them.

Even the games they played lacked the happiness they had once shared at the Third Directorate. It was like they dimly recalled what it was like to enjoy one another's company, but weren't actually experiencing it.

But then Cinder had come, and everything changed. The brothers, dour even in the midst of laughing, had launched themselves at Hotgate, excited in ways Estin hadn't remembered them behaving since their final days at the Third Directorate. It was like years of struggle had spilled off them like sand washed away by clean water, leaving behind the happy young men Estin had loved during his final year at the academy.

He hadn't expected Cinder to cause such a change. The last time he'd seen Hotgate, the man had seemed a shell of his former self. That vast confidence in his abilities and skills had appeared less sturdy. No doubt much of it stemmed from learning that he wasn't actually Shokan but merely the recipient of the Blessed One's memories.

Leaving that aside, there was also a sorrow to Hotgate, and Estin didn't need anyone to tell him why. It was Cinder's strained relationship with Anya. Neither of them was certain about who they were to each other, and it left them in an emotional quagmire—stuck in place with no clear or easy way out.

Well, watching them at breakfast, seated next to each other in the kitchen, it was pretty obvious what needed to happen. Cinder and Anya loved one another, but something had caused them to believe they shouldn't. As a result, fingers of bitterness had pried them apart and mildewed their feelings for one another.

It was probably because they'd been stupid enough to let a rakshasa change them. Estin recognized they thought it was necessary, but was it really? Surely, there must have been some other way to achieve what they had needed.

And when that change was no longer necessary, Estin hoped Anya would accept what she felt for and wanted from Cinder. Maybe then the two of them could put all this drama away. Anya would be happy again, which had rarely been the case prior to Hotgate.

And even if Cinder wasn't Shokan—Estin still wasn't sure that was true—during their years apart, his prior idolization of the Blessed One had transferred to Hotgate... which only made sense. After all, even before their last meeting at Fort Carnate, there had been an air of destiny around Cinder. It had been present from his first day at the Third Directorate, shown in how he had developed by leaps and bounds as a warrior, better than anyone Estin had ever met at a similar age. He'd even earned the loyalty of an untamed Yavana stallion, who had spoken to Cinder seemingly from the beginning.

Estin grimaced at Hotgate's relationship with his horse. Byerley hardly ever spoke to him. Usually, Estin couldn't even sense his Yavana's emotions, and he wished it were otherwise. He wished he and Byerley had a deeper relationship.

There were plenty of regrets Estin had, but at least his last two years at the Directorate hadn't gone to waste. In that time, he had learned much of what was important in life, and it began with the acceptance of others. Although Estin was still immensely proud of his elven heritage, he recognized that other people could be proud of theirs as well, and it didn't lessen the history and glory of his own.

He was pulled out of his meandering thoughts when Mirk—of course Mirk—cursed upon burning his hand.

"Was the skillet hot?" Sash asked.

"No, you fucking moron, it was cold as your sister's ti—"

Bones interrupted. "Sisters are—"

"Off limits," Mohal finished for the leader of the Shokans.

The room broke into warm laughter, and even Estin cracked a smile. That joke never got old.

"You're being awfully quiet, oh great and wonderful Prime," Riyne said, drawing Estin into the conversation.

"I was just thinking how nice it was that we're all together," Estin said.

"Who'd have figured you wouldn't mind spending time with a bunch of humans," Wark said. "You used to think we were dirty, stupid warriors unworthy of the name."

Estin quirked a grin. "And who says I still don't think that? And who says you aren't?"

The others hooted.

"That sounds like a challenge," Ishmay said. "You better fucking bring it if you want to defend your position."

Estin laughed. "Dirty, stupid human," he said addressing Ishmay, "you are the one who better fucking bring it. Riyne and Mohal might give me a run but not any of you lot."

"You might be surprised," Bones said, stretching extravagantly and flexing his muscles, something he always did when he was being cocky. "We've been out in the field fighting while you've been back at the Directorate, doing what exactly? Polishing a chair with your ass?"

"Besides," Ishmay said, "I wasn't talking about just us or Mohal and Riyne." He pointed to Cinder. "You're going to have to face Hotgate."

Estin blanched. Cinder was also a member of their class. He had started off in their year, and during his time, he had been their unquestioned Prime. Which meant if Estin wanted to maintain his position, he'd have to contest the man.

How had he forgotten that?

The answer came as soon as he considered the question.

It was because Cinder was above and beyond him. He'd been out experiencing adventures Estin could have never even imagined. Traveling to the depths of the Daggers, to Mount Kirindor itself, and seeing Shet. Defeating *hashains*. Journeying to Mahadev and surviving. Meeting

Manifold Fulsom and learning his Yavana stallion was actually Sapient Dormant.

Estin had yet to fully grasp everything Cinder had experienced. It was just too remarkable and unbelievable. *Cinder* was too remarkable and unbelievable. Estin would never admit it, but it was true. And in thinking about sparring against him, he had no doubt that he'd lose and lose badly.

But he also wouldn't back down.

"Before he left, he *was* the Prime," Estin said, staring Cinder in the eyes. "But if he wants the ruby-brooch, he'll have to earn it."

Cinder never dropped his gaze. "Whenever you're ready. Whenever you want it. I'm here."

Estin smiled, inwardly pleased. Cinder being serious meant he was taking the sparring seriously. In some ways, it was a tip of the hat, an acknowledgment of Estin's own worth.

"I'm ready now."

"Let's go." Cinder rose, stepping toward the courtyard.

14

Cinder stepped outside. The air was cool with the day's mugginess yet to manifest. Or maybe they'd get lucky and the weather would be dry for once. He doubted it, but there was always hope. As if in answer to his unspoken prayer, a mild wind tugged at his clothes, carrying the scent of the briny sea and intermixing with the sweet aromas from the courtyard's lovely wisteria and jasmine. The flowers grew in profusion, creating an arbor over the pergola. A pair of bluebirds sang from their perch upon a dwarf maple Cinder hadn't noticed last night.

Why did he always have these observations before a spar? Rather than focus on the match to come, he tended to be distracted by his environment. Or maybe it wasn't a distraction. Maybe he just needed to know the setting in which he fought, understand anything that might interfere with his movements or that of his opponent.

Whatever the case, once satisfied that the courtyard was relatively flat and there weren't any obviously loose bricks, Cinder rolled his shoulders and neck. He did some quick lunges to get stretched and limber. It had been too long since he'd done anything more than practice his forms. After Liline had dropped them off, he and Anya had ridden hard to get here, and during that time, they'd not done any sparring. Cinder felt rusty, and regaining his keen edge was important.

Anya stood close at hand. "Don't humiliate him," she warned before stepping away.

Cinder shot her an uncertain look. Why would she think he'd humiliate Estin? He'd defeat the prince—no question about it—but he wouldn't toy with him. He'd beat Estin quickly, and afterward, if the boy was smart, he'd ask how to improve.

He smiled to himself then. Who was he to think of Estin as a boy? The prince was decades older than him, even if his relative age as an elf was similar to Cinder's as a human. And yet, in their comparative experiences, Estin still reminded Cinder of a boy.

Shortly after, Gorant returned with a pair of shokes, the practice swords favored by the elves. Riyne also brought gear, padded armor, and governors—leather helmets that dampened the use of *lorethasra* and *Jivatma*.

The Shokans stood clustered under the rear porch next to the entrance to the kitchen.

"What are the rules?" Cinder asked. Since Estin was the Prime, no matter what military rank any of the others had, the prince was still their senior. And as their senior, it was for him to decide the rules of this match.

"Like a normal spar," Estin said. "Deadly hits count for two. Getting knocked out of…" He glanced around. "There's no ring." He frowned, hands on his hips. "We need a ring."

Cinder had a suggestion, and an instant later, several low-lying planters were quickly shifted about to form the corners of a square. "It's not a ring, but it should do."

Estin nodded. "Right. One point if you get knocked out of the square. First to four points wins."

"As the leader of the Shokans, I'll officiate," Bones declared, stepping toward the square.

Anya cut him off. "As a princess of Yaksha Sithe, I outrank you. I'll officiate."

"But you're his sister," Depth complained.

Anya arched an elegant eyebrow, and the wiry warrior drooped. "Any other objections?" she asked.

No one voiced any other complaints.

"Then the rules will be as Estin stated." Anya paced to just inside the ring.

Cinder did so as well, perpendicular to her. He took a deep breath, another roll of his shoulders. He could have sourced *lorethasra*, sending it into *Muladhara*, and in another circumstance, he might have done so. But on this occasion, *Jivatma* alone was sufficient.

He conducted, and the early morning sunshine seemed to increase beyond noon-brightness. The song of the bluebirds melded with the murmured conversations from the estates on either side of their own. Servants were out, cleaning rugs and complaining in good nature. The horses in the stables whickered. The fragrance of the wisteria and jasmine was briefly overwhelming, and Cinder almost imagined he could see the scent.

He controlled his senses then, focusing inward to where his muscles twitched, wanting to blur him into motion. He had to hold in the energy, though. Another breath, and Cinder steadied. Another, and he raised his shoke to the ready. He flattened his features, deadening all expressions.

Estin faced him from a diagonal, showing no obvious hint of nerves. But Cinder noticed one of the prince's eyes twitch. He blinked a bit too rapidly. Estin did have nerves, but for the most part, he was controlling it.

Good.

But Estin was less able to hide his intentions. Based on his balance, the barely visible rocking forward of his weight, he was figuring on opening with a thrust.

Cinder caught Anya move her gaze from Estin to him. One final look over, and she shouted, "Go!"

Estin surged forward. His shoke was aimed in a thrust, just like Cinder had guessed. The prince's body was extended, and his form was impeccable.

But Cinder had already shifted to the side, angling his body to present a smaller target. A single vertical chop, and his shoke slammed into Estin's forearms. Had they been using actual swords, it would have been a literal disarming strike. Instead, it merely caused the prince to drop his shoke, fall to his knees, and clutch his arms in obvious agony. Estin held in the scream, though.

Cinder viewed the prince, feeling vaguely guilty. Maybe he should have gone with a less painful way to win the two points. Anya made to help her brother, but even as she took a step toward him, Estin was back on his feet, shaking out the last of the phantom pains.

"Sorry about that," Cinder said to him.

Estin's brow creased. "Sorry for what? I never knew you could move that fast. Now I do."

"Two points for Cinder," Anya stated. "Get to your places."

Once again, Cinder set himself across the square from Estin, studying the prince. It was laughably easy to figure what the other man intended. Sparring against Anya all these months had given him a deep insight into combat. And that was even before he'd unlocked Shokan's memories and experiences. The Blessed One had developed a preternatural ability to decipher the likely flow of combat before swords were even crossed.

Seconds later, Anya called the start of the next engagement.

Estin was more careful this time. He edged to his right, seeking to maintain distance.

Cinder didn't allow it. He cut off the prince. A slash led to a side-kick. Estin didn't even try to block Cinder's attacks. He simply dove left, seeking distance. Before he could get to his knees, a straight thrust took him in the chest.

Once again, Estin had dropped his shoke and was hunched around himself. He held his chest this time, holding in a scream of pain.

"Victory to Cinder," Anya stated. This time she did go to Estin, helping him rise to his feet.

"Anybody see what Hotgate actually did?" Mirk asked in a carrying voice. "Because I couldn't see a fucking thing."

Cinder went to the prince, too. "You did well," he said.

"I don't need your condescension," Estin said with a scowl.

"It wasn't condescension," Cinder replied. "You did well. Ask your sister."

"You lasted three blows on the second engagement. That's actually a lot considering how good he is now."

Estin didn't seem sure whether to believe them.

"Let me show you." Cinder turned to the Shokans, who were talking amongst themselves.

"Riyne," Cinder called out. "You ready?"

Riyne grinned. "Absolutely."

The match against Ryne didn't go much differently than the one against Estin. After that, every other Shokan wanted a chance at Cinder.

None of them lasted longer than three strokes, though. Most only managed two. And even as Cinder sparred against them, he inwardly gaped at how much he'd improved. Not just his form but also his understanding of posture and stance. Even more, he could use that information now to counter at a speed the Shokans simply couldn't match.

After finishing off Mirk, Cinder stepped away from the sparring square. "Enough."

The Shokans weren't learning anything by going against him. Even with the governor, Cinder was moving too swiftly for them. He needed to slow his pace; let the others send out an attack without instantly defeating it; allow them to get a defense in place and have a chance to reset.

"How the fuck did you get so fast?" Mirk asked, genuinely curious rather than upset.

"And so good," Estin said. "The few times you moved, your form was perfect."

"*Jivatma*," Cinder replied. "I've spoken about it before." He also had an idea on how to help the Shokans gain some of his skills and Talents. Jozep had learned to use *Jivatma* by training in the Lucid Foe, and the wraiths, who had once been human, had access to it as well. So why not the brothers? They could go to Shalla Vale and train with the holders, possibly learn in Verity Foe. Maybe even the wraiths could help. Fastness had said they would.

He smiled on thinking about his Yavana stallion, who was both a mythical hero and a gluttonous brat when it came to apples.

Anya stepped forward, shoke in hand and wearing padded armor. "Let's see how that *Jivatma* does against someone who has it as well."

Cheers and hoots met her challenge.

Anya smiled at him, strapping a governor in place.

Cinder studied her. She had once been far better than him, but then he'd outpaced her ability—significantly so. That changed again after Mahadev. Once she'd gained *Jivatma*, she'd closed the distance between them, but over the past few months, that distance had opened again. Their matches, once competitive, were now lopsided in Cinder's favor.

But why? He'd continued to get better, done well at incorporating Shokan's memories into his own techniques. But why not Anya? Why hadn't she done the same with Sira's memories?

Anya seemed to recognize the question in Cinder's gaze. "Humor me. I want to test something."

Cinder eyed her a moment longer. Test what? An instant later, he shrugged off his question. She'd tell him later. He nodded her way, conducting *Jivatma*. All his senses heightened, and his muscles twitched, prepared to rush him forward in a blur of motion.

He could sense Anya doing the same as she seemed to move in fits and starts, ready to take him on. Her posture indicated she planned to rush forward. A vertical chop maybe? He couldn't tell for sure. Anya was skilled at concealing her intentions. A rebalancing, and he had a new certainty, a greater one. She'd defend.

Estin stood off to the side, ready to serve as their official. The prince glanced in Cinder's direction and then Anya's.

Cinder filled his lungs, scenting her mountain-stream *lorethasra*.

One final look over from Estin, and the prince shouted. "Go!"

Anya surprised him with a dash forward. Cinder wasn't caught back-footed, though. He smoothly parried a vertical slice and shifted to her left. She shuffled to cut him off. Cinder aimed a lazy swipe. She blocked, but he managed to get his lead leg to her outside. But only for a moment. Anya corrected. Another vertical slice from her led to a line of Fire.

Cinder blocked both, one with a parry the other with a Shield. He countered with a thrust of his own, pulling back when she slid aside and sent another line of Fire. He no longer had to see the color of her sclerae to know what braid of *lorethasra* was coming. A slap of his shoke got hers out of the way, leaving a break in her defense. Cinder launched a frontkick, but it met air. Anya had angled away. He landed, flexing to make it seem like he was off balance.

She didn't bite on the obvious opening. Instead, she eased away, smiling slightly, swirling her shoke and gesturing him forward.

Cinder offered a crooked smile of his own, taking the invitation. He circled, and this time, he sped his attacks. A rising slash transitioned into a horizontal strike followed by a straight thrust. He checked a kick aimed at his knee, countered with a short chop and lance of Air. Anya blocked, Shielded, and barely evaded when he finished his attack by trying to smash the pommel of his shoke into her wrist.

They reset and went faster. A handful of blows were exchanged, but by now, Cinder had her timing. She wasn't able to keep up, not like she could a few months ago. Afterward, the end came swiftly. Anya put too much force into a slash. It left her off-balance. Just a little, but a little was all Cinder needed. A kick she tried to check left her out of position, and a short thrust to the chest finished her off.

Anya grunted, going to a knee, sucking wind as she controlled the agony of what no doubt felt like a chest wound. Cinder watched, waiting for her pain to ease. Once it did, he helped her rise, almost congratulating her on doing better. At the last moment, wisdom kept his mouth shut. Anya wouldn't accept his praise as being anything other than condescension.

She slapped his shoulder. "You've come far."

"Not far enough," Cinder said. Shokan's memories told him of what the man had been able to do against Shet and his Titans, solo defeating nearly all of them. That was where Cinder needed to be.

Anya, though, rolled her eyes at his comment. "Accept the compliment." She then faced the Shokans, who remained gathered under the porch leading to the kitchen. "Why did you lose to him?"

Cinder waited, wondering where this lesson was going.

"Because we didn't think we'd win," Gorant eventually said.

Anya nodded. "Partially true, but there's a lot more to it than that."

"Timing beats speed. Precision defeats power," Bones said. "Cinder used to say that all the time."

Cinder smiled, surprised. He hadn't expected anyone to remember the phrase.

"Is that what you think happened?" Anya asked.

"Not just that," Bones said. "Cinder has both. He has timing and speed along with precision and power."

"So does Anya," Estin said.

"Not like Cinder," she replied. "No one does."

Cinder viewed her with a frown. That wasn't right. She should have similar abilities as him.

His considerations were interrupted when Anya addressed the Shokans again. She quoted from *Forever Triumphant*, the elven religious book. "'*Accept your fate, but never embrace certainty other than your love of Devesh.*'"

Silence met her declaration.

"I don't get it," Ishmay said.

"You never get it," Depth replied.

"Your mother got it."

"That's what your sister said."

Cinder bit back a laugh. It seemed the years apart hadn't stifled the Shokans love for insulting one another's mothers and sisters.

"Boys," Anya called out, shutting down the conversation. "What it means is that you should never enter a fight thinking you'll lose. You weren't just sure you wouldn't win. You were certain you'd lose. Don't ever have certainty about that."

Cinder tuned his mandolin while Riyne did the same with his fiddle. They sat in a pair of chairs in front of the windows while the rest of the Shokans were spread throughout the drawing room, the area beyond the kitchen where Cinder had discovered his brothers yesterday.

It was late in the afternoon, and sunlight streamed through the western facing windows that gazed out at the glistening waters of the Onus Sea. A cool breeze puffed Cinder's clothes and hair, billowing the curtains and freshening the room.

Someone wandered into the kitchen while Cinder gave his mandolin an experimental strum. He frowned. The D-string was flat. While Cinder worked on his instrument, he listened with half an ear to the conversations going on in the rest of the room.

Currently, there were two games of euchre going on with Sash leaning in now and then to provide commentary and advice, neither of which seemed needed or appreciated.

"Go away," Bones said to Sash, pushing him off. "I know what I'm doing."

"Doesn't look like it," Sash said, but he did as Bones told him and moved over to the other game. He immediately made a comment to Mohal. "You should have led with your king."

Mohal gave a long-suffering sigh. "Why don't you go play some darts? Maybe stab yourself in the eye?"

Sash chuckled. "Why would I do that when you need my help playing this game your elven brain is clearly unequipped to handle?"

Riyne glanced up upon hearing that. "Something must be wrong with the world; Sash spoke two sentences that sounded halfway intelligent."

"Which is still stupid for most anyone else," Wark said with a chuckle.

"Yes, *most* anyone else," Sash said. "For you, it's still twice as smart."

"Where's Anya?" Estin asked, glancing around. "She likes to sing."

"In the garden," Cinder said, giving the mandolin another exper-imental strum. "You know how she is." He recalled the many times he'd seen her in the garden behind Krathe House, pruning her flowers while he, Riyne, and Jozep played music.

Estin grunted at Cinder's answer. "She's always gardening. If she wasn't a princess and a ranger, I think she'd be happiest as a farmer."

Cinder blinked. The exact same thing could have been said about Sira.

"Ready?" Riyne asked.

"Give me a second," Cinder replied. A final tune and strum of the open strings, and he had them right. "You want to lead?"

Riyne shook his head. "Not this time. Surprise me."

"Try this one." Cinder started off in a soft, slow melody. He hoped Riyne knew it. It was one of Cinder's favorites, and he loved playing it with Anya. Her voice was perfect for it since she was able to hit the high notes. Riyne played her part, his fiddle mimicking her singing.

"Sounds like a love song," someone muttered.

"A fucking love song," someone else corrected.

Cinder smiled in fond longing even as the tempo built... rising... cresting... falling off again. He closed his eyes and let the music slip him away, falling into something that was beyond a simple feeling. This one filled him with longing.

The last notes trailed off, but seconds later, he and Riyne were off to the next melody. They played on, and the Shokans continued their games of euchre, chatting with one another or playing darts. Occasionally they even fell quiet and listened to the music. It was like the years had fallen away, and they were back at their quarters in the Third Directorate.

Devesh, Cinder wished it could be so. The next song was exactly about that, about reaching back into the past, living precious moments that were gone but never forgotten. Or freezing the inevitable motion of time and living in the here and now.

Finally, hours later, with night having fallen and their fingers starting to ache, of silent accord, Cinder and Riyne decided to take a break.

"Who was it that laughed like a jackass?" Bones asked.

"It was you," Cinder said, recalling that long ago conversation. "Mohal brays like a donkey."

"I bray like a fragging donkey," Mohal corrected.

"You smell like one, too," Estin said, waving a hand in front of his nose like something stank.

"Something most definitely is wrong with the world," Riyne said. "Estin just made a joke, and it wasn't terrible."

"Speaking of someone who makes terrible jokes," Bones began, "that has to be Cinder. His jokes are the worst."

Mirk nodded agreement. "Always has to explain them because they're so fucking stupid."

"Or worse," Ishmay said. "They're puns."

"What is wrong with puns?" Gorant asked Ishmay. "Are they too clever for you?"

"Riyne might be right," Bones said with a sage nod. "Something *is* wrong with the world when Gorant is the one making fun of someone else."

Sometime while Cinder and Riyne had been playing, Anya must have reentered the house. She had cleaned up and currently stood framed in the doorway leading deeper into the manor, arms akimbo. Her posture and expression reminded Cinder of a teacher about to give an unpleasant lesson. Sure enough…

"I know you want to stay up late," Anya began, "but we have an early day ahead of us. Our ship leaves before first light. We'll have to be up and moving well before then."

The room quieted, and Bones rose to his feet, his prior frivolity gone. "Yes, ma'am," he said with a respectful incline of his head. "We won't let you down. The Shokans know what it is to be on time."

That's right. Bones was in command of the Shokans. *Bones.* Cinder gave himself a rueful shake. Who could have ever imagined him as the leader of these men and elves? Cinder viewed the room, amazed once more by how much his friends had changed. They had gone from boys to men, and he hadn't been a part of that seemingly endless road.

"I expect you will," Anya said in reply to Bones' promise, leaving them then and heading upstairs.

Afterward, a contemplative quiet fell upon the room.

"We're shipping out to Bharat," Wark eventually said. "To the Island of the Saints."

"Saints, my ass," Mohal said with a scowl. "They're nothing but damn sorcerers."

"Bharat," Ishmay said, concern evident on his face. "Devesh, I hope we all come out of it on the other side."

Cinder shot Ishmay a look of dismay. Was he trying to court bad luck?

"Don't say that," Gorant hissed to Ishmay.

"It's bad karma," Sash said with a sage nod.

A grim mood settled over the Shokans as everyone seemed to draw inward, focused on their own thoughts.

It wouldn't do. Their last night alone shouldn't have room for moroseness.

Cinder picked up his mandolin, gesturing for Riyne to grab his fiddle. They began playing a song that all of them knew and that used to drive Sriovey to distraction... mostly because Cinder figured the grumpy dwarf actually liked it.

Within just a few notes, Bones recognized the tune. "It's a love song," he said with a laugh.

Cinder glanced up from the mandolin, grinning. "Looks like Bones still laughs like a jackass."

Bones made stupid noises like a jackass, and the others laughed with him.

15

"Can you believe this?" Bones asked.

Cinder knew the reason for his question. The ship that would take them to Bharat was *Whispering Tanned Fox*. It was the same vessel that had transported the two of them along with Wark and Depth to Revelant as rising Firsters and being aboard felt like stepping back in time.

Currently, Cinder stood alongside Bones on the top deck of the ship, and together they watched the calm waters of the Onus Sea, which was spread out all around them. The weather was looking to be fine since the early morning sun revealed no heavy clouds, and a stiff wind blew steadily. Hopefully, it would continue to quicken their passage south. In fact, they'd already traveled far enough for Char to have been lost over the horizon.

Cinder observed Captain Swell, who was still in charge of the ship, approach them. An impressive mustache drooped like a golden caterpillar around both corners of the captain's mouth, and he also had the heavy build, fair skin, and light hair of those from the Savage

Kingdoms. However, he wasn't as tall as Cinder remembered. Not even close.

Then again, maybe that was because Cinder's perspective was different. Back when he'd been a rising Firster, he had been shorter than he was now, slighter of frame, too.

"Remember to stay out of the way," Captain Swell warned. "Do that, and you'll be fine." His words spoken, he set off to make his rounds.

Bones chuckled after the man was gone. "Some things never change. Irritable captains being one."

Cinder smiled. "A good thing. It's for people like him that we do this. People who have no idea how terrible their lives will be if we fail."

Anya arrived on deck, wearing a yellow dress that reminded Cinder of summer sunshine. It hung off her shoulders and included a lacy white fabric that reached down to a scooped neckline where an emerald pendant on a slim, silver chain rested against her chest. The hemline, etched in gold stitching, caused the dress to hug the ground. However, with every step, Cinder noted the flash of elegant white shoes, which weren't practical. Then again, nothing about the outfit was.

Cinder's eyes went back to the emerald pendant, and he viewed it for a moment, wishing Anya was wearing a black beaded necklace instead. A *thaali* might be what it was called, but he wasn't sure.

Regardless, the reason for the dress rather than her usual warrior's garb had to do with how Cinder and Anya had decided to approach Bharat. They hoped that news of what they'd done in Surent and Revelant hadn't yet made it to the rishis. If so, then Anya and Estin could maintain this pretense of being a delegation representing both Rakesh and Yaksha Sithe. And while on the island, they could also steal the Orb of Undying Light.

It should be possible. Most everyone who knew anything about Bharat figured the Orb rested atop the tall spire centered in Black Jackal House, the fortress and temple at the heart of Bharatian life. It was guarded day and night by a group of rakishis and one rishi at all times. However, that wasn't entirely true. Rather than resting atop the spire, the Orb was actually housed at the structure's base. From there, its light was reflected and refracted by a cleverly positioned series of mirrors until it burst forth from the spire's pinnacle.

As for the rakishis, Cinder figured his team could overwhelm them. He knew of their reputation—they were said to be as good as holders—but he was also confident in his brothers. And as for the rishi, they were someone either he or Anya could handle. After that, it was a simple matter of escaping the island.

Whispering Tanned Fox would play a role in that as well, and it all began with not letting the sailors think on Anya as anything other than a princess, hence her dress.

Bones seemed to take her arrival as a signal. "I'll see you later." He dipped his head to Cinder, doing the same to Anya on his way to the hatch leading belowdecks.

"Thinking about Bharat?" Anya asked upon reaching Cinder's side.

Cinder smiled. "Good guess. But you probably know by now how I'm always thinking about what we're about to face. It's what I do."

"It's what we both do. It's our shared sin."

"Maybe we should pray for forgiveness," Cinder suggested with a grin.

Anya tilted her head. "You think we should pray not to worry?"

"Pray to not *have* to worry."

Anya laughed lightly. "I would love a world like that."

Cinder's eyes went again to the pendant, to where it shook lightly with her laughter. An instant later, he darted his gaze away, trying not to blush. She always knew when he was looking at her, and just then, he'd been all but staring at her breasts.

"We have a strange relationship," Anya said, drawing his attention back to her.

That was putting it mildly. Two people who had once believed themselves the Blessed Ones and in love. But then had come the hard truth, hating it, and nearly each other. And yet they'd decided to work together, toward a goal the rest of Seminal would think an impossible fraud. Strange would have been an improvement over what they had.

"Estin has an *insufi* blade," Anya said, shifting the conversation.

"When did he receive it?" Cinder asked. "And how did he earn it?"

An *insufi* blade took months or even years to forge and was gifted to only the finest of swordsmen, sublime warriors like Anya and Lisandre—and in the future, possibly Riyne—but not someone of Estin's caliber.

"A few months ago," Anya answered. "Mother had it made for him. She even held an *upanayana* ceremony, although from the way Estin talks, it was more political theater than a religious offering."

It sounded like something an empress would do: give an unwarranted accolade to one of her children. "What does Estin think about it?"

"He doesn't like it, but what can he do? It's his now, forged to his reach and need."

Cinder grunted, glad Estin at least recognized that he didn't deserve an *insufi* blade. It was another measure of the other man's growth and maturity.

A flash of memory raced across Cinder's mind as he recalled a ceremony from Shokan's past where a matte-black weapon, forged and formed of *sathana* grass until the blade was harder and more limber than steel, had been gifted to him. It had been after a night of solitary meditation. His *upanayana* ceremony, so different than that of the elves, especially Estin's.

As if talking about him called the prince forth, here he came, wearing his warrior's leathers. He didn't need to hide who he was onboard the ship, but once they readied to dock, he'd have to change into finery, too.

"What are you two talking about?" Estin asked. "It won't do our plan any good if the sailors gossip onshore about how much time the two of you spent together. We have to maintain our roles."

He was right. Cinder knew it, and he'd been on the cusp of departing from Anya anyway. But since Estin was with them, he might as well stay and enjoy the fresh air. As he stared at the prince, a wager from long ago occurred to him. It was a bet that he had made with Estin and neither had collected. He smiled, wondering if he should remind the prince.

"What's so funny?" Estin asked.

Cinder told him. "We said that whoever lost the bout after our second year had to call the other person 'Exalted Lord and Master.' We sparred yesterday, and I won."

"But it wasn't at the end of our second year."

"But it was heard and honored," Anya reminded him.

Estin wore a worried grimace. "True, but—"

Cinder took pity on the prince and laughed. "Don't worry. I'd never make you do that." Estin sagged in relief. "At least not in public. In private, though…"

He laughed again at Estin's rising alarm. It was just so easy to tweak the prince. He knew it was beneath him, but sometimes it was just fun.

Later that evening, hours after supper, Cinder called a meeting of the Shokans. Night had fallen, and hooded *diptha* lanterns pooled dim illumination on the deck. The spread of stars winked in the night sky, shrouded by the occasional cloud. Dormant—high in the heavens— cast a ghostly, ivory light while golden Fulsom hung lower, illuminating the waters along the horizon's edge. A lonesome bell rang out, signaling *Whispering Tanned Fox*'s position to any nearby vessels.

Otherwise, the ship was quiet. Many of the sailors were turned in for the night. This included Captain Swell, who had mentioned that they should arrive at Solace, Bharat's port and capital, late tomorrow morning.

Before then, the Shokans needed to finalize their plan. It was why they were gathered on the top deck, well away from any sailors. Anya was present as well, standing front and center. It was she who was reviewing what they intended.

Questions were asked, and Cinder let her handle them. It was better if the Shokans gained practice now in looking to her as the leader of their delegation. Once they reached Bharat, the rishis, the so-called

Upright Ones, would certainly expect it.

"You're certain about the skill of the rakishis?" Bones asked. As the commander of the Shokans, it was his responsibility to learn the answers to these kinds of questions.

"We can't be absolutely certain, but I'm fairly confident," Anya said. "And you've likely also heard about the *hashains*—about their prowess."

"We heard," Riyne said with arms folded. "But we also heard that Hotgate defeated twelve of them on his own. There can't be much truth to the *hashains* supposed skill if he took out so many."

Cinder stirred upon hearing about the *hashains*. He kept catching impressions from Jeet and Stren. They were pleased with themselves and their work. And it wasn't the butchery to which they'd been trained. Through the leash he held on them, Cinder wouldn't allow them to murder. Instead, it was something religious in orientation. Something about him. The Grimyogi.

"Or maybe the legends *are* accurate," Bones mused, "and Hotgate really took down that many. We sparred against him. None of us lasted long."

"But that was against us," Ishmay countered. "We're only human."

"Speak for yourself," Riyne said.

"You know what I mean," Ishmay replied. "None of us are legendary warriors."

"We might not be, but the *hashains* are," Mohal said.

The argument appeared ready to spiral out of control, which wasn't how Cinder wanted the meeting handled. Bones needed to rein the others in, and if he didn't, Cinder would. He didn't want to step in and supplant Bones' station, but they couldn't afford the meeting to get sidetracked.

Just then, Bones did what Cinder was hoping. He knocked his knuckles on the railing, stifling the discussion. "You're missing the point. Cinder killed twelve *hashains* who are legendary warriors. That means their true ability either isn't the equal of their legend, or Hotgate is greater by far than their legend. Both cases, we might be fine against the rakishis." He indicated Anya. "Maybe the princess can shed some light on their abilities. She's battled all kinds, after all."

"First, you are correct. It was twelve *hashains* that Cinder defeated," Anya said. "Second, I've spoken to the holders about the rakishis. They've sparred against them, and the holders believe themselves to be better. Just as one rakishi is said to be the equal of three elven warriors and five humans, holders believe they are the equal of at least two rakishis. I believe them. In addition, I've sparred against the holders as well. I'm better than them now, and you've all seen Cinder." She scanned the Shokans, meeting their gazes. "It means we aren't going in outnumbered when we're facing the rakishis at the Spire of the Saints."

"What about the rishis? The Upright Ones?" Wark asked. "They're supposed to have four open Chakras."

"It's not true," Cinder said, speaking for the first time. "They likely have two, and even then, they don't have *Jivatma*. Anya and I do, and we've got more open Chakras than any of them."

"But they won't be limited by the blue-and-green lightning you're always on about," Depth said. "Wish I could see that lightning," he muttered as an aside.

Cinder wished the same thing, elves included.

"Damn sorcerers," Mohal said, uttering again the curse by which the Yaksha elves referred to the rishis.

Riyne appeared on the verge of adding his own diatribe, but Bones smoothly cut him off. "Elves or not, Depth is right." He gazed from Cinder to Anya. "Can you handle a rishi? Defeat him or her and also help us with the rakishis?"

This was where Cinder and Anya's plan would be put to the test. They had good intelligence on the rakishis and the current number of guards protecting the Spire of the Saints and the Orb of Undying Light. But the rishi was the wildcard. Cinder figured he could take one, but could he do so while the Shokans and Anya were also battling the rakishis?

"We'll find out," Cinder said. "But we also won't leave it to chance. It's why we're going to create havoc in that chamber. Make it as confusing as possible. We'll take down the rakishis during the chaos and then the rishi at the end."

Riyne nodded acceptance, but apparently, he still had questions. "And you're sure we can get admittance onto the island with this plan?"

Cinder let Anya answer, and she did so without hesitation. "Estin and I are royalty. That alone should gain us admittance. And we'll explain the Shokans as being our guards. You're a mixed unit with two members coming from Yaksha's nobility. If we say we're a delegation representing Rakesh *and* Yaksha, the rishis shouldn't have any reason to distrust us."

"And Cinder?" Bones said with a mischievous gleam in his eye. "He's an adjutant assigned to the Shokans?"

Cinder could tell where this might be going. "No. You don't get to order me about." He smiled at Bones. "If anything, I get to order you about."

"When haven't you gotten to order us about?" Mirk asked. "Even as a fucking runt at *Steel-Graced*, you ordered us around."

Cinder simply grinned.

Before the meeting drifted away again, Anya called out. "Does anyone have any other questions?"

They hadn't discussed how they were going to get free of Bharat, but that was the simplest part of the plan, so there was no need. Otherwise, the Shokans muttered amongst themselves, glancing about and raising no further questions.

"In that case, I'm going to sleep," Anya said. She glanced at her brother, with whom she was sharing a cabin. "Try not to wake me when you get in."

"I won't," Estin promised.

Anya departed, and Cinder wished he could join her. When by themselves, they would usually spend the evening discussing any issues either of them thought important. They couldn't do so here, though; appearances had to be maintained.

Meanwhile, the Shokans remained on deck, soft conversations drifting about.

"Water looks cold," Mirk said, gazing out over the sea.

"You remember when Estin screamed when we went swimming that day?" Ishmay asked Bones with a grin.

Cinder chuckled. He remembered. It had been back when they had been Seconds. Sriovey had discovered a lovely pond in the hills above the Directorate—a clear blue jewel, the kind made for swimming on a hot summer day.

Back then, Estin hadn't been the kind to listen to anyone else's opinion. Before anyone could warn him off, he'd launched himself off a rope swing, landing in what was actually frigid water. The shock of the cold had caused Estin to shriek like a banshee.

"It wasn't that funny," Estin muttered.

"Yes, it was," Depth said in disagreement. "You sounded like a girl."

Bones laughed. "I swear, you scared off half the birds in the trees."

"The water was cold," Estin protested.

"Probably cold enough for your nuggets to disappear," Wark said.

Estin squawked. "That's gross."

As the silly argument brewed, Bones moved over next to Cinder. "I wish this was what our lives could be like all the time. Us just being people, laughing and not having to carry so many burdens."

Cinder nodded. He had many wishes but giving peace to the Shokans was definitely high on the list.

16

The next morning, *Whispering Tanned Fox* pulled into Solace, and compared to Revelant or even Swift Sword, it wasn't very impressive, at least not in terms of size or how many ships were in the harbor. However, it was beautiful. Steep hills, forested by a tropical jungle, ringed the aqua waters of the bay, and brightly colored homes of red, yellow, green, and even pomegranate hues pressed close to one another. The houses and other buildings were framed by broad, clean streets that led into the surrounding heights.

"It's lovely," Anya said, standing at Cinder's side next to the railing.

"Almost as pretty as Revelant," he said, knowing she'd appreciate the comparison.

Anya smiled. "Wisely chosen words."

"Why are they wisely chosen?" Ishmay asked, standing close at hand. "Ow." He rubbed the back of his head, glaring at Bones, who had just smacked him. "What was that for?"

"For still not knowing when to stay out of it," Bones replied.

"Well, stop hitting me." Ishmay scowled. "Next time just tell me."

"Sad part is there's going to be a next time. Come on." Bones drew Ishmay off, leaving Cinder and Anya in a small window of privacy.

She was shaking her head. "Do they ever grow up?"

Cinder doubted it, and in some ways, he hoped they never would. He viewed the Shokans, and his jaw tightened when considering what he was asking of them. He was about to place them in danger, and there was no way around it. He needed their help. The world did. This was their Trial; this and more to come if Seminal was to ever rid itself of Shet and Zahhack.

Anya tapped his elbow, drawing his attention. "It's too lovely a day to think morose thoughts."

She was right, and Cinder faced the city again, feeling the soft wind, rich with a mineral scent rather than a briny tang. Large cotton-white clouds seemed to hang motionless in the sky. He lifted his face, eyes closed and letting the warm sunshine pour down on him like a benediction.

And when he next opened his eyes, he'd found a serenity in his heart.

"See," Anya said. "Too lovely."

Estin approached them. "Captain Swell says there's a delegation waiting for us on the dock."

Cinder nodded in appreciation of the good news. The rishis had received the message Estin had sent to Bharat from when he'd first arrived in Char.

"We should go," Anya said. She stepped away from the railing, pausing to glance back at Cinder. "Remember your place?"

Cinder nodded. "Bones and I walk ahead of you while the Shokans maintain a distance two paces behind." He grinned. "Just like you're the empress."

She chuckled. "If I'm ever the empress, it would be a tragedy for everyone. I would make a terrible ruler. Besides, we were made to be servants."

With that, she turned away in a swirl, indicating for Estin to follow. Cinder watched as she gracefully made her way toward the gangplank in spite of the sari she wore, which was a royal purple. Her hair was caught in a diamond-laced net, and heavy gold bangles graced both wrists while the same pendant as yesterday rested on her chest.

Estin had similar finery, and both he and Anya gleamed from all the precious gems they wore.

Cinder reached the Shokans, who wore their best dress uniforms but had well-used swords in battered scabbards belted at their hips. Anya had reached the gangplank first, but she stepped aside for Cinder. He conducted *Jivatma* and sourced *lorethasra*. Diplomatic mission or not, there was no knowing how they would be greeted. It was also why he had Anya's *insufi* sword sheathed at his side. It wouldn't make sense for her to have it on her when wearing a sari, but she also wanted to at least have some access to a weapon.

Bones joined him, and together they paced down the gangplank toward a dozen warriors waiting at the dock. *Rakishis.* They had a striking appearance with skin dark enough that it seemed to glow blue and coarse hair that was as black as Cinder's. Armored in a mix of buffed steel and polished leather, they had short swords at their hips and held tasseled spears that rose several feet above their heads. And based on their posture and flat-eyed, studious gazes, these were men and women who knew how to use their weapons—they weren't ornamental warriors.

But Cinder's attention locked on a woman standing in their midst. She was plain in her features, but there was a commanding air about her, a weight to the way she stared at the world. Was she a rishi? Were they all like this?

One of the rakishis stepped forward. He was older than the others, clearly seasoned based on his confident stride and the pale scars on his cheeks. "I am Tobias Rentwing," he said, bowing at the waist to Anya before moving aside and indicating the woman Cinder had earlier marked. "This is Rishi Persistence."

Cinder's eyes narrowed as Rishi Persistence marched forward. She was graceful, controlled, and based on her movements, she knew how to use the sword on her belt. He studied her anew, recalling everything he knew about this woman. The rishi was a warrior of note, several centuries old, and said to be a genius even at a young age. She would make a dangerous foe, and he hoped she wasn't the rishi they'd have to face in the Spire of the Saints.

"Welcome to Bharat," Rishi Persistence said. Her voice had a rich timbre, as clipped and authoritative as her bearing.

"Thank you," Bones said, dipping his head to the rishi. As the leader of the Shokans, they'd decided he would be the one to make the introductions. "I am Bones Jorn." He stepped out of the way—Cinder doing the same—bowing low as he indicated Anya and her brother. "Her Royal Highness, Princess Anya Aruyen of Yaksha Sithe and His Royal Highness, Prince Estn Aruyen."

Cinder had also bowed during Anya's introduction, and he straightened as she stepped forward. Her gaze never left the rishi's. "It is my great pleasure to meet you, Rishi Persistence. I believe we have much to discuss." Her voice was just as cool and commanding as the rishi's.

"In time," Rishi Persistence said. "I'm sure your travels have left you tired. We can have conversation once you've rested. We've made arrangements for you and your... honor guard. We will host you."

"Thank you," Anya said, with an incline of her neck.

Cinder's eyes narrowed. That hesitation on the rishi's part hadn't been a mistake; it had been intentional, a way of stating that she knew the royal family of Yaksha Sithe was normally protected by the Sun Guard, all of whom were elves.

Tobias glanced about. "Where are your horses?"

Anya was the one to answer. "We left them in Char."

Which was true. And if all went well, they'd be able to retrieve them later. However, they did disembark the pack mules, although most of their gear remained in Char as well.

"Then we should be off," Rishi Persistence said. She glanced at Anya. "I'm curious. Perhaps you can tell me of your travels over the past few years. Rumors abound about you and a certain human male. Your mother is said to be unhappy with you. It makes me wonder why she chose you for this delegation."

Anya smiled easily. "I'm sure you know better than to listen to rumors. And what mother isn't occasionally upset with her daughter? As for the human…" She shrugged. "Who can tell what happened to him?"

"And your mother's unhappiness?" the rishi asked. "That wasn't a rumor."

Again, Anya waved aside the comment. "Whatever I may or may not have done, before Sala Yaksha acts as my mother, she rules as my empress. In this regard, she will always do what is right for the sithe."

Rishi Persistence eyed her a moment. "So you say," she allowed before setting off with Anya. Estin trailed alongside the two women as they discussed the weather and economy while the Shokans and rakishis arranged themselves behind the rishi and elven royalty, eyeing one another.

Cinder did more than eye, though. He studied every motion the rakishis made, even when they entered the crowds, who gave way with silent bows as Rishi Persistence swept past. He watched and noted how the rakishis handled their weapons, their spacing, where they placed their hands when having to shift about. Cinder wanted every last scrap of information.

"I know the name of your commander," Tobias said, striding next to him. "But I haven't heard yours."

Cinder had caught the man viewing the Shokans in the same way he had been examining the rakishis. Tobias would make a formidable opponent, and a warning flared in Cinder's mind to give the man as little information as possible. "I'm known as Hotgate. Simple adjutant." He made a note to spread the word among the Shokans. They were to give away as little as possible to the rakishis.

"Hotgate?" Tobias sounded doubtful. "An interesting name."

Cinder flashed him a smile. "Not really. Nothing like Persistence. That's a name worthy of honoring."

It seemed to be the correct thing to say because Tobias straightened. "I'm glad to hear you say so."

"I've seen to the delegation from Rakesh and Yaksha Sithe," Tobias said.

He had only just arrived and stood a single pace behind Rishi Persistence, who had waited for him on a balcony outside her quarters. From here, within the Spire of the Saints, they had a view of Restitution Chalice, the manor where Tobias had settled the delegation from Rakesh and Yaksha Sithe.

Tobias stared at the building—one of many—within the grounds of Black Jackal House, the palace from which the rishis ruled.

"What did you learn?" Rishi Persistence asked. She, too, stared toward Restitution Chalice, and as always, the sense of her presence dominated whatever space in which she stood.

"The unit guarding the royals call themselves the Shokans." He mentally snorted at the name. *Who were they to give themselves such a powerful title?*

Rishi Persistence smiled at him. "I sense disapproval."

He heard the mild rebuke in her tone, and Tobias knew better than to whitewash the truth. "The name is offensive."

The rishi shrugged. "Regardless. What else?"

Tobias described the command structure of the Shokans, starting with the officer who had first introduced himself. "He leads, and the others respect him, even the two elves in the unit."

"What do we know of him?"

"He's from Swift Sword, but a graduate of the Third Directorate in Yaksha Sithe. All of them are." Tobias went on to tell what he and the other rakishis had learned in speaking with the Shokans. "They're a veteran unit. Their scabbards aren't polished and pretty, and they have that way about them. They've battled zahhacks, possibly even necrosed, and been victorious every time."

"They said this?"

"One of them—Ishmay, a boastful sort—let it slip."

"Then they didn't come to serve as decoration. They are Rakesh's best?"

Tobias nodded. "That would be my guess. They were chosen over the Sun Guard because they don't simply look good on the training ground. They have practical experience." He ventured a question of his own. "What about the princess and her brother?"

Persistence's attention went back to Restitution Chalice, staring as if her sight could pierce the walls of the manor. "Anya is the older sibling, and as is the case with those from Yaksha, the prince always gives way to the princess." She sniffed. "In truth, I don't think he said more than a handful of words."

"And Anya?" Tobias hadn't missed how she walked and moved. It seemed the reports of her abilities as a warrior might not be in exaggeration. Of course, the only way to tell for true would be to test her in a training hall.

The rishi confirmed his opinion. "She may have some skill, but in the end, she's still just an elf. They aren't our equal." She faced Tobias again, and this time, a slight frown marred her otherwise calm features. "What of the other one? The adjutant? Before she disappeared, Anya was said to have traveled extensively with a human male. Cinder Shade was his name, the ones those fool *hashains* had farcically declared the Grimyogi."

"He calls himself Hotgate. No surname. Remarkably close-mouthed about his background, but based on his appearance, he's not from Rakesh."

"He could be a *hashain*."

"It's possible, but the way the others from Rakesh and even the elves defer to him, I find that hard to believe. *Hashains* are hated in Rakesh, and Yaksha elves wouldn't allow such a dangerous individual so close to their royalty."

"Defer?"

Tobias nodded. "The Shokans didn't say much about him. Just his name, but the respect they held was obvious. I would venture to say even awe."

"Anything else?"

"He had an odd aroma about him. It was almost of blood."

Persistence pulled a moue of distaste. "I noticed it, too. But regardless of his lack of hygiene, could he be Cinder Shade? The one who defeated the *hashains*?"

Tobias snorted in derision. For those who weren't rakishis, the *hashains* were fine enough warriors, but during his visit several years ago to Chapterhouse Bedwin, they hadn't impressed him. They lacked discipline and proper breeding. *Uncouth louts.*

"Cinder Shade was also said to have been the Prime of his class at the Third Directorate," Rishi Persistence reminded him.

"True, and even elves are superior warriors to mere humans." Tobias pondered the matter. Was this Hotgate truly Cinder Shade? And what did it mean if he was? A human who could challenge elves, dwarves, and *hashains*?

"He might be a danger."

Tobias' gaze sharpened on the rishi. She rarely spoke words that were meaningless. "You don't trust them?"

This time it was Persistence who snorted. "Of course not. I find this entire farce distasteful." She exhaled heavily. "But we must do as we're instructed."

Tobias hid a scowl. Then it was politics from Shrewd Hall—the assembly where the rishis met—that had forced Persistence to meet with these *naajas*.

"They claim to be a delegation from Rakesh and Yaksha," Rishi Persistence mused. "Which makes no sense. The sithe doesn't fear Shet. Only the human nation does."

"We don't fear Shet either," Tobias said.

"No, but we respect him, and when the time is right, we will end him." The rishi shook her head as if removing unimportant thoughts. "At any rate, I have been tasked with dealing with this delegation, and I will do so, in my own way and at my own pace. And it will be quick. There is no need to hear them out because rumors, despite what the princess might believe, can provide insight into both friend and foe."

"Do the rumors say they are foes?"

Persistence didn't answer at once. "Maybe. But the rumors definitely state that Anya is disfavored by her mother. And yet here she arrives, with all the proper diplomatic papers, signed by the empress herself."

Tobias shifted, uncertain what to say.

Meanwhile, Persistence continued to stare at Restitution Chalice. She abruptly faced Tobias. "We need to test this delegation. I want to see Anya Aruyen in action as a warrior. Same with the Shokans and this Hotgate."

"I doubt they will take part," Tobias said. He stiffened when the rishi's penetrating gaze landed on him. He had closely observed many of the other rishis, and of them all, Persistence was the wisest and most generous—seeing to the needs to their people—but she was also the most deadly and decisive. It was a challenging combination, which led Tobias to both adore and fear her in equal measure.

"What makes you believe so?" Persistence asked.

Tobias again explained the close-mouthed nature of the Shokans. "I don't think they'll want us to see how weak they actually are."

Persistence might have muttered in disappointment. "Then we need to make them an offer they must accept. They want an alliance with us? We'll tell them that our tradition is to ally with no one but our equal."

It was true. Bharat had no allies, and in truth, the notion of allying—of accepting a position of equality with any other nation—sat poorly with Tobias. Were their people not the inheritors of the Mythaspuris? By his calculation, Bharat should lead, and the other nations should follow. That was the natural order of things.

And yet, Tobias wasn't sure how any of this was relevant to the delegation and what Persistence wanted from them. "How will this convince them to spar against us?"

She faced him again, smiling. "Because, as I said, if they want us as allies, they need to prove themselves worthy, and the only way is to show us their skills."

Tobias offered a slow nod of agreement, already thinking on those he'd want to face the Shokans. No true rakishi was needed. He could show the Shokans the folly of their ways by having them battle some older Accepted, children really.

However, Rishi Persistence seemed to have another idea in mind. "I want you to take part," she said. "Defeat whomever they choose as swiftly as you can. Embarrass them."

Tobias frowned. It sounded like Persistence didn't want a tournament. "Just me?"

She nodded. "They will choose one person to serve as their champion, and so will we. And when this delegation is found wanting, they will be escorted off the island forthwith. We have no need for the weak."

17

A knock at the door caused Cinder to glance up from where he was seated in a large, luxurious room, along with the rest of the Shokans. Soft leather furniture and tables inlaid with elegant marquetry decorated the space while chocolate-colored walls served to make the room cozier. Windowed doors were left open onto a broad balcony, from which could be viewed the towering Spire of the Saints and the shining blue light of the island's Orb.

The knock repeated, and he went to the front door. Tobias, the commander of Rishi Persistence's warriors, waited outside.

"Sorry to disturb," the rakishi said, "but might I speak to the princess?"

Anya was already close at hand, and she and Tobias conversed briefly, the discussion ending when he passed her a folded document.

Cinder followed Anya as she reentered the room where the Shokans were situated, scanning the paper.

"What is it?" Cinder asked upon seeing her grimace.

"It seems the rishis won't meet with us unless we demonstrate our worthiness to serve as allies."

She passed Cinder the document so he could read it for himself. He quickly perused the missive, immediately making note of the neat, consistent penmanship. Whoever had written this had an ordered mind. And based on the contents and their few interactions, he guessed it was Rishi Persistence.

"What do they want?" Estin asked.

The rest of the Shokans seemed to lean in as Anya explained, and when she finished, it was Estin who said what was on all their minds.

"We're sending Cinder, right?" the prince asked.

"He's the obvious choice," Anya agreed.

"But why send anyone at all?" Gorant asked. "Were we not trying to keep Hotgate's abilities secret?"

"He has to fight," Estin said. "Other than Anya, he's the only one who can beat one of their rakishis. It wouldn't look good if the princess leading this delegation is also the one who has to fight so we can stay on Bharat."

"It doesn't matter," Cinder said, ending the discussion. Their plan to get on the island had worked. They just had to remain on it until this evening. "I'll spar whomever they send, and the rest of the plan will be the same."

"You're sure you can take whomever you have to face?" Estin asked.

Nothing in battle was ever certain, but there were layers to the uncertainties. In this case, Cinder had none. "We'll be fine."

Several hours later, with the late afternoon sunshine warming the island to a baking intensity, a pair of rakishis came to guide the Shokans to where the sparring match was to be held. It was a place called Retribution Hall, a large, open-air edifice where those young men and women who would eventually become rakishis were taught. The building consisted of a number of courtyards and training areas, and it was to one such space that the Shokans were delivered.

Upon their arrival, Cinder swiftly recognized the true purpose of the sparring match: it was meant to humiliate Rakesh and Yaksha. The space was an arena, filled with hundreds of rakishis sitting in silent regard, none of whom appeared too friendly. There also appeared to be a trio of rishis—Rishi Persistence and two others. They stood alongside one another in a private bubble granted by the other warriors.

Cinder tried to identify them. The small, unobtrusive one might be Patience, the rishi healer, while the one with the slim, elegant build of a vampire was likely Guile, the spymaster known as the Bloody Needle. In the midst of his examination, Persistence seemed to notice his attention, and she faced him with a cold expression.

In other circumstances, Cinder might have given the three rishis an impudent grin, but now wasn't the time. Right now, he had to concentrate. And that concentration brought to him various scents: crushed grapes seemed to emanate from Persistence; loamy moss from Guile— their *lorethasras* maybe. From Patience, though, there was nothing.

Cinder briefly broke off his examination when the Shokans were shown to their seats, while he, as the one who would represent their interests, was led to a square sparring area. It was floored with hard-packed sand, about fifty feet on each side, and he gave an experimental scuff, satisfied by what he found. The footing was solid.

Gazing ahead, he wasn't surprised at whom he would be sparring against—Tobias. Facing him with a smirk of supreme confidence, the rakishi stood alone in the center of the square. The smell of hot sand was overwhelming, and it wasn't just from the arena floor. It was Tobias' *lorethasra* as well.

"We weren't sure you would show," the rakishi said.

"Wouldn't dream of missing it," Cinder replied, staring down the rakishi. His gaze never wavered, and he stepped forward, getting within inches of the other man. "I'm here. What are you going to do about it?"

Tobias snarled, shoving Cinder away.

Cinder made to dart back at the rakishi but was pulled short by the rakishis who had guided him here. The audience shouted in outrage.

"Filthy barbarian." Tobias spat. "No wonder your kind are so weak. You have no self-control."

Cinder smirked, not bothering to reply. In truth, his actions hadn't been due to lack of control. During the entire encounter, he hadn't felt the slightest bit of anger. What he wanted was information. Tobias was several inches shorter but had a similar reach. He was also fast but not deadly so. And based on his shove, he wasn't as strong as Cinder had expected.

Persistence shouted, calling for their attention, explaining the reason for the match and the rules, which were the same as what Cinder was used to from *Steel-Graced Adepts* and the Third Directorate: first warrior to four points was victorious. Any non-lethal blow counted for one point and a lethal one was two.

"The warriors will take their positions," Persistence said.

Cinder found Tobias giving him a last scathing look before the rakishi went to his side of the square. The other man rolled his shoulders, cranked his neck, and unsheathed what looked to be a shoke. Cinder did the same, standing at the diagonal of Tobias, just like when he'd sparred the Shokans back in Char. And while warming up, he went over everything he knew about the rakishis one last time.

The most important item was that the rishis—and by extension, possibly the rakishis—claimed to use *Jivatma,* but it was a lie. They used *lorethasra.* Cinder knew it, could smell it, which meant he should have an edge in speed and power. But skill would likely still be the determining factor.

In reality, this sparring match was a good chance for Cinder to gain information on the rakishis. How well he performed against Tobias would give him greater clarity on the likely success of their plan.

Tobias eyed the man called Hotgate in anger. *How dare he?* The filth had dared challenge him before the match had even been declared official. Originally, Tobias had intended to teach these Shokans a quick but brutal lesson.

Not now.

Now Tobias intended on inflicting punishment, pain to go along with the lesson of Bharatian superiority. Just enough to hurt but not necessarily to injure. An injury wouldn't be just, and if there was one thing that separated Bharat from the other peoples of Seminal, it was their sacred belief in justice. However, when Tobias was through with Hotgate, the man would think twice before ever acting so arrogant.

Persistence, standing just outside the sparring square, raised her hands.

Tobias sourced *lorethasra*, flowing it through his one open Chakra—*Muladhara*—where it exited as *prana*. The world was cleaner, brighter, and his senses enlivened. Braids of Fire, Earth, and Water, his most powerful weaves, were ready.

Persistence dropped her hands. "Go!"

Tobias burst forward. He stabbed at half-speed, expecting Hotgate to block. Using the distraction, he sent a braid of Earth to trap the other man's feet while a line of Fire crackled at him.

Hotgate surprised him, though, twisting away from the entangling Earth and moving just enough to evade the Fire. Tobias blinked. It had been done as quickly and perfectly controlled as Rishi Persistence might have managed.

Possibly a fluke.

Tobias sourced more deeply from his *lorethasra*. He attacked, eschewing his braids for the moment. He wanted to test the man, to see if his earlier evasion had truly been a fluke. A thrust was parried; a slash slapped aside. A frontkick missed entirely. Tobias quickly gathered his balance and reset. Those had been hard, fast attacks, enough to defeat any human, and yet Hotgate had defended beautifully. The man stood there waiting, calm as a winter lake.

Maybe not just a fluke, then.

So be it.

Tobias attacked faster, moving as swiftly as he would against a late-term Accepted. Again, his blows were turned aside or simply missed.

Each of Hotgate's motions was crisp and well timed—no wasted movement. Not even in how he placed his feet.

Even when Tobias added weaves, he was unsuccessful. Fire was evaded. Earth caught nothing, and Water was somehow cut in half. The man must have *lorethasra,* although Tobias scented nothing other than sunbaked sand and his own sweat.

He reset again, trying to reckon how Hotgate was keeping up. Intending to take a few seconds to think over his next plan of attack, Tobias was nearly caught unawares when Hotgate came at him. Until now, all the man had done was defend.

Fine. Let's see what skill the man brings.

Tobias blocked a diagonal slash. Pushed off a vertical chop. A side-kick nearly cracked his knee, but he angled it aside at the last instant.

Hotgate gave him no time to regain his balance. He strode forward, his blows coming faster.

Tobias sourced more deeply from his *lorethasra,* keeping up. By now, they were moving with the swiftness of a newly graduated rakishi. Again, Cinder raised the pace, and Tobias—starting to worry—matched him. Just how much speed did the man have? Tobias prepared to send another braid of Fire, knowing it would miss. But Hotgate always evaded by going to his right.

Tobias would catch him this time. An ensnaring braid of Earth would hold him in place long enough to claim victory.

The line of Fire roared forward. Hotgate evaded to his right. The trap was sprung, and Tobias used the weave of Earth he'd earlier placed along the other man's line of motion to—

He backpedaled when Cinder stepped over the weave and darted forward. Again, Tobias found himself on the back foot, defending.

A short thrust transitioned to an elbow that would have taken Tobias' head off. He rolled out of the way, regaining his feet in time to slap aside a slash. A wall of Water caused Hotgate to pause, gaining Tobias valuable time.

But it wasn't enough. Hotgate leapt through the Water as if it wasn't there and attacked. Once again, he increased the pace, moving at a speed that left Tobias struggling to keep up. He sourced *lorethasra* to his deepest extent possible.

And still, Hotgate showed no sign of slowing.

How was this happening? How was Hotgate so strong? So fast? And, most worrisome, so skilled?

Tobias wasn't holding back. He was giving it his all, and still Hotgate seemed nonplussed. He fought as if he were standing in a meadow and butterflies were the only danger he faced.

He shocked Tobias by rushing forward. A thrust slammed home. Tobias collapsed to his knees. It felt like he'd been stabbed in the abdomen. He clutched his stomach but refused to release a cry of agony.

An instant later, the pain receded, and Tobias found that a murmuring of shock had spread throughout the arena.

And there stood Hotgate, ten feet away, face cold. "You cannot win," he said, before turning on his heels and stepping back to his starting position.

"Two points for Hotgate," Persistence said, sounding as shaken as Tobias felt.

It shouldn't have been possible. Hotgate, a mere human, had kept pace with him, and worse, Tobias could tell, the man hadn't needed to demonstrate the full width and breadth of his skill.

No matter.

Tobias leaned on a lifetime's worth of experience and shoved away the loss. He hadn't taken Hotgate seriously before, but this time he would.

He would still win the match.

Filling himself with confidence, Tobias studied his opponent anew. The man was as fast and skilled as any rakishi, but did he have the same level of experience? Unlikely, given his youth. Tobias had decades of fighting on Hotgate, and he knew how to defeat the young and powerful.

"Be ready," Persistence called out, arms raised again.

Tobias inhaled deeply, sourcing *lorethasra* as deeply as he could manage.

"Go!"

He feigned darting at Hotgate before abruptly pulling back. Again, he did it. A third time. Tobias circled to the right, ready to pretend another attack. He wanted Hotgate to burn energy by chasing him.

Tobias' hands moved before his mind was aware of what was occurring. He barely blocked a blistering attack. Instinct rolled him under another slash. Another slash from his right. Tobias rolled again, gathered himself. And here came Hotgate, sending attack after attack. Precise and powerful. Showing no signs of slowing, the man pounded at Tobias' defenses.

Tobias cursed. He couldn't gain distance to figure out what was happening, and worse, his *lorethasra* was flagging.

The end came with a stunning abruptness. A simple slash that knocked aside his shoke. A follow-on thrust to the chest, and the match was done.

The pain. Again, Tobias found himself on the ground, teeth clenched to hold back a scream. The pain finally left him, and he rose shakily to his feet, finding the shocked mutterings grown to become loud exclamations of incredulity, a disbelief Tobias shared. He'd lost to a human—the shame.

Meanwhile, Hotgate faced the crowd, arms outstretched as he spun in a slow circle. "Is it done? Or are there others who wish to test me?"

"Victory to Hotgate," Persistence shouted, silencing the man's antics.

The princess, who had been seated with her guards, rose to her feet. "Will this serve to demonstrate our worthiness in negotiating with Bharat?"

Tobias' humiliation crested upon seeing the sour expression fill Persistence's features. "It will serve," the rishi said to the princess. "Collect your men and return to Restitution Chalice. We will consult with you in the morning."

Cinder bowed low to the rishi before making to depart the sparring square.

A question blaring in his mind, Tobias held him back. He had to know. "How did you win?"

Hotgate answered in an esoteric fashion. "Wisdom is the acceptance of what can be achieved and what cannot. Learning this brings understanding, if not peace."

18

Captain Swell had his vision locked on the dark waters up ahead of his ship. *Whispering Tanned Fox* was nearly out of Solace's harbor—thank Devesh!—but ahead of them was the most treacherous part of the passage. The Bharatian Narrows, a choked opening that was only wide enough for a few vessels to pass through at a time.

Crossing it at night was especially tense, but in spite of the darkness, the captain was confident. The rishis might be arrogant pricks, but they knew how to organize their harbor, having placed bright lights on buoys near rocks, shoals, and other dangers. There was also the lighthouse at the harbor's mouth and the twin moons in the sky.

Nevertheless, even with the extra illumination, it didn't mean a good crew couldn't find their vessel in danger. It was never wise to take the sea at her word, which was why Captain Swell had his eyes focused on the dark waters and his senses attuned to the feel of the wind. He occasionally flicked a glance at the sails, noted the way his ship moved, and called out orders to his first mate and bosun. *Whispering Tanned Fox* was a sweet vessel, but all it would take was an unaccounted rogue wave or a gust of wind aimed in the wrong direction to see his beauty crashed on the rocks.

Just as dangerous were the fools who shouldn't have command of a rowboat, much less a deep-water ship. Those kinds of 'sailors' made life on the ocean dangerous for anyone.

"Rocks to starboard!" the barrel man shouted. "A hundred yards."

Captain Swell had already seen it, and he called an adjustment to the sails, and *Whispering Tanned Fox* heeled slightly to port.

They entered the Narrows then, leaving plenty of room ahead for *Dory's Rainbow*, which Solace's harbormaster had cleared to exit directly ahead of *Whispering Tanned Fox*.

An edgy half-hour later, the wide-open sea bloomed before them, and they were free. Captain Swell shouted further orders for the shifting of rigging. The bosun transmitted the commands and the sails billowed with a crack. *Whispering Tanned Fox* surged forward, catching the wind.

Only then did Captain Swell relax, and he found himself staring back at Bharat. The rocky island was directly astern, and the lights of Solace twinkled while the glowing Orb atop the Spire of Saints blazed forth, heralding the power of the rishis.

Captain Swell continued to stare at the island, contemplating the Yaksha royals. What was their real reason for journeying to Bharat? They had traveled there aboard *Whispering Tanned Fox,* but they weren't returning by way of his ship. And their demeanor had indicated a purpose that had nothing to do with meeting the rishis.

There was something else going on. But what?

Captain Swell had heard stories about the princess when he'd been through Plinth. About how she and the human with whom she traveled, Cinder Shade, had stolen the Orb of Eretria from the dwarves of Surent Crèche.

Was that why they had gone to Bharat? To steal the Orb of Undying Light? Was that why they'd been so strict in insisting that he depart the island on the same evening in which they'd disembarked?

Hopefully, that wasn't their plan. If so, death would be their kindest punishment since the rishis would likely make an example of them first.

Captain Swell grimaced, giving a final examination to Bharat, along with a prayer on behalf of the Yaksha royals and their entire party: *Devesh, see them safe. no matter what those idiots have planned.*

It was in the midst of his prayer that the Orb of Undying Light went dark.

Both moons were out tonight, shedding soft light through clear skies on the large plaza in front of the Spire of the Saints. A slight breeze whispered, and the steady tromp of patrolling guards echoed about. Those same warriors could be easily seen under the bright glow of a vast array of *diptha* lamps that illuminated much of the plaza.

It wasn't ideal conditions for a Trial like this. Better if it had been cloudy and overcast or even rainy, with the guards clustered close and not wanting any part of the weather.

But summers in Bharat were warm, hot, and dry, and the conditions were what they were. The Shokans, currently split into two teams, would simply have to work around them. Cinder's unit, consisting of Estin, Riyne, Wark, Depth, and Gorant, led the way while the trailing squad—commanded by Anya—included Bones, Mirk, Mohal, Sash, and Ishmay.

Thus far, the Shokans had made a mad dash from Restitution Chalice, where the rishis had housed them, across the grounds of Black Jackal House—scaling walls, descending them, and darting along the shadows—before finally reaching the broad mall directly outside the Spire of the Saints.

Several hundred yards in length, they'd have to make a final run along the plaza's perimeter and count on the guards not noticing their presence.

So far, they hadn't, and Cinder figured they wouldn't here either, not with the Blend he was holding. He had it as tight as possible, which was significantly richer than when he had first recovered the Talent. It was due to the destruction of the Orbs. With the ending of each one, his abilities had increased enough in power, utility, and efficiency that his Blend could now encompass the entirety of his unit, just as Anya's covered hers.

Which was why none of the guards had raised an alarm. None of them even knew to suspect the presence of the Shokans in their midst. It didn't matter that the rakishis were patrolling in force with numbers far greater than Cinder had expected or wanted. They were blind and deaf to the Shokans racing past them.

At a short wall, Cinder had his unit leapfrog forward.

Only fifty yards to reach the entrance and then would come the most difficult part of their plan.

But it would work; Cinder had to believe so.

After Blending his way through Fort Carnate and Revelant, he had learned a valuable lesson, one that once again confirmed Shokan's teachings: Blends—or any abilities, for that matter—that were powered by *lorethasra* were of no comparison to ones created by *Jivatma*. And one created by both? Impossible to detect, except by those trained to recognize them. Such warriors had been far more common in Shokan's time, but in today's world, the only ones who were properly schooled to penetrate such a Blend were Cinder and Anya.

At a pause directly outside the Spire, Cinder had the Shokans halt. Included as they were in his Blend, they could see each other just fine, and right now all of them were staring at the closed doors. None appeared nervous. They were ready to get inside and complete this Trial.

But Cinder wouldn't simply allow them to rush ahead. They'd come too far and done too well to slip up because of a stupid oversight.

He held up a hand, halting them, quickly whispering his concerns to Estin, who passed them on to the others. In the meanwhile, Cinder peered ahead, sourcing and conducting, flooding his senses. More booted steps coming from inside. He counted them.

Five guards outside and fifteen within. The ones inside tracked back and forth, down a long corridor that led through the heart of the Spire.

And at the end of the hallway should be a door leading into a single room. There, the Orb of Undying Light was supposedly kept. That and the Gate of the Saints.

The rishis likely knew the function of the Orb, but they'd apparently forgotten what their Gate could do. Just like the Yaksha elves, they only used it to access the attached Arrival Foe, which was said to lead to a mountain lodge and hot springs where they learned healing. It was probably the reason the rishis were such skilled physicians.

Anya's team reached them, waiting just behind with their Blends Linked. A whispered explanation was quickly passed along.

All the while, Cinder kept his senses locked on the open door. The faintest smell of crushed grapes drifted to him, only noticeable due to his enhanced senses from *Jivatma*. He'd tasted the aroma during his fight with Tobias, and it had come from Rishi Persistence. She was in there, and given the scent of hot sand, so was Tobias.

What about other rishis, though? There were more guards than expected warding the Spire of the Saints, and Cinder figured it might be a response to his display from earlier in the day. His defeat of Tobias had surely stung Bharatian pride.

Demanding to know the scent of Cinder's *lorethasra* during their match, they would have debriefed Tobias, and the rakishi wouldn't have been able to tell them anything. A conundrum for the rishis and also the rakishis, who were arrogant as elves and as certain of themselves as holders.

And yet a mere human had defeated one of their best warriors. How, they would demand to know. It would stick in their craw, but the wiser ones, like Rishi Persistence, would have recognized truths about Cinder. Certainly, she would have guessed his name, probably even before the sparring match.

But she might have also realized a possibility: Cinder could use *Jivatma*. And if she did suspect what Cinder could do, would Persistence have told anyone else?

Guile, the spymaster, certainly. He was here. The scent of loam and moss—Guile's *lorethasra*—drifted to Cinder.

It proved that there were at least *two* rishis to go along with the rak-ishis waiting for them inside.

Cinder nodded to himself. They were odds he figured he could han-dle. He recalled again what Manifold had once said about how a war-rior with a single open Chakra was equal to one thousand who had none available and how that advantage continued to evenly scale with each open Chakra.

Well, he and Anya each had five open Chakras, and the rishis only had two. And even as limited as they both seemed—him because of the remaining Orbs and Anya for a reason that had him suspicious—he was still confident in their chances. He only hoped they didn't have to kill anyone in order to accomplish this Trial. Such a notion made him ill.

It wouldn't stop him, though. He'd do whatever was necessary and deal with the consequences afterward.

Regardless, he prayed no one would die tonight.

With a last-second study of the way ahead, Cinder passed on the in-formation he'd gleaned. "We can bypass them," he said to the Shokans, Anya's unit included. "Stay alert. We'll want to be fast. If there's trouble, leave it to me and Anya."

There were four entrances into the Spire of the Saints, each one lead-ing to a corridor that ended in Indrun's Chamber, the room where Persistence waited with Guile. And each hallway was currently guard-ed by fifteen rakishis, over twice the usual complement and a similar number waited in here as well.

As Persistence calculated matters, it should be more than enough to handle the Shokans, unless Hotgate was who she suspected. She would have never considered such a possibility except for what had happened this afternoon.

Tobias had been soundly beaten, which should have never hap-pened. Only a holder or a rishi were the equal of or better than a rakishi.

And yet it had occurred, and most troubling of all, Tobias had insisted that the human had no odor of *lorethasra* about him.

So then how had Hotgate won?

Persistence had reviewed everything she knew about the man along with every member of the delegation from Rakesh and Yaksha Sithe. And it hadn't taken her long to confirm her previous educated guess. There was one man who was said to command the respect of every one of the Shokans. One man who was the reason for Anya Aruyen's fall from grace. One man who was said to easily best elves, dwarves, *hashains*, and any other woven.

That man was Cinder Shade, the man who rumors claimed had been born a cripple, had lived as one for many years before his miraculous rebirth at the bottom of a well. From there, he'd achieved astonishing greatness, first in Swift Sword and later at the Third Directorate. And Cinder Shade was also said to source *Jivatma*. No, not source; he *conducted* it. That was the proper term.

Until this afternoon, Persistence would have put little stock in such stories. She had thought it far more likely that Cinder Shade was like the *hashains*—an unexpected child of a powerful woven and a human, nothing more. And the hearsay about him as a cripple? Simple fabrication and exaggeration, as were his achievements in his various martial schools.

Now, though, she was faced with a very different possibility, because what if the stories were true? It might mean the *Book of Flight* was seeing its final and most important words echoing across the world.

It spoke of Shokan, the Lord of the Sword, known by his proper name of Rukh Shektan. Was he reborn? There were ways to tell. Tests that could prove the matter, and Persistence was determined to perform them. She wouldn't simply hang her hopes on the words of prophecy alone. She intended to challenge Cinder Shade. He was coming to the Spire. It was almost certain. It was where the Orb of Undying Light was kept and guarded. She expected to receive word of battle against the Rakesh delegation at any moment. Because if some rumors about him were true, then another simpler one was likely to also be true: Cinder's vow to destroy the Orbs of Peace.

Just like Persistence's true purpose was to await Shokan's coming. Prior to today, she had lost faith in that purpose, that of her ancestral line. It had been a slow erosion of belief from those rishis who had been called 'Persistence' prior to her; a wearing away of a hope that stretched back to the time of Mede and the creation of the *hashains*, who should never have existed.

But after seeing the weakness of the Titans, Liline Salt and Rence Darim, Persistence had reluctantly come to believe that the *Book of Flight* had been corrupted in some way. Shokan, Sira, Shet, and his Titans were myths who would never live up to their fame.

And yet, just this afternoon, a seemingly normal human man had defeated a rakishi and did so without use of *lorethasra*. There were others in history who might have managed it, but none had the innate nobility that Cinder Shade—Hotgate—was said to possess.

But was he really Shokan? Persistence had to know. Her rishi line was the only one who properly understood and recognized Shokan, all the way back to his first appearance in the fabulous Realm of Earth. Hence, the name they had chosen: Persistence. Her ancestral line *persisted*. They remembered and lauded Shokan, and they also knew how best to determine the validity of his rebirth.

It all relied on a simple test, and Persistence would provide it, just as others in her lineage had done for other pretenders to Shokan's name. Unimportant men who were forgotten by time and their own people but not by those called Persistence. After all, it was those of her line who had been the ones to destroy those charlatans.

And the testing would begin with the evaluation of Cinder's character. How would he react to the rakishis preventing him from entering Indrun's Chamber? What would he do? Kill to get inside? Sacrifice his Shokans—no doubt named for who he believed himself to be—in order to reach the Orb? Or would he somehow sneak his way here?

A young rakishi, frazzled in appearance, entered the chamber and rushed to her side. "*Whispering Tanned Fox* applied to leave the harbor. She's already out at sea."

Persistence frowned. Had the delegation already departed the island? Why? The Orb of Undying Light was here, and they clearly wanted it. Or had she completely misinterpreted the situation?

Guile, having overheard the report, dismissed the rakishi. "This changes things," he said to Persistence.

"Have you received word that the delegation went to the harbor?"

Guile shook his head. "The last report from Restitution Chalice was an hour ago. The lights were off, and they were inside, asleep."

"Check again."

Guile nodded. Although he was the elder rishi, his ancestral line had always served hers, a closely guarded secret amongst their lineages. The Persistences persisted, whereas the Guiles understood the *Book of Flight* better than anyone.

And as they waited on word about the delegation and Restitution Chalice, Persistence paced before the broken halo-shaped Gate of the Saints, lost in thought. She pored over every facet of her information about Cinder Shade; every detail about his encounter with the *hashains* when they'd labeled him the Grimyogi, reviewed Hotgate's immaculate sparring match with Tobias. What had she missed?

While she paced, her gaze landed on the Orb of Undying Light. It glowed bright, almost painful to look upon, with blue-and-green lightning etched within its center. Persistence marveled again at the cleverness of her people. They had placed the Orb within a hollow on a broad pedestal made of mirrored glass, which reflected and refracted its light to the very top of the Spire's needle-thin tower. There, it shined out like a beacon of hope.

And yet, it all started here, with a small globe the size of a plum. Such a small thing to provide so much for the world. Without it, the people of Seminal would have broken and gone mad.

Persistence wouldn't give the Orb away to anyone. They would have to earn it. She stroked the hilt of her sword. And that cost would be dear.

19

Cinder paused when he and the Shokans were halfway through the corridor, reassessing the way forward.

Four more rakishis lined the hallway directly ahead, armored and armed, hands on their spears as they stared outward. In addition, the corridor narrowed up ahead, and the metal door into Indrun's Chamber was barred. Cinder pondered: *How to get inside without alerting the guards?*

The best way would be through distraction.

Just then, the door leading into Indrun's Chamber opened, and a rakishi came running out. He spoke to one of the guards and left the door open.

Cinder quickly signaled Anya, who stood not more than twenty yards away and was Linked.

She knew what he wanted and had already readied a *nomasra* they'd earlier created. She tossed it toward the corridor's far entrance, where it bounced once and exploded. It was all light and pressure but with no heat, but still, the entire corridor shook. An instant later, Cinder's own *nomasra*—he'd thrown his just an instant after Anya's—landed a few feet from hers. Another explosion. His was of smoke, and it billowed.

Dust rained from the ceiling, and momentary chaos filled the hallway as questions and commands were shouted. But the rakishis quickly responded. They rushed past where Cinder and the Shokans were pressed against the wall and formed a perimeter line.

And the door leading into Indrun's Chamber was only now closing.

Dropping his Blend and pouring every bit of *Jivatma* into speed, Cinder blurred forward. He left his feet and smashed a Shielded shoulder into the closing door. The rakishi who had been shutting it was flung backward, launched into the room. Cinder landed ten feet away, rolling to his feet.

Fourteen more rakishis and two rishis filled the chamber. They gaped in shock—a mistake. They should have attacked. Anya and the rest of the Shokans dashed inside. They barred the corridor they'd used while Cinder sent Fireballs to fuse shut the other three entrances. The rakishis dove aside from the flames, which was fine. Cinder hadn't really been trying to kill them. He just didn't want them letting in any other guards.

"Cinder Shade," Rishi Persistence said, striding forward. "We've been expecting you."

Persistence hadn't predicted that Hotgate would literally barrel his way into Indrun's Chamber. As soon as the twin explosions had set off, she knew he was coming. But she also thought the rakishis she'd set to guard the way forward would have at least slowed him down.

Apparently not.

Hotgate had arrived so quickly, acted so decisively that Persistence never had a chance to order the other guards inward. Now they were locked outside. Cinder's Fireballs—of an intensity Persistence had never dreamt—had basically welded the doors to their frame.

Examining him, she stared at the man she believed and feared might be Shokan. He appeared fresh and unconcerned, as composed as a ruler in his garden, not even the slightest bit winded.

But he should have been. Those explosions had come from near the entrance to the Spire, and he'd arrived less than a second later. How had he covered so much ground so quickly?

Her attention next went to Anya, who was dressed in grays and blacks and looked every bit the fit warrior. The princess met Persistence's gaze and had the audacity to lift a challenging brow. Then there were the Shokans. They, too, appeared fresh, no blood marring their clothes and no signs to demonstrate that they'd recently battled their way into Indrun's Chamber.

How was this possible?

Persistence bit back a scowl, refusing to show her unhappiness. Instead, she more deeply considered the matter. With all the extra security, someone should have seen the Shokans and raised the alarm. Word of their approach should have been passed toward Persistence and Guile. Instead, the Shokans looked like they might have strolled into Indrun's Chamber after walking through a tame forest.

Or had they used more of whatever had caused the recent explosions? Even so, Persistence would have expected to hear them.

The only answer that fit tonight's criteria was if the killing had been done quietly—poison or some other means.

It was sickening. Unless…

What if Cinder Shade was Shokan? What if his Blend was as equally deep as his Fireballs? Could he have hidden his entire unit and brought them here undetected?

Persistence's jaw briefly tightened. She hoped so. Her people weren't as fruitful as some races. Every one of them who died was a gut-wrenching loss, and if this need to test Cinder Shade proved a disaster, she'd have no one to blame but herself.

This time, Persistence allowed the scowl.

The only other question was why Cinder and Anya had sent *Whispering Tanned Fox* away from Bharat? How would they flee? Or could they? Maybe that hadn't been part of their plan. The captain must have left early.

Persistence's scowl transitioned to a cold, pitiless expression. It didn't matter. She'd do whatever her people required of her, even if it meant killing all the Shokans and the Yaksha royals. Anya and Estin had signed their own death warrants by invading her island.

"You say you expected us," Cinder said. "By the way, that was quite a dramatic statement, and I'm glad you figured out who I am. I would have been disappointed if you hadn't. What happens now?"

"What happens now is I will end you." She gestured to Guile. Together, the two of them would take out Cinder while the rakishis dealt with the Shokans and the princess.

"Think it through," Cinder said. "We only want the Orb. Hand it over, and we'll leave. No one has to die."

Persistence wasn't persuaded. "You offer peace after having killed so many of my people."

Cinder appeared honestly puzzled. "We didn't kill anyone."

Guile scoffed. "You expect us to believe that you simply walked all the way here undetected. Through all our guards?"

"We were Blended."

"We can detect Blends," Persistence replied. Nonetheless, a hope flowered in her heart. Could he—

Cinder disappeared. One instant he was present, and the next he was gone. Persistence inhaled sharply, shocked. She sourced *lorethasra* as deeply as she could, desperately cast her senses. Where was he? She twisted about, searching, unable to find a single trace of him.

The Orb of Undying Light vanished, and Cinder reappeared.

By the greatest of efforts, Persistence managed to hide her dismay.

"What did you do?" Tobias cried.

Persistence gestured, indicating for the rakishi to be silent. She also wanted to know what had happened.

"You can't detect my Blend," Cinder stated.

Persistence stared at the man, whose features had gone inscrutable. She would have preferred if they were insufferably smug. Emotions could be read and played. "Where is the Orb?"

"Safe. And we didn't kill any of your warriors. We Blended past them all."

Persistence's hope rose, and she couldn't contain it even if she wanted. The *Book of Flight*… "And the explosions?" she asked.

"A diversion. The door was open. It was a way inside without having to fight your guards."

"You fear fighting our rakishis?" Guile asked.

Anya paced a single martial step forward. "You already saw him beat your best."

Persistence shook her head, smiling now as she unsheathed her sword. "No. I did not." She gestured Cinder forward. No matter what this man said, actions spoke louder than words.

And his actions so far were that he'd arrived here undetected and stolen the Orb of Undying Light. How he'd accomplished the former would indicate much about him, but for the latter, there could be only one punishment. Unless…

Persistence prepared a strike, a mix of weaves and her own skill. Guile unsheathed his weapon as well, moving to support her. They'd trained so many times together. He knew how to defend her blind side.

Just then, the smell of blood came to Persistence, and she frowned. What did it mean?

Even as she considered, the rakishis readied themselves, Tobias ordering them into place. It was the same with the Shokans, Anya foolishly taking point. The room looked ready to explode into violence.

"It doesn't need to go like this," Cinder said, sounding imploring. He hadn't yet drawn his blade.

"It does," Persistence said. "You think you defeated our best, but our best is me. I'll take you into the deep waters and drown you."

Cinder smirked. "A good friend said something similar to me once. I loved him and hated having to take away an opportunity he held dear." He finally unsheathed his sword. "I won't be feeling so charitably toward you."

Persistence almost rolled her eyes. "And you say I'm dramatic." She hoped the needling would cause him to lose concentration. "Come then and cease your prattling."

Cinder blurred toward her.

So far, Cinder hadn't been forced to kill anyone. He and the Shokans had made it to Indrun's Chamber undetected, and thus far, the raid into the Spire of the Saints had gone better than he could have imagined.

For that, Cinder was grateful. None of these men and women deserved to lose their lives for simply doing their duties. They weren't evil, and even the vast majority of the zahhacks truly weren't. In fact, if there was a way to defeat Shet and not have to kill his armies, Cinder would want to take that approach.

Of course, he might still be able to, but not until after the Orbs were destroyed and Shet—the only being with six open Chakras—had closed the anchor line leading to whatever cruel, dark realm Zahhack called His own.

With a mental sigh, Cinder pushed aside his future hopes. It was a Trial for another day, one to be confronted after this one was completed. He already had the Orb of Undying Light secreted in his *null pocket*, but unfortunately, the way out of Bharat wasn't so easy to obtain. Not with Persistence, Guile, and their rakishis blocking their departure.

"It doesn't need to go like this," Cinder said, praying for Persistence to see reason, even while he recognized she probably wouldn't. Her reasoning would be other than his and equally sound in her own judgment.

As if in confirmation, Persistence frowned. It was only a slight downward bend of her lips, but for someone who had learned to decipher the flattest of affects, it was a resounding scowl.

"It does," Persistence said. "You think you defeated our best, but our best is me. I'm going to take you into the deep waters and drown you."

In spite of the severity of the situation, Cinder had to smile. He had heard that kind of threat before—about being pulled into the deep waters—and it had come from Dorr, of all people. Back when Cinder had been young and unsure of himself, and the words had been intimidating. But now, they only caused amusement, especially because his mind was unburdened by the outcome. In his estimation, this fight was already over. He had already overcome Persistence.

So when she called him forward, he was happy to oblige. After all, in his heart Cinder was and always would be a predator.

He attacked.

Persistence smoothly defended against Cinder's assaults, and he just as efficiently turned aside her counters. Attacking when able, Guile defended her blind side. Together they managed to deflect Cinder's initial charge. Only barely. How did he move so—

Cinder rushed them. His sword distorted with speed. Persistence leaped backward, covering twenty feet. Guile went with her. Together they unleashed lines of Fire.

A green webbing flared around Cinder—a strange kind of Shield. They were usually gray in color, but whatever the case, his worked. Cinder was able to shrug off their attacks as if they were of no consequence. Persistence sought to snare Cinder's feet with thorny vines while Guile shot bolts of Air.

Neither was successful. Cinder's sword twirled, trailing light, and he cut through their attempts. Then there was room for nothing but blades.

Persistence slipped a thrust, countered with one of her own. Guile, on the other side, tried to trap Hotgate, who leaned away, parried, parried again, and countered with a sidekick. Cinder swirled away from Persistence, trying to get Guile in between the two of them. Another rapid shift, and he succeeded, launching a set of blistering blows aimed at her fellow rishi.

No!

At the last instant, Persistence turned aside a slash that would have put Guile down.

Cinder's attention was now on her, and this time it was she who fought unsupported. Cinder battered her defenses. Even the *lorethasra* weaves she tried to utilize, he slapped aside as if she was nothing more than a young Accepted. His moves came faster.

Persistence gritted her teeth. She and Guile only had to hold on long enough for the rakishis to kill the Shokans and bring them relief. But even then, she wasn't sure how they could defeat Cinder. He didn't seem like he was going full out against them. Not exactly toying with her and Guile, but also not fighting at his utmost best.

Guile was back in the fight. He launched a strike and tried a loop of Fire that would have decapitated Cinder. Both missed badly. Cinder easily parried the first and allowed the second to disperse against his Shield.

Persistence tried to take advantage. She sent every pattern she knew, moving as fast as she could manage.

And every time, Cinder deflected, defending with shocking grace and ease.

Shokan. Was it him?

The question punctured her concentration, nearly cost her. At the last instant, she managed to disengage and gain space. Guile shifted to fall back with her. Panic and a strange joy threatened, but Persistence crushed them down. Never had she felt so helpless before a warrior.

"How is he doing this?" Guile asked, sounding as shocked as she'd ever heard.

Persistence didn't know, but the question from earlier remained in her head. In addition, she quickly replayed the battle thus far, and an understanding of Cinder's attacks became apparent. "He doesn't want to kill us."

"Well, I want to kill him," Guile muttered.

There was no more time to talk. Cinder ended their brief interlude. He came at them again. Persistence parried, blocked, shifted. Cinder had moved her out of position. He feinted a diagonal slash. Guile bit. The slash transitioned to a leaping, spinning back kick. It punched through Guile's Shield.

And Guile's head snapped around like it threatened to be torn free. He collapsed, unconscious.

"Enough!" Persistence shouted. She took a calculated risk and let her sword droop until the tip touched the ground. "Stand down," she ordered the rakishis.

Cinder pulled up, eyeing her warily. At least he wasn't attacking.

Silence fell across the rest of the room, and Persistence quickly scanned about, realizing that the Shokans had only lost two of their own, both alive but looking rough. The rakishis, on the other hand, were down five warriors. None of them had immediate critical injuries, but they needed Patience's healing, or they wouldn't last the hour. The two groups, Shokans and rakishis, drifted apart, viewing one another with distrust.

"What would you have us do?" Tobias asked, addressing Persistence. He had taken damage. Blood dripped from a cut to his off-arm, and a bruise bloomed on his cheek.

"Stand down," Persistence said, repeating the command.

"How are you?" It was Anya, and the question had been directed to Cinder.

"Fine. You?"

Anya smiled. "I wouldn't want to do this all day, but…" She shrugged. "I doubt I'll have to."

The princess was right. The rakishis were ragged. They wouldn't have lasted much longer. In comparison, Anya and the Shokans appeared fresh. Had Persistence not called a halt to the battle, there would have been a lot more than five injured rakishis.

Which was just as nonsensical as a single human holding his own against two rishis. An instant later, Persistence corrected herself, forced to admit the truth. No, Cinder hadn't simply held his own against two rishis. He'd defeated them. Just like the Shokans had defeated a larger force of rakishis.

Persistence found herself studying the princess. She'd done well as the tip of the spear. In fact, based on her positioning, she had fought essentially unsupported. Had she been the one to put down five rakishis?

A startling possibility caused her eyes to widen. *Sira?*

"I asked you before," Cinder said. "What happens now?"

"You cannot leave Bharat with the Orb," Tobias said, his voice a growl of outrage.

A sharp gesture from Persistence cut him off. But he was also right. "You mistimed tonight's misadventure. Your ship has already departed our harbor. You have no way off Bharat."

"Will you continue fighting us?" Anya asked.

"Will you kill us if we do?" Persistence asked.

It was Cinder who answered. "If need be." Although reluctance undercut his firm tone, Persistence knew he'd do it. He'd kill her and her rakishis if given no other option.

"Then we are at an impasse," she said. "We cannot let you leave, and as much as I hate to admit it, I know you can best us. But even after you do, you'll face the full might of the Army of the Saints. You can't win."

"We don't have to defeat your army," Cinder said. "We just need to get off your island."

He sounded so sure of himself. "How?"

"We have a way," Cinder said, gesturing toward the Gate of the Saints, which had been forged of yellow-stone and was shaped like a broken halo.

It was the final piece of evidence. He knew how to travel by anchor line.

"Put down your weapons," Persistence ordered her warriors.

"Rishi?" Tobias dared ask.

"You heard me. They are beyond us. I will not have you die for no reason. The invaders will depart this chamber, and either the army will kill them or…" She held off on saying anything else. *Let's see if Cinder Shade can do what he implied.*

The man Persistence hoped was Shokan nodded to Anya, the woman she hoped was Sira. Without speaking a word, the princess and her warriors moved to the Gate of the Saints, carrying their moaning injured. Persistence didn't fail to note where Cinder placed himself. He stood as a defense between her people and his.

In the meanwhile, Anya utilized *lorethasra*, swift braids that Persistence had never seen and couldn't replicate. The princess pressed the runes in a seemingly random way. But once finished, she stepped aside, and a crackling crawled across the broken halo, completing the circle. Persistence's attention fixed on it. She had memories of this from her rishi lineage but had never expected to see it actually happen. A white line split the circle, expanding to fill it like a film of milk.

"It's always different," Anya murmured as if speaking to herself.

She nodded to Bones, and the Shokans stepped into the Gate of the Saints, gathering their injured and departing into the film. *Where would it take them?*

Cinder backed away toward Anya while his unit exited. Neither of them appeared afraid, and Persistence knew it wasn't a pose. These two could take her and the remaining rakishis and likely do so without much trouble. In fact, if Cinder had unleashed his Fireballs, that alone would have sufficed. Persistence's Shields wouldn't have slowed them one bit.

She made a decision then. If no rakishis had died during tonight's raid—and she would trust him when he said they hadn't—then Cinder would have proven himself. Persistence tossed him a pair of vials, not missing Tobias' hiss of alarm when she did. She'd have to speak to him about his loss of decorum later.

"Those should see to the healing of your men," Persistence said. "They are of my own creation, and although I'm not the best of healers, I think you'll be happy for the help."

Cinder appeared confused. "Why?"

"I have my reasons."

Cinder stared at her in examination, then the vials, before finally passing them to Anya. He nodded to Persistence, and as one, he and the princess made to step through the Gate of Saints.

"Abomination!"

A spear was hurtled at Cinder and Anya. The weapon followed them, just as they exited Indrun's Chamber, an instant before the milky-white substance filling the Gate of Saints crackled out of existence.

Persistence stiffened in alarm. She had no means to know whether the spear might have punctured Cinder's Shield, but if it had… Her gaze snapped around to the rakishis. One of them had thrown the spear after a rishi had declared a cessation to the battle.

Tobias was already seeing to the disobedient rakishi. He would be punished. But first, she had to warn her people.

"Empty the room!" she shouted.

The rakishis hustled through the one door that still worked. And once they were clear, Persistence had them bar the exit.

"What's wrong?" Tobias asked.

Persistence's gaze landed on the fool of a rakishi who had dared attack Cinder when his back had been turned. "If the spear didn't land, and Cinder Shade takes offense to an attack in the middle of a truce, he'll come back."

Tobias' gaze went to a still unconscious Guile. He barked out orders for reinforcements. Even as he did so, Persistence hoped Cinder wouldn't come back. If he didn't, it would be even greater proof of his true identity. A bubbling joy filled her heart.

Did I just meet Shokan and Sira? Rukh and Jessira Shektan?

20

Anya saw the incoming weapon out of the corner of her eye. A spear launched by a treacherous rakishi at Cinder's back. She tried to divert it but was too late. They were both already entering the anchor line. Even then, the spear should have been stopped by Cinder's Shield.

And yet, it wasn't. When Cinder stepped onto the rainbow bridge, his Shield weakened. According to Sira's memories, it was a normal occurrence. Weaves, braids, and anything of *Jivatma* was temporarily disrupted by passage through an anchor line, reconstituting upon exit.

As a result, Cinder's Shield slowed the spear but didn't stop it. Then they were in the anchor line, and Anya couldn't tell what had happened. But she grabbed Cinder, holding him with her tether since he'd lost his own. The screaming and shaking of the trip through the rainbow bridge, the biting cold… none of it held her attention.

Only Cinder mattered.

They exited the anchor line through Twilight Gate and into Shalla Valley. Cinder collapsed into her arms, limp. The spear had cut a deep blow along the side of his neck. Blood spurted.

Devesh, no.

213

Anya surged *Jivatma* and *lorethasra*, driving every bit of Healing into Cinder. But she struggled to reach her power. Something hindered her.

A ball of smoke, drifting, wreathing within her mind. Malignant tendrils tied to her *lorethasra*. Watching. Aware.

With a shock, Anya knew what it was. Knew who it was. *Rabisu*. She snarled. All this time, the rakshasa had been hiding within her, ever since Mahadev. Feeding on her *lorethasra*. Growing stronger. He was the reason for her weakness; the reason Cinder might die.

Not losing a second, Anya tore the tendrils tying Rabisu to her *lorethasra*. It felt like ripping off her own skin, and she had to bite back a scream.

While dealing with the pain, her thoughts grew vague. What was she doing? Where was she? A voice whispered, urging her to sleep, seeking to cloud her thoughts. To forget what she had recognized…

Anya resisted the siren call. Cinder needed her. She ripped through the fogginess, restoring her sense of self.

Her eyes snapped open. Less than an instant had passed. The ache in her mind of tearing free of Rabisu lingered, but she disregarded the pain. *Deal with it later.*

First, she had to save Cinder. His jugular vein and carotid artery had been nicked. He only had seconds to live, and Anya poured Healing into him, the golden glow surging into his body like streaming lightning.

She peered closely once she was finished, with senses other than just her eyes. The bleeding had slowed to a crawl, but Cinder wasn't safe yet. Anya prepared another Healing.

"Nut and root!" For some reason, Sadana was waiting for them. "Get him in Verity Foe! We can heal him best there." The tree maiden quickly pressed the runes upon Twilight Gate.

The Shokans silenced at a single shouted order from Bones.

While waiting for Verity Foe to open, Anya continued Healing Cinder. It was rough and dirty, causing him to jerk in her hands.

"Follow." Sadana reached down and plucked Cinder from Anya's arms. A single stride took her into the milkiness of Twilight Gate.

"Use this on Sash and Mohal," Anya ordered the Shokans, passing them the healing vials Persistence had given them. She could sense their purity. "Someone will come for you." There was no more time for words, and she jumped through Twilight Gate. Once again, she disregarded the cold on traveling and the nausea on exiting.

Sadana had set Cinder on the ground. Quick impressions hit Anya. A ring of large boulders standing like sentinels framed a small clearing of grass. A stream gurgled close at hand, glistening under the light of a single moon.

Anya took a step toward Cinder. She blinked. *No.* His name was Rukh, and hers was Jessira.

Vertigo stole her balance. Fear loomed in her mind. Her heart hammered. What was happening? Who was she?

"Calm yourself," Sadana said, her voice soothing. "You are in Verity Foe. Lies cannot be maintained here. Hear me." The yakshin hummed a low note of peace.

Anya closed her eyes, refusing to panic, listening to the yakshin. She couldn't afford to give in to fear. A long breath in and out, and she disregarded all the turmoils of the past year, the doubts and confusions. Rukh needed her. Clarity smoothed aside the uncertainties. Her husband needed her. All the while Sadana hummed, the tone calming her mind until she opened her eyes.

Jessira saw the world of Verity Foe. She knew herself. And she knew what was required.

And yet in the back of her mind, there still slithered the liar: the Rakshasa of Dissolution, Rabisu.

Prior to allowing the rakshasa's initial touch in Mahadev, the weave she and Rukh had placed upon themselves had protected them in ways Rabisu didn't know. There were a dozen ways it could have been activated. Verity Foe was merely one. The weave itself should have trapped the rakshasa. Jessira briefly thought of killing Rabisu but decided against it. He might be needed later.

But first…

She ripped the last bit of stolen strength from the rakshasa, the drips of *lorethasra* he'd used to rebuild himself. And he had no defense. In her body and mind, he only had whatever power she had unknowingly granted. With her full knowledge and awareness restored, she granted him none.

A countdown in her head. Less than three seconds since she'd entered Verity Foe. Distantly Rabisu screamed, but Jessira's attention was on Rukh. His face had taken on a blue hue. Blood no longer poured from his wound, but a large hematoma distorted the side of his neck. It was compressing his jugular.

She knelt at his side and tested his pulse and breath, cupped his face, searching with *Jivatma*. His carotid had dissected, and his pulse was faint, but she could still save him. Death wouldn't steal her husband away.

Jessira conducted *Jivatma* and sourced *lorethasra*, pouring it into *Anahata*, the Heart Chakra. It exited as *prana*, scintillating along the web of her *nadis*. A stabbing pain formed in her chest, but she kept at it. More *lorethasra*. She focused on her intent, what she wished of her *prana*. This was different than weaving *lorethasra*, both harder and easier.

A glow built in the back of her vision, and tiny lightning rippled across her knuckles.

Devesh, let this work.

Jessira released her *prana* and her intent. The lightning sparked, buzzing and roaring like a breaking wave, straight into Rukh. He jerked, his entire torso coming off the ground. The hematoma tore, draining thick blood, but afterward, his breathing steadied. The dissected carotid was sealed.

Not completely healed, though.

Another quick-and-dirty Healing, and once again, Rukh jerked, mouth opening in a painless scream. The moment he settled on the tall grass, Jessira searched again. The carotid was healed, but it was a fragile thing, like a newborn bird in a nest. But at least Rukh's blue hue was gone, and his skin had recovered its normal color.

Jessira almost smiled then, thinking of how he always thought of his skin's hue as being tea-touched with milk.

"Will Maynalor live?" Sadana asked.

Jessira nodded in distraction, her attention locked on Rukh. His breathing was steady, and his pulse stable and strong. The worst was over, but he wasn't yet free of danger, not with his carotid still bruised and apt to rip once more. She needed to Heal him a final time.

"I have this," she told Sadana. "But he needs food."

"How much food? What kind?"

"Any kind will do," Jessira said. "Just make sure there's lots of it. As much as a holder might eat in two days. He'll be as hungry as a starved tiger when this is over." She smiled again when a comprehension flickered across her mind. "And tell Aranya that her joke is appreciated. I'm proud of her."

Sadana startled. "Sira?"

Jessira looked to the yakshin, who loomed over her, ancient and powerful, but in that moment, the tree maiden seemed young and fragile. "We'll speak on it later. Get the food."

"By your will." Sadana bowed low and departed Verity Foe.

Only then, while Rukh recovered, did Jessira feel like she finally had a moment to breathe, a moment to accept the profound changes poured on her like a thundering waterfall. So many lost memories, truths, and awarenesses of who she really was. And poor Anya, having to deal with it all with a broken memory and failed understandings.

Of course, Jessira was Anya and Anya was Jessira. They were one and the same. Or were they?

Jessira considered the matter and realized Rukh had been right all along: they weren't ever the same person from one moment to the next. Presently, she was Jessira Shektan, which was the same as saying she was Anya Aruyen with her memories restored, whereas the elven princess was Jessira Shektan without those same elements.

It was confusing and not worth considering in the moment.

Her glance fell to Rukh—Cinder, Shokan—her husband. The confusions never included him—her love for him—and she tenderly kissed his forehead. "We have a long journey still." Understanding of what she might yet have to accept nearly undid her composure, but she held on to it. She could weep when Rukh was able to hold her.

For now, he still required her help.

In the back of her mind, Rabisu momentarily distracted her with his ranting. She lashed out at the creature, abruptly furious with his treachery. Her barbed whip of anger cut into the rakshasa, and he howled in anguish. An instant later, he silenced when she softly threatened to repeat the pain.

Good. He could hear her, just as she could hear him. And even a fool could learn.

Her mind quiet now, Jessira conducted *Jivatma*. As before, she let it build within, and a golden glow encompassed her hands. She measured it out until it was a thread, as fine as a spider's strand but as precise as a Duriah's measurement. The final Healing would require a much more delicate touch.

Once ready, Jessira let the glow bleed out of her hands, where it flowed like liquid lightning, streaming into Rukh's chest.

Again, he arched his back, mouth agape. But this time when he settled and Jessira examined him, she was heartened to see his carotid dissection completely Healed. As for the wound on his neck…

Jessira unstopped her canteen and liberally poured water over Rukh's wounds, cleaning away the blood. He didn't even have a scar to tell where the spear had cut him. Only then did Jessira exhale in relief, leaning back on her arms. Rukh would be weak for a while, but at least he'd be fine.

She stared at the night sky of this strange world, grateful for Rukh's survival. Minutes later, she straightened, peering at him, running fingers through his hair. When he awoke, they'd have much to discuss. Until then, she'd steal this moment of peace.

Jessira bent, kissing his forehead again.

Jessira gazed on her sleeping husband. Sadana had returned with the promised food, and on recovering from his Healing, Rukh had consumed it all. Afterward, he'd fallen asleep again, the food leaving his stomach bulging like a snake that had swallowed more than was wise.

Of course, Rukh was anything but a snake, but the image still caused Jessira to smile in warm affection. She sat next to him, both of them still in the rock-ringed glade of Verity Foe, stroking his forehead. It had been so long since her mind was clear enough to understand who she was and what Rukh meant to her. *Priya.* Her beloved. And she had no doubt he felt the same for her. In spite of everything they'd endured, she had no questions about that.

But still, Rabisu had done damage to them, their hateful behavior toward one another, and that hurt wasn't done with them yet. They still had an upcoming battle against Shet, and in it, her past self had witnessed something Jessira was terrified might still come to pass. Now more so than ever.

And it was all because of that fragging rakshasa. Jessira wasn't yet sure what to do with Rabisu, and while Rukh wasn't a person meant to hate, she couldn't always say the same about herself. She hated the rakshasa, and elaborate punishments of what she might want to do to the fiend flitted through her mind.

She made sure to let Rabisu know them, and it caused him to quiver and shake, coward that he was, but it didn't help Jessira feel any better.

Rukh stirred, blinking blearily. His eyes, unfocused at first, eventually landed on her, awareness entering them. *"Priya."*

Jessira smiled, cupping his face. "How do you feel?" She'd been examining him minute by minute since she'd last Healed him, and while she couldn't find anything wrong, she needed his words to fully settle her fears.

He frowned, head tilted as he was likely taking a mental inventory. "Still a bit hungry and weak, but otherwise fine."

She exhaled in relief. "Do you remember what happened?"

He shook his head, levering himself upright with a groan. "Not really. But it must have been bad." He winced, hand going to his neck where he'd been wounded. "Actually, I do remember. And remind me to do something painful to whichever rakishi backstabbed me."

Jessira chuckled softly, a brittle sound. Now came the important question, and her mouth went dry. "What about me?"

He smiled. "Of course, I know you. Anya Aruyen. Jessira Shektan." He drew her into his arms, and she was lost when he kissed her. She melted into him, her senses focused on the feel of him pressed against her. She gripped him when he ran his fingers through her hair. Nothing else mattered but to hold him.

He pulled away after a timeless interval. "This isn't new," he said, still smiling as he stroked her peaked elven ears. "But is it you?"

Jessira smiled back, pressing her forehead against his. "It is for now." She forced herself to meet his eyes. "I'm sorry."

His smile faded. "So am I." He took her hands, kissing her fingers. "We were arrogant, and it cost us."

The weave meant to protect them from Rabisu.

Jessira didn't want to have this conversation, but there was also no putting it off. "He's still with us." She tapped her mind. "In here."

Rukh's features sharpened. "Why haven't you killed him? Does he have a way of hurting you?"

Jessira nodded. "He's wound himself throughout my mind. I can kill him, but his counterstroke will hurt. He might even be able to rip apart my memories of you and our family. And even if he can't, it'll take me months to heal. I wouldn't be able to help you. You'd have to fight Shet on your own." She shook her head. "I won't risk you."

Rukh exhaled heavily. "I'm so sorry you have to keep him inside you. He's a rakshasa. He deserves to die."

Jessira smiled wanly. "You won't get an argument from me."

Rukh stood then, offering a hand to help her rise. "Let's go for a walk. We deserve a moment of peace."

Jessira took Rukh's hand, and they strolled along the stream.

They spoke, haltingly at first, discussing their regrets from the past year. There were too many to catalogue, but it didn't take long to accept and forgive what they'd done to each other. For Jessira, it didn't matter that so much of her behavior hadn't been under her control. There would always be guilt and shame in how she had behaved toward Rukh, and she recognized he felt the same way.

Their discussion shifted toward their children: Jareth, Wren, Sindar, and Brinatha.

Jessira smiled wryly. "Wren and Sindar… those two stretched my patience."

"I worried they'd lose their ears, given how often you had to tug on them to get them to stop whatever trouble they'd concocted."

She laughed. "Do you remember when they found those two puppies? Brat—Black Rat—and Shadow? I swear those dogs had the patience of a guru, dealing with our children."

"No," Rukh said. "It wasn't patience. It was love. Brat and Shadow loved Sindar and Wren. And they loved them back. It's why the dogs insisted on sleeping in the children's rooms every night, why they followed them on every adventure, no matter how stupid."

They reminisced some more about their family, about their nephews and nieces from Rukh's sister, Bree, his brother, Jaresh, and Jaresh's wife, Sign. But they shied away from speaking much about Jareth and Brinatha, their children who had died during the war with Shet's daughter.

"I'm glad they stayed in Arisa," Rukh said. "Our family."

"Wren came here," Jessira reminded him.

He laughed. "Aranya, 'of Anya.' What a little pest, choosing a name like that."

"You know how much she enjoyed jokes, and I won't say she was your favorite, but…"

"She wasn't my favorite. I don't have one, but I do love her." Rukh's smile faded. "What a brave girl. She left Arisa to save us."

Jessira fell silent, fear for her daughter stealing her words. "I wish she hadn't," she whispered. "This world has seen too much death and tragedy. I don't want Wren to become a part of it. I want her free to live and love. She should have stayed safe on Arisa."

"But even Arisa wasn't always a Realm bathed in Devesh's love.

Even after we killed the Sorrow Bringer, it didn't rise as high toward Devesh as we expected."

Jessira nodded. "It only happened after we defeated Mistress Arisa."

"Mistress Arisa," Rukh said in contemplation. "She's daughter. She came here. We thought we'd killed her, but she survived long enough to pollute this world with her presence."

"Titan's Reach." Jessira patted her *null pocket* where she still had the Withering Knife. She hoped they wouldn't have to ever use it again. Once had been terrible enough.

Rukh squeezed her hand in support. "I hope so, too," he said, speaking to her unvoiced fears.

Jessira let out a small laugh of disbelief. "You can say that after what we've already endured? We almost made a huge mistake with Rabisu."

"But we didn't," Rukh said, voice soft and empty of anything but regret. "And I'm still so sorry about that."

Jessira hesitated but felt it necessary to speak her honest assessment. "I'm not sure we should trust our judgment... About what to do with Rabisu, the Orbs... any of it."

"We don't have to make these decisions on our own," Rukh told her. "We have Wren, the yakshins, and so many others who might offer advice."

"We had Manifold and Sapient," Jessira reminded him. "They advised we go through with that fool plan with Rabisu."

"And they weren't entirely wrong. We left pieces in place that would have undone his weave at some point. I already checked, and his braid on me was already coming apart. He wouldn't have destroyed us."

"But what we did..."

"Is over."

But was it?

By then, they had returned to the small, ringed glade next to the stream, and the moon beamed down in a wash of ghostly light.

"I like this glade," Rukh said. "We should make one like it when we create our own Realms."

Jessira wasn't sure if he was being serious. Rukh would sometimes bring up the most ridiculous proposals, things to which she usually said, *"But it can't be done."* More often than not, though, he somehow managed to see it through. Was this one of those occasions? If so, Jessira didn't have the slightest idea on how to make real what he'd just suggested.

"We aren't Devesh, to create Realms," she finally told him.

Rukh grinned, not appearing disheartened in the slightest. "But if we *were* like Him, don't you think creating Realms would be so much more relaxing than saving them?"

She laughed. "I think that injury did more than drain your blood. I think it drained your common sense."

"It's still a good idea, though."

"We'll see. Let's get through this current disaster before we aim so high." But could they actually get through their current problems? Defeating Shet and then Zahhack? Could they actually succeed? Jessira had always lacked Rukh's supreme confidence, and as a result, despondency stole her enjoyment of the moment.

Her reminder seemed to end Rukh's humor, and his smile slid away. "I wish we didn't have to do it," he said.

Jessira smiled wanly. "Is that your only wish?"

He faced her, head tilted as he smiled teasingly. "What did you have in mind?"

"We're alone in a moonlight glade." She stepped closer to him, wanting to be held, particularly since the fears of the future continued to fill her with despair. The battle against Shet, when she hated Rukh… She didn't have the courage to give away her love for him.

Rukh tilted her chin, so she was staring him in the eyes. "You quoted this to me once:

'Doubt thou, the stars are fire,
Doubt, that the sun doth move,
Doubt truth to be a liar,
But never doubt I love.'"

He stared into her eyes. "I never doubted your love. You shouldn't either. We will endure."

There was such certainty in his words that Jessira's hesitations weakened, disintegrating under the spell of his conviction. She pulled him toward her, kissing him softly at first, more deeply after.

For Rukh, the knowledge of his proper name and past still struck him as surreal. So long had he been Cinder Shade, living amidst a crooked melody of falsehoods and half-truths. But now those falsehoods and half-truths had been cleansed like he'd showered them away under the glorious waterfall formed by River Namaste on Arylyn.

That island had been such a lovely place, and thinking on it, Rukh wondered how William and Serena were doing. He hoped to see them again at some point in his strange life.

Of course, love for them had been amongst the many other truths he'd discovered upon awakening. And those discoveries had felt like trying to take a sip of water from that same raging waterfall formed by River Namaste. Jessira had saved him from drowning, though, giving him the needed lucidity in those initial minutes.

That precious time to readjust to his true nature also let him realize that, while he'd always be Cinder Shade just as much as he had once been Shokan, the Lord of the Sword, he would first and foremost consider himself Rukh Shektan. It was the name given to him at his birth, the one affirmed during his *upanayana* ceremony, and the person he wanted to remain.

He also wanted to remain with Jessira, and he held her close, the soft grass pillowing them as they rested against a smooth, low-lying boulder in the small glade ringed by stones. Sadana had yet to ask to re-enter Verity Foe—no one had—but Rukh figured he and Jessira would soon have to rejoin the world.

"I wish I could kill Rabisu," Jessira said, idly stroking his forearm.

Rukh wished the same thing, but thinking on how much it would hurt Jessira, possibly steal away everything of worth, didn't bear considering. He shifted the conversation. "That anchor line is the key to what we do next."

He knew he wouldn't have to explain what he meant, and as if proving his point, Jessira sat up with a frown. "We already know what happens."

"We only think we know. That's not the same as actually knowing for sure." He, too, recalled the battle on the anchor line, but from the perspective of who he'd been on Arylyn. And just like Jessira, he also recognized the dislike—or was it confusion, like Aia and Shon had insisted—that her future self had seemed to feel toward him. But why? What did it actually mean? Because in no Realm could he believe Jessira would ever betray him.

Jessira chuckled bitterly. "Aren't we in Verity Foe? Isn't this supposed to be where we learn truths about ourselves?"

Rukh shifted until he could peer into her face, into her hazel-flecked green eyes, which he never wanted to forget. "The future isn't predestined."

"And you think we should change it?"

Rukh didn't answer at once. "I'm not sure."

"We eventually crushed Shet on Earth," Jessira said. "And some of that is because I saw my future and hated myself for it. But that vision also inspired me. I became a better person and warrior because of that future meeting."

Rukh didn't want to hear that. He had always loved Jessira regardless of whatever flaws she saw in herself, and this notion that she had to offer a sacrifice on behalf of others turned his stomach. Jessira had already sacrificed enough. She deserved happiness. He deliberated on the matter, finding himself locked on a surety as immutable as the sun. "You didn't hate me," Rukh responded after a few moments of thought. "It's not in you to feel that way."

"I could never hate you," Jessira agreed. "But there was something in me that made it look like I did."

"Rabisu's weave?"

"Or some other kind of weave."

Rukh grunted, trying to figure on what to do. Why would Jessira have acted that way toward him? What was the point?

They fell silent until Jessira spoke. "We can't lose that victory we had over Shet," she said. "Two worlds will suffer if we do."

Rukh grimaced. There it was again: Jessira having to sacrifice. "Can you really see yourself becoming that person on the anchor line?"

"Never."

Inspiration struck him like a bolt. "Wren. She might have an answer."

Jessira frowned. "Wren?" An instant later, she smiled with tremulous hope. "We know Wren as the little prankster, but on Seminal she is Aranya, Mahamatha, and Mother Ashoka. She's been alive for three millennia."

Rukh smiled in reply. "She's older than us. Vastly so. Even you." He tapped Jessira's nose, and she rubbed at it furiously, feigning a scowl.

"Rukh Shektan," she said, still scowling. "Why do you vex me so?"

"Because you're never really vexed."

"Really? You think bopping me on the nose does what exactly? You think it makes me want to do this?" She cupped his face, leaned in like she was going to kiss him. But at the last instant, she grabbed his lips, moved them about like he was talking while she mimicked his speech as if he was a dullard. "My name is Rukh, and I am infuriating."

He tugged away, amused more than irritated. "I only bopped your nose. I didn't call you names."

"I'm sorry," Jessira said, trying to sound penitent, but doing nothing to hide a lurking smile. "Truly. Maybe I can make it up to you." She leaned forward again, eyes hooded like she was really going to kiss him this time.

But Rukh was ready. When she reached to move his lips, he dumped her off his lap, laughing when she squawked. "It's time to rejoin the world."

Jessira stood, offering him a helping hand. "Fine. But you'll wish we hadn't."

Rukh took her hand, rising with a grunt. "I already do," he said, bending to gather his clothes.

"Then let's go talk to our three-thousand-year-old tree goddess of a daughter," Jessira said with a warm chuckle.

"After three thousand years of living, she probably sees us as children."

Jessira smiled, her eyes growing distant. "She'll always be my little girl." Her sight returned to the here and now. "I only hope she has a good idea on what we should do. After all, Manifold is also three thousand years old and look where his advice landed us."

"Yes, but he was around Heremisth for all those years, next to an anchor line leading to Zahhack."

Jessira's brow furrowed in a frown. "You're right. I wonder if that changed him." Her gaze sharpened. "That wouldn't explain Sapient, though. He agreed with Manifold's stupid plan."

"But he wasn't entirely wrong, either." Rukh shrugged. "We'll have to ask them the next time we see them."

Jessira held up a cautioning hand. "Before we exit, we need to end the weave Rabisu placed on us. Otherwise, we'll forget everything we just talked about when we leave Verity Foe."

Rukh nodded agreement, ticking off what they needed to do on his fingers. "End Rabisu's weave, speak to Wren—hopefully she'll know what we should do—and then collect the rest of the Orbs."

Jessira snapped her fingers, like she just had an epiphany. "And when we speak to Wren, it'll be in her personal Foe, the meadow where she dances. She can control Rabisu there, completely and utterly."

A burgeoning hope filled Rukh, and his heart began racing. "She might even be able to pull him out of you without you being harmed." More than anything, that's what he wanted for Jessira.

She grinned at him, and a moment later, her smile grew even happier, like she'd discovered something unexpected and wonderful. "Wren is the mother of the yakshins and all the Ashoka trees."

Rukh chuckled. "That name—Ashoka. It's just the city of my birth, but it keeps following us around—Ashoka, Shokan, Ashoka trees."

"That's not what I mean," Jessira said. "Our daughter has children."

Rukh finally understood, and he reached for her, laughing in delight as he spun her about. "I'm a tatayya, a grandfather" he said, setting her down.

"And I'm an ammamma."

21

Enma had never seen Mother so angry as when she discovered the loss of the Orb of Moss. She had been furious in a way that even Father hadn't been able to soothe.

On and on she had raged, but it wasn't enough to make Enma wish that she had turned in her sister and Cinder Shade. Their story of this Dark Lord, Zahhack, had been terrifying at the time, and even after a night's rest, with morning sunshine pouring down, that fear hadn't abated.

Anya and Cinder had been so certain, which Enma had to believe was of importance. They weren't Shokan and Sira, but they had the memories of the Blessed Ones. Or so they claimed, which would have been a ridiculous notion at any other time in Enma's life, but it wasn't so ludicrous now given the reemergence of Shet and his Titans.

Regardless, in the end it didn't matter how much Mother raged. Anya and Cinder were gone, and it hadn't been difficult figuring out who had helped them—Estin. Nor had it been hard to figure which ship they had taken and its destination of Swift Sword. But the discovery had occurred too late since by the time one of Yaksha's naval vessels could reach Rakesh's capital, the pair of fugitives—and Mother had declared them exactly that—had already fled.

As for Estin, he had enlisted as an advisor to Rakesh's High Army, which shouldn't have protected him from their mother's long reach. However, that was in the past. Rakesh's leaders, the so-called Loyalty Cabinet, had steadfastly refused to hand over her brother in spite of Mother's increasingly threatening missives. Worse, Estin was said to have shortly left Swift Sword, and again, it was for parts unknown.

In thinking on the three of them—Anya, Estin, and Cinder—Enma certainly commended their passion, but she dearly wished the fallout hadn't left Mother lashing out at anyone she believed might have aided them.

At times, that anger included Enma, and by extension, Redwinth. So far, he hadn't received a tongue-lashing so much as hard, pointed questions. And in answering Mother's questions, Enma had discovered Redwinth had a heretofore unknown talent: he could deceive without actually lying. It was an admirable skill, and she leaned into it, learning how to phrase her own answers in a similar fashion.

Currently, she and Redwinth stood alone on the balcony outside their quarters, quietly discussing what next they should do, but only after making sure there weren't any eavesdropping braids on the patio, since there had been one within the main room of their quarters. How had Anya known of them? Did she truly have Sira's memories?

Enma shook off her thoughts, not sure what to think and seeking peace as she faced night's cathedral. Both moons were in the vaulted heavens, glowing their ghostly illumination, and a night hawk crossed the sky, flashing out of view as it passed near a cloud. Fragrant blossoms perfumed the air while from well below came the sounds of the guards on patrol. Ever since the Orb's theft, their numbers had been bolstered.

"That was some dinner," Redwinth said, sounding shaky.

"Yes, it was," Enma replied, empathizing with Redwinth. It had been a difficult meal. During it, Quelchon Ginala had made a passing reference to one of Enma's old lovers, who she hadn't seen in several years.

But at the time, Enma had been passionate in the affair. Indecorous some might even say, and Ginala had mentioned one such embarrassing incident.

It had been said as if in amused recollection, one friend reminding another of when they'd acted foolishly. But given Redwinth's presence, it had clearly been meant to knock him off his stride and make it easier to expose any secrets he might have.

It hadn't worked, although Redwinth pretended it had. He had reddened and sputtered as though upset by what he was hearing. After all, what husband, even elven ones, wanted to hear stories of their wife's former lovers. Eventually, Redwinth had collected himself and pretended to laugh over the matter.

And not once did he give away any information about Anya and Cinder.

He had done well, and Enma viewed him with a renewed speculation. She had done far better than she initially realized in marrying Redwinth. He was a skilled enough warrior as well as a talented negotiator—cunning in business. But this ability at pretense was unanticipated and wonderfully helpful.

Enma wandered to the edge of the balcony, staring at the city she would one day rule. Revelant was preparing for a celebration. The Summer Gala, held in honor of the Grey Lady, to Sira, whose birthday was said to fall in Vahasth. The people would offer prayers and tribute in her name, pleading for healing, rain, and the growth of crops. Enma quirked a smile. There were even some who caught and caged wild cats and fed them for a month.

Such odd devotions, and it might all be in honor of her sister, who had Sira's memories. Enma cocked her head in thought. Wouldn't that mean she was Sira's older sister?

She smiled at the possibility.

The smile faded when the notion led Enma to questions about Shokan and his other name: Ash, the Winter Lord. Was that Cinder Shade? Was that why his presence in Mother's private throne hall had spurred such strange emotions in her? In hindsight, Enma recognized what those feelings were: terror and possibly lust.

Thinking about her embarrassing reaction to Cinder curdled the last cream of her humor at considering Sira to be her younger sister.

"You're awfully quiet," Redwinth said.

"I was thinking about the Summer Gala," Enma stated, going on to explain her thoughts on the matter. She was wise enough to keep her feelings about Cinder Shade private, though.

"I'm surprised your mother isn't cancelling the celebration."

"Even she doesn't have the power to do something like that. The people wouldn't stand for it."

Redwinth grunted. "It would be so much easier if we could tell her what we've done and why."

"After the weeks and weeks of her shouting and screaming about Anya and Estin, do you think she'd actually listen? No matter what we said, she'd take it as a betrayal."

"I think Quelchon Ginala is the reason for her anger."

Enma turned to him in surprise. She knew Anya didn't like the quelchon—and truthfully, the feeling was mutual—and Estin had also begun to distrust their old advisor, but why would Redwinth reach the same conclusion? "Ginala has counseled our family for decades. Centuries."

"And I'm sure she's provided excellent advice." Redwinth frowned, appearing like he was searching for the right words to explain his thinking. "But in Apsara Sithe, we have a saying. The gist of it is this: after a time, an employee will provide the advice they think their employer wants to hear rather than what they need to hear."

Enma didn't answer at once. Instead, she examined the phrase. It made sense. "And you believe this of Ginala. That she's saying whatever it takes to keep my mother's outrage stoked?"

Redwinth shrugged. "I don't know for sure, but it certainly seems that whenever your mother's anger cools, Ginala will say something, and shortly thereafter, your mother's fury will reignite."

Again, Enma didn't reply at once. She remembered those few occasions when she thought her mother's rage was finally cooling. She replayed the conversations in her head, and the study caused her to frown. Redwinth was right. Ginala was the one who triggered the anger to flare again. It was subtle, just a reminder here and there along with a rueful chuckle.

But why? It couldn't be accidental. Ginala was too shrewd, too cognizant of elvish behavior to make such mistakes.

There could be another reason, but it wasn't one Enma wanted to voice. She had held Ginala in high regard for all her life. But ever since the quelchon's recitation of Cinder Shade—and Enma still struggled to make sense of what it might mean—her sharpness had faded. Was her mind finally slowing? It was possible given her age.

Enma said as much. "Which means you might be right. She's giving information she thinks Mother wants to hear rather than what she needs to know."

"Or it means she has her own plans for Yaksha."

Enma shot him a sharp look that gradually faded to one of acceptance. "We shouldn't consider old women to be harmless just because we want them to be."

Salt stared at the others who were gathered in this private room, deep in the heart of Jade's Moon. It was an old storage space, unused and empty, dusty and filled with the lingering smell of dried flowers that might have once been stored here. It was also where the ones seeking to save Surent Crèche had taken to hold their meetings.

Jozep, seemingly gentler with each passing day, sat in a corner, gazing about with a slight smile, like he thought even this dark, dank room was a source of amazement—so calm and sweet.

Salt wanted to smile back at him, to just be around him. Him and the other dwarves who had rediscovered their true calling of providing serenity and comfort to others.

Sriovey, seated next to Jozep, had most certainly *not* rediscovered that true calling. Right now he scowled, clearly irritated, and it was likely because of his allergies. As if in demonstration of his problem, he sneezed.

Then there was Willa, Sriovey's pretty sister. For a long time, she had been the black sheep of her family. Promiscuous and unwise in her choices, but it seemed her poor decisions had largely been driven by the fact that she simply didn't fit into the martial mindset that had permeated Surent Crèche over the centuries. Willa hearkened back to a time when dwarves and peaceful contentment were synonymous. And when Jozep had returned with knowledge of how to restore who their people had once been, Willa had learned from him. She was currently seated on his other side, and from her emanated a focused tranquility.

Wisdom Simla was seated next to Salt, and she appeared anxious, constantly wiping her hands on her long skirt. It wasn't a surprise. Simla had reason to be nervous, constantly surveilled as she was. It wasn't easy for her to make it to these meetings unnoticed, which was an insult given how the wisdoms used to guide the crèche.

Unfortunately, though, the influence of the wisdoms had faded, especially over the past few years, supplanted as they were by the Baptisers, the warriors controlled by Stipe Jasth—Sriovey's father. His faction continued to grow in prestige and power, especially after the theft of the Orb of Eretria.

Salt worried for Surent's future in the hands of a man like Stipe.

The final person present was Derius, and it seemed like he stood on the brink of a choice. On one side was the heart's ease promised by Jozep's way of being, and on the other was his warrior training. It was unclear which path Derius would choose. Part of it had to do with his father, who controlled that portion of Surent's military that still answered directly to the wisdoms.

These days, there weren't nearly as many of those warriors as there were of the Baptisers, whose plans on allying with Shet would surely lead to disaster, not just for Surent Crèche but for the entire world. And how could anyone actually believe the false god's promises? They were fools to do so.

Of course, Salt had once been exactly that kind of a fool, born of a people—the *Shetawarin*—who had worshiped Shet, so much so that the most important members of their community—the Forebears—were named for his Titans. Hence, Salt's name. She was named for Liline Salt.

But what was her purpose at this meeting? What advice could she offer? Several years ago, she wouldn't have wanted to offer anything. Among the *Shetawarin*, all woven were considered to be inherently immoral and of lesser worth than a human. But Salt's time at Mahadev had knocked such stupid beliefs out of her head.

Nonetheless, what was she doing here?

Salt mentally shrugged. She'd listen and learn, and if she had something to add, she would. While Sriovey called the meeting to order, Salt's attention caught on her right hand. By now, it was fully restored, all because of Jozep's remarkable healing ability, a talent held by all dwarves like him. Salt flexed her hand, forming a fist. At the time of the injury—from the battle against Rabisu—she had been certain it would never again work correctly, so deformed and burned had it been.

"News arrived today from Yaksha," Sriovey said. "Cinder and Anya stole the Orb of Moss. The empress is fucking furious."

"And Flatiron?" Derius asked. "Have we learned anything about the Temple of Prana?"

"A few months ago, a large earthquake shook the region," Sriovey said. "But who knows if that had anything to do with the temple."

"It was Cinder and Anya," Salt said, speaking up for the first time and certain of what she was saying. "They are *thoraythons*—people of destiny."

"More properly, *thoraython* means 'people around whom fate is woven,'" said Wisdom Simla. It made sense she would know the correct definition. Few, if any, knew how to speak or read *Shevasra*, but some of that knowledge had been retained by the wisdoms of Surent.

"We can't assume the earthquake had to do with them," Sriovey growled.

"I think we can," Derius said. "They stole the Orb of Eretria and told us where they planned on going afterward—the Temple of Prana.

And now, months later, they've stolen the Orb of Moss. Given the time between when we last saw them, the occurrence of this earthquake, and when the Orb of Moss was thieved, I think they got the Orb of Flames as well."

Sriovey grunted. "Maybe. I just don't like trying to figure on things without knowing what's really happening." He scuffed the floor in agitation.

Salt had to hide a smile. Sriovey looked like a scolded little boy when he did that.

"You need to come to Tympany," Jozep said, speaking to Sriovey.

Tympany was one of Salt's favorite ceremonies. The dwarves held it on the first night of every new month, and during it, they prayed for peace and deliverance. But ever since Jozep had started teaching who their people used to be, it had taken on the feeling of something holy. Salt didn't even mind the azalea-flavored water at the end.

"The fuck for?" Sriovey asked Jozep.

"Because of that," Jozep replied. "You're too angry. As it says in the *Crèche Prani*, we must seek that which was lost."

"The translation is that we must *reclaim* that which was lost," Simla corrected in a prim tone. "Not simply seek it. But otherwise Jozep is right. It is about peace, and you lack it."

Salt hid a smile. Simla could be so pedantic, but in this case, she was right, both about the translation and about Sriovey.

"I'm a warrior first," Sriovey said, not backing down. "I'll never become like Jozep."

"You might need to," Simla said. "We can't stay here. We need a place of safety. The wisdoms are too weak. We may not be able to hold out against the Baptisers."

Her words sparked shock. Salt had no idea matters were so dire.

"Is there no way to defeat him?" Derius asked. "My father—"

"There is no way," Simla cut in. "Too many warriors agree with Stipe, but even worse, the vast majority who would normally support us are too afraid of him and his Baptisers. And we know about Stipe's warriors. They are quick to judge, quick to anger, and refuse to understand."

"Those dog-like creatures are an abomination."

"Ur-Fels," Salt said, recollecting a story from Titan's Reach. It was one featuring Mistress Arisa, who had been the one to lure their small village into heresy. And in the tale, a species of creatures had been described. Ur-Fels had been their name.

"What do you know about them?" Sriovey asked.

Salt shrugged. "Just the name."

The conversation fell quiet for a moment.

"Who will have us?" Willa asked. "If we cannot stay here?"

"Cinder and Anya," Jozep said. "They'll find us a place."

Sriovey scoffed. "That would only work if we had a way to contact them."

Derius snapped his fingers as if he'd just remembered something important. "Shadion. He's had contact with Cinder's brother. He might be able to get them a message."

"And if that doesn't work?" Simla said. "Shadion has also been to Shalla Valley, he and his donkey."

"Pretty," Willa said. "The donkey's name is Pretty."

Simla nodded. "Right. He can ask the yakshins for asylum on our behalf."

Salt stared at the young wisdom in admiration. All along, this was the direction she had intended for the conversation.

"Only the purest are allowed in Shalla Vale," Sriovey reminded them all.

"Which is why you'll need to become like Jozep and Willa," Simla said. "They are what we once were and should have always been. We brought tranquility and peace to anyone who encountered us. The *Crèche Prani* even says we changed the nature of dragons, starting with Antalagore. We made them kind and good. If that isn't pure, then nothing of this world can be."

"In that case, we should send more than just Shadion and his donkey," Derius said. "We should send Jozep and Willa. We need them safe."

Jozep shook his head in disagreement. "No. There are too many here who still need our instruction." His gaze locked on Sriovey. "*You* need my instruction."

"You just aren't going to let this fucking go, are you?"

Jozep smiled. "Not until you stop cursing."

"Being peaceful means I have to stop cursing? Fuck."

Salt grinned at the interplay, and as the others planned what they needed to do, she realized she could help. "I can go with Shadion," she said. "If I can't make it into Shalla with everything I've learned and everything Jozep's given me, then I'm probably hopeless anyway."

"You're not hopeless," Jozep said. "And the yakshins will accept you."

Salt shot him a look of gratitude, glad to have his support.

"You've all read the missive from Estin?" Absin asked, glancing around at the others.

They were meeting in Duchess Cervine's study, which was muggy right now since the doors and windows were closed. They couldn't risk anyone listening in on what was said today, including anyone lurking in the gardens outside. It was always the case with those gathered here, the senior members of the *Lamarin Hosh*.

Seated behind her desk was Duchess Cervine, a lovely elf of middle years with only the first faint traces of crow's feet at the corners of her eyes and golden hair that was absent of even a single strand of gray. In contrast, her aunt, the Dowager Duchess Simone Trementh, was ancient—possibly as old as Quelchon Ginala—with seamed features, parchment-thin skin, and a head of white hair wrapped in a bun. She sat in one of the armchairs, tapping her ironwood-handled cane, a faint scent of lavender wafting about her.

Surely, the dowager didn't think those here didn't realize the aroma was from her *lorethasra*? Or that she used it to influence people?

Absin shrugged to himself. Using her *lorethasra* amongst those here in such a way was a waste, but who was he to judge?

The final member was Karthalyn Shoma, the spymaster for the duchess. The plain-faced elf who the world reckoned to be a merchant of middling success had also been Estin's *Isha* within the *Lamarin Hosh*.

"We've read it?" Duchess Trementh asked. "They went to Bharat, but we've yet to learn if they were successful."

"Let's assume they were," Duchess Cervine said.

"Why would we?" the dowager asked.

"Because they've yet to fail anywhere else," Karthalyn said. The man had a mousy way about him, but there was also a repressed sense of deadliness. Absin didn't doubt he could take the spymaster in a straight-up fight, but that was the key, wasn't it? A straight-up fight. He doubted Karthalyn would ever allow himself to be put at such a disadvantage.

"This is Shokan and Sira we're talking about," Duchess Cervine said by way of agreement. "If they're unable to complete this task that they believe is so imperative, what hope do we have?"

"You still cling to that notion?" the dowager challenged. "That Cinder and Anya are the Blessed Ones?"

The duchess nodded. "Of course. You read Estin's letter."

The letter had been written when Estin had been in Char, sent to Swift Sword in code, and passed on to Absin. He'd translated the missive and shared it with the others. The prince's letter indicated his ongoing certainty that while Cinder and Anya claimed that they only had the memories of the Blessed Ones, he believed they actually *were* the Blessed Ones. His judgment was based on close observation of their behavior, which wasn't that of two people leaning on borrowed memories, Talents, and skills. Their feelings weren't borrowed either. Estin felt that every aspect of Anya and Cinder were genuine, but they were simply confused somehow.

"The boy may believe they don't know themselves," Duchess Trementh countered. "But that isn't the same as it being the truth."

"Perhaps not," Absin said, willing to go against the sharp-minded, sharp-tongued dowager duchess. "But the facts argue against your doubt."

"What facts?" Duchess Trementh scoffed.

Absin hated when she spoke to him like that. He wasn't a child; nor was he a simpleton. Nevertheless, he suppressed his annoyance. "Cinder's abilities. His *Jivatma*. Anya's as well. And their claims to have the memories of the Blessed Ones."

"His abilities could simply mean he's a savant," the dowager said. "Anya as well."

"And her *Jivatma*?" Absin asked.

"We have no proof of it."

Absin inwardly sighed. The dowager seemed intent on waving aside everything he said. It was her way—test everything assumed and believed. They'd once had a conversation about this, in which the dowager had spoken of her philosophy: *"We all live off of received wisdom, but what if it's wrong? Shouldn't we doubt?"*

There had been and still was wisdom in what she had said, but sometimes it was just an excuse for unending scrutiny. Paralysis by analysis was how Absin would have phrased it. But it wouldn't be polite to say that to the dowager duchess, so he had to settle for a mild barb. "And I suppose you'll also say there's no proof they actually have the memories of the Blessed Ones?"

Duchess Trementh shrugged. "There isn't."

"But we do know they can create *nomasras*," Absin said. "That is a long-lost skill, and you can't simply shrug it away because it's inconvenient."

"I shrug nothing aside," the dowager exclaimed, rapping her cane against the oak flooring. "But what I am saying is that we have to be clearheaded in our approach."

"I'm sorry, but I agree with Absin," Karthalyn said. "We don't have a choice, especially since there are other facts involved in our calculus. Shet is real. That is truth. The Titans are awoken. That is truth. Cinder and Anya have likely seen to the destruction of the Orbs of Eretria, Flames, and Moss. That isn't absolute truth, but it is claimed truth, and I believe it. And those aren't the actions of lunatics. Every one of their actions has been toward a singular goal, and they haven't been shy in stating it. This story about a darker god. Our question is whether to believe them. Are they speaking the truth?"

"I think they think it's truth," Duchess Cervine said.

Absin nodded. "Which takes us back to my original point. If we think Cinder and Anya are Shokan and Sira, or at least have their memories, then whatever they're doing, we should also think it's the truth."

"I agree," Duchess Cervine said, which essentially ended the conversation. "Now what do we do about it?"

"What can we do?" Karthalyn asked. "We'll receive word in the next few weeks as to whether they managed to steal the Orb of Undying Light from the sorcerers. After that, there's Mede's Orb. I doubt Genka will turn that over to them, and I doubt we can help them retrieve it. And there are still two more Orbs of Peace besides—the Orb of Wings and the Orb of Regret. Both vanished shortly after the *NusraelShev*."

"Which means we do nothing different," Duchess Trementh said. "We continue to support Rakesh's High Army. We build our own forces. We continue speaking about Shokan and Sira returning."

"Even if Sira is a princess of Yaksha Sithe?" Absin asked.

The dowager duchess grinned. "Anya, an elven princess of Yaksha Sithe, as Sira reborn?" She cackled. "I can't think of anything that would rally the people so well as that."

22

Genka let the beauty of Cord Valley soothe his troubles. He'd gone out for a ride, and while his guards ringed him, there were no courtiers or politicians begging for a moment of his time. There was only the peace and tranquility of the wilderness. He needed it. Life the past two years, especially the past two months, had been difficult. There were so many issues that needed attending. Rebuilding his army, keeping his fractious empire in one piece, and ensuring that the farmers, the nation's bedrock, could still plant and harvest their crops.

The last was the most challenging. The herd of wraiths in the north persisted, and Genka couldn't overlook their threat. It was why he needed his army rebuilt. He needed thousands of young men, who should be in the fields with their fathers and working the land, as soldiers to save Shang Mendi if the worst came to pass.

Hopefully, it never would, but if it did, the Sunsets would be on their own. Genka's overtures to Shima Sithe and Aurelian Crèche had fallen on deaf ears. His ambassadors had been given the cold shoulder by both of Shang Mendi's southern neighbors. And in the case of

Shima Sithe, the elves had proclaimed their joy at Genka's troubles and laughed at his diplomats.

Their reactions hadn't been a surprise. Genka had held little hope that anything good could come of entreating with the southern nations. After all, he hadn't exactly made a secret of his desire to conquer their countries. And when the wraiths had nearly destroyed his army several years ago, they had been pleased.

Still, Shima Sithe's and Aurelian Crèche's decisions were shortsighted. If the herd blew through Shang Mendi's reconstituted army—which they very well could—what was to stop them from rampaging south?

Nothing.

Which raised the importance of Vel's mission. Genka hadn't been able to change the opinion of the southerners, but maybe his most trusted advisor could. The old man had been sent south with the hope that he could get Shima Sithe and Aurelian Crèche to see reason. Vel probably wouldn't succeed, but he had surprised Genka time and time again, and he hoped to be surprised again.

In the meantime, Genka had decided to take a short respite by coming to Cord Valley, the home of his heart. On initial inspection, this narrow strip of land, not more than seven miles wide and twenty-five miles long, didn't seem like much. Rugged mountains ringed the lush valley, which consisted of a broad expanse of green fields and grass. In addition, a bevy of streams and rivers emptied into a lovely central lake. And across the blue sky—deeper in color than anywhere in the Sunsets—clouds currently marched, heavy, pregnant, and regularly providing rain. Otherwise, the valley was generally sunny.

It was likely that Seminal held many such areas as Cord Valley, but this was a special place, a sacred one.

While the elves proclaimed the glory of Revelant and the dwarves the obdurate beauty of lost Hinane Crèche, humanity had this valley. It was the only place where the Yavanas, the most noble of steeds, could breed true, and the gift of husbanding and honoring the great horses was given only to the people of the Sunsets.

Some claimed that the secret to Cord Valley had to do with the blue-hued grass, which was felt to be a special cultivar that grew no-where else. Others insisted it was the water, which was purer and rich-er than could be found in any other location on Seminal.

Genka figured both answers might be correct, but he also didn't care. It was enough to know that Cord Valley belonged to the Sunsets, and he would do anything to protect it. In some ways, it was the true heart of Shang Mendi, possibly the true heart of Seminal itself.

Just then, impressions of chasing after brash colts and fillies broke into Genka's thinking. They came from his beautiful Yavana stallion, Midnight's Silence, who was as gentle as a father with his newborn and yet as deadly as that same father against anyone who dared threaten his child. In all the ways that mattered, Genka felt the same way toward his stallion—his boy, the child of his heart.

He grinned when Silence offered more impressions of catching the colts and fillies. Of racing past them and having them eat the dirt of the one whom they had mocked as being an 'old horse who should be put out to pasture.' At least that had been the impression given to Silence by the younger horses, and how the black stallion had enjoyed proving them wrong. He had long years on those colts and fillies, but they had nothing on him when it came to speed and stamina. In this, Midnight's Silence was unmatched.

The stallion whinnied in agreement, rearing like a colt.

Genka smiled, patting his boy, rubbing the only place on Silence's coal-dark coat, which wasn't black, a teardrop white patch right below his forelock.

Once the Yavana was done with his antics, he also seemed done with passing on his impressions. It was like that with him. Silence spoke to Genka but only when he was in the mood. In fact, they could go days without conversing, but what of it? It was a Yavana's prerogative to decide when to speak and who was worthy enough to hear their voice.

Genka relaxed as they continued back to *Kronon pa Ralia*—Horses Home—the massive stables in Cord Valley, where the Yavanas were housed and protected. As they came closer, a white Yavana flashed into view, a yearling colt just finding his hooves. He raced along the long line of fencing keeping him safe, faster than others his age. If the colt developed, he would be a jewel of a stallion.

Silence agreed with a proud toss of his head.

Genka smiled. Of course Silence would be proud. The yearling was his child.

As Genka stared at the white colt, his mind went to another white Yavana. The one originally named Sunbane—who had later been called Fastness. The stallion who'd chosen Cinder Shade as his rider. In all ways, he was Silence's equal.

So why had he chosen a simple warrior as his rider? Because regardless of Cinder Shade's supposed skill, in the end, that was all he was: a simple warrior no matter how many *hashains* he'd defeated. He wasn't the *Zuthrum lon Varshin*.

Then again, other than speed and power, was Fastness himself truly special? In Silence's case, the Great Annals—the genealogy of the Yavanas—had predicted he would choose a rider of a special nature. In fact, the phrasing had been similar enough to the *Medeian Scryings*, particularly sutra five hundred twenty-nine, to fully convince Genka of his destiny. Those sutras had spoken of Mede's rebirth: *He will come from the land of the sun's dying, birthed in blood and bathed in tears to bring forth peace.*

And Silence had been fated to choose a special rider of destiny, a warrior from the land of the setting sun, sent to demand obeisance for the peace that was lost. Two prophecies, close enough to easily recognize their links.

Of course, there was also the one professed by the cursed Errows. In their version, that same sutra had been altered. It still spoke of the sun's dying and the bathing in tears, but it also said that the risen Mede would act as the herald for Shokan—the Deathless Hero. And that fool, Jeet Condune, the heretic *hashain*, said the same, gathering followers and evading Genka's best attempts to find and kill him.

"Why is the prophecy you believe the right one?"

Genka started, hands tightening on Silence's reins and pulling him short. The stallion had spoken to him with words on only a handful of occasions. And for him to challenge Genka's faith in his fate sparked a disquiet.

While he pondered the matter, a messenger swept toward Genka. He was briefly halted by the guards before being let through. A haggard expression held across his face.

Genka didn't like the looks of that. "What news?"

"The wraiths are stirring."

Corvid Drem had once been a person of little repute. After her father's passing, she'd inherited and run the small mercantile shop he'd founded in Drow. There, like her father, she had sold goods and services to those adventurers from Drow who dared the badlands.

They would come in, sell their wares, and she would sell them supplies. She had even been honest in how much she cheated them. Only rarely did she take more than her due, and the adventurers had appreciated her for it.

Or so she had thought. There were always a few who griped, but that's all Corvid thought it to be—gripes. She hadn't thought the adventurers would see her in anything close to a despicable light.

Her life had been good. It didn't matter that she didn't have a husband or children. First, she didn't want a man in her life. Always getting underfoot and thinking he knew better than she. And second, she didn't want children; didn't want the trouble and dangers of a pregnancy. Besides, she could always adopt a smart young street urchin as her own. There were dozens of them in Drow, and one of them would surely do.

So Corvid had maintained her business and her pleasant life, paying for company when she felt the itch and otherwise keeping to herself.

But then a man whose name she couldn't even remember had come into the store, and for whatever reason, he just couldn't fathom that a woman should tell him *no*. It began when she had gotten the better of him on the sale of some furs, and he'd taken the loss as a challenge, stopping by every few months and being bested on every occasion. He never took the defeats well, which Corvid had found amusing. Later, as he got progressively angrier, her own annoyance had flared, and she'd kicked the man out of her store, telling him to never come back.

He'd done so but not before spouting what she took to be nonsense and threats. At the time, Corvid had given it little thought. By then, she had heard it all. In fact, she had long since hired four guards to protect her at all times.

But that night, that same individual had used her own guards against her. They had attacked Corvid in her home, securing her in the basement, where they did her unspeakable violence. And in the midst of her torment, Corvid had screamed for help, reaching out to anyone who would listen.

It was from the void that a voice had answered, promising vengeance for a small price. Corvid had accepted, and when it was over, she had visited gruesome death upon the man and her faithless guards. Their blood dripped from the walls, their entrails lay on the floor, and yet they lived, long enough for Corvid to feed and feast.

Even now, thinking on it brought a smile to her face.

Corvid had become a wraith, and in the many, many decades since, she'd never had reason to regret her choice.

That included several years ago when the Hungering Heart, the voice answering Corvid during her time of torture, had ordered the wraiths to attack the Sunsets. Corvid had feasted then like she hadn't in many years, wallowing in the lovely killing and blood of thousands of weak humans. Toriaz had been the one to lead them, the one closest to the Hungering Heart, their Master.

It all ended when Residar the Treasonous betrayed them. He'd killed Toriaz and, in so doing, broken the binding between their Master's will and His chosen one. The wraiths, aimless and with no voice to guide them, had fled the Sunsets, heading north for the WraithLands.

Weeks later, though, Corvid learned of Residar's treachery, and upon doing so, she had immediately led the wraiths in attacking the traitor, intent on killing him.

She'd failed.

Residar and a score of others had fought back, many of them had died, with fewer than a dozen escaping the battle. They'd left the WraithLands for parts unknown, but they wouldn't live long. Without the Hellmaw, they were fated to die a long and miserable death.

Good. They deserved worse, and Corvid had the means to see it happen. Because after Toriaz's death, the Hungering Heart had begun speaking to Corvid. She was now the leader of the wraiths, and the Master wanted the herd to remain together. He wanted them to attack the Sunsets again, to head to Cord Valley and utterly destroy and despoil it. There was also a strange orb to collect and an order to kill Genka Devesth. That man was marked for death.

Those had been the final instructions that Corvid had heard prior to resting.

But she was awake now. The time for vengeance would soon be at hand.

A cold wind blustered, rustling and fingering its way through Forebear Mael's coat and clothes. It chilled him, and he shivered. The icy breeze might have acted as a mirror of what life had been like in Titan's Reach since Salt and Jury had gone after the man known as Rukh—the man who had the appearance of one of their own and a skill with the blade that had left Mael in awe.

That same man had likely killed Salt, Jury, and those with them. Mael couldn't fathom any other explanation on what must have happened. It had been nearly three years since Salt and Jury, named for the glorious Titans, had set out to seek vengeance against Rukh and his companions.

But they'd never returned, and by now, they likely never would. They were dead and gone, two of Titan's Reach's best and brightest.

Mael sighed as he trudged through the well-kept village.

Winter gripped the hamlet, and his breath plumed. Icicles hung like spears from the eaves and roofs, and smoke breathed out from hearths. The sun looked to set soon and warm light shined out from many windows. The cold had driven everyone inside, where they shared the blessings of a fire with family and friends.

As for Mael, he had no one waiting for him at home. He was a widower who had outlived his wife by over twenty years now, and as if the streets reflected his solitude, they were empty. He was alone.

It was only Salt who Mael truly considered a friend in these latter years of his life. The young woman had an old soul, and she had understood him in ways his own wife never had. Then again, his wife hadn't been named for a Titan. She'd barely survived her first trepanation, much less the three Mael had endured. It had been that final one that had allowed him to access *Jivatma* and earn his name.

The same as Salt, which was why the two of them got along so well. Old and young, they shared the same responsibilities.

"This is a nice village you have," a voice whispered from the shadows.

Mael started. He'd sensed no one, but he did now, a powerful presence. He conducted *Jivatma*, enhancing his thin limbs and bringing the darkening night to brightness.

What he saw standing in the shadows of an alley left him cold and angry—a dwarf. The woven's eyes, dark in the night, held a mockery that urged Mael to give in to his anger and crush the foul creature.

"Do not call out," the dwarf said, stepping forward. "I bring word about one of your own. Salt Tangent."

Mael held his attack. Old he might be, but he was still more than a match for this woven perversion. He didn't fear the dwarf, and more, he was curious what the creature might have to say. "How do you know Salt?"

"Because she resides in Surent Crèche. She has lived amongst my people for nigh on a year."

Mael scowled. He didn't know this dwarf or how he knew of Salt. Likely he'd been told of her by the other dwarf who had visited Titan's Reach, the one with Rukh. But saying her name wouldn't save this one.

"She spoke of her people here, at Titan's Reach," the dwarf said, seemingly unconcerned with Mael's anger. "Of your beliefs in Shet. We share those beliefs."

Mael scoffed, barking laughter. "You believe that the woven are an abomination?"

The dwarf shook his head. "Not that. But we do believe Shet's teachings are right. That the weak should step aside for the mighty. That those with power should wield it for their betterment."

Mael tilted his head. The dwarf sounded sincere, but it was also lunacy to accept anything he said. "Tell me again how you know Salt."

"As I said, she lives in Surent Crèche." The dwarf went on to describe her appearance and upbringing, her relationships and family, things only someone deeply familiar with her could have known.

"Why are you here?" Mael asked, convinced now that the dwarf had known Salt. Whether she lived or not was another matter. He also reckoned she would have never told those details to a dwarf except through torture. Salt would have never betrayed Titan's Reach.

"I seek an alliance," the dwarf said. "I represent Stipe Jasth, the leader of the Baptisers, those who would see Surent shift to a better way of thinking—Shet's way of thinking."

"But not to worshipping Shet?" Mael was further curious on where this was going.

"We leave the worship to you, but his teachings are worthy of emulating. There are many in our crèche who cling to the old ways, and it doesn't help our cause that Salt, a human, loves and supports them."

Mael had heard enough. "You speak nonsense. Salt wouldn't support any dwarf, much less love one."

"And yet she does, as a sister might a brother. The one who came here before, Jozep, son of matron Virala Anwar."

Mael stared at the dwarf, trying to decipher his actual purpose in traveling to Titan's Reach from Surent Crèche. Or was that even true? Might he actually be from Ardent Crèche? A spy sent to learn their weaknesses?

That seemed the more likely scenario, which meant Mael would need to bring the dwarf to the council's attention. Scouts would be needed to backtrack from whence he'd come. They'd likely need to bolster the guards for a while, too.

His decision made, Mael sought to entrap the dwarf's feet with a webbing of *Jivatma*.

The woven rebuffed him, backing away hastily. "Wait! I can prove what I say."

The dwarf threw his arms to the side, cried out then as his limbs deformed, audibly snapping and breaking. A muzzle extended from his mouth. Hair thickened to fur along his body. A further transformation until the dwarf stood on legs belonging to a wolf.

Mael breathed out. Mistress Arisa, the one who had taught the *Shetawarin* the truth, had described these creatures—Ur-Fels. They were her servants, which meant the dwarf might not be lying when he said that those he represented believed in Shet's teachings.

"We were fashioned from something purer into the dwarves you know," the Ur-Fel said around a mangling of teeth. "I am one of those who wish to reclaim our holy shape and our holy state. We can be allies to see both our peoples achieve our ends."

Still in shock, Mael stared at the creature. An Ur-Fel. They were real, and he was speaking to one. The moment felt heavy, as if great fortune had reached out to touch him. He wouldn't fail that offering. "Tell me more."

23

Before exiting Verity Foe, Rukh searched deep within his mind, looking for any and all traces of Rabisu's weave. It turned out there was only one, but the malignant braid had done far more damage than he had initially suspected. While active, it had touched on his emotions, memories, and judgment, and in all ways, tried to change his nature.

But Rukh's own weave had protected him from the bulk of Rabisu's malevolence, and he could see that it was already erasing the rakshasa's braids. In fact, just another couple of months and the worst of Rabisu's damage would have already largely been mitigated and extinguished.

Relieved that their decision at Mahadev wouldn't have left them unable to recover, he explained his discoveries to Jessira.

"But Rabisu is still within me," she said. "He was leeching *lorethasra* and growing stronger. He would have used it to enhance his weave."

Rukh's relief disappeared, and he gave a pensive nod. "And set you back to where you were before." More than ever, they needed Wren's advice on what to do with Rabisu. As Rukh figured matters, it would be best to kill the rakshasa and, failing that, contain him in some way.

They continued deliberating on the matter, even as they exited Verity Foe and entered Twilight Gate's meadow, which stood bathed in sunlight. The tall flowers swayed beneath a soft wind, intermittent and perfumed. Thick white clouds paraded across the sky, and the world was beautiful.

For Rukh, however, it also felt completely different. He was himself again, and it was like a shroud had been lifted from his thoughts, emotions, and abilities. He smiled when he noticed Sadana waiting for them.

"Mahamatha wishes to speak with you," the yakshin said, cocking her head as if seeing them for the first time. "You seem different."

"We'll explain later," Rukh said, gesturing for Sadana to lead the way. Now wasn't the time to discuss their fresh discoveries with anyone but Wren.

Sadana grunted acceptance, not bothering to press the matter. Instead, they walked in silence through the forest and out into the savanna. Hours of quiet traveling later, the Shriven Grove loomed ahead, and soon enough, they were walking beneath the shading boughs of the massive Ashoka trees. Rukh smiled, eagerness building. In some ways the Ashoka trees could be considered his grandchildren, just like Sadana and the yakshins. His family was suddenly much larger.

Jessira grinned, reaching for his hand. "When this is over, I want to get to know them better."

He nodded agreement, chuckling a bit. "But they're all so much older than us."

Jessira sniffed. "Speak for yourself. I have over a century of life on Seminal."

Sadana pulled up short when three young foxes dashed across their path. The little animals yipped happily.

"An auspicious sign," the yakshin noted.

Rukh smiled, recalling a similar event when Deepak Moral, the old village priest, had guided him from Swallow to Swift Sword—a time when Rukh had been a young, crippled boy called Cinder Shade and had no notion of himself—no name, no history, no true purpose. Back then, three small foxes had run across his path during the beginning of his trek to Swift Sword, and their presence might have actually been auspicious back then. He hoped it would be the same now.

His smile broadened when he caught Jessira's cinnamon scent. He'd noticed it ever more strongly since waking from her Healing.

"It makes me wonder what you achieved in Verity," Sadana added.

"You'll learn if Mother Ashoka thinks you should," Rukh replied.

Another grunt, and Sadana strode off.

Soon, more yakshins became visible, going about their tasks, while others stood rooted in the dirt, their limbs thrown wide to soak in the sunshine. Farther in the distance, framed against the scintillating blue waters of the long lake centered in the vale, holders trained the Shokans. Bones saw them, and he waved.

Rukh replied in kind, glad to see the young men he still considered his brothers. How could he not? Yes, he had experienced so much more than them, lived far longer, but in the end, none of that mattered. These were the men with whom he'd shared so much, walking under skies of joy, skies of tears, skies of terrors, skies of mercy, skies of sorrow, and skies of love. They were his brothers, no matter the Realm.

His wave caused the other Shokans to pause briefly and respond with overjoyed smiles, but none of them broke off their training.

A wise decision. The holders would have responded poorly. To them, when training, there was room for nothing else.

Shortly thereafter, they reached their destination: Mahamatha, Mother Ashoka, Aranya—their daughter, Wren. Rukh grinned again at Jessira, anticipation bubbling, heart pounding out his excitement. They hadn't seen their family in so long, and soon they would.

"Place your palms upon Mother Ashoka's trunk," Sadana instructed. "Close your eyes and rest your head against her."

Rukh and Jessira did as instructed, and the tree maiden chanted:

"Goddess of the wild forest,
Who vanishes from our sight.

Seeming to sound like dancing bells,
The Lady of the Wood exults.
The Forest Queen frees our wains."

A twinkling of bells chimed across Rukh's mind…

… And he stood with Jessira on the edge of a wildflower meadow. A conifer forest spread around it, like hands cupping something precious. The air held still and cool, pregnant with the scents of moss, lightly scented flowers, and impending rain. Clouds and sunshine dappled the field in splashes of shadow and light while butterflies and bumblebees flitted about the blossoms.

And just like the last time he had been here, a woman danced in the middle of the clearing. She twirled and swayed, moving with an impossible grace. Then again, Wren had always loved to dance. When Rukh had seen her before in this place, her skin had been pale as fresh snow with hair so blonde he'd mistaken it for being white.

This time, she had skin of a dusky hue, a mixture of color between his own and Jessira's, and her hair was a deep brown, lush and long. She'd replaced her dress, too, which had been made of roses but was now a simple blue sari trimmed in gold. However, a circlet of purple jasmine still graced her brow, woven into the long locks of her hair while wrapped around her ankles were the same thin chains tinkling with silver bells.

Rukh smiled. Jessira used to weave jasmines in her hair and often wore a silver-belled chain around an ankle. Their daughters had copied the habit.

Wren came to a stop, and Rukh had his first clear view of her in what felt like a millennium. His throat tightened, and his eyes went wet with tears. *Wren.* It felt unreal, but it was truly her.

Jessira's hands had gone to her face, covering her mouth. Her eyes shined, and she shook with the same suppressed emotion that Rukh was feeling.

Wren offered a welcoming smile, and her teeth flashed white rather than pearlescent, like before.

It was enough. Rukh took a step forward, still struggling with accepting the reality of the situation. *Wren. His child.* It had been decades since he'd last seen her. Why had he ever left home?

Jessira reached for him, and hand in hand, they approached their daughter. Faster they went, running. Wren had her arms wide open, and Rukh let Jessira embrace her first.

"I'm so sorry," Jessira said, clutching their daughter like she thought she might disappear. "We should have never left you. I'm so sorry."

"You don't have to apologize, Amma," Wren said, stroking Jessira's hair. Although their daughter was shorter, she had a sense of majesty and purpose that lent her a grave air. She was their child, but she was older than them, and the truth was especially evident in her eyes, which were ancient and wise but also fresh and inquisitive as an infant's.

Rukh didn't care about any of that. He hugged Wren, enfolded Jessira as well. He had nothing to say. Words were useless. More regrets than he cared to count might have flickered through the back of his mind, and he wished he could express how deeply he felt the grief of leaving Arisa, of leaving Wren and Sindar and the rest of the family. At the time, the reasons had been sound, but the price…

Why did we leave?

It was a question whose answer wasn't important. Not now when Rukh was holding two women he loved.

Wren pulled away then and bowed slightly to him. "Nanna."

The word nearly undid Rukh. A thousand memories filled his thoughts. Wren's first smile. The first time she rolled over. Her earliest words. When she learned to crawl and then walk. Feeding her rice for the first time. So many recollections spinning through his mind, all of them meaningful and good. Wren's *upanayana* ceremony. The powdery sweet smell of her as an infant. Her and Jessira gardening together.

Wren held their hands, tears on her face. "Amma. Nanna. Don't be sad. We're together, just as you promised. And leaving Arisa was the right decision." Her voice remained lilting but resonant. "You did what the Realms needed. You saved them just like you saved Arisa. I loved and honored you for it. So did Sindar, Uncle Jaresh, and Aunties Bree and Sign. Even Nayanamma and Tatayya would have approved."

Rukh's parents. Fresh tears threatened. It felt like he hadn't thought of them in so long.

"You don't hate us for leaving you?" Jessira asked.

Wren laughed. "You didn't leave me and Sindar when we were children. We were grown adults, and you didn't abandon us. Don't you remember how much we spoke about this? Sindar and Kopha were the ones who planned on leaving for Earth. You went in their place."

Rukh *had* forgotten, and he shared a startled glance with Jessira. Based on her expression of surprise, she hadn't remembered either.

And like a lantern, Wren's words shined a light into the dim recesses of his past. What she said was true. After the devastating war against Marnel—Mistress Arisa, Shet's daughter—Sindar and Kopha had been intent on seeking out the fiendish woman's father. Many had raised their voices in agreement. Marnel had done incalculable harm, and she'd also let slip that her father was of the same mind as she, but even more powerful.

He had to be found and prevented from doing to others as Marnel had done to Arisa. And in order to keep Sindar safe, Rukh and Jessira had gone in their son's and Kopha's place, leaving their home and everyone they loved to search for Shet.

"We never hated you," Wren said, gripping their hands. "Truly. We honored you. We will always honor you."

Rukh let out a shuddering breath, profoundly relieved. They spoke then, learning what had happened to Arisa following their departure, of their family and friends, their children, and why Wren had descended to Seminal.

"After you defeated Shet's daughter, Arisa was made anew," she explained. "We rose closer to Devesh and learned more about the anchor lines that bind the Realms in the Web of Worlds. But by then, those connections between Arisa and Earth and Seminal were not so easy to travel. The distance was too great."

"Then how did you manage it?" Rukh asked, hating that his daughter might have risked her life for him. "Why did you manage it?"

"I managed it through the help of Himaya and Koresh."

"Bree's children?"

Wren nodded. "They have their mother's intelligence and found a way. And as for why, blame Rukhi, Jaresh's son. He is what Seminal might label a quelchon and Earth would call a prophet. He saw your future and your need, especially when Indrun and Sachi left Seminal with the work not complete. They couldn't have known, but it is the truth." She grinned suddenly. "Rukhi also saw the names you would hold in this Realm, which is why I chose mine as Aranya."

"Yes," Jessira said with a wry chuckle. "We figured that one out on our own."

"You'd be surprised by how few people have," Wren replied. "In fact, no one has. Not even the yakshins. It seems like it should be easy. 'Ar' in Shevasra means 'of' and Anya is self-explanatory. Aranya. Of Anya. Just like the temple of Ardevesh in Mahadev means of Devesh."

"You mean even our grandchildren didn't figure it out? The yakshins?" Rukh asked. He laughed when Wren startled.

"Your grandchildren," she breathed. "I never thought of them in that way." An instant later, she appeared to throw off her consideration. "We could talk for days, but your time here is limited. You need my help?"

Rukh shelved his disappointment. He wanted to spend more time with his daughter. There was so much to learn: everything she had done; her life; more about their family on Arisa; Ashoka, the city of his heart...

But Seminal's needs took precedence. "We need your advice."

"With Rabisu." Wren's lips pursed. "What to do with him since the Orbs still need to be destroyed. And you still need to remain unknown to Shet."

Rukh remembered whenever Wren had tried to keep a secret from him. It was a simple thing, but a father noticed. She would tuck a lock of hair behind an ear and have trouble meeting his gaze. She did so now. "We have to forget ourselves again," he guessed.

Wren dipped her head. "I'm sorry. It is the only way to preserve the past. Your past is written, and I've found that the past is almost like a living entity. It will seek to preserve itself regardless of our wants and wishes."

"There is no other way?" Jessira whispered, eyes wet with tears.

Wren took Jessira's hands. "I'm sorry, but if there's any comfort, know that the weave you and Nanna wanted wasn't a mistake. It was necessary. The past cannot be changed, and too many rely on what happened in that moment when you hated that prior view of herself. It has to be. Call the rakshasa. He and I need to speak."

Jessira didn't want to forget Rukh. It didn't matter if he wore the name Shokan or Cinder Shade; she loved him. In addition, she didn't want to release Rabisu. The rakshasa shouldn't be allowed anywhere near her daughter. Better if Jessira could simply kill him.

She held in a sigh, knowing she couldn't, knowing the price to pay if she destroyed the rakshasa.

But if he tried to harm her daughter in the slightest, that calculation would go out the window. Jessira had sacrificed plenty and would sacrifice even more in order to save entire worlds full of strangers. But she wouldn't allow another of her children to sacrifice themselves. Wren would live no matter what else happened to Seminal.

"This is my Foe," Wren said, seemingly recognizing her fear. "The rakshasa cannot hurt me here."

Jessira knew that in her mind but not in her heart. This *was* a kind of Foe—similar to Verity, Lucid, and even the one attached to Misery Gate—connected to Wren's form as a massive Ashoka tree, but still…

"Bring him out," Rukh said. "He won't hurt her. We won't let it happen."

Jessira stared at their daughter. Wren wasn't a child any longer. Hadn't been even before she and Rukh had departed Arisa. Most important, Wren had wisdom they lacked. They would have to trust her judgment.

She nodded to Wren, exhaling heavily before closing her eyes. Reaching inside to Rabisu, she told him what she wanted, glowering when he refused her summons. "A moment," she said. "He won't come out."

Jessira knelt on the ground, buried her sword between her knees, and closed her eyes. She sourced and conducted, and wisps of green Earth rustled and collected around her hands, pooled around her sword. "Come out," she ordered the rakshasa within her.

Rabisu refused again, but this time, Jessira latched on to him with her power, knowing her touch would hurt. He screamed, cursing. But she had him. Jessira's eyes snapped open then. So did her mouth, and from it, smoke issued forth, gathering with a noise of metal grinding. It took the shape of a massive, red-eyed dog looming behind her. *Rabisu.* He growled, the sound of steel shearing, and the stench of burning pitch and seared meat filled the air.

An instant later, the sound and stink were gone, silenced and washed away by a single motion from Wren.

"This is my Foe," Wren stated. "You will not make your mark upon it."

Rabisu made to growl again, but no voice issued from his mouth. He howled silently.

"I know I cautioned you to stay away from him," Wren said to Jessira. "But the choice you made was likely better in the long run than the advice I offered."

Jessira viewed her in surprise. She recalled Wren's warning, but with Manifold arguing otherwise, she and Rukh had taken what they had later on thought was an unwise decision. Apparently not.

"What would you have done instead?" Rukh asked.

Wren shrugged. "One possibility was that after your time in the Lucid Foe, I would have also placed a braid upon you. But I'm not as knowledgeable about such matters as Rabisu. I would have done my best, but it likely would not have been good enough to hide you from Shet. At best, I would have 'frozen' you as Cinder and Anya, and while you would still have your abilities and memories, they would feel like they belonged to someone else."

"And at worst?" Jessira prodded.

Wren sighed. "Let's just be thankful Manifold was more cunning than I. And also more cunning than Rabisu." She faced the rakshasa. "Are you ready to talk?"

She gestured, and Rabisu stretched his mouth like he intended on swallowing her. She never flinched, and eventually the rakshasa settled his shape. "Aranya," he said, apparently familiar with their daughter. "I should have known it was you. The stench of purity fills the air." His voice was a mill wheel churning wood.

"And I promised you would not appreciate our next meeting," Wren said.

"I am bested for now," Rabisu agreed. "But you know as well as I that all victories and setbacks are only temporary."

"Unless they are permanent," Rukh said, entering the conversation.

Rabisu sneered. "Shokan. I do not fear you. I know your weakness." The dog-form nosed at Jessira. "You love her too much to see her damaged."

"But I don't fear that damage," Jessira stated. She stepped forward, pushing close to Rabisu. He didn't like that, and he edged away.

"I won't be banished," he declared, clearly trying to rally his courage.

Jessira walked him down. "You have no choice. I will end you if you do not leave."

Rabisu attacked in a storm of fangs and claws.

Jessira slipped to the side and backhanded him. Her hand glowed white, a mix of Talents. The blow connected, and Rabisu was sent hurtling. He landed in a lump, a white spot the size of Jessira's fist glowing on his smoky black frame.

"What did you do?" Rabisu asked.

"Test me again, and you'll find out," Jessira declared, walking the rakshasa down once again.

He crouched low, growling. "I can hurt you. From inside. You might heal from it, but it won't be easy. It will take years, which you don't have."

"You're wrong," Wren said. "It would take months at most. You forget the Marat Archipelago."

"What can the kapis and pixies do?" Rabisu scoffed. "They cannot heal whatever damage I cause."

"They cannot," Wren agreed. "But at Coral Gate and Interval Foe, time moves differently. What takes a year of recovery in the rest of the world would only take a month there."

"But even still, he's right," Jessira said. "We don't have months for me to heal. I won't have Rukh face this world's dangers on his own." She viewed the rakshasa with distaste. "What do you want?"

"And think carefully," Rukh warned. "Remaining where you are now is not an option."

"Sanctuary," Rabisu quickly declared. He spoke to Wren. "You can create what I need. An Aushadha fruit is similar enough. Place me within it. I'll be safe there. Then drop me off in a Realm of my choosing."

"Absolutely not," Jessira declared. She'd never allow Rabisu free in a world that had no defenses against him. She didn't want to free him in any Realm, period.

"We will free you in a Realm of our choosing," Rukh stated.

"An empty Realm, then," Rabisu said. "One not yet touched by Devesh or the Empty One. Find me one, and I'll leave Sira. Either that or a Realm of your creation."

"Done," Wren said. "But we have needs as well."

Jessira caught Rabisu smirking, and she made her features go blank. "Do not be so pleased with yourself. You haven't won anything yet."

"We will do as you asked," Rukh said by way of agreement. "But this time, the weave will be to our exact specifications. No deviations."

"And since you are in my Foe," Wren said, "I will know if you deviate in even the slightest way. You will teach me what you intend."

The rakshasa continued to smirk. "And let me guess—you'll destroy me. You forget who I am. I am the Rakshasa of Dissolution. I do not fear death."

He was lying. It was his greatest fear. Jessira knew it. She was connected to Rabisu. He existed within her, and in the short time since she'd truly awoken, she recognized much about what drove the rakshasa. Fear of his own demise was chief among them, followed closely by an intense hunger.

And while it was true that he could hurt her, it wasn't to the same degree that Jessira could hurt him. It was time he understood that. She reached for him, touching him with the Wildness only.

Rabisu writhed, screaming in pain, begging for it to end.

Jessira didn't listen. Instead, she intensified the agony. Rabisu needed to recognize where matters stood. "You won't be killed, but if you fail me—if you fail us—if you try again to harm us, I will remember. I will keep you inside my mind, and this pain is how you will be housed. Simply nod if you understand."

"You don't have the will to—"

Jessira ignited the rakshasa with the Wildness.

Again he screamed. Jessira noticed that Rukh and Wren stood in silent regard, features flat. She hated having to do this, especially disliked that her daughter was seeing her behave in this way. On Arisa, she and Rukh had redeemed all five species of Chimeras—creatures who the vast bulk of Humanity had declared incorrigibly evil—and they'd done so without torturing them into submission.

It made no difference that Rabisu was a special case. Jessira took no pleasure in hurting him—it actually made her sick—but it was also necessary.

She let off the Wildness, and Rabisu collapsed, whimpering. Jessira viewed him in a mix of sorrow and contempt. Like most evil creatures, the rakshasa was used to doling out pain but not to receiving it.

"Do we have an understanding?" Jessira asked him. "Simply nod if you do. Do not talk."

Rabisu gave a shuddering nod.

It seemed even a fool could learn.

"Before we begin, I need to speak with you first," Wren said, addressing Jessira. "I need to know everything about what happened on that anchor line." Her eyes went to Rukh. "From both your perspectives."

They spoke for several minutes, with Jessira dredging every last memory she could recall. Next, it was Rukh's turn, and he, too, spoke to Wren about the events in the Web of Worlds.

"It's about Nanna," Wren said to Jessira afterward. "That's where your anger originates."

The observation sparked a recollection. "When I was under the influence of Rabisu's weave, I would sometimes remember Rukh as my husband, and I would always think he betrayed me. That he was supposed to come to Seminal with me, and he didn't. It would make me so angry." She immediately knew what was needed, and she had to swallow a bolus of loathing. "I have to feel that way again."

"Unless you can pretend to feel that way?" Wren asked, a hopeful tone in her voice. "Trick him and your past self?"

Jessira smiled sadly. "Not in a thousand lifetimes could I pretend to feel that way about your father." She frowned as an idea occurred to her. "But does it have to be this way? We need the braids in order to remain hidden from Shet. But that's it."

"The world can't know your true names, either," Wren said. "Not even you can know them."

"At all times?" Jessira asked. "What if we simply don't know ourselves when we're in Naraka?"

"We've told everyone we're not Shokan and Sira," Rukh agreed. "For now, no one needs to know any different."

"It won't be enough," Wren said. "With three Orbs destroyed and a fourth soon to be, Shet's skills will increase. He might be able to see through a weave that only activates in his presence. You have to wear a deeper weave."

Jessira scowled. It had been worth the attempt.

Wren gripped her hands, sympathy in her eyes. "I'm sorry, Amma."

Jessira gave a pursed-lipped expression of feigned nonchalance. "Don't be. I love your father. I always have, and I always will. But acting hateful toward him will hurt."

"Him or you?"

"Both."

Wren sighed. "You know, I used to envy your love for him. I had always hoped for something like it."

Jessira had never expected to hear such an admission. "Used to? What changed?"

"Arisa rose closer to Devesh. His love is enough." Wren smiled. "And I have all your grandchildren to keep me company."

Jessira laughed. "I hope to get to know all of them."

Wren laughed with her, but her humor eventually failed, replaced by seriousness. "You'll love him again."

"I'll always love him," Jessira agreed. "You know why?"

"Because love is the finest of things."

Jessira smiled, hugging her daughter. "You listened."

Wren chuckled. "I always listened. I just didn't always do what you wanted."

Jessira grinned. "What child does?" She stepped away from Wren. She could have spent days talking to her daughter, but work awaited. "See to Rabisu?"

"I will."

Wren addressed Rabisu, describing her plan. The rakshasa reluctantly bobbed his head in agreement.

"We have to forget again," Rukh said, sounding despondent while their daughter talked to the rakshasa.

"Only somewhat, and only temporarily," Jessira replied, hating to see the sorrow etched on his face. "But on that anchor line, it won't be me. Just a hateful version."

"A confused version."

"You think that's all I'll be on that anchor line? Confused?"

Rukh nodded. "You never hated me. I also saw you on that anchor line, and it wasn't hate you were feeling so much as self-loathing."

Jessira pursed her lips, recalling again the events to come on the anchor line, reconsidering them from a fresh perspective. Maybe he was right.

"The truth is," Rukh continued, "you're not a person meant to hate."

Jessira chuckled, taking one of his hands in both of hers, kissing his fingers. "That's my line."

"It's still true."

Jessira's humor faded. "This should scare me, but it doesn't. I'm not giving away my life. Until the destruction of the Orbs, I'll not know myself as Sira or Jessira, but I'll still love you as Anya. And that confused version will only exist when we're in Naraka and on that anchor line. At best, that poor version of myself will be a temporary avatar."

"A temporary avatar," Rukh said the words like he was tasting them. "And since we're in our daughter's personal Foe, her own Way into Divinity…"

"What's that?"

He shrugged again. "Just a phrase. Thought it sounded inspiring."

"Way into Divinity." Jessira tested the phrase. "I like it."

"And since we're in Wren's personal Foe, she'll be the one to braid the weaves. We'll survive, just like we have everything else."

Jessira took heart from his words, even as fears chewed away at her optimism. In all the battles she and Rukh had fought, Jessira had been the one to defend his blind spots. It was what she'd always done, and she wouldn't allow any flaw to breach her duty.

"We've planned in exacting detail how to proceed," Wren said. "I can see how it will work. You'll be safe. You have my promise as your daughter."

This was it, then. Jessira blinked back tears. In a few minutes, she'd once again forget herself. Worse, she'd forget Wren and Sindar. *Rukh.* Fear heaved within her. She wasn't sure she could do it.

"Trust me, Amma. I will protect you," Wren promised. "I know what's needed. This is not your end."

Jessira closed her eyes tightly, praying. *Please, Devesh. When this is over, let me remember my loves.*

She opened her eyes. "I'm ready."

24

Cinder stared at the matte-black stone, which was smooth, round, and the size of a plum. Otherwise, it was nondescript. He tossed it a few times. Even in its weight, there was nothing untoward about the object.

But it held Rabisu, who had been hiding within Anya all this time and leeching her *lorethasra*. And the fiend *had* altered their emotions. His weave had been the reason for Cinder and Anya's inexplicable anger towards one another.

Thankfully, that was no longer the case. The braid was gone, removed by Mother Ashoka and replaced by a better one. In addition, Rabisu had been removed from Anya and was now trapped in this stone that they were to carry out of Shalla Valley and keep with them at all times. Mahamatha had stressed the last, stating it was due to a promise made.

Why Mother Ashoka had agreed to such a term—or why Rabisu had done so—was beyond Cinder. But if that was the agreement, then so be it. He slipped the stone containing Rabisu into his *null pocket*, patting it out of habit, and as usual, having no sense of its presence.

Anya, standing next to him, viewed the *null pocket* in disgust. "I can't believe that fragging monster was inside me all this time."

"I can," Cinder said. "We were too sure of ourselves after gaining Shokan's and Sira's memories." He shook his head. "They were legends who could handle someone like Rabisu. We are not."

"Not yet," Anya said, flashing a cocky smile. "But we will be. It's why we've been granted permission to Path directly into Shalla Vale."

"We don't know how to create a Path," Cinder reminded her.

"But we will," Anya said with breezy confidence.

Cinder laughed. "I don't doubt it. Or at least you'll figure it out." When it came to learning new uses of *Jivatma* and *lorethasra*, Shokan's memories told him that Sira had always been quicker than him.

"It is time for you to leave," Aranya said, interrupting their conversation. She stepped toward them, her silver-belled anklets tinkling and her dress fashioned from roses of many colors swirling.

Cinder peered at Mother Ashoka in concern. Her blue eyes—so incongruously young and ancient—appeared filled with sorrow, and clouds covered her skies. "What's wrong?"

Aranya smiled faintly at his disquiet, her pearlescent teeth flashing. "I am sad because those I love have to leave," she said, her resonant voice lilting and echoing. Her smile firmed, and the sun came out from behind the clouds, reflecting off her pale skin and white-blonde hair. "We will see each other again."

She flicked her hand, and Cinder felt himself thrown backward, hastily flung from her glade. The meadow became a small pinpoint, and then the light was gone, replaced by a bleak emptiness, one that mirrored Cinder's heart. He already missed Aranya—he wasn't sure why—but a weight of sorrow settled across his chest, and he sensed it wouldn't be so easy to dislodge.

A second later, Seminal resumed, an energetic return to the world of Shalla Valley. Reality warped and curved, shivering like liquid before a bass note sounded time's recovery. Nausea had Cinder stumbling away from Mother Ashoka, and he bent at the waist, hands on his knees, struggling to maintain focus. Several minutes passed before he felt able to stand, and his eyes went to Anya. She rose unsteadily to her feet, her face reflecting Cinder's sorrow.

"I'm going to miss her," Cinder said, blinking back unexpected tears. What was it about Aranya that put him at such ease? There was a familiarity about her, something deeper than the few meager conversations they'd shared.

"I wonder why she likes us so much?"

"She loves us," Cinder corrected, reminding her of Mother Ashoka's last statement to them.

"Right. I don't know what we've done to earn it, but it's also probably why she invited us to the *shraddha* for Holifer."

Cinder feigned puzzlement. "I can understand why she'd love me— I'm adorable—but what about you?"

Anya shoved him, chuckling lightly. "Here we are, finally past our arguments, and you say something like that. And calling yourself adorable might be the most ridiculous thing you've ever said." She waited a beat. "And you've said plenty of ridiculous things."

Cinder rolled with the push, disregarding Anya's words while pretending to muse over his earlier question. "Maybe she loves you because you remind her of a well-mannered stray she picked up somewhere."

"No. That would be you. You're the stray. You're the one who wandered into Swift Sword, the Third Directorate, and my life."

It was actually a good point, and Cinder was momentarily silenced. "So, am I a well-mannered stray?"

Anya viewed him sidelong. "You've behaved well enough."

They exited the area under Mahamatha, walking into sunshine and the peaceful quiet of the Grove. Close at hand, the yakshins were focused on their tasks, and past them were the holders, training. But where were the Shokans? Cinder searched about, not seeing them. He mentally shrugged. They were around somewhere, probably enjoying the beautiful weather.

"Even though we just left Mother Ashoka, you seem happier than before," Anya noted.

On the reminder of Mahamatha, a pang of regret once again stabbed at Cinder's heart, but he also realized that Anya was right. He was happy—content, actually—the first time he could honestly say so in many months, probably since Mahadev. And it was mostly because he could look at Anya without any regret. They had fallen in love based on a mistake, but what if he'd never stopped loving her?

It felt right to draw Anya toward him and kiss her cheek. "I am happy, and I'm also sorry."

Rather than pull away, which he feared she might do, Anya looped her arms around his neck and gazed at him. "What are you sorry about? About all the times you yelled at me? Shouted at me? Made me want to cry?"

She said the words in a light tone, but Cinder could hear the darkness and hurt underneath. "For all the pain I gave you."

"You wouldn't have done any of it if it wasn't for Rabisu."

"But it was still my words and deeds."

"It was my words and deeds as well," she said, gently stroking his face. "I'm also sorry for what I said and did. Truly."

The words were heartfelt, and Cinder found himself unable to meet her gaze. He sighted the ground, chuckling softly. "I feel like my head keeps getting jerked about."

"What do you mean?"

"When we arrived at Char, I liked you. I already thought of you as a friend. Wanted to think of you as more than a friend."

"And now? You don't think of me as a friend?"

There was a teasing note in her voice, and Cinder sped his explanation. "I liked you, but I was afraid of you, too. We argued so much."

"Not after Flatiron," Anya reminded him. "We got along better after that."

She was right, and Cinder had long since recognized it. "I wish I had been braver," he whispered. "I wish I'd told you how I was starting to feel before we reached Char. I wish—"

She put a finger to his lips. "You weren't the only one who was confused. I didn't know what to feel about you either." She tilted her head as if in consideration. "No. That's not right. I knew what I felt. And I also wish I had the courage to tell you the truth."

Cinder blinked, not sure what to say. He knew what he felt for Anya, but was she saying she felt the same way about him?

"Cinder." Anya had her head tilted, and as if she had come to a decision, she cupped the side of his face and pulled him close, kissing him. For a moment, shock held him stiff. He didn't know what was happening…

But then understanding and emotion bloomed, a warmth for Anya flooded his being. He kissed her back, enfolding her in his arms, never wanting to let her go. He held her tighter when her body rose, her chest pressing into his. All he knew was the feel of her, the touch of her soft lips.

In the end, it was she who released him. "Love is the finest of things," Anya said, sounding breathless as she stared him in the eyes. "Never forget it. And never forget that I love you."

"You still love me?" Stunned amazement and delight filled Cinder's mind. He hadn't dared hope that she might feel the same as he.

"I do," she replied, breaking away from him and staring off into the distance. She clutched herself, shivering. "Devesh save me, but I do."

Cinder tipped her head, making her meet his gaze, seeing the fear-filled question lurking in her eyes. "I love you, too."

Her relief and beaming smile could have been the sun and the moon and the stars… Again, she looped her arms around his neck. "We're together again. Shet won't have a chance."

"Oh my," Sadana said, entering their privacy. She wore a knowing grin, one that was only a shade less than a leer. "I guess everything went well. Cinder is healed. Mother Ashoka spoke to both of you." Now the smile did become a leer. "And if you two aren't careful, who knows what might happen eleven months from now."

Rather than blush in embarrassment, Cinder frowned in confusion. "What's so special about eleven months?"

"It's how long an elven pregnancy lasts," Anya answered.

After the gentle interlude at Shalla Valley, Cinder and Anya had been politely but firmly asked to depart, and the reason was Rabisu. The rakshasa was no longer shrouded and bound within Anya, and even the *null pocket* didn't suffice in containing Rabisu's polluting aura, which threatened Shalla Vale's harmony and security. And all this was further stressed by the Shokans.

Cinder and Anya had to make haste and depart.

In fact, it was only because of the once-wraiths defending Shalla's eastern entrance that the Shokans could remain in the vale at all without compromising Mother Ashoka's ability to keep the borders secure.

The knowledge of how the once-wraiths were maintaining the valley's safety gave Cinder heart. There were so many others upon whom he and Anya could ask for help. They weren't battling Shet on their own. Plus, it seemed as if Fastness' plan to redeem the wraiths was succeeding. The holders trusted Selin and the others, which was as strong a recommendation as they could have expected to receive.

Hopefully, the wraiths could also help the Shokans. After another week or so of extra training with the holders, Cinder's brothers would leave Shalla Valley and head off to see Fastness, who would continue their tutelage, teaching them the basics of conducting *Jivatma*. The world needed them to be stronger. Everyone needed to be stronger.

Naraka's armies were increasing daily, and worse, an anchor line to the new Realms of the Rakshasas had been established. Mother Ashoka had learned of it, stating that Shet would likely start recruiting from their denizens. The rakshasas would be the so-called god's most powerful allies, barely under his control. In fact, without Shet, they would murder everyone they could. Rakshasas were similar to *aether*-cursed beasts in that they grew stronger with every kill they made and every bit of *lorethasra* they stole.

That made it even more imperative for the Shokans to learn what was required from the wraiths, especially since Cinder and Anya wouldn't be able to help them, not when they were off trying to acquire the Orb of Regret, which Mother Ashoka informed them was in the Webbed Kingdom, confirming Manifold's information.

Who knew how long that would take? And with their mounts still in Char, they'd first have to walk most of the way back to Naraka. It was why a week after leaving Mahamatha, they were still afoot, walking clear of Shalla Valley. They had taken the eastern entrance and currently traveled a wide trail. Below, a broad valley, alive with the verdant colors of summer, was spread out before them while beyond it and in every other direction, the Dagger Mountains soared. A rough wind swirled, and Cinder did his best to disregard the cold after Shalla's warmth.

Just then, he came to an abrupt halt. He'd sensed something.

"*Roar,*" Brilliance said, hopping off an overlooking rise and onto the trail they followed.

With her was Kela, the dog. "*Whoof. I mean growl and growl.*" His tail gave a hesitant wag. "*Are you afraid?*"

Cinder dropped his rucksack, laughing. "What are you two doing?"

Brilliance cocked her head. "*You get so mad when we try to scare you. I thought maybe I could make you laugh. Did it work?*"

"What do you think?" Cinder asked, still laughing. He rubbed the giant snowtiger's forehead, and she leaned into his hand, eyes slitting. A recollection had him scratch her chin, and she lifted her head, rumbling in pleasure.

Meanwhile, Kela was on his back, tongue lolling and tail wagging as Anya energetically rubbed his belly.

"*That's enough,*" Brilliance said, righting herself. "*How long are you staying? Fastness and I sensed you coming earlier in the day.*"

Something like that from Fastness, Cinder could understand. They had been bonded, Yavana stallion and rider. But what about Brilliance? He asked.

"*We've been connected ever since I almost killed you,*" Brilliance said. "*Your blood bonded us.*" She shuddered. "*And it's a good thing I didn't kill you. Just stealing the lorethasra from your parents nearly killed me. It*" *was almost too much."*

"But you don't actually regret killing them, do you?"

Her response was a puzzled tilt of her head, which didn't surprise Cinder. Brilliance might have developed some semblance of empathy, but in the end, she was mostly still a predator. Would she ever become something greater?

Anya spoke. "In answer to your question, we're only passing through," she said to Brilliance.

"A good thing," Brilliance said. *"I was thinking of hunting you."* She quickly ducked her head. *"I was just joking."*

Cinder's gaze hardened. "No, you weren't. You were being serious."

Brilliance's ears wilted. *"I like to hunt,"* she said in a whining tone.

"I'm sure you do but you don't hunt friends."

Her ears perked. *"I'm your friend?"*

Cinder sighed. "Talk to her," he said to Anya. "Let me say hello to Kela."

"For a cat, you are remarkably dense," Cinder heard Anya say to Brilliance. "Some might even say you're stupid."

He bent then, staring Kela in the eyes. "And what have you learned while we've been gone?"

"That Brilliance is remarkably dense?"

"Traitor!" Brilliance snapped.

Cinder laughed.

"I see the children are playing again," Fastness noted, his clip-clopping hooves heralding his arrival. He crested a rise, and with him were two wraiths—a big man who might have been a farmer—and based on her build and gait, a woman who knew how to fight. Both looked to have originally been from Rakesh.

They were vaguely familiar, but Cinder didn't immediately recognize them. An instant later, he knew whom he faced: the wraiths who had almost killed him and Anya—twice.

He stood, setting a Flame in his dominant hand. The world slowed, and his muscles bunched. A reticle filled his vision, and he was ready to unleash a barrage of Fireballs.

The wraiths halted, but otherwise did nothing to defend themselves.

"This is Residar and Brissianna," Fastness said. *"And they aren't the people who once tried to kill us."*

"I am sorry for what we nearly did," the man, Residar, said. "Zahhacks had just killed my family. My wife and children. I wasn't thinking right."

"Neither of us were," Brissianna said. "Our minds were... cloaked. We thought we weren't worth anything other than to commit darkness and evil."

Cinder let go of the reticle, but he didn't ease off his state of readiness. Fastness had vouched for these two, but he wasn't yet ready to give them his full trust, especially since every memory of Residar and Brissianna had been filled with mortal danger.

But as he studied the wraiths, he realized they weren't the same beings as before. Just like Selin Heron, their eyes had recovered a more human appearance, with dark irises in place of the pure whites. And right now those eyes viewed him with curiosity and nervousness.

Anya moved to stand beside him. "I'm Anya Aruyen," she said, greeting Residar and Brissianna. Both once-wraiths shook her proffered hand.

Cinder stepped forward as well, overcoming the last of his reserve. "I'm Cinder Shade."

Residar shook his hand, smiling. "We know who you are," he said. "Both of you. Your cat won't stop talking about you."

"I'm not his cat. He's my boy," Brilliance declared.

"He's not a boy," Kela said. *"He's a man."* He tilted his head. *"Are you sure you can see correctly?"*

"Quiet," Brilliance hissed.

Cinder stared at the snowtiger and dog, bemused by their behavior. "Are they always like this?"

"This is them on their best behavior," Brissianna said. "Every one of their conversations begins and ends with an argument."

Residar nodded. "And then Brilliance usually apologizes, tells an outlandish lie, and it starts all over again."

"Why don't you take Brilliance and Kela elsewhere," Fastness suggested to Residar and Brissianna.

"It was good to meet the two of you," Brissianna said. "And I really am sorry we tried to kill you."

Residar echoed her words, which earned a laugh from Anya. "That may be the strangest apology I've ever heard," she said.

Brissianna chuckled ruefully. "And how much stranger is it for a wraith to be redeemed?"

"Not strange so much as wonderful," Cinder said to her before addressing Fastness. "This is one of the greatest things you've ever done. And I should know." He tapped the side of his head. "Shokan's memories, remember?"

The wraiths and Kela made to move on, but Brilliance paused. *"Can I talk to you afterward, Shokan?"* she asked.

Cinder nodded. "Before we leave, I'll find you."

Fastness waited until the other four had left. *"You've accepted Shokan's name as your own? I thought that's not who you were?"*

Cinder shrugged. "It's not, but I'm also the closest this world will have to him. If that is what people need me to be, then I accept."

Fastness glanced from him to Anya. *"Something is different about the two of you. What is it?"*

Anya stepped close to Cinder, giving him a quick wink.

He grinned, knowing enough to play along with whatever game she had in mind.

She put her arms around his waist, gazing lovingly into his eyes. "My sweet *priya*, should we tell him now or after the baby is born?"

Fastness whinnied in shock. *"What!"*

Training against the holders had done the Shokans a world of good, and Bones was grateful for the work. His unit had tightened up so many deficiencies that had crept into their techniques.

And the holders were willing to help them out even more. Four of them had been dispatched to fetch the mounts and equipment the Shokans had left behind at Char, and with them had gone a visiting troll and a yakshin. The combination of various woven should see them easily able to handle any troubles they might encounter on their journey.

Hopefully, the trip shouldn't take too long either. According to Sadana, the limits of Shalla Valley could be bent outward toward Swift Sword, shortening the traveling distance to a bit more than several weeks. Add in pausing to pass on any messages to Lisandre and Captain Dorr at Fort Carmine, travel to and from Char and back to the Vale... All told, Bone's men should be fully kitted in a couple or three months, including Byerley, who Estin couldn't stop whining about.

And while they were waiting, the Shokans wouldn't be lazing away. They'd set to train with a different set of warriors, ones that were supposedly as good as the holders. At least that's what Cinder and Anya had said before they'd left the vale. Then again, they'd also said that the ones to train them would be Fastness and a group of wraiths.

Bones mentally snorted. The Shokans were to be trained by a horse and creatures the entire world counted as evil. It sounded ridiculous, but then again, Fastness wasn't just a horse, and Cinder and Anya insisted the wraiths were redeemed. If anyone would know, it would be those two. They'd handed out their instructions a week ago and left shortly thereafter.

Bones only wished he and the Shokans could have spoken to Cinder and Anya some more. There was still so much to say, so much to learn.

"You really think some fucking wraiths are waiting to teach us?" Mirk asked as the Shokans walked out of Shalla Vale.

"Quiet," Mohal hissed from where he strode ahead of their column. "We're being watched."

"Where?" Bones asked even as swords were loosened in their scabbards.

Everyone peered about, searching for movement.

"Dead ahead." Mohal indicated with his chin to a place where their downward sloping trail narrowed into a channel between two stony rises.

"He's right," Riyne said. Even more than Mohal, he was their best scout. "*Aether*-cursed. I don't see them, but that's the feeling I get. To the right side of those rises."

"Shit." A wish for spears flickered across Bones' thoughts, but his unit didn't have any, and there was no use wanting for them now. "Bows out." He split his group, signaling for Mohal, Ishmay, Mirk, Sash, and Gorant to climb a rocky incline and flank the *aether*-cursed.

The rest of the unit edged forward. As they did, Bones wished he had the senses of an elf. He wished it for every member of the Shokans. And maybe one day they'd have it.

"There's two of them," Riyne whispered.

The Shokans prepared to receive the enemy.

A white stallion bugled, rushing up the slope. "*Stop! Don't hurt the idiots.*"

Fastness?

Bones recognized Cinder's Yavana, but even after being told who he was actually supposed to be, he had trouble matching the pesky stallion—a greater glutton for apples, he'd never met—with the mythical Sapient Dormant.

Still, that's who Cinder insisted the stallion really was.

Bones whistled sharply, signaling for the flanking team to stand down and hold position. In the meantime, he waited on Fastness, who had halted in the middle of the narrowed passage.

"What's he doing?" Depth asked, coming up next to Bones.

"*Come out, you idiots,*" Fastness ordered, directing his words toward the heights. "*And be quick about it!*" He stomped a hoof, looking angry.

Bones shook his head. "No idea," he said in answer to Depth. "But what I want to know is how the hell we can hear what he's saying?"

Just then, slinking down the slope, came a massive snowtiger and a dog of nearly equal size, both with the glowing white eyes of an *aether*-cursed. The cat he recognized from the battle during his Autumn Trial and also because Cinder had described the beast. She'd killed his parents but was somehow... maybe tame? He wasn't sure, but from his end, she was big and dangerous.

As for the dog, Cinder had told them about him, too. He didn't look like much. Sure, he was large, but describing him as ugly was being kind. The dog might as well have been an oversized goblin with his ganky teeth and a right leg that flopped but didn't cause him to limp.

Still, ugly or not, neither beast seemed like they'd be easy to put down.

And Bones didn't know for sure, but it seemed like both creatures were scared of Fastness—embarrassed, too. The stallion looked to be berating them, going so far as to nip the cat in the hind end, eliciting a yowl.

"Apologize," Fastness said to the snowtiger and the dog.

The *aether*-cursed animals crept forward, the dog seemingly humiliated, but the cat clearly pissed. Bones gave a signal, and everyone got their bows ready.

"That's close enough," he called out once the *aether*-cursed were about twenty yards away. He had no idea if the beasts could understand him, but Cinder had said they could. "Name yourselves and state your business."

The cat drew herself up, proud as a queen. *"I am Brilliance. I would not have killed you. Cinder won't allow it. But scaring you would have been fun. Fastness says it wouldn't, and I'm sorry you wouldn't have understood the joke."*

Beyond the shock of hearing the *aether*-cursed actually speak in response, the apology was sorely lacking.

"I'm sorry, too," the dog said, tail pulling out from between his legs as he offered a tentative wag. *"I told you this was a bad idea,"* he added, apparently speaking to the cat, since she was the one who replied.

"Predators need to practice their hunting."

"I thought we were supposed to find aether-*cursed and teach them to serve."*

"We will, but until we actually find one, we should keep our claws and teeth sharp. Cinder would tell us to train."

"That doesn't sound right."

Bones shared a wide-eyed look with Estin, who merely shrugged.

What the hell were those animals going on about?

An instant later, two more individuals approached—humans, likely. Nevertheless, the Shokans remained alert.

"We're in trouble," Estin hissed. He sourced *lorethasra,* and Elements pooled in his hands: sulfurous Fire, rustling Earth, and hissing Air.

"What is it?" Bones couldn't see anything off about the two people.

"Wraiths," Estin said. "The same ones who nearly killed me and Cinder during our Secondary Trial."

Bones could see it now. The creatures had dark brown eyes, but they were covered in a haze of white, just like an *aether*-cursed. "Bows up! Target the wraiths!" While he recalled Cinder's instructions about these supposedly redeemed wraiths, he wasn't planning on taking any chances.

"You don't need to target anyone," Fastness said.

The female wraith appeared puzzled. She paced forward, and the groaning of drawn bows met her march. She didn't seem to care. On she came, and Bones realized she was staring at him. He also realized there was a familiarity to her gait, to her features. Someone he'd never thought to ever see again.

His face went slack. It couldn't be. She was dead.

And yet, here she was, standing fifty feet away.

"Bones?" she said in a trembling voice full of hope.

A single word and it felt like the world was crashing down. Memories coursed through him; of his childhood and this woman, his sister, who'd been like a mother. "Briss?"

Her face broke into a smile, and she rushed toward him. Bones went to her as well, hugging her, not believing Brissianna was alive. He had a thousand questions. More than a thousand.

Brissianna leaned away, staring up at him. "You've grown," she said with a laugh.

"Who is this?" Estin asked, arriving then.

"This is my sister," Bones answered.

"Your sister is a wraith?" Sash asked. "No wonder sisters are off limits."

25

"**B**e careful," Anya reminded Cinder, momentarily holding him back. She flicked a nervous expression. "I guess we'll find out now if these new braids will actually work."

"They'll work," Cinder said, knowing she needed to hear him say so. Anya trusted Mahamatha, but right now, just before entering the serpent's lair of Naraka, she was feeling the same anxiety that he was.

Just like their old braids, the new ones kept the world from recognizing them, but there was also this second one. This one was different. This one brought falsehoods to the forefront of their minds; untruths that—while the weaves were active—Cinder and Anya wouldn't know to be wrong. They would believe them, totally and utterly, and according to Mahamatha, the odd deception was a necessary deceit because with every Orb destroyed, Shet's Talent at detecting lies—spoken or by omission—would continue to improve.

As a result, neither Cinder nor Anya could approach Shet with their true motives in mind. They had to truly believe that Cinder had been born a cripple. That he'd been discovered to have an ability to bond metal. That humans were enslaved by the Yaksha elves. And that he'd been abused by them during his training at the Third Directorate.

All of those lies, so well-known by Shet at this point, would be the easiest means by which to hide their truths—truths that would see them dead if the god ever sensed them.

Easy enough, but Cinder knew the real reason for Anya's concern. The braid was untested, and he'd be taking the greater risk by standing directly in front of Shet.

Anya ran fingers through his hair, resting her forehead against his, but saying nothing. A quick kiss on the lips, and she stepped back. "Ready?"

"Let's get this done."

They activated their braids, and a watery sensation settled over Cinder's thoughts. He could have fought it, but he let it find purchase. His thoughts quickly reordered, a vertiginous sensation. And when he next viewed Anya, it was in dispassion.

"It's time to call her," he said, his deadpan voice reflecting his lack of emotion.

They stepped out from where they'd been hidden and Blended, directly onto the plains of Darand's Gap. Before them towered Mount Kirindor, the Piercing Heart, and hunched upon its slopes was Shet's black palace of Naraka.

Anya retrieved the *divasvapna*, speaking into it. A few moments of conversation, and shortly thereafter, an anchor line split the world with Liline towering over them.

"You have the Orb of Undying Light?" she demanded.

Cinder drew it forth in answer.

Liline threw her head back and laughed. "Will you tell me how you escaped the island?"

"We went into the Spire of the Saints," Cinder said, "fought the rakishis, and ran out before they could catch us."

"And the rishis?"

"There was only one," Anya lied. "We took her unawares, and the rest was easy. A boat in the harbor, and we were free."

"And your swift journey back to Naraka? You've discovered how to use the Gates?" Liline glanced around. "Or did you walk all the way here?"

"Or maybe we've learned to create our own anchor lines," Cinder offered, remaining fearless in the face of Liline's sudden scowl.

"If you had figured out the means to create your own anchor lines, then why call me?" the Titan asked.

Cinder didn't bother responding. Let Liline think what she wanted. But the less she and Shet actually knew, the better.

Liline shrugged. "Prepare to deliver the Orb." She turned about, gesturing for them to step upon the still-open anchor line.

Cinder tethered to it, quicker than before. So did Anya, and an instant later, they were in the same outdoor alcove as usual. They paced beyond its bounds, turned a corner, and exited onto the broad courtyard that led to where Shet sat atop his throne. The tawny dragon remained slumbering at the foot of his dais.

"Wait here until he calls for you," Liline said. "The Lord has a visitor." With that, she strode away, leaving them alone.

Cinder peered forward to where a man stood before Shet while the self-proclaimed god listened in apparent boredom, twirling a loosely gripped rune-marked black spear.

But it was the man who captured Cinder's attention. He'd seen him before. A powerfully built individual with dark hair and eyes, gripping a white spear with white knuckles. His square-cut jaw was clenched tight, but to Cinder, rather than indicating anger, the expression indicated fear. And based on the dark amusement glimmering in Shet's good eye, he noticed it, too. Their voices carried, and Cinder was able to tease out the man's name: Adam Carpenter.

"Rakshasas," Anya hissed, alarm in her voice.

Cinder had already noticed, but nevertheless, he returned his attention to the courtyard. The zahhacks were arrayed as before. Farthest out were the scourskins, followed by the tattered-clothed ghouls, and then the elegantly arrayed vampires. But where were the unformed, ketus, goblins, and ajakavas? They were nowhere in evidence.

Not so the necrosed, who remained present although in lesser numbers than before. In addition, they were quiet in the face of the handful of figures standing closest to the throne.

Rakshasas, just like Anya had said. They stood nearly as tall as a Titan, black-winged like a bat and armored in dark chitin. Smoke intermittently drifted from their nostrils and the occasional fire flared around their horned heads. An overbite of fangs protruded from their jaws, and claws like daggers tipped their fingers.

Cinder viewed the rakshasas in curiosity rather than fear, which was for him a foreign feeling. If he'd ever experienced that emotion, he couldn't recall when it might have been. And the rakshasas certainly didn't inspire it. More, he wanted to test himself against them to learn if they were the equal of their legend.

He continued examining the rakshasas until Sture Mael entered the courtyard.

Heavily muscled, he only wore a kilt and a set of broadswords on his back. Pushing straight through the zahhacks, including the rakshasas, he halted next to Adam Carpenter. "The human wishes to speak with you," Sture stated. "Again."

"Our time is ended," Shet barked to Adam. "Leave us."

Adam bowed low, making ready to leave, his relief obvious.

However, Shet halted him. "Before you depart, tell me, how goes the construction of the firewagers? I told your Servitor how to build them when last he visited us."

"We work to create that which you taught us. It will not be long now."

Shet smiled, cunning and pleased. "That is good. Be off now."

Shet viewed Cinder Shade with distaste. There was something about the man he simply didn't like. Perhaps it was how bold and fearless he carried himself. The man never gave the slightest hint that he found Shet intimidating. Which just wouldn't do—not after the delicious terror of Adam Carpenter.

It wasn't that Shet enjoyed inspiring fear in others, but he expected it from those he didn't respect or considered significantly lesser than him. And although he respected Cinder Shade, the man was most definitely his lesser. After all, what kind of a fool would take up with an elf? Such weak creatures they were, and yet this man had been stupid enough to love one.

And she sometimes hated the man, which was the most ridiculous aspect of their relationship. Disgusting as well. Which was why he had Cinder Shade remain on bent knee for longer than usual. Shet leaned back on his white throne and considered how long to leave him there.

He finally relented when Sture shifted about in impatience. His general had other tasks to manage and resented the wasted time. Sture glowered at Cinder, leaning toward him in an aggressive posture since he certainly couldn't angle his discontent toward Shet.

Fine. In order to humor his oldest friend, Shet relented. "Rise."

Cinder stood smoothly, and when he faced Shet, not a tremble marred his inscrutable features. His expression and his eyes were as dead as a shark's, and he peered at Shet with an unflinching gaze.

Sture didn't like that. Neither did Shet.

"The human grows bold," Sture growled.

Cinder twisted his head, and now his gaze was locked on Sture. He even dared to offer an appraising glance before sniffing in dismissal.

Shet's brows went up in shock at the human's arrogance. Who was this man to have such confidence?

Sture was equally outraged, and a hand went to the hilt of one of his massive swords. He appeared ready to draw the blade and cut the human in twain. Upon seeing his reaction, Shet wanted to laugh. Sture looked so angry.

"Bold indeed," Sture growled. "Allow me to instruct him on the proper etiquette of humility."

The zahhacks, including the rakshasas, shifted closer, excited by the prospect of violence and blood. Shet wouldn't have minded seeing some of both, too—the day so far had been utterly dull—but alas, now wasn't the time to see Cinder's innards spilled.

Instead, he chuckled lightly, like he found the entire situation amusing. "Set aside your anger," he said to Sture before leaning forward. "What news do you bring, slave?" The last was said merely to see how Cinder would react. Would his icy demeanor finally crack?

It didn't. Cinder viewed him with that unflappable expression, and Shet found himself wondering what it would take to see an emotion upon the man's face.

"Anya and I have discovered another Orb," Cinder said.

This was unexpectedly good news, and Shet steepled his fingers. "Where is it? I don't sense it upon your being."

"The spiderkin possess it," Cinder declared. "They hold it deep in the heart of their mountains."

Shet grimaced. Good news turned bad. "I share the mountains with those vermin." And how he hated to admit that even as he gestured around him to the various peaks surrounding Naraka. "The Dagger Mountains are mine, but the spiderkin refuse to accept my authority. They will pay." He hissed the last, angry on account of Sheoboth's defiance. He would fillet her carcass and eat her liver… Assuming she had one.

"Only after we destroy all the Orbs," Cinder declared in a voice of utter certainty. "Until then, you can't move against them. You lack the power."

There was mocking Sture, and then there was mocking Shet. Death was the price for such an affront.

But even as Sture cried out in outrage, and the zahhacks made to rush closer, Shet considered the situation. He needed Cinder Shade and Anya Aruyen. They had obtained four Orbs thus far. All within a year when he had reckoned it might take a decade to gather so many.

As a result, he suppressed his anger, his features went as flat as Cinder's, and he raised a hand, calling for calm. Before slaying this man, he'd have an explanation for this insult. The scent of gardenias filled the air as he sourced *lorethasra*, using it to form a weave of Fire powerful enough to burn Cinder to his namesake cinders. "Be very careful of your next words," Shet said.

"I meant no insult," Cinder said, head cocked as if confused. "I merely speak truthful advice, doing as you instructed in your holy book." Shet inwardly gaped when the outrageous man dared quote from *Shet's Council*, his very own book of philosophy. "*Fear not to speak the truth. Your true friends will always hear your words.*"

Shet didn't reply at once, somewhat impressed. Cinder had memorized his teachings, and it spoke well of him. Perhaps he had greater worth than Shet had originally measured. He offered the man a crooked smile. "You think me a friend?"

"I think only a fool would ever lie to you," Cinder replied, careful in his word selection.

Another good response. "All too true." Shet let go of his braid. "How do you and your elf princess plan on obtaining the Orb?"

Cinder smiled. "I was trained to fight the spiderkin."

"Ah, yes," Shet said with an answering smile. "Your training in the Third Directorate." It was said the elves especially trained their warriors to battle the spiderkin, who year by year, steadily encroached on lands claimed by Yaksha Sithe. Which was patently absurd. An elf claiming any land was as nonsensical as a donkey claiming to be handsome.

Sture, however, didn't see the humor. He snorted in derision. "I know not why you require this human scum. I could accomplish the same as he in half the time. Let me serve in his place."

Shet wouldn't have minded doing exactly that, but the Orbs were beyond both his reach and that of his Titans. None of them could seek them out. It was part of the laws placed upon the globes by the cursed Indrun and Sachi.

Even while Shet considered the futility of sending Sture in place of Cinder, he realized the man hadn't responded. Instead, he simply stared at Shet, as if waiting for him to come to a conclusion that was obvious to them both.

Shet bristled, disliking anew the man's attitude. In that moment, he decided to end Cinder Shade when his usefulness was over. He didn't care if the man could recite *Shet's Council* backward and forward. His arrogance was unforgivable.

Until then…

Shet slowly shook his head at Sture's offer, not having to pretend regret. "I will not waste you when a worthless human can do the task." He rapped his steel-shod spear against the floor of the dais. "You will attend our needs and recover the Orb held by the spiderkin."

Cinder bowed low, but his eyes remained on Shet. "As you command."

Shet found the regard uncomfortable, and he glared at the man. "What about the Orb of Undying Light? Produce it."

Cinder did so, and for the first time since the man had entered his presence, Shet finally felt pleasure. He lifted the Orb off Cinder's hand and brought it to his own. With a flexion of his forearm along with *Jivatma* and *lorethasra*, the deed was done. He crushed the Orb to powdered light.

And immediately a weight lifted from his shoulders as the blue-and-green lightning that trapped his true power became that much thinner.

The dragon tried to stand, but with his thoughts fogged, the most he could manage was to shift about. Even a yawn was a challenge.

It was unacceptable, but there was also no breaking through to the light. The weave of the one who had bound him continued to hinder his mind, and sometimes it was so bad that he could barely remember his name.

But he did remember his human. She was foremost in his mind, and he hoped she would soon find him. If anyone could free him of his binding, it would be her.

Her mate, a powerful warrior, could probably manage it, too, but in the dragon's mind, his human was the better individual. She had to be since he had chosen her as his own particular person.

And how he missed her, desperately wishing he could recall her name. He missed her mate, too. Same with his sister. She also might be able to free him from his entrapment.

A man paced toward the one who held the dragon's mind in thrall. He had a familiar gait and appearance, but the dragon couldn't muster enough energy to search his memories. Instead, he simply observed the man through slitted eyes.

Impressions came quickly. The man was a warrior. He moved like one, with control and leashed power. Like a predator. No fear clouded his features, and when he bowed to Shet, the gesture was meaningless since the man demonstrated no sense of humility. It was clear he didn't think of the dragon's master as *his* master.

Seeing Shet tweaked like that caused the dragon to chuckle to himself. He liked the warrior. The man reminded him of a truth he desperately wished to remember, and although he struggled to draw it forth, the most he could accomplish was to formulate a single question: who was this person?

The scar-faced fool who served Shet stood close at hand, and he didn't like something the warrior said. His hand went to a sword, looking as furious as a tiger with its kill stolen by a crocodile.

But the warrior was a Kesarin. He easily stared the fool down, and the stalemate only broke when the master said something to them both.

It had the flavor of an order, and the warrior produced a familiar-appearing glowing globe from somewhere in his cloak. It floated from the man's hand and into the palm of the dragon's master. Seconds later, the globe was blown apart into shards of drifting light.

That seemed to please the warrior. He breathed easier, and so did Shet and the scar-faced fool. All three of them were relieved by the globe's destruction. But why? What had been so special about it?

The answer meandered to the very edge of the dragon's mind before scattering apart. He didn't know the reason for the orb's importance, but the failure didn't dishearten him. That had been the closest he'd come to breaking the wall separating who he was now and who he knew he should be.

The man spoke a little longer, and the dragon found himself wanting to go with the warrior. Even a few shared words might mean everything. What if the man knew the dragon's human? Or even his human's mate?

A bit more conversation followed, all of which sounded like meaningless noises. The dragon wished he could understand the words, but his ability to speak and understand speech had been erased like it had never existed.

But he could reckon emotions, and what he reckoned from the warrior even as he walked away was satisfaction. The man was pleased, and it wasn't from parting the wretched creatures around the master's throne like an orca through minnows. It was because he felt he'd come out ahead during the exchange with the master.

The dragon watched the man leave, wondering anew who he was. Did he know Aia? It was the one name the dragon could dredge from his recollection, that of his sister.

Shet rolled the *nomasra* ring on his right forefinger. Plain and unadorned, it was an alloy made of a bone-white metal and gold and was how he could protect himself from the Orbs of Peace. The seven Titans had received similar rings, stolen *nomasras* of unknown creation and likely thought lost by their dwarven forgers in their halls of stone.

But they were of limited utility: Only three uses for Shet's master ring and two for each of the rings gifted to the Titans. And now the *nomasras* were nearly empty. Repopulating the zahhacks and rebuilding Naraka to Garad's exacting specifications had required all their efforts. All their rings now contained only a single charge, their best defense against the Sisters if those three ever came against them in force.

"I don't like that man," Sture observed.

Shet, drawn from his thoughts, stared to where Cinder Shade departed the outdoor throne hall. The zahhacks rustled around the man, but for whatever reason, they gave him a wide berth even while promising death and torment.

"He is necessary," Shet said, knowing the real reason for Sture's antipathy. Possibly because of how Cinder walked, like his sword wasn't a weapon so much as an extension of himself, Shet's general wasn't sure he could take the human.

Shokan used to have the same bearing, but what good had it done him? Shet had crushed the fool. Shet's mastery of the Beautiful Art—the melding of *Jivatma* and *lorethasra*—had allowed him to destroy his foe. He mentally sneered. The so-called Lord of the Sword should have spent more time learning the greater skills instead of wasting so much effort twirling his pointy bit of steel. If he had, maybe he and his wife wouldn't have died so easily.

Shet smiled to himself. But dead was dead, and there was no such thing as resurrection except in the fables.

"Our allies in Surent Crèche, the Baptisers, are gaining ground," Sture said. "They might soon be able to grant us access to their inner cities."

Shet's attention returned to his general. "And Surent will then fall." It was a good first step. The dwarves were an abomination. Peace wasn't how the Realms were ordered. They were ordered through the mailed fist of those who should rule. "And Yaksha?"

"We've made overtures, but they've yet to bear fruit," Sture replied. "I have hope, though. Their arrogance will be their undoing."

Of that, Shet had no doubt. The elves had always been an overly proud race, and their arrogance had only increased since the Holy War of Liberation. In many ways, that conceit had been justified. Prior to the destruction of any of the Orbs of Peace, Shet would have found it hard to overcome Yaksha Sithe.

But now, with four of the Orbs gone, he could manage the feat. Certainly, it would come at great personal cost, but he was also gathering other options. For instance, he'd sent a call out into the Web of Worlds, and it had been heard. A plucked string, penetrating time, space, and Realms. Something only an individual with access to six Chakras could manage.

The sound had rung out, echoing to Earth, his original home, where even now, the powerful unformed Primes of that Realm were rallying, making ready to travel to Sinskrill. And in unexpected luck, Sapient Dormant had also answered. But this was a Sapient who remained a loyal necrosed. Shet couldn't yet communicate directly with the Overward, but soon enough, he'd manage it.

A loyal Sapient would be invaluable, and Shet wondered which other necrosed had survived the millennia. They'd be powerful. They'd have to be, living as long as they had, far deadlier than the other necrosed who currently populated the Drakar.

Still, Shet couldn't help but wonder why and how it was that another version of Sapient Dormant had erupted into Seminal three thousand years ago as a Mythaspuri. What had Indrun and Sachi promised to seduce him from Shet's side? What inducements to convince the once-loyal creature to take up arms against his true master in the Holy War of Liberation?

Shet had never learned, but as to *how* a different version of Sapient could have existed in Seminal's past, that was an easier explanation. The various Realms of reality didn't necessarily share the same boundaries of time and space. Instead, each existed separate and apart from the others, thus allowing a person to travel from one Realm to another and then return to their original one but at a completely different place and time. In fact, they could return years, decades, or even centuries before their birth.

Of course, doing so meant that same individual had also been foolish enough to fall off an anchor line, which was utterly dangerous. Shet knew no one who had survived such a misadventure... no one but perhaps Sapient Dormant and Manifold Fulsom.

"What about the *lorethasra* of this world?" Sture asked, interrupting Shet's deliberations.

"What about it?"

"Does it still drain to Earth?"

Shet nodded. "It's what I warned the people of this foolish world of during the Holy War. If the anchor line to Earth isn't severed, Seminal will eventually wither and die. I won't allow it. We will be the ones to save them."

"We will, but the world won't care. The majority of the races will continue to see us as villains when they should be lauding us as heroes."

Shet chuckled. "Oh, they'll be lauding us as heroes. By then we'll have crushed them—and they'll have no option but to praise us."

"I like the sound of that," Sture said with a predatory smile. His humor slowly departed, and a pensive expression stole across his face. "I still don't like that human."

Shet scowled. This again. "You're only angry because he dares stare you in the eyes."

"He dares stare you in the eyes as well. He thinks he's your equal."

"You stare me in the eye," Shet reminded his general.

"That's because we've fought together, bled together, nearly died together. Same with the other Titans. We've earned the right to stand at your side. But none of us are daft enough to believe ourselves your equal."

Shet grunted. Sture's statement was only right and proper. "I will make you this promise, then. When the seventh Orb is destroyed, I give you free rein to kill Cinder Shade. Will that make you happy? I wanted to kill him myself."

Sture laughed. "If you planned on doing him in on your own, who am I to deprive you of your pleasure?"

"In this, I can be generous," Shet said with an answering smile. "There are plenty of enemies whom I wish to personally end. Cinder Shade can be yours. I'll happily slay the Sisters."

"Those three women should never have been birthed," Sture said.

His words reminded Shet of another issue he wanted to see settled. "Liline and Rence... I see them talking all the time. What do you know of this?"

Sture shrugged. "They're close. They think of themselves as sisters."

"Sisters." Shet grimaced. "I don't like that notion. See them separated. And what of the Sunsets and their supposed military genius and emperor?"

"Genka Devesth," Sture provided.

Shet nodded. "Once we have the eastern nations under our heel, we'll want to begin overtures with him. Make him an offer he can't refuse."

26

No longer babbling their curses at him, the zahhacks finally left Cinder in peace, but even had they kept on with their comments, it would have made no impact on him. In truth, he found their behavior amusing. It was the same with the necrosed and rakshasas.

Even more humorous had been Sture Mael's threatening posture. The Titan had acted like a savage dog straining at his leash, and while Sture was more than twice Cinder's height, in the end, he wouldn't have posed much of a challenge. Not when Shokan on his own had very nearly defeated all the Titans *and* Shet. And the only reason he hadn't succeeded in his victory was because of a mix of hubris and overwhelming grief, specifically, the Blessed One had believed that Shet had killed Sira.

It was largely true, but Sira had also lived long enough to pass her memories on to Anya, and this time, matters would be different. This time, as soon as Shet closed off Zahhack's emergence into Seminal, Cinder planned on putting a final end to the false god and his Titans. And afterward, he could deal with the weave that altered who he was as a person.

He knew of its presence, and although he didn't like it weighing on his mind, it was necessary.

For now.

However, it did raise the question he and Anya had discussed in Mahadev. Were they really the same people when their memories were distorted? Or to take it to an even more extreme example, what about now? When it wasn't just his memories that were altered, but his emotions? How could he say that this aspect of himself wasn't actually the truest one? Why believe that some other version that might feel differently about Anya—right now he considered her an ally but not a friend—was the correct one? Why not who he was in this moment? Wasn't he worthy of existing?

The possibilities led to another question: Why ever let go of the braid? Maybe he was already the best version of himself.

Cinder's thoughts continued circling in this fashion, leaving him ever more certain that he should never give away his purpose and his persona as he and Anya paced through the halls of Naraka. She had a question on her mind but was wise enough to keep it to herself until they were in a place where they could converse—their quarters within Shet's palace.

Their boots clicked off the black marble, but otherwise, the corridor was eerily quiet. It was also cold and chilly—their breaths plumed—and with no one else about, the dark hallway had the air of a mausoleum. Indeed, the patches of bright sunlight peering through the widely scattered windows did little to relieve the gloom.

Minutes later, he and Anya reached their quarters, and she looked ready to discuss what had happened at Shet's outdoor courtyard, but Cinder remained distracted by the idea of who he really was as a person.

He was finally drawn out of his thoughts by the wafting of Anya's mountain-fresh stream of *lorethasra*. She had formed a bubble of Air around them, a distorting braid that should keep anyone from hearing their conversation or even reading their lips.

"What happened during the meeting?" Anya asked, a burr of annoyance in her voice.

Reluctantly, Cinder set aside his ponderings on the meaning of self, but prior to answering, he cast his senses about. He hadn't forgotten the eavesdropping braid in Estin's rooms. It would make sense for Shet to have something similar in place here.

"Are you looking for a weave to let Shet listen?" Anya asked. "There is one, but it can't penetrate my braid of Air."

A disquieted frown creased Cinder's brow. How had she made that determination so much quicker than he? Had he been so preoccupied with his thoughts that he'd grown unaware of his surroundings?

"Because my braid interacted with the one already here," Anya replied, guessing at his thoughts like she could, smirking with a smug attitude. "I knew of it as soon as I created my weave."

Cinder grunted in reply, glad for the explanation.

"Now, what happened?" Anya asked. She held up a hand before he could respond. "Wait." Her eyes flashed white as an *aether*-cursed beast or a wraith. An instant later, they cleared, resuming their normal brilliant green. "That's better," she said, wearing a warm, expectant smile.

Cinder stared at her, unsure what she wanted.

Her smile faded. "Let go of your braid."

He continued to stare at her, the questions he'd asked of himself reverberating in his mind. Why should he? Wouldn't doing so be a form of suicide? Why wasn't who he was currently good enough? Worthy of life?

Anya took his hands, gazing into his eyes. "It will be clear if you let go of the braid." She spoke softly, as if he was a frightened colt.

But fear had never touched him. At least, not in this version of himself. In fact, he realized that he could hardly contain any emotions. Satisfaction and amusement, but not true joy. Worry and mild concern, but not fear. Affection but not love.

"Please."

Anya's plea sparked a truth. In his current state, Cinder was most certainly different, especially with his changed emotions. And while this version of him might deserve to live, so did that richer, fuller aspect of himself. And it was that person who Anya needed; not this truncated identity. Viewing her, Cinder couldn't maintain himself, didn't even want to. Even if he lacked much of his emotional range, he couldn't see himself hurting Anya. It just wasn't in him.

Cinder let the braid dissolve… and a buzzing sensation rippled across his thoughts. He had no defense as it swept across his mind, re-establishing his thoughts and patterns of thinking. Banished memories as well as emotions were restored. When he next opened his eyes, he viewed Anya with a glad smile made even happier when her worried expression transformed to one of relief.

"It's good to see you again," he said, drawing her close.

"It's good to see you, too," Anya said, her voice muffled against his shoulder. She pulled away from him, cupping his face, staring into his eyes. "What happened?"

She wasn't talking about the discussion with Shet, but about why he hadn't immediately let go of his braid at the same time that she had.

How to explain?

Cinder decided on the truth. "Do you remember when we spoke in Mahadev? About whether we're the same people if our memories are altered?"

"We've had that discussion in other places, too, but yes, I remember. And I said I didn't think we were."

"And I didn't take your worries seriously enough," Cinder admitted. "We aren't the same, and if you add in the change in emotions, it's even more apparent." He chuckled ruefully. "The version of myself with the braid was thinking about those same ideas, and he didn't want to die."

Anya tilted her head in contemplation, eventually nodding understanding. "It must have been hard for him."

"You didn't have the same trouble?"

She shook her head. "I didn't like who I was with the braid. I couldn't wait to be rid of it."

This time it was Cinder who eyed Anya in contemplation.

"Your version is fearless, has flattened emotions, and recalls oddities," Anya explained. "But mine is bitter and angry." She grimaced. "I don't like her, and she doesn't like herself."

Cinder sighed. "So many convolutions to keep our memories of Shokan and Sira hidden from Shet."

"It'll be worth it when we succeed."

A tinkling of silver bells echoed briefly in Cinder's mind, causing him to recall Mahamatha. He smiled on thinking of her. When he and Anya succeeded in this Trial, Aranya would live, and so would her children, the Ashoka trees and yakshins.

"What happened with Shet?" Anya asked, recollecting him to her original question. He told her, and she frowned when he finished his account. "Tweaking Shet like that, Sture, too. You have to be smarter."

"It wasn't tweaking," Cinder said. "It was a distraction. I didn't want him to ever guess whose memories I have inside of me. You've never had to stand so close to him. He doesn't even see you as a person. But he does me. And me, he's always studying. I didn't like what was in his eyes. It wasn't recognition, but there was consideration." He shrugged. "So I gave him something else to consider."

Anya crossed her arms, still frowning. "I still don't like it, but I also know it can't be helped." She sighed. "I'll be so happy when all this is over."

Cinder glanced over when Anya stirred in the bed. She had been asleep for hours—he hadn't realized how fatigued she must have been—and they were still in their quarters in Naraka, where they had chosen to remain following their long days of travel in journeying to Shet's palace. They needed to plan how to enter the Webbed Kingdom, and for that, Liline might be able to offer some insights. Cinder and Anya had already discussed the matter, including the help they would need from the Titan.

In the meantime, while waiting to meet with Liline, they had decided to get some rest. Cinder had taken an earlier nap with Anya watching over him, and right now he was simply repaying the favor.

However, his hours alone had left him with plenty of time to think, and not unexpectedly, his mind went back to the idea of who he was as a person. By now, he'd come to accept that he *was* a different individual whenever he wore that heavier braid, and the idea didn't sit well with him. In his mind, *he* was Cinder Shade—no one else—and there was only room for one version of him in all the Realms.

He exhaled heavily. What he wanted also didn't matter. Seminal required this strange sacrifice from him, where he destroyed himself whenever he was in Shet's palace, and he'd continue giving what was needed until he no longer had to.

Devesh, let the last Orb's destruction be the moment when I can just be myself.

He glanced at Anya when she stirred again, rolling over this time. Once more, she stirred, but on this occasion, she yawned mightily, and her eyes cracked open. She stretched her arms above her head and sat up. "How long was I asleep?" she asked, covering another yawn.

Cinder wove a bubble of Air. "A couple hours," he answered. "It's late afternoon. How are you feeling?"

"Rested. I had the loveliest dream. I dreamt we were camping in Shalla Valley." She exhaled heavily in disappointment. "And then I wake up, and here we are, still in Naraka." A soft shake of her head. "I wish we didn't have to stay here."

Cinder wished the same thing. "While you were asleep, a messenger stopped by. Liline is busy until tomorrow morning. She'll meet with us then."

Anya sat up. "Hopefully, she can do more than just transport us from one place to another."

Again, Cinder hoped the same thing, but there was no need to say so. He and Anya had discussed much of what they'd need from Liline earlier in the day, and in truth, without the Titan's aid, they might not be able to steal the Orb of Regret. It would be the most challenging one yet.

Not only was it held deep in the heart of an enemy nation, but one of the Three Sisters, Sheoboth, was its holder. Besides which, no one knew exactly where the Webbed Queen had the Orb secreted. And simply wandering around her kingdom wouldn't do. It could take years to find the Orb if they didn't have a better plan than that.

Hopefully, Liline would have a way of shortening their search, a way to guide them to Sheoboth's hiding spots. There were *nomasras* that should allow for it. Both Shokan's and Sira's memories stated it was the case, but their creation was beyond them. The blue-and-green lightning hindered their capabilities, but apparently, it didn't fully limit those of the Titans and Shet. Witness the rapid work that had gone into rebuilding Naraka.

In addition, a personal knowledge of the person in question, such as what Liline or one of the Titans might have with Sheoboth, the so-called Crooked Branch, often also helped.

"Do we have anything to eat?" Anya asked. Still wearing her armored clothing, she kicked over to the edge of the bed and tugged on her boots.

Cinder indicated a platter full of fruits, cheese, and dry bread. A goblin had dropped it off when Anya had fallen asleep. Cinder had already eaten a good chunk of it, but he'd also made sure to leave enough for Anya.

"Thank you," she said, digging in. She paused, holding an apple and staring at it in contemplation. "Where do you suppose Shet gets his fruit?"

Cinder shrugged, not knowing or caring. "Probably steals it. He steals everything else."

Anya glanced toward the ceiling, searching.

"I wove a bubble of Air when you woke," Cinder said. She must not have noticed, still half-asleep like she'd been.

"Sira remembers when Shet was married, how his son died and his world seemed to change."

"Sentin chose death," Cinder said. "He was ashamed of his father, of what he'd done to those who didn't have the gift of *Asra*."

"I know, but I wonder how Sentin's death changed Shet. The same with his wife leaving. Shet always used to go on and on about how

Shokan was wrong to create the dwarves, and Sira was wrong to create the elves. And when his son died and his wife left him, it only got worse. That's when their war with him started."

Cinder waited for her to elaborate, not sure where she was going with her observation.

"It makes me wonder is all," Anya said. "Just like we're different people when we wear those heavier braids, what might Shet have been like if his son hadn't died?"

Cinder didn't think it would have changed matters. "I think the heart of Shet's arrogance and cruelty was already baked into him by then. He wasn't some noble person whose grounding was through his spouse and children. He didn't become who he is because of their absence. He lost all sense of propriety and honor long before all that."

"And us? What would you do if I died?"

Cinder didn't want to think about it. A future without Anya wasn't a future worth contemplating. He'd rather be placed back on the wheel of life.

"Cinder?" Anya prodded.

He still didn't want to think about it. "What about you? What would you do?"

"I would accomplish whatever task you needed of me, and then I would set down my life's burdens."

"And hope for the providence of a sparrow's fall?" Cinder asked.

"You're asking if I think Devesh truly has a plan for even the smallest of us?" Anya pursed her lips. "It seems unlikely given the evil in the Realms. That it's only His hand on the rudder."

"But you'd like to believe it was true?" Cinder wanted to have the same faith.

Anya nodded. "Otherwise, what's the point? If what we do isn't seen or known, why bother? Why struggle so hard at all that we're doing—at all Shokan and Sira did—if we don't have a purpose beyond our own narrow lives?"

"We do have a purpose, though." It was actually a somewhat vague hope, and in truth, Cinder wasn't really sure.

"But the purpose is through the lens of our importance to Devesh."

Cinder chuckled. "This is quite the deep conversation to have here in Naraka. Not the likeliest place to do so, is it?"

Anya shrugged. "I don't know about that. What better place than a palace given over to evil?"

"Nice alliteration," Cinder said with a chuckle. "Just don't let our host ever hear you saying what you just did."

"As long as your braid of Air is working, he won't."

Just then, there came a gentle rapping on their chamber door.

Anya froze, likely fearful for a moment that Cinder's weave had been breached. Cinder momentarily shared her uncertainty, but he shook it off. No one could have pierced the braid without his awareness. Nonetheless, he ended the weave and went to answer the knocking.

Standing outside was a young goblin—his chitin still soft—and clothed in clean servants garb. He held a covered platter, trembling. "Your supper, masters," the small creature said, staring at the floor, a shiver going through him.

Cinder took the platter from the trembling goblin. "Thank you. You may go."

The creature ducked his head, bobbing it a few times before rushing off.

"Why were you so curt with him?" Anya asked.

Cinder placed the platter of food—from the drifting aromas, it was some kind of seared meat and vegetables—on a small table before re-braiding the weave of Air. "I wasn't. I was as kind as I could be where he would still recognize it. He was afraid I would abuse him."

"More types of people that need saving," Anya said, her voice soft and filled with sorrow. "Do you think the goblins have been abused for so long that they see themselves as being worthy of nothing better?"

"It's the culture Shet wanted for them," Cinder replied, sharing her empathy and sadness.

What had been done to the goblins—and all the zahhacks—was awful, especially since Cinder still recalled Shokan's creation of the dwarves. It had been one of the Blessed Ones' finest achievements, transforming the doglike Ur-Fels into one of the most peaceful people in all the Realms. He—"

"Ur-Fels," Cinder breathed in disbelief. "We fought Ur-Fels."

Anya frowned in confusion. "Sira and Shokan did, but we…" Awareness spread across her face. "The Orb of Eretria. The creatures that came after us. They were Ur-Fels."

A hollowness pitted Cinder's stomach. "Someone resurrected them, transformed dwarves back into the Ur-Fels." He paced the room, abruptly furious. "It has to be Shet. He's always hated the dwarves more than any other kind of woven. Either him or one of his fragging Titans."

"It wasn't him," Anya said, her eyes were wide with horror and alarm. "Shet had nothing to do with it."

Cinder shot his gaze to her. "Then who?"

"The dwarves. They did it to themselves. They're choosing to become Ur-Fels. They're choosing violence."

Cinder halted his pacing, chewing over her explanation. Why would the dwarves do such a thing? It was nonsensical.

But then he recalled the meeting in the Hall of Wisdoms in Surent. Sriovey's father, Stipe, all but running the crèche, when throughout all of history, dwarven society had been matrilineal. The violence inherent in that man…

The hollowness in Cinder's stomach widened, sickening him. Anya was right. The dwarves had somehow found a way to undo the gift Shokan had given them.

"It can't be all of them," he whispered, praying it was true.

"Not even most of them," Anya agreed. "Only enough to cow the others into obedience or convince them that only Stipe's people can provide the crèche with safety."

"Sriovey said his father's group had a name—the Baptisers. He said there were several hundred of them, and that they'd achieved influential positions throughout Surent Crèche. That's who we fought—the Baptisers."

Anya slowly nodded. "The question is what do we do about it?"

Cinder didn't know, and after a moment of deliberation, he realized there wasn't anything they could do. "Nothing for now, but we need to be prepared to save as many dwarves from Surent as possible. Stipe will want to partner with Shet."

"How do you figure?"

Cinder began pacing again, needing to be in movement. He couldn't sit still after learning something so terrible. "Stipe will see Shet as a worthy ally. He, too, believes in power and domination. That was the sense I got from our time in Surent, which is about the same as a certain human who fancies himself a god."

"But if Jozep can teach others to be like him, they can go to Shalla Valley. Mahamatha can shelter them there. A dwarf like Jozep, like what Shokan originally wanted for them, has to be pure enough for the Vale."

Cinder halted his pacing, hope rising as he considered Anya's words. *Shalla Valley*. Jozep and others like him should have no trouble entering it; nor would they make it difficult for Mother Ashoka to keep her borders sealed. Best of all, the holders could use some contentment in their lives.

He laughed at a stray thought. "Can you imagine Sriovey not being able to curse? I think he'd pull a hernia if he wasn't allowed to spice at least one sentence out of three with a *fuck*. He's almost as bad as Nathaz."

His laughter faded to a longing smile. He'd loved Nathaz and recollecting him—his absence. It still hurt.

"I'm sorry," Anya said, squeezing his shoulder in support as she recognized the nature of his grief. "I wish I could have known him as well as you did."

"I wish you could have, too. I wish you could have known all of them."

She kissed his cheek. "I'll get to know the Shokans. We'll see your brothers again."

Cinder nodded at her words, but another vagrant thought caused him to view her in speculation. "It doesn't bother you? Being surrounded by men all the time?"

Anya pursed her lips in a faint frown. "By now, I'm used to it, but I wouldn't mind spending time with women. It's just..." She shrugged.

"There aren't a lot of women like you?" It couldn't be easy being the only one of her kind.

"There aren't any." The simple statement contained a world of loneliness.

This time it was Cinder who squeezed her shoulder in support. "We need to widen our pool of friends and family."

"And how do you propose we do that?" Anya asked. "With everything we have going on."

"It won't always go on," Cinder said. "And once it's done, we should settle down." He had to believe in the likelihood of their success since failure wasn't an option worth considering.

"And what? Get married?" Anya raised her brows, smirking. "Can you imagine how the world would react? The elves of Yaksha Sithe? Or even the humans of Rakesh and Gandharva? I doubt there's a place in all Seminal where a human and an elf can be married and live in peace."

"The human nations wouldn't mind." Cinder was pretty certain about that. "It's the elven customs about your women never touching a male who isn't an elf that would be the biggest obstacle."

"A prohibition I break all the time," Anya said.

"And even your people wouldn't probably care all that much."

"Oh?"

Cinder quirked a grin. "Saving the world earns a lot of forgiveness."

"Yes, it does," Anya agreed with a laugh.

"I'm hungry," Cinder announced a moment later. He lifted the cover off the platter, exposing a pot of heavy stew, two bowls, a hunk of bread, and set of spoons.

"You're going to eat now?" Anya asked. "After everything we

discovered about the dwarves? It didn't steal your appetite?"

Cinder paused in the midst of filling a bowl with the savory stew, viewing her in confusion as he deliberated on her question. He discovered that, no, his appetite wasn't stolen. He wanted to eat and, for just a while, not think about the world's troubles. In addition, no matter Shet's too-long-to-list of vices, his kitchens never produced anything but fine cooking. "I'm hungry," he repeated. "And we can't do anything about the dwarves right now anyway."

Anya grunted acquiescence. "I suppose you're right."

Cinder's ears perked. "What did you say?"

"I said you're right."

Cinder drew himself up straight, as if to make an important declaration. "On this, the third day of Agniasth in the year 3028 of Sapro Yan, Anya Aruyen declared that I was right."

Anya rolled her eyes, which merely caused him to grin.

"You are allowed to think I'm charming," he said.

"Is that what you think of yourself? That you're charming?" She smiled in condescension. "How sweet."

"I thought you said I wasn't sweet." It was something she'd mentioned to him once or thrice.

"You're not. It's your behavior that's sometimes sweet, like an infant making a mess is sweet." She patted his cheek, kissing it. "Sweet Cinder."

27

The next morning, the same goblin who had brought them their meals also led Cinder and Anya to their meeting with Liline.

The little zahhack scampered along, his hands clasped before him, and his head ducked low. "This way," the goblin urged. "The mistress can be impatient for those who are late."

Cinder, having braided the weave meant to hide his truths and deaden his emotions, didn't fear Liline's impatience—at least, not on his own behalf. But what about the goblin? Or anyone else? They didn't deserve to catch the brunt of her anger because of his actions.

As a result, he hurried after the goblin, Anya alongside him as they rushed through the quiet corridors. It was early, well before sunrise, and the hallways were dim with the *diptha* chandeliers still turned down. The fresh scent of potpourri and cut flowers in their tall vases filled the air, and the corridors were silent, except for their racing footsteps. Most of Naraka had yet to awaken, but Cinder knew that the forges and ironworks down under the massive black palace were likely already hot and running. Shet's engine of war never slept.

A stench gave him warning, and he hauled back the suddenly squawking goblin as a necrosed stepped into the corridor.

"You stole my breakfast," the tall, gruesome zahhack growled, eyes locked on the cowering goblin.

Cinder stared upward at the necrosed, who had a tremendous reach advantage given his ape-like arms that ended in the claws of a bear. His mangled teeth looked like they could chew through stone, and his muscles bunched, appearing sturdy enough to crush that same rock.

"Didn't you kill this one already?" Anya asked.

Cinder had. During the run back to Shalla Valley when he and Anya had first discovered a newly arisen Shet. "What do you suggest we do with him?" he asked the goblin, not expecting an answer.

"Kill him if you are able." It was Liline who answered, striding down the hall. "Hurry up about it."

Cinder unsheathed his *isthrim*-forged sword and reached into himself. If the Titan required the death of the necrosed, then so be it. In Liline's presence, he couldn't afford to show mercy. She'd consider it a weakness. So would the goblin and the necrosed.

White lightning sheathed Cinder's blade—the Wildness.

The necrosed had an instant to demonstrate shock before bellowing. He rushed forward, clawed hands extended. Cinder launched to meet him. The necrosed didn't even have time to get his arms in defense before his head was separated from his body. It was a clean decapitation, one powered by the Wildness. This time there would be no chance for the necrosed to restore himself.

Cinder viewed the dead zahhack without expression, but nonetheless, a sense of loss rippled through him. Sapient Dormant and Manifold Fulsom had been necrosed, and yet, they'd also been redeemed. Why not this creature whom he'd just killed?

"Now that that's out of the way," Liline declared, going on to address the trembling goblin. "Have his remains repurposed." Next, she faced Cinder. "Come with me. We have much to discuss."

Cinder glanced to Anya, who shrugged minutely. The two of them followed Liline. Towering above them, she set a rapid pace, and they had to trot to keep up with her.

Thankfully, they didn't have far to go. Liline brought them to a pair of double doors that opened into a large meeting space. A massive live-edged table—made of a dark wood and fit for a Titan—dominated the room, and a matching set of chairs were spaced evenly about it. The walls were a neutral gray, except for one, which held a mural of the tawny dragon in flight. Both the furniture and the painting were of fine quality, and Cinder found himself appreciating anew the skill of the goblins, Naraka's craftspeople.

If this was the kind of art the little creatures could accomplish, then surely they deserved a better fate than to serve a master as monstrous as Shet.

"I've learned some useful information," Liline began, seating herself in one of the large chairs. "The Orb of Regret is kept deep in the vaults of the Webbed Kingdom. No matter how much you might believe the task within your abilities, we—my fellow Titans and I—are no longer so sanguine. You'll never find it without a plan." She waited expectantly.

Cinder and Anya remained standing. Seated in one of the chairs, they would have appeared as children.

"It can be done," Anya said. "But it begins with food. We can eat and trap if we need to, but we also know the spiderkin harvest their own crops and food. We'll steal what we need."

"True, but how will you enter the Kingdom without the spiderkin noticing? Or steal the food?"

"We'll be Blended," Anya replied. "And we also need *nomasras* that can enhance those Blends." This time it was she who waited expectantly.

Liline stared at her, unspeaking for a moment. "You possess strange knowledge," she eventually allowed. "*Nomasras* aren't well known in this age. But, yes, what you describe can be fashioned."

"We also need a *nomasra* that looks and feels like the Orb of Regret," Cinder said, joining the conversation.

Liline scoffed. "How many different types of *nomasras* do you expect us to provide?"

"As many as we need to complete this mission," Cinder answered in an even tone. "We all want the Orb destroyed, and we'll need your help to see it done."

They had to have the *nomasras*; otherwise, the Trial would be a failure before they even left Naraka. And while Shokan's and Sira's memories told them how they could create the needed *nomasras*, they lacked the ability: Cinder because of the ongoing blue-and-green lightning, and Anya because of her weakness as an elf. Or at least that's what Mahamatha had mentioned when they'd last seen her.

"Our help comes with a cost," Liline said.

"So does ours," Anya replied. "If we're to succeed, we'll need those two *nomasras* and others."

Liline waved aside her words. "Why do you need a *nomasra* that mimics the Orb?"

"So when we steal it, no one will immediately know," Cinder replied, thinking the answer should have been obvious. "We'll also need other *nomasras*, something to prevent us from sticking to the webs, one to let us see in the dark, and another to let us communicate with the spiderkin."

"All wise choices," Liline said. "It won't be easy, though."

"And another one to make us look, smell, and taste like a spider," Anya stated.

The last one might be the most difficult, and Cinder knew it. "We have to have that one. Can you combine it with the *nomasra* that enhances our Blends?"

"Perhaps," Liline mused, idly tapping her teeth. "I'll give it some thought."

"We need them as fast as possible," Cinder said. "We're already deep into summer. We don't want to be trying for the Orb of Regret when the autumn snows start to land."

Liline froze him with a hard stare. "Be very careful. I am no one's lackey."

Cinder inclined his head. "I'm only telling you the truth. Our task in the Webbed Kingdom has a time limit."

"Understood," Liline said. "But do not dare speak to me in such a tone ever again. I am no one's servant."

Cinder inclined his head a second time, surprised at the Titan's patience. In Shokan's memories, she had never possessed such forbearance. "Please forgive me if my words sounded demanding."

Liline continued to stare at him, finally removing her gaze when she looked to Anya. "Will you have trouble controlling your emotions in the Webbed Kingdom? Your people and the spiderkin have a deep hatred."

"I can keep my temper," Anya replied coolly. "You don't have to worry on my account. I know what's needed."

"Even though the spiderkin have killed so many of your people over the millennia?"

Anya shrugged. "Like I said, I know what's needed. The spiderkin want to spread everywhere, and this is the best way to stop them."

"It is their way," Liline said. "The need to spread and enslave."

"And their way is antithetical to our own," Anya stated. "We won't be slaves."

A smile curled Liline's lips. "No being of worth should be, and in this regard, the spiderkin are like their mother."

Cinder didn't recall ever speaking to the Titans or Shet about Sheoboth. It would be another piece of strange information for him and Anya to know about the rakshasa duchess—another nugget of knowledge by which Shet might determine their truths. "Who is their mother?" he asked.

"A rakshasa duchess. Sheoboth is her name. The Crooked Branch. The Webbed Queen. You would do well to avoid her."

"A rakshasa duchess." Cinder stroked his chin, as if in contemplation, but in reality, Liline's explanation merely allowed for an update to the plans he and Anya had in mind. But he couldn't speak of it too soon. Patience first. When sufficient time had passed, he pretended to have been struck by inspiration. "If we're in trouble, will you come get us?"

"That might be considered a breach of the non-aggression pact between Naraka and the Webbed Kingdom."

"Does it matter?" Cinder asked. "Shet only made that agreement because he was in a position of weakness. His position is now strengthened, and once we have the Orb, his position becomes even stronger."

"What do you have in mind?" Liline asked, her expression curious, but not yet committed.

"We'll want you to ask Sheoboth for parley," Cinder said. "It'll be at a time of our choosing. We'll contact you through the *divasvapna* right before we're about to steal the Orb. If Sheoboth is off parlaying with you, our likelihood of success becomes that much greater."

"It might be best if you mass armies a few times at the border of the Webbed Kingdom," Anya added—all part of their plan.

"How interesting," Liline said. "Tell me more."

Liline saw Cinder and Anya off from the meeting room, and as she departed to her own quarters, she considered the two of them.

Anya wasn't so impressive. She was a fine-enough warrior and had some skill with *lorethasra*, but it was clear she followed where Cinder led.

Which was sad. Why did the woman always have to tread softly while the man stole all the thunder and glory? In this, Anya's situation struck Liline as similar to her own.

Shet was the master of all the Titans, and although Liline was honored to shadow his lead, she wished—

She cut off that line of thinking.

Without Shet, she would have languished as an ugly, no-account *asrasin* on Earth. Instead, her master had changed the trajectory of her life. He had taught her how to perfect her form, granted her a chance at true power and influence, and gifted her a greater purpose in life than she could have ever imagined.

For all that he'd done on her behalf, Liline would always be grateful.

But what about the other Titans? Why did Shet treat her and Rence like they were lesser than the others? It shouldn't be the case, especially since Liline was more powerful than any of the others, except Sture and Rence could nearly say the same thing. Shet should have—

Again, Liline silenced her near-traitorous contemplations. She owed Shet everything, and she'd never criticize him—not in thought, word, or deed.

Instead, she focused her mind once more on Anya and Cinder, and this time her deliberations went to the man. He was certainly sure of himself, and given how well he had performed so far in obtaining the Orbs, he had that right. The plans he concocted were clever, some downright sneaky, such as simply waltzing into Taj Wada, the imperial palace in Revelant, and making off with the Orb of Moss with no one the wiser.

And then this proposal of using various *nomasras* for specific purposes, ending with a deception of Sheoboth through a feigned parlay… ingenious.

It was too bad Cinder seemed to have no sense of self-preservation. His behavior when speaking to his betters would get him in trouble. In fact, it had nearly cost him his life just the other day.

Liline had heard it from Sture, about how Cinder had all but challenged him to a duel. Only Shet's intervention had saved the foolish man's life, but immediately after, he'd then compounded his arrogance. Cinder had dared speak poorly to Shet. Of course, he'd instantly backtracked, tried to explain away his rudeness as if his words were inspired by *Shet's Council*, the holy book given out to those of weak wills.

Liline hadn't been fooled, though, and neither had Shet. She had heard, again from Sture, that their master intended on seeing Cinder dead as soon as he was no longer of use.

A pity.

Cinder Shade, for all his faults, had his uses, and Liline had suspicions on how he had become so useful. Shet believed Anya had discovered some unknown use of *lorethasra* that allowed her to unlock Cinder's abilities. She had then taken him as both a lover and an apprentice.

Liline, however, had a different view on the matter. She didn't think Cinder was entirely human. More likely he was akin to the rishis or the *hashains*, a child of a powerful woven and a human. Either that or he was like the people from Titan's Reach. If the dwarves were to be believed, there was a lost village of humans who had maintained the proper obeisance to Lord Shet, and even more fantastical, the one who had taught them was named Mistress Arisa.

Hearing the name had sent a shockwave through the Titans. They all recollected Shet's daughter, Marnel Asuring, and also remembered the name she had taken in the Realm to which she'd disappeared: Mistress Arisa.

Upon the discovery, hope had filled their hearts. Shet's daughter was powerful. She could help them close the anchor line leading to Zahhack. Although Shet had six closed Chakras, it wouldn't be enough. Her master lacked the requisite control of *Jivatma*—they all did—but with just one or two more individuals with Titan-level powers lending their assistance, Liline was sure they could close Seminal away from Zahhack.

But that assistance wouldn't come from Marnel. She was dead, deceased shortly after coming to Seminal. The World Killers had defeated and destroyed her, although it had taken years before she had succumbed to her wounds. Worse, Marnel had brought the Withering Knife to Seminal, and it had been left in the care of Salt Tangent, a young woman of Titan's Reach who had been named in honor of Liline.

And that same individual had apparently betrayed her people and Shet. She'd taken to living with the dwarves, hewing to their beliefs and now honoring Shokan and Sira. There was some confusion about how she might have helped in the theft of the Orb of Eretria from Surent or what long game Cinder and Anya—the thieves in question—were actually playing, but what wasn't in contention was that Salt no longer had the Withering Knife.

Liline grimaced. If only Marnel had been able to pass along information on how she had created such a weapon. Stealing *lorethasra* was its simplest effect, but when used properly, the Withering Knife could also close or open Chakras. With it, all the Titans could have become like Zahhack Himself. They could have challenged the Son of Emptiness for supremacy in whatever Realm they chose. Possibly even challenged the Empty One and Devesh.

But it wasn't to be, and there was no use navel-gazing over regrets.

"We have everything we need?" Cinder asked. He was checking the contents of his rucksack one last time. It was the only pack he was taking. He couldn't labor under anything heavier. Going into the Webbed Kingdom meant he and Anya would have to personally carry all their supplies. Horses or pack animals would simply give them away.

"It looks like it," Anya replied, tying off her own rucksack and settling on the bed. "I'm glad we were able to get some information out of Colifrond."

Cinder smiled her way. "Is this your way of fishing for a compliment?"

"I wouldn't say I'm necessarily fishing for anything," she said with a grin, "but if you feel like complimenting me, I wouldn't mind."

Cinder laughed. "In that case, consider yourself complimented. You were very smart to think of talking to him." It had been Anya's suggestion to discuss the Webbed Kingdom with Colifrond, the little goblin who had served them so well. In hindsight, it was also obvious.

Spiderkin and goblins hated one another. They had fought for space in the same caverns of the Dagger Mountains for millennia now. And neither side had truly been able to get the upper hand. Of course, if the spiderkin hadn't been so intent on spreading south into Yaksha Sithe and north toward Surent Crèche, they might have managed to annihilate the goblins.

Instead, they were at a stalemate, with the small zahhacks actually pushing the Webbed Kingdom back on some occasions.

As a result, the goblins had information about the spiderkin that not even Anya's people possessed. They even knew the rough location of the main chamber, where Sheoboth was said to lair, with maps on how to get there and knowledge about the various tribes and castes making up the Webbed Kingdom and their long-running, long-simmering civil war.

Yet another reason why the spiderkin hadn't been able to overwhelm Yaksha Sithe, Surent Crèche, and the goblins: they were too busy fighting each other.

Let them kill one another and never notice us, Cinder thought.

It wouldn't happen. He knew it, but thanks to Colifrond and his goblin friends, at least he and Anya had a chance. They had everything they needed, including a map on where best to enter the Webbed Kingdom, how to proceed toward Sheoboth's location, and the politics driving the spiderkin wars. In addition, with Liline coming through and providing the various *nomasras* they needed, success actually seemed like a possibility.

"Will we need the braids for tomorrow morning?" Anya asked.

Cinder scowled. "I hope not." Beyond the distaste of having someone else seemingly inhabit his body, Cinder also recollected every conversation, emotion, and thought held by his other self while Mahamatha's heavier braid was active.

He didn't like the choices that other person made, and when he really considered it, he realized he also didn't like that other person very much. Blandly certain of himself was the best he could say about him. Arrogant if he wasn't being kind. And strangest of all, that other version rarely considered Cinder as he was now; only the moment seemed to matter to him.

"He's not that bad," Anya said, guessing his thoughts. "He's not nice, but he's kind."

"What's the difference?" Cinder was honestly puzzled. He'd never heard that comparison before.

"He doesn't soften his words. He's blunt, which can seem cruel. But he's generous and willing to risk himself on behalf of others. To that other version of me, he's kind."

"Really?" Cinder quirked a grin. "Even though that other version of you isn't too bright?"

Anya narrowed her eyes. "It was that other version who thought of talking to the goblins. So if you don't think she's too bright, especially after saying it was smart, then what does that say about you?"

Cinder blushed. "I guess I didn't think that one through."

Anya smiled. "No, you didn't."

Cinder exhaled heavily then, abruptly overwhelmed with the need to be gone from Naraka. He rose to his feet and paced the suddenly stifling room. They'd been here a week now, the longest stretch of time they'd ever stayed in Shet's imperial palace, and he longed for the open road.

The only benefit of staying in Naraka had been the opportunity to explore the palace and learn everything they could about the Drakar, Shet's army. They'd learned its composition, structure, and organization, along with the training and competence of the zahhacks, and even the army's food stores, complaints, and hopes.

They'd also discovered that Shet was seeking more rakshasas to help train his fighting force. The necrosed—the previous commanders— were competent at inspiring fear but not at teaching the fundamentals of unit cohesion; of how to effectively fight even without the direct guidance or supervision of the leadership; and the tactics and strategies that could play to the strengths of the zahhacks, specifically their overwhelming numbers.

That last still puzzled Cinder. How had Shet bred such a massive army so quickly? How did he feed them? Or even create Naraka? He shouldn't have had the strength to manage any of those feats. No matter how he fancied himself, Shet was still a human, and the Orbs should have reduced his abilities the same way they hindered Cinder's.

But the fact that Naraka stood, the army barracked within was vaster than any other on Seminal, and there was food aplenty to feed the zahhacks indicated a truth: Shet wasn't entirely hindered by the Orbs. He had a means of negating their effect. But it also wasn't a perfect solution; otherwise, Shet wouldn't need to have the Orbs of Peace destroyed.

"Cinder." He glanced to where Anya sat on the bed, patting a spot next to her. "I know you want to leave Naraka. I feel the same way, but pacing won't help. Sit with me. Pray, meditate, or both. Just sit."

She was right. Cinder had an overabundance of nervous energy, and although his body wanted to work it off, the better notion would be to do as Anya had suggested. He settled himself next to her, thinking on how she really was quite smart. He smiled to himself, recalling how some might even call her wicked smart.

"And don't you forget it," Anya said, responding to his unspoken words. She lifted one of his arms, wrapping it around her shoulders.

"I'll try to relax," Cinder promised. "But I wanted to talk about something first." He went on to describe what they'd learned about the rakshasas being brought in to more properly train the zahhacks. "I'm worried about their effectiveness."

"But they aren't more effective," Anya responded with a frown of confusion. "In all the training areas, we never saw the members of the Drakar demonstrate a true fighting spirit. They went through the motions of training, but it was half-hearted at best. They lack the grit that inspires soldiers to *want* to fight for their cause."

Cinder could see it, a dawning realization. How had he not noticed it before? "The zahhacks worship Shet, but they don't love him. They fear him."

"Exactly. But the reason you might have thought the rakshasas were better is because their discipline is better than that of the necrosed. They don't threaten and mutilate their charges. It helps, but it also won't be enough."

No, it wouldn't, Cinder vowed.

28

Bones listened closely as his sister—sometimes he still couldn't believe Briss was alive—tried to teach him and the brothers how to conduct *Jivatma*. It was all about balance and reaching past oneself. About listening to the wind flowing through one's heart and meditative bullshit like that.

At least that's how Bones would have categorized the instruction if it had come from anyone else. But this was Briss, and if she told him to press his head against the ground and speak gibberish, he'd have done it. Because Briss wasn't just his sister, she was pretty much his mother.

"You're not listening," Residar chided.

Bones glanced to the large wraith. Well, he wasn't really a wraith any longer. His eyes didn't have the solid whiteness anymore. There was a rich brown to his irises, and he no longer had a mouth filled with fangs. He still had his claws, though. Not the six-inch red ones that dripped poison, but something more natural: simple tan ones that extruded from his fingers.

However, none of that interested Bones. Instead, he was concerned about Residar's relationship with Briss. Bones wouldn't have minded if the once-wraith and his sister had some kind of romantic notions for one another. He'd have actually approved, but Devesh's light, Residar was as dumb as a stump in not noticing Briss' obvious interest in him.

"I'm listening," Bones said to Residar. "I just don't know how to fix my mind on what you're talking about. Cinder tried to tell us the same thing. He even tried to teach us like you've been doing. But so far, all I'm seeing is the back of my eyelids."

"*Which is the problem,*" Fastness said. "*You shouldn't be seeing anything but your true heart. Your Jivatma.*"

The stallion stood close at hand, next to the narrow stream cutting through their campsite, a small meadow wrapped in a grove of evergreens, and the place where the Shokans had decided to settle in while trying to learn *Jivatma*. It was a good location, containing a fresh source of water and close enough to defend Shalla Valley's entrance if the need ever arose. In addition, the holders still allowed them access to the vale so that they could hunt and gather food for winter.

This now was the life of the Shokans. Mornings were given over to learning what they could of *Jivatma*, afternoons were spent gathering food, and evenings were focused on their martial training.

Fastness snorted. "*If Aia were here, she could teach you. She had a way of educating people that would have made all of this simple and easy.*"

Estin cracked open his eyes, and like it was a signal, the rest of the Shokans did the same. "Aia?"

"Shokan's steed?" Gorant asked. He leaned forward, a hungry expression on his face.

Bones smiled to himself. Gorant loved a good story, especially if it had to do with Shokan and Sira.

Briss sighed, rising to her feet. "I can see we're not going to get any learning done today." She went to the fire and stirred the stew in the cook pot.

"*Aia never thought of herself as Shokan's steed,*" Fastness said in reply to Gorant's question. "*She always considered him her human.*"

Brilliance, lounging on a large, sunny rock, sat up. *"Her human?"*

"She was a cat," Fastness said, humor in his voice.

Brilliance arched her back and leapt to the ground. *"I like her already."*

"I said she was *a cat,"* Fastness corrected. *"That's who she was in her original form, but here on Seminal, we knew her as the Calico."*

"The Calico?" Estin said, sounding shocked. If Gorant loved stories about Shokan and Sira, the prince was obsessed with them. "You mean the Calico dragon?"

That got Bones' interest. Did that mean that the Calico dragon had once been a kind of giant cat? How?

"Yes," Fastness said in answer to Estin. *"In the very first Realm, where she and Shokan fought evil, she was a giant cat."*

"How giant?" Brilliance asked, a challenge in her voice.

"Every bit as big as you."

Brilliance stared unblinking at the stallion for a moment. *"I could have taken her,"* she finally declared. *"But it also doesn't matter. She had her human, and I have mine. So long as she never tried to poach my boy, I'd have let her live."*

"Doubtful," Fastness said. *"Aia was faster than me and every bit as powerful."*

Brilliance might have sniffed. *"I would have found a way."*

Bones rolled his eyes. He was wary of the large *aether*-cursed snow-tiger, but she sure liked to brag, a habit he found annoying.

He blinked an instant later. He used to brag all the time, too. *Did others find him equally annoying?* He shrugged away the question. If they did, that was their problem.

Just then, Selin, who'd been on guard duty, entered the campsite. "He's back."

Before the once-wraith could announce who it was, Kela pushed through the underbrush. Bones frowned. The dog was clearly exhaust-ed. His head drooped, his fur was matted, and he'd lost weight. What had happened to him?

Kela had been gone for the past few weeks—some kind of argument with Brilliance. *Of course.* What else did those two do but argue? Bones shook his head. On first meeting the two *aether*-cursed beasts, he hadn't been able to make any sense of them or their purpose. What did they want? Why did they remain with Fastness?

In truth, the snowtiger was nothing but a pain in the ass, always wanting to play pranks on people and doing little more than lounge around in the sun. That and claiming some magnificent destiny, which Bones had never bothered to learn. Meanwhile the ugly dog simply followed after her like a… well, a dog.

But the two of them also fought like an old married couple, and several weeks ago, after their latest dustup, Kela had left, proclaiming something about one of them finally doing what they'd always promised.

Bones hadn't bothered learning the reason for the dog's departure. He was just glad not to have to listen to their constant bickering. Apparently, that glad interlude was about to end.

"I found one," Kela announced, speaking to Brilliance.

"Found what? And what happened to you? You look terrible. When was the last time you slept?"

"I did what we promised. I found another aether-*cursed. She needs to be taught."*

That got everyone's attention, including Brilliance's. *"What kind of* aether-*cursed did you find?"* She stood upright, her nostrils flaring, and her pupils wide.

Something had triggered her hunter's instincts. Bones signed for the Shokans to be ready. Violence threatened. He didn't know the cause, but he wouldn't have his men caught with their pants down.

Residar, farmer that he was, didn't notice anything; not at first, but even his thick instincts finally kicked in. He faced Brilliance, claws out.

Fastness, of course, had picked out the warning signs at the same time as Bones. The stallion had already moved to stand with Kela. *"Stand down,"* he ordered Brilliance.

"I'm a hunter, and I wish to hunt."

"Even though it breaks your vow to Mahamatha?"

Brilliance whimpered. *"I'm hungry."*

"No, you're not," Fastness said, his voice sympathetic. *"You're just frightened."*

Kela stepped aside, and a young doe entered the campsite. Her eyes glowed white, but the canines protruding from her upper jaw were what gave Bones pause.

"Is that cat really wanting to eat me?" the doe asked. *"Why? What did I ever do to her? Kela said she would love me. He talked and talked and talked about her like she was someone special. But she just wants to eat me. Everyone wants to eat me. Why can't everyone just eat leaves and nuts like I do? They taste delicious. That's spelled d-e-l-i-s-h-u-s. That's pretty smart, right?"*

Bones boggled at the stream of words.

"Hello?" Fastness offered, sounding unaccustomedly diffident.

The doe blinked, meeting Fastness' gaze. *"Hi there. You sure are big. Did you get so big from eating leaves and nuts? Or did you eat something else? I'd like to try some of that if you don't mind."*

"Her name is Hima," Kela said. *"And now you know why I'm so exhausted."* He collapsed and fell asleep.

The doe was now addressing Residar, who wore a slightly panicked expression on his face.

Bones took one look at the scene and knew what was needed. "Shokans. Make haste! We're heading into Shalla Valley. Now!"

His men never moved so quickly.

Jeet sighed, glad to be finished with the preaching. He stood with Stren in a winter-bare field a mile distant from Shuming, a hamlet in Devesth, several days south of Cord Valley. The sun stood a few hours past noon in a cloudless sky, and the light reflected off the inch-thick snow covering the stubbled field. The wind gusted cold, tugging at Jeet's coat, and he clutched it closer about himself.

This fallow farmland was what passed for a house church. Or at least that was what Jeet and Stren had taken to calling the meetings, which had the flavor of a revival with farmers and folks coming in from the nearby villages, sharing food and song and listening as Jeet, the one-time *hashain*, described his revelation and truth, and Stren spoke of supporting the Grimyogi.

It was their chosen life, traveling the small villages of the Sunset Kingdoms in order to spread the word about Cinder Shade, the Grimyogi. Theirs was the existence of a wanderer, never resting in one place for more than a week since Jeet and Stren had no home and no place they could name as their own. Some might have called it a sad, desperate life—certainly Jeet would have back when he'd been a *hashain*—but nowadays, he awoke every morning with a fresh sense of excitement and purpose. He enjoyed what he was doing more than he could have ever dreamed.

It would have been perfect if not for Genka's spies. They'd discovered them hiding in Querel, necessitating their flight from that small village. In fact, Jeet and Stren had barely escaped with their lives since a sect of *hashains* from Chapterhouse had also been sent to kill them.

But being free of Querel meant that at least Jeet no longer had to listen to his annoying sister. Hopefully, the sect had roughed her up some— maybe even cut off a few of her fingers—when they'd discovered he and Stren had escaped. It would serve her right and maybe teach her to keep her mouth shut when talking to her betters.

Jeet immediately chided himself for such unworthy thoughts. His sister had housed him and Stren, and although he didn't like her much, she didn't deserve torture or torment on his account. More importantly, the Grimyogi would expect better of him, in both deed and thought.

"That was a better sermon," Maize said. The troll had paced over to stand next to Jeet, his two holders shadowing his movements. For reasons only known to them, Maize and his guards had decided to journey with Jeet and Stren through the Sunsets, which was a good thing. Early on, the troll had provided a great deal of insight and advice about what exactly to teach those who needed teaching.

Jeet wouldn't have figured on it himself, but Maize was a patient instructor. He was also wise and understood why the coming of the Grimyogi would be such a glorious event for the peons of the world.

Jeet immediately corrected his thinking. They weren't peons. They were people, worthy of respect in their own right.

Or so he tried to tell himself. It wasn't easy, though, trying to overcome a lifetime of teachings that instructed him on the natural superiority of some in the eyes of Devesh. Teachings that told of a Grimyogi who was the most fearsome of warriors. Someone who destroyed his enemies without hesitation, gave no quarter to those who dared wrong him, and was the epitome of what it meant to be a *hashain*.

But that Grimyogi also wasn't real. The holy book of the *hashains*, their version of the *Medeian Scryings*, wasn't correct. Maize himself had declared it so, although he hadn't made an actual Judgment on the case. However, his explanation also made sense.

Cinder Shade, the man Jeet knew to be the Grimyogi *was* a fearsome warrior. He did destroy his enemies without hesitation. But he also gave quarter to those who had wronged him. After all, he had allowed Jeet and Stren to walk away with their lives when he would have been well within his rights to see them dead. And although Jeet had given Cinder his leash, the only restriction the Grimyogi had placed upon him was to disallow murder.

"How can I do better?" Jeet asked the troll.

It was Stren who answered. "You need to focus more on why the Grimyogi would be a better ruler than Genka."

The advice wasn't as surprising as the fact of who had offered it. "What do you mean?" Jeet asked, wondering where the younger man was going with his line of thinking.

"Exactly that. The Sunsets have been ruled by the Lords ever since Mede. It's all we know. The wars that have occurred, the famines, the destitution… Nothing has changed in all these ages. Poverty breeds sorrow. It's all our people have ever experienced."

Jeet viewed the younger *hashain* in faint surprise. Early on and for months after, Stren had resented their fallen status in the world. Even after moving to Querel, he hadn't bothered hiding his distaste for what they had been forced to accept.

That attitude had slowly improved following Maize's arrival. The troll had taught them both what he knew of the *Medeian Scryings*, as written and interpreted by the Errows, a tribe Jeet had long considered heretical fools.

And yet it had been they who had best known the mind of the Grimyogi, the *Cipre Elonicon*, the Destroyer of Falsehood. In addition, Maize had also spoken of what he knew of Cinder Shade from a personal perspective. Maynalor was how he called him, and it wasn't surprising that the troll's view of the man coincided with what the Errows described in their version of the *Medeian Scryings*.

Maize's teachings had slowly altered Stren's attitude, and the young *hashain* had developed a greater generosity to the lesser folk in their nation: the farmers, craftsfolk, and peasants, who strained under the weight of Genka's needs. The supposed *Garnala lon Anarin* had drafted many of the poor, young men of the Sunsets into his army, giving an excuse that another herd of wraiths threatened.

Jeet mentally snorted at the notion. More likely Genka was bent on heading south and conquering Shima Sithe and Aurelian Crèche, two nations who had never done anything of significance to the people of the Sunsets. The situation had Jeet believing that his people deserved someone better to lead them.

He smiled. *His people.* When had he become such a soft-hearted romantic?

"What did I say?" Stren asked, probably mistaking Jeet's humor for something else.

"Nothing," Jeet said, going on to explain what he'd been thinking on.

"You've come far," Maize said. "You aren't there yet, but you're heading in the right direction."

Jeet's smile broadened, pleased to have pleased the troll. "So you agree with Stren? About what needs to be explained to the people?"

Maize nodded. "I do. And I know it makes your fierce *hashain* heart race faster whenever you discuss Cinder's battle prowess, but it also doesn't help your cause. The people don't care about how good the Grimyogi might be at killing. They have other needs."

"But telling them about his strength… won't it give them peace that someone powerful is protecting their interests?"

It was an old conversation between the two of them. Jeet didn't think Maize placed enough stock on the importance of safety, whereas the troll felt like Jeet placed too much emphasis on need for control rather than on freedom. But what use was there in living the life you thought you wanted if you weren't safe enough to do so?

Stren stepped between them, which at one point, he would have never done. That single stride of the younger man drove home a point: if Jeet had come far, then Stren had traveled around the world.

"Peace," the younger once-*hashain* said. "It is what the people want. An end to wars and a chance to live without a heavy foot bearing down on their necks."

Jeet sighted Stren in deeper surprise. When had the young man learned such eloquence?

Stren flushed, indicating Maize. "He and I have been talking."

"And you think that's what people want?" Jeet asked. "Peace?"

"I think they ultimately want the freedom to live the lives they wish. And while it begins with safety, it doesn't end there. The requirements of a good life are broader."

Listening to Stren and Maize, it finally occurred to Jeet that he had been arguing out of habit and heart rather than rationality. They were right. The people needed a reason to follow the Grimyogi, and the knowledge of his magnificent skills as a warrior wouldn't be it. Even the name should be different. Grimyogi was a name to inspire fear, but it didn't inspire hope.

"We'll do it your way," Jeet said in the end to Stren. "And I also think we should use a different name for Cinder. Something other than the Grimyogi."

"There already is one," Maize said. "In the *Crèche Prani*, he is known as the *Cipre Elonicon*."

Of course. Jeet wanted to smack himself in the forehead even as

Stren viewed him in confusion. "You really never thought of that until now?"

Jeet shrugged, not wanting to admit the truth.

"I have something for you," Maize said. He passed each of them a walking staff, similar to his own and sized for their height. "These will serve you better than swords, if you so choose."

With trembling hands, Jeet took the proffered staff, touched in ways he couldn't describe. And yet Maize's last words triggered a note of caution. "If we so choose what?"

"If you choose to become my apprentices. You have it in you to become as me."

"It is good to see you again, Master Fincher," Rence said, not entirely sure of the dwarf's name, but guessing it was the one she'd met a few other times. He was said to be a member of the Baptisers—Shet's secret supporters in Surent Crèche—but if so, she couldn't tell. In truth, all dwarves looked alike to her, and the only reason she could figure out the name of this one was because of his attire, specifically his axe.

Rence had a penchant for weapons, and this dwarf's axe was particularly well crafted. Her eyes traveled along its lines, picking out the metal knob merging with the dark oak handle, the leather wrapping along the grip and throat, the brilliant half-moon of *isthrim* steel with a counterbalancing spike on the other side. A lovely weapon indeed.

The dwarf kowtowed, bringing a smile to Rence's face as she viewed the little woven. Despite her distaste for most people, no matter their race, she fancied this little fellow. He always offered appropriate obeisance, which she found delightful.

It was also rare. The zahhacks, mindless and pathetic as they were, didn't count, and the other Titans would never bend the knee to her. In fact, they barely respected her; a flaw Shet shared, treating her like a lackey rather than as his equal. It was an insult that would one day cost him dearly, especially since he should know better. Rence was the best of his followers, not the least.

In fact, she wasn't so far behind Shet's glory, and in the end, she would catch him. Sometime in the not-too-distant future, she would close a sixth Chakra, then a seventh, and possibly the mythical eighth. And on that day, she would arise as the new queen of this Realm and any other she chose to honor with her rule. Of course, when that happened, there would be changes. Rence would suffer no rivals. Shet and all the Titans would have to die since she would do away with any who were near her own level of power.

She reconsidered the last. Liline she would allow to live. Rence couldn't see herself killing the woman she considered a sister. The Water Death had always been loving, honest, and supportive. In addition, they both suffered the same lack of respect under Shet, chafed under it, although Liline was too kind and loyal to say so. In the end, though, Rence's chosen sister would likely be just as glad to see the so-called god destroyed as Rence herself.

She mentally nodded to herself. *Yes. Liline would be pleased with Shet's death.* It wouldn't be too far off now either, but until then, patience and a simpering attitude would be her best allies.

"I bring good news," said Anulth Fincher.

The little dwarf drew Rence's attention back to the here and now, to the private audience chamber near Shet's throne hall, the place in which visitors were first questioned and assessed. A rectangular table, well-crafted and carved, stood centered within the room while a vase full of perfumed, dried flowers rested upon its surface. Several Titan-sized chairs were spaced about its length, the dimensions meant to humble any who came here since they would appear as children within those seats.

In addition, flames roared in a broad fireplace, bringing warmth to the chamber, while on the wall opposite hung a fanciful painting of Shet defeating Shokan upon the Web of Worlds. A massive window allowed an expansive view of the Dagger Mountains, specifically the slopes of Mount Blankenshield, where Shet had captured Charn, the red dragon who was now tawny.

What that change meant, Rence didn't know. Shet believed it a natural process where the dragon recognized him as its master, but Rence
didn't think that was correct. She also didn't have a better explanation,
however, and was wise enough not to directly contradict Shet when he
claimed certainty on a matter.

"We continue to gain ground in Surent Crèche," Anulth continued.
"It will be ours soon."

A part of Rence wanted to leave the little woven bent low before her,
but it wasn't easy hearing his words when they were muffled against
the ground. Add in Rence's stature—she towered a good four times
above Anulth's height—and the difficulty was exacerbated.

"Rise," she ordered.

"Thank you, my lady," Anulth said, mopping his face. "The wisdoms
are daily losing prestige and power. Soon, the Baptisers will have control of the entire crèche. On that day, we can offer our open support to
Lord Shet."

Rence offered a pleased smile. Having the support of the dwarves
aided her own plans since it kept Shet's eyes away from her true de-
signs. Let him battle for small nations, while she sought out the larger
prize of all of Seminal.

The only stone in her boot was when Zahhack managed to break
free and enter the world. Could he do so before the destruction of the
Orbs?

Rence didn't think so. Time wasn't on his side, not with how quickly
Cinder and Anya were gathering the Orbs of Peace, which might be
entirely destroyed by this time next year. And Rence intended on having her sixth Chakra closed by then as well. It all depended on her will,
especially her resilience in accepting pain.

Pain brought growth and opportunity, and what better pain was
there than continually punching through the blue-and-green lightning surrounding her *Jivatma* and laced throughout her *lorethasra*?
Utilizing that pain, focusing it upon her Chakras, forcing them shut
ever tighter would allow Rence to reach heights of power no one else
could even conceive.

"How soon will your master be able to bring the crèche to heel?" Rence asked in reply to Anulth's statement.

The dwarf hesitated. "I wouldn't think it much longer than six months."

"And he will be in a position to open Surent's doors to our zah-hacks?" That was the key. If given a choice, allies could be fickle, but having zahhacks quartered within the crèche would take that choice away from the dwarves. Then they would be slaves inside their own nation.

A delicious irony since dwarves had been Shokan's greatest achievement, and seeing his creatures brought low gave Rence indescribable happiness. Just imagining that self-righteous fucker marinating in horror when the zahhacks made a mess of his special people… It was a delectable dream.

Too bad Shokan wasn't alive to witness it though. Him and his bitch wife, Sira. Rence detested Shet for how little he respected her, but she hated the so-called Blessed Ones, and it was for an entirely different reason. It was because they had dared pity her. Contempt and disrespect Rence would pay back in kind, but pity… that was something she would never accept. And any who dared offer it, she would see burned and dead.

Rence realized her mind had gotten away from her again, and the room had fallen silent. Had the dwarf replied to her question? She replayed the scene in her mind and realized that only a few seconds had passed, and he hadn't. "Well?" she prodded, going back to her prior question.

"I am sure we can open the doors of Surent Crèche to some zah-hacks," the dwarf said. "But I can't make promises that anything beyond a small force of the Drakar can be afforded housing. Stipe will be focused on bringing a restive nation under his authority, and it won't be easy, especially if a foreign army is seen as an invading force."

Rence's eyes narrowed. It was a wise decision on Stipe's part, not to make too firm a commitment. It was also rather unfortunate.

The dwarf licked his lips in nervousness. "There will always be lingerers who defy Stipe's rule," he explained. "I hope you understand."

Rence smiled thinly. "I understand. Now tell me, how can we help?" Her smile thinned further. "And be clear in what you need. I am in no mood for having my time wasted."

The dwarf licked his lips again, terror evident, which Rence found delightful.

29

Into an isolated clearing, Sture Mael created an anchor line where he'd agreed to meet a small contingent of elves from Yaksha Sithe. They awaited him, already encamped on the meadow in a scattering of brightly colored tents.

Upon the meadow, sunshine beamed, but it provided no warmth, not at this elevation where cold reigned and an icy wind gusted. The breeze rippled through Sture's short hair, but he paid it no heed even as it carried away his fogging breath. For a Titan, neither heat nor cold was worth acknowledging. He and the rest of his brethren were above such mortal complaints.

However, he did note the scent of wood fire and seared meat. Even as a Titan, he had to eat, and his stomach rumbled. In order to attend this meeting, he'd skipped breakfast, and he wouldn't have minded a plate of whatever the elves were cooking.

Not that he'd ever ask. A Titan asked for nothing. A Titan simply took.

Sture made a mental sigh.

But he couldn't take anything from the Yaksha elves. After all, this was a diplomatic mission and certain niceties had to be maintained. His lip curled at that. Diplomacy was a weakness he was forced to endure, but there would come a day when the world would be ordered to Shet's will, that of his friend and master, and none of the Titans would ever again have to accede to the desires of their lessers.

Until then... Sture plastered a false smile on his face when several elves approached him. He'd met them before. This delegation from their empress to enact a supposed peace agreement between their people and Naraka.

While the elves walked closer, including a high noble surrounded by a coterie of ineffectual warriors, Sture did his best to maintain his pleasant façade, even as he inwardly seethed. These puffed-up elves thought so highly of themselves. Look at them preening and viewing him as if they were his betters. So sure were they of their power and prestige.

Fools.

Their safety was only assured because his friend and lord required their assistance, that and the damnable Orbs of Peace, which limited the skills and Talents of all the Titans as well as Shet. Otherwise, Sture would have long since taught these elves the true meaning of power and prestige.

"It is good to meet you again, Lord Mael," the leader of the contingent, Duchess Cervine, said. She inclined her head as one equal to another, this despite the fact that she didn't even reach as high as his waist and had to crane her neck to meet his gaze. Her golden hair was caught in an intricate braid with her peaked elfin ears rising tall, an indication of her beauty, which Sture had to admit she possessed. She was a lovely woman.

It was a shame she was an elf, though, a lesser breed of being, and this one was too stupid to know it. There she stood, wearing a proud visage, although she had never achieved anything worthwhile in her useless life.

"You as well," Sture lied, not bothering to incline his head. "Has your empress given thought to our last offer?"

"The one where you defend our borders from the spiderkin?" the duchess asked. "I was under the impression that your nation and the Webbed Kingdom had forged a non-aggression pact."

Sture held back a blink of surprise. How had the elves learned of that? He quickly reordered his thoughts. "Regardless of what rumors state regarding Naraka and the Webbed Kingdom, we are still willing to defend Yaksha's borders."

"But only if we grant your armies access to the headwaters of the Gideon River." She shook her head. "We cannot allow that. It would potentially split our lands on the mainland."

Sture waved aside her words. "It would do no such thing. You would still control your territory. We won't be able to move our armies along the Gideon without your approval."

"Unless you chose to ignore our directives. Which you could if you had a sufficient force in place."

This wasn't the conversation Sture had expected, and once again, he was forced to reorder his thoughts. Once they were in place, he offered a cheery smile followed by a light laugh as if the duchess' words were silly. "You're so suspicious."

"You taught us to suspect you during the *NusraelShev*."

Sture maintained the witless grin, even though he wanted to grind his teeth. He hated these diplomatic missions. Liline was better at them. So was Garad, but he clearly couldn't be the one to speak to the Yaksha elves, not after they'd displayed his frozen form in their military school as a kind of trophy for the past three thousand years. As much as Sture disliked the Yaksha elves, Garad hated them with the heat of a hundred forest fires.

"Then what would you have us do?" Sture asked, dropping the smile. "What is the point of this meeting?"

"We are willing to make concessions," Duchess Cervine allowed. "Trade between our nations, but not free travel, especially for armed personnel. We find it unusual you would even ask us to consider such an offer."

"Lord Shet is not the fearsome tyrant portrayed in your histories," Sture stated. "Histories defame his good name. It is true. Much of the *NusraelShev* was simply Naraka defending our borders against the incursions of the Mythaspuris." It was no such thing, but who cared if he lied to the elves?

"So you claim," Duchess Cervine said, her voice cool.

"I claim nothing. It is the truth. I was there. I should know."

Duchess Cervine offered a thin smile, stepping forward to hand him a sheaf of papers. "Deliver this to your lord. It is the trade my empress is willing to allow between our nations. Anything more will have to be developed through trust."

Hiding his distaste, Sture took the papers. The missives were useless. Nonetheless, revealing no evidence of his irritation, he met the duchess' eyes. "We'll consider them." He made to turn around but paused first, head tilted as if in consideration of a matter. "Shall we meet again? In two months? In this meadow?"

"Only if you're willing to consider the trade initiatives the empress will allow, and forgo this notion of your zahhacks moving through our lands unimpeded."

"I will be sure to discuss your decision with my lord," Sture replied. And although it was petty, he also made sure to get in a small dig. "You should get started for your home soon. A long ride awaits." His words spoken, with a gesture, he opened an anchor line back to Naraka and grinned at them. How it must curdle their pride to see him able to travel so effortlessly. "Next time if you wish, we can meet at my home."

Duchess Cervine's jaw clenched slightly. "So you say," she said, offering a bow.

Sture laughed inside at her anger even as he tethered to the anchor line. Shet wouldn't like the decision of the Yaksha empress, but it was also expected. Which meant that Apsara Sithe would have to be their next target. One of the elven nations would bend the knee.

It was only after he recovered from the icy chill and gut-curdling nausea that Jozep was able to gaze at Shalla Valley. It was his first time here and also his first time traveling by anchor line. It hadn't been a fun trip, but it was also worth it. What would have been at least a month-long journey from Surent Crèche to the vale had spun by in seconds, Noon Gate to Twilight.

With him were Salt—on hands-and-knees and still struggling with the travel's discomfort—and Sriovey, who had yet to fully embrace his dwarven heritage. He was coming along, though. Jozep only wished they could have brought along Derius. He was also relearning what it meant to be a true dwarf—faster than Sriovey, in fact—but it wasn't his time. Derius' father still needed him to help save their people.

And if today's meeting with the yakshins went well, maybe they actually could.

The Baptisers had gained control of Jade's Moon, and the wisdoms were fearful of what might come next. Rumors abounded that Stipe planned on allying with Shet. Few regular folk agreed with such insanity, but they were also too afraid to speak out.

Examples had been made of those who disagreed too loudly with the Baptisers; suspicious deaths of dwarves who argued against Stipe. Even the wisdoms weren't safe. Wisdom Palav had been found hanged in her quarters, leaving behind a note stating that she couldn't live with herself after being so wrong about Stipe's brilliance.

It was an obvious lie, but her death had served its function, cowing those who might have fought against the Baptisers.

Jozep shook his head, unable to comprehend how his people could have fallen so far so fast.

"It's warm," Sriovey noted, glancing around. "And the trees are all wrong. They're too many hardwoods."

"The weather is whatever the yakshins want," Jozep reminded him. "The rest of the Daggers might be covered in snow, but in Shalla Valley, it's always spring or summer."

"What about Shadion?" Salt asked. "He was supposed to have left Surent a month ago. You think he's arrived already? Or is he holed up somewhere because of the snow?"

"That fucker is—" Sriovey corrected himself. "I mean Shadion is probably safe. He's got all sorts of places to ride out the storms." By the end, Sriovey's face was red, and he looked to be straining not to curse.

Jozep laughed. "You'll get there."

Sriovey sighed. "It's hard not to curse. I love cursing."

"As long as you're not angry when you do, then go ahead."

"Really?" Sriovey wore a bright, hopeful expression.

"Really." Early on after leaving Mahadev, Jozep had thought that cursing would hinder the dwarves from learning their true heritage, but now he didn't think it mattered. Only achieving serenity was important. After that, the cursing would probably end on its own anyway.

A tree-like being approached, disrupting his thoughts, and Jozep gaped. She was twenty feet tall if she was an inch, and he had to blink to ensure he was actually seeing something real.

"Is that a yakshin?" Salt whispered, sounding as awed as Jozep was feeling.

The tree maiden halted, bending as low as possible, but even then she was several feet taller than any of them. "Hello, young dwarves. My name is Sepia. Do you know Maynalor?"

Jozep frowned. He didn't know anyone named Maynalor—someone of interest with a secret. *Wait.* Wasn't that Cinder? It was. The realization lit a smile on his face. "I'm Jozep," he said to the yakshin. "And this is Sriovey Kalenth and Salt Tangent. And we all know Maynalor. He is our friend, Cinder Shade."

The yakshin grinned. "If he's your friend, then so are we." She tilted her head in consideration. "There's something pleasing about you, young Jozep. I like you." Sepia straightened to her full height. "Are you ready to see the vale?"

Salt's shoulders were tight, and her eyes darted about like she was nervous. "I thought Shalla Valley was only for the purified. Will I be welcome?"

The yakshin laughed. "Of course you are. Can you not tell? Mahamatha has already decreed it so."

Sepia strode off then in the direction from which she had arrived, and they chased after her long strides, leaving behind the field surrounding Twilight Gate. Moments later, they entered a forest of soaring oaks, maples, and walnuts. The entire time, Sepia spoke over her shoulder, telling them of the vale and the various climates found within it. It was much like Jozep had earlier said—it was always spring or early summer in Shalla Valley—but rather than due to the magic of the yakshins, it was because of the magic of the Ashoka trees.

Jozep had heard about them, giant trees the size of hills. Their shade was supposed to cover acres, and he couldn't wait to see them.

His hopes, however, were dashed when Sepia told them they weren't going to the Ashoka grove but were instead heading to the northwestern bounds of the vale. Jozep asked her why, and she simply smiled, telling them it was a surprise. Sriovey, of course, mumbled some curse about hating surprises, which elicited a laugh from Sepia. Nevertheless, she never did tell them what was waiting for them at the end of their trek.

Not that it mattered. Although Jozep had only recently met the yakshin, he trusted her. She just had that way about her.

As a result, he and the others followed Sepia without complaint, and they hiked through a savanna rich with life.

Days passed, and they kept at it, heading ever eastward with something new to discover seemingly upon every mile. And if there wasn't, Sepia filled the trek with stories of the world she'd seen and the life of Shalla Vale, including the wise, ancient Ashoka trees, especially the mother of them all, Mahamatha.

"And Cinder and Anya actually got to talk to her?" Salt asked upon learning about Mother Ashoka. She shook her head as if in disbelief. "They always get the best experiences."

Sepia halted, gazing at her. "Do not discount your own experiences, child. Your struggles are noteworthy. Setting aside terrible teaching. Accompanying a dwarf with the ancient magic. You have been made whole in ways that no human in millennia can claim. You are pure."

The yakshin's words sparked a furrow on Salt's brow, and she stared downward, lost in thought. "I guess it just seems like exciting things always happen to other people."

Sriovey grunted. "Excitement might sound wonderful, but it's usually fucking terrifying." He scowled. "I mean—"

Sepia's peal of laughter cut him off. "Young Master Sriovey, you and your cursing."

"It's a condition," Sriovey muttered. "I'm trying to find a cure."

"And I'm sure you'll succeed," Sepia said.

On they hiked, and on the afternoon of their fifth day, they crested a rise. There, they reached their destination.

Jozep came to a stop, staring down into a shallow bowl where a group of men were training. His eyes watered.

So did Sriovey's. "I wish Derius was here," he whispered. "I wish Hotgate was, too."

It was Salt who pushed them forward. After all the stories they'd spoken about the individuals down in the bowl, she must have recognized them. "Your brothers are waiting. Go to them."

It was Riyne who spotted them first, and he shouted with joy, sprinting to greet them, the rest of the brothers following close behind. Jozep found himself captured by their embraces, their laughter, and their love. He'd missed his brothers, but until now, he hadn't really understood just how much. Tears flowed, and Jozep couldn't stop grinning.

After the hugs were done, Ishmay gazed at him in concern. "It's strange being around you. I feel better inside, and I don't want to curse so much. Like it would be wrong."

"Tell me about it," Sriovey deadpanned.

With an early cool spell settling on the island, the crackling fire in the hearth was the only sound in Mother's offices. Father, meanwhile, sat upon the couch, perusing his own documents, while Enma sat next to him, facing Redwinth, who'd settled into one of the high-backed armchairs.

His inclusion in this morning's meeting was a high honor. In the months after Anya's theft of the Orb of Moss, Redwinth had eventually earned some semblance of Mother's acceptance. It wasn't yet trust, but it also wasn't dismissiveness. In other words, it was a start.

Enma glanced at her husband, wondering what he thought about the report he was currently reading. It had been sent by Duchess Cervine and documented her meeting with Sture Mael, including what the Titan and his master wanted from Yaksha Sithe and what they were willing to give. Based on Duchess Cervine's notes, it was too much and not enough.

Then again, the noblewoman disagreed with the empress on how Shet should be handled. Enma's auntie—she wasn't a true aunt, but that was the familial rapport she felt toward the noblewoman—believed that no agreement should be made with Shet. Duchess Cervine hated the so-called god, and in her estimation, Yaksha should ally fully and completely with Rakesh and Gandharva against him. She believed Yaksha shouldn't stand aside as the human nations prepared for war against Naraka, and Surent Crèche should have been included in that self-defense partnership, but with Stipe Jasth, the leader of the Baptisers, likely admiring Shet, that was an impossibility.

"What do you think we should do?" the empress asked Redwinth. She was seated behind her desk with a kind yet curious expression on her face.

Enma wasn't fooled. The question was a test, and the expression on Mother's face a means by which she put a person at ease so they'd give their honest opinion. Seeing it, Enma wanted to warn Redwinth, but she couldn't. Her husband had to pass this examination on his own.

"I think we should be careful," Redwinth said after some deliberation. "So far, we've accepted these overtures, so to turn them down immediately might not be wise."

Enma agreed with him. Yaksha Sithe skirted on the edge of catastrophe. They weren't ready for open conflict with Naraka, and continuing these diplomatic meetings might grant them the time needed to reinforce their armies and navies.

"You think so?" Mother asked, still wearing that curious expression. But Enma didn't miss her perched-forward posture of a hunter.

"I do," Redwinth said, going on to explain thoughts similar to what Enma had been thinking.

Mother leaned back in her chair, hands templed beneath her chin. "We will see," she replied, offering neither a compliment nor a disagreement.

Nonetheless, Enma could sense the satisfaction and pleasure in her bearing.

"Where's Ginala?" Father asked, glancing up from his papers. "She should have been here to discuss the situation."

Redwinth caught Enma's eye, and she nodded. They'd discussed this before, and now would be the perfect time to enact their plan. Using Anya's instruction, the two of them had managed to untangle the eavesdropping braid they'd unearthed in their quarters, and they'd come across the same weave in Mother's office—an unsettling finding, which they'd dissolved just prior to this morning's meeting. In addition, the discovery had led them to a near certainty about the quelchon.

Enma rose to her feet, taking Duchess Cervine's report from Redwinth, and approached her mother. "Ginala usually receives these documents before we do," she said. "Perhaps she's putting together her own assessment."

It was a blunt hint as to what Enma was actually thinking, and her mother quickly understood the unspoken undertones. So did Father.

"You don't trust Ginala," he said, speaking for both himself and mother.

The quelchon had long been an influential force within Yaksha, especially in Taj Wada and, even more so, within this chamber. As such, Enma wasn't yet ready to make plain her accusations against the ancient elf. She needed to tread lightly. "I'm merely stating a possibility."

Her mother stared hard at her. "This is why you insisted Cervine send two sets of missives, one directly to me and another to the First Directorate."

Redwinth spoke in Enma's place, something else they had discussed prior to today's meeting. "Is Anya still considered a traitor to the crown?"

Father shot a glance to Mother. They had never been in agreement when it came to deciding what to do about Anya. Father wanted to give her a chance to freely return to Taj Wada and explain herself; Mother wanted her returned to the palace in chains, if need be. No doubt, that was Ginala's influence.

"What does my daughter have to do with distrusting Ginala?" Mother eventually asked Redwinth.

"Nothing," Redwinth said, "but whenever I think you'll relent and let her come home on her own, you decide against it."

Mother eyed him coldly, but Redwinth didn't shrink in the face of her anger. He faced her, bold and brave, and once again, Enma found herself grateful that he'd ended up in her life. Redwinth was courageous, intelligent, and believed her worthy of his attention. Few did in Taj Wada, although some of that had been due to her own… inartful dalliances.

"You have a clear reason for why you brought this up right now," Mother said. "Why?"

Redwinth glanced to Enma. This, too, they'd discussed. "I think it might be of interest to see how closely the missive Duchess Cervine sent to you matches whatever information Ginala presents."

A flicker of an approving smile ghosted across Mother's face. "So be it."

30

Ginala left the empress' office, feeling as though she had missed something important. Upon giving her version of Duchess Cervine's report, a chill seemed like it might have fallen upon the room. If Ginala didn't know better, there could have even been a sense of suspicion wafting off the others.

But surely not. Ginala had forged unbreakable bonds of trust with the members of the royal family. After all, she'd all but raised them, guiding them during these long decades and centuries, and in the entirety of that time, Ginala had never been given reason to doubt that she had the imperial family exactly where she wanted them. Surely, at this late hour, they wouldn't find some reason to harbor skepticism about her?

True, Redwinth was an outlier, a bit of an enigma, but that was only for the present. Ginala would figure out his wants, needs, and fears soon enough. Then she would twist him around her finger so that he would always do as she wanted.

Such had always been the case since Ginala had first landed on Yaksha proper's shores following the devastating end to the *NusraelShev*, and the number of royals who had slipped her collaring grasp could be counted on one hand. One was obviously that thief and betrayer Anya, but otherwise, it had been generations since she had felt any fear that her advice might go unheeded. And even in that particular situation, it had been Ginala's unwarranted worries that had caused her to kill an empress.

No doubt, such was the case even now. Of all the many rulers Ginala had guided in Yaksha's history, Sala was the one she felt was the most securely in hand, and if not, there was also the *thaalis*.

Giving herself a firm nod, Ginala set aside her concerns. She had other issues to which to attend, such as the recent conversation with Sheoboth. Her sister, the Crooked Crone, had to maintain vigilance. They couldn't allow the theft of the Orb of Regret, but when Ginala had pressed the matter, her sister had laughed in her face.

"*The Orb is safe,*" Sheoboth had sneered. "*You would do better to watch your own place in the world. Did the thieves not simply wander into your domain and steal away the Orb of Moss?*"

"*They made their theft when we were unsure of their plans,*" Ginala growled in response. "*The information from Surent Crèche had yet to be verified.*"

"*But you knew what Shet would want. You knew he'd want the Orbs destroyed, and you failed to secure yours.*"

Ginala had wanted to growl at her sister, but she had maintained her temper. "*Be that as it may, the past is written, and it cannot be unwritten or changed. Is your Orb secure?*"

"*Perfectly so,*" Sheoboth stated, going on to needle Ginala. "*But the bold thievery in your palace does make me wonder how much control you actually have over the elves.*"

"*I have all the control I need,*" Ginala replied, fingering a black ring.

"*Your thaali that's supposed to kill any elf you desire, including the entire race, if you so choose?*"

"*Exactly.*"

"*A blunt and stupid plan,*" Sheoboth sneered.

"It's better than your mindless hordes."

Sheoboth had smiled across the connection. "Keep believing that of my children. Keep believing that when I send them to consume your weak and foolish elves. But not your women. Those we'll impregnate to birth our queens. Just as we've always done."

That had been the end of the conversation, but the Crone's threat had Ginala worried. The Yaksha elves had no means to stop the tide of spiderkin Sheoboth could unleash. It had her wondering how best to blunt her sister's armies as she made her way back to the First Directorate, all the while feigning the limp of an old woman and the visage of a kindly grandmother.

"It confirms nothing," the empress said upon Ginala's departure.

Redwinth hadn't been a member of Yaksha's royal family for very long, and he only knew his mother-in-law in the vaguest of ways, but in that time, he'd learned to read some parts of her temperament and expressions. And right now what he was reading was that the empress was disquieted by Ginala's explanation of Duchess Cervine's report.

The quelchon hadn't actually lied very much. Instead, she'd merely omitted certain sections and twisted others, but in the end, her report made it sound as if Duchess Cervine hated Shet—which was true— and that she considered him a threat—also true—but that she considered the spiderkin to be the graver danger.

Perhaps that was true as well, but that wasn't what the duchess' missive had stated. She'd never spoken about the spiderkin.

"It confirms nothing," Enma's father agreed, "except that matters with the quelchon are not as straightforward as we thought just an hour ago."

The empress grunted, rising to her feet and pacing to the window overlooking her gardens. She crossed her arms. "She has been a trusted fixture in my life since I was a child."

Redwinth flicked his gaze to Enma, indicating the corner where they'd discovered the braid.

She nodded, understanding, rising to her feet as well and making her way to her mother's side. "There's something else."

Residar stood bathed in the very first rays of sunlight. The nearby creek burbled, and dew glinted on the meadow where the Shokans had decided to settle in. A crispness suffused the air—like the first bite of a tart—and the smell of loam and pinecones wafted on the faint stirrings of a breeze. The wind rustled trees that would soon go bare as autumn took hold of the highlands.

The world was otherwise quiet and peaceful, not yet awake—just the way Residar liked his mornings.

He glanced to where Hima slept next to Brilliance, with Kela sacked out in the sunshine. Of course, as soon as the doe woke, the peace would be ruined. It wasn't that Hima was a bad sort, but light in heaven, did she talk some, all the time yapping and asking questions and forgetful as a birdbrained child.

Truth was, after their initial rough meeting, Brilliance was the only one who could keep the doe quiet: something about her intimidating expression and oddly maternal behavior. The last still shocked Residar. Brilliance was a lot of things but a sweet mother hadn't been something he'd expected from her.

Residar glanced over again, seeing how the big snowtiger was curled around Hima with a paw resting on the doe's shoulder. A strange sight, seeing the great cat behaving kindly to what she wanted to hunt and kill. Residar nodded to himself. Yes, Brilliance had surprised him, grown mature after months of acting like a fool.

The snowtiger had even asked Brissianna for advice on how to teach Hima. And again, it showed wisdom on Brilliance's part. Brissianna— "Briss," as her brother called her—had once been a stone-cold killer, but prior to that, she had been a mother and a teacher, loving and devoted.

This time, Residar's eyes went to Brissianna. She lay in her rolls, breathing lightly. He smiled, admiring her loveliness. After the murder of his wife, Marin, and his transformation into a wraith, he never figured he'd ever admire another woman like that, not with lust, but with love and affection. And he had sure never figured that his love and affection would be directed toward the woman who had been his Isha in the world of wraiths.

Soft clip clops drew Residar's attention away from Brissianna. Fastness was coming.

"Come with me," the white ordered, not halting as he cut across the camp and headed into the surrounding woods.

With no thought of questioning the stallion, Residar paced after the white. He implicitly trusted Fastness. If not for the white, he'd still be a wraith.

At a short distance, in a small clearing barely large enough for the stallion to turn around, Fastness stopped. *"I need your help."*

"And you'll have it," Residar said. There wasn't anything he wouldn't do for the stallion.

Fastness appeared troubled, though, and he didn't right away say what was on his mind.

"What's wrong?" Residar asked.

Fastness whiskered softly. *"How close are you to opening Muladhara?"*

It wasn't the question Residar had expected. "I'm close. Another few weeks, and I should have it."

Having his Chakras closed meant Residar's *Jivatma* had reflected the absolute darkness of the Empty One, the father to Zahhack, the Hungering Heart. It had been He who had transformed a willing Residar into a wraith, several years ago now, during a time when he'd been at his lowest, right after his family had been murdered by Shet's monsters, and when he'd been on death's door. That was when Zahhack had sneaked His way into Residar's life, the Master offering a path to vengeance, which in hindsight was a pointless endeavor.

But Residar had taken that offer, and he had hated himself for it ever since. That hatred had only grown after the battle against the army of the Sunset Kingdoms, when Residar had killed and killed and killed, destroying people who were only wanting to defend their families.

That's when Residar had broken from the Hungering Heart, fully expecting to die without the nourishment a wraith could only find in the Hellmaw.

But Fastness had come into Residar's life and showed him a different path. It was all about returning his Chakras to neutral and eventually opening at least one of them, which Residar would do. If Fastness said it was important, then so be it. He'd see it accomplished.

However, in full honesty, just having his Chakras return to neutral was enough. Doing so had lifted away so much of Residar's pain and heartache. His *Jivatma* was no longer black as sin. Instead, it glowed under Devesh's steady light. And while getting it done hadn't been easy—it had been harder than anything Residar had ever attempted—it was also worth it. *So worth it.* Residar was at peace with himself and the world.

It didn't mean he still didn't struggle with the pain of his family's murder. That never faded. But sometimes the events of that terrible evening felt like they might have happened decades in the past or even in a different lifetime. Then there were other moments when the memories would catch Residar like a fish on the line. When it all came rushing back. Just a smell to remind him of Marin or a sound to recall how Tola used to love when he tickled her.

"*Good,*" Fastness said, returning Residar to the here and now. "*I need you, Brissianna, and Selin to head north. There's a town in the Savage Kingdoms. You should be able to reach it in a few months of travel. Titan's Reach is its name. A village full of humans who believe that Shet is a true god worthy of worship.*"

Looking for the joke, Residar stared at the stallion. While Fastness was wise and knowledgeable—he'd have to be since he was also Sapient Dormant—he also liked to play pranks. Lord Brat as Cinder Shade called him.

And his claim about a village full of Shet worshipers had to be some kind of joke. What kind of fools would be stupid enough to actually worship the false god? Deluded didn't begin to describe that kind of idiocy. And Residar would know better than most about the delusion of following evil.

But this didn't seem to be a joke. Fastness was deadly serious.

"What do you need me to do?"

"Convince them of the folly of their beliefs. We can't let Shet gain their aid."

"What's so important about this village?"

"They practice a type of trepanation, and through it, they've learned to access their Jivatma. There is no blue-and-green lightning hindering them either. Not like it does the Shokans and every other human on Seminal."

"They sound dangerous. A village full of people already trained in using *Jivatma.*"

Fastness nodded. *"You're right. The people of Titan's Reach can be dangerous, but they can also be a great ally. They can be the missionaries who help rebuild the BrightLands, the part of the world now known as the Savage Kingdoms. They can even become the next generation of Mythaspuris."*

It sounded like a glorious idea, but there was still a large problem. "And if I can't convince them to turn aside from their worship?"

Fastness might have sighed. *"Just do your best. But whatever you do, don't kill them. We'll deal with them in some other way."*

Residar exhaled in relief. He'd do anything for Fastness, but killing the innocent—no matter how ridiculous their beliefs—wasn't something he would ever again do.

In the temple of Ardevesh, Heremisth circled the anchor line leading to her Lord, Zahhack. The tarp that Manifold had placed upon it billowed now and then—a flapping of canvas—but otherwise, with it being the depths of the night, the nave was quiet. Not even a mouse moved, which Heremisth reckoned was wise of the small critters. If they approached Zahhack, either He would kill them with the mere horror of His presence, or she would consume the little rodent.

Soft footfalls broke the quiet, and Heremisth grimaced. Manifold was coming. This on a night when she'd been hoping for some privacy. Only rarely could Heremisth manifest a physical form, and whenever she did, she wanted time alone. Mostly because she'd never been pleased with her appearance in this Realm. It was embarrassing. She was pretty enough until she grinned and exposed a shark's mouth of jagged teeth. As for the girl-child raiment she sometimes wore, that was equally disturbing.

But then again, it was also humorous, especially how it scared Sapient.

She chuckled to herself when thinking about the last time she had seen the traitorous Mythaspuri. He'd been a white stallion, running flat out in full terror as she'd giggled and chased him through Mahadev.

"You couldn't sleep either?" Manifold asked.

Heremisth faced the restored Mythaspuri. Appearing to be a tall, powerfully built human, he paced toward her. Ruggedly handsome with a strong jaw and full lips. All told, he was so much finer than when he'd been a necrosed, well enough that she wouldn't mind a tumble with him.

In the millennia since they'd been forced into this détente, they hadn't formed a friendship—she hated Manifold, and she was sure the feeling was mutual—but they had become well acquainted with one another, and that included an odd kind of respect.

"I could sleep, but I didn't want to." The lie slid out before Heremisth could even think to alter it. By now, lying to Manifold was an ingrained habit.

Manifold grunted. "Your Lord slumbers?" He gestured to the tarp, which had fallen still.

She shrugged. "Zahhack never rests. He's probably thinking about something else."

"What about you? What are you thinking about?"

Heremisth smirked. She knew this game. She and Manifold had

been playing it for more years than she could count. He wanted to know what she had planned, which was another way of saying he had too much time on his hands and was busy thinking.

Well, let him think on this.

Heremisth transformed into a little girl wearing a blue dress with a yellow ribbon. Her dark hair was collected in a pair of ponytails.

Manifold breathed a tired sigh. "Why?"

It was a single-word question that indicated his frustration and confusion, and Heremisth laughed in delight. "I knew Sapient would find it terrifying. I didn't think you would, too."

"I don't. I find it revolting."

Heremisth pouted. "You don't think I'm cute?"

"I think you are a psychopath who's afraid of her own shadow."

The pout deepened. "What a cruel thing to say."

"I'll leave you alone, then." Manifold dipped his head and made to leave.

A strange sensation rippled through Heremisth's chest. Regret, an emotion she hadn't felt in so long and one that she detested. She doused it in anger. "Why did you really come down here?"

"I heard you moving about and thought it might be worth talking to you. We haven't done so very much since Rabisu left."

Rabisu. Heremisth scowled to herself. That little deviant. When she got her claws on him, she'd tear him into pieces. How dare he depart Mahadev without her permission. He was the one creature who had united her and Manifold. It had taken both of them to keep him out of the temple. But now that he'd escaped the city, there was little reason for her and Manifold to ever converse.

Rather than display her irritation, Heremisth schooled her features to stillness. "Rabisu will be dealt with in his own time."

Manifold shrugged. "As you say." He made to exit the nave once again, but he paused on the threshold, speaking over his shoulder. "You want power, but it will never fill your heart. You want to love Zahhack, but how can you love something that is incapable of reciprocity?"

He left before Heremisth could offer a scathing retort.

Sriovey stood within the deepest heart of Jade's Moon, amongst his crèche's holiest objects, which were gathered together in this nondescript vault. Included in this was Noon Gate, which had the rough shape and appearance of a billet of steel with a hole carved through the center. It was also how Sriovey had come home undetected. The vault was nearly always unoccupied since the treasures down here were considered too valuable to be brought out for public viewing.

A stupid thing, but right now, it worked to Sriovey's advantage.

He grimaced as he stared about. There were so many weapons on the walls: war hammers, axes, swords, knives, and armor. So many statues to his people's most illustrious wisdoms and warriors, all of which meant less to him than they once had.

Sriovey still honored his forebears, but the fact that they were so martial in orientation no longer sat without complaint within his gut. The wisdoms of the past had guided their people as best they could and the warriors had fought to their utmost to keep them alive, but for Sriovey, it was no longer what he wanted for himself. He didn't think those honored here should have simply known better—an insulting prejudice of the present. Instead, he had changed the way he thought.

Or rather, he *wanted* to change. He wasn't all the way there yet, but he'd taken the first, hard steps along that road. And in the process, how he figured he could help his people was different. Sriovey wanted to see his people escape to a better way of life, a more meaningful one.

It was why he was back in the Surent Crèche, meeting in secret with Derius down here in this vault. It was a plan they'd concocted before Sriovey had left for Shalla Valley. Once every two weeks, he'd come home to meet Derius and learn what was going on with the crèche.

This was the second time, and the news, it turned out, was getting steadily worse. Sriovey's father still had full control of Jade's Moon, and the wisdoms remained powerless to oppose him.

"That's where things stand now," Derius finished explaining. "And I see no way to stop your father."

Sriovey didn't either, and the lack of a plan galled him. If only he could talk to Cinder. If anyone could figure out a means to save Sriovey's people, it would be Hotgate. But they hadn't heard word from him in many weeks, and by now, he was probably in the Webbed Kingdom.

It didn't mean he was dead, though—Devesh, don't let him be dead. He couldn't be. After all, this was the same dumbass…

Sriovey corrected his thoughts.

The same *person* who had entered Mahadev, the cursed city from which no one had successfully escaped since the *NusraelShev*. But Cinder had managed it. Several years after going into Mahadev, he'd come back to his friends, right around the time when most of them had thought him dead and gone.

So why not believe that he'd also survive the Webbed Kingdom?

Of course, until he showed up again, Sriovey and everyone else would have to figure things out on their own.

"We can't bring everyone to Shalla Vale," Sriovey said. "It's a big enough place, but I doubt the holders would allow that many unclean people near the yakshins and Ashoka trees. They'd have a fucking fit—I mean." He flushed. He wanted to become a better person, but why did it mean he shouldn't curse? Why did that matter so much?

Derius laughed. "It's good to see some things haven't yet changed. You're cursing for one." He sobered a moment later. "But you are coming along. I can tell. You're already different compared to when you left a few weeks ago."

Sriovey grumbled. "I'd be farther along if I could curse."

"Then maybe you shouldn't fight your nature. Go ahead and curse."

"That's what Jozep says, but it still feels wrong," Sriovey said. "I'm trying to become gentle and meek." The entire time, he tried to keep a mocking tone out of his voice. Of course before all this, he'd never been or wanted to be gentle or meek.

"You're supposed to be calm and caring, not necessarily gentle. And being meek doesn't have anything to do with it anyway. Can't we still be fierce in opposing evil?"

Sriovey shrugged. It didn't seem possible. If he was calm and caring, how could he also be fierce? Right now it also wasn't of any concern. He and Derius had other things to discuss. "The Baptisers greatest strength lies here, in Jade's Moon. We might want to give it over to them and defend the outer cities and villages. Evacuate those opposed to the Baptisers."

Derius didn't like that notion. "Most of our people live in Jade's Moon."

"I know," Sriovey said, "but what other option do we have? Your father doesn't have enough soldiers to directly oppose Stipe." Mentally, he refused to call the man his father. "And that doesn't even account for that new force of dog-like creatures Stipe is supposed to have bred."

"Ur-Fels." Derius scowled in disgust. "The ancient ones from which we're supposed to have been created."

Seemingly of its own volition, Sriovey's sight went to a painting of Shokan, the Blessed One who had formed the dwarves. In the image, Shokan knelt, surrounded and loved by his creations. But like nearly all paintings of him, his features were blurred, and no one could properly say what he looked like.

"The Shokans are coming along," Sriovey said, wanting to give Derius some hope. "Your father's forces can defend Surent's outer villages and towns, and when our brothers are ready, we'll have them and the once-wraiths to help us take back Jade's Moon. It's the best way forward that I can see."

"What about the wisdoms?" Derius asked.

Sriovey had thought long and hard about this. He didn't like the wisdoms, but he couldn't stand back and let them be killed. "We should safeguard them, but I also think they need to be replaced. They were the ones who gave the crèche away to Stipe."

Derius grunted in agreement. Apparently, he'd already come to the same conclusion.

Sriovey rubbed his head. All this thinking was giving him a headache, and he found himself longing to return to the peace of Shalla Vale.

"There's something else," Derius said. "Simla had a recitation. She thinks that we need to go to Titan's Reach."

"Salt's old village?" Sriovey asked in surprise. "Why? Did she say when?"

"She wants to leave soon. In a few weeks. She thinks we'll be needed. That the people there need Serenity more than any others." He vacillated a moment. "She wants to take me and Willa, too."

Sriovey's headache was suddenly pounding much harder.

A warm wind blew through the grounds of Ardevesh. Coming from the south, it carried the briny scent of Mahadev Bay along with the gritty texture of the city's many granite buildings. The breeze groaned through a stand of trees, rattling the leaves and branches, and from there it gusted its way across green fields to where Manifold worked his crops, picking at weeds even in night's stillness. And finally, the wind reached the temple's entrance, swirling Heremisth's long, lank hair as she watched the darkness.

The wind reminded her of when she had been a Duchess of the Rakshasas, ancient centuries ago, back in her original Realm. Of her home overlooking the ocean. How she missed it. Her slaves and the torture she could inflict on those who dissatisfied her. The exquisite pleasures of administering punishment and pain. The glory of ruling her lessers.

All gone now, and she sighed in longing, her breath coming out in a heavy huff.

Heremisth had decided on taking a physical form this evening. It was the safest means of speaking to her Master. He had called on her several nights ago, stating He had orders for her.

She grimaced, hating her forced servitude.

Zahhack was reaching deeper into Seminal. Several years ago when Heremisth had chased Shokan and Sira from the city, her Master had but a finger's hold in Mahadev, His voice silent, but now he could touch her thoughts. Not easily and not often, but frequently enough to give her pause. She didn't like His voice echoing in crypts of her mind. Zahhack had the ability to alter her thoughts until they were no longer her own. All too easily, He could enslave her to His wants, and that wouldn't do.

While Heremisth was loyal enough to Zahhack, that didn't mean she trusted Him. Only a fool ever would.

She smirked at the thought, realizing that was exactly what she was: a fool. Only a fool would have taken on an incorporeal form or split her consciousness in three directions. But Heremisth had done so; all so she could maintain the three anchor lines that Zahhack had demanded of her and her sisters. True, it was now down to two anchor lines, but even then, it wasn't safe. All because of poor choices she had made millennia ago.

Fool.

Why hadn't she forced Sheoboth or Jesherol to accept some of the burden? Why hadn't she pretended to be unable to do as Zahhack had commanded? Why hadn't she raised her own empire like her sisters? No doubt, they laughed themselves silly thinking of how they'd tricked their foolish, younger sister and left her caged to their shared Master's dictates.

And until recently, Heremisth had been able to lie to herself, pretend that there would come a time when Zahhack would honor her above all others because of her faithfulness in maintaining His requirements.

Not anymore. Heremisth's mind and eyes were open. She was a slave, no different than the idiots who had sought to earn her approval back in the original Realms of the Rakshasas. But how could she free herself?

It was a question to which her thoughts endlessly circled.

And while considering the answer, her mind drifted to Manifold. He represented safety of a sort, but in trusting him, she'd simply be trading one sort of enslavement for another. It didn't matter how much Manifold proclaimed that Devesh's yoke was light. Any yoke was too heavy for what Heremisth wanted.

In this regard, she was much like Shet. She, too, wished to become like Zahhack, a force in all the Realms, not just here or amongst the rakshasas, but throughout all creation. A power, free to do whatever she wished.

Of course, there weren't many of those around. There never had been. In fact, the last able to make such a claim had been born several thousand years ago, an actual incarnation of the Divine. The son of a woodworker who Indrun had been unable to seduce; Indrun who had been loyal to her and her sisters at the time, and oddly enough, through failure had eventually achieved greatness.

Heremisth wished she had killed him before any of his glory had occurred. Either that or she wished she'd joined him.

It was too late now, though.

A whispering sound from deep in the temple threw off her deliberations, causing Heremisth to spin about, dread shivering along her spine. She knew what that sound heralded. Her Master was stretching His will toward her, pushing at the barrier preventing His emergence into Seminal. Manifold would feel it soon enough, and he'd do his best to shove away Zahhack's scratching finger from this world.

Nevertheless, it wouldn't be until after the Son of Emptiness, the Hungering Heart, had penetrated Heremisth's thoughts and made manifest His will.

"Heremisth. I have sight of you." His voice was as soft as a lover's caress, as cold as a knife sliding into her ribs. "Come closer, child, and know My command."

Heremisth could have refused Him, but she lacked the will. There was no denying Zahhack, not here nor anywhere. With the dread turned to terror, Heremisth shuffled toward the black hole centered in the floor of the altar. Toward the pews arranged around a tarp flapping under the influence of an unfelt breeze. And while she trudged, her heart raced. Her thoughts emptied of all but the need to escape, like a mouse walking toward a cunning cat.

She reached the tarp, withdrawing it from a section of the yawning hole leading to end of all. Her mind seized.

"You shall open wider the anchor line to the newly fashioned Realms of the Rakshasa," Zahhack stated.

Heremisth shivered at his voice, feeling a pain grip her heart. Her jaw ached. So did her left arm. She disregarded the pain. "Yes, my lord."

"Reach you to the rakshasas. I require a two and one-half score of them for a fell and righteous duty."

Two and one-half score? A dim, terrified portion of Heremisth wondered why Zahhack couldn't just speak with normal words.

She quickly silenced the traitorous part of her consciousness.

"I shall instruct the rakshasas in their task, merge them to the forces commanded by Corvid Drem, the leader of My wraiths. She rouses in the Sunsets."

"Only fifty?" Heremisth noted herself asking.

"That is my limit. I cannot control a larger number." A pause. "For now."

Some force hurled her aside. Heremisth smashed into a pew, numb and unthinking. She distantly noted Manifold replacing the tarp over the hole, a fierce expression of concentration on his face.

Her thoughts started to come clearer. The link to Zahhack had been interrupted. Manifold was trying to push the Son of Emptiness away from Seminal. And he was succeeding, but not to the same extent as he had once managed. The Hungering Heart was too powerful.

"Help me," Manifold begged, staring her way.

Heremisth shook off the last of her lethargy. Help Manifold lock Zahhack away from Seminal? What foolishness. She rose to her feet, ready to leave Manifold to his task.

"Please."

It was the please that halted her. If she helped him, would she not also be helping herself? Zahhack would conquer this realm, but she and her sisters had always planned on removing themselves from this plane of existence, continuing onward until they achieved the power they so desperately needed.

And by delaying the Son of Emptiness... wouldn't it give her a better chance at accomplishing her dream? Of remaining free of her Master?

It would, but that didn't mean she could utterly disobey him. She would still have to do as Zahhack commanded and send fifty rakshasas to the Sunsets. But after that...

Her decision made, Heremisth moved to stand next to Manifold, watching as he strained. "What do I do?"

31

"There it is," Anya said, gesturing with her chin.

She and Cinder had crested a steep mountain pass and were currently laying on their stomachs, staring downhill. This was their first view of the deepest part of the Webbed Kingdom, a place to which Anya had never before expected to travel. Even as a ranger, she had rarely pressed into the home of the spiderkin and certainly not these northern bounds, which were the agreed upon border between Naraka and the lands controlled by Sheoboth. Anya continued to study the land, looking for some sign that it was under the control of her people's great enemy.

But there was nothing.

The Webbed Kingdom looked no different than any other part of Seminal. Down below the rocky slope upon which they perched, the land flattened into a broad valley where a conifer forest glowed verdant under sunlight lancing through thin clouds stretched across a blue sky. The trees edged a high mountain lake that gleamed mirror bright, but most importantly, there were no obvious signs of spiderkin.

Anya frowned in thought. Why weren't there any guards or scouts warding the way into the kingdom?

"What do you think?" Cinder asked, apparently waiting on her lead, which he hadn't always done—certainly not when Rabisu's weave had interfered with their memories and emotions.

It only made sense that he would now. Cinder was a warrior without compare, but he wasn't a ranger. He lacked the full set of skills needed to examine the landscape and see what wasn't obvious.

And something *was* down there, setting off Anya's warning instincts. As a result, she held off from answering Cinder just yet. They were Blended as deeply as they could manage, using also the *nomasra* that enhanced their Talent and gave them the scent of a spiderkin. They had time to surveil the situation.

After a few more minutes of inspection, Anya saw it—a rustling in the trees lining the western edge of the lake—*spiderkin*. They herded a drove of hogs to the water. Upon seeing them, Anya created a weave that mimicked a pair of spyglasses and set her sights along the lakeshore, looking for any large trails. Several more came into view, and tracing them, she viewed what she had initially taken to be a scattering of simple meadows but which might actually be farm country. It certainly seemed that way once she accounted for their regular spacing.

"We'll have to be careful around those fields," Anya said, pointing out what she'd noticed.

"Do we go down now?" Cinder asked.

Anya nodded. "Slowly and carefully." She rose to her feet, easing down the mountainside.

Cinder followed, and they kept to the edges of the downhill slope, remaining in shadow as much as possible. An hour later, the path leveled, and Anya led them west, circling the lake where they entered the forest. The sunshine cut off like a pulled drape over a window.

Anya kept her senses on alert, easing forward, careful not to break or bend any boughs. She did her best to leave the needle-covered forest floor undisturbed since Blending wouldn't hide signs of their passage. They soon came across a game trail and were able to push forward a little faster. All the while, Anya let her gaze wander, searching for movement, listening for the rustle of spiderkin, smelling for them, too.

A half-mile later, they came across one of the larger trails she'd earlier sighted from the ridge.

Anya crouched low, holding up a hand, ordering Cinder to halt. She let her senses roam. Was there anything untoward?

Cinder waited patiently. His senses were generally more acute, and if he hadn't noticed anything, there likely wasn't anything of concern close at hand. But senses could be fooled, and Anya relied on instincts as well.

There. A hundred yards distant, deeper into the woods. An unnatural swaying of the pine boughs. Anya pointed in the direction of the disruption.

Cinder peered at the indicated area, nodding slowly.

Seconds later, a pair of spiderkin chittered as they made their way toward the lake, and Anya activated the *nomasra* that allowed her to understand their speech.

Soon enough, the spiderkin passed close enough for her to make out their words. "I hate scouting," one of them said to the one closer at hand. "Nothing ever happens here."

"It's better than farming," the other replied.

"Too right, Sister," the first one replied in approval. She chittered in a way that reminded Anya of laughter. "Lettuce work like that should go to the males."

"Useless chits," agreed the second.

They wandered along the path, heading for the lake, discussing the weather and complaining about their leaders. Bemused, Anya watched them go. In every encounter she'd ever had with the spiderkin, they had never displayed the slightest sense of having any emotion other than outrage and fury. All they did was scream mindlessly and charge. It was the spiderkin way. All rage and ferocity with no hint that they might have any other motivating emotions or even intellect—definitely nothing like complaining about mundane topics such as work, weather, and leaders.

Anya shook off her reverie, spending another couple of minutes to study the large trail where the spiderkin herded their farm animals. This time her instincts didn't warn her off.

One last examination, and she darted across the trail. Cinder followed on her heels, and they pressed deeper into the trees. On they went, the forest unchanging around them, rarely talking as they steadily made their way south and west.

During their trek, they circled around the clearings, which Anya confirmed were farms and fields where hogs, goats, and sheep were contained. Generally, male spiderkin worked the land while a small group of female warriors stood watch.

As dusk settled across the forest, Anya finally found a game trail heading west, and several miles later, she came across an undisturbed brambled thicket—blackberry, dewberry, and silver birch. It was massive, stretching a hundred yards in either direction.

Anya sourced *lorethasra*, creating a weave from Sira's memories. A portion of the briar patch creaked outward, leaving open the beginning of a thin trail. It was barely wide enough for a single person, but it would do.

She eased forward, with Cinder close on her heels. The thicket continued to open before them, while behind, it closed as she let the weave resolve. They pressed deeper into the briar patch, and many yards later, Anya came across a small clearing, only a dozen feet in diameter, but it would do.

"Looks like a good place to stop for the night," Cinder noted, glancing around. "Better than out in the open." He groaned as he eased his rucksack on the ground. "I miss the mules."

"So do I," Anya agreed. "At least we know there really are farms inside the Webbed Kingdom. We'll use them to resupply instead of eating our stores."

"Where are we?" Cinder asked. He pulled out a map supplied by the goblins. It highlighted the areas controlled by the various nests of spiderkin along with the area where the most powerful queens lived. That was where they would likely find Sheoboth.

Anya settled next to him, tracing an area on the map. "We came through Carnin's Pass and covered a couple miles this afternoon. I'd say we're about here." She tapped a location. She noticed Cinder's eyes flicking about the map, and in the way they had, she knew what he was pondering. "We're about two weeks from reaching the entrance to the main cavern."

Cinder grunted. "Figured as much, but we're also coming up on a boundary between two tribes. It would be a good place to resupply, and if we have to fight any spiderkin, we can maybe make it look like it was the work of the other nest."

It wasn't a bad idea, but Anya wasn't yet ready to commit to such a plan. "Before doing that, let's see how they man the borders first."

"It would be *woman* the borders. Their warriors are all female."

Anya chuckled. "Just for that, you get to make us dinner."

Cinder replied by handing her a length of jerky and a selection of dried fruit. He smirked. "Dinner is served."

"Devesh, it's cold," Cinder said, pausing to warm his hands. Gloved though they were, they felt like blocks of ice, and he shoved them under his arms, trying to imbue them with some heat.

"Too cold for your warm Pureblood?" Anya asked with a smile.

Cinder wasn't fooled. Her smile was strained. She didn't like this weather any more than he did. But still, what did she mean by her question? What was a Pureblood?

Cinder asked her, and Anya's smile fell, replaced by an expression of uncertainty. "I don't know."

He stared at her a moment longer, eventually shrugging away the question. They still had a long climb to make and standing around wouldn't get it done. He pushed on.

It had been a little under two weeks since they'd entered the Webbed Kingdom, and they currently trudged along a steep trail toward a cavern high in the mountains. Boulders littered the path, and scree made the footing slick. The world was white as the wind whipped, swirling snow in sheets. It moaned through the narrow passage that they struggled to climb, chilling them to the bone. At any moment, Cinder felt like the wind's claws might hurl him off the mountain.

He glared as he stared upward, searching for their destination: the entrance to a cave system. Once inside, they would at least be out of the weather. He'd be so happy when they reached it.

Hours longer they trekked, one plodding foot in front of the next. Despite the double layer of thick socks and the heavy boots, Cinder couldn't feel his toes. Snowflakes clung to his eyelashes, and he had a wool scarf wrapped around his face and head. Even then, the knifing wind cut through his protections. He'd long ago lost sensation in his ears. Frostbite could be a real possibility if they didn't get to the cavern soon.

He might have created a bubble of Air and heated it with Fire, but the skill required eluded him. *The fragging Orbs.* While for Anya, the answer was different. She wasn't strong enough to maintain even one such weave in the face of such hostile weather.

Regardless, once they reached the cavern, they could build a fire—it would be their first since entering the Webbed Kingdom——and warm themselves. Just as wonderful, they could sleep in peace since there were no spiderkin at this elevation. The creatures couldn't survive the thin air.

On they went, one slogging step up the mountain.

"Cinder."

It took him a moment to realize Anya had called for him to stop. On a steeply sloped ledge, she stood off the trail. He blinked, trying to make sense of why she had halted. Another blink and he finally understood.

Directly above her was a narrow cave. They'd have to crawl to get in there, but Cinder didn't care. It was likely a lot warmer within than out here in the wind.

He shambled back to Anya, waiting as she scrambled up the sloping ledge. She paused to take off her backpack, shoving it into the cavern before she hauled herself within. He followed on her heels, crawling inside on elbows and knees. Every so often, his head would bump the ceiling, inspiring a vague hope that the cave would eventually rise.

A hundred yards later, just as he started to wonder if this was the right cavern, the floor began a gentle slope downward.

"Hold on," Anya said. She had a glowing globe floating in front of her to light their way. "The floor falls away a few feet ahead."

Cinder coughed, the dust of their passage irritating his sinuses. Several seconds later, Anya had her gloved hands braced against the cavern walls. She dropped out of view, landing with a soft thud.

"Come on down," she urged.

Cinder shoved his rucksack forward. "Catch." An impact followed by a soft grunt indicated that Anya had managed to do so. Cinder then braided his own glowing light and set it floating forward.

Anya stood about ten feet below him, already setting down his rucksack as she viewed him expectantly.

Cinder examined the area in which she stood. It was a roughhewn space, round in shape and strewn with small rocks and boulders. Best of all, behind Anya the cavern continued, appearing tall enough that they could walk some of the way at least. *Thank Devesh.* This was the right place, after all, just the way the goblins had described it. A perfect place to rest and recover.

Cinder dropped down to where Anya waited.

Of silent accord, they got to work. Cinder gathered some rocks and formed a fire pit. It didn't matter where he placed it since there would be no flames, but nonetheless, by habit, he built it close to where the cavern exited out onto the mountain's slopes. In the meantime, Anya unpacked the fresh meat they'd earlier stolen.

It had been the fifth farm they'd ransacked, but this time, they'd been forced to kill the guards and farmers who had discovered them in the midst of their thievery. Hopefully, any investigating spiderkin would take the deaths to be an attack from a rival nest.

Regardless, Cinder figured they were flush with food, enough to last them for several weeks if they were careful. But that didn't account for the water they'd need. He hoped they ran across some underground streams since it was a minimum of three more weeks to get to Sheoboth's lair.

Three weeks of tense travel, where a single mistake could see them doomed. The entire time, they'd be surrounded by enemies with no easy way to retreat.

Sure, they could call Liline and hope she would create an anchor line to bring them out, but who knew if she'd actually follow through. Just as easily, and for whatever short-sighted reason she chose, the Titan could hang them out to dry.

Minutes later, Cinder had the firepit completed. Then set to gathering a grouping of likely rocks, stacking them. Next, he punched through the blue-and-green lightning—much easier now with four Orbs destroyed—and created a graceless braid of Fire. His fine control was still lacking, but despite his struggles, he was able to send the weave rushing in an uncontrolled fashion into the gathered stones. They quickly grew hotter, glowing red, but Cinder wasn't done. He continued to pour Fire into them until they were blazing yellow.

"I think it's hot enough," Anya said. She'd discarded her gloves and had her hands stretched out over the hot stones, sighing in satisfaction.

Cinder followed suit, going as far as to unwind his scarf and rub heat into his ears. The air in the cavern had warmed considerably, and it felt like he was slowly thawing and coming back to life. After a while, he felt comfortable enough to take off his boots and socks and roast his feet over the hot stones. Neither he nor Anya spoke, both of them intent on restoring lost warmth.

Eventually, Cinder sat back, putting his socks and boots back on. "Let's not do that again." He went to the food Anya had laid out and began planning what to do with the provisions. Jerky and roasted vegetables would probably be the best solution, undoubtedly easier to carry that way, and just as important, this might be the last time they would have the safety to actually cook their food. The rest of the trek into the Webbed Kingdom would have to be without a stone fire.

"Do you need help with that?" Anya asked.

Cinder glanced at her, smiling. "You actually think you can help?"

Anya shifted, appearing embarrassed. "Well, I can try."

"Just keep your pretty self out of the way. We don't want you burning the food."

Anya shrugged, smiling slightly as if she knew a secret and couldn't wait to reveal it. "You know I'm a ranger. I've cooked for myself plenty of times in the field."

"And how many times did the food taste good?"

"Good point."

Steaks seasoned with nearly the last of their salt and pepper were what Cinder prepared for dinner. He also roasted corn and potatoes, and after they'd eaten, he created an oven to slow-cook the rest of the fresh meat and vegetables. It would take hours, but the food also wouldn't require much of his attention.

He went to Anya then, who sat on her bedrolls, studying their map. Her braid of light shone down on her.

"Find anything interesting?" he asked, settling next to her.

"Nothing new," she said. "I just want to make sure I know the landmarks. This cave system is endless. We could easily get lost in here."

Cinder grunted, moving to situate himself in his bedroll. He closed his eyes, wanting an hour of rest. It had been a hard day. "Tell me if you find anything interesting." He scratched at his beard, giving a faint notion to shaving.

"I like it," Anya said.

He cracked an eye, viewing her in question.

"The beard. I like it." She moved to snuggle next to him inside his bedroll. Her arm lay across his torso, and she peered intently at him, a vulnerable expression on her face.

Cinder stared back, understanding what she wanted since he longed for the same thing. He drew her close, kissed her softly at first, more passionately after. It had been too long since they'd been alone and safe.

The descent into the heart of the Webbed Kingdom took most of several days, and once they reached it, Cinder discovered a world unlike anything he had ever expected to see. Rather than dank caverns covered in mold and dust, the tunnels were clean and swept clear of debris. The walls were smoothly sculpted and with clear thought given to where supplies and stores were to be kept. Best of all, the corridors weren't dark and cramped. Instead, they contained dim lighting and were tall enough for Cinder to walk upright.

It was nothing like the nest that Cinder had encountered during his first Trial as a member of the Third Directorate.

His considerations cut off when Anya held up a hand, indicating for him to stop. She gestured to a branching tunnel. The opening was largely sheathed in a thin webbing. Cinder nodded understanding. From within the corridor came a questioning chittering.

A spiderkin guard was likely on patrol. Cinder and Anya had encountered a number of them so far, but always before, they had been in groups of five or six. Too many to successfully attack and keep their presence hidden. On one occasion, they had even encountered groups of spiderkin engaged in combat.

But if this was a lone spiderkin, then maybe they could capture and interrogate the creature. It should be possible. Cinder and Anya were Blended, and so far, it had served them well. They hadn't come close to being found out, and he figured it would be the case here.

And even if they were seen, they could always just kill the spiderkin.

Cinder got Anya's attention, indicating what he wanted. She nodded.

They entered the corridor, careful around the webbing. It would have alerted more of the guards. Anya flicked her hands at the ground—more webbing. This was also a problem they'd encountered, and they activated another of Liline's *nomasras*. This one granted them the ability to not stick to the webbing.

They paced on toward the chittering. Yards later, they discovered a spiderkin male unloading a large cart, moving stores into a room while a female watched. Cinder glanced back in the direction they'd come, forward as well, questing his senses for signs of any other spiderkin.

There were none, and these two evidenced no notion of Cinder and Anya's presence.

They observed the spiderkin a few seconds longer. By now, the efficient male had nearly emptied the wagon whereas the female stood close at hand, appearing bored.

Anya gestured to the male. *She was going to kill him.* Cinder's job would be to engage the female. He conducted *Jivatma*, creating a bubble to hide the stink of his *lorethasra* when he sourced it. Seconds later—accepting the pain of the blue-and-green lightning—he was ready, nodding slightly to Anya.

She crept forward. Cinder timed her movements. As soon as she struck, he'd attack the female. An instant later, she stabbed, and the male was dead. The female spun about, mouth agape. She made to lunge toward Anya, but Cinder pulled her short with a weave of Air. He collapsed her legs, pressing them tight, shoved her mouth closed.

It wasn't easy holding her in place. Would have been simpler if the blue-and-green lightning didn't hinder his full use of *Jivatma* and *lorethasra*.

"Burn the male," he said, teeth clenched with effort. "I'll learn what we can from this one." Cinder pushed the helpless spiderkin into the room into which the male had been unloading the stores. It was a large space, square and with walls lined with shelves full of grains and flour. A single, straight path, wide enough for the cart, cut through the chamber.

Anya must have already noticed it as well since she quickly pulled the wagon inside and closed the door behind her. The same dim lighting as in the hallways illuminated the room. An instant later, the tension of holding the spiderkin in place was relieved when Anya added her own braid of Air to Cinder's.

"This won't be fun," she said, sounding as unhappy as Cinder felt.

He didn't want to do this. What they'd have to do in order to gain the information they required disgusted him. Cinder stared at the spiderkin in regret, recognizing her shivering for the terror she obviously felt.

Why couldn't she have just been a mindless monster? That way, he could kill her without too much remorse. Instead, she knew what was about to happen, and… Cinder swallowed his empathy. This was necessary, but by Devesh, he wished it wasn't.

"I'm going to let her speak," he said, slowly lifting the braid around the spiderkin's jaws. She chittered, and he immediately snapped shut her mouth.

"Let me," Anya said, activating the *nomasra* that allowed communication with the spiderkin. Through it, she spoke to the creature, making no promises, but simply stating what they needed to learn.

"You want to see the Great Mother?" the spiderkin asked. She chirped laughter. "She'll eat you before you even have a chance to chitter a question."

"How do we reach her?" Anya asked, doing the talking while Cinder maintained his braid.

Surprisingly, the spiderkin gave them detailed instructions, speaking of the different territories of the Webbed Kingdom, including the higher caste nests and tribes that bordered Sheoboth's lair.

Cinder viewed the spiderkin in surprise. She no longer shivered, and instead she viewed them steadily with her multitudinous eyes. A sense of leering amusement emanated from her.

"Why are you so willing to tell us how to reach your Great Mother?" Anya asked, speaking the same question on Cinder's mind.

"Because you will die," the spiderkin said. "The Great Mother will consume you. Or other sisters and mothers of mine. You are walking corpses. You will kill me, but in the Great Weaving, I will be reborn and laugh at your pathetic deaths."

Cinder disregarded her humor. They had to make sure she wasn't lying. "Repeat what you said," he ordered. "Tell us again how to reach the Great Mother."

"Why?"

"Because I said so." Cinder hardened his heart and tightened his weave, cutting into the spiderkin's body. She groaned in pain, lines of ichor oozing from her legs. Seconds later, he eased off.

The spiderkin glared at him. It was clear despite their obvious differences. "I will speak. There is no need for pain-giving."

Once again, she spat out the detailed instructions, and as she did so, Cinder compared what she was currently saying with what she'd already told them. The information was the same.

"Thank you," Anya said, her voice solemn.

"And now you will kill me?"

Anya nodded, although Cinder doubted the spiderkin understood the gesture. "I'm afraid so."

"Why did you kill Dan'ack?"

"The male?" Anya asked.

"A gentle one. He was never chosen as a mate, but he was full of vigor. He made me laugh. I hope he's reborn in a better world."

"So do I," Anya said. A single thrust, and it was over.

Cinder stared at the dead spiderkin in guilt and regret. "Why do I feel like we did something wrong?"

Anya faced him, her visage echoing his sorrow. "Because we did. And we'll have to do it again. You know this?"

Cinder nodded. He knew, but he wished it wasn't so.

32

Anya knew exactly how long she and Cinder had been traveling the Webbed Kingdom, but some days it was hard to care. Some days it felt like they'd been within these brooding caverns for years on end and with no end in sight. Nothing but gloomy corridors with bare lights to illuminate their way; the ear-aching sound of spiderkin chittering, and the stink of dust, blood, and some inexplicable odor that Anya took to be that of the creatures who inhabited these halls. And all the while there was the shoulder-clenching tension where at any moment a troop of guards might sense them.

In any case, for an elf, the unending darkness and setting felt like a stygian nightmare. Worse, their journey was about to grow harder. Thus far, they had traveled along the outer edges of the kingdom, the less inhabited portions where the lower caste nests held sway. Now, though, they would have to enter the deeper parts toward the more densely populated, higher caste regions.

Cinder, who currently had the lead, raised a hand, calling for a halt.

Anya immediately spied the reason. There was a different stench pervading the corridor in which they found themselves, an area that looked to have once been a vast prison. It was deep underneath the living areas of the Webbed Kingdom, a set of unending, largely unused hallways. Three levels tall and containing a seemingly endless number of barred cells. Thick dust coated the floors.

They'd decided to come this way after interrogating a spiderkin, this one a male. He'd claimed only a single tribe—the Madri-Ma Clan—made their home here, a place below the heart of the higher caste regions and Sheoboth's lair.

They'd trusted the spiderkin male because, strangely enough, the creatures always answered honestly and did so without hesitation whenever they were questioned. They were often clearly afraid of being killed, but Anya was surprised by how courageously they met their end and how oddly protective the females were of their males.

With the males being so weak, she had always figured the females would treat them poorly, but it wasn't the case. The males had names and personalities, and the females genuinely wanted what was best for them.

In this—learning more about the spiderkin—Anya found herself feeling empathetic toward them. They deserved a better life, to understand that there were ways to greatness that didn't require killing in service to the nest—or even in service to the world, which is the only way Anya could accept her own actions in the Webbed Kingdom.

The spiderkin should have a chance to receive grace, and Anya found herself wanting that for them. Although they were the great adversary of her people, the Yaksha elves, she leaned on what she felt sure Sira would have sought out for the spiderkin. The Blessed One would have wanted to see them saved.

A moment later, that higher ideal was put to the test when Anya looked to the prison cell where Cinder had halted. So far, they'd only come across rotting, old bones that might have been down here for centuries. But within this cell, there was a pile of fresher corpses. From the score of them emanated the putrid stench of rot. They retained flesh on their frames and had likely been dead for only several years.

Into this room, they'd been tossed like trash, their limbs flung in every direction like kindling. Pools of blood had dried beneath them, and they gazed sightlessly, lacking eyes and ears, but Anya knew them for what they had been in life.

Elves. Females. Tortured, with abdomens ripped open. They'd been used as breeders for the spiderkin, just like the very first spiderkin whose queens had been implanted inside the wombs of elven women.

Anya swallowed heavily. What pain these poor women must have endured. Alone, tormented for months that must have seemed endlessly long. Then killed during a torture of delivery. She wept for them.

"Why?" Cinder asked. The question held an ocean of fury and outrage.

"Because that's how their greatest and most powerful queens are often birthed," Anya said, her voice toneless. She couldn't express the heartbreak she was feeling. To do so might cause her to lose control and scream incoherently. Right now, she had no empathy for the spiderkin. She wanted to burn this whole prison and kingdom down.

Cinder got them moving past the horrifying sight. "That male said that a lower caste nest rules this prison, the Madri-Ma Clan," he said. "They live directly above this level."

Anya forced aside the images of the dead elves, focusing instead on Cinder's words, what he was parsing his way through. The two of them still had a Trial to complete, and grieving over the dead right now wouldn't do them any good. She made herself think. "What if the Madri-Ma Clan was trying to breed a more powerful group of ruling queens? That's why they needed the elves back there."

It was a regular occurrence. As a ranger, Anya had come across spiderkin raids deep in the heart of Yaksha, and almost always, some of the women would be missing.

"Will they really be that much more powerful?" Cinder asked.

Anya nodded. "They'll not only be larger and stronger, but also more charismatic. Other spiderkin will be drawn to them, including those from higher-caste nests."

Cinder grunted. "We can use that."

"What are you thinking?"

"I'm thinking that the safest way for us to get into the heart of this kingdom is if the spiderkin are too busy fighting each other."

Anya wasn't seeing it.

Cinder explained. "If the Madri-Ma Clan has twenty hungry young queens leading them. Twenty hungry young queens who are bigger, stronger, and more charismatic, I'm sure they'll just be aching for a reason to invade the regions controlled by a higher caste. We'll give them that reason."

Cinder dropped his Blend and used the *nomasra* that would give him the appearance and scent of a spiderkin—a high caste one, it turned out. He rushed toward a score or so of clustered spiderkin warriors, who'd come to a milling halt. *That wouldn't do.* They'd been pursuing him for the past fifteen minutes, only catching a brief sight of him now and then, and he wasn't yet ready for them to give up the chase.

A reticle in his eyes, he sent a series of underpowered Fireballs bursting into the spiderkin. The subsequent explosions caused little damage, just tossing the creatures around, but it did what Cinder wanted; it got the spiderkin royally angry. They screamed outrage, swarming in the direction from which he'd attacked.

But he was already gone.

He'd darted away from the line of their angry ranting down a wide corridor, and took a right. Dodged a bunch of males rushing about in confusion and fear. Pressed into an alcove, waiting for the back end of the females he'd recently attacked to pass him by. He pushed out, trailing them, Blending hard, utilizing the *nomasra* that hid his scent and also the one to listen in on the conversations going on.

Nothing new to learn. Another set of Fireballs got the spiderkin further enraged, and they spun in the direction from which he'd assaulted them.

Again, Cinder was gone like a ghost. This time he didn't want them persisting on the chase. A few turns, and he lost them. But he didn't stop.

On he went, evading males and females as well as the grasping tendrils of webbing meant to trap the unwary. At this point, the latter was merely a cause for minor concern. He had grown used to avoiding the strands of webbing, especially since his *nomasra*-enhanced boots allowed him to traverse the silken threads without getting entangled in their sticky binding.

It was too bad he couldn't use the gloves meant for the same purpose. But the Fireballs would burn right through them.

On Cinder went, careful and quick, until he reached the less-lived-in sections of the Madri-Ma Clan's nest. A hundred yards later, he was heading down a narrow corridor. Another left and right and he was back to the unused storage room that he and Anya had chosen for their base of operations. Double checking to make sure no one was there to witness, he hustled inside.

He sensed Anya already within, and before doing anything else, he linked his Blend with hers.

She had a Fireball in hand, letting it wisp away once she saw him. "How did it go?"

Cinder breathed out a sigh of relief. He'd been rushing around for the past hour, dodging spiderkin and leading them on a dangerous chase. "Good enough," he replied. "Another day of attacks, and I think we might get them to muster their warriors to head upward."

"And draw them into attacking the higher caste nest."

It was the plan he'd concocted upon seeing the corpses of the elven women a week ago. He still struggled getting that image out of his mind. In getting to know the spiderkin, he could see their potential—they didn't have to be as they were—but visualizing the dead elves threatened to snuff out that desire. Forced him to think of the spiderkin as nothing but the enemy; to kill them in whatever numbers were necessary to complete this Trial.

To do so, he and Anya had started by interrogating members of the Madri-Ma Clan and learning all they could about the nest: its composition and leadership, its plans for the future, and where its stores were kept. They'd even learned the exact location of Sheoboth's lair as well as that of the Orb of Regret, an unforeseen stroke of luck.

Following on had been a series of low-level hit and run attacks. They'd used the *nomasra* that gave them the appearance of a high-caste spiderkin, killing a few warriors but always careful to leave a witness. That witness would hopefully go on to report that the ones attacking were of a higher caste. Over time, their assaults had grown more brazen. They'd taken to burning supplies and provisions, still making sure that a high-caste warrior was seen doing the attacking.

And based on the conversations Cinder had overheard over the past few days, that's exactly what the queens of the Madri-Ma Clan believed, especially the younger, more aggressive ones, the ones bred from the elves.

"We'll want to call Liline again before heading upward," Anya said, interrupting Cinder's musings.

This was also part of their plan: having the goblins and ghouls mass along the borders of the Webbed Kingdom was bound to get Sheoboth's attention. Liline should have already had the zahhacks do so at least twice so far. On the third occasion, the Titan would seek a parlay with the Crooked Crone, luring her out of her lair. And that was when Cinder and Anya would attack Sheoboth's home, sneak into her cavern, and steal the Orb of Regret while the high-caste spiderkin nests were engaged in putting down the Madri-Ma Clan. Afterward, it would just be a matter of getting clear of the cavern, calling Liline, and having her anchor line them away to safety.

Cinder breathed out a sigh. "Let's call Liline tomorrow. Give it another couple of days to get the Madri-Ma Clan properly furious." He flashed a wry grin. "That's when our lives will become interesting."

Anya quirked an eyebrow. "That sounds like a curse."

"I'm pretty sure it is."

Senabeth was old by spiderkin standards, wise and of great influence in all the clans, but compared to the ancient knowledge and puissance of Sheoboth, she was but a child. Not that such was a sin. All were fresh from the egg in comparison to the one who had created their race: The Great Mother and Queen, Sheoboth.

And right now, the Mother needed to learn of the disaster caused by the execrable Madri-Ma Clan.

Senabeth sped forward, claws clicking on the smooth white marble of the throne hall, eager to pass on the information. She passed the line of sentinels monitoring the massive cavern, the finest warriors of the Pentad, the five nests who held preeminence in the Webbed Kingdom. The guards stood arrayed amongst the tree-trunk thick stalactites and stalagmites that columned the space, carefully observing Senabeth as she rushed along. And high overhead, a single light beamed directly upon Mother's throne, while everywhere else it was properly dark, the air filled with the delicately musky aroma of the People.

Senabeth reached Sheoboth's dais, and she bowed low before giving her troubling report.

When she finished, Mother sat silent, staring downward from where she sat atop her throne, no expression betraying her thoughts. Senabeth tried to control a shiver of nervousness. Mother's brooding attention was never easy to absorb.

The Queen was ancient, deadly, and wise, and from her emanated the sense of the inevitable. She was a rockslide, massive enough that if she chose to step down from her dais, she would still easily overtop Senabeth, twice her size and able to meet the eyes of a Titan without having to gaze upwards. The Great Mother dominated everything, including the massive cavern that served as her home and throne hall.

The Queen stirred at last, speaking. "Why is the Madri-Ma Clan invading the regions of the higher castes?"

"We do not yet know," Senabeth answered. "Early information indicates they believe *they've* been under continuous small-scale assaults from a small group of higher-caste warriors. They've suffered many losses to their food supplies and stocks."

Mother unfolded her limbs, rising to her full height. From her flooded the pressure of leashed anger. "And who approved this attack on the Madri-Ma Clan?"

The guards arranged around the hall, stirred upon seeing Mother stand. Generally, when she did so, someone died… usually the bearer of bad news.

Senabeth knew such might be her own fate, but she stood upright, brave and bold, refusing to cower. Death, after all, was a part of life. The guiding light of the spiderkin was to fearlessly accept it when it arrived. Senabeth wasn't sure she'd live through this audience, but she also figured she'd lived well enough already. "No one," she answered in reply to the Queen's question. "At least no one is admitting to it."

"And the Madri-Ma Clan? What do they have to say?"

"Only that they won't be driven to extinction through treachery."

Sheoboth hissed. "Have the scents spread throughout the caverns. I want to meet with their queens. Same with the senior queens of the Pentad. They are to cease all hostilities. We will discover the cause of these troubles."

Senabeth bowed low. "As you will." She didn't bother feeling relief yet. There was more to relay.

Mother noticed. "What else?"

"An army of goblins and ghouls have gathered on our northern border. Again." The scents transmitted had been clear.

Mother hissed in irritation. "What do they want this time? It's the third massing in the past six weeks."

"They won't say, but Titan Liline wants a parlay." It was the second time she had asked for one since the goblins and ghouls had started massing on the border. This time the communication had come through the *divaspana* that the Titans had a year ago provided and which Senabeth still mistrusted.

"Of course, she does," Mother grumbled.

Now was the reason for Senabeth's nervousness. "Liline demands that it be in person. She was quite adamant about it."

For several long seconds that seemed to stretch to hours, Mother didn't respond. But in the end, she did. "So be it. Contact the Titan. I will meet her in the same location as before." She resettled on her throne. "And if that upstart child dares demand anything else, I'll devour her."

Senabeth bowed low a third time. "As you will." Her words spoken, she sped out of the throne hall, grateful to have survived the audience.

Cinder ducked his head and ran, arms pumping, legs lifting, *Jivatma* powering him forward. The spiderkin were on him and Anya, right on their tail. Something must have gone wrong with their Blends since the fragging creatures seemed able to see right through them. It was the same with the *nomasras* meant to give them the appearance and scent of a spiderkin. For the past ten minutes, the creatures had chased them down. It had been an unexpected encounter when Cinder and Anya had turned a corner and nearly run into twenty-five of the monsters, not counting the brute out front.

The spiderkin had immediately set off in a cacophony of excited screeches, and it hadn't taken long to realize the Blends weren't working. After that, Cinder and Anya had hauled off at a dead sprint.

Unfortunately, the fragging spiderkin were able to keep up, and nothing Cinder and Anya did was able to shake them loose. The creatures stayed with them, racing through the corridors, past males and females alike, picking up more outraged spiderkin along the way. Killing a half-dozen did nothing to thin their numbers since by now there were over five hundred tearing after them.

Of course, Shokan could have handled that many, but the Blessed One hadn't been debilitated with the fragging blue-and-green lightning.

Anya signaled a change in direction. Given her skill with reading and memorizing maps, she knew the layout of this part of the nest better than Cinder did. Glancing back briefly, he followed after her. There was that big mother of a spiderkin still after him.

"I will eat you, you deceitful elf!" she shouted when she noticed him looking back.

Deceitful elf? What was she going on about?

Cinder shook off the question. All that mattered was getting free of the spiderkin. These were the higher-caste kind, bigger than the ones of the Madri-Ma Clan, and that big one out front was likely a queen. Maybe that was why they'd been able to see through the Blends.

If so, running through the narrow hallways of the Webbed Kingdom, dodging webs and the flung tendrils, or cutting down any spiderkin impeding their way wouldn't get the job done. They needed a different plan.

"We can't keep running," Anya shouted, recognizing their plight, the same as he. Perspiration dripped in streaks down her dirt-crusted face. She was reaching her limit. In their time in the Webbed Kingdom, they'd discovered a truth: as an elf, Anya was simply weaker than him, both physically and spiritually, regardless of the blue-and-green lightning that impeded his Talents.

They had to get clear of the spiderkin, and a last stand would do them no good. A distraction was needed, that and a place to hide.

A distant cacophony of screeches, cries, and screams interrupted his thinking. The din of battle echoing from up ahead. A couple of turns, maybe. Sending his senses outward, Cinder recognized it as coming from what sounded like a large cave. Faint for now, barely heard over the chittering of the fragging spiderkin pursuing after them. But it might just do.

Anya had the same thought. "We're heading for that battle."

Cinder nodded agreement, and without hesitation, Anya had them take an angled left-hand turn. Five spiderkin warriors stood in the way. Cinder sent a single Fireball roaring into their midst. It blasted the spiderkin apart, exploding them backward. Charred chitin was flung about. The shards impacted off their hastily raised Shields, but Anya never slowed and on they went.

A sharp left turn, but this time the crash of battle grew quieter. They were moving away from it. But Anya would get them there. A hard right was followed by a hundred-yard sprint.

A cluster of spiderkin emerged from up ahead, another big mother leading them. This time Cinder set a reticle to his eyes, sent a salvo of Fireballs. A rain of burning thunder destroyed the spiderkin. The large one had raised a Shield, but in the end, it didn't do her any good. The fifth Fireball overwhelmed her defenses, and the sixth did her in.

Less than two seconds and Cinder and Anya were through the burning corpses. From behind them rose outraged screeches.

A slight right, and the earlier sounds of battle reached them.

"Reform your Blend," Cinder ordered. "We'll bring this group into whatever's up ahead. Let them fight each other. Just get us clear of it."

Anya nodded understanding. She had them take a diagonal right, which led down a long, empty hallway, straight and with a slight up-ward slope. Her breathing was coming harder. Sweat poured down Anya's face, and her features were set in a rictus of will and pain. She didn't have much left.

Fifty yards later, the corridor leveled, widening up ahead. The sounds of battle were clearer. They sprinted toward it. Seconds later, Cinder could see it. The spiderkin of the Madri-Ma Clan, identified by their smaller size, battled creatures of similar heft to the ones chasing Cinder and Anya. He couldn't tell who was winning. Nor did he care. It was a wild melee, and that was good enough for him.

They burst out of the corridor into a large, vaulted hall, as tall and vast as Swift Sword's library with carved columns holding up the ceil-ing. The space was cast in shadow, barely any light, but Liline's *nomas-ra* to give them sight in the dark made the chamber as bright as day. And in that space, the spiderkin within were fighting in wild abandon, on the ground, on the walls, and on their webs.

Perfect.

This wasn't quick, but Cinder figured it the best place to break free of their pursuers, lose them in the midst of this chaotic battle. Cinder and Anya sprinted straight into the heart of it, their *nomasra* boots allowing them to race across the strands of spider silk. The larger spiderkin noticed them, but they were too busy killing their smaller brethren—or being killed—to do anything about it.

A thunderous screeching followed by chittering announced the arrival of the large spiderkin who'd been leading their chase. "What is this madness," she screeched. "You battle each other when two elves cause all our troubles."

She tried to get the attention of the battling spiderkin, but thankfully, wasn't all too effective. The creatures fighting in the large cavern never paused their conflict.

Cinder and Anya waded deeper into the battle. They dodged threads of webbing, evaded spiderkin twisting and spinning as they attacked one another. Raced past any creatures that tried to stop them. Put more distance between themselves and the spiderkin queen who'd been hounding them all this time.

Halfway across the cavern, Anya broke right then angled left. She ran toward a hallway that was relatively clear.

Five large spiderkin, who noticed them despite their Blends, moved to intercept. From Anya came a stuttering set of howling Fireballs to blow them apart.

The battle then halted as every spiderkin in the cavern peered at what had just happened. An instant later, a tremendous scream resounded in the cavern followed by a single roar. "Kill the elves!"

"Keep going," Cinder shouted to Anya.

They reached the hallway, and twenty feet in, Cinder turned around and formed a concussive barrage of Spears. He unleashed the golden rods, one after the other—ten, twenty. He kept going until the ceiling collapsed. Chunks of rocks and large boulders crashed down, a din like an endless peal of thunder. A billowing cloud of dust and superheated stones blasted outward.

Cinder's Shield blocked it all. And when it was over, he grunted approval. The debris had filled the hallway, blocking the spiderkin in their pursuit.

Anya had halted farther up the corridor. She was sweaty, tired, and covered in filth. Her braided hair hung limp and dirty. He knew he looked no fresher. Both of them stank. Neither having had a chance to clean themselves since descending into the Webbed Kingdom.

"What's the plan?" Anya asked, sucking in great lungfuls of air.

Their original idea of stealing into Sheoboth's lair and making off undetected with the Orb of Regret was out the window. They'd have to take a more direct approach.

"We get to the throne hall, make sure Sheoboth isn't there, kill anything inside, steal the Orb, and get the fragging unholy hells out of here."

33

Cinder kept his focus behind and around them as Anya led them toward Sheoboth's lair. The corridor he'd pulled down was miles in the rear, and since that time, they'd run flat out through dark passages and shadowy halls. All the while, battling. By this point, Cinder had lost track of the number of spiderkin he'd encountered and killed.

Thankfully, at some point a signal must have gone out because the hallways were now empty. Only powerful spiderkin remained on the hunt, and it made their journey toward the throne hall that much faster. Every so often, they still had to stop and engage some queens, but at least it wasn't an overwhelming number.

Which was a relief. Cinder had drawn deep on both *Jivatma* and *lorethasra*, and his reserves were running low.

As they ran, he briefly wondered how Sheoboth was ignorant of the battle going on. They'd roiled her entire kingdom. Set a lower-caste nest to invade the areas controlled by the higher-caste ones. And yet Sheoboth wasn't aware?

The only answer he figured was that Liline must have come through and had the Crooked Crone in conference, far distant from her kingdom.

Whatever the reason, Cinder was grateful. Having to confront Sheoboth would have been a disaster. Defeating the higher-caste queens was challenging enough since Fireballs did minimal damage to their stout Shields. Instead, Cinder had to rely on heavier attacks—Bows and Spears—infusing his sword with as many damaging weaves as possible. Even the Wildness was only useful to strengthen the steel. Otherwise, it did the queens no harm.

A scuttling from behind had Cinder casting his senses outward, counting. "Nine queens coming up on us," he told Anya.

"Ambush them?"

"Let's do it."

At the next intersection, Anya took a right. Seconds later, another right. They raced down an empty corridor that was webbed in places.

Cinder nearly pulled up short when they broke into a large hallway where hundreds of spiderkin were huddled close together in webs high off the floor. *So, that's where they went.*

The spiderkin murmured and rustled but never noticed as Cinder and Anya raced through their midst. Within the chamber, the two of them didn't bother with Blends but relied instead on Liline's *nomasra* that gave them the appearance and scent of a spiderkin. Only the more powerful queens could apparently see through the deception, and none were present—

Anya yanked Cinder out of the way when a surge of Fireballs billowed his way. His inattentiveness had nearly cost him, but Anya was on it. She fired a Spear, a bar of golden light that cracked into a large queen, who likely ruled this nest. It was she who had attacked Cinder. She was now a smoking ruin.

"Blend," Anya ordered.

The nest was riled, chittering and screeching, surging down their webs. Before dying, the senior queen must have pointed out Cinder and Anya. A Blend would hopefully conceal them.

Cinder followed Anya, and they dodged spiderkin, who'd dropped to the ground, rolled under wildly slashing limbs, and evaded any fresh strands of entangling silk. None of the strikes came close. The spiderkin couldn't see them, and their attacks had been unfocused.

Anya had them take a right-hand exit, and they quickly left the enraged spiderkin behind. Yards down another empty corridor, they ducked into a darkened alcove near an intersection, continuing to both Blend and use Liline's *nomasra*, waiting.

There. The scuttling of spiderkin claws—the queens he'd heard minutes prior. Within seconds, they were rushing past Cinder and Anya's location. Nine massive queens, larger than any others they'd encountered thus far.

After they were gone, Cinder held Anya back and listened for any stragglers. *None.* This time he took the lead, racing after the spiderkin and planning how to kill the high-caste queens. He'd have to use Bows and Spears even if it further drained his abilities. Or maybe it would be better to avoid the queens altogether? But that seemed unlikely. The queens were going in the same direction that Cinder and Anya were headed: toward the throne lair.

Fully strengthening his sword, Cinder approached the rear-most queen. She must have sensed his approach, spinning about. Too late.

Cinder's blade crackled with the sun, howled like a wolf as it nearly bisected the queen through her thorax. A Spear hammered another spiderkin, leaving her a smoking ruin. Anya let loose with a fusillade of Fireballs that screamed across the short distance. It was only a distraction.

The queens roared, and one of them shouted. "Kill them!"

Cinder could have attacked them all at a distance, but he felt certain he'd need as much *Jivatma* as possible later on. Instead, he attacked at close quarters.

Sliding on his knees under a barbed limb, he amputated it. Vaulting upward, he spun, his blade momentarily brightening. He severed more limbs. A rustle of sound, and Cinder backflipped over another queen's attack; landed on her back. A quick pierce to her head, and he leapt off of her, seeking distance.

More Fireballs thundered, exploding, echoing, and shaking the corridor. Those came from the queens. Cinder shifted about, taking the brunt on his Shield. It flared a brighter green as more impacts hit against it. He answered, a wide barrage of Fireballs. It relieved the pressure.

A line of silk attached to his leg, wrenching him off balance. He sped toward a gaping maw. Cinder braided Air, blasting forward. The queen with the wide-open mouth never had a chance. Cinder reached her too quickly. A vertical chop, and he cut her head in half. Her thrashing corpse battered him, punching through his Shield, cutting him in places. He'd add them to the list of injuries. A flick of his sword and he cut the silk thread attaching him to the dying queen.

Anya had downed two more of the spiderkin, including the one he'd badly injured.

Three left, and though the queens showed no signs of quitting, there was a slight pause to the battle.

One of them stepped forward. "The fuck are you doing in our kingdom? You may kill us, but our children will feast on your corpse." She gestured to Anya. "And she'll be bred to birth a spectacular queen."

Cinder rolled his neck. *Frag them.*

He launched himself at the one who had threatened Anya. He swayed through the attacks of her barbed legs, pushed off against the hallway, flew over her, and blinded her with a Fireball. His sword enhanced once again, he angled a slash and removed a leg. The queen squealed in rage.

Cinder landed behind the other two spiderkin. One spun to face him. Another Fireball to blind her. He stepped forward, prepared to attack. At the last instant, he pulled back, rolling. A shifting of air snagged at his clothing. It didn't penetrate, but it flung him aside.

He slammed into a wall. His Shield held, but his ears rang. His vision went in and out of focus. What had just happened? Memories flitted, formed, and faded... then came solid. It was the same with his sight.

Cinder had to get up. The queen who had threatened Anya was

coming. He clambered to his feet, balance unsteady. The queen was on him.

Desperate for distance, he parried her attacks. One of her sisters wanted at him, too. Without conscious thought, Cinder shifted his position. Moving, getting the queens knotted together. They wrenched about, trying to get themselves unentangled. *Too late.* Cinder leapt at them, launched off one of the queens. Airborne and with the right angle, a single golden Spear ended them both.

Cinder landed on crouched knees, sword at the ready. There were no more enemies. The hallway was quiet. Anya had put down the final queen. Cinder breathed heavily. His heart pounded in his chest. His limbs weighed heavy. He wanted nothing more than to lie down and take a nap.

But that would have to wait. Maybe he'd rest when he was dead.

Cinder rose to his feet. "How much farther to the throne room?"

Anya pointed down the hallway. "We're almost there. Straight down this corridor, a left turn, and we should be in front of the doors."

Another heavy breath. "Let's get it done."

Anya slid against a wall, and peeked around the corner. She quickly drew back. She and Cinder huddled in a long, empty corridor that dead-ended into a larger one. The hallway was dimly lit like the rest of the Webbed Kingdom. The ceiling towered high above them, tall enough for even a Titan. After the non-stop battles, it was quiet except for the faint crackle of fire with the smell of ichor and burned chitin filling the air.

Cinder rested next to her. Dirt, grime, and ichor covered him, along with a multitude of nicks and cuts. His hair was matted and filthy, and he appeared as wrung out as Anya felt. But right now, he stared back the way they had come, at his handiwork. He'd killed dozens of spiderkin, and their corpses lay strung out behind them, some smoking and burned, others cleaved in two.

How was he still able to fight so hard? Was this then the difference between elven strength and that of a fully trained human? Or was it unique to Cinder? And if so, what were his limits?

Anya had no idea as to any of the answers, and rather than ponder the matter, she looked inward, knowing without searching that she was down to her last dregs. She hardly had any strength left. Her breathing was ragged, and her heart pounded against her ribs. Lifting her sword was a challenge. Every parry nearly sent her weapon flying from her hand. And running at a sprint… her boots felt like they were encased in bricks.

She shook off her self-assessment. Her fatigue and weakness didn't matter. If Cinder was still game for the battle, then so was she. She wouldn't fail him.

"How many?" Cinder asked, indicating the queens up ahead.

"Thirteen," Anya answered.

Cinder glowered. "How many fragging queens does Sheoboth have?" His face cleared. "Never mind. We kill them, and we'll have a clear path to Sheoboth's hall. One final battle after that and we should have the Orb." A heavy exhalation. "Fragging unholy hells, I'll be happy when this is over."

Anya pulled the *divaspana* from her *null pocket*. "I'm going to call Liline. Update her on our status."

They'd been keeping the Titan apprised throughout the running battle. Liline had to keep Sheoboth occupied—that was of utmost importance—and away from the Webbed Kingdom.

Anya smirked to herself. It really should be called a *queendom*.

Cinder nodded, not noticing her humor. "We'll be needing an open anchor line as soon as we have the Orb."

Anya activated the *divaspana*, speaking into it. "We'll need a quick departure."

An unfamiliar woman responded. "You have the Orb?"

Anya frowned. "Who is this?"

The voice tsked. "Your savior. How else do you think you'll get free of the Webbed Kingdom?"

An instant of thought and Anya knew who had answered her call. "Rence Darim."

"Exactly. Now, do you have the Orb?"

"Not yet. We'll be in touch again inside fifteen minutes. We'll have it then. Get us out as soon as you hear from us."

"So demanding," Rence said in mock disbelief.

Anya didn't have time to play games. "Just be ready."

"Don't fail us, and I will be." The Titan shut off her connection, and Anya replaced the *divaspana* within her *null pocket*. She quickly explained the details of the conversation with Cinder.

"Then we wouldn't want to keep her waiting," Cinder said. "Stay behind me. Cover our backside. I'll handle the guards." He rose to his feet.

Anya did the same, preparing herself for another rush into danger. A deep breath to calm her nerves. Another few to control her racing heart. "The spiderkin are getting more powerful. I've had to go full out to put them down." Anya hoped Cinder *hadn't* been going full out. She hoped he had enough reserves left. Otherwise, they were in trouble.

"We can take them."

Not a shadow of doubt touched Cinder's voice, and Anya took heart from his confidence. The iron-tang of his *lorethasra* came to her, and he also readied a Talent. Anya did the same although she was working on nothing but the last bit of her strength. In the throne hall, she feared she'd have no other weapons but her sword.

"Let's roll." Cinder sprang out from around the corner. A thunderous set of explosions lit into the spiderkin queens at the far end of the hallway. The corridor rattled. Dust and stone obscured the air.

Cinder set a reticle to his eye, drew from *Jivatma*. Fireballs, hot as he could make them, roared off his hand. They slammed into the thirteen spiderkin guarding the doors leading into Sheoboth's lair. The attack did little damage, but it also wasn't the point. The Fireballs threw the queens off their stride, causing them to stumble about. It was all he needed.

Anya launched a Spear. The golden bar expanded off her hand, punched through Shields, and two of the queens were down. She fired off more Fireballs. They weren't as bright as his, but they did the job.

Cinder rushed in behind their thundering clamor. A spiderkin reared before him. Dodging left, he bypassed her. The queen tried to crush him. It only got her in the way of her sisters. Cinder was close in, within the cover of her Shield. A Fireball pounded into the spiderkin, punching through her. It slammed into another queen, too, knocking her over. She wasn't out of it, though.

A whistling alerted him. A quick slash cut a silken thread. More came at him. Cinder defended. He spun through the entrapments, cutting them apart. Defended against Fireballs and weaves of hardened Air and Earth. They pounded at his Shield, causing the green webbing to brighten, crackle, and sizzle like meat over a fire.

A shift to his left and the bulk of a dead queen protected him. Cinder went at the spiderkin he'd earlier knocked over. She was just getting back to her feet, lurching at him, fangs extended. Ducking low, he angled a chop, removing half of her head. The queen thrashed, and one of her legs snagged on his clothes.

Cinder jerked away from her. At the same time, he leaned backward at the waist, under a line of spider silk. And followed the motion into a backflip. Landing, he launched himself at another queen. She was facing off against Anya, who stood at a safer distance. The spiderkin never saw him. A vertical chop of his sword, heavily enhanced, severed her at mid-thorax.

Cinder distantly noted his sword was taking nicks and damage. Even made of *isthrim* steel and suffused with *lorethasra*, it wasn't holding up against the spiderkin chitin. Not a good sign. But how many spiderkin were left? Cinder took an instant to count and collect himself. *Seven*. Testing his resources, he nodded inwardly. He could handle them.

He only hoped he had enough left over to handle however many queens were in the throne hall.

The moment ended, and Cinder cut two threads threatening to latch on to his feet. More Fireballs and braids. He gave ground, pouring more effort into his Shield. It was threatening to buckle.

Cinder sheathed his sword and leapt upward. From a higher vantage, he thrust two golden Spears, one from each hand. Three more queens were down. He unsheathed his sword and landed on a spiderkin who had been standing close by. She stood unmoving, possibly shocked or terrified into stillness.

He didn't let the opportunity go to waste. The Wildness crackled, giving strength to the steel of his sword, making it too bright to look upon. The blade whined as it pierced her chitin. The spiderkin died, a pithing thrust from the top of her head through the bottom. The final two queens were put down without incident.

This left the doors leading into the throne hall available.

A roar from somewhere deep in the Webbed Kingdom echoed through the hallways. It was the incandescent scream of something other than a queen—something greater.

Cinder exchanged a horrified expression with Anya. *Sheoboth was back.* They were almost out of time. Without a second thought, Cinder shoved open the doors leading into the throne hall. Thankfully, they opened inward, giving him a precious instant to assess what lay within.

A score of queens waited, paired and ten deep within a vast cavern with a ceiling lost to the heights, dim and musky, like the rest of the Webbed Kingdom.

"You cannot win," one of the queens intoned, a momentary pause. "The Great Mother is coming. She will end you if we do not."

Cinder shrugged to himself. It didn't matter what these queens thought. The pause ended. Cinder rolled beneath a bombardment of Fireballs, Spears, and Bows, accepted a number of them on his Shield. The green webbing crackled, brightened to a gray, then a white. He jerked about, searching for a way to get off his own attack. It would come.

Anya brought the relief, sending a Spear sweeping across the room.

Underpowered as it was, it did little damage. But it did enough.

Unburdened from having to defend, Cinder took the momentary reprieve to calculate. He couldn't afford to waste his energy. He'd have to be precise in how he handled these spiderkin. The best he'd ever managed.

In less than an instant, his calculations were completed. Cinder drew nearly to the depths of his Talents and skills. He held nothing back as he attacked.

Starting close at hand, a flash of a Spear took a queen in the head. Turning away before she fell, Cinder launched at another spiderkin. He conducted *Jivatma*, sending it and *lorethasra* through his Chakras— *Manipura* and *Ajna*—he nearly flew. He utilized Bearing—a Talent to pull objects together—a Talent he'd not yet used. It crushed two queens against one another. Their heads pulped.

Three down in the span of a second.

Cinder continued his assault—another Spear. He twisted away from a strand of spider silk. His Wildness-infused sword screamed and crackled, cutting apart more threads. Halting less than an instant, Cinder lined up another queen. Another Bearing, and she collapsed, her head imploding.

More attacks landed against his Shield. It sizzled and shrilled in protest. Cinder disregarded it. The Shield would either hold or it wouldn't. But fear wouldn't slow him. More threads were severed. He raised a hand. A blast of Air hurled a queen aside into another of her kind. A clench of his fist, and a plucked Bow stabbed through them both.

The queens retreated from him, terrified. More of them died.

"What kind of monster is he?" one of them screamed.

"Kill him!" another shrieked.

Cinder's heart raced like it was the instrument of some mad drummer. Sweat poured off him like water. His breath wanted to come in gasps. His arms were heavy, and his legs felt sluggish.

But he displayed no weakness. Instead, he walked the queens down. With his sword, he blocked a set of braids that would have burned him to ash. His blade glowed hotter, whiter, looking like the metal might melt.

So be it.

Cinder darted forward. A thrust and slash and two more queens were dead. A follow-up Fireball from within the range of a Shield blew another queen apart. Two rapid flashes of a Bow, and there were only half a dozen queens left. Surrounded, Cinder was in the midst of the spiderkin. He launched fifteen feet upward. A spar of a Spear spun downward, cutting through half their remaining numbers.

Three left.

Fireballs lit into the last queens. The spiderkin flinched.

Cinder was there, inside a Shield. Cutting the queen through her head. The other two retreated, huddled close—a mistake. Drawing nearly the last of his *Jivatma*, a final Bearing crushed them together, crunching chitin and ending the fight.

The throne hall was quiet but for Cinder's panting. He sagged, barely able to stay upright. But he stiffened his legs when from without the chamber came a scream of fury. Still distant, but Sheoboth approached, and they had better be gone when she arrived.

34

Silence filled Sheoboth's lair. Anya still couldn't believe what she'd seen. Cinder had crushed twenty powerful spiderkin queens. And he'd done so after having already taken plenty of damage while fighting most of the day.

His fortitude and will… She'd known he was driven unlike anyone she had ever met, but still. What he'd done should have been impossible. They both possessed the memories of a Blessed One, but Cinder was clearly stronger than her.

Anya was an elf, and her people were meant to be healers of land and people, not warriors like Cinder. His use of *Jivatma* and *lorethasra* simply wasn't in their nature. Her elven heritage would forever limit what she could accomplish as a warrior, a fact she now fully recognized. The gap between the finest elven warriors—or even holders—and humans who were able to fully use their abilities might be vast beyond measure.

Was Seminal ready for such a change?

Anya wasn't sure, although she implicitly trusted Cinder with such power.

And although he was powerful, right now he looked ready to collapse. His legs buckled, and she rushed to his side, supporting him. Even during the battle, she'd supported him, defending his blind spots while he'd attacked…

And the support he currently needed was getting clear of the throne hall.

But first…

Anya passed Cinder the *divaspana*. "Call Rence. I'll get the Orb."

It was clasped in an iron scepter that rose above Sheoboth's throne, and she rushed to collect it. Only a little longer, and they'd be free of this dark, dismal place. She raced up the stairs of the dais, disregarding the weakness in her legs, the heaving of her lungs, and the thudding of her heart. Nor did she bother to pry the Orb free from the scepter. Rather, she simply used a braid of Fire to cut it free, not bothering to replace it with the *nomasra* meant to mimic it.

The Orb of Regret in hand, Anya ran back down the stairs, handing it to Cinder. He'd be the one to deliver it to Shet anyway, and she'd die if that's what it took to see him free of Sheoboth's throne hall.

His expression, however, gave her pause.

"Rence says that she can't create an anchor line into the throne hall. There's a *nomasra* that prevents it. We need to get a mile or so free of here before she can latch on to the *divaspana* and get to us."

Terror clenched at Anya's racing heart. A mile? Her eyes darted to the doors of the throne hall. From that direction came the enraged shouts of what had to be Sheoboth.

Anya cast her sight about, looking for another exit. *There.* She pointed to a broad and tall set of double doors on the far side of the lair behind the dais.

Cinder nodded, and without another word, they rushed toward the only other exit. Anya had no idea where it would take them, but anywhere was better than here.

The doorway led into an arched corridor, wide enough for a farmer's wagon and tall enough for a Titan. Given the size and the murals on the walls—all of them featuring a massive spider—the hallway like-ly led to Sheoboth's private quarters. What were the odds that it was outside the range of the *nomasra*?

Even as they hustled down the passage, Anya continued to search for another way out.

The booming of the doors to the throne hall resounded into the cor-ridor. Sheoboth had arrived. Cinder and Anya redoubled their speed.

"Wait." Pointing up, Cinder halted her. High in the ceiling was a grate—an air vent. It was how fresh air was pulled into the depths of the Webbed Kingdom. By now, they'd seen plenty of them.

"Can you reach it?" Cinder asked.

Anya searched inside herself. "Yes."

Cinder leapt upward, punching the grate into the air vent. It reset-tled on his Shielded back as he grasped the tunnel's lip, scrambling inside. The door leading from the throne hall was thrown open.

Anya was already airborne. Cinder grabbed her arms and pulled her inside, replacing the grate. An enraged shriek reached them.

"Come on," Cinder said.

Cinder ran as fast as he could despite his hunched-over posture and the pitch blackness of the air vent. Anya followed directly behind, and both of them had activated the *nomasras* that allowed them to see in the dark. Cinder realized he might have to thank Liline for all that she'd done after this was over. Without her *nomasras*, none of this would have been possible.

But they weren't free yet. They had a mile more to cover, rushing along when both of them were on their last legs. Nonetheless, they couldn't afford to slow down. They'd heard Sheoboth's scream of fury when they'd escaped into the air vent. She was too big to follow, but her children weren't. No doubt there would soon be a horde of spiderkin rushing after them.

Thankfully, the more powerful queens wouldn't be amongst that number. They, too, were too big for the ventilation shafts. And in this momentary peace, Cinder did his best to conserve energy.

If only he were just a bit fresher, he would have liked their chances of escaping the Webbed Kingdom. Too bad he wasn't. But there also was no use in wishing or complaining now. They just had to grit their teeth and do the best they could.

They ran on, the vent echoing with their harsh breathing and the chittering cries and screeches of the spiderkin from down below.

Minutes later, a rumbling shook the vent. An explosion sounded, and dust and small stones powdered them. Cinder spared a wondering glance with Anya. She shrugged. The rumbling repeated, closer this time. More dirt fell upon them.

Cinder didn't know what was happening, but whatever it was, he wanted no part of it. He sped up, no longer bothering to conserve any energy.

"Left turn," Anya said, pointing to an upcoming T-intersection.

"You sure?"

"Positive."

There it was again—the rumbling. The closest one yet. Stones blasted into the vent, and something huge emerged from the wreckage. Cinder didn't bother waiting to see what it might be. He took the left-hand turn, Anya right behind him.

"There you are," a voice said. It was deep and imperious: *Sheoboth.* It had to be her.

Cinder reached back and hauled Anya in front of him. "Go!" he shouted.

She didn't slow, and neither did he. They needed distance from whatever Sheoboth had planned. By now, Cinder had recovered some *Jivatma*, enough to form a weak Shield.

"Stairs," Anya warned. "Going down."

A massive roar, like a mountain breaking, filled the air vent. Something slammed into Cinder. He launched into Anya. A blast furnace opened. His Shield instantly went white. They tumbled down the stairs. Cinder twisted, landing first. He took the fall on his Shield. Just then, it failed.

Anya was on her knees, arms outstretched, a rictus of strain on her face. She'd also Shielded. It, too, had gone white, the only thing keeping them safe from a Spear so powerful it had the stones red-hot and already melting. They needed to get clear. Cinder scrambled away from the heat, Anya tugging him along.

His mouth went dry. The heat was boiling. Finally, the Spear ended.

"We have to go back," Anya said.

Cinder shot her an expression of horror. "Why?"

"Sheoboth will do the same thing as she just did but farther up the air vent. She knows where this one leads."

His expression resolved, realizing she was right. "Lead us."

They reengaged their Shields, which fluttered and barely held their integrity, and climbed pitted stairs that threatened to crumble underfoot. The heat billowed from the glowing stones, hotter as they climbed. But this was their best option.

Once they summited the stairs, Anya sped along, retracing their steps. Back to the original corridor. A glance to the right showed the rubble left by Sheoboth's rupture into the air vent.

Just then, like Anya predicted, there came a rumbling from the direction in which they'd just escaped. Sheoboth was already trying to track them down.

"She'll figure out where we are," Cinder said.

"We need stairs heading upward," Anya said. "As much stone between us and these lower levels as possible."

"Let's hope we come across it soon."

They ran on. Another shaking of the air vent—thankfully still distant and in the wrong direction—caused debris to fall on them. They approached another intersection, and Anya went right this time.

A scuttling of claws reached Cinder. The spiderkin were in the tunnels and coming on fast. They needed that mile from the throne hall. Surely, they were closing in on that distance. *Devesh, please let it be so.*

Anya passed under a vertical air vent.

A spiderkin fell atop her, biting, stabbing. Anya screamed, slamming a foot to hold the creature's head in place. She Fireballed it but not before her leg was shredded. Blood leaked in rivulets down her calf. She tried to stand but was unable.

Cinder reached her and glanced upward. *Clear.* He slung Anya's arm around his shoulders, carrying most of her weight. "Come on."

More scuttling, louder this time. Another rumbling with a further raining of stones—Sheoboth, closer this time. A fog of dust shrouded the way forward. The Crone would be on them soon. They might only have seconds. Anya clenched her teeth, hobbling along, her face pale.

For the first time, Cinder worried that he and Anya would die here. It had always been a possibility, but he'd never allowed it to press on his thoughts. It did now.

Another shaking of their narrow tunnel. Cinder glanced back. It was only a hundred feet behind them. Just as bad, there came the mad scrambling of claws.

"Look," Anya directed his attention forward.

A blessed staircase, rising upward, appeared out of the dusty haze. Cinder hurried as best he could. The scuttling neared.

Cinder set Anya down. A Fireball illuminated what was approaching. A swarm of spiderkin. They crawled on the tunnel's floor, walls, and ceiling. Cinder had nothing left but heart and determination and the barest dregs of *lorethasra*. It would have to do. Sending everything he had, he tore into the spiderkin. But given their numbers, it wasn't enough.

"Cinder!" Anya had somehow gritted her way to the top of the stairs. "We're clear!"

It was the words he'd been hoping to hear. Reaching past his limits to something that had left him feeling like he'd carved open his chest, he conducted the last dregs of *Jivatma*… and then some. A singing light filled him but so did power. A single Spear collapsed the tunnel entirely, blocking the spiderkin and crushing dozens of them.

His chest aching, coughing great globs of blood, Cinder lurched toward the stairs. Collapsed on his back, mouth agape as he stared at the tunnel's ceiling. He had no strength left.

Anya was back, hauling him upward, somehow pulling him along despite the ruin of her leg. Up the stairs. She kicked aside a grate opening into an empty room. Cinder barely clung to consciousness. *Divaspana* in hand, Anya whispered urgently.

An instant later, an anchor line opened. Liline stepped out of it. She took one look at them, gathered them in her arms, and stepped back through the anchor line.

Cinder was about passed out, but he heard Liline whisper. "Well done, my brave ones. Well done."

35

Residar, Brissianna, and Selin stared intently at Titan's Reach from amidst a large thicket. They'd reached the village earlier in the day, but prior to entering into its environs, they had decided to scout it out—a *wise decision.*

Something odd was happening in Titan's Reach. Looking like upright dogs, a small group of bizarre creatures walked the village's streets. Three of them in total, but what were they? Some kind of zahhack?

That's what Residar believed, especially if the people here really did worship Shet. Wouldn't it then make sense that zahhacks would be allowed to wander their village? Brissianna thought the same thing, but Selin disagreed. He felt like the creatures were something else, but what they were, he couldn't say.

It was why the three of them were currently hiding in a tall stand of brush, Blended like Fastness had taught them, while they observed the village.

"There," Selin pointed to the dog-like creatures that had left the village. "Look at that. They're changing."

Residar watched, slack-jawed, as the creatures transformed into dwarves. "What are they?" He looked to Brissianna, who had the most experience of them all.

She shook her head. "I don't know, but whatever we're expected to do here, I want to see it finished as quick as possible. We're too close to the Hellmaw."

"The Hungering Heart," Residar said, making a noise of disgust. He'd felt the call, constant, insistent, and grating. The promises were the same as always: power, vengeance, and the seduction of not caring. It was the lifeless husk of existing as a wraith.

"I've heard it, too," Selin confirmed. "But we still have to figure out what to do about the dwarves turning into those dog-like creatures."

Residar disagreed. "No, we don't. Fastness wanted us to convince the people here that Shet is evil. And if we can't, we have to figure out what to do about them. The dwarves, or whatever they are, aren't our problem."

Selin shot him a disappointed glance. "You don't think Fastness would want to know about them?"

"He's right," Brissianna said. "Dwarves becoming zahhacks, in ca-hoots with the people here… Fastness will want to know. Even more, he'll want to know where those dwarves come from."

"If they're even dwarves," Selin said.

Residar grimaced, but it was two votes against his one. Besides which, Brissianna was right: they had to learn whatever they could about the dwarves. "Then this is what we'll do. Selin follows the dwarves while Brissianna and I try to learn what we can about Titan's Reach and whether they can be saved."

Brissianna shot him a sharp gaze. "And if they can't?"

Residar shifted. He didn't want to think about it. Fastness had said the people of Titan's Reach weren't to be killed, but the white also wanted them convinced to change their ways. It left Residar in a pre-dicament. How could he convince idiots who consorted with Shet and dwarf-zahhacks? And if he couldn't convince them, was he really sup-posed to not do anything about it?

"I think they're leaving," Selin noted, pointing out the dwarves, who were striding off, heading west.

Residar stared in the direction of the departure. *Why west?* He would have expected them to head north to Ardent Crèche. And how could he be sure they were leaving?

"Follow them," he ordered Selin. "Stay out of sight. Just find out where they're headed."

"They'll never know I'm there," Selin promised, shuffling noiselessly out of the stand of brush. Seconds later, he was gone like a ghost.

Residar stared after the man.

Selin might act like a mousy prig, but his heart was in the right place. Even more important, the man knew his business. Of all the wraiths who'd thrown off the shackles of the Hungering Heart, Selin was possibly the deadliest. Underneath his unimpressive exterior was the heart of a killer. Before becoming a wraith, Selin had been an assassin.

All of this was to say that Selin could trail the dwarves, and they'd never know he was there.

But what to do about this cursed village? Residar faced forward, prepared to venture forth, but a disturbance in the brush had him glancing behind. Was Selin back already?

But instead of his fellow once-wraith, three dwarves—two women and a man—entered their thicket. Of the women, one was younger while the other appeared scholarly. The man had the bearing of a warrior.

The pretty dwarf smiled brightly at them, and when she did, the voice of the Hungering Heart died, replaced by a peace and contentment the likes of which Residar had never known, not even when his family had been alive. He felt light enough to fly.

"Hello," the younger dwarf female said, still smiling. "I'm Willa. A friend of mine thought you might need my help with the people down there."

It was late at night, and Rishi Persistence stared at the empty pedestal that had once held the Orb of Undying Light. She'd come to Indrun's Chamber on many an occasion, ever since that battle where Cinder Shade and Anya Aruyen had done the impossible and defeated a force that, on paper, should have been so much deadlier than the two of them.

Her gaze went to the Gate of Saints, recalling the anchor line that Anya had opened—another impossibility. Then there was the fool of a rakishi who had thrown a spear at Cinder after Persistence had agreed to the cessation of hostilities. That rakishi could have killed them all if Cinder had decided to come back through the anchor line and claim his justified vengeance.

But he hadn't, and Persistence feared what it might mean: Was Cinder dead? No one knew. No one had heard word about him or Anya in several months now.

Devesh, let them be alive. They had to be. A dozen times, Persistence had replayed her battle against Cinder, and in every assessment, she'd come to firmly believe that he had granted her and Guile their lives. He could have killed them if he so chose, but he hadn't.

Why?

"What are you thinking about?" Guile asked. He was the only other person present in Indrun's Chamber. "Cinder and Anya?"

Persistence smiled at her closest ally in Shrewd Hall, the assembly of rishis. She and Guile had always supported each other even prior to the Orb's theft, but afterward, events had forced them to work together even more closely. The other rishis blamed them for the loss of the Orb, and that blame showed no signs of abating.

In fact, Persistence and Guile had nearly been stripped of their titles as rishis, escaping a death sentence by the barest of margins. And while they still retained their positions in Shrewd Hall, they had little influence. Rather, they were pariahs.

"I think so," Persistence said in reply to Guile's question. "You've reviewed our fight against them, the testimony of the rakishis who battled Anya. Those two, Cinder Shade and Anya Aruyen, are the ones to whom our lineages are pledged."

"I believe you," Guile replied. "But that still doesn't say what we should do next." He scowled. "We were meant to bring Bharat into the Last War on the side of the Blessed Ones. How can we do so when we're so clearly ostracized by the other rishis?"

Persistence had long considered the matter, and she finally had an answer. "We must ask for a Holy Mission."

"We?" Guile cocked his head. "And where would *we* go?"

This, too, Persistence had determined. "Shalla Vale."

Guile frowned. "Why?"

Persistence took a moment to gather her reasons before responding to Guile. "Shalla Valley. It is known to be the holiest place in all of Seminal. We will ask for a mission there as a pilgrimage and penance to wash away the sins of our failure."

Guile's eyes narrowed. "What else aren't you telling me?"

Persistence exhaled heavily. "Call it a premonition, but we also need to send a rishi to Shima Sithe. Mortar would be best. He knows their empress."

Guile's eyes remained narrow. "A premonition or a recitation?"

Persistence wasn't sure. And her sense of uncertainty was an annoyance that had begun when Cinder and Anya had entered her life. She was heartily sick of it. "I don't know," she allowed. "But my heart tells me we need him there."

"And the real reason for our journey to Shalla Vale?"

Persistence could finally face him with a smile of surety. "Because of what I saw on the other side of the anchor line that Anya Aruyen opened. It was a momentary flash, but it was there, on the other end of the rainbow bridge—a yakshin. That is where the Blessed Ones went."

Jeet strode forward in the martial way that he'd long ago been taught at Chapterhouse Bedwin: upright posture, one foot after the other, perfect timing and length between each step. He could walk endlessly like this. So could Stren, who marched at his side.

However, for both of them, there was also now a difference in how they paced. It was because of their staves—Maize's gifts—which set the tempo of their gait, striking the ground like a drumbeat with every right-footed step that they took on the hard-packed dirt of the rural road. In addition, nowhere in evidence were their swords, which they'd cast aside on agreeing to become Maize's apprentices.

Currently, their group—Jeet, Stren, Maize, and the holders—were less than a mile out from Querel. And although Jeet hadn't liked his sister all that much during the time spent at her home, there was in him a desire to see her again, to ensure that the *hashains* hadn't harmed her. In truth, he should have done this months ago. Brena was family, and she'd taken him in when no one else had. She was undeserving of his ungrateful behavior, and she certainly shouldn't receive punishment from the *hashains* on his account.

Hashains. The word still resonated in Jeet's mind, but not in the same way it once had. No longer did it ring as a synonym to brother.

"There it is. The ugliest scarecrow in several districts," Stren said, pulling Jeet out of his reflections. His fellow apprentice was smiling as he pointed to a scarecrow in a nearby farmer's field. It loomed tall, and its shadow slid long with the sun hanging low at dusk.

Jeet grinned at the scarecrow, an expression that was becoming easier and easier to manage. In his life as a *hashain*, he'd rarely smiled because in Chapterhouse there was no such thing as humor. Dealing out life and death left no room for frivolity. "I do believe you're right," he said to Stren. "That scarecrow actually won an award for how ugly it is."

"There was a competition?" Stren asked.

Maize, pacing behind them, chuckled. "I hadn't realized the ugliness was intentional."

Jeet shrugged. "Brena said there was."

Only now did he realize that, in telling him the story about the scarecrow, his sister had actually been trying to draw him into the life of Querel. She wanted him to know her people, and his response had been a dismissive sneer. How had she endured his presence for so long without demanding he leave? It spoke to her generosity that she hadn't. And Jeet hoped that it also spoke to his own growth as a person that he recognized that internal change.

Those changes might alter him still in ways he could have never imagined. Currently he was physically the same, but Maize said it didn't have to always be the case. It all depended on what Jeet and Stren wanted to do with their lives.

They could continue as Maize's apprentices and eventually become holders, who were born like all other races, but some woven—like the rakishis and apparently the *hashains*—could also transform into them. The other option was even more fantastical: to become a troll. Jeet would have never imagined either possibility during his life as a *hashain.*

But which one was right for him?

A holder spoke to his martial heritage, his years of training and sacrifice as a *hashain.* And a warrior's heart still beat in his chest.

But what about a troll? His entire form would transform. He'd grow two feet in height, add hundreds of pounds in weight, and horns would curl off his temples. The very way he thought would be different.

Jeet glanced at Maize. And how much did that really matter? In becoming a troll, what would he really be giving away? Marriage and children? They'd never before interested him, so was it really that much of a sacrifice?

He shook off his considerations. Honestly, while Jeet wasn't sure what he wanted, he also doubted he'd ever have to make such a decision. The *hashains* had marked him and Stren for death, and so had Genka Devesth. He would likely not live out the year, and if he did, certainly not the next.

None of which mattered to Jeet. As long as he served Cinder Shade, the *Cipre Elonicon,* and spoke of his coming, he would have achieved his life's goal. He'd have informed the people of the Sunsets of Cinder's presence and explained why his arrival was to be celebrated. The *Cipre Elonicon* would save them and their sons. He'd defeat the wraiths. He'd restore order and justice. He'd smooth their hard lives with peace and prosperity.

Ten minutes later, their small group crested a rise and halted, taking in the sight of Querel. The village was busy with a dozen people, mostly women going about their late-day tasks, walking with purpose while the men headed in from the fields. Shadows spread across the land, and a wind whispered.

All the while, Jeet stared. He didn't have many good memories of this village, but he hoped to change that. Just as much, he hoped to change Brena's poor opinion of him. And for some strange reason, a nervousness filled his stomach at the notion.

"Are you ready?" Maize asked.

Recognizing the layers to the question, Jeet stared at the troll. He shrugged. "Only way to know is to get it done."

Maize grinned. "That it is."

They set off, garnering stares and shouted questions as they proceeded into the village. Before long, a crowd of people had gathered at their backs, with Stren asking for patience and promising that all would be explained. The noise drew Brena to her front door. She stood, arms akimbo and an unwelcoming expression on her face.

Jeet studied her. Her posture seemed a bit more stooped than before, and deeper lines than from before creased her face. A flash of pain flickered across her features when she stepped off her front stoop, hobbling a bit as she moved in their direction. Was the limp because of what the *hashains* had done to her?

"Never expected to see you back," she said.

"I never expected to be back," Jeet replied. He stepped closer to his sister. "I'm sorry, Brena. Sorry for how poorly I treated you the last time I was here. Sorry for that limp. Is that because of the *hashains*?"

She spit over to the side. "Food's on the table. Come in if you want some." Her words spoken, she hobbled back toward her home.

Impressed by her stoic demeanor and generosity even as he viewed her in a fresh light, Jeet watched her go. As a *hashain*, he would have considered the sharing of her bounty to be nothing more than what was his by right. Brena was a peasant, and peasants served their betters.

But his travels and instructions with Maize had taught him how wrong that sort of thinking truly was. And seeing Brena offer her food to him and Stren like that, without even a second thought… it was humbling.

Jeet realized then just how long a road he had to travel if he wished to become worthy of his sister's charity.

36

Dorr leaned back in his chair while reading the latest report from the Ramoni and its recent set of graduates. In each case, the matriculated soldier had been an experienced and competent sergeant from the ranks who was now advanced to lieutenant and expected to bring another unit of the High Army to the required readiness state. So far, it had been working remarkably well, and Dorr was pleased with the improvement to Rakesh's military. It was already far deadlier now than it had been even just six months ago. Add another six months, and it would be deadlier still.

Give him a year and they'd be able to fully defend every inch of Rakesh's territory against any army of zahhacks. That's assuming it was only zahhacks they faced. If it was the Titans and Shet, then the High Army was doomed. In that one regard, Dorr's work would eventually reach its limit. To defeat Shet's true power, they needed Shokan and Sira—*Cinder and Anya.*

Beyond that, the one other snag was what to do with the elves. Sure, they were fine warriors—far better on a one-on-one basis compared to a human—but their ability to maintain focus when under pressure was lacking. They kept making stupid mistake after stupid mistake, like the only tactic they knew was to scream and leap like a rabid raccoon. Worse, they seemed incapable of correcting those errors.

It had led to some uncomfortable conversations with elves who in Yaksha Sithe were considered high nobility. They should have been granted some kind of command role in the High Army, but who would ever trust them in such a position? And smoothing those ruffled feathers was part of Dorr's job as a captain in the High Army. He was an administrator, a role he didn't necessarily want, but one at which he was pretty good.

He was involved in exactly that kind of work when a knock on the door interrupted his reading.

"Yes," he barked, glancing up to see who was there. However, as soon as he recognized his visitor, he rose to his feet. "Riner. What are you doing here?"

"I thought you might find this interesting," Riner answered, withdrawing a dusty, old tome and a thick notebook from a leather satchel. "It's a set of battlefield accounts from the *NusraelShev*." He patted the tome. "I translated the older language into something more modern. It's about the defense of what's now Rakesh by an army of elves against a superior force of zahhacks. I might not have gotten the words right, and I was hoping you could take a look."

Dorr held in a sigh. He didn't have time for this. He doubted Riner had actually found anything useful, but he wouldn't squash the boy's attempts at doing good. His forbearance wasn't just because Riner was Coral's brother, but because Dorr liked the lad: Riner had a good heart.

So, to humor him, Dorr accepted the notebook and perused it. There wasn't much there, just an explanation of unit strengths and positioning, weather, commanders, and time of year. There was some historical information, such as how, when, and where the forces had faced each other. Also included was an endless description about streams forded and the landscape around them and the clothes worn by the various officers.

He rolled his eyes about the illustrative passages. While the writing in the book was poetic enough, did the author really need to describe every leaf on every plant or go over every button on a commander's uniform?

There was one sequence, though, that caught Dorr's attention. He straightened with a frown. "Is this part true? You translated it correctly?" He pointed to the page in question.

Riner leaned over to briefly read it before nodding. "Yes. That part was easy to translate. It didn't make sense to me either, and there are others like it in the book."

Dorr recited the passage. "The commander of the goblins sent food and heavy clothing to the elves when they were fighting in the high passes of the Daggers in the winter, because he hated to see such honorable foes laid low by weather and bad planning."

"If you read on, you'll find out they didn't have winter gear, and the elven commander wrote a letter of acknowledgment and thanks." Riner reached into the older book. "I even found a possible copy of the letter tucked inside the back pages. Whether it's real or not is another question."

Dorr's frown deepened. "But that doesn't make sense. Why would the goblins or any zahhacks help the elves? They're mortal enemies."

"Maybe it has to do with what Shokan and Sira used to teach—about how helping redeem evil people is the highest act of holiness? It's like a song of freedom… *redemption*, I mean. Like something Cinder might sing."

Dorr leaned back in his chair, not ready to accept what was written in the book Riner had found or the supposed teaching that he mentioned. Instead, his mind went to Jarde Linger and Stard Lener. Those young men had been unholy terrors to Riner and Coral back at *Our Lady of Fire*. Cinder had even fought the two Errows, laying them out bad, a rough beating that should have led to lifelong enmity.

But later on, the Errows had become better people, and Cinder had forgiven them, but only after they'd apologized to Coral and Riner. In truth, if Jarde and Stard hadn't shown that bit of remorse, Dorr would have never accepted them into the Ramoni.

So maybe there was something to what Riner was talking about, especially if Cinder really was Shokan.

"You see it, don't you?" Riner asked with a triumphant smile. "About Cinder and the Errows."

Dorr snorted. "Anyone ever tell you how annoying a know-it-all can be?"

Riner's grin widened. "Does that mean I know all?"

Dorr laughed. "I don't know if you know it all, but you know something." He glanced at the wall clock, noticing the late morning hour. "Do you want to get some lunch?"

Raj Klepiun Jorow, prime minister of Gandharva, steepled his fingers as he stared at Ambassador Harima Mathe from Rakesh and considered how best to respond to the blasted woman's entreaty. He mentally snorted. It wasn't an actual entreaty. Rather it was a demand couched in the language of a request, which was too often the way of matters between their nations these days.

Klepiun hated it, this feeling of subservience of Gandharva to Rakesh. Especially since only twenty years ago, their countries had stood side by side as equals, but with his nation's rising internal strife, that was no longer the case.

All because of the damned Moralists—fucking busybodies, always complaining about what they wanted and telling folks how to live their lives. Why couldn't they just accept their lot in life and stop their whining?

It would have made Klepiun's life a large way easier and would have also made this current meeting more palatable.

As Klepiun contemplated what to say, Ambassador Harima fanned herself.

The autumn sunshine was beaming through narrow-paned windows, lighting the space and bringing blessed warmth. Typically, such wasn't the case. This time of year, even with the fireplace blazing, it was perpetually cold in the drafty old building that served as Gandharva's capital and seat of power.

Built of thick walls of stone and brick, it dated back some seventeen hundred years, from when Gandharva and Rakesh had been a single country—Brinane—ruled by King Polland Brinane, founder of the nation and first of his name. He had also been one of Klepiun's direct ancestors. There was a portrait of the old king hanging above the hearth; a regal appearing man, he was said to have been a fine warrior—supposedly a descendent of one of Mede's high commanders—and an even finer politician.

Too bad his descendants had wasted what he'd achieved. Within seventy years of King Polland's founding of a unified Gandharva and Rakesh, it had all fallen apart.

As Klepiun reckoned matters, it had all started when the Moralists of the time insisted on equal representation in the Parliament. And that demand had been granted by King Polland IV, a fool of man whose only claim to rule was that he was the least foolish great-grandson of the original King Polland.

And as the sun rose in the east, upon obtaining their demands, the Moralists had made fresh ones, escalated their wants until it culminated in a civil war that saw Brinane torn asunder. Rakesh had broken free as its own separate nation, with Gandharva forged from the remaining pieces.

It didn't matter that the Moralists and their Devesh-damned rebellion had been crushed since they had eventually risen again, whining once more for better treatment. And now, in this terribly late hour, when Shet was ready to spill out of Naraka and destroy them all, here came the fucking Moralists and their fucking complaints.

If they wanted better treatment, then maybe they could start by not fomenting rebellion at every perceived slight. All they had to do was shut their stupid mouths and do as they were told.

"Prime Minister Klepiun," Ambassador Harima said, interrupting his thoughts. "Have you been listening to a word I've spoken?"

Klepiun drew himself out of his reflections. "Yes, I heard you." He stared afresh at the ambassador, hating her smug expression. How it galled him to see the woman's conceit. But such an insult would have to be accepted for now. Gandharva couldn't survive without Rakesh. The Moralists and their civil unrest ensured that humbling fact.

"We will do our best to provide more officers and units to defend our shared northern borders," Klepiun promised.

Ambassador Harima nodded her head in supposed thanks. "We need those soldiers. Our scouts tell us that the zahhacks have new leadership, powerful figures we fear might be rakshasas."

Klepiun had heard the same, and he hid a shiver of fear. Rakshasas were Shet's most terrifying commanders: Ancient demons who drank the blood of infants and sucked the marrow of virgins. Or so it was said, and who knew if any of it was true?

Then again, five years ago, Klepiun hadn't believed Shet was real.

"As I said, we will do our best to send more units north." Klepiun offered a grim smile. "But I'm sure you're aware of our troubles in that regard."

Ambassador Harima smiled faintly in return. "We hope those… issues can be peacefully resolved."

As Ambassador Harima exited the prime minister's offices, her mind was already stepping past the man's obstacles. He was doing his best to maintain the best fortunes for his people, but in this, his thinking was limited. He still thought of himself as the first among equals, the principal leader of a set of noble families who ruled Gandharva. And it was to them, not their figurehead emperor, that Klepiun truly answered.

Which wouldn't do much for the suddenly changed world in which everyone found themselves. Klepiun's way of thinking was that of the past, and while his noble families still mattered, it wasn't in the way they once had.

A danger unlike any other threatened the world, and in the face of that peril, the puffed-up needs of some obscure aristocrats didn't matter. They could burn for all Ambassador Harima cared.

She was an Errow, and she understood what it meant to suffer under a society's bigotry. It was what the Errows had known throughout the vast majority of their existence, and although they'd largely taken command of Rakesh, none of them were stupid enough to believe that the general populace was happy over the matter.

Most Rakeshians went along with it because the Errows were better administrators than the Shrewds who had previously ruled—successful at making sure bellies were fed, streets were kept in good repair, and the High Army was made ever more lethal. The last fact was what had earned the Errows their greatest reprieve. That and the knowledge that Shokan—Cinder Shade—had befriended a number of them, all members of the High Army.

And Harima didn't care about any rumors of Cinder claiming he wasn't Shokan. It didn't matter. Cinder Shade was Shokan because that's what the world needed him to be. With enough and proper influence, Harima was sure that he would eventually see it the same way.

Beyond that, the only reason Harima's people were willing to work with Klepiun was because they had no choice. Shet had forced their hand. In truth, under different circumstances, the Errows would have supported no one from Gandharva. The Moralists might have been oppressed by the current noble families, but it hadn't always been the case. At one time, it had been the Moralists who had been the oppressors and rulers of Gandharva. They certainly had oppressed the Errows when her people had lived within their nation.

As far as Harima was concerned, if not for Shet, they could get on with their civil war and kill each other to their heart's content.

Lost in thought, Liline walked alongside Rence. The two of them skirted the bounds of the black palace of Naraka, late at night and with no one about in the darkened corridor. It felt grim, the walls an unrelieved black, but for the various murals, frescoes, and assorted paintings of

Shet in heroic poses.

All the art was meant to inspire the zahhacks and spark fear in the hearts of any of Naraka's visitors. Whether it actually did so was a matter for debate… assuming anyone was stupid enough to actually raise that sort of a topic. Shet wouldn't take kindly to it.

Liline eyed Rence askance. Her sister Titan was supposed to have left for the Sunset Kingdoms, but instead, she had been recalled before her departure and tasked with coordinating with the Baptisers—the dwarves who wished to become Ur-Fels.

Liline couldn't figure why they would want such a change in their lives. Were they not happy as dwarves? Weren't dwarves, by their very design, happy?

Apparently not. They certainly hadn't been happy during the *NusraelShev*, the Holy War of Liberation, as Shet insisted it be called. Liline mentally rolled her eyes at the phrase. Was it really necessary to give the war such a bespoke name?

Regardless, the dwarves of the time hadn't been happy when their human protectors had fallen to the slaughter. Those humans had known nothing but peace for an age prior to Shet's emergence into Seminal and had been ill-equipped to fight him. Liline recalled the many conflicts and conflagrations in which she had taken part. Her rage after the final battle against Shokan had been great, and she'd enjoyed killing those who had failed to bow before her glory.

So why was she unsettled by the notion of the dwarves becoming Ur-Fels? They couldn't believe in reincarnation, could they? Or did they believe that by reclaiming their prior forms, they would regain their past lives as warriors?

Of course, if they knew the truth, they'd want nothing to do with those past forms. The Ur-Fels had been created as nothing more than expendable soldiers. Their only task was to die in great numbers while whittling down the enemy until others who were more useful could come along to administer the killing strike.

But even if the dwarves did seek some sort of reincarnation, it was a fool's mission. Devesh was real, but even if He was a Loving Lord, it didn't matter. Love was a hindrance. Love bound a person to the needs of others. Love provided nothing, certainly no defense against an enemy wielding a weapon.

The same held true with the Empty One and His son, Zahhack. The latter two might be great powers, but they weren't the unbeatable engines of evil that they claimed. They had their flaws. Their need to rule others, for instance. It was a shackle. Ruling others was just as limiting as loving them. In both cases, they served as a restriction on the wants, needs, and desires of a person.

In Liline's estimation, an individual's force of will was all that mattered. As Shet was fond of saying, *I will form my own success rather than pray for it.* For Liline, that aphorism meant she would never pray to anyone ever again.

"You're thinking heavy thoughts," Rence said, drawing Liline out of her wonderings. "What is it?"

Liline answered without a moment's hesitation. She held many secrets from her sister, but this wasn't one of them. Instead, she described what she'd been contemplating: the dwarves reverting to Ur-Fels, the notion of reincarnation, and Shet's phrase.

But even as she said the statement, she wanted to smirk. Shet had stolen the adage from Shokan.

Rence must not have noticed the humor because she merely nodded in agreement. "It is a wise statement. Rule your life and never bend the knee. Devesh and the Empty One aren't some timeless beings of love and evil, and we don't owe them anything. They were once just like us, raised to godhood through force and will."

Rence's statement went without saying, and the two of them walked on through the darkened halls of Naraka, past more frescoes, murals, and figurines of Shet posed in images of greatness. There were also some of the Titans, but Liline didn't like the ones cast of her. In some of them—not many, but enough—the goblins had taken liberty with the size of her breasts, making them look positively bovine in size. And her lust-filled expressions… absolutely grotesque.

Liline had ordered the artist to rectify the situation, and while he had done so, there were some he couldn't, such as the ones in which she gazed longingly at Shet. Although Liline found them insulting, her lord liked them.

Maybe that was why she found herself out of sorts lately. Or was it because of Cinder and Anya? The words she'd spoken when rescuing them from the Webbed Kingdom had been meant to earn their trust, but in the moment, they had also felt right. She only realized it later. But why? Why would they feel right to say?

Her meanderings ended when they came across another image that Liline found less than flattering. She scowled. In it, her form-fitting silver armor hung off her like lingerie, accentuating every curve. Stare hard enough, and a pervert could imagine her nipples.

Rence noticed, and she wore a tight-lipped smile of commiseration. "It won't always be like this."

Liline folded her arms across her chest. "It should have never been like this." She continued to stare at the image, abruptly wishing this fresh war was already over. She heaved a sigh. "I can't wait until we're free of the Orbs."

Rence smirked. "If we're ever free of them."

Liline faced her in surprise. After what Cinder and Anya had managed, she had thought the destruction of the Orbs was a foregone conclusion. There was Mede's Orb with Genka Devesth, which should be easy to obtain. The only remaining challenge after that would be the Orb of Wings, and that only because the location wasn't yet known. "You don't think we will be?" Liline asked.

Rence shrugged. "I know you're impressed by the human and the elf, and they have been impressive, but the Orb of Wings is hidden. We will be powerful enough to rule this world without its destruction, but we won't be powerful enough to stop Zahhack or progress to the point that we can do whatever we want and have no one tell us otherwise."

Liline got them walking again. "You're right. We need the Orb of Wings. But we'll find it. And no matter where it's hidden, Cinder and Anya will obtain it."

Rence stared her way as they paced along the quiet and dimly lit hallway. "You truly have that much faith in them, a pair of simple warriors?"

"Shokan and Sira always claimed to be simple warriors." Liline mentally frowned. Why would she say something like that, comparing Cinder and Anya to her greatest enemies?

"Yes," Rence said. "And look how well that turned out."

"This won't be like that," Liline countered. "Cinder isn't Shokan, and Anya is only an elf. And neither are *asrasins*."

"Thankfully so," Rence muttered. "How is their healing coming along? I didn't stop by to check on them today."

"They're coming along. Anya is functional if limited, but Cinder is yet to awaken."

"I wonder what happened to him?" Rence mused. "Was it really *lorethasra* he strained?"

Liline eyed her sister Titan askance. It was the very question she had pondered as well. What if, instead, it was *Jivatma*? Then might it be that Cinder Shade could one day claim the title of *asrasin*? It seemed incomprehensible, but the notion stayed with her, leaving her strangely troubled.

37

Cinder awoke with a throbbing headache. His entire body hurt, especially his chest and his throat, and he felt as weak as he could ever remember, worse than when he and Anya had survived Flatiron Death, pain that maybe even compared to when he'd awoken in the well back in Swallow.

He stared at the ceiling, trying to remember what had him feeling so puny. Slowly the memories returned—the last minutes in the Webbed Kingdom.

Anya!

He sat up with a groan, vision going in and out of focus, finally settling, and once he could see, Cinder cast his eyes about. *There.* Asleep, she lay in bed next to him. He leaned over, checking her breathing and pulse. Both were strong. One of her legs was wrapped. He recalled the spiderkin that had mauled her calf. Hopefully, whoever had tended to them had properly healed her. At least there was no redness beyond the bandages. No swelling that he could see either.

Only after checking on Anya did he gaze about. They were in their quarters in Naraka, and nothing seemed out of place. A tray of food and a pitcher of water rested on the low-lying table fronting the couch. However, before doing anything else, Cinder glanced in every corner. In moments, he sighted the braid meant to spy on them.

"Cinder?" Anya's eyes flickered open. "You're awake."

He smiled. "So are you." His voice was raspy, and he cleared his throat, annoyed at the pain of doing so. "How are you feeling?" He cleared his throat again.

"Better than you," she sat up on her elbows. "We've been in Naraka for two days. You only woke up now."

Two days? Cinder felt his chest, which wasn't tender to the touch, but there remained a deep-seated pain within it. "What happened?" he asked, flicking his eyes to the braid in the corner.

She caught on, nodding. "You strained your *lorethasra*, sourced it too deeply."

Cinder frowned. They'd never before confirmed to Shet or his Titans that he actually could source *lorethasra*, and here was Anya blurting out the truth. He grimaced. Then again, did it matter? By now, he'd demonstrated enough abilities that could only be accounted through *lorethasra*, so what difference did it make if she confirmed their suspicions?

Anya formed a bubble of Air, cupping his face as she stared into his eyes, frowning in silent scrutiny. Apparently satisfied, she looped her arms around his neck, drawing him close. "They had guessed already, and I had to tell them something. They couldn't find anything physically wrong with you."

Cinder made the final connection. If Shet and his Titans couldn't find out what was wrong with him, they'd figure it was either *lorethasra* or *Jivatma* that he'd strained. It was both an educated guess on their part as well as a needling for information. In the face of such an intrusion, Anya had made the right decision. Shet could never learn of Cinder's *Jivatma*.

"I understand," he whispered to her, cheek pressed against hers. "But it wasn't *lorethasra*. It was *Jivatma*. That's what I strained."

"You conducted too much?"

Cinder nodded.

"Say no more." Anya eyed him in worry. "Rence is their most knowledgeable healer, and she thinks you'll be a month or more recovering from this."

Cinder viewed Anya in consternation. A month. It was too long. They didn't have a month to waste while Shet grew stronger and stronger and exerted his influence throughout the eastern world. And that was assuming healing from whatever he'd done to his *Jivatma* didn't require more than a month of recuperation. He scowled to himself. What a disaster.

He lay back with a fresh groan. He needed more information, and he searched Shokan's memories. Did he know of anything like this? Had he experienced it?

As it turned out, the Blessed One did in fact know about overuse of *Jivatma* and *lorethasra*. And from his memories, Cinder gleaned that a month *was* the likely length of time it would take for him to heal. But he wouldn't do it while lying in bed.

Cinder made to rise.

"Don't," Anya advised, clutching at his arm. "You need to rest. You pushed yourself past your limits, physically, mentally, and spiritually."

A huff of frustration. Lying around doing nothing was not in Cinder's nature. It was the last thing he wanted to do. He glanced at Anya, at her wrapped calf. "What about you?"

She noticed the direction of his gaze. "That spiderkin got me in a pretty bad way, but Rence knows what she's doing. She neutralized the venom and cut away whatever muscle tissue had gone necrotic. There wasn't much, but I'm still in the same state as you. I need to heal and rest." She offered a wry smile. "I'll only be out of commission for about two weeks."

"Two weeks? Is that all?" Cinder chuckled mirthlessly. "Well, aren't we a pair."

"The best pair."

Cinder shoved aside his grim humor. "And the Orb?"

"In your cloak. And no one can reach into the *null pocket* except you. Unless they want to destroy the cloak."

"I imagine Shet will want me to present it to him."

"As soon as you're able," Anya confirmed. "He enjoys the spectacle of you marching through his zahhacks and presenting the Orb."

This time, Cinder's chuckle was evidence of true humor. "A good spectacle isn't to be missed," he said with a grin. His eyes lighted on Anya again, and he viewed her with a silent query. There was something else he recalled in the Webbed Kingdom: What Liline had said to them. Had that been real?

Anya, in that way they had of knowing what the other was thinking, minutely shook her head. "It was real, but I don't want to talk about it right now."

Meaning she *did* want to talk about it, but only after they were stronger and gone from Naraka.

Five days passed before Cinder was well enough to present the Orb to Shet. Possibly, he could have gone sooner, but Liline wouldn't allow it. She didn't want him overexerting himself or risk doing lasting harm. But why Liline cared was a mystery that the Titan never bothered explaining.

Nevertheless, during his convalescence, Cinder learned much, all of it coming from Liline, who explained what had been going on during the time when he'd been unconscious.

Sheoboth had been furious at the loss of the Orb, especially after discovering the storage room from which Cinder and Anya had made their escape. A line of their blood had led into the space, but then it was abruptly gone. The Crooked Crone had known it meant they must have left by anchor line. Add in the by-now widespread knowledge of a human and an elf who had stolen the Orbs of Peace from Surent Crèche and Yaksha Sithe, and the Webbed Queen had been certain Shet had reneged on their pact of nonaggression.

However, Sheoboth didn't have proof of her claims, and when she'd presented her demands to Shet—the return of the Orb at the top of the list—he had adamantly refused any knowledge of what had happened in the Webbed Kingdom. Further, Shet had demanded to know if Sheoboth had actually seen a human and an elf. Or had it been two humans? Or two elves? And had there even been a man and a woman? Or two men? Two women?

Sheoboth hadn't been able to say for sure, apparently never getting a clear look at Cinder and Anya. Regardless, she had threatened to end the nonaggression treaty between the Webbed Kingdom and Naraka.

Shet, though, had told her to think clearly before making such a threat, intimating that her children stood to lose far more than he did if she attacked. According to Liline, with five Orbs destroyed, Shet felt sure he could defend his empire against the spiderkin and even against Sheoboth if she took the field.

In the end, despite all her rumbling and complaining, the Crone did nothing.

Which was a shame as far as Cinder was concerned. To have two enemies—Naraka and the Webbed Kingdom—at one another's throats would have served the world far better than to have them as allies.

There was more to learn from Liline, such as the repair of Manifold's clothing. They'd been battered and torn, but Drak Renter, the youngest Titan, had mended them. He had wanted to know where they had obtained them, but stony silence had met his question. Regardless, right now they looked as good as ever, and Cinder currently stared at his image in the floor-length mirror.

His cloak's gilt edging shined, and the rest of the white fabric was clean, unmarred, and perfect. The only difference was that his clothes hung loose on his frame. He'd lost a lot of weight. Hollows caused his eyes to bulge, and now that he'd shaved, his cheeks appeared sunken. He stroked his chin, annoyed at the slight tremor in his hands and wondered at how long it would take to regain his strength.

Anya moved to stand behind him, hugging him as she rested her chin on his shoulder and kissed his cheek. "I don't miss getting a mouth full of beard whenever I do that," she said with a laugh. The mountain-fresh scent of her *lorethasra* perfumed the room as she formed a bubble of Air, her gaze flicking to the eavesdropping braid in the corner.

They had privacy.

Cinder turned into her embrace, his arms going around her waist. "I thought you liked the beard," he said, disliking the ongoing raspiness to his voice and the soreness in his throat.

"I like you." She ran her fingers through his freshly close-cropped hair, which had grown shaggy and unruly during their time in the Webbed Kingdom. "Beard or no beard. Long hair or short."

Cinder smiled. She always knew the right thing to say. He dipped his head, kissing her.

"Liline will be here soon," she said when he pulled back. "And Shet will be waiting for the Orb."

Cinder scowled, knowing what she meant. He'd have to wear the weave that stunted his emotions.

"We'll let them go as soon as we leave Naraka," Anya reminded him.

"I just don't like using it."

"It'll only be for a few hours. We are still planning on leaving after this meeting, right?" She peered at him in concern. "Is something wrong? Rence was sure you'd be in bed for at least a few weeks. It's only been five days. You don't have to push it. We can stay."

Cinder cut her off. "I'm fine. I'm not fully healed, but you know how much I hate staying here."

She continued to gaze at him in concern.

He found himself flinching under her regard. "Honestly, I'm fine. I heal faster than I used to. I think it's from having so many Orbs destroyed. It's making me stronger in all sorts of ways."

She eventually gave a slow nod of acceptance. "Just don't push yourself. I know how you are."

"Speaking of healing, how is your leg?"

Anya shrugged off his question. "It's still sore and aching," she said, her tone dismissive. "But if you're ready to leave, then so am I."

"I'm ready," he said with feeling. A hesitation followed, leading to a question that had bothered him ever since their escape from the Webbed Kingdom. "Liline saved us. And she said things. Do you remember?"

Anya nodded. "I don't know if she knew we could hear her."

"Or maybe she was counting on it. What if that was her plan all along?" It would make more sense than for Liline to actually care for them. The Titan was evil personified—all the horror she'd inflicted.

Anya moved out of his embrace, frowning. "What are you saying? She wanted us to hear so we'd trust her?"

Cinder didn't reply. Anya needed to reckon this on her own.

She had her head tilted in thought. "And she's been nothing but kind and considerate ever since. She's the one who saw to the repair of our clothes. I didn't even have to ask her. And then there was the information she gave us about the meeting between Sheoboth and Shet. She didn't have to tell us that."

"She's a Titan. Sira's memories should have told you who she really is."

"Someone we shouldn't trust. I never forgot, and I never will." Anya moved away from him. "There's something else I wanted to show you." From her *null pocket*, she withdrew her *divaspana*, passing it to him. "Liline gave me another one of these. She wanted us to each have one."

Cinder examined the *nomasra*. It looked slightly different from the original, felt different, too. He lifted his gaze to Anya, a furrowed question on his face. There was more going on with the *nomasra* than Liline demonstrating generosity.

"It works as a *divaspana*, but it can also track our movements," Anya explained. "With it, Liline will always know our location, possibly even when it's in our *null pockets*."

Cinder smirked. "Meaning she's hoping we'll be careless."

"Exactly," Anya said. "But having two of them to compare to one another, Sira's memories gave me a theory on how they might be made."

Cinder's smirk became a hopeful smile. "And?"

Anya replied with a smug grin. "And I know how to make them.

That, and maybe a Path, the Talent used to make an anchor line."

Cinder's attention locked on her. Forming their own anchor lines would change everything. "How?"

The sun shone without heat in the outdoor courtyard, and wispy clouds stretched across a pale blue sky. The wind whipped about, moaning and cold and carrying the dry smell of winter that caused Cinder's nose to itch. His feet crunched on packed snow as he paced through the gathered zahhacks.

Even frail as he was, they didn't impress him. What could they do? Attack? So what? Death was to be avoided but it wasn't to be feared. In Cinder's mind, the one who would suffer the most would be Shet.

The so-called god had no means to obtain the Orbs of Peace without Cinder and Anya. That much was clear by now. Otherwise, Shet or his Titans would have gone to Bharat and through brute force obtained the Orb of Undying Light. They could have done the same for the Orb of Moss in Revelant and the Orb of Eretria in Surent.

But they hadn't, which meant they couldn't. Which also meant all the snarling and dark promises were nothing but sound and fury but signifying nothing.

Cinder smiled to himself on recalling the mangled quote. It had been one of Shokan's favorites. Sira had appreciated it, too.

The reminder of Sira caused Cinder to nearly step wrong. Was she actually Anya? Was he actually Shokan? He had the Blessed One's memories, skills, and Talents, and wasn't that the mark of a person? Having their memories and abilities?

Possibly so, but what of emotions? In that regard, Cinder as he was now—fearless and without feeling—was most certainly not Shokan.

It left a hanging question that always seemed to crop up whenever he wore this particular braid. Who was he really? Was he merely the avatar of a greater being—of a Cinder Shade who had all the emotions he currently lacked—a Cinder Shade who *was* Shokan Reborn? And how much did it matter anyway? Did the answer dictate his purpose?

Cinder shook his head. Now wasn't the time for this.

He'd entered the clustering of necrosed, and they crowded him. He shoulder-checked the nearest, flexing his barely recovered *Jivatma, and glaring the other ones down*. Even weakened, he needed to appear strong here in this den full of villains.

Next, he neared the rakshasas, who stared at him in grim but silent scrutiny.

Cinder appreciated their quiet. They were the more intimidating for it. They let him through their ranks without a single word spoken until it was only Shet who was ahead, seated on his black throne, twirling his black spear carved with red runes. At the base of his dais rested the tawny-furred dragon, Charn, sleeping as usual. Did the beast ever rouse?

At the proscribed twenty-foot distance, Cinder went to a knee. There, he waited patiently for Shet to bid him rise. It took a while, and Cinder recognized what was happening. Shet was testing his patience, waiting to see if he could maintain his equanimity. In that case, the supposed god was in for a long wait.

Finally, Shet called on him to stand. "You've been feasting on my good will for nearly a week now," the false god said. "I expect more from my servants."

Cinder bowed his head, eyes facing the ground. "My apologies, Lord Shet. I'll labor to ensure it never happens again."

"See that you do. Give me the Orb."

Only then did Cinder raise his gaze. He reached into his *null pocket*, withdrawing the Orb of Regret and holding it out for Shet.

Moments later, it was done. The Orb was destroyed, and as with the others, a weight seemed to lift off of Cinder. Each time it was of less quality and quantity than the last, but it was removed, nevertheless.

"You may go," Shet intoned, giving a lazy gesture of his hand as if waving off a pest.

Cinder responded in the way he knew would bother the god the most: by not reacting. Instead, he bowed his head once again and prepared to leave Shet. As he straightened, he noticed Charn staring at him through a cracked eye. The dragon blinked once, and an instant later, he was asleep.

Shrugging away the importance of Charn's brief awakening, Cinder faced away from Shet and marched toward the courtyard's exit.

"Rukh?"

Cinder nearly halted his progress upon hearing the whispery thin noise. He listened close as he strode onward, but it didn't repeat, and he couldn't tell if it had even been real. The word, though... it had a haunting familiarity to it.

His deliberations cut off when he reached Anya.

"It went well?" she asked, peering intently at him.

"It went well enough. I survived, after all."

Minutes earlier, the cursed fifth Orb of Peace had finally been destroyed, and the blue-and-green lightning had additionally thinned. Unfortunately, the other two still impeded Liline's skills and Talents, but soon enough, she would be free. Even now, as someone with five closed Chakras, the only beings on Seminal who could contend with her were her fellow Titans, and the Sisters. Otherwise, no one else stood a chance.

It felt good to be nearly whole, and Liline wanted to luxuriate in the coolness of her *Jivatma*, which was dark as night, with only the fewest vague lights to indicate Devesh's role in her life. Certainly, He was her creator, and she respected His reach and power, but in the end, He had His mission, and she had hers. And hers was to become free of all constraints, no responsibilities to chain her.

But to accomplish such an ideal, she wondered if Shet was correct in his belief that their Chakras needed to be completely closed rather than completely open, like her *asrasin* brothers and sisters used to claim? Wouldn't Shet's way simply trade the power of Devesh for that of the Empty One?

Shet didn't believe so. He was sure that his way would lead to a third option, becoming apparent when he closed his seventh and eighth Chakras and he would finally stand on equal footing to both Devesh and the Empty One.

It was a lofty goal, and if anyone could achieve it, Liline figured it would be her lord and master. And once he did, she would follow in his footsteps.

But still, was he right in his advice? Should she keep her Chakras closed? It was a question that was millennia in the making, one she had never doubted until now. On Earth and during the *NusraelShev*, Liline had always followed where Shet led; never considered that closure of her Chakras wasn't the better means to true power. After all, look where it had led her. Freedom to do as she wished, with no one able to judge her.

True, she had killed and tortured an uncountable number of people, but that was the price paid by those who weren't sufficiently powerful. The strong ruled, and the weak prayed to be overlooked.

But to whom did they pray?

Such odd doubts, and Liline wondered at how and why they had arisen.

She glanced aside to Cinder and Anya, who strode silently at her side. After delivering the Orb of Regret to Shet, they had decided to immediately tackle the next one. It was held by Genka Devesth, the Warlord of the Sunsets, the *Garnala lon Anarin*—the Sower of the Wind—and holder of many other lofty titles. But rumor suggested his power was broken ever since the herd of wraiths had ravaged his empire several years ago.

Whether it was true or not was immaterial. Of greater import was that Liline couldn't anchor line Cinder and Anya all the way to the Sunset Kingdoms. She'd never been there and, thus far, a worthy subordinate hadn't either.

Therefore, she would have to take Cinder and Anya to the oasis in which she'd saved them following their time in Flatiron Death and the Temple of Prana. They could even take the camels they'd brought to

Naraka: Fellow, Bellow, Mellow, and Callow. Liline had named them, and she knew they would enjoy returning to the desert's heat. The cold and high climes of her lord's citadel certainly wasn't for them.

From there, Cinder and Anya could travel to Devesth, which should take about three months, and then obtain Mede's Orb.

But Liline had no doubt as to their success. They'd already achieved the near-miraculous on several occasions. The Orbs at Surent, Yaksha, and Bharat had required cunning and foresight, while the one in Flatiron had required a steel will. Liline shuddered on thinking how difficult their journey must have been. She had recently gone into that hellscape, and even a single day inside its bounds had tested her resolve. And yet Cinder and Anya had withstood its borders for several days, lasting long enough to obtain the Orb of Flames before escaping to tell the tale.

Then there had been their dive into the Webbed Kingdom. Even at the peak of power, Liline wasn't sure she could have accomplished what Anya and Cinder had. The spiderkin queens would have posed no challenge, but Liline wouldn't have wanted to battle Sheoboth. She was a true power.

Then again, maybe Cinder and Anya were as well. Liline was coming to understand that. She hadn't at first, not even after their impressive display at Flatiron or their clever planning at Yaksha and Bharat. But she realized it now even though it hadn't been the case prior to the Webbed Kingdom.

Everything changed, though, when Liline had received that shocking message from Anya about how close they were to obtaining the Orb. To say that she had been stunned would have been to say that Flatiron was dry. Until then, Liline hadn't figured she ever need to actually contact Sheoboth and demand a parlay. Sure, she'd massed the goblins and ghouls a couple of times, but that was easy. Goblins and ghouls existed to be ordered about.

But upon hearing that message from Anya, all attention from every Titan had been given over to supporting her and Cinder. They had all dropped any other business and focused on the Orb of Regret. The goblins and ghouls had been massed, but the Titans had also bolstered their forces. It had forced Sheoboth to leave her lair and parlay with them.

The exact opening Cinder and Anya had needed.

Again, Liline glanced askance. It had been due to him, Cinder Shade. He'd killed powerful queens. She knew it. Anya was an elf, deadly in her own way, but not powerful enough to have defeated whomever Sheoboth had guarding her throne hall. Only a human—an *asrasin* with a full arsenal of *lorethasra* at their disposal—could have managed it.

And here he was walking the halls of Naraka after suffering injuries that should have had him abed for at least another week.

All of which raised a troubling question: how was Cinder Shade so strong? And what would he be like once the inhibition from the Orbs of Peace was fully lifted? Would he be a match for a Titan? Was his secret his lack of emotions whenever he required fearlessness in battle? Did it allow him to fully commit to any attack without worry over the consequences?

And what was the source of his injuries? Was it really overextending his use of *lorethasra*? It was what Anya had claimed, but Liline couldn't get it out of her head that it might be *Jivatma*.

The matter raised a troubling possibility, and although Shet—who considered Cinder and Anya nothing more than extremely competent vassals—disregarded it, Liline did not. Her lord was blind when it came to those two, but she wouldn't let emotions cloud her judgment. At this point, only a fool would overlook them.

Which was why Liline had wanted Cinder and Anya to hear her soft words when she'd collected them in the Webbed Kingdom and why she was so kind to them during their healing here at Naraka.

Earn their trust, and they might tell her the truth about Cinder's abilities.

It wasn't a foolish endeavor, either. Rence and Drak shared her concern, but none of the other Titans—the same shortsightedness they shared with Shet. Liline refused to fall victim to such limited vision.

For that reason, she plastered a bright smile on her face when they reached the stables, addressing Cinder and Anya. "After you recover in the wilds, contact me. I'll gather the camels and whatever pack animals you might need." She tossed each of them a heavy pouch of coins. "This should pay for whatever else you might need when you travel to Devesth, whenever you decide to head in that direction." She let her smile become faint and longing. "Let me know if you need anything else." She offered a practiced hesitation. "I hope you both know that I am your ally." She'd almost said friend, but that would have been a step too far.

It was Anya who replied, smiling in response, briefly inclining her head like the elf was an empress. "We won't forget how you saved us in the Webbed Kingdom."

38

What should have been a two-day journey to reach the edge of Shalla Vale ended up taking five. It was because of Cinder. He still struggled with his injuries—more the spiritual kind than the physical. Draining his *Jivatma* had left him with a dull pain, weakness, and a distinct lack of stamina. His mind didn't want to work right either. Riding set his aching chest aflame, and any Healing Anya provided didn't seem to help. His spirit, mind, and body needed to recover on their own.

However, recuperating in Naraka was out of the question. Neither Cinder nor Anya was comfortable remaining in Shet's black palace.

Just as importantly, they wanted to reconnect with the Shokans, who might be needed in the Sunset Kingdoms. Rumor circulated east that the wraiths who had destroyed Genka Devesth's army were reorganizing, bent on invading Shang Mendi and leveling it. There likely weren't as many this time, but it also didn't matter. Genka's green army couldn't handle any sized herd.

But that's where Cinder and Anya were eventually headed, to bring relief to the Sunsets. The Shokans might be able to help, too but only if they managed to open at least one of their Chakras. Their support could then prove critical, aiding while Cinder and Anya took down the wraiths. He figured they could handle the hundred or so that likely remained in the world.

It was with these thoughts in mind that Cinder heeled his gelding up the slopes to where Fastness and the Shokans were said to be camped. He and Anya crested a rise, entering a plateau where the trail they'd been following angled to the left. It led them into an evergreen forest with a few interspersed aspens, their limbs bare of leaves.

Cinder and Anya had spent more than two months in the Webbed Kingdom, and by now summer had transitioned into autumn. The weather in the highlands had grown chill and the days shorter. The first snow had fallen with icy patches scattered throughout the forest and trails. And although it was only late afternoon, the sun was already bending behind the western mountains, leaving stark shadows stretching large. Twilight wasn't too far off, and the temperature was likely to plunge additionally with nightfall.

Cinder scowled as his breath frosted in the cold. He clutched his coat tighter about himself, grateful that a newer snowfall hadn't caught him and Anya out here. That would have made travel through the mountains nearly impossible.

Shortly afterward, a woman stepped onto the trail, hindering their way forward. Cinder didn't recognize her, but based on the white sheen over her otherwise dark pupils, he guessed she had once been a wraith. He reined his gelding and offered her a smile, introducing himself.

Head tilted in consideration, the once-wraith stared at him. "Are you really as deadly as Fastness says? I'd like to see that."

As meager as Cinder was feeling, he doubted he could take on a newborn puppy, much less someone as deadly as this woman was likely to be. But he also didn't want to admit to such weakness, especially to a once-wraith.

Thankfully, Anya took the matter out of his hands. She heeled her horse forward, addressing the woman barring their way. "To challenge him, you'd have to best me first." Dismounting from her mare and hiding her lingering limp, she approached the once-wraith with a warm smile. "Fastness probably told you about us. Why don't you go find him, and afterward, if you still want, I'll be happy to spar with you."

The words were said with kindness and generosity, but they seemed to have little effect on the once-wraith, who continued to scowl at Anya. "I'll get Fastness, but come toward our camp, and you'll have trouble. Run back the way you came, and you'll have trouble. Take a step off the trail—"

Anya nodded understanding. "I get it. We'll have trouble."

The once-wraith glowered, taking offense for some reason. "Don't push it. My name is Shella Marsh. Remember it for when I kick your ass." She pressed close into Anya's personal space.

But Anya never blinked, and she never backed down. Instead, she shook her head in disappointment. "Is this the lesson Fastness taught you? To show ill will toward strangers? I said I would be happy to spar against you, but your anger has me feeling decidedly less charitable. I'm Anya Aruyen. This is Cinder Shade. We should be friends, not adversaries."

Again, the words seemed to have no effect on the other woman. She continued to scowl, and Cinder was beginning to wonder if Shella had gotten any of her Chakras to neutral. It seemed unlikely.

"She always speak for you?" Shella asked Cinder after another few seconds of staring hard at Anya.

He'd had enough, and he dismounted the gelding, hiding any discomfort and the slight tremble in his hands. "She does the talking when it's necessary," Cinder said, clearing his throat of its raspiness. "Now do like you promised. Go get Fastness."

Shella smirked. "I'll be right back. Don't run away." She departed, heading up the trail.

"What was that about?" Anya asked after Shella was out of sight.

"Someone just wanting to show they're in charge," Cinder replied.

There wasn't much else to say after that, and they waited in silence until soft hoofbeats announced Fastness' approach.

Cinder found himself smiling, looking forward to seeing his old friend. There were also questions to ask, such as why Fastness had agreed with Manifold's suggestion about Rabisu's weave. Cinder and Anya had made the decision on their own, but only because they trusted the stallion and the Mythaspuri.

Seconds later, there he was: Fastness, the white. With him was Shella, but she halted in the near distance, giving them privacy.

Cinder stepped forward, hugging his old friend and rubbing his forelock.

"It is good to see you again," Fastness said. *"Come to our camp and tell me what you've been doing."*

Cinder remounted the gelding Naraka had provided while Anya did the same with her mare, and they set off.

Shella glowered at them as they passed her by. "I'll be waiting for that match, Princess. And afterward, I'll take him down." She gestured to Cinder.

Anya smiled thinly. "I look forward to it."

Shella might have responded further, but a sharp snort and a glare from Fastness hauled her up short. She sneered. "I'll see you soon."

Anya didn't bother replying.

"You'll have to forgive Shella," Fastness said. *"In her previous life, she was a mercenary, and the fighting arts is what she knows best. Amongst the wraiths who wanted to return to Devesh's love, she was easily the most physically capable. It hurts her heart that the skills that she worked so hard to hone aren't as useful in this new life of hers."*

"And what kind of life is that?" Cinder asked, genuinely interested.

"A life of peace. That's what Shella wants."

"Peace?" Anya asked, her voice holding the same surprise that Cinder was feeling.

"Jozep and Sriovey are here," Fastness said. *"The serenity they bring inspired Shella to want to become like Salt and release herself from the way of the warrior."*

Cinder shared a wondering look with Anya. "If she wants to follow the path of peace, she's not doing a very good job."

"I know. But following the path of peace doesn't mean that she can't practice her martial skills," Fastness said. *"She just can't use them in the ways she once had. She can't seek war and conflict, which at one time, was all she wanted. For some, it's a hard transition."*

Cinder mentally shrugged. It was a lovely way to live, but it was also one he couldn't imagine living. While he longed for tranquility in his days, he also recognized there would always have to be stalwarts who defended those who couldn't defend themselves. The warriors who fought so others didn't have to.

At one time, such a recognition would have left him feeling despondent, but by now, he had come to accept his lot in life. He'd one day know peace, but he would always ensure that he could fight if it was ever required. Maybe that was the hard transition Shella still had to make.

"She has to accept and understand that her skills might not always be useful," Anya said, knowing his unspoken considerations in the way they shared. "But she needs to let go of the belligerent attitude."

"Let's hope she manages it," Cinder said with heartfelt emotion. He addressed Fastness then, asking the question that had been foremost in his mind ever since learning of Rabisu's betrayal.

Fastness didn't answer at once. *"I had my reasons,"* he said at last. *"I trusted in Manifold. I trusted he could see through Rabisu's deception. I trusted in your Talents to protect you from the rakshasa."*

"They were Shokan's and Sira's Talents," Cinder reminded him.

"Of course. And I trusted those as well. For those and any other misjudgments, I truly apologize, and I'm sorry for what you had to endure. I just didn't expect Rabisu to find a way around all our protections."

"He didn't," Anya said. "He was hiding within me, but the weave he placed on Cinder was already coming apart."

"And in Verity Foe, you learned everything you needed," Fastness said with a firm nod of his head. *"So everything worked out in the end."*

Cinder scowled. Fastness' answer was nearly worthless. Actually, it was worthless. He sighed a second later. Then again, they weren't likely to receive anything better. Besides, what was done was done. However, moving forward, he'd have to think carefully before accepting advice from Fastness. He trusted the stallion, but he also couldn't help but wonder if the white had his own motives.

"Any news from the Sunsets?" Anya asked, shifting the conversation.

"A new herd is forming. One and a half times the size of the last one, and it, too, is aimed at Genka Devesth's empire."

Cinder startled. "One and a half times? I thought most of the wraiths were killed during their last incursion into the Sunsets."

Fastness whickered. *"The Hungering Heart, the one who rules the wraiths, apparently only sent a third of his forces."*

Cinder frowned. There was no chance that he and Anya could stop a herd of that size on their own? Nothing could. But before worrying over the matter, was it even true? "How reliable is this information?"

"Very. It comes from the once-wraiths—they call themselves the re-deemers, by the way—who left the Hungering Heart. The redeemers can still hear him, and from what they can tell, the herd is likely to march into the Sunsets in the northern climes early summer, almost certainly in the next three or four months."

It wasn't what Cinder had wanted to hear. The trek to the Sunsets was always going to be long, but now the pressing of time weighed upon their journey. "What about the southern nations? Shima Sithe and Aurelian Crèche?"

"From what I've heard—"

"How exactly did you hear?" Anya interrupted.

"The troll, yakshin, and holders who went to Char—they brought back Barton, Painter, and your other mounts—they learned it there. Genka hasn't been able to convince the southern nations to fight their common enemy. They're happier seeing him fail."

Cinder grimaced. Shortsighted idiots. "We can't let the Sunsets fall."

"It won't be easy to save them," Fastness replied.

No, it wouldn't, and Cinder pondered how to convince the leaders of Aurelian Crèche and Shima Sithe to aid the Sunsets. His sight fell on Anya, and an idea formed. He smiled. "We need Jozep and Sriovey. And you, too."

"What do you have in mind?" Anya asked.

"Shima Sithe will send their warriors if Anya Aruyen, princess of Yaksha Sithe and Sira Reborn, demands it. And the same will hold true in Aurelian Crèche if Shokan Reborn and a dwarf like Jozep, someone they all want to emulate, asks it of them."

Fastness chuckled laughter in their minds. *"Clever. I like that."*

Cinder shrugged. "They don't have to know that we're not actually the Blessed Ones."

They rode on, and Cinder heard surprising information about Titan's Reach.

"I sent Residar, Brissianna, and Selin to Salt's old village," Fastness said.

"Why?"

"To save them. They worship Shet. If he has a chance to answer their prayers, their community will be destroyed and many others with it. He'll send them to war."

Cinder grunted. He doubted Residar and the other once-wraiths—no, the redeemers—could do much for the people of Titan's Reach, but miracles did happen. A notion occurred to him. "What's Salt doing during all this?"

"She's in Shalla Vale, training with the holders and yakshins."

"Training to do what?" Anya asked.

Fastness whickered. *"Training in the ways of humans before the NusraelShev."*

Cinder followed Fastness into a small clearing, and the first sight that met his eyes was Brilliance grooming a young doe with glowing white eyes. He blinked, trying to make sense of what he was seeing.

"Ow. That hurts," the doe complained.

"Then you shouldn't have played in the dirt with Kela," Brilliance said, holding the doe between her paws.

Cinder shared a wondering expression with Anya.

"*Ah, yes,*" Fastness said with a nervous nicker and a shiver of his coat. "*The newest recruit to our little band. Kela found her.*" He mentally muttered under his breath. "*I sometimes wish he never had.*"

"What?"

"*Nothing.*" Fastness made to trot off. "*Good luck. I'll talk to you later.*"

"Wait," Cinder called after the white.

"*No time,*" Fastness shouted, picking up the pace as he sped off.

What was going on? Cinder's attention went back to Brilliance and the doe.

"*But Kela said it would be fun,*" the doe was saying. "*And it was fun. I don't see why you can't clean him instead of me. I'm not that dirty at all.*"

"*Then you should have joined him for a swim in the pond. It's how he's getting clean.*"

"*I don't like swimming.*" A swipe to the side of her head caused her to squall. "*I said ow. That really hurts.*" She blinked. "*And it's still hurting.*"

"*Shush,*" Brilliance replied. A few more swipes and she seemed satisfied. "*Now stand up and meet our guests.*"

"*Guests?*" The doe sounded excited as she jumped to her feet, hopping forward, quivering in excitement. "*A human and an elf.*" She tilted her head. "*Or are you a holder? Bones says holders are the best warriors in the world. Is that true? He says the only one better is someone named Cinder Shade.*" She shivered. "*That's a scary name. I bet he's a scary person. My name is Hima. What's your name?*"

"Cinder Shade."

The doe leapt away with a squeak of fear, darting behind Brilliance. In the corner of his vision, he caught Anya laughing. He rolled his eyes, addressing Brilliance. "Is there something you feel like telling us?"

Rather than answer, the big snowtiger paced forward, tail lashing, eyes narrowed. "*Do you have another cat named Aia?*"

Cinder frowned at her unexpected question. "Shokan did."

"*And since you're Shokan, that means you do, too.*"

Cinder didn't bother correcting the snowtiger. "Why don't you tell me about your new friend?"

Brilliance glanced back at the doe. "*She's cute, isn't she? Kela found her. I'm teaching her what it means to serve like you serve."*

"She's a good teacher, so you better be nice," the doe said with a flash of her teeth. *"I'm deadly dangerous. Don't you forget it. If you try to eat me, I'll bite you to death. I'm not afraid of your scary name, and if you think—"*

"Hima, this is my human. Be silent."

"Oh? Cinder is your human? This Cinder? The one Bones and the holders say is so powerful? I didn't know they were the same person. Why didn't you say so? I've been so—"

"Hima," Brilliance said with a warning growl.

"Oh, right. Sorry." The doe settled on the ground.

Brilliance faced Cinder again. *"There's a lot I have to teach her, and because I'm doing such servantly work, I expect some delicious food tonight along with a back rub, a belly rub, and some rubs around my ears."* Leaning forward, Brilliance rubbed the side of her head against the top of Cinder's before departing with a swish of her tail, taking the doe with her.

Cinder stared after the *aether*-cursed animals in utter confusion before addressing Anya. "Do you have any idea what that was about?"

"I think Brilliance finally has a child to teach. She's always wanted one, but being as she's both a mother and a child, it's likely to be an interesting demonstration in child-rearing."

Cinder rubbed his chin, considering her explanation. After a moment's deliberation, he grunted. He supposed it made sense. His reflections were interrupted when voices that he recognized approached. A trickster and testing part of him had him Blending lightly. He hoped Anya would catch the hint. She did.

"I got fussed *and* cussed," said Ishmay, pulling into view.

Bones was walking alongside him. "That seems to happen to you a lot. You might want to fix that."

The rest of the Shokans trailed after the two of them.

"It's a problem with his personality," Riyne declared.

"There's a problem with your mother," Ishmay shot back.

"You're thinking of your sister," Mirk said.

"Go stuff yourself," Ishmay said with a glower.

A pair of familiar dwarves came into sight: *Jozep and Sriovey.* Cinder's eyes watered.

Bones held up a fist. The Shokans halted, crouching, hands going to their weapons.

"What is it?" Riyne asked, stepping forward, eyes darting about.

"There's a Blend somewhere," Bones replied.

Cinder grinned to himself, pleased that at least one of the Shokans had noticed his presence. He dropped the Blend.

An instant later he was embraced by his brothers, much like he had been at Char. And like at Char, he couldn't stop grinning and laughing.

"What have you been doing?" Estin asked, addressing Anya. "You both look like you've gone through the hard end of it."

"We have," Anya replied, going on to tell of their trek through the Webbed Kingdom.

When she finished, Sriovey whistled in admiration. "You went straight to the heart of the enemy and survived? That's some serious badassery." He flushed a moment later. "Sorry, Jozep."

The other dwarf laughed. "You don't have to apologize for cursing."

Having already learned from Fastness what was going on, Cinder stared from Jozep to Sriovey. Sriovey was learning what it meant to be a true dwarf. Cinder clapped his friend on the shoulder, not knowing how to properly express how proud he was, afraid any words to that effect would come across as condescending.

"How long can you stay?" Bones asked.

"Just the night," Cinder replied. "Liline has a way of tracking our movements. We left the device behind in Naraka, but she'll get more suspicious than she already is if we go too long without it."

"But if she's already suspicious, why worry about what she thinks?" Gorant asked.

Anya answered. "Because we don't want her looking for where we've been resting and recovering. She might locate your camp if she looks hard enough. And we also don't trust just staying somewhere in the Daggers, either. Sheoboth and Shet still have their alliance, but it won't do us any good if we're discovered by any spiderkin."

"Why not stay in Shalla Valley then?" Bones suggested. "That would be the best place to regain your strength. We'd be around, too. You'd be with friends."

Cinder tightened his lips. He wished it could be just like Bones was saying. "We can't. There's also Rabisu. He's trapped and can't go anywhere, but his very existence is a pollution. Having him in Shalla Vale would make it hard, maybe impossible for Mahamatha to keep her borders secure."

Groans and disappointed mutters met his pronouncement.

"Isn't there anything we can do to help?" Sriovey asked.

Cinder smiled. "As a matter of fact, there is. I think you'll like it."

The next morning, with the sun barely peeking over the mountains and pinking the sky, Shella made sure to challenge Anya before she even had breakfast. The Shokans were gathered in a line, bowls in hand, as they waited their turn to scoop food from the cook pot. Sriovey, in charge of breakfast this morning, stirred it over the fire, and he glanced up as the once-wraith—the redeemer—confronted Anya.

"You owe me," Shella proclaimed. "Show me what you got or call yourself a coward."

Anya stifled a sigh. She wasn't fully recovered, not by any stretch. Her leg was still rubbery, especially the ankle, which twinged and ached, threatening to give way without a moment's notice. And stressing it in a sparring match wasn't likely to do it much good, either.

But she also couldn't see herself giving way to Shella. First of all, the redeemer needed humbling. Thus far, her comportment and attitude had been atrocious. Second, the warrior in Anya would break before it bent to this woman who claimed to want to follow the path of peace. Let this supposed peace-lover taste defeat.

"Fine, but no weapons," Anya said. "Just fists, feet, and anything else you got."

"Agreed." Shella said with a smirk.

And Anya knew the reason for the redeemer's confidence. Shella still had her claws. They were as long and sharp as a bear's, and she likely thought it would give her all the advantage she'd need in the sparring match. Yet another reason to teach her humility. Anya had her Talents and skills, and even with a less-than-sturdy ankle, she wouldn't lose. There was no fear in her at such a possibility.

"You can use one of our sparring circles," Bones said.

"I'll adjudicate," Estin said.

"I want Fastness," Shella stated.

"And you'll have him," Fastness said, sounding annoyed. He'd been standing off to the side, talking to Kela, Brilliance, and Hima. *"I'll decide the victor. Now go to your marks, and let's get this done. I'm still sleepy."*

Anya concealed a limp as she passed Cinder. He wore a blank expression, but she could tell he was worried. The concern was apparent in the tightness at the corners of his mouth and the frown he was trying not to show. Anya nodded his way, letting him know she was fine, but his gaze flicked to her ankle, and she smiled inwardly. It was only fair. Just like they could tell what the other was feeling or thinking, they could sense each other's injuries.

She gave him a small headshake, letting him know it was good enough, which it was. Anya didn't fear the redeemer. In her view, this match would be nothing more than a teaching lesson.

Throwing off her deliberations, Anya reached the sparring circle and stood opposite Shella. Fastness called for them to bow to one another, which they did, neither of them breaking eye contact.

"Go!"

Shella rushed forward, trying to use aggression to push Anya out of the circle.

It didn't work.

Anya circled away, maintaining distance, using just the barest amount of *Jivatma* to power her motions. She checked a hard kick, the slap echoing as she evaded a powerful right hook. Another hook.

Ducked it this time. She stuffed a takedown, hitting for a knee on the way out.

She missed badly.

Shella grinned. "You have to be faster than that, Princess." She bull-rushed, getting low.

Anya got even lower—or tried to. Her ankle tweaked, gave out. *Fragging hells.* There went the easy, quick lesson she wanted to impart on the redeemer.

Shella shot in for a single-leg. Anya tried to block, but her ankle wouldn't hold. It buckled. Anya cursed to herself when the redeemer got in deep. She wasn't in trouble, but this wasn't going to be as simple as she had hoped.

The redeemer tried for a trip, but Anya stepped over it. Shella didn't let up, though, pushing forward. Anya gave ground, maintaining her balance until she could plant her back leg. An overhook to Shella's right arm led to a sprawl. The other woman tried to crawl through it. Anya blocked, keeping the overhook and pushed down on the back of Shella's neck.

A flare of power as Shella tried to explode forward. Anya kept her under control and waited. *There.* Shella's hand started to slide down the back of Anya's leg. She posted the other woman's hand to the ground, broke the hold, and came around the corner. Anya's hands went around Shella's waist, and she flared her own power. The redeemer went airborne when Anya suplexed her, dumping Shella on her back.

Anya immediately slid out, landing a heavy elbow before surging to her feet.

So did Shella, who didn't slow one bit. She sent a questing jab, slow and lazy.

Anya knew its intent. She shifted off the center line and powered her Shield. Just as expected, Shella's punch intentionally missed by four inches, and at the end of the blow, her claws extruded, ready to rake. Anya took it on her Shield, snapped off a kick. It popped like a drum, rocking the other woman in the jaw.

Shella growled, eating the shot. Anya blinked. That kick could have put down a bull. A mental shrug. *Oh, well.* They circled, exchanging jabs. Anya's ankle throbbed, and she knew she had to end this match soon.

Another snap kick to her opponent's jaw, more powerful than the last, got Shella's attention. The other woman hammered an uppercut. Again, Anya took the blow on her Shield, but it still rocked her backward. She gave ground as Shella sent punches and kicks. Anya sought to drift away but was cut off from retreating.

If that's how she wants it. If she wants to stand and bang…

Anya stopped circling. Shella cracked her, the punch partially getting through Anya's Shield. But she answered with a right-left-right combination. Each punch landed, but Shella still plowed through the shots.

Anya grimaced. She didn't truly want to hurt the other woman, but seeing no other option, she dug just a bit deeper into her *Jivatma.* Her punches and kicks came heavier, faster. She ended a combination with a bruising knee to the stomach that buckled her opponent.

Shella grunted in pain, her legs going weak. She stepped back, looking for room to clear the cobwebs. Anya didn't give it to her. She clutched the back of Shella's head, grabbing a plum hold, and battered the woman's ribs with pounding knees. A final one to Shella's temple, and the redeemer collapsed to the ground.

"*Victory for Anya,*" Fastness declared.

"Are we done?" Anya asked Shella even though she'd been declared the winner. Waiting for an answer, she stared down at the other woman.

"We're done," Shella said, sounding both groggy and angry.

"You'll need healing," Anya said. "And in the future, if you truly wish to follow the path of peace, listen to Jozep. Ask him if he would have spoken to strangers in the way you did. Ask him if he would have challenged those who should be your friends the way you did." Her words spoken, she spun on her heel, exiting the sparring circle.

"Wait."

Anya turned around, facing the redeemer.

"I had to know if you were as good as Fastness said. It's important."

Anya quirked an eyebrow in question. "And?"

"You're good," Shella allowed. "But you're not that good."

The comment earned a smile. "I was barely using my *Jivatma*, and my ankle is injured."

The wraith stared in disbelief.

Anya sighed. She closed her eyes, mildly shaking her head. *Fine.* She conducted more deeply from her *Jivatma*, though it was still a strain after the Webbed Kingdom. Using a Talent to power her muscles, she darted forward, fisting Shella's shirt and lifting the other woman into the air. The redeemer struggled to free herself, but it was to no avail.

Anya casually flung Shella aside, careful so she didn't land on her head. "Do you need another demonstration?" she asked.

Shella shook her head, eyes wide, slowly regaining her feet. "Why didn't you just do that from the beginning?"

"Because if I just beat you, you wouldn't have learned anything. Sparring the way we did, you'll learn to tighten your defenses."

Shella continued to stare at her wide-eyed.

Anya placed a hand on the woman's shoulder. "The path you wish to walk is hard, but it is worth traveling. I hope you realize that. And I hope you also realize that for some of us, our paths require that we defend those who can't defend themselves. We have to fight against those who would do our loved ones harm. Think about it. It might give you some peace." She left Shella then. She caught Cinder smiling her way, and she grinned in reply.

"How the fuck did she get so good?" Sriovey whispered to the camp at large.

"She's always been that good," Estin said.

"No, she wasn't," Ishmay stated. "Anya was good before, but now she's like the Lady of Fire good."

39

After visiting the Shokans, Cinder and Anya had returned to Naraka, meeting with Liline, who had immediately anchor-lined them here, to a familiar oasis south of Flatiron.

And upon stepping on to the sand, Cinder had rocked on his feet. He was used to the late autumn cold of the Daggers, not the blistering temperatures of Flatiron, even at the edges. Right now, the heat hit like an anvil, and sweat immediately dripped down his brow. He fanned himself. Devesh, it was hot.

He glanced to where a set of red hills rose in the distance while, closer at hand, palm trees and a field of grass covered several rolling acres. Large boulders, each one at least Cinder's height, lay scattered about, lining the blessed pond centered within the oasis. The water fluttered as a dry wind passed across its glistening surface, carrying the smell of hot sand.

Cinder inhaled deeply, and a stray recollection caused him to imagine the stench of death also wafting on that breeze.

Flatiron. There weren't any good memories of that place. The heat haze, arguing with Anya, the broiling sun, and the utter lack of life and water were the least of the miseries found in that desert. Worse was the lack of *lorasra*—aether, as the rest of the world called it. Whatever the name, it was the source of life, matched to a person's *lorethasra*, and for some reason, Flatiron had no *lorasra* at all. What disaster could account for such a terrible lacking?

At least they would never again have to go into that killing heat. Once was more than enough.

He shook off his ruminations, taking further stock.

From this oasis, which was toward the western edge of Flatiron, Liline had said it was a week's journey to the city of Grind. And from there, another two months to the Sunsets. Liline would have anchor lined them closer to their destination, but she couldn't. No zahhacks under Shet's command had yet managed to reach that area of the world.

But before any of that traveling occurred, Cinder had to recover, and since he couldn't stay with the Shokans or enter Shalla Vale for any length of time, this place would serve as well as any other.

"It's so bright," Anya said, squinting into the depths of the Flatiron. She'd wrapped a green shawl around her head to keep off the heat.

Cinder was about to respond to her comment, but just then, he noticed something different about Anya's eyes: they were slitted like a cat's.

"You like?" Anya asked with a smile as she batted her eyelashes.

Cinder viewed her in bemusement. "How did you do that?"

"Liline keeps teaching us new tricks that she doesn't mean to."

"New tricks?"

"When she rescued us from the Webbed Kingdom, she had these kind of eyes. I was awake long enough to watch them transform back to normal. It's a simple weave."

"Does it help you see better in low light?"

Anya nodded. "I can see deeper into dark reds, too."

"Can you teach me?"

"Of course. It's going to cost you, though." She stepped close, a teasing smile on her face as she tapped him on the nose.

Cinder rubbed his nose, pretending a scowl. "What kind of cost?"

Anya settled her arms around his neck but didn't answer. She merely stared at him, head cocked, and an indecipherable expression on her face. She eventually drew him down so she could kiss him, soft, deep, and fierce before stepping back.

They broke apart. "I like making that kind of payment," Cinder said with a breathless smile.

Anya stared at him, running fingers through his hair. "I love you, Cinder Shade," she eventually said. "I always will. Never forget that."

Cinder stared at her, perplexed by her statement. "I love you, too."

Anya pursed her lips. "I know, but..." She blinked, eyes grown misty, and Cinder finally understood the fear that was in her heart. He tightened his arms, deepening their embrace. They had survived the Webbed Kingdom, but it had been a close-run thing.

And if Anya had died... Cinder didn't want to think about a world without her. He would have fulfilled his mission, but after defeating Shet and Zahhack, what further purpose would he have to his life? It was a terrifying question, one Anya had been considering just now.

"What are you thinking about?" she asked, her voice husky as she stroked his chin. He told her, and she smiled wanly. "Not the most romantic thought to have, is it? Our first time safe and alone in months." She shuddered, laying her head against his shoulder. "Let's never do that again."

While Cinder agreed with Anya, the mood was too saturnine for the moment. He offered a joking question. "You don't think it's sweet?"

She lifted her head, peering at him with a frown. "Are you serious? Of course not. How—"

He grinned, causing her to huff in exasperation. It only made him smile wider.

Anya noticed, and she rolled her eyes. "Don't be so pleased with yourself. We both know that I knew that you knew that I'd be annoyed by your teasing."

"But we also both knew that I knew that you knew—"

Anya held up a hand. "For the love of Devesh, please stop."

Cinder laughed, feeling like he'd won something. "Weren't you go-ing to show me how to transform my eyes?"

"Not after that."

She wasn't really upset with him. They both knew it. There were words to say, though. Cinder drew her close again, making sure to stare into her eyes, which had resumed their normal shape. "I love you, Anya Aruyen. There's no power in any Realm that will keep me apart from you."

Searching, she simply gazed at him. An instant later, she smiled, warm and inviting, pulling him down for another kiss.

He could have stayed in her embrace, wanted to, but like always, there was work to be done. With a discontented sigh, he stepped away.

Anya wore a half-smile of longing. "We never have enough time, do we?"

"Never," Cinder agreed. He wondered when they would. And un-til that blessed era… "Two things," he told her. "First, how did you change your eyes like that? And second, I'll need another week before I'm recovered enough to set off toward Grind."

Anya frowned. "Are you sure you only need one more week?"

In truth, Cinder wasn't sure, but as was generally the case, time didn't wait on his wants. "I'll be fine."

"Fine isn't good enough," Anya said, her frown deepening. "The Ring Road is dangerous. There are bandits about. Remember Orinin? We both need to be at our best before we attempt it."

"We can't afford to wait," Cinder argued, although his heart wasn't in it. He knew she was right.

"And we can't afford for either of us to suffer a preventable injury. If you need more than a week, then you'll have it."

Cinder nodded, although he was determined that a week would be all he needed.

Anya offered a slow smile, one that was of the cat-that-ate-the-ca-nary variety. "At least we won't have to stay stuck in this oasis the whole time. Get stronger, regain your skills, and I might have a present for you."

Cinder inhaled sharply. "You've figured out the anchor line? How to create a Path?"

Anya answered with a frown of concentration, and a simple gesture. Where she pointed, a black line split the air directly in front of her. It rotated, exposing a tall doorway filled with all the swirling colors of a rainbow that eventually settled into a bridge extending into infinity. And at the far end, Cinder could just barely make out the Shriven Grove. "It's not easy. Actually takes a lot out of me, but it works."

A notion occurred to him. "Can we go from here to the Shokans?" Cinder asked, trying to tamp down his excitement.

"We could," Anya said, "but not for long. There's the camels. Who would take care of them?"

Cinder glanced at Fellow, Bellow, Mellow, and Callow. They wouldn't do well in the cold heights of the Dagger Mountains.

"Besides, didn't you see? Our presence wasn't good for your brothers. They were tight when they sparred. Stiff, nervous, like they were performing for you. We were hindering them just by being there."

Cinder considered her observation, and with a disappointed sigh, he realized she was right. Still, there was an opportunity in what she'd demonstrated. He viewed her, his expression earnest. "Can you teach me to Path?"

She quirked a challenging brow, arms folded. "I can, but it's still going to cost you."

Cinder chuckled. "I already told you. I like making that kind of payment."

Cinder stepped out of the tent and stretched to his fullest extent. The sun had just risen, pinking the cloudless sky, and a wind rustled amongst the palm, date, and coconut trees of the oasis, which caused the fronds to clatter like a rattle. The breeze stirred the boulder-strewn pond, and the mineral-fresh scent of water filled the air.

One of the camels groaned while the others shuffled about.

Cinder grinned, walking to the line of animals. "What's wrong, boys? It's such a beautiful day."

The original camel who had groaned shook his head, seemingly in disagreement, or possibly gesturing to the Flatiron Death.

"What a pretty day," Anya said, exiting the tent while buttoning her blouse.

Cinder glanced back, interest piqued when he caught a flash of golden skin and her taut abdomen, and disappointed when it was covered. No matter how much time he spent with Anya, her beauty endlessly fascinated him.

"Turn those eyes elsewhere," Anya chided.

He offered a shameless grin, knowing he shouldn't have been staring, but she was so easy to stare at. "It is a lovely day, isn't it? Almost as lovely as—"

Anya pressed a cautioning finger to his mouth, laughing lightly. "Don't say anything sappy. You and sweet aren't—"

She didn't get to finish her thought as Cinder kissed her, softly at first, but then deeper.

It only ended when Anya pushed him off with a warm chuckle. "What's gotten into you?"

"I feel good," Cinder said. A moment's reflection told him how true his statement was. He did feel good, for the first time since coming to the oasis, less than a week ago now.

"How good?" Anya asked with a challenging quirk of her eyebrow.

Cinder examined himself more thoroughly, inhaling deep, searching. The weakness, soreness, and lingering fatigue from the Webbed Kingdom were gone. He felt fit and strong. Good enough to try himself against Anya. "Do you want to spar?" he asked.

"You sure you're up for it?"

Cinder examined himself again. He'd been pushing harder every day—stretching deeper, running farther, lifting more—and this morning was the first he could recall in some time where he awoke without any issues. Nevertheless, maybe it was best if they eased into the sparring. "Let's take it slow. See how it goes."

"Start with stretching. Work into a long run and some sprints. Spar afterward."

Cinder nodded agreement, and after loosening their muscles, they set off at a slow jog. The oasis was large enough that a single circuit around its perimeter consisted of close to a mile.

It didn't take long—three slow laps—before Cinder was struggling to get enough air. His heart raced and sweat poured off him like someone had upended a bucket of water over his head. But he didn't stop. If he wanted to regain his fitness, he had to embrace the grind.

He joined Anya in wind sprints—five sets of three with a short break in between each one, and by the time they finished, Cinder's legs were jelly-weak. His lungs heaved. His heart pounded too fast for him to accurately count each beat. His vision was hazy, and he collapsed to his hands and knees, unable to remain standing.

Anya silently passed him a canteen of water, and he briefly dipped his head in acknowledgment. "I don't think we should spar right now," she said. "You pushed too hard."

Cinder grunted in agreement, too weak to argue. He *had* pushed too hard. Sparring would have to wait until he'd recovered some. But they would be sparring this morning. Of that, there was no doubt. He said so, sipping the water, even though he wanted to drain the canteen in one gulp. But if he did that, he'd get stomach cramps.

Anya stared at him, concern on her face. "We'll spar, but no *Jivatma* or *lorethasra*. And if I see you struggling, we stop. No arguing."

Cinder didn't reply, his attention focused inward. His breathing was starting to settle, but he couldn't say the same about his heart. It continued to pound rapidly, not having slowed in the slightest.

He rubbed his chest. It didn't hurt, but his heart… he didn't like the way it was beating.

Anya crouched by his side. Worry had replaced her concern. "Let me see." She placed a hand on his chest. He felt a surge as she pressed her Talent for Healing into him; testing, searching, and evaluating. She sat back, relief evident. "Everything looks fine, but I don't want you out in the sun. Can you stand?"

Cinder got his legs under him and rose with a groan, but they barely held. He stumbled, threatening to collapse. His heart continued to hammer against his ribs, thudding like a runaway horse. He couldn't get enough breath. He had never before been this feeble, not since… well, since his time in Flatiron, but this was a different sort of feebleness.

In either case, Cinder didn't like it, hated being the weak link. He grimaced when he almost fell and Anya had to shift to support him. A short shuffling set of steps, and he reached their tent, shifting aside the flap before stumbling inside, falling rather than levering himself to the ground.

"I'll be fine," he said to Anya's ongoing worry. "Just pushed too hard, like you said. We're still sparring."

She shook her head. "No, we aren't. Not until you get your strength back. Show me you can stand without assistance. Run one lap around the oasis without needing to lie down. Then we'll see."

Cinder stared at her a moment before falling onto his back with a groan. Once again, she was right. He had to pace himself if he really wanted to regain his strength. His mind was willing, but right now, his body wasn't. But that would change. He promised it would.

Several hours later, Cinder was finally feeling fit enough to crawl out of the tent. Anya had brought him more water along with breakfast— he'd had two helpings, and he'd also drained two canteens of water. The combination of water, food, and rest had him feeling nearly back to normal, and he wanted to spar.

He told Anya, but she didn't agree. Instead, she had him complete a slow lap around the oasis, and only when he showed no evidence that he'd collapse did she relent. She had their shokes at her feet, but no governors, still insisting that they wouldn't be using *lorethasra* or *Jivatma*.

"We're going to take it easy," she said. "One-quarter speed. Nothing more."

She handed him his shoke, and they started off with forms. As they progressed, Cinder shook his head at how much he had deteriorated: his slashes were too broad, his recovery lax, and his initiation too hesitant and slow.

It was all because of his weakness, but it wouldn't always be the case. He'd just have to work through it. As his strength and stamina improved, so would his abilities. *Embrace the grind.*

After the forms, they sparred. Here, Cinder did better. His skill at reading Anya's movements remained intact, and he was able to execute his counters without any difficulty. Of course, they were only moving at one-quarter speed. Any quicker and Cinder wouldn't have been able to keep up.

An hour later, Anya called a halt.

Cinder was breathing heavily again, and while his heart raced, at least it wasn't anywhere near as bad as this morning.

"What's the verdict?" Anya asked. "And be honest."

"Half a week, and I'll be ready to go."

"Full strength?"

Cinder shook his head. "It'll be a while for that. I've lost a lot of weight."

Half a week later—five days—and Cinder wasn't yet himself. He didn't have any lingering pain, but there was still the lingering fatigue and weakness. They kept him from feeling right with the world and himself. And while he could once again keep up with Anya—even surpass her on rare occasions—his frequently racing heart and lack of stamina held him back. Worse, neither showed any sign of improving.

At least his throat wasn't sore anymore. That nagging discomfort had finally faded away, and his *lorethasra* and *Jivatma* had also recovered for the most part. There was still a ways more to go, but in a few days, he figured he'd likely be fully restored.

He unconsciously rubbed his chest when his heart began ticking faster. Anya hadn't found anything wrong with him, and he wished it would just settle down so he could recuperate. It wasn't just his *Jivatma* and *lorethasra*, but his weight, strength, and stamina—everything. And although the best way to earn it back was hard work, thus far, it wasn't working. His mind was willing, but his body remained unable.

Still, laziness wouldn't see him reach his goals, which was why at the end of the day he was still practicing his forms. It had already been a long day, but with the sun still in the sky, Cinder figured on using every minute of daylight available to him. He and Anya remained at the oasis outside Flatiron, preparing to move on once Cinder was fully himself.

Then they'd journey west to Grind before trekking southwest toward Shima Sithe. That was where Anya would need to work her influence and convince that empire's royal house to send warriors north to the Sunsets.

The herd of wraiths had to be defeated. They posed a risk to every nation of the northwest, and Cinder wouldn't allow such a disaster to go unchallenged. Yes, his Trial to the Sunsets was, first and foremost, about obtaining Mede's Orb, but he'd also do whatever it took to stop the wraiths. He'd even save Genka Devesth; not least because if the man was equal to his legend, he might be exactly who Cinder and Anya needed to help lead the eastern nations against the innumerable zahhacks of the Drakar, Shet's army.

With those considerations in mind, Cinder continued his forms, occasionally feeling Anya's eyes, even as she practiced alongside him.

Minutes later, Cinder's heart began stuttering, and he came to a stop, annoyed with the fragging betrayal of his body. His muscles remained strong and ready. His lungs drew air easily enough. But the racing of his heart couldn't be ignored.

Anya ceased her forms, worry for him evident. "Let me see."

For whatever reason, having her concern irritated him further. A small part of him wanted to lash out at her, but he kept the words inside. She wasn't the cause of his problems. The cause was his frailty.

Cinder despised it, was furious over it.

But what if this was to be his lot in life from now on?

He silently prayed that it wasn't the case, holding still when Anya placed her hands on his chest. Her eyes closed, and he felt her Healing thread coursing through his body and searching like it always did.

A discontented frown appeared on Anya's face. She still couldn't find whatever was wrong with his heart, which was simultaneously a relief as well as disappointing.

"At least my throat doesn't hurt anymore," Cinder said in the midst of her examination.

Anya's eyes flashed open. "Your throat?" There was something in her gaze: hope.

Now it was Cinder who sighted her with a frown. He'd mentioned this before. For most of the past three weeks following their escape from the Webbed Kingdom, his throat had been sore and his voice raspy.

He had no time to state any questions because Anya moved to stand behind him. She palpated fingers into the hollow of his throat, massaging. "Is it sore when I press here?"

Cinder swallowed, noticing a mild but tolerable soreness where her fingers pressed. "A little. Not much."

"Don't move." Again came Anya's questing Healing and palpating hands. "Ah." There was a smile in her voice.

"What is it?"

Cinder went to face her, but she tsked, holding him in place. "Stand still. I think I know what's happening to you."

An instant later, the lightning warmth of her Healing raced into him. His vision blanked, and he stiffened. His mouth gaped in a silent scream. On it went. Lasting only seconds but seemingly for hours.

It ended, and Cinder slumped, staying erect only because Anya held him upright. His heart pounded as fast as it ever had, but within moments, it began to slow, and strength steadily returned to his limbs. He stepped away from Anya, took a deep breath and heaved out a sigh, willed his heart to slow.

And it did, settling down to its normal rate.

Wondering what she'd done, Cinder shot a glance at Anya. He took another deep breath, focused inward, waiting. But his heart retained its slow, steady rhythm—its usual pace. "What did you do?"

"It worked?"

Another deep breath. Still no change. "I think so."

She smiled. "It was something in your throat. Sira's memories call it a thyroid gland. She Healed someone who had a similar problem."

"And this was the cause of my heart racing?"

"And your weight loss, agitation, feeling hot all the time, and your tremor. All of it."

Cinder touched his throat in wonderment. "All this from some small thing in the neck?"

Anya shrugged, still smiling. "Sira always thought of our bodies as a union of miracles from Devesh."

Cinder abruptly laughed, relieved and overjoyed. His body wouldn't fail him. He'd be strong again, just like the world needed. "Thank you, Anya." He infused his words with every bit of gratitude he could manage.

"You're not Healed yet," she corrected. "From what I can tell, it'll take another few days of multiple Healings for that to happen."

He didn't care how many Healings it took. "We always meant to go to Fare after I recovered. Why not go to there now? We can leave Liline's *divaspana* here so she'll never know we're gone. Meanwhile, we'll be in Fare to sell the camels and afterward we can visit the Shokans and get Barton and Painter?"

Anya tilted her head in consideration. "We'd need a Path. I can only manage one every couple of days. It takes everything I have to create one."

"If you don't think it's worth it…"

"I didn't say that. I actually think you're right. You need to recover still, and we need to do something about the camels. We can do both in Fare, and after a few days, we can come back here. A couple more days after that, and we can get Barton and Painter." She peered at him.

"You'll be recovered by then? And don't lie."

Cinder shrugged. "I should be?" He wasn't sure, but taking any longer than that wasn't ideal. Between recovering in Naraka, traveling to see the Shokans, and waiting here at the oasis, they'd already wasted nearly three weeks waiting for him to regain his health. And now another five or six days before finally heading toward Grind?

It seemed like it was too long, but what was the alternative? Cinder couldn't make himself get better more quickly.

"I suppose going to Fare won't be so bad," he said after deliberating a bit longer. "Better than staying here where our only companions are a quartet of flatulent camels." He offered a wan grin. "Not a tough choice, *priya.*"

40

The next evening saw Cinder holding open the door for Anya, waiting for her to enter Café Marakent, supposedly the finest restaurant in all of Fare. They found themselves in a lushly appointed foyer. To the right, a beautiful mosaic depicted an oasis in the middle of the desert, while to the left were leather couches, provided for those waiting to be seated inside. An expensive crystal chandelier provided soft illumination and a luxurious ambiance while a fragrant incense perfumed the air. The floral scent mingled with the spicy aromas wafting from the kitchen.

However, Cinder and Anya didn't have much time to take in the beauty since the host, a slender man with a thin mustache and wearing a floor-length robe, quickly directed them to a table centered within the restaurant. He offered a practiced smile and well wishes for the enjoyment of their meal before returning to his station in the foyer.

Once seated, Cinder looked about, noticing immediately that the restaurant resembled an interior courtyard. Twenty-foot walls enclosed an open-air space with olive trees planted directly into the ground, the soil topped by fine white gravel. A large bowl of water—two yards wide and one tall—was centered in the room and decorated with floating rose petals and water lilies. Pink sandstone walls reached down to a floor consisting of a perimeter of bright blue tiles that edged white marble veined in green. Quartets of columns, slender and ornately carved, were strategically placed around the room, but rather than merely providing architectural support, the columns also gave the restaurant a certain opulence. That same atmosphere was further enhanced by softly glowing *diptha* lamps set in elaborate wall sconces and the trio of musicians situated next to the dance floor.

Seeing them had Cinder swallow back a sudden longing. He missed playing music with Jozep and Riyne. He missed his brothers.

"You're thinking about the Shokans," Anya said, knowing his thoughts in that way they shared.

Cinder merely nodded. "I never get to spend enough time with them."

"Someday, you will." She took his hands, kissing his fingers. "Someday, we'll be free."

It was a wonderful dream for the future, and not for the first time, Cinder longed for it to come true. But rather than brood over the matter, he recognized that he would do better to live in the present. Lamenting the absence of his brother warriors wouldn't make them suddenly appear. Besides which, why should he grieve, especially in this particular moment? Here he was, about to share a wonderful meal in a fine restaurant with the woman he loved. In the face of that, shouldn't he focus on what was, rather than wish for what wasn't?

"Maybe so," Cinder said, kissing Anya's fingers in return. "But right now, this day is enough."

Anya offered a slow smile of pleasure, which was all Cinder could have hoped to see. "Thank you for bringing me here."

"Thank Comp Salingit," Cinder said with a chuckle, deferring Anya's approval.

Their decision to come here had been on account of the merchant to whom they had sold Fellow, Bellow, Mellow, and Callow. Comp apparently had a soft spot for camels—something to do with one of them saving his life during his youth.

After asking around the souks—the city's maze of marketplaces—for a likely buyer, Cinder and Anya had learned about him, and upon that meeting, both had felt sure Comp would do a better job caring for the camels than Dromin Tarn, the man from whom they'd originally bought the animals.

In addition, Comp seemed to have good taste when it came to fine dining, and glancing about the restaurant, Cinder momentarily wondered how they could afford a place this expensive. Then again, there was the money Liline had gifted them. With it and whatever coin Anya had, they could easily pay for a meal here.

Their waiter arrived, quick and efficient, he reviewed what was on the menu along with the available beverages, took their orders, and departed with a promise to return shortly. Minutes later, he was back, a goblet of red wine for both of them.

Cinder took a tentative taste, not really having a palate for the drink. But with that first sip, he found himself appreciating the beverage's full-bodied flavor along with its hint of cinnamon and plum undertones. There was a complexity there that he hadn't anticipated, and he took another sip, capturing a buttery note underneath the acidic tannin.

His perception of the wine's qualities caused him to smile inwardly. Since when did he know about wines? It probably had something to do with Shokan and the Blessed One's knowledge.

"This is nice," Anya said, also taking a sip. She made to unwrap her green shawl meant to conceal her ears, but upon looking about, she left it in place.

Cinder understood the reason for her reticence: better to leave her ears covered than to draw any unnecessary attention.

"To us," Cinder said, raising his glass.

Anya clinked her goblet against his. "To us."

They sipped their wines, and shortly after, their food arrived. They ate in companionable silence even as more people entered the restaurant. But when the music became more boisterous, and Cinder noted several couples occupying the dance floor, he viewed Anya with an unspoken question.

She grinned in a hint of challenge. "I thought you'd never ask." She rose to her feet, taking his hand and sauntering as she guided him toward the dance floor.

Cinder smiled to himself. In his mind, Anya was always lovely, but it was especially the case tonight. She wore a sunshine-yellow dress that she'd purchased earlier in the day at one of the souks. It clung to her form, reaching to her knees and trailing her every motion, her swaying hips.

She caught his gaze, and there came a knowing grin. Her eyes flicked him up and down. "You look nice, too."

After buying the dress, Anya had insisted that Cinder also buy appropriate clothes for a fine restaurant. Rather than the *nomasra* garb gifted by Manifold, he wore soft cotton pants, snugly fitted but still allowing free movement. The locals called them chinos, and they were a shade of terracotta. As for his shirt, it was also made of cotton, cream-colored with black piping, and buttons of a similar hue to his pants.

With a single twirl, Anya entered the dance floor, settling next to him. Her cinnamon aroma drifted, richer than usual, and Cinder filled his lungs with her fragrance, letting his worries slip away. He wasn't a practiced dancer, but he still had his martial instincts. They'd guided him before when he'd danced with Anya back at the Winter Gala. He smiled to himself. Had it really been only a few years ago? So much had happened since then.

He set aside his remembrances, willing himself to only consider the music and his partner, to lean on his martial instincts. That and Shokan's memories. The Blessed One had loved dancing with Sira.

The song started, and Cinder fell into the rhythmic flow of the music's tempo, let himself fall into the seductive melody that called for close dancing. He held Anya's hand, resting another to support her shoulder. She stared into his eyes, wearing a faint smile of challenge.

Cinder smiled back, accepting her test. He inclined Anya into a quick dip before she slowly straightened. She lifted her left leg, slid it along his side, stretched it fully to touch her ankle to his shoulder. Lowered it to wrap around his waist and spun into a graceful twirl.

Cinder followed her motion, letting her lead. This time it was her right leg that slid along his side. Another twirl led to a layout. Anya rose, deftly swaying away from him, one hand in his and another on his bicep, guiding him forward.

He stared into her eyes, never breaking contact, mesmerized. It felt like he was simultaneously rising and falling. Excitement thrilled through him, but he didn't let it control his movements. Rather, he moved in time to Anya's needs, making sure his attention was always on her.

A complex series of twists and stepovers ended with Cinder bending low at the knees, gliding forward, his thighs pressed close to hers.

Anya matched his motions, all elegance as she paced backward, one hand on his chest. This time, he spun under her arm, moved so he faced her again. They shifted across the dance floor, feet striking the ground in time to the music's staccato rhythm.

Cinder sensed what Anya wanted to do, and he slammed to a halt. She lifted her leg in a slow rise and fall. Another glide of her foot along his side led to a twirl and a layout. When she rose, Cinder spun her so her back was pressed to his chest, one arm around her waist, holding her momentarily still.

Not once in his life had he trained to dance like this. But it didn't matter. It was as if his instincts for battle had merged with Shokan's gentler ones of dancing. It left his body knowing the proper motions better than his mind ever would—as if he and Anya had danced this dance a hundred times.

They stood still for a few seconds, both of them breathing easy but deep. Anya's chest rose and fell, and Cinder waited on her, his arm still around her waist.

She broke the tableau, slowly, gently swaying her hips against his thigh, back and forth, back and forth. Then they were off again. More spins and tapping of their feet. Anya pulled away. But Cinder strode with her. She spun around him as he continued to hold her hand, their bodies close.

Cinder distantly noted that the other dancers had stepped away, giving him and Anya space to roam. The floor was theirs. And while Cinder remained aware of everyone else, for him, there was only Anya. And he gazed into her eyes, at her maddening ineffable smile. What did she know?

They continued around the floor, and Cinder noticed that somewhere along the way, Anya had lost her green shawl. The glory of her unbound blonde hair moved with her every motion, swaying and twirling, and still hiding her ears.

The music readied to stop, and Cinder ended their dance by guiding Anya to a final, slow layover. Her hand dragged the ground. The other around his neck as he braced her.

Her breathing came fast, and a slight sheen glistened on her brow. Her golden hair touched the flooring, and her earlier enigmatic smile had been replaced by a delighted grin.

Cinder lifted her upright, trying to collect his breath, willing his heart to slow. Dancing wasn't sparring, but it was enough to get his heart racing. His breathing came heavy, and a glisten of perspiration had formed on his forehead.

"Do you still want to dance?" Anya asked with a breathless chuckle, stroking his cheek.

Cinder needed another few moments to collect himself, and while he did so, he bent down to regather her shawl, which she wrapped around her hair. "I wish I could, but…" He sighed, expressing his regret. "It's probably better if I didn't."

Only then did he catch sight of the other patrons applauding, and the musicians beaming with pleasure. And no one seemed to have noticed Anya's elven ears, but if they had, it might have made their evening remarkably different and sad.

But Cinder set aside that vague sorrow. It wasn't worth considering, not tonight.

Cinder viewed Anya in amusement as she adjusted the green shawl about her head, tucking in a few strands of hair. She still didn't want to draw unnecessary attention to either of them, to which Cinder agreed, but still...

Anya looked good in the shawl. In truth, she looked good in anything, and Cinder looked forward to the day when they didn't have to worry about what others might think about their relationship. When they could just live and love one another as they chose.

She glanced his way, offering a wistful smile. "I wish that, too," she said, picking up on his unspoken thoughts.

He responded by drawing her into a brief hug, kissing her forehead. He kept an arm around her waist as they strolled through an area of large warehouses where drovers shouted orders while unloading their wagons. Dust floated like a cloud, camels groaned, and the streets were packed with the noise of people heading to whatever tasks they'd been assigned. Fare never slowed. Even now, in the hottest part of the day and with the sun gliding to early afternoon, the city was forever awake and bustling, especially in areas such as this.

Thankfully, just a short distance away stood the opening to one of Fare's two souks—the maze of alleys and streets—and a reprieve from the sweltering heat and noise. It wasn't necessarily their destination—Cinder was certain Anya would want to do some browsing—but it should lead them to their intended goal: a park along an aqueduct-filled lake in the center of the city; a place for couples and lovers to stroll at the end of the day.

They reached the souk, and it felt like entering a different world. Gone was the dust and din, replaced by a different kind of energy with hordes of people milling about, looking for items to purchase. Strings of *diptha* lights crisscrossed the alleys like a running stitch, giving the souk the air of a festival. Merchants called out for attention, hawking their wares.

And everywhere Cinder looked there was something new to explore. Unfinished textiles as well as well-crafted clothing: leather cloaks, coats, and armor, silk saris with gold etching, and elaborate dresses with piping all intermixed with small mirrors. Ceramic pots of nearly all shapes and sizes mounded next to plush and meticulously crafted carpets and rugs and exquisitely shaped lanterns. Piles of spices, such as dried coriander, crushed cumin, turmeric, ground red pepper, dahls of every sort, and various masalas were on display. Close at hand, a trio of musicians busked, and their music and song melded seamlessly with the market's overall exuberance.

Cinder breathed in the music and the heady scents, smiling when another inhalation brought him Anya's warm, familiar cinnamon aroma.

Unfortunately, as expected, she made a beeline for one of the stalls selling clothing. She claimed she didn't like impractical garb, but the dress she had bought yesterday said otherwise. Until last night, Cinder couldn't recall seeing Anya so relaxed when wearing something other than the *nomasra* garb gifted to her by Manifold.

As she began perusing some delicate clothing, Cinder watched for a moment, boredom quickly taking hold. Standing around doing nothing was so tedious, and he sighed in disappointment. For Cinder, shopping had a single purpose: find what he needed and leave.

"What do you think?" Anya asked. She held a slip of clothing—a white camisole—up to her chest. It hung no lower than her waist.

Cinder could visualize her wearing it all too well. The camisole would leave little to the imagination, and if she wasn't wearing anything else…

With a shudder of effort, he cut off his thoughts, not wanting to say what was truly on his mind. She'd laugh at him, smirk in that knowing way, and—

He held in a groan. She *had* figured out what he had been thinking. A tinkle of laughter was followed by exactly that knowing smirk.

Cinder closed his eyes, doing his best to suppress his irritation at her enjoyment. "I'm going to listen to the music," he declared.

In truth, he really didn't care about the song being played, but as he reckoned the situation, it was a far better option than standing around like an idiot while Anya perused lingerie.

"I'll be right here," Anya replied, amusement still in her voice.

Cinder wandered away but remained close enough for Anya to find him if she needed. He frowned in thought. Maybe if he shot her impatient looks now and then, she'd speed up her shopping.

He shook his head. The shopping would still feel endless. With a final unhappy sigh, he joined a pair of disconsolate-appearing men, who stood next to the buskers; a man playing the tabla; a woman with a shehnai—a lovely type of reed instrument with a nasal quality—and another woman on the guitar, singing a song about rowdy friends and a rough-and-tumble game.

Cinder hummed along to the tune, until one of the disconsolate-looking men got his attention. The man, likely in his mid-to-late twenties, was of medium height and build. He had a thick mustache that drooped to a patchy beard and wore a slightly stained white robe that draped over a slightly protuberant belly. "Is your woman shopping?" the man asked.

Cinder nodded, gesturing vaguely toward Anya. "She's over there looking at clothes."

"They're always looking at clothes," another man grumbled. "My father warned me about this. He told me, *'Marcan, whatever you do, marry a woman who can cook and hates to shop.'*" He sighed. "So what did I do? I married a woman whose cooking is poison and who loves to shop."

"Losia's cooking isn't so bad," the first man disagreed. "I've used her food to kill plenty of rats."

The two men laughed good-naturedly, clearly familiar with one another, and Cinder felt himself warming up to them. He might have said something about Anya's cooking, which was admittedly terrible, but he couldn't see himself insulting her behind her back.

"At least Losia's cooking keeps me slim," Marcan said, patting his trim belly. "I can still chase after her like when we were courting."

"Calowim's cooking does not keep me thin," the first man said with a dry chuckle. "I swear that woman wants me as fat as the king of Rakesh."

There was no king in Rakesh, but Cinder didn't bother correcting the man. What would be the point? Instead, he listened to the gentle ribbing amongst friends, and like last night, he found himself missing the Shokans, especially when some of the comments devolved into insults about parentage, sisters, and the unattractive qualities of some of the women with whom the men had been previously involved.

"What about your wife?" the first man asked Cinder. "How is her cooking?"

Cinder smiled. "Road rations taste better."

This earned a hoot of laughter.

"And next you'll tell us that your wife is ugly and covered in warts," Marcan said with a chuckle.

"See for yourself." Cinder pointed to Anya, who stood out like a vibrant sunflower, beautiful and unlike any other woman in the souk.

A heavy silence fell across the two men and a few others standing close by, broken when Marcan spoke in a strained voice. "You must be some kind of warrior"—he pointed to Cinder's sword—" to have earned the love of a woman like that."

Cinder grinned. "I don't think it was my skill with the sword that impressed her. I think it's because I make her laugh."

The first man grumbled. "Then you must be the funniest damn person in all of Seminal."

"What were you and those men talking about?" Anya asked several hours later. She'd shopped and strolled throughout the souk, which in hindsight wasn't a bad idea. If nothing else, it kept them out of the midday sun. Dusk approached, a time when Fare was far more comfortable.

"About music and women who like to shop." Cinder replied.

"Is that all?"

There was a note of suppressed humor in her voice, and Cinder eyed her askance, wondering what had her so amused. It came to him a moment later. She'd noticed when he'd pointed her out to Marcan and his friend as well as their reactions. He grinned her way. "They did seem surprised, didn't they?"

"And you seemed like a proud father."

"Is that what I looked like?" Cinder shuddered. "I hope not. The last thing I'd want is to look at you like I was your father."

Anya elbowed him gently in the stomach. "You know what I mean."

Cinder laughed, kissing her on the cheek. "Yes, I do."

She smiled, tucking herself against him, and they walked in silence past a final few stalls, full of clothing, glass jewelry, and furniture. This part of the souk was quieter than the area near the warehouse district, but there were still many people milling about the market's narrow alleys and streets.

Within moments, they reached the end of the souk and exited onto a busy boulevard. Drovers guided wagons pulled by bullocks. Warriors and guards trailed fine carriages, and pedestrians went about their tasks, calling out to friends and acquaintances.

Cinder and Anya darted across the street, and on the other side, through a narrow alley between a set of tall, narrow buildings, they discovered another world: Shunting Park. Anya inhaled sharply in appreciation, and they paused, taking in the scene.

A park spread out upon rolling hills with copses of oak and maple gathering cool shadows. Benches were set beneath them, and men and women, dressed in the tan robes that were so prevalent in Fare, played a game using small, rectangular, white tiles with various black dots. Dominoes was its name, and although Cinder had tried to learn the rules, he preferred chess and euchre.

In the center of the park was a large pond, blue and glistening and fed by a set of streams into which emptied the aqueduct that brought water to the city. A number of stone bridges arched across the various brooks and rivulets.

The setting sparked a stray memory, caused it to flicker across Cinder's mind. A remembrance of taking a similar walk with Anya. But when? He couldn't recall ever strolling in a park with her.

A wind blew then, distracting him, and with the sun lowering past the horizon to twilight, it was actually mild, not the scirocco to which Cinder had grown accustomed here in Fare. The breeze brought with it the scent of lilac and hyacinth, and his eyes went to the colorful bushes growing in profusion in different parts of the park. The flowers seemed to reflect the bright hues of the sky that were lit with sunset oranges and reds.

"It's beautiful," Anya whispered.

Cinder nodded agreement, throat tight with the emotion triggered by his vagrant memory. He took her hand. "Let's walk."

"As you wish."

They strolled along a brick path that followed a brook. It would be dark soon, and the folks playing dominoes were soon gathering their games and heading home. In preparation for night, *diptha* lamps on black posts were brought to light by men hustling along the various walkways.

In silence, Cinder and Anya ambled hand in hand, alone along the brick path, passing over small bridges, circling the central pond. Birds and bats soared across the darkening sky. Frogs croaked, crickets chirped, and fireflies briefly brightened the night. The gentle breeze continued to blow, somewhat chill now, which wasn't a surprise. In the areas near Flatiron, the nights were often cold.

Cinder halted when Anya tugged on his hand. They stood at the crest of a bridge overlooking a brook, and along the edges of the water, cattails swayed and lily pads floated. A owl hooted, and something plumped into the stream. The park spread out all around them.

Anya removed her shawl, facing him and taking both his hands in her own. She wore a serious expression. "This is what we fight for: so places like this can flourish and people can live in peace. So they can appreciate their arts, museums, restaurants, and plays. I want their lives to be more than a struggle for survival. For us, too."

Her words reflected everything that was in Cinder's heart, and he took a steadying breath, surprised by the depth of his emotions. He'd felt the same way ever since coming to Fare. Everyone should have that peace and that opportunity.

"A serious endeavor," he said.

"But it's also the best kind."

Cinder nodded, although there was a part of him that wondered if that same safety and happiness would ever be afforded to him and Anya. Over the past few days, they'd been gifted a small view of what their life together might be like without having to always worry about wars and dark gods. In truth, coming to Fare had been a window into what they wanted for their lives together as well as an emotional reprieve that they both needed, although neither had known of it prior.

But like all reprieves, this one was destined to end, and Cinder regretted its passing well before its conclusion.

He had recovered well enough for them to go back to the oasis and from there, head toward Grind. There was no reason to wait. He had most of his strength back, and while his stamina was still lacking, he figured he had plenty for any bandits they might encounter on the Ring Road. They even had mounts to carry them, purchasing a useful pair of sturdy horses that would suffice until they could collect Barton and Painter.

Anya ended his wandering contemplations by touching his face, stroking it gently, her eyes reflecting her awareness of his thoughts. "This will be our life one day. I promise. We deserve it." She kissed him on the lips.

Cinder smiled, brought out of his melancholy by her vow. He believed her. She'd make it happen. He was also amused by the sense that all of this had happened before. It was like his subconscious self was warning him never to take Anya for granted. It was a lesson he didn't need.

"What's so funny?" Anya asked, appearing perplexed and maybe affronted. He explained, and she lifted her brows in surprise. "That's what you're thinking about?"

Still amused, Cinder drew Anya closer. "You don't think what I just said was romantic?"

Her eyes gleamed. "Maybe if you kiss me right, I'll know for sure."

41

The next morning, Cinder and Anya returned to the oasis near Flatiron and immediately departed the place. They headed west on the Ring Road before turning south at the town of Grind, shifting toward Shima Sithe. They'd eventually bring Sriovey and Jozep with them, but now wasn't the time. This part of the world was dangerous, filled with bandits, and although Cinder and Anya didn't fear for themselves, they couldn't say the same about the dwarves.

Sriovey and Jozep were no longer warriors. They couldn't defend themselves like they had once been able. Theirs was no longer the warrior's path.

A week south of Grind, they stopped for the evening, and Anya stretched out her back with a grateful groan. She had just finished unpacking the mules they'd purchased in Fare, and once she straightened, she more fully examined their setting.

The oasis in which they'd made camp was a half-acre of green life in the otherwise red and brown desert. Small pockets of grass grew in clots amongst a score of frail-appearing coconut and palm trees. A tiny pond, small enough for Anya to leap across without any assistance from *Jivatma*, stirred under a steady wind that might have carried the scents of Shima Sithe's forest.

The latter could also have been Anya's imagination. They were so close. Only a day longer and she and Cinder would reach the edge of the desert and head into Shima Sithe proper.

Anya couldn't wait. The desert had its own beauty—there was no denying that fact—but it wasn't one that she appreciated. Anya longed to be shrouded beneath the protective, heavy boughs and shading limbs of broad trees. The wooded slopes of deep mountains with their greens, blues, whites, and grays—not the angry reds and browns of the desert and its endless sky and scorching heat—were where she yearned to be.

In that moment, when Anya breathed deep, she imagined herself inhaling the heavenly aromas of moss mixed with that of the dark, living soil of a healthy forest.

She sighed away her desires, her attention going to Cinder as he went through his forms, alert and mildly concerned. He appeared nearly back to his normal self, but that alone didn't rest Anya's heart. Cinder lied all the time about his well-being. He downplayed his injuries, pushing through them, giving and giving so others could live, no matter how it might injure him.

It was part of why she loved him—his generosity and courage—and also why she feared on his behalf. And that fear wouldn't go away just because she had figured out what was wrong with him—his thyroid, of all things. Nor would it go away because Cinder seemed to have mostly recovered. Once again, he exceeded her abilities, and although there was no longer a strain to his movements, skills, and Talents, he didn't yet have that effortless grace that he'd possessed prior to the Webbed Kingdom.

He struggled every now and then, and because of that, Anya's fear for him remained. She wanted Cinder healthy and hale, not for what he could do for the world, but simply because she loved him. More than anything else, she hated seeing Cinder hurt and hurting, such as in those weeks when he'd been injured following their time in Flatiron and his worse injuries after the Webbed Kingdom.

Both occasions had been hard on him, both physically and emotionally, and watching his hardships had been awful for Anya, knowing that she couldn't take away his pain or help him in any way.

Thankfully, the last wasn't true. Sira's memories had told her what to do, and she'd managed to Heal Cinder—this time. But what about the next? And there would be a next time. Would she be capable then as well? She worried it wouldn't always be the case.

"Do you want to spar?" Cinder asked, interrupting her reverie. He had finished his forms, and he breathed easily with only a slight sheen on his forehead.

"Maybe in a bit. Let me get our tents organized."

"Do you want some help?"

He made to join her, but she shook him off. "I can do it. Go ahead and repeat your forms."

He flashed her an easy smile, one that always made her glad. "Let me know if you change your mind." With that, he went back to practicing.

While Anya got their packs sorted and their tents raised, she observed Cinder out of the corners of her eyes. At the same time, she deliberated on what was to come.

In the next few days, when they exited the last of these badlands and entered Shima Sithe proper, they would need to collect Sriovey and Jozep. Hopefully, the presence of the two dwarves could calm the waters so she could convince Empress Aqueem Shima to send warriors to the Sunsets.

Of course, it would be so much easier if the empress simply believed Anya's statement of being Sira reborn, but that was unlikely. The elves of Shima had a prickly relationship with the older sithes. Empress Aqueem's line had been started by Shawl Brooks, a duchess of Sonail Sithe, and the noblewoman had been assigned to take regency of what was then a quiet, out-of-the-way land of rough hills and rugged slopes. But rather than simply biding her time there, Shawl had fallen in love with her new home. She had gone on to found a sleepy capital and declared her freedom from Sonail's imperial line.

The news hadn't gone over well, and war might have broken out if not for the intervention of Yaksha and several other sithes. Instead of war, a treaty had been reached. Or rather, one had been imposed on Shima Sithe. It didn't sound like much: every generation, a single warrior was to be assigned to Sonail's army. However, that warrior had to be a son of the Shima empress. To this day, the treaty held force, and the elves of Shima Sithe hated it.

Nevertheless, Empress Aqueem would meet with Anya because of her station as a princess of Yaksha Sithe, but that title wouldn't earn her as much influence as she needed. In order to convince the Shima elves to support Genka—and their own best interests—she would have to lean on her status as a princess of Yaksha Sithe, the presence of Jozep and Sriovey, and the claim that she was Sira, a possibility she found more and more likely with each passing day. It might just be enough to get the job done.

Anya had to hope so because she didn't know of any other way to bring Shima Sithe into the brewing war in the Sunsets. And all of these machinations were necessary so she and Cinder could obtain Mede's Orb. In the end, that was what was of greatest concern.

She scowled. The calculations of war were an ugly math. A single Orb versus the cost of countless lives in the Sunsets. She sighed at the notion. Gaining this particular Orb would require nothing less than her best efforts at diplomacy, which for her was a challenge. Until this Trial, she hadn't given much thought at what was needed to bring together those who weren't already friends.

Anya was a warrior, and for most of her life, enhancing her skills in battle had been her sole focus, which was a shame. Wielding a sword was wonderful, but she realized now that she should have spent just as much effort in learning the finer points of statecraft. It was a skill Sira had certainly possessed, and Anya was determined to master it as well: the art of bringing together those who weren't allies.

Even now, she regularly searched through the Blessed One's memories in order to shore up her weaknesses, determined to reach Sirasent, Shima's capital, and achieve her part in what was needed.

True, it would stretch her abilities, but Anya welcomed the challenge, and on further reflection, gathering every Orb so far had already pushed her and Cinder past their limits. In gaining the Orb of Eretria, it had been the skill of simple thievery. For the Orb of Flames, enduring unimaginable hardship. In Revelant, the mastery of old skills and Talents. Bharat had required overwhelming power against some of the deadliest warriors in all of Seminal. In the Webbed Kingdom, they had journeyed through a terrifying dungeon-like environment and defeated an uncountable number of enemies. And for Mede's Orb, it would be diplomacy.

But what about for the final Orb—the Orb of Wings? What would be needed there?

"How about that spar?" Cinder asked, once again interrupting her thoughts.

Anya set the last anchor for her tent and rose to face him. "Give me a moment." She put on her padded leathers, unwrapped her shoke, and stepped to where Cinder had marked out a sparring circle in the desert's dirt. He set himself, and Anya did the same.

"Full abilities?" Cinder asked.

Anya knew what he meant—conducting *Jivatma* and sourcing *lorethasra*—and she nodded. The world brightened, all of her senses enhanced, the dimness of twilight shone bright as midday.

Her observations ended when Cinder sent a questing thrust. Anya parried, content to defend. A slash met air as she shifted aside.

"You can go faster than that," she told him.

Cinder's answer was a combination of a rising diagonal slash, a blow aimed at her legs, and an elbow that would have caught her ribs. She blocked the first two and slipped the last.

He came at her faster, and she kept pace with him, still content to merely defend. Faster still, and finally Anya was finding herself pushed. Sparring against Cinder always took her full concentration.

Yet again, Cinder increased his speed.

Anya kept pace.

He tried to get outside her lead leg, but she wouldn't let him. Cinder lunged, a feint. Anya took a single step back… only to discover that his lunge wasn't a feint. He accelerated at the last instant, and his shoke took her in the chest.

Pain exploded. Stabbing agony wrenched through her chest, and for a few seconds, it was impossible to get a proper breath. Anya hunched over, waiting for the agony to end. The pain wasn't important, but learning from it was.

Anya straightened with a frown of concentration. "Go again?"

Cinder called her forward.

Several days later found Cinder and Anya trudging along a series of knolls that had originally begun as a line of humped rises marching out of Flatiron. However, once past the borders of that deadly place, the rises had become rugged, bare mounds, and in Shima Sithe, they'd transitioned again. Life started to make its presence felt with pockets of faded grass and sagebrush gathering along the rocky slopes.

Cinder glanced around. Several stunted trees—ragged pines and cypress with a modest covering of needles—clung to the hillsides, but in the distance, he sighted the same mounds transitioning to rolling hills, forested in places. The air sat still and heavy, and the sun hung high in the sky, beaming warmth that wasn't much milder than the desert's scorching heat. And although it was only early afternoon in these hills, at the place where they needed to go, it was already evening.

"What about here?" he asked Anya while wiping the sweat from his brow.

"It'll do," she said, briefly gazing about before quirking a single eyebrow. "Think you can manage it?"

Cinder smiled. "The better question is how you will react when I *do* manage it? Maybe make a bet? The loser has to take second watch?"

Anya flashed a grin. "Show me."

Cinder's eyes went unfocused as he centered his mind. Forming a Path—the name of the Talent Anya had learned from an unsuspecting

Liline—required *Jivatma* and *lorethasra* sent through *Manipura* and *Anahata*, and all of it in a stepwise fashion. First, he opened the necessary Chakras. Next, he sourced *lorethasra* and sent it through *Manipura* and *Anahata* where it exited into his *nadis* as *prana*. Finally, once he had the correct framework of a braid in mind, he infused the structure with his will and *Jivatma*.

No concern over failing marred his concentration. In his mind, he'd already succeeded, and there was no room for worry about any kind of lack of success.

An instant later... *There.* The Path flashed into being, a single black line splitting the world, rotating to form a doorway full of chaotic colors. Cinder remained tied to his nascent braid, feeling through what was needed. The sensations. The connection to his brothers and what he recalled of the field where they'd been camped. Moving faster than the speed of thought, the colors brightened, organizing into a rainbow bridge.

And on the distant end, Cinder could see Bones and the rest of the Shokans briefly staring at the anchor line before moving to take positions behind cover, swords unsheathed and bows ready. *Good.* Better that they assumed an enemy was coming at them through a Path rather than expect a friend. Of course, once they could more easily see past the rainbow bridge, they should be able to tell for sure who approached.

Cinder pondered the anchor line he'd created. Once he regularly practiced this Talent, he imagined the necessary steps would require the same level of concentration as when he went through his sword forms. But it wouldn't come easy. He'd have to work at it until the comprehension was as straightforward as a thrust leading to a parry, and he was determined to make it so.

In the meantime, he could form a Path, and although this was only his third attempt at creating one, he felt certain that inside of a day, he could form another one. Anya, on the other hand, required days of recovery before she was able to create a second Path.

The knowledge was a sad reinforcement of what Cinder had come to accept: as an elf, Anya would always be weaker than him. It was a restriction the ancient *asrasins* had placed on the Blessed Ones when they had first set out to create the woven from the disparate creatures Shet had forged as his first zahhacks: the Baels, Ur-Fels, Tigons, Bovars, and Balants.

The *asrasins* of the time hadn't wanted the creations of the Blessed Ones to ever challenge them, which meant all the numerous kinds of woven would be forever restricted in what they could accomplish compared to a human. It had been shortsighted on the part of the *asrasins*, but nonetheless, Shokan and Sira had been forced to work within those strictures.

And seeing Anya steadily fall behind him only proved that those strictures were still in effect, even for someone who held all the memories, skills, and Talents of the Lady of Fire.

"Do you want me to come?" Anya asked.

Cinder shook his head. "It shouldn't take long. I'll just stop over, share the information we've learned, and get Sriovey, Jozep, and our mounts. I'll be right back."

"Don't forget to learn how the Shokans are progressing," Anya reminded him. "We might need them against the wraiths."

"Yes, dear," Cinder said, mentally rolling his eyes at her obvious advice.

Anya narrowed her gaze into an annoyed frown, arms folded. "Don't pretend you're not mentally rolling your eyes at me. I'm not the only one who offers useless advice. You do it all the time."

Cinder flushed, knowing what she meant. It had been while they'd been setting up camp. He'd told her not to put the tents too close to a dead pine tree because it looked like it could fall over at any moment. It was advice given to a woman who had served as a ranger in Yaksha Sithe's Imperial Army for many decades. If anything, she should be advising him on those sorts of matters.

"Can we pretend that my anchor line will come apart if I don't leave right now?" Cinder asked.

"You mean before you put your foot in your mouth again?" Anya asked, still frowning and her arms still folded. "Just don't roll your eyes at me like I'm stupid."

Cinder considered her request. "Can I roll my eyes at you like you're smart?"

Anya huffed. "Cinder Shade. Why do you vex me so?"

"It's a gift?" he suggested, hoping to see her smile.

"It's something," she said, arms uncrossing and her frown fading. However, she still wore an air of annoyance.

Cinder wiped away his smile. "I don't think you're stupid. I never have."

"I know that. I'm just saying don't roll your eyes at me like I am. And also, you better get going. The Shokans are waiting."

Cinder glanced at the Path, looked back at her. "I really am sorry, *priya*." He kissed her quickly before tethering to the anchor line. "See you in a few minutes."

42

"**D**evesh, it's hot out here," Sriovey complained.

"Yes, but it's a dry heat," Jozep said with a smile.

"Oh, fuc—I mean." Sriovey's jaw worked, but no sound came out as he tried to collect himself. In the end, he simply grunted, sounding disgusted. "Never mind."

Cinder grinned at the interplay. He and Anya had fetched the two dwarves a couple days back, and neither of them liked the baking heat in this area of Shima Sithe, which was down in the lowlands. Jozep kept his discomfort to himself, but Sriovey couldn't help but complain about the ongoing heat. What made it even worse was his inability to properly say what was on his mind. Sriovey wanted to curse but also felt like he shouldn't.

He had journeyed far in becoming a true dwarf—Jozep's name for what his people had once been—but his journey was far from over. Sometimes he was as serene as he was supposed to be, but on other occasions, he remained the irascible, hard-charging, foul-mouthed dwarf Cinder recalled from their first meeting.

Anya moved to help Cinder unburden the pack mules. Late in

the day, with the sun only a few fingers from setting, they'd reached a meadow in the center of a small valley. It was spring in this part of Seminal, but a warm spell shivered the world with heat shimmers. A desultory breeze stirred the air, softly trembling the surrounding scrub trees and brush and causing their limbs and branches to shake like rattles.

They got their gear unpacked and led the mules to a small brook burbling close at hand. Guiding Painter, Cinder rubbed her forehead and smiled fondly. "Who's a pretty girl?"

Painter whickered, nudging his shoulder.

Cinder's smile widened. "I missed you, too."

"He's coming along," Anya noted, indicating Sriovey. "But he might be better off just letting himself curse."

Considering his situation before responding, Cinder glanced at Sriovey. Anya was right: Sriovey might be better off cursing as much as he wanted, but it wasn't that simple. Holding in his curses or letting them out. There was more to what he was attempting. Something fundamental in terms of what he hoped to be as a person. And while there were many who didn't think that a person could really change after a certain point, Cinder had to believe that wasn't true. Otherwise, how would the dwarves ever return to their true state?

Besides which, Jozep had accomplished it, and so had a number of other dwarves in Surent Crèche. So why not Sriovey and others like him?

"You're probably right," Cinder allowed. "But I also think that after a certain point, he won't have to fight himself so much. He won't need to curse."

"Who won't need to curse?" Sriovey asked, arriving then.

"You," Cinder said.

Sriovey scowled. "Jozep and Derius think I should give in and curse all I want. You don't think so?"

Cinder shook his head. "I didn't say that. I think what you're trying to accomplish means you need to focus on the things that are important. Holding in your curses isn't one of them. And I also think there will come a time when you won't need to curse or even worry about it."

"That's what I keep telling him," Jozep said, also having come to them while they watered the animals. "He needs to let himself be, and—"

"That's easy for you to say," Sriovey snapped. "You've got it all figured out, trained by Manifold Fulsom in Mahadev." A second later, his features fell into a crestfallen expression. "I'm sorry. I shouldn't have said that."

Cinder's heart broke for his friend, at his obvious despondency. But what could he say? And was it even his place? Shouldn't this be something Jozep handled?

A long moment's deliberation followed, and Cinder realized he was wrong. It wasn't Jozep's place. It was his, like what he said would be heard more readily than whatever Jozep might tell him.

"I think the animals have had enough water," Cinder said to Anya and Jozep. "Maybe get them settled?"

Anya stared at him a moment, knowledge of what he was really asking clear on her face. She nodded agreement, squeezing his arm in support as she and Jozep led the horses and pack animals back to where they'd set up camp.

Sriovey kicked a stone into the water, scowling. "If you're going to tell me what to do—to go ahead and curse or that it'll get better—save your breath."

Cinder drew his brother into a sideways hug. "I won't tell you what to do. I just wanted you to know that I'm here for you. That's all."

They stood in silence as the water babbled and the sun crept below the horizon. Wide swatches of red, orange, and plum spread across the cloudless sky like spilled paint. The wind kicked up, growing stronger, ebbing the day's heat moment by moment. A half-hour passed, and insects chirped as the night prepared to come to life. The sound of a crackling fire and the smell of spiced stew drifted from the camp.

Sriovey had settled on a low-lying boulder. "It isn't easy," he finally said, breaking the silence, his voice was quiet and strained.

Cinder stared at his friend, trying to figure what to say. Sriovey's three words reflected a lifetime of changes that he was struggling to accomplish. And he was right; it wasn't easy. It was hard, likely the hardest thing Sriovey could ever hope to do.

The quiet lingered, and Cinder deliberated on what might settle his friend's sorrow. Maybe the truth? "Will you look at me?"

Sriovey twisted about, facing him.

Cinder squatted so he and Sriovey were nearly at eye level. "I want you to know how much I admire what you're doing. I've always loved and admired you. All the brothers." He flashed a grin. "Except for Estin. It took me a while to figure him out."

Sriovey tilted his head, the self-directed frustration still obvious, but there was also a hint of curiosity. "You didn't have many warm feelings for Riyne, either."

Cinder nodded agreement, recalling his first year at the Third Directorate and all his run-ins with Riyne. Their relationship had improved substantially after the tragedies of the Unitary Trial, and for that he was grateful. "I suppose I didn't, but like a fungus, he grew on me."

Sriovey chuckled. "A fungus. I like it."

Cinder seated himself next to Sriovey, and a gentle silence fell across them again. They stared into the gathering gloaming. The hills and surrounding trees grew vague, blurred. Brilliant stars lit heaven's dome with cold crowns of illumination.

After a period of time, Cinder spoke again. "What you're doing isn't easy, but it is worthwhile. It's beautiful, and you're amazing for making the attempt. Even more, you're amazing for coming as far as you have."

Sriovey finally faced him. "Amazing?" He offered a hesitant smile.

"Amazing," Cinder agreed.

"Now you're going to make me blush," Sriovey said with a stronger smile.

The purity of his expression calmed Cinder's heart and caused it to soar. From Shokan's memories, he recalled it was the nature of a true dwarf to bring peace and contentment through a simple smile. He grinned at Sriovey. "See? Without even trying, you're able to show your true colors. They shine through."

Sriovey stared at him, uncertainty and hope warring on his features.

"Come on," Cinder encouraged. "If you don't believe me, then believe the memories of the Blessed One. Believe Shokan. He created your people, and everything I know from his thoughts say that he would approve of you. He would love you."

Sriovey's expression flitted between disbelief and a terrible longing. He blinked back tears. "Shokan would love me?"

Cinder pulled his brother into a hug, feeling Sriovey shudder with emotion against his chest. "Of course he would. You're brave, bold, and beautiful." He grinned. "Well, maybe not beautiful, but the other two will do."

Sriovey wiped at his eyes. "It really isn't easy becoming like Jozep—a true dwarf."

Cinder cleared his smile, his face settling into seriousness. "No. But, like I said, you're amazing for coming as far as you have. More importantly, you should forgive yourself for failing when you do. Love yourself. You deserve it."

Sriovey's expression grew pensive. "Is that Shokan speaking or Hotgate?"

Cinder didn't reply at once. Instead, he stared at heaven's glory, breathing in the night's embrace. "Sometimes, it feels like they're one and the same."

Sriovey nodded. "I think they are one and the same. Just like I need to accept myself, so do you."

His statement echoed in Cinder's mind as they continued to stare into the night. Was Sriovey right? It was a question Cinder had begun to wonder about himself. Was he more than just the repository of Shokan's memories? It seemed impossible, but what if it was true?

"How did it go?" Anya asked, moving to stand when Cinder rejoined her after talking to Sriovey.

Cinder's sight went to his friend, watching as he spooned a bowl of stew, blowing to cool it. Had their conversation really done his friend any good? Or had it simply been words that sounded important and influential in the moment but truly didn't mean much? He wanted to believe it was the former. Otherwise, what was the point? "I think it helped," he said.

Anya's eyes had also gone to Sriovey, and an undefinable expression stole across her face. "I know what it's like to go against everything you've been taught," she whispered at last, a simple statement that was full of a lifetime of heartache and longing. "It's terrifying. Everyone telling you that what you're doing is foolish or immoral."

Not knowing how to respond, Cinder hugged Anya from behind, his arms around her waist. Holding her close, rocking her softly, the two of them faced the fire. She rested her head on his shoulder, placed her arms atop his, stroking his forearms.

"You are so much wiser than me," Cinder said. "All I've ever known is pushing on and on in order to become a better warrior. You have always sought what's best for others."

Anya twisted about to peer at him. "That's not true. You've always wanted the best for others. Who else could have convinced a group of humans, elves, and dwarves to think of themselves as brothers? That was you."

Cinder didn't immediately reply. She was right, but it wasn't enough. Becoming a warrior worthy of the name had once been his only goal. Then he had wanted to become the equal of the woven, surpass them. Now, Cinder had other aspirations—protecting those who needed defending, and afterward, further goals. Finding a life of peace for him and Anya and becoming a better person. He also wanted to be someone who created. "I'll keep it in mind."

"See that you do." Anya shifted in his arms, laying her hands on his chest. "In this, I speak as your Isha." She lifted a cautioning finger. "And if you say a single word about me being old or somehow insert the adjective *simply* into our conversation, your bedroll will be mighty cold tonight."

Cinder eyed Anya, waiting for her to figure out what she'd just said. Seconds later, she did, but rather than blushing, she grinned. "You only warm my bedroll on some nights, when we're safe and alone."

"Some nights, when all this ends," Cinder said with a longing sigh.

"Some nights," Anya agreed.

Minutes later, Sriovey and Jozep approached.

"We were talking about this plan of yours," Sriovey said, indicating Jozep. "About having us help you convince the dwarves of Aurelian Crèche, and we're not so sure it'll work."

"Why not?" Cinder asked, not expecting this late-minute disagreement. He and Anya had discussed the matter at length, and both felt like it should work.

"Because our people have become naturally obstinate," Sriovey said.

Jozep smiled. "You might even say we're ornery."

Cinder glanced from one dwarf to the other, recognizing that the two of them might not be in consensus. "You think the dwarves of Aurelian Crèche are set in their ways as warriors and won't want to change?"

It was Sriovey who nodded while Jozep merely shrugged his shoulders.

"Or are you worried we might find a faction there similar to the Baptisers?" Anya asked, speaking to Sriovey, who grimaced.

"It would make sense, as war-hungry as dwarves have become." Sriovey said, kicking the ground in frustration.

Cinder disagreed. "Your people aren't hungry for war and conquest. They're afraid. Even the Baptisers are ultimately afraid. They're afraid of a world that's grown more dangerous, of having their people face those dangers without protection. It's natural, but our response to those fears is what defines us. It's why the Baptisers are ultimately cowards. They want to crush into silence anyone who disagrees with them. It's the only way they can survive. They know it, and their brutality is the only reason they have any strength. People of good will don't act in such a fashion. And I can't believe any of the other crèches will follow the path of the Baptisers."

Eyes wide in surprise, Sriovey stared at him. So did Anya and Jozep. Only then did Cinder realize that he hadn't simply made a point, he'd pontificated. And no one liked a pontificator. He closed his eyes, preparing for the mockery to come. But seconds passed, and nothing happened.

He cracked open an eye, seeing Sriovey, Jozep, and Anya still gazing at him in questioning regard. "What?" he asked.

"That was a sweet sentiment," Jozep said.

"And you're never sweet," Sriovey added.

Anya rested a hand against his cheek. "But he can be."

43

It took two more weeks for their small band to reach Sirasent, the capital of Shima Sithe, and their arrival took place early in a late spring afternoon. They settled into a suite of spaces in a fine hotel, the dwarves sharing one room and Cinder and Anya having another. When the clerk at the front desk had learned the last, he'd flustered and blubbered, clearly not wanting to acquiesce to their request.

But eventually he'd agreed, still uncomfortable and unhappy, but at this point, neither Cinder nor Anya cared about his reaction. As far as they were concerned, it was time to stop worrying about the attitudes of the close-minded.

Just as important, Cinder had other worries on his mind—this Trial, for one. In its own way, it would be as challenging as any they'd undertaken, and the reason was clear: *politics*. Cinder wasn't good at statecraft, but he'd have to learn, especially since Shokan's memories—the Blessed Ones had both been skilled diplomats—could teach him what he needed to know.

That knowledge would soon be put to the test since word of Anya's arrival had already been forwarded to the palace, and Empress Aqueem had quickly responded, calling on them to visit her tomorrow morning. Once again, the forged diplomatic documents that General Arwan had managed to procure for them were proving invaluable.

Until then, they had the evening to themselves, and Cinder stared out the windows at Sirasent.

Like all elven cities, it was beautiful. A narrow river separated the city into a northern and southern district, and buildings of vibrant colors, tall and flat-roofed, nestled next to each other on clean, broad streets that ran in straight lines across a flat expanse of land. Parks, copses of hardwood trees—some of them in bloom—and flowering meadows imbued the city with a sense of the natural, and so did the rice paddies growing upon terraced hillsides in the near distance. Opposite of southern seasons, here in the northern climes, spring was soon to give way to summer.

Anya moved to stand next to him. "I'm hungry."

Cinder smiled. "You're always hungry."

She elbowed him. "Take me to a restaurant?"

"You don't want to eat here at the hotel?"

"There's a restaurant that's supposed to serve spicy food like what we have at Yaksha."

"And you're not worried what the elves here might say about a human man having dinner with an elven woman?"

Anya shifted, moving behind him and wrapping her arms around his waist, head on his shoulder. "Let them whine. Besides which, I'm pretty sure that ship has already sailed. We're sharing a hotel room, after all, and if there's one overriding truism about any people—humans, elves, dwarves, or even yakshins—it's that they love to gossip. By now, everyone from here to the imperial palace probably knows about the scandal of that degenerate Anya Aruyen sharing a room with her human lover."

"Well, speaking about yourself in the third person *is* the sign of a degenerate," Cinder said with a grin.

Anya shrugged. "Then consider me a degenerate. Now take Anya

Aruyen out to dinner."

"This is a pretty place," Anya said, glancing about after they'd been seated.

The restaurant to which she'd led them sat upon a main road and took up the first two levels of a tall brick-faced building painted indigo blue. A dozen wrought-iron tables with matching chairs provided outdoor seating for those who wanted to enjoy the beautiful weather and observe the carriages, mounted travelers, and pedestrians making their way along the tree-lined street.

Currently, with it being late afternoon, the restaurant wasn't yet busy with only one other party—a couple—sitting outside. Cinder had briefly glanced over at them—a man and a woman, clearly wealthy— but the majority of his attention was on the staff. The waiters and waitresses stood like a cluster of gossiping hens, shooting him and Anya sneers, which they likely thought he didn't notice. He should have realized having a public meal with Anya wouldn't be a straightforward matter.

"I don't think we should eat here," he told her.

Anya briefly glanced in the direction of his gaze. "You're afraid they'll spit in our food," she said, guessing his thoughts.

"And our drinks."

She frowned at the staff, who quickly dispersed upon noticing her regard. A quick pursing of her lips gave away her discontent. "I guess it was too much to hope for a peaceful meal."

"Order dinner to our room at the hotel?"

Anya nodded. "I guess we don't have any other choice." She stood, and Cinder rose as well.

"Don't tell me you're leaving," sneered a young elf around Anya's age—part of the other couple seated outside. "Especially after making such a spectacle of yourself." He pointed at Cinder, disgust evident.

Cinder flicked his eyes over the man and dismissed him as a threat.

Handsome like the rest of his kind, he had a sword belted at his hip, but it looked like it might have never been drawn. Besides, the man's build wasn't that of a warrior. He had the slim shoulders of someone who rarely concerned himself with physical labor. His only remarkable feature was his dark skin, similar in hue to those of Bharat, different than what was seen in Yaksha.

Cinder's sight landed next on the woman. Dark-haired and dark-skinned like her companion, she viewed him with a cutting smirk.

He might have said something he would have regretted, but Anya responded before he could do so. She dipped her head in acknowledgement at the couple. "Princess Cerin Ripple. It's a pleasure to meet you." She also addressed the man who had spoken to them. "Prince Tura, a pleasure as well."

Cinder took a harder look at the couple. Princess Cerin, heir to the throne and Prince Tura, her husband. Long odds, running into the two of them in public like this. Regardless, the meeting represented an unexpected opportunity.

"You have me at a disadvantage," Princess Cerin said.

"Anya Aruyen." She indicated Cinder. "And my companion, Cinder Shade of Rakesh."

"Anya Aruyen? Princess Anya Aruyen of Yaksha Sithe?" Princess Cerin repeated in a tone of disbelief. "I heard you were in Sirasent, but I didn't expect to meet you out in the open like this."

"What brings you so far north?" Prince Tura asked.

Anya offered a faint smile. "A long journey, many troubles and toils, and unfortunately, grim tidings."

"Grim tidings," Princess Cerin said rather than asked, a neutral expression on her face. "These days, the world is awash in grim tidings. What worse news do you bring?" Her eyes flicked to Cinder, the contempt obvious. "And what role does this human play in all this?"

Cinder kept his gaze on the other party, but he noticed the restaurant staff had grouped nearby, listening in. So did a number of pedestrians on the sidewalk. None of them appeared particularly friendly, but he kept his hand away from his sword. *Diplomacy.* Besides which, it was probably best to let Anya handle the situation.

"I've heard rumors about you and a human male," Prince Tura said. "Unsettling stories, unfit for public consumption." His flat gaze went to Cinder, scowling when the prince received nothing but an impassive expression.

Anya didn't take the bait. "Rumors rarely speak the truth, which is part of why I'm here. I have much to discuss with your empress."

A brief quiet met her statement.

"You dance around the topic, but you mean Shet, don't you?" the princess asked.

Hisses of fear arose from the restaurant's staff.

"He is risen," Anya said. "And he must be stopped."

"And what does Shima Sithe have to do with this mission?" Prince Tura asked. "Naraka is closer to your nation, thousands of miles distant from our own."

"So is Shalla Valley," Anya said. "And yet only a single step separates it from Shima Sithe. Your nation is not so safe as you believe."

Scoffs of disbelief met her words.

"You jest," Princess Cerin said with a mocking laugh. "We are far distant from Naraka."

Anya kept her eyes on the other party. "Cinder."

He knew what she wanted. They'd discussed doing exactly this, but in their conversations, it was to have happened in the throne hall of Empress Aqueem. But this might serve even better. Whatever it took to convince the royalty of the dangers posed by Shet and the wraiths.

Cinder stood, quickly forming the necessary weave. The iron tang of his *lorethasra* filled the air, and if the Shima royals had any kind of training, Cinder knew they'd recognize the source.

Apparently they did. Both of them went white.

"It's him," Prince Tura said. "He's sourcing *lorethasra*." His tone went strained. "How is this possible?"

"You've heard the other stories about him," Princess Cerin said, appearing as equally unsettled. "They're real."

Focusing on the task at hand, Cinder blocked out their conversation.

Seconds later, out in the street, a black line split the air, rotating into a doorway filled with swirling colors—a *Path*. An image formed within the anchor line, that of a massive tree: Mahamatha, Mother Ashoka.

Gasps of shock and awe filled the area immediately around the restaurant.

"What is it?"

"It's a trick!"

"It can't be real!"

Anya stood as well. "It's real, and it's not a trick," she shouted to the gathered crowd, although she continued to stare at the princess and the prince, whose faces had gone ghastly. "It's an anchor line to Shalla Valley and Mother Ashoka. She is inimitable."

His point made, Cinder let go of the Path. It was also time he entered the conversation. "Shet has this ability as well. He will come for you. You need to be prepared. But I can't defend you if you aren't willing to fight."

"Who are you to say you can defend us?" asked Prince Tura with a snarl. "No one can make that claim."

Cinder smiled at the opening, wanting to thank the other man.

Anya saw it as well. "You say you've heard rumors about me and the man with whom I travel. And I told you his name is Cinder Shade, which it is. But he has another name, an older one. His true name is Shokan. The Lord of the Sword is also risen!" She stared down the other princess. "After all, what other human can source *lorethasra*? And who else but the Lady of Fire would accompany him?"

If Cinder's demonstration of the anchor line had caused shock, Anya's words caused chaos.

Cinder winked at the wait staff. "It was lovely dining here." He Blended then, deeper than any elf could detect, not wanting to deal with the ensuing commotion.

An instant later, Anya Linked to him, looping her arm through his. They stood to the side, watching as members of the crowd sourced *lorethasra* and searched for them. The throng of people stirred like a beehive, buzzing about as they shouted in fear and disbelief. Anya shook her head in sorrow.

"It's not necessarily a lie," Cinder said, recalling what Sriovey had said to him a few weeks ago. "I have Shokan's memories, and I know his way of thinking. I am him as well as myself."

"I know," Anya said, in an unsurprised tone. "And I think the same about Sira." She gestured to the fear-filled crowd. "But look at them. They only want to live in peace, and here we are bringing a nest of trouble to their homes. Is this our lot? To disturb the comfort and solace of everyone we meet?"

Cinder feared it would be so. He tugged on Anya's arm, getting her moving. "Let's go back to the hotel. I wouldn't be surprised if we're called to the palace tonight."

Cinder placed a supportive hand on Sriovey's shoulder, offering comfort as the dwarf shivered with nervousness.

"I don't like this," Sriovey muttered.

"It'll be over soon," Cinder said. "I'll be with you the entire time."

"I still don't like it." Sriovey's concern was understandable.

It was the early evening of their arrival to Sirasent, and just like Cinder had guessed, a message had come from the imperial palace for the four of them to attend the empress. Anya and Jozep led the way while Cinder and Sriovey trailed after, the four of them pacing along the length of Shima's Sithe throne hall.

Cinder held in a frown as he took in the thirty guards warding the way forward. Their faces were creased with worry, and their hands lay upon the hilts of their swords. Some stood upon balconies overlooking the hall, arrows aimed.

"What did you do?" Jozep asked, addressing Cinder over his shoulder. "The guards look terrified."

"Hotgate probably fought someone," Sriovey muttered. "Always causing trouble, that one."

Cinder smiled. Sriovey was trying so hard to be brave without reverting to his usual feigned anger.

An instant later, Cinder set his gaze forward, studying Empress Aqueem, who sat atop a pile of plush red cushions on a white-marble throne that matched the walls and flooring. Fanciful columns, slender and decoratively carved, held up a vaulted ceiling, and from it dangled a half-dozen crystal chandeliers, each one massive. Their light supplemented that of the late-day sun, which cast colorful shadows as it poured through the stained-glass windows lining the walls.

The empress sat calmly while waiting for them, but Cinder could see the tension in her shoulders. Bracketing her on the right were Princess Cerin, her only child, and Prince Tura while on her left stood an older man that Cinder recognized was likely her husband, Prince Consort Forage Ripple.

There was one other individual, however—a man, possibly human. He was slim, elegant, and a manicured mustache swept down to his chin. Dark-skinned like a rakishi, he stood at the foot of the dais and had the bearing of a warrior. Cinder marked him. In response, the man offered a terse nod.

Cinder addressed Jozep and Sriovey, whispering so his voice wouldn't carry. "Maybe the two of you can calm the waters?"

Jozep offered an open-hearted grin. "Of course." He fell back to pace beside Sriovey, and a moment later, a sense of peace wafted off them.

As it did, Cinder felt his worries slowly recede. The same easing of concerns also seemed to work on the guards. Though still alert, they no longer appeared quite as tense. Similarly, the royals might have taken a relieved breath. Prince Tura, who had been scowling, no longer did so. Instead, uncertain curiosity filled his features, while the unknown man appeared puzzled.

No one moved, and the room remained silent except for the footsteps of Cinder's party as they neared the throne. And when they reached the dais, Sriovey and Jozep bowed, but Cinder and Anya did not. The world needed to believe they were Shokan and Sira, and the Blessed Ones bowed to no one.

The slight wasn't missed. The guards stiffened, and the scowl returned to Prince Tura's face. His wife, Princess Cerin, merely lifted a brow, while the prince consort glowered momentarily before his features settled into an inscrutable expression.

The empress didn't respond at first, staring down at them for a long moment, fingernails clicking on the arm of her throne. At last, she spoke. "Is Yaksha Sithe so devoid of good manners that her visiting royalty no longer offers proper respect to their hosts?"

"No slight was intended," Anya said. "But currently, I represent both Yaksha Sithe and myself. And in representing myself, I will not bow before anyone. I think you know why."

The empress smirked. "My daughter mentioned your claim. But it's only a claim. You have no proof."

She was right. They didn't have proof, and while this afternoon's demonstration with the princess and prince should have helped their cause, it apparently wasn't enough.

"It's the dwarves," Princess Cerin stated.

"What about them?" the empress asked.

"Calmness pours off them. Can you not feel it?"

"She's right," said the man at the base of the dais, his scrutiny landing on Jozep and Sriovey.

Cinder viewed the man in a fresh light. If he'd noticed the serenity from Sriovey and Jozep, then it meant he wasn't human. So what was he then? A rishi? Cinder centered himself, reaching for *Jivatma*... Just in case.

"They are true dwarves," Anya said, going on to explain about Jozep and Sriovey.

Her account caused the man at the base of the dais to shrug. "It's possible."

"And I'm sure you've heard of the events of this afternoon," Anya continued. "Who else but the Blessed Ones can forge an anchor line and have dwarves with the old Talents as their companions? We are who we say we are, and we need your help."

The as-yet-unidentified man grunted. "Whatever ability the dwarves possess has nothing to do with you."

"It has everything to do with them," Sriovey disagreed, speaking in a soft yet carrying voice. "Shokan created the dwarves." He indicated Cinder. "*He* created the dwarves."

The man blinked in apparent surprise. "Shokan was also the deadliest warrior in history. That boy doesn't look like much."

Cinder had heard enough. The man was trying to get a rise out of him, and he understood why. It wouldn't work. But that didn't mean that Cinder would let matters lie. "Who are you?"

The man smiled, like he'd been waiting for Cinder's demand all along. "Rishi Mortar. We've heard much about you, Cinder Shade." He bowed mockingly to Anya. "And you as well, Princess of Yaksha Sithe. You stole something precious from us."

"And your reason for being here?" Cinder asked.

"Call it a lucky happenstance."

More likely the rishis had a quelchon who had guided Mortar here. No doubt the man was now hoping to either regain the Orb of Undying Light or obtain vengeance for its theft.

Cinder faced the empress. "And does a rishi rule in Shima Sithe? Does he speak for you?"

"I speak for Shima Sithe," the empress said, knuckles rapping hard on the arm of her throne. "No one else. Not a rishi. Not true dwarves. Not even Shokan and Sira."

"Of course," Cinder said with a mild incline of his head.

"May I speak plainly?" Anya asked.

"I would appreciate it," the empress said.

"We need your help. A herd of wraiths is ready to pour into the Sunset Kingdoms. Genka Devesth will need your support if he's to defeat them."

"If you're Shokan and Sira," Mortar said, "why not defeat the wraiths by yourself?" He addressed Cinder. "That is if you really are who you say you are."

Cinder had been forced to forgo any weapons for this late-day meeting, but it didn't mean he was unarmed. A dash forward, and he had Mortar by the throat, straight-arming him off his feet. He stared the empress in the eyes, ignoring the rishi's ineffectual clawing and weaves. A harsh lesson was needed. "I could defeat the wraiths but not before they destroy much of the Sunsets. No people deserve to die because others hate their leaders."

He set the rishi down, letting the man fall on his bottom. The guards stationed throughout the hall had drawn their swords, advancing while others had arrows aimed. Cinder stared about. It seemed he had a long way to go as a diplomat.

Thankfully, Anya was able to salvage the situation. "We are not your enemy," she declared. "Your enemies are the wraiths. Help us stop them or they'll come for you next."

Rishi Mortar sat in a high-backed chair, swirling a cup of wine as he stared into the flames crackling in the hearth.

"You are certain of what you saw?" Empress Aqueem asked her son-in-law.

The prince nodded, maintaining his admirable poise and patience, something his mother-in-law too often lacked. "We're certain. We saw him form an anchor line. Cinder Shade. Nothing else makes sense."

The empress scowled, pacing about her study. It was a square space, tastefully appointed with a large desk overlooking her gardens and a seating arrangement fronting the fireplace and mantle. An eclectic collection of books was carefully, but seemingly casually, arranged on the many shelves lining the golden oak-paneled walls. And from the coffered ceiling hung a crystal chandelier to provide light at this late hour.

"He had me at his mercy," Rishi Mortar said, finally looking up from the fireplace. He still couldn't believe it. Never before in his life, even as a young rakishi, had he ever felt so helpless. Cinder Shade could have snapped his neck without any effort, and just thinking about it caused Mortar to shiver in terror. The man's speed... One moment, he had been a score of feet distant, and the next, Mortar had been seized and held out at arm's length. Worse, his strength and weaves had made no impact on the fearsome man.

It left Mortar simultaneously terrified and exultant. What if Cinder truly was who he claimed: Shokan? As Mortar reckoned matters, it was actually a prospect now worth entertaining. After all, Shet and his Titans were real, so why not Shokan and Sira?

In fact, the possibility of the Blessed Ones was the entire reason Mortar was in Shima Sithe to begin with. Persistence, who had some talent as a quelchon, had suggested the journey, and at first, Mortar had been unwilling. Why help her? Persistence wasn't exactly his favorite rishi, even less so after her fall from grace.

But she had worked at him, and Mortar had finally agreed to make the mission, mostly because he was tired of Bharat. He hadn't left the island in decades, and he desired to again see the world.

Nonetheless, although Mortar had agreed to journey to Shima Sithe, he'd never believed Persistence's promise that his future would be decided here. After all, Persistence had recently made many ludicrous claims, such as her explanation about what had happened during the disastrous battle in Indrun's Chamber. When the Orb of Undying Light had been stolen from directly underneath her and Guile's noses.

Prior to this evening, Mortar would have scoffed at her account. A single man able to hold off two rishis and fight in such a way as to save those same rishis from injury? Impossible.

But then had come this evening when the impossible had been made flesh.

"He had me at his mercy," Mortar repeated to the empress, a woman he had known since his years as a rakishi, although he doubted she remembered him from that time. He'd changed so much since then, both mentally and physically.

Still, she'd been kind to him, and he had always had a warm place in his heart for her, trusted her enough to attend this evening's meeting without his rakishis. He wondered if they might have made any difference, or would Cinder Shade have crushed them like Persistence stated Anya had done to the rakishis in Indrun's Chamber?

"What does that mean?" Princess Cerin asked.

"It means that his power far exceeds mine—by the same factor that mine exceeds yours."

Mortar's response caused a silence to fall on the room, one broken by the prince consort. "Other than Shet and his Titans, are there any who can match you in this world?"

Mortar briefly eyed the man. He was a good match for Empress Aqueem, both intellectually and emotionally, steadier and far smarter than her. In truth, the empress was somewhat dull.

"No one," Mortar answered the prince consort.

"No one except apparently Cinder Shade and Anya Aruyen," Prince Tura said by way of correction. "Who may or may not be Shokan and Sira."

"They are not," the empress stated in a tone of absolute certainty. "But what I want to know is this: are they lovers? A human and an elven princess?" She pulled a face. "Disgusting if true."

Mortar wanted to roll his eyes.

"They appeared to be quite close when we saw them," Princess Cerin said. "But if they're Shokan and Sira, then it also doesn't matter. They are wed."

"But a human male and an elven woman," the empress persisted.

Prince Tura was the one who responded. "As Shokan and Sira, they are beyond our elven conceits about propriety."

The empress continued to wear a mulish expression.

Mortar sighed, addressing the empress. "If they're Shokan and Sira, do you really think any of your limitations are of concern to them? Prince Tura is right. The Blessed Ones stand well above and beyond such restrictions."

The empress continued to wear a disturbed countenance, but in the end, she came to the right conclusion. The disgust left her features. "Then what do you advise?"

What did he advise? Prior to this evening, Mortar would have advised that Aqueem have Cinder Shade thrown in prison and Anya Aruyen delivered in chains back to her mother. In truth, prior to this evening, Mortar would have wanted nothing to do with this entire situation.

But this evening had come. Princess Cerin and Prince Tura had confirmed the forging of an anchor line by Cinder Shade. An action apparently similar to how he and Anya had escaped Indrun's Chamber. Combine that with what Cinder had done this evening—lifting Mortar off his feet and holding him helpless.

How had he done it? What trick? Because despite these impressive feats, there had to be some deception involved, and—

Mortar stiffened, eyes wide, when a realization struck him. In his two centuries of life as a rishi, Mortar had been surprised on only four occasions. This night marked the fifth.

There had been no *lorethasra*. Cinder hadn't used any weaves— nothing at all. His speed and strength… Had it been *Jivatma*, like Persistence stated?

Mortar faced the empress, explaining what he was only now recognizing. And from their shocked expressions, they hadn't noticed it either. "This is what I think you should do," he said. "Exactly what Cinder Shade asks. His plan to support the Sunsets is a good one. It may save your sithe regardless of whether he's actually Shokan."

"You advise that my wife place our warriors under the command of a man who vowed to end our sithe?" the prince consort demanded.

Mortar shrugged. "If Genka can't hold off the wraiths, they may destroy your sithe anyway. This way, at least you'll have built some goodwill with the warlord."

"And if Cinder and Anya are the Blessed Ones," Prince Tura said, "we'll have built goodwill with them, too. They can protect us from Genka."

Mortar gave the prince an approving nod before glancing around the room, seeing that everyone had quickly come to the same conclusion.

Everyone but the empress. She stared out the window, conflicted. Finally, though, she faced them. "As you will. We'll help the Sunsets. We'll send a legion north with General Spalinkar to command. I only pray they aren't needed, and that Genka doesn't try to hold them hostage."

44

Sunlight beamed through the hotel restaurant's wall of windows, illuminating and warming the space. The spicy scents of masala dosa, idli, sambar, and chapatis filled the air while wait staff rushed about, taking and delivering breakfast orders, all of which came on banana leaves that served as plates. Given the number of patrons—not a single table in the restaurant was empty—it was clearly popular, and Anya was glad she and the others had come down early rather than late.

Right now, it was just she and Cinder since Sriovey and Jozep had already finished eating and retired to their room. The two of them had gathered a few stares—an elven woman and human man—but no one had cast them scowls or glares. If anything, those present seemed to find them fascinating. Rumors about what had happened yesterday afternoon—the creation of an anchor line to Shalla Vale—must have made the rounds, and it wasn't too hard to figure who stood front and center in those stories.

Cinder pretended like he didn't notice the attention, keeping his head down and focused on his food like it was a battle he had to win.

But he ate so slowly. Anya had finished her breakfast many, many minutes ago—she tended to gulp down her food—and only now was Cinder using the last of a dosa to gather his final bit of ginger pachadi. "I think the masala dosa could have used some more heat," he noted after finishing.

Anya smiled. "You think everything could use some more heat. And heat isn't the only spice, you know?

"I know. But I like my food hot."

She arched her brows. "Aren't you the one who grew up eating bland food in the mountains of Rakesh?"

Cinder shrugged. "I didn't know what I was missing."

"At least not until I introduced you to proper spices. Now that's all you can talk about." Anya pretended exasperation. "I think I created a monster."

"Maybe. But how was your idli and sambar?" Cinder indicated her empty banana leaf with a perceptive smirk.

Anya didn't want to answer. His question was a trap, but after a heavy exhalation, she replied. "It could have used more heat."

She cut off whatever else she might have said when she saw who was coming through the restaurant's front door: Princess Cerin and Prince Tura. Their presence at the restaurant must have been fairly common since only a few patrons glanced their way.

Anya set her napkin on her plate, waiting on their arrival. Hopefully they were here to announce the empress' intentions regarding the Sunset Kingdoms. Would she support them? Anya wasn't sure, and that ignorance had her anxiety ticking up a bit.

Cinder had also noticed the princess and prince as well, and he rose to his feet in greeting.

"Don't stand on our account," Cerin said when she reached their table. "You didn't bow before my mother, so you shouldn't stand for us."

Cinder eyed her a moment before shrugging and resuming his seat.

Cerin cleared her throat. "We came here to tell you my mother's decision. The empress has agreed to your plan of sending support to the Sunsets. We'll be sending the Ninth Legion."

Cinder frowned. "I thought the Ninth was lost in the wilderness a couple hundred years ago."

Anya glanced his way, not expecting him to know so much about Shima Sithe's history, especially the unexplained tragedy involving the Ninth Legion. All that was known was that they had gone north for some reason, into the wilds, and not a single warrior had made it home.

"It's a reconstituted Ninth," Cerin explained.

Anya found herself praying that bad luck didn't travel with this new legion's name.

"They'll be under the command of General Spalinkar," Tura said. "We won't turn them over to Genka Devesth."

Anya nodded. "I wouldn't expect anything different. When will the legion be ready to muster?"

"They were already preparing for a shakedown tour," Tura said. "They can leave within three days. Four at the most."

Anya glanced at Cinder. "Head on over to Aurelian Crèche while I march with the Ninth?"

"I'll take Jozep and Sriovey to the crèche, and between the three of us, hopefully we can convince them to send a unit north as well."

"And by the time you're ready, I'll be in the Sunsets. We can meet there."

"Jeet and Stren are in Querel," Cinder said. "Go there first?"

"You're sure they're trustworthy?"

Cinder tilted his head in consideration. "Yes." His voice held no hint of indecision. "They're changed. I think you'll like them a lot more this time than I did the last."

Anya smiled. "And once I reach Jeet and Stren, you can Path to my location through the *divaspana*."

Cinder grinned. "It'll save me weeks of travel."

Anya broke off when she noticed the princess and the prince staring at her and Cinder in baffled surprise. "What is it?"

"Do you always speak like you know what the other person is already thinking?" the princess asked, Tura nodding along to her question.

Anya laughed. "You'd be surprised. The first time it happened—when

Cinder guessed my unspoken thoughts—it was… unexpected. Then it kept happening over and over again, and I did the same to him." She shrugged. "Now it's just become part of our relationship."

"And you still refer to each other by your names from this age?" Tura asked.

Cinder answered. "The names we currently carry—Anya and Cinder—those are the ones by which we were first introduced to one another. Those are the ones by which everyone we love knows us." He shrugged. "It's what is easiest."

Cerin and Tura nodded acceptance, still hovering over their table.

Anya had enough of that. She gestured for the other couple to sit. "If you haven't eaten, please join us, and if you have, there's still no reason to stand over us. At least have some coffee."

The princess shared an uncertain expression with her husband. He shrugged minutely, and they settled themselves at the table. But having delivered their news, the other couple appeared reticent.

"We don't bite," Anya said with what she hoped was a soothing smile. "Say whatever is on your mind."

Nervousness flitted across Tura's face before his features firmed into resoluteness. "Are you really Shokan and Sira?"

Anya smiled. It was the very question she had expected of the princess and her husband. It was also the one to which she and Cinder would have to respond more often than not. Everyone would want to know the answer, wanting some measure of proof, regardless if the claim was true or not. And maybe it was. Anya wasn't sure, but this is what the world needed from her and Cinder.

"We are who we say we are," Anya said. "It is hard to believe, I know. At first, we didn't believe it ourselves."

"When did you know?" Cerin asked.

Again, Anya glanced to Cinder in question, waiting for his response.

He addressed Cerin. "In Mahadev, after we entered the Lucid Foe. It gave us insight into our truths, which until then had been masked by time, dreams, and loss of memories."

"The Lucid Foe in Mahadev," Tura mused. "How did you survive the place? Ever since the *NusraelShev*, Mahadev is a name synonymous with death."

Anya tried not to wear a sour expression. "There was an evil in the city that killed any who entered."

"Was?" Tura pressed.

"Was," Anya confirmed. "We defeated him, and when he challenged us, we broke him. Eventually." Her sight went to Cinder, her eyes latching on the *null pocket* in his cloak. She couldn't see or sense it, but she knew its location—the globe that held Rabisu's essence.

What would they do with the Rakshasa of Dissolution? They'd promised to release him at some point, but where would that be? And how could they do so in good conscience? No people deserved to be terrorized and tormented by the rakshasa.

But it was also a question for the far, distant future. They had so many more important issues and journeys ahead of them. Anya heading with the Ninth Legion to the Sunsets, and Cinder going with Jozep and Sriovey to Aurelian Crèche. Which meant she might as well get ready now instead of waiting for later.

Anya took a deep breath. She might have wished for more hours with Cinder, but it wasn't to be. It was time to get to work. She stood, addressing Cerin and Tura with a smile. "It's been lovely chatting with you, but we have to prepare for our travels."

"Of course," Tura said, rising to his feet as well.

"I hope to see you before you leave," Cerin said, a beat later.

Anya briefly viewed the royals, wondering when it was that everyone started to appear so young to her.

After the prince and princess made their departure, Cinder sighed, sounding as tired as she felt. "I wish I could stay longer, but it's best if I left today. Within the hour."

Anya moved to stand next to him, taking his hand and kissing his fingers, not bothering about the scandal of an elven woman touching a human man. "Travel safe, *priya*."

Jozep and Sriovey bracketed Cinder as they marched through the heart of Tashkar, the capital of Aurelian Crèche. It had taken them nearly a month to get here from Shima Sithe, and a full week of that journey had required passage through the heart of the Trendil Mountains.

They had set a hard pace throughout, but there had been time enough to observe and reminisce. If nothing else, the travel through the mountains reminded Jozep of Surent Crèche—not just the architecture and buildings but also the way those of Aurelian lived and loved. It brought an unexpected lump to Jozep's throat. He missed his people, and he missed his home. Not because of the similarities here but rather because of the subtle differences.

The dwarves of Aurelian Crèche were kinder and gentler than the ones in Surent, more at peace with themselves. The preparations for war didn't consume them. Instead, they loved art, peace, and laughter. They were closer to what dwarves had originally been intended... everything except their views of the Sunset Kingdoms. In that regard, the dwarves here were too much like the ones of Surent: they had nothing but contempt for their northern neighbors.

It was unsurprising, though. Aurelian Crèche, having seen various warlords ravage south every few centuries, had always held a tense relationship with the Sunsets. It colored their attitude toward all humans, including Cinder, to whom they were at best cold and distant—and at worst, contemptuous and sneering.

And it would make their mission here all the more difficult.

Just then, a harried-appearing young dwarf with the air of a messenger hustled to reach them. He whispered to their guide, who nodded once in acknowledgment. The messenger then spoke. "The wisdoms have been made aware of your presence. They wish to see you. Now."

"No chance to rest and recover?" Sriovey asked, miraculously not scowling or cursing. He'd come far.

"I'm afraid not," the young dwarf responded, warmth in his voice as he addressed Sriovey. An instant later, a glower filled his features as he viewed Cinder. "The wisdoms want to meet your human companion and see him gone from our lands as quickly as possible."

Cinder peered at the dwarf with an inscrutable expression, but Jozep could tell his friend was irritated. He held in a sigh. Yes, their mission would be difficult.

Moments later, the young dwarf and their guide ushered them into a small chamber. Jozep blinked in surprise. Instead of deep within the mountain, it seemed they were now along the very perimeter.

A large window—mullions green with age—and a pair of window-paneled doors peered out at a walled and private garden where several dwarves were weeding and tending to flowers and shrubs. The glass also allowed the light of the late afternoon sun, which illuminated the chamber and made redundant the three chandeliers hanging from stout wooden trusses. The walls of the room were white-washed brick and contained a number of paintings and murals. Most were bucolic scenes from dwarven life, but the one that dominated the space was one familiar to Jozep. It was the creation scene of Shokan bringing the dwarven people to life. As usual, his face was obscured.

Rising to greet them were five dwarves, four women and one man— the wisdoms and likely the leader of Aurelian's military. They sat along the length of a polished black-marble table that was set crosswise to the entrance. A lectern—the place where those addressing the council would speak—was set at a distance of ten feet from the wisdoms, and twenty or so guards warded the room, poised and alert

"Welcome to Aurelian Crèche," the eldest of the wisdoms said. "I am Rune Tremble." She gestured, identifying the others. "These are the other wisdoms. Lazus Quaint, Trail Swift, and Junina Rose." She indicated the only man on the council, smiling at him with genuine warmth. "And, of course, we would be remiss if we didn't include General Wilder Propst in today's meeting."

Jozep studied the council. They ranged in age from one who wasn't much older than himself to another who had a similar ancientness to Wisdom Derilee in Surent. The general, on the other hand, was of middle years, red-haired like Sriovey, and viewed them through narrowed eyes, stroking his beard.

"We know your names," Rune continued, "so there is no need for introductions on your part. We also know the nature of your visit." She shook her head. "I hate to tell such fine dwarves as yourselves that you've wasted your time, but it is the truth."

Jozep swallowed when Cinder momentarily set his sight upon him. There was an undeniable heft and charisma to his friend's company, one that spoke of his restrained power and a forceful personality. He was the *Cipre Elonicon*, and the wisdoms and their general would soon feel the weight of that heavy regard.

Cinder moved to the lectern, facing the council with a smile. Not unexpectedly, they shifted in their white marble chairs, appearing uncomfortable. "I know you don't have the warmest regards for humans," Cinder began. "And I can understand and respect that. The Sunsets haven't been kind to your people." His jaw firmed. "Nevertheless, I need your help."

"*You* need our help?" General Wilder asked. "Not the Sunsets?"

Cinder nodded. "I need your help to save the Sunsets."

The general leaned forward, having the appearance of a raptor, and in that moment, he reminded Jozep of Stipe, all aggression and a want for violence. He hoped that wasn't the case. If something like the Baptisers had gained a foothold in Aurelian, then their mission was already doomed.

"Genka Devesth promised to conquer our lands," the general said. "To enslave our people to his empire. And we are supposed to save him from the wraiths?"

"If you wish to save yourselves, then yes," Cinder replied.

Wilder leaned back in his chair, hands folded across his stomach, wearing a smile of satisfaction. Jozep didn't like his reaction. So far, the general had been the only one to speak. None of the wisdoms, other than Rune during her welcome, had bothered to open their mouths. It had Jozep wondering just how much power the military had in Aurelian. Was it like what had happened to Surent?

Jozep hoped not, and if there was a way, he'd fight to prevent it. He caught Sriovey's eye. They reached for their *lorethasra* and *Jivatma*, utilizing *Anahata* and their *nadis*. A moment later, their Talent for

Serenity imbued the air, calming emotions. Maybe it would be enough for the wisdoms to gain courage and for the general to find some peace.

"His diplomats stated the same thing," Wilder said in response to Cinder's declaration. "And while I can understand why they would, I have yet to be convinced as to why we should fear the wraiths. They want to ravage the Sunsets? Let them. And if they come south, we'll close our home forts and wait them out, just like we have for every other unwelcome northern army that entered our mountains."

Cinder shook his head. "You cannot hide behind your walls. This is a war unlike any other. Seminal will not have seen anything like it since the *NusraelShev*. All nations must come together now, or we will surely be torn asunder separately. Shet has risen. The word must have reached you by now. And I tell you, it is true. I witnessed it."

"You are the human who travels with Anya Aruyen?" Trail, a middle-aged wisdom, asked.

Jozep wanted to cheer. A wisdom had finally spoken. Plus, he got the sense that of all the wisdoms, she might be the one most apt to listen with a charitable ear to what Cinder was telling them.

"I am," Cinder said, "and I'm here to tell you worse. Shet is not the gravest threat your crèche faces."

Cinder went on to speak of Zahhack, the Son of Emptiness. Jozep shuddered on simply hearing the name. He'd heard this before, but it still impacted him, shivered him with fear. He believed Cinder, but then again, he wanted to believe his friend. No doubt that colored his judgment, but he also didn't care about that.

What about the Council of Wisdoms, though? Would they also believe?

"Some of these tidings have reached our ears," said Junina, the youngest of the wisdoms. She took a tone between Wilder's unvarnished doubt and Trail's willingness to listen. "Vague misgivings. And you say it is true?" She shrugged. "Who are you to make such declarations? You, a mere human, no matter what legends and myths you're said to have witnessed."

"Who am I?" Cinder smiled faintly, but there was a deadly

earnestness to his simple utterance. He seemed to swell with power. "The people of Surent Crèche have named me as the *Cipre Elonicon.*" A sharp hiss met his statement. "So have some of the *hashains* of the Sunsets. But the world knows me as Shokan."

The Council of Wisdoms broke into cries of derision and anger.

Their reaction didn't cause Jozep any worry. Peace and acceptance was his greatest attribute, and the greatest gift he could provide. Once again, he gathered Sriovey's attention. And once again, they imbued Serenity into the air, more distinct and powerful this time. The dwarves of Aurelian might notice, likely would.

But General Wilder didn't. He railed at Cinder. "Who is this late-come, so-called warrior? This unwelcome guest who seeks to frighten us with nightmares of some evil greater than Shet?" He gestured to the line of guards. "Have this jackal removed."

The guards made to move on Cinder, who stood relaxed and seemingly unworried.

But a sharp gesture from Rune halted the warriors warding the council chambers. "It's them," she said, wearing a smile of wonder and joy as she pointed at Jozep and Sriovey. "Can you not feel it? Serenity."

Chaos ensued.

Sriovey stiffened when he felt everyone's eyes land on him. Having people stare his way had never bothered him much, but nowadays, with the person he was trying to become, it didn't sit so well. He might have cursed under his breath, but he managed to knuckle it under. It wasn't that the cursing was wrong, but more that it just didn't feel necessary like it once had.

Instead, he straightened, listening as Rune spoke about him and Jozep... especially Jozep.

"How are you the way you are?" she asked. Her gaze darted between Sriovey and Jozep, disregarding Cinder altogether. How foolish. Cinder was the reason for the existence of all dwarves. He was Shokan, and it didn't matter whether he actually believed it or not. It was the truth.

Jozep moved to take the lectern from Cinder. "You know how," he said, answering after the bustle and shouts had died down. "I accompanied Shokan and Sira to Mahadev—"

More shouts and exclamations.

Sriovey sighed to himself. At this rate, he'd run low on his *Jivatma* if the folks here insisted on yelling over every matter. "Maybe you can let us explain ourselves before you start asking questions?" he suggested into the tumult.

His advice was met by silence.

Seconds later. "Perhaps that would be best," Wilder said, glancing at the wisdoms.

Wisdom Trail nodded minutely. "If we don't, we'll be here all night."

Sriovey straightened, viewing her in a positive light. It seemed like at least one other person wanted to figure out what to do without spending so much time crying over every surprise.

"I agree," Rune said. "Please continue." She glanced around the table, even to the guards. "And we will keep quiet this time."

Jozep nodded acceptance, and he spoke then about his journey to Mahadev; Fastness as Sapient Dormant, which elicited a number of hisses and indrawn breaths; and then Manifold Fulsom's long and lonely vigil.

This time, the general couldn't contain himself. "Manifold Fulsom? *The* Manifold Fulsom?"

Jozep nodded, going on to talk about the Salutation Gate, *Jivatma*, and his friendship with Salt Tangent, learning to conduct, recreating Serenity, Rabisu, and the escape from Heremisth.

So much to tell, and when he was done, silence filled the chamber.

"That is much to accept," Rune said.

"Too much," Wisdom Junina said. "Where is your evidence? And it had better be exemplary."

Cinder moved to stand again before the lectern. "And you have that exemplary evidence in what Jozep and Sriovey can do. Their Serenity." He gestured to them. "You can let it go now."

With a groan of relief, Sriovey let go of his *Jivatma*. Time and practice had allowed him to create Serenity ever more easily, but it didn't mean it had become *easy*.

"And what of you?" Wilder asked Cinder. "What evidence do you have? Why should we believe you are Shokan?"

Cinder smiled. "There are words under that painting." He pointed to the mural of Shokan creating the dwarves. "It's written in Shevasra, a language known only to Shokan and Sira. The same as the untranslated version of the *Lor Agni*. Do any of you know what it says? The words under the painting?"

Everyone at the table raised their hands, and Sriovey noticed that some of the guards appeared aware of the wording as well.

"It states that Shokan created the dwarves as a promise," Rune said.

Sriovey narrowed his eyes at her. That wasn't all that it said. He didn't know for sure since he couldn't read Shevasra, but there was something in her tone. She'd left out part of the translation.

"What else does it say?" Sriovey asked. "You know there's more."

Rune smiled. "Maybe there is, and maybe there isn't. But for someone claiming to be Shokan, the creator of our kind, surely he can read the words and tell us himself."

Sriovey grumbled but lapsed into silence.

"A promise to whom?" Cinder asked.

The wisdoms and the general shared uncertain looks.

"The promise is made, but the words used aren't ones that we know," Rune said.

Cinder nodded. "Fair enough. Then I will tell you. The writing actually says that Shokan, son of Ashoka, from the Realm of Arisa—"

Shocked intakes interrupted his words.

"How does he know?" Junina demanded.

"Is that what it actually says?" one of the guards asked, unable to help himself.

"It has to be a trick," said Wilder. "He's lying."

More exclamations and shouts, but Sriovey couldn't tell who was talking since they were all speaking over one another. And as the argument threatened to spiral out of control, Cinder ended it.

"Enough!" His shout caused the dwarves to quiet themselves. "I know what it says because I can read it. *Shokan, son of Ashoka from the Realm of Arisa created the dwarves as fulfillment of his promise made to the Ur-Fels of Arisa. His promise of for them to reckon peace.*" He gazed about the room in challenge, meeting the eyes of those who had previously viewed him with contempt and now held burgeoning hope.

Sriovey wanted to cheer Cinder on.

"How can we know you speak the truth?" Rune asked in a whisper. "That your translation is true? Your friends," she indicated Jozep and Sriovey, "could have told you that word."

"We didn't," Sriovey replied. "That name—Ur-Fel—isn't one that's commonly known. We don't just bandy it about to strangers. Shokan already knew it."

"What other proof do you need?" Jozep asked. "We have Serenity, and Cinder has the name of our progenitors."

"He does," Rune said, "but it isn't enough. We—"

A vertical line split the air to Cinder's right. It rotated, widening into a rainbow-hued doorway leading into anarchy. The colors settled, becoming a bridge, and at the far end stood the Shriven Grove. A pair of yakshins passed into view, pausing as they stared at Cinder.

Sadana seemed to understand what Cinder wanted. She even knew how to tether, and she stepped upon the anchor line, entering the chamber. Her presence dominated the room. "Maynalor," Sadana said. "It is good to see you again."

"You as well," Cinder said with a grin. "Can you tell my name to these dwarves?"

Sadana peered at him in confusion. "Your name?" She stared at the dwarves with a frown. "Has he not told you? He is Cinder Shade. Also known by my people as Maynalor. And Mahamatha confirms he holds the memories of the Blessed One, Shokan."

Further cacophony threatened to erupt, but Cinder quieted the room with a single barked command.

Sriovey wondered how he was doing it. What was it about him that had the wisdoms holding still when he told them to?

"If that is all you need, then I will go," Sadana said. Cinder gestured to the anchor line, and without another word, she departed the room.

"Exemplary evidence," Cinder said to the quiet council.

No one responded for a moment.

"Then I think we have all the information we need," Rune said, breaking the quiet. "We will send a brigade to the Sunsets, commanded by one of our own. Not by Genka."

"He is Shokan," the general said, awe and stunned amazement on his face, indicating Cinder. "Our lord should have command."

"If you think that would be best," Rune replied.

"I do."

"Then it will be so," Rune said, hesitating as diffidence seemed to steal her courage. She cleared her throat, gathering herself. "Then we have one final request. Can Jozep and Sriovey stay and teach our people?"

Jozep replied with an accepting smile. "Of course."

There were more issues to decide, but the general stood then. He approached Cinder, tears and a miserable hope in his eyes. "You are truly Shokan."

It was a statement, not a question, but Cinder treated it like one. He gave a single grave nod. "I encompass all the wisdom and knowledge of the Blessed One."

Wilder bowed low, voice quavering. "It is an honor to meet you, Lord Shokan."

Cinder, whose visage and posture had been rigid and unyielding until now, relaxed. He went to his knees, viewing the general at eye level. "It's an honor to meet you as well."

He opened his arms, and the dwarf stepped into his embrace.

Sriovey muttered under his breath, and this time a curse felt right. "Why do my eyes sweat so fucking much these days?"

45

Genka stood amidst the disarray of an army ready to make camp. Soldiers dashed about, carrying out orders, screaming curses, demanding clarification, and shouting at idiots who didn't do as they were told. The entire army looked overwhelmed, but there was an underlying order to the madness.

It was through the sergeants, the heart and soul of the army. They stood as calm eyes amongst the storm, barking commands and seeing to the army's proper arrangement. It was the sergeants who got the tents arranged in straight rows and trenches dug. The sergeants who got the new recruits sorted out and in position. And it would be the sergeants who kept those same new recruits fighting when the enemy threatened to crush them all.

Alone and unbothered for now, Genka stood before his command tent, watching, evaluating. The army had come far, but they hadn't come far enough. They were still unblooded, and he worried at the first foe they would face. Would they hold when confronted by such a terrible enemy? Would they fight?

Three scouts thundered into the camp, catching Genka's attention. Travel-stained and worn, fatigue seemed to weigh them down. Fresh mud and dried dirt obscured their faces and forms. Same with their horses.

Genka watched as the scouts were confronted and shared words with the soldiers warding the camp. Their leader dismounted, flashed his papers and said something else before he was allowed forward. Genka realized the scout was heading his way. What news did he bring? It had to be about the wraiths.

The scout reached him and slapped a firm salute, which Genka returned. "What word, soldier?"

"My lord, we've contacted the enemy."

Genka took a settling breath. *It begins.*

"We count approximately four hundred of them."

By the barest margin, Genka prevented himself from rocking back in shock. A full twenty-five percent more than the last herd. How would they stop them? It was impossible. Even if Shima Sithe and Aurelian Crèche sent the entirety of their armies north, there would be no way to do so.

The Sunsets were doomed. His empire fallen. His myth stillborn.

"Four hundred wraiths?" Genka asked, knowing he'd heard right, but still needing confirmation.

"Yes, my lord. They're traveling in loose packs. Never slowing down. Not even to pillage."

"Where are they headed? Can you tell?" Genka asked, finally getting his mind working properly. Four hundred wraiths spelled oblivion to his army and maybe his people, but he wouldn't go gently into the dark. He'd fight the fuckers until the bitterest end.

The scout shook his head. "South and then west. That's their general direction. Nothing slows them down. Our weapons don't do nothing to them. Even the Immortals aren't having no luck. Weird thing, though. Sometimes they chase us, but usually they leave us be."

"South?" Genka mused. He gestured the man into the command

tent, shouting for his generals to join him. They'd arrive in minutes, but Genka had questions that he wanted answered now. He wouldn't wait. The others could learn what they needed afterward.

Inside, *diptha* lamps lit a tent that was far larger than those of the soldiers, but otherwise unremarkable and plain. A cot in the corner. A footlocker for his clothes. And a large map-and-chart-strewn table of the Sunsets. That was all.

Genka thumbed through the maps, finding the one he wanted. He slapped it to the forefront. "Show me where you contacted the wraiths."

The scout stepped to the table, leaning forward, frowning as he studied the map of the Sunsets. He tapped a place. "Here. Just south of Grain River. We paced them, day and night until we reached River Moon. They went west then, but I think that's so they could find a place to cross. Grain River was swollen with spring floods."

Genka stared at the map, measuring, gauging. "How long did it take for them to reach River Moon from the Grain?"

"Four days."

Genka stroked his chin in thought, staring at the map. "Four days to travel thirty miles? That's not nearly as fast as they can go." He glanced at the scout. "Was there a reason for their slow travel?"

"Not that we could tell. It's why the captain had us split off and report. In case the pigeons didn't reach you."

"You traveled from River Moon in what time?"

"A full week."

"You covered seven hundred miles in ten days?" Genka tried to keep the disbelief out of his voice.

The scout nodded. "We rode flat out. Changed horses every twenty miles at one of the forts. Barely stopped for sleep."

Genka grunted, pleased at getting the information so quickly. "We have to assume the wraiths will eventually pick up the pace." He continued to frown as he stared at the map. The headwaters of Grain River were three hundred miles north of the army's current position. His eyes flicked about, figuring on the most likely route the wraiths would take.

"We've had contact?" Vel Parnesth asked, standing at the entrance.

Genka straightened, facing his friend. "We have." He indicated the scout, pausing. He didn't know the man's name.

"Sergeant Palden," the scout supplied. "My commander is Captain Hailnit."

"The sergeant's unit contacted the enemy at River Moon." He went on to explain what he'd learned so far.

And by the time he finished, more officers had come hustling into the tent—generals, colonels, and their aides. All were quickly brought up to speed, and while they discussed and argued about what next to do, Genka pored over the map, wondering.

The wraiths had gone west instead of east along River Moon. Why? West was rougher terrain, a harder crossing. Ten miles east, and the river gentled. There was even a bridge a couple of leagues past it. By going west, they'd have to go fifteen miles before reaching a safe crossing.

He grimaced. Then again, these were wraiths, so maybe a hard river crossing wouldn't bother them so much. His eyes scanned the terrain. There was the capital, Devesth, if they continued southwest, but the city was walled. Even with all the physical abilities the wraiths possessed, that would be a nearly impossible nut for them to crack.

His eyes tracked… south of the capital. Traced a line, distantly noted the argument of the officers had quieted down. Genka hadn't even needed to say anything. His officers, the veterans and new ones alike, had noticed him studying the map. They knew to be quiet while he scanned for the likely avenues of attack that the wraiths might take. Of course, once he figured where he wanted to shift the army, the officers could then provide insight and help on getting them to that proper position. But until then, he needed quiet.

"We also saw something else, sir," Sergeant Palden said. "There were taller creatures in with the enemy. We counted roughly forty or fifty of them. Twice the height of a man, armored in black and red-eyed."

A wave of shocked gasps followed the sergeant's description. Everyone knew what he thought he had seen, and Genka viewed the scout in private alarm. *Rakshasas.* Could it be? He'd have to adjust his plans, but first he needed to know where the wraiths and this new foe intended on going.

He set aside his fear and stared anew at the map, the location of River Moon. Why west? It still had him bothered, like a piece of gristle between his teeth. The battle against the first herd had taught him that the wraiths weren't just ravenous monsters. They could think and plan. They had thought and planned, even in retreat after their leader had been killed.

West, though? He fingered the map, at the relief, measuring locations, distances. Roads and bridges…

His eyes widened. "Cord Valley. That's where the wraiths are headed."

Stipe, son of his mother, Chalice, and father to a pair of traitors—his son, Sriovey, and his daughter, Willa—strode with purpose down the hallway. Other dwarves scrambled to get out of his way. Which was as it should be. This section of Jade's Moon was the headquarters of the Baptisers, and a hustle of martial activity filled the corridors even as the warriors raced about to complete their work and stay out of Stipe's way.

He gave a satisfied nod as he passed by the unadorned walls. There were no murals or frescoes to ruin the clean lines of the stony corridors. *Good.* He'd always detested his people's artwork. So treacly. Nothing about the glory of battle in the defense of the sacred. Only scenes about gentle home life, wisdoms doing wisdom shit, or some stupid mountainscape with some dumbass happy tree.

In fact, the final murals had been covered over yesterday afternoon, and the smell of fresh paint still lingered. An odor that was a damn sight better than having to view those fucking bucolic paintings.

This section of Jade's Moon was a place for warriors, and warriors had no room in their hearts or homes for weak shit like art and music. In Stipe's view, the world was a rough place, and only rough men could bring it to heel. That couldn't happen if those rough men were constantly fighting the taming influence of women and their damnable soft arts.

And speaking of soft arts, there were no paintings of Shokan and his supposed creation of the dwarves either. That had been the first thing Stipe had removed when he'd taken over these hallways. While others in Surent might find images of the so-called Blessed One iconic and beautiful—they were everywhere in Surent Crèche—Stipe wanted nothing to do with them. Not in the heart of Baptiser power.

His men didn't worship Shokan. They didn't honor him either. In fact, just thinking about the Blessed One made Stipe's mouth want to curl into a snarl. That bastard, Shokan, hadn't created the dwarves. He'd destroyed the Ur-Fels.

Fucker. Who was he to have done that to Stipe's people? Leave them passive little bitches, unable to defend themselves?

Well, that time was over. Recovering their killers' hearts was what Stipe had always been about, ever since he'd joined Crèche Dawn and learned the truth about his people's past. Later on, he'd founded the Baptisers, and now he had a chance to make it real.

The transformative powers of the Orb of Eretria had been the key. Through careful study of the globe, of learning how similar it was to Mede's Orb, which could grant humans the powers of a woven, Stipe had discovered what was needed. He'd used the Orb to recreate his warriors into what they should have always been. A more powerful breed of killers, one with the strengths of both dwarven might and Ur-Fel speed.

But then the Orb had been stolen.

Stipe still cursed his lack of foresight at having the Orb protected. Cinder Shade and Anya Aruyen had come to Surent Crèche with some damn fool warning about a dark god or some stupid shit like that. Whining little bitches, afraid of their own shadows. *Shet. Zahhack.* Oh, those terrifying gods!

Fucking idiots. Disgusting, too. An elven princess fornicating with a human. Everyone knew it. Filthy assholes.

Stipe ground his teeth, furious at himself for what had come next because those bastards had managed to escape their prison. They'd made their way into Surent's most important vault and hied off with the Orb of Eretria, right out from underneath his fucking nose. And trying to reclaim it had only led to the death of nearly a score of his Baptisers.

Stipe paused momentarily in his stride, thinking about the battle. While he didn't respect Cinder and Anya as individuals, he did respect their fighting prowess. Especially Cinder's. The man was a Devesh-damned rakshasa when it came to fighting.

He shook off his angry thoughts. In the end, losing the Orb hadn't mattered. While it had been key to what Stipe wanted for his people, it wasn't instrumental. The information gained through studying the Orb had been far more valuable, learning the stresses and torture needed to induce the changes where a dwarf could shift to an Ur-Fel—a skill similar to what the unformed could do.

Which only made sense. Originally, the Ur-Fels had also been a kind of zahhack. Stipe's work was merely restoring what his people should have always been.

He pulled to a stop when a junior aide, Rulick Granthe, halted in front of him, throwing a hasty salute.

"I have what you need," Rulick said, grinning proudly.

Stipe blinked. The fuck was Rulick on about?

"The means to bring the wisdoms to heel," Rulick said. "You wanted me to find a way to break their power. I have it."

Stipe stared hard at Rulick, wanting him to know better than to waste his time. "Tell me."

"Wisdom Derilee is dying. Everyone knows that. Even better for us, the death of Wisdom Palav caused the others to shut down their stupid mewling."

"What about it? Before she ran away, Wisdom Simla was the only one who still spoke against me." And it still chafed his nuts how the little bitch had slipped out of Jade's Moon—her and a full quarter of the populace, a steady trickle that Stipe couldn't yet stop.

What use was it to have command over Jade's Moon if no one lived here? People were leaving the capital, heading to Surent's outlying districts. No doubt the fools thought they were safe from his rule out in the hinterland villages and towns, but soon enough, they'd learn the hard truth. Stipe intended on ruling all of Surent: every hallway, corridor, chamber, and pisspot. He'd reign over it all, like Shet did Naraka.

Rulick cleared his throat. "Dermit Corrend also speaks against you," he said in reply to Stipe's earlier words.

It was also a reminder that Stipe didn't need. He let Rulick see his displeasure, satisfied when the arrogant little shit went pale and pasty with fear and swallowed heavily.

Dermit Corrend was a boil Stipe couldn't yet lance. The man had a group of warriors, good fighters. Stipe couldn't yet take them on in a frontal assault. Doing so would bleed his men. The Baptisers would win but not without a grim cost. Enough for the fucking wisdoms to rally their people from Surent's peripheral towns and cities and put Stipe's people under their thumb once more.

"You said you had a way to break the power of the wisdoms," Stipe said. "What is it?"

"They're waiting in your office. It wasn't easy getting them into Surent, but I managed."

"Them?" Stipe didn't like the sound of that. Marching swiftly, he brushed past Rulick. His office was only a few corridors away. There was a cluster of dwarven warriors, tense and alert, standing close by. A whole bunch of them, with more hustling in to join them by the second.

What the fuck had Rulick done? He shot the junior aide a furious glance, not caring this time when the little fucker wilted.

Bearain Waleg, his senior aide, moved to intercept. The man looked upset, which caused a pit of worry to open up in Stipe's gut.

"What's happening?" Stipe demanded.

"We're in trouble, is what's happening," Bearain said. He gestured to Rulick, who was cowering now like a beaten dog. "The stupid shit let them in, and there won't be an easy way to keep this under control."

"Let who in?" Stipe asked, fear clutching his guts like a spiderkin.

"Better if you saw," Bearain said.

Stipe snarled. Why the fuck wouldn't anyone answer his questions? He pushed past Bearain and the line of warriors, all of them armored and with their axes and war hammers in hand. He shoved open the door to his offices, only surprised in the slightest at the sight that confronted him.

Standing in the middle of his quarters was a quartet of necrosed. Massive, deformed, powerful, and smelling of rot. They loomed. One of them was gnawing on a gangrenous limb. Based on the size and shape, it was likely that of a dwarf.

Rulick, you dumb fucker.

"Ah," the limb-eating necrosed said. "You're here. Then I won't have to repeat myself." His voice was the grating of bones, and he gestured with the limb. "Shet has agreed to ally with you." He grinned, bloody meat clinging to his teeth. "But you need to understand your place. You will serve, or you will be served like this one."

He gestured, and another necrosed flung a corpse at Stipe. Staring sightlessly at him were the vacant eyes of Wisdom Derilee.

The pit in Stipe's gut became a yawning hole. Nausea threatened to see him lose his breakfast, and he struggled to hold down his gorge. As much as he had detested Derilee, she hadn't deserved to meet her end in such a despicable fashion.

"We killed her in her chambers," the apparent leader of the necrosed said. "Understand what this means."

Stipe nodded, not needing it spelled out for him. His people were fucked.

The winter sun shone wan and weak through a pale blue sky empty of clouds. The late afternoon light glinted, blindingly reflective on snowfall that crested the ragged peaks of the Dagger Mountains. An icy wind moaned through the evergreen trees surrounding a bare hollow where the Shokans trained alongside the four redeemers—the once-wraiths—all of them seeking to improve themselves as warriors.

Estin stepped away, moving to a slope where he dropped heavily to the ground, needing a break. He groaned, muscles tired, lungs heaving, and heart thumping. Conducting *Jivatma* took everything out of him. It was so much harder than sourcing *lorethasra*. But if he wanted to become the best version of himself, he had to master its use.

He sighed. And even then, he'd still be far weaker than a human, a truth made apparent when Bones, Ishmay, Depth, and the others had learned to conduct *Jivatma* and source *lorethasra*. It was also a truth that Estin had never expected to face. Ever since the *NusraelShev*, humans had been the weakest of all races, easily defeated in one-on-one combat.

That was no longer the case.

By learning to conduct and source, the humans of the Shokans had become powerful. They were now faster and stronger than the elves—likely the dwarves as well—and able to cut through any weaves or braids with surpassing ease.

Estin sipped water from his canteen, watching as three of his brother humans—Bones, Ishmay, and Wark—sparred against a redeemer. The match was proving a close contest, which was a massive improvement compared to when the Shokans had first journeyed to this part of the Daggers.

Back then, it had required every one of them to defeat a single redeemer. Even now, it took a minimum of four elves to accomplish the feat, but for the humans, they only needed three.

Bones, Ishmay, and Depth eventually defeated the redeemer, and as soon as it was finished, Fastness bugled a halt to the contest. The stallion—the mythical Sapient Dormant and their instructor—called out advice, pointing out mistakes and lost opportunities. He spoke to Bones, the best of them; Ishmay, who wasn't far behind; and Depth, who'd come the farthest. All three men accepted their instruction, nodding respectfully before departing the sparring square.

Then a new set of contestants were called forward, and it began again. Others faced off as well, and there was a frenetic pace to all their engagements. It was swift, certainly, and seemingly wild, but it was also far from it.

There was control amidst the mess, something Fastness demanded. In his view, the Shokans were expected to train like they would eventually fight: with focused determination and self-control. Only fools fought with hotheaded abandonment. Sure, it might give them a brief moment of heightened strength and speed—a sense of invulnerability—but in the end, such warriors were easy meat for a skilled warrior.

Estin continued to sip water, waiting to recover as he watched his brothers. He wanted to get back down there and train. He couldn't afford to sit out for too long. None of them could. They'd be called into battle soon. All of them knew it. Anya and Cinder would soon need their help against the herd of wraiths that threatened to destroy the Sunset Kingdoms.

And Estin was determined to be ready when that call came.

Riyne dropped down next to him, breathing hard, and Estin studied his fellow elf. They had once been the best of the Shokans, but that time was long past. Estin wondered if Riyne felt the embarrassment of their diminished status the same way he did.

He had to. They shared much in their outlook on life, and it wasn't simply because Riyne was also a noble elf—Mohal was one, too. Rather it was because the two of them had been close since childhood, weighed down by expectations that neither had been sure they could manage.

For Riyne, it had been living up to the legend of his family name and their warrior heritage, especially as exemplified by his older brother, Lisandre. For Estin, it had been the presumptions of what it meant to be a prince of the blood.

And yet, here they were, members of a brotherhood that had already earned acclaim throughout Rakesh. The Shokans, a scouting unit that even the elven warriors of Yaksha Sithe spoke about in a reverent hush. And it was because they were members of the Shokans that Estin and Riyne had accomplished more than their younger selves, stupid and cocksure, had ever expected; namely, able to claim the friendship and respect of the Blessed Ones Reborn.

But were he, Riyne, and Mohal truly worthy to be part of the Shokans? Given who the humans were becoming—restored to the power of their *asrasin* ancestors? Of this, Estin was less sure, but it also wasn't his decision to make. That judgment was in Cinder's hands.

"When do you think they'll come for us?" Riyne asked, interrupting his reflections.

"I'm not sure," Estin replied. "But it's probably soon. They said that it would take them a couple months to get to the Sunsets, and..." He shrugged, not needing to spell it out. It had been over two months since Anya and Cinder had come for Jozep and Sriovey, which meant they were likely in the Sunsets by now.

Riyne grunted. "You think we're ready?"

It was a question a younger Riyne would have never voiced. The idea of being unprepared would have been as foreign to him as the possibility of the sun rising in the west. However, hard teachings had burst Riyne's bubble of surety, just as it had done for Estin's arrogance.

Which in hindsight was a good thing. In the not-too-distant future, the Shokans would have to battle all manner of fiends: a herd of wraiths, armies of evil, Shet and his Titans, and possibly even some greater horror named the Son of Emptiness.

"I'm not sure," Estin said in response to Riyne's question. "But we've done all we can. We've trained harder than we ever have, even at the Directorate. We've become finer warriors than I think either of us could have ever imagined becoming." He rose to his feet, holding out a hand to draw his friend upright as well. "So if we aren't ready, it won't be because we didn't give it our all."

Riyne grinned. "That sounds like something Cinder might say."

Estin feigned a shudder. "Anything but that. No one should be so unabashedly good and upstanding. So giving and forgiving. So—"

Riyne's grin widened. "I think you're just jealous of our brother."

Estin halted his pretend diatribe. Was Cinder still their brother? The question had him blink in doubt.

Yes, Cinder was Shokan, no matter what the man might think about the matter. Yes, he was also likely Estin's brother-in-law, anciently wed to Anya, who was also Sira. And yes, Estin had the utmost respect and veneration for Shokan. But was *Cinder* still a brother to the Shokans? To him? Had he ever been Cinder's brother?

Estin wasn't sure, and he frowned at the lack of clarity.

Riyne clapped him on the shoulder. "He's your brother as much as mine," he said, figuring on Estin's discontent. "Never doubt it. Now, come on. Let's go kick some ass. I'm tired of losing to the humans."

Estin grinned, setting aside his doubts and unease. "That's the best idea I've heard all day."

46

The night sky might hold an uncountable number of shining stars and the brilliance of two moons, white Dormant and golden Fulsom, but such heavenly lights would only be visible if the curtain of ragged, scudding clouds broke apart. And that seemed unlikely. Rain threatened, the smell of moisture in the air evident on a breeze that blustered.

But despite the inclement weather, the tidy and well-planned streets of Titan's Reach were alive, lit as they were by *diptha* lamps that shed golden light from tall posts. The smell of fresh-baked goods and meat on the grill drifted on the air, coming from Wanderer's Respite, Salt's old inn and tavern. Farmers and craftsfolk walked about, visiting with their neighbors, laughing, carefree and happy, calling out to Mael with a hearty cheer.

He feigned a smile, waving to them. Inside, though, he seethed. The glory of Titan's Reach was being steadily eroded. His people's faith in Shet was dying away as swiftly as flowers washed away in a spring flood. And Mael couldn't figure on how to stem the tide.

Just then, a stiff gust tugged at his clothing, rippled through his thinning hair, but he refused to give way to the wind. He leaned into the breeze, not wanting to be late for this meeting. It might be his last, best opportunity to save his people. If his voice wasn't heard tonight, he'd have to resort to other means. But what that might be, he couldn't yet reckon…

Which was absolutely infuriating.

Following his meeting with the dwarves of Surent Crèche—the Ur-Fel kind—and making his people aware of their presence along with Shet's rising, Mael had felt sure that his path forward would be straight and unencumbered. The Shetawarin would ally with the Ur-Fels, travel to their crèche, and from there go to Naraka, where they would serve their god.

Everything had been going well. The promise of prophecy seemed ready to be made manifest, and his people's future secure.

But then had come the new dwarves, Willa Kalenth, Derius Lawin, and Simla Carrend. Two women and one man, and from them had emanated a calm unlike anything anyone in Titan's Reach had ever experienced. It was a tranquility that inspired a person to set aside the sword and take up the plow and peace. Many had been seduced by that promise, including the majority of those who had been given a Titan's name.

Worse, Mael had been unable to harm the dwarves. Three wraiths protected them. Three wraiths, who claimed to have broken with their Master, something called the Hungering Heart. They stood guard around the dwarves, and their words carried a great deal of weight. Everyone knew that wraiths were humans who had been transformed into monsters of boundless hunger. And yet these wraiths didn't hunger.

Other than their strange eyes, which seemed to be covered in a film of white, they were utterly normal. More powerful than any Shetawarin, too. A simple demonstration from their meekest-appearing member, Selin Heron, had demonstrated that the legend of the wraiths wasn't an exaggeration. Selin had handily defeated two of the best warriors from Titan's Reach as swiftly as Rukh had beaten Jury Mast.

And his demonstration had left a mark. For the Shetawarin, power-ful humans carried great influence, and the wraiths, with their teach-ings and views on *Jivatma,* Devesh, Shokan the Traitor, and Sira the Whore, threatened to shatter all that was right and holy.

The wraiths had even claimed that Rukh Shektan, the degenerate who fornicated with an elf, was actually Shokan himself, and that the elf was Sira, their coming promised in the *Lor Agni,* a book of heresy. And despite Mael's best efforts, too many were heeding the wraiths… all because of the dwarves and their damnable ability to calm a per-son's thoughts.

How could he rouse his people to righteous anger if they answered the possibility of extinction with a slouching disregard?

It was impossible. Rukh claiming to be Shokan was impossible. The elf as Sira— Well, maybe she was Sira. After all, she was beautiful and whorish enough to be the great temptress.

Mael briefly wondered what had become of the two of them. Hopefully, a slow, painful death because ever since their intrusion into Titan's Reach, life in the village had never been the same—Jury and his warriors killed while chasing Rukh and his elven lover. Salt, corrupted by Jozep, the dwarf who had accompanied Rukh and Jessira to Titan's Reach. And now, these new dwarves, whose mere presence had utterly shifted the attitude and thinking of his people.

He had to stop them, defeat them somehow.

Such were his thoughts as he took a left-hand turn, cutting through an empty alley. From there, he reached a quiet lane where the sounds and smells of Titan's Reach grew distant. There was no one else about.

"Where are you headed to in such a rush?" Reuelus Midth asked.

Mael jumped in the air, nearly shitting himself. Where the hell had that old man come from?

Reuelus chuckled, puffing on his pipe even while Mael grimaced.

"None of your business," Mael said in reply to Reuelus' question and doing his best at holding off from taking his staff and beating the other man over the head.

"You should tell me," Reuelus persisted.

Mael sighed. The old man was a wen on his arse, always regaling the idiots in the community with his stupid stories about rings and wee folk. Childish prick. But not answering him would only have the old fool following him. "I'm headed for an important meeting."

"An important meeting, you say?" Reuelus said, pretending to sound impressed. "You wouldn't mean that important meeting with Lull, Renter, Darim, and Jury." He meant the other Forebears, the leaders of their village, the ones with the names of Titans.

Mael pulled up short. "How do you know about that meeting?"

Reuelus laughed. "Have a good meeting," he said, heading down the alley Mael had recently exited.

Staring at the old man for a little longer, Mael eventually shook his head and shortly made it to the council's cottage. He halted outside the door, eavesdropping before entering.

"What are we to be?" asked Darim, an elder in name only. She'd barely reached her ninth decade of life.

Mael's heart dropped when he heard a familiar voice reply.

It was Residar. "You've always wanted to be missionaries. You shall be such. It's as Fastness told me. When the time is right, Mahadev will be restored. Same with the Savage Kingdoms, which were once called the BrightLands."

No, no, no. That wasn't what the Shetawarin should do. They needed to go to Naraka.

"And once we're there?" Darim asked.

Although he couldn't see him, Mael sensed a smile from Residar. "Then you will open your Chakras and become true humans."

"How?" Darim asked.

Mael had heard enough. He barged inside.

And promptly dropped his staff. He tried his best to hold on to his rage, succeeded some, but when three pairs of dwarven eyes met his own, he knew his hopes for tonight's meeting were dead.

"Come and sit down," Simla said. She patted a place next to her. "We've never had a chance to talk."

Mael swallowed down a bolus of fear. He wanted to do nothing of the sort, but of their own accord, his feet seemed to carry him to the dwarf. He sat, his anger simmering but not all-consuming. With every breath he took, it drifted out of him, slowly leaving a sense of completion behind.

He'd never allowed himself to be in such close proximity to the dwarves. The serenity soothed his worries, and when he looked in Simla's face, all he saw was caring and compassion.

She patted his hand. "This isn't easy for you, and I'm truly sorry. But open your heart, and it will be so much better."

Aia rose to her feet, paused to stretch out her forelegs, leaned forward to limber her hindquarters. A hard shake with her wings outspread was followed by a yawn. Then she felt ready to face the day. A sense of relief filled her at executing the simple set of movements because when she'd first awoken, even shifting her wings had taken dedicated concentration and effort.

Thankfully, that was no longer the case. Aia's strength and stamina had steadily returned, but she remained lesser than she had once been, lesser than she expected of herself. She had to be able to fight Shet and his Titans, something she wasn't yet capable of doing. It would be weeks before she actually was.

Then she could finally go seek Rukh. She had sensed his presence several times now, and that sensation had grown stronger with each occasion. He was traveling west, in her general direction, but well north of her current location. She cocked her head, eyes closed, searching for him. Sometimes she could feel him when she least expected it.

A long stretch of seconds followed before she grimaced in frustration. Where was he? And where was Shon? She had also sensed her brother a couple of times, dim and distant, like he was far away or asleep.

Shaking off her ruminations, Aia padded to the cave's entrance and peered out at the dawning day.

The early morning sky was pink and orange, accented with a few clouds, while the sun highlighted the ocean that smashed against the heavy stones of her island home. Spray splashed high, nearly reaching her cave, and rainbows glistened, rising up the cliff face. The clean tang of the salty waters filled the air, and Aia inhaled deep, appreciating the pleasing smell. Only Rukh's scent, that of Jessira—his mate—and the humid redolence of the savanna were better.

She sighed, missing Rukh and Jessira and looking forward to seeing them soon.

Then again, any view might be better than what currently filled her vision: the wide red-and-brown escarpment and barren terrain of the Coalescent Desert. Breezes shifted the dunes, trickling the sands, but in the far distance, well past where her once-Kesarin eyes could have seen, there stood an oasis. It was a narrow island of life that would soon be overtaken by a sandstorm.

Shifting her attention downward, Aia spied large fishes swimming about. She never bothered learning their names since all that mattered to her was that they tasted good, and that they would make a good breakfast.

Another yawn, and Aia launched herself off the ledge fronting her cave. Snapping open her wings, she glided, carried on the rising currents of wind. Her tail automatically compressed its long length and soft flaps expanded out from the sides. It made her tail wider, which gave her additional lift and control.

A twist and shift, and Aia swept left. Her eyes locked on the fishes below. She'd need a number to fill her appetite. Either that or a large shark. She didn't favor their taste, but she also didn't care to hunt for too long. Better to kill one beast and rest and recover afterward then wing about for hours on end in order to sate her hunger.

Aia continued to circle on the thermals, seeking likely prey. A trio of dolphins launched through the air, swimming swiftly, but not swiftly enough. Aia could have easily overtaken and killed them, but she also couldn't see herself eating a dolphin. Mostly because they always looked like they were smiling.

And what kind of monster ate an animal that seemed so friendly?

Looking more closely, Aia spied the reason for the dolphins rapid swimming and leaping out of the water.

She smiled. A shark. A big one with a strange head like a hammer. *Perfect.*

Aia tucked her wings, descending like a bolt, tail additionally shortening. Her shadow passed over the water, over the dolphins. The shark had no idea what was coming. She snapped open her wings, tail flaps widening more.

She plunged into the ocean, claws snagging the shark. Heavy thrusts of her wings, and she heaved out of the water. The shark struggled, but she killed it with a quick squeeze of her claws. Aia swept her wings harder, rising higher. The wind helped, but not enough, and she continued to struggle at gaining altitude. But it wasn't anything she couldn't handle.

Finally, she caught a thermal and relaxed, wings fully open, gliding, circling as she rested from the hard climb. Her racing heart slowed, and she angled back to her cave. She'd eat the shark, rest some, and maybe go seek more prey later on.

Hunting the shark hadn't taken much effort, and killing another meal today could help shorten her recovery even more. Shorten the time to when she finally got to see Rukh again. He was somewhere northwest, a few days' flight, and as soon as she had the strength, she'd go see him.

47

Anya reined Barton to a halt at the lip of a shallow rise. Below them nestled a small hamlet, lit in preparation for the evening to come, although dusk had yet to settle upon the land. Streamers of smoke drifted from chimneys, and a mild wind carried the smells of the suppers cooking by the villagers below, intermingling it with the loamy richness of the surrounding farmlands.

She ran fingers through her unbound hair and breathed out in satisfaction, happy to have reached their destination. Barton whickered, sounding like he was in agreement, and she patted his shoulder in fondness. She was glad to have him with her. She'd missed him plenty during the trek through the Webbed Kingdom.

"Is this it? Querel?" asked General Spalinkar, who rode at her side.

"It is," she said, turning to face the general and behind them, the dusty, tired elves of the Ninth Legion.

Once Empress Aqueem had agreed to aid Genka, the Ninth—a mix of cavalry, infantry, and dedicated archers—had been swiftly outfitted and pushed to reach the Sunsets as quickly as possible. A five-week journey had been cut to three, but they'd have a chance to at least catch their breaths here.

This was the village of Querel, the place where Cinder said Jeet and Stren could be found. He wanted to re-engage with the *hashains* and find out for sure what they had been doing. Once she learned, she—

Anya abruptly straightened when she saw a huge form exit one of the homes.

"What is that?" General Spalinkar asked, having seen the figure as well.

Anya didn't answer at once. Instead, she formed a quick weave— one Sira used regularly—and was able to see the figure as clearly as if she were using a spyglass.

A vaguely familiar troll and five smaller figures. Two were holders; one was an older woman, hunched and limping. But the final two… Anya narrowed her eyes. Unlike the holders and the woman, they had Cinder's coloring, height, and similar features. Those must be the *hashains*. Cinder had said they had joined a troll. They trod at the front of the group, holding staves matched to their heights.

"See to your men," Anya instructed the general, who had a spyglass to an eye. "I'll talk to the troll."

"You don't want an escort?"

He appeared concerned, but Anya shook her head. A troll was of the same trustworthy nature as a yakshin. She had nothing to fear from one. She could say the same about the holders. About Jeet and Stren, however… Cinder was certain the two *hashains* had reached a turning point in their lives. They were no longer the assassins he had met in Swift Sword.

But could she trust them? Of that, she wasn't entirely sure, nor was she particularly concerned. Even if Cinder was wrong, they posed no risk to her. She explained as much to the general, adding a final reason. "We also don't want to frighten the villagers with a large escort of armed elves marching on their town."

The general wore a conflicted expression. "Allow me to at least send five warriors to accompany you. Surely, that won't spark the fear of these villagers."

Anya considered his request, nodding agreement in the end. "See to it."

The general turned his horse about and began barking commands. Five riders broke away, surging forward, and once she'd been introduced to them and they'd been given their orders, Anya heeled Barton forward.

"Just a little farther," she said to the gelding, who snorted in reply.

Easing her way down the rise, she let go of the braid that brought the trolls and those with him in sharp relief, not needing it any longer. And despite her words about trolls and not needing to fear anything from them or those with them, nonetheless, she wove a Shield powered by *Jivatma*, which was far sturdier than one created through *lorethasra*.

And at a distance of twenty yards from the other party, she drew to a halt and braided another weave. This one projected her voice. "My name is Anya Aruyen. I seek two *hashains*, Jeet Condune and Stren Coldire."

It was the troll who shouted an answer. "Your name is known to me. I am Maize Broad. You may approach closer."

Maize Broad. The name sparked a recollection.

Anya nudged Barton forward, her escorts wrapped on either side, even as she delved her memories. Cinder had first run across the troll at the Third Directorate, and then they'd briefly met Maize at Surent Crèche. The troll certainly traveled around a lot.

Currently, he was gesturing to the side, indicating the two Anya had guessed to be the *hashains*. "These are Jeet and Stren. What is your purpose in seeking them out?"

Jeet spoke before she could reply. "She comes on behalf of the *Zuthrum lon Varshin*."

The old woman seemed to stiffen in either shock or alarm, and Anya spoke quickly, wanting to soothe her worry. "I'm not here to hurt Jeet or Stren," Anya assured the old woman and the others. "Cinder Shade, the *Zuthrum lon Varshin*, asked me to meet with the *hashains*, and learn how they are doing."

The old woman relaxed, and Maize smiled, speaking. "They are no longer *hashains.*"

Before Anya could process the information, Jeet and Stren stepped forward, setting aside their staves, and prostrated themselves. "Sira, Lady of Fire," they intoned as one. "How may we serve you?"

Several of the elves in her escort inhaled sharply, and she caught all of them staring at her in disbelief. Apparently, her claim of being Sira hadn't been as fully accepted as she had hoped. Maybe Jeet and Stren's unexpected reaction would change that perception, especially because it was probably true.

"You are truly she?" one of her elven escorts asked, his tone hopeful. "The Lady of Fire?"

"So it seems," Anya said, smiling his way.

The elf's mien grew slack, awe and reverence filling his features. The rest of the escort had a similar reaction.

Anya hid a sigh, disturbed by their veneration. In this, she was very much like Sira, who had hated the near worship by which the ancient *asrasins* had held her and Shokan.

Maize spoke. "As you can see, Jeet and Stren are doing well, but what your eyes can't tell you is how far they've come. They are my disciples, agreeing to follow the path of peace."

Anya quirked a brow in surprise. Cinder had mentioned that the *hashains* had changed their outlook on life, but until hearing it from Maize, she hadn't been sure what that actually entailed. Regardless, the change in Jeet and Stren had only occurred because Cinder had shown compassion to his enemies. Rather than kill them, he had given them an opportunity to become better versions of themselves.

"That is wonderful to hear," Anya said, realizing she'd been staring at the small group. She also realized Jeet and Stren remained prostrate. "Have them rise."

A disturbance on the far side of the village captured her attention. Once again, Anya formed the spyglass braid, frowning as riders came into view. Her eyes widened a moment later. There were sixty or so of them—warriors—and they were making their way toward the village from the direction roughly opposite of the Ninth. Worse, they shared many of the same features as Jeet and Stren.

Hashains.

Anya twisted about to address her escort. "Get back to the general. Tell him to ride for the village and prepare for battle." Next, she withdrew her *divaspana*. Cinder needed to know of this. He was supposed to have joined her here anyway. She spoke to him, telling him of the situation.

"I'll be there right away," he said. "I can bring the dwarven unit later on."

"No need to rush," Anya said. "I have the Ninth backing me up. We can handle the *hashains*. Come whenever you're ready." She faced the *hashains* again. What were the odds the two groups would arrive at Querel at the same time?

The question must have been obvious because Maize chuckled. "We were staying in Querel until we found out about those *hashains* coming to kill us. Then we fled. They gave chase, but once we discovered your elven army and the direction it was headed, we returned to Querel and decided to wait for both of you here." He grinned. "Thankfully, you arrived first."

"You drew the *hashains* back to Querel," Anya said. "Knowing we could protect you if you needed it."

Maize nodded. "A good enough plan."

It was a good enough plan, but still... Anya observed the *hashains*. They had yet to advance, likely having seen the Ninth on the other side of Querel. She only hoped the assassins would stay where they were, at least until General Spalinkar got a contingent of his warriors closer to her position.

"Perhaps we should retreat," one of her escorts suggested.

"We will if we have to," Anya said. "Right now we're far enough away that they can't threaten us. Let's see how this plays out." She glanced to Jeet. "They're here for you?"

He nodded. "For me and Stren. They've been searching for us ever since we brought word of the *Zuthrum lon Varshin's* emergence. We were declared apostates for what we witnessed. We should have been put to death, but some of our former brothers retain some shred of their honor. They left open the doors to our cells and gave us an opportunity to escape."

Anya considered his explanation. It had been nearly three years since Jeet and Stren had returned to the Sunsets, and in all that time, the legendary *hashains* had never managed to figure out where they had gone to ground? It didn't make sense. Either they were monumentally incompetent, or the erstwhile *hashains* still had friends in the brotherhood.

Jeet's sister, the older-appearing woman, spoke. "The emperor's soldiers came through here, too. They had no trouble figuring out where Jeet and Stren had gone away to hide."

"But not the *hashains*?" Anya asked. "Strange, don't you think?"

Jeet shrugged. "Ever since Maize found us, we've been traveling. Never staying in one place for more than a week. We've covered the width and breadth of the Sunsets."

"Maize found you?" She set her sight on the troll. "How?"

"I am a troll. It is in my nature to find that which is interesting. And something linked to Maynalor, to Cinder Shade, is bound to be interesting."

Anya grunted. It still didn't make sense. Even with the traveling, the *hashains* should have easily been able to run down Jeet and Stren.

"I know what you're thinking, and you're probably right," Jeet said. "We had help. We've discussed it. My former brothers should have found and killed us a long time ago. The fact that they didn't tells me it was intentional."

"Then why chase after you now?" Anya asked. "What's changed?"

No one had an answer.

Anya returned her focus to the *hashains*, who continued milling about on the distant knoll, staring at their small group. She stared right back. There was an older *hashain* giving out orders—their commander, then. She described him to Jeet and Stren. "Wrinkles all over. Bald, except for a fringe of white hair, like a tonsure. Stooped posture. Scar on his right cheek."

Jeet grimaced. "Mahav Benk Roon."

"Mahav? That's his title?" Anya asked.

"It is," Jeet answered. "He is a member of the Council of Sabala, one of those who said I lied about Cinder."

"Politicians," Stren added with a sneer.

Anya glanced backward upon hearing a commotion. The Ninth was on the march and would arrive in a few moments. She faced forward again, noticed the mahav calling out more orders. She found herself wishing she had a weave that could bring the *hashain's* words to her. Sira had known one, but it was currently beyond Anya's skill with *lorethasra.*

She frowned when she noticed the *hashains* edging forward—all of them. But by then, the Ninth had nearly arrived. The entire legion, over five thousand elven warriors, and this was without the drovers and support personnel. What were the *hashains* planning?

"They aren't thinking of attacking, are they?" Stren asked.

"Not unless *hashains* are suicidal." Anya looked to Jeet, addressing him. "They aren't, are they?"

He shrugged. "They can be if that's what the mission requires."

It wasn't what Anya had hoped to hear. She had no desire to kill the *hashains.* But what if they came back when the Ninth left? What would they do to the villagers after she left? Even if she took Jeet and Stren with her?

General Spalinkar arrived then, along with a large force of cavalry. The rest of the Ninth set a perimeter, blocking any advancement from the *hashains.*

"Should we kill them once they're within range of our archers?" General Spalinkar asked. "Or should we ride them down with a straight charge?"

Before replying, Anya momentarily closed her eyes, breathing out her annoyance. As always, her people's inability to plan when it came to combat reared its ugly head. They had a massively superior force. They could destroy the *hashains* whenever they wished. But more importantly, they needed information, and corpses couldn't be interrogated.

"No," Anya said. "Maintain the perimeter. Have everyone weave a Shield. Three lines of infantry. Archers directly behind them. Two wings of cavalry to the sides."

The general slammed a fist to his heart. "As you will, Your Highness."

A member of her escort indicated Jeet and Stren. "Those two called her the Lady of Fire, and the troll never denied it," he said to the general.

His words sparked shocked murmurs that spread outward like a wave, and once again, Anya stifled a disheartened sigh. While having the elves follow her lead without question—and they would certainly do so if they thought her to be Sira—would be useful, she hated the worshipful gazes she already sighted on those near at hand, especially from General Spalinkar, who, until now, had treated her with professional courtesy.

"Is this true?" the general asked, wide-eyed hope dawning on his face.

"It is," Anya replied, staring straight ahead. The *hashains* had halted just out of range of the elven archers. "But let's take care of business first, and then I can answer any of your questions." She held up a hand when the general appeared on the verge of speaking. "I need to hear what's being said."

This time, the *hashains* were close enough for her to cast a crude form of the weave that brought the words of the mahav to her. He wanted to talk to Jeet and Stren. Something about the *Medeian Scryings*, the Grimyogi, and prophecy. The *hashain* commander also wanted to know what the Ninth was doing on Sunset soil.

Anya narrowed her eyes. There was more going on here than the *hashains* merely wanting to talk to Jeet and Stren. They'd come here for a different reason.

She addressed the general. "Let your men allow Mahav Benk and one other through the lines. I want to talk to them. They're to come on foot. No weapons. Those are the rules if they want to speak to Jeet and Stren."

It took several minutes before the mahav accepted Anya's dictates. He and another *hashain* marched, all pride and poise through the elven lines, graceful in their own way.

Anya waited on them, Barton stirring, likely sensing the air of potential violence.

The men of the Ninth continued to open their lines for the two *hashains*, but Anya called the assassins to a halt when Benk and his aide were twenty feet distant. "That's close enough. What is your purpose here?"

The mahav flicked her a dismissive gaze before offering a shallow bow to General Spalinkar, calling him out by name. "I know your kind are ruled by women, but I wasn't aware that such control extended to what is a man's prerogative. The world of war."

Anya smirked at his words, not bothering to respond. Let the general handle matters for now.

"You have me at a disadvantage," General Spalinkar said. "Who are you?"

The *hashain* introduced himself and his aide.

"And your purpose?" the general asked.

"Those two"—Benk indicated Jeet and Stren—"were declared apostates by the Council of Sabala, but they also spoke the truth. The Grimyogi is arisen." He glanced to Maize. "Others tracked their movements through the Sunsets, documenting what they preached—the peace and equality to be brought forth by the Grimyogi. But in this, Jeet and Stren erred. The Grimyogi is a warrior without equal, peerless, unforgiving, and a firm taskmaster. We came to speak with them about their heresy."

Anya did her best not to roll her eyes at the blather.

"What we preach is truth," Stren declared, voice confident.

"So, you may think, child. But Chapterhouse believes otherwise."

"You say that you believe the Grimyogi is risen," Jeet said. "What about the rest of Chapterhouse?"

Mahav Benk shrugged. "Their beliefs are not the same as ours. We have broken with them."

Which meant he no longer thought of Jeet and Stren as apostates? Anya wasn't sure, and theology wasn't important now anyway. "Why didn't you withdraw when you saw our forces?" she asked.

Benk viewed her in obvious distaste. "You are?"

"The wife of the Grimyogi," Anya said, finding an emotional resonance to the words even as she spoke them.

Her *divaspana* warmed. Cinder wanted to talk. She withdrew the device from her *null pocket.*

Cinder offered terse words. "I'm coming."

48

Mahav Benk patted the dagger hidden under his clothing. He'd been told to disarm, and while he missed the comforting weight of his sword, there was no chance he'd ever be completely without a weapon of some kind. He spied those close at hand, preparing how he might fight his way free of the elves if that became necessary. He would—

His plans cut off when a black line spun on its axis, opening a portal into a world of rainbows. The frenzied hues gained shape, forming a bridge, and upon it strode a man with the bearing of a warrior.

Benk stiffened, eyes wide as he realized what he was seeing. It was a mythical means of travel, an anchor line. And based on the surprised exclamations of the elves and even the troll, they were just as stunned as he. Benk's gaze shot to the woman, noticing her lack of reaction. She had known of the anchor line, expected it.

Who was she?

Benk didn't know, and he certainly didn't accept her claim of being the wife of the Grimyogi. Not even an elf as pleasing to the eye as this one was acceptable. Of greater import was the fact that she lacked the finer qualities expected in the Grimyogi's bride. There was no modesty in her bearing—far too much pride in the way she sat atop her Yavana gelding—and she dared to speak to men as if she were their equal.

And while it was true that the Grimyogi's prior mate had been a warrior, that had been a special case. In her next incarnation, his wife was meant to convey the very height of feminine modesty, of humble comportment, and quick to see to the needs of her husband and his children.

Those were the thoughts racing across Benk's mind even as the elven army shifted away when the man stepped through the doorway. They drifted farther when a number of dwarves—clearly warriors— followed on the man's heels. One hundred… two… The elves continued to give ground as four hundred dwarves eventually exited the doorway before it closed.

Benk briefly studied them before arresting his attention again on the man. The way he moved through the dwarves… it was like a king moving through his subjects, an orca swimming the deep. The lord of all he surveyed. All knew it and bent before his power.

"Am I late?" the man asked, addressing the woman before glancing around. "I take it this is the Ninth and their commander, General Spalinkar."

"Lord Shokan." The general had slid off his horse, bowing low, head parallel with the ground. Many of the elves did so as well.

Only then did Benk realize that Jeet and Stren had prostrated themselves. "*Zuthrum lon Varshin.* What service do you require?" they asked in a worshipful tone.

Shock followed shock—that title. Lord Shokan. *Zuthrum lon Varshin.* They were the Grimyogi's proper name and another of his titles.

Benk realized in whose presence he stood and terror gripped him. He collapsed to his knees, face pressed to the dirt. His aide, Lood Vion, did so as well. Neither spoke. The Grimyogi hadn't given them leave to do so.

"So this is how it will go," the Grimyogi said, exhaling heavily.

"Everyone stand up and tell me what's going on."

Benk risked a glance, noticing Jeet and Stren had risen to their feet. The elves had unbent themselves, too. Only the woman hadn't bowed before the Grimyogi. Instead, she strode to his side, a smile on her well-formed face.

Benk nudged Lood, and together they stood, dusting off their clothing.

"You're right on time," the woman declared. "I think you know Maize and his holders. Jeet and Stren." She indicated Benk and Lood. "And these two are *hashains*. There are another fifty-eight of them on that hill. We were just getting to know each other."

Sweat beaded on Benk's brow, and he had to lock his knees from shaking when the Grimyogi turned his attention on him.

"You wanted to talk to Jeet and Stren about me? About my purpose here?" the Grimyogi asked.

Benk girded his courage. He was about to converse with the Grimyogi. A monumental occasion. "That is correct."

"Fair enough," the Grimyogi said. "Send for your men. All of them. I don't plan on explaining what I have to say twice."

"Let them through," the woman ordered.

The line of elves and dwarves widened, allowing Benk and Lood to exit back to their men. The mahav shouted orders when he arrived amongst the brothers, and minutes later, they were returned to the Grimyogi, all five sects of *hashains* grouped behind him, none of them obviously armed.

Benk initially listened with rapt attention when the Grimyogi began speaking of his mission to the Sunsets, his desire to save them from the herd of wraiths. And Benk had no doubt that the Grimyogi would accomplish it. He was, after all, the greatest of all warriors; the one against whom all others were measured.

But then the Grimyogi began speaking about his highest philosophies, such as fraternity with all people, walking the path of peace, and service being the highest ideal of a leader.

Benk did his best not to frown. The path of peace? Servitude to the unworthy? Fraternity to those who were lesser? What madness. He scowled. This wasn't the Grimyogi. This was a charlatan with nothing but illusions and tricks.

The Grimyogi smiled then. "You don't believe me. Jeet and Stren didn't understand what I was talking about either. Look at them now."

He gestured toward the two in question, who Benk was coming to realize truly were apostates. How else to explain their ridiculous garb. No armor at all. And where were there swords?

"Will we have a problem?" the false Grimyogi demanded. He approached, wearing a countenance of anger mixed with a promise of violence.

But by now Benk's fear of the man had left him. Not needing to glance aside or signal, he could tell Lood, who was closest at hand, was ready. They had come to this remote village for Jeet and Stren, who had been protected by unknown allies in Chapterhouse ever since their escape several years ago. Those same allies had kept secret the movements and teachings of the apostates from the rest of the brothers. Only recently had the deception been discovered.

And seeking the truth about the Grimyogi, Benk had taken the lead in tracking down Jeet and Stren. The once-*hashains* had claimed to have met him, and they had spoken true in their belief. The brothers had some of a troll's ability to sense that which the speaker felt to be accurate. But accurate beliefs didn't necessarily translate to reality, a situation highlighted by Jeet and Stern's declaration regarding this man, Cinder Shade.

Drawing on a lifetime of experience, knowing Lood would do the same, Benk withdrew his dagger. He aimed the blade unerringly at the fraudster's chest.

The dagger never reached its target. Neither did Lood's. Both their wrists were gripped in an unbreakable hold. The breath was blasted from Benk's lungs, and he found himself lying on his back. Pain burst from his hand. His own dagger was punctured through his palm, pinning it to the ground.

He held in a groan, trying to decipher how he'd been injured, replaying the events in his mind. *Cinder Shade*. He had done this. Moving faster than any man could. He'd stopped Benk's attack, kneed him in the gut, and hurled him down. He had done the same to Lood and stabbed their hands to the ground with their own daggers, all in the single flicker of a hummingbird's wings. How did he move so fast? His strength?

The questions crashed to an end when Cinder stood over them, the hard look of a proper warrior on his face. "Stand up. Face your end like a man."

Benk did as instructed, grunting as he tugged his dagger from his hand, clutching the injury to his stomach, staunching the blood flow even as he clambered to his feet. "What will you do with us?"

The elves and dwarves had unsheathed their weapons with arrows trained on Benk's men, who were poised for violence as well, tense and ready. A single gesture, and they'd Blend, Shield, and enact vengeance. But Benk held them back for now. He needed to learn what had just happened.

"You wanted to know if I'm the Grimyogi," Cinder demanded. "I am. You can sense my truth?"

The words broke through Benk's anger. They were the truth, or at least the man believed they were. "I can sense you think you speak the truth."

"And as the Grimyogi, I should kill you for attacking me, especially during a time of parlay. I won't."

Benk smiled, confident in his righteous judgment. More than anything else, this man's forbearance proved he wasn't the Grimyogi.

"Kill the chicken to scare the monkey. Have you ever heard the phrase?" Cinder asked.

"Kill something weak to intimidate something strong," Benk said.

"Correct. And while I won't kill your men, you'll watch me hurt them."

The mahav scoffed. Not even the true Grimyogi could defeat—

Cinder Shade blurred. Cries of pain arose. Benk spun around. His men were falling, like wheat cut by the scythe. They unsheathed hidden knives, but their blades hit nothing but air.

Benk gaped. Less than fifteen seconds, and all his men were down—some unconscious, others with broken bones. What had just happened? How? The questions swirled, and Benk had trouble formulating any coherent thoughts.

A nightmare come to life; Cinder Shade stood before him. "I am the Grimyogi, and if you value your life or those of your men, you will obey my every command. Am I understood?"

Benk prostrated himself, recognizing some modicum of this man's terrible power. Was he really the Grimyogi? His heretical philosophy said it was impossible, but who else could have destroyed so many brothers and done so without using a single weapon? "What would you bid us do?" Even as he asked the question, Benk got his mind organized, and he sought a way free of his predicament. Chapterhouse had to learn of this man. They—

"Leash yourself to me."

Benk startled, but on consideration, he recognized why the man would demand such a stiff punishment. They had attacked him, after all. "And if I do not?"

"Then your men will die. If killing the chicken won't work, I'll kill the monkey and everything he loves."

There was a chilling promise to the man's words. A declaration that he would do exactly that. Maybe he really was the Grimyogi.

Benk swallowed heavily, hating having to do so, but seeing no other option that would see his men live. "It will be as you say." He closed his eyes, creating a leash and granting it to the man, and in doing so, leashed all of the *hashains* under his command, including all the ones here and a dozen more in Chapterhouse. Curious, he shot a glance at the Grimyogi's woman. "And her? Who is she truly?"

"I am the Grimmeryogi," the woman declared.

Later that evening, Anya finished walking the Ninth's encampment and made her way back to her own campsite. After decades as a princess and a ranger, doing so was an ingrained habit, making sure that those under her command had what they needed, and just as importantly, letting them grow used to her company. After more than three weeks on the road, she'd learned some details about the Ninth, enough to form bonds—or at least some aspect of one.

And while she understood that as their ultimate commander, there would always be a remove between her and everyone else, that remove yawned ever wider now. Once Maize had declared her to be Sira, the soldiers of the Ninth began viewing her in nothing less than awe and even worship. This included General Spalinkar. The man had barely been able to stutter out his explanation for how the Ninth had been dispersed around Querel.

The same situation held true for the dwarves Cinder had brought with him from Aurelian Crèche—the Fortieth Infantry and their commander, Colonel Green Bollind. When Anya had met with them, they'd bowed to her, shuffling about in clear nervousness. And getting them to engage in conversation had been a near impossibility.

She sighed, thinking about their reactions while approaching the campfire she shared with Cinder. It was set apart in an island of solitude, centered amidst the Ninth and the Fortieth, but at a distance that allowed them privacy. Conversations murmured on the humid summer breeze, occasional laughter as well, and while some of the warriors moved about, most had settled in for the night.

Cinder, who had apparently already finished his tour of the Ninth, sat on a sawn-off log, staring into the flames, and Anya settled down next to him. She meant to kiss his cheek, but he turned to face her, and she ended up kissing his lips.

Hisses of surprise and possible alarm arose from amongst those of the Ninth, but they were quickly hushed with murmured explanations of how they were Shokan and Sira.

Anya smiled to herself. At least there was one personal bright spot to being considered Sira. Her people would no longer give her grief whenever she touched Cinder. Or when he touched her, like he did now, drawing her close.

"How did it go?" she asked, resting her head on his shoulder.

He snorted. "About as well as it did for you. The elves are terrified of me, and the dwarves…" He shook his head. "They were already on the edge of worshiping me, and after this afternoon, it's just so much worse."

Anya lifted her head, glancing at the *hashains* of Mahav Benk. The assassins were camped at a distance and on their own, quiet and appearing lost. Most had been healed of their injuries, but their hurts likely extended to the emotional after what Cinder had done to them today.

"Defeating *hashains* and leashing them seems like it's becoming a habit," Anya noted. A beat later. "Would you have really killed them?"

Cinder didn't answer at first, staring into the fire, pondering. "I wouldn't have wanted to, but I also couldn't have trusted having them at my back like that."

It wasn't a full answer, but Anya also recognized that Cinder likely didn't want to give one. Speaking it out loud might have made it seem too real.

"And the leash was the only way to ensure their loyalty," Cinder continued. "The *hashains* don't believe in peace or the fraternity of people. It'll take time."

"If they succeed at all."

"Jeet and Stren did."

Anya knew this, but she felt it important to play devil's advocate. Cinder forgave and loved like no one other than Sira's memories of Shokan. But Anya worried how that would leave him open to betrayal. "They had a troll to teach them."

"So will these other *hashains*. I spoke to Maize. He'll instruct them." He smiled at her, laughing in soft disbelief. "And he also said that Jeet and Stren can become trolls, too."

Anya startled. "What? How?" Cinder explained the choices available to Maize's disciples, and when he finished, she shook her head in amazement. "I never knew."

"I doubt anyone does. Jeet had intended on becoming a holder, but after today, he and Stren both plan on completing their transformations into a troll. They'll come back here for when it happens. It's supposed to be a painful process, weeks to complete. And afterward, they'll travel to Chapterhouse and share what they've learned."

A smile of joy bloomed across Anya's face. Hope—absent for months—was restored, all because of a single act of charity: Cinder's kindness that allowed remorseless assassins to become trolls, a byword for trustworthy allies. "What a wonderful dream," she said, viewing the *hashains* again. "I'm guessing we'll take them with us."

Cinder nodded. "We need them against the herd. Those who survive will go with Stren and Jeet to Chapterhouse and protect them there."

"And Genka? Have you thought of how to approach him?" From the *hashains*, they had learned that the warlord had taken his army to Cord Valley. It was where the herd of wraiths was supposedly heading. In addition, Anya had her own ideas on what to do with Genka, but she wanted to hear Cinder's thoughts.

"It'll have to be from a position of strength. Having the Ninth and the Fortieth should help. But I want Fastness and the Shokans with us, too. Same with the redeemers, who will have to fight their once-brethren." Cinder snorted, a sharp, bitter sound.

Anya shared his resentment. How many of those around them would survive the coming battle? How many would die? Too many, and every death would be a tragedy she and Cinder couldn't prevent. "Where are Sriovey and Jozep?" Anya asked, wanting to shift the conversation to happier matters.

"Aurelian Crèche. They aren't warriors any longer, and their best good is done in teaching their people." He chuckled ruefully. "I doubt it will be easy extracting them from Aurelian anyway. Once the wisdoms realized what Jozep and Sriovey represented, they latched on to them like…"

Anya waited on him to finish his statement. "Like what?" she asked when he showed no signs of completing his thought.

He wore a wry grin. "I don't know. I couldn't come up with a good enough simile."

Anya laughed. "And you call me simple."

"What do you mean?"

"You know what I mean. And there were plenty of similes you could have used."

He arched his eyebrows in challenge. "Such as?"

"Oh, I don't know. How about latched onto them like a mother onto her newborn? Or latched onto them like a wolf onto its prey? Or latched on to them like a bad habit?"

He laughed. "Those are terrible."

Yes, they were, but that hadn't been the point. Until now, an air of sour melancholy had held over Cinder. With his laughter, some of it had lifted—Anya's goal all along.

49

The main body of the Army of Shang Mendi was centered in an area north of Cord Valley, organized into quadrants with rows of identical white tents spaced with precision. Each section had areas given over to infantry, cavalry, and auxiliaries, along with specific locations where soldiers could get their supper. Latrines lined two sides of the camp and farther out, trenches had been dug and lined with sharpened stakes.

But it was to the central area of command tents to which Cinder and Anya, accompanied by General Spalinkar, Colonel Rum, Benk, and several of their officers, made their way. The Ninth, Fortieth, and the *hashains* had arrived only minutes before and had already been asked to attend a meeting with Genka Devesth and his senior staff. They'd barely had time to dismount before the message had reached them, which told Cinder that their presence had been noted long before they had set foot in the camp.

"They certainly are organized," General Spalinkar said, drawing Cinder's attention.

"Wouldn't have expected anything less from the Sunset Warlord," Colonel Rum stated.

There wasn't time for any more words. They'd reached the command tent.

A single man—tall, dark-haired, and with features similar enough to be an Errow—stood at the forefront of a group of officers. It had to be Genka Devesth. The officers huddled behind him gave away his identity. So did his air of command and arrogant bearing—the haughty lift to his chin, a slight smirk, and the folded arms as if the world waited on his needs. It couldn't be anyone else. Intelligence glinted in his eyes, and the Sunset Warlord assessed them even while Cinder did the same.

"A proud man," Anya noted.

Cinder nodded agreement, unsurprised by Genka's posture. After all, this was the man who had conquered all of the Sunsets, believed himself to be Mede's Heir, and was intent on rebuilding Shang Mendi. It would have been shocking if he wasn't proud. "Hopefully, his conceit won't overcome his good sense. We need the Orb. He needs our help."

Anya shrugged. "Arrogance has been known to overwhelm good sense. It's been known to happen—emotion bettering rationality. No matter what we offer, it won't be easy convincing him to give over Mede's Orb."

Cinder grinned her way. "Then we'll just have to ask nicely. Be at our sweetest."

"You aren't sweet," Colonel Rum muttered.

The tension broke as the small group chuckled.

So, this was the *Zuthrum lon Varshin*. Genka watched as Cinder Shade marched forward. He certainly had a warrior's bearing—unintimidated and sure of himself, matched with a fluid grace. Even if his reputation was exaggerated, he was clearly dangerous. There was a firmness to his comportment, as if whatever he desired, he would produce through strength of will alone.

Genka could appreciate that. But he still wouldn't bow before this man, whether or not he truly was Shokan. Nor would he bow to the elven woman by his side, Princess Anya Aruyen, who rumors now stated was Sira Reborn, the Lady of Fire.

His gaze flickered over the rest of the group, pausing at the *hashain*. What was this? Had more assassins gone over to Cinder's side?

"Genka Devesth?" Cinder Shade asked.

Genka set aside his contemplations. "I am he. I assume you are Cinder Shade?"

"It's good to meet you," Cinder said, flashing a smile. He held out a hand, one man to another, as if they were equals.

Genka viewed the hand in fleeting distaste, setting aside his aversion. He needed Cinder's forces. He had a use for them even if this battle against the wraiths was likely fruitless. There was still a chance for victory, and he'd fight for it, regardless if it required a mild act of humility. He grasped Cinder's hand, appreciating the calluses and firm grip. "It is good to meet you as well."

Cinder indicated the elven woman. "Anya Aruyen, princess of Yaksha Sithe."

She, too, offered a handshake, which Genka forced himself to accept.

The others—the general of the Ninth, Colonel Rum of the Fortieth, and the *hashain*—were also introduced, and they knew enough to offer a measured bow.

Genka held in his dislike for Cinder and Anya—what they represented—gesturing for them to follow him into his command tent. "We have much to discuss."

Once inside, he went over the plans he had made for the upcoming battle.

"And you're certain they're headed for Cord Valley?" Cinder asked after the presentation.

"They've shown no signs of wavering," Vel answered. "We've had scouts shadowing them this entire time."

"And the rakshasas," Anya said. "You say fifty of them have been spotted. Have you accounted for how to defeat them? They're much tougher than the wraiths."

Vel answered once again. "We have siege engines in place that should stop the rakshasas."

"They might," Cinder said, peering at the map of Cord Valley. "But we might have a means to counter them."

Genka listened as Cinder and Anya offered suggestions on how to defeat the wraiths and rakshasas. Shockingly, most of them were reasonable. It made him view the two in a fresh light. Whether they were or weren't Shokan and Sira, they had a mind for battle, and when this was over, he'd have to remember that.

"That was a good meeting," Cinder said as they departed from Genka's command tent.

Anya and the others paced alongside him as they strode through the quiet camp. With the sun having set, most of Shang Mendi's army had largely settled in for the evening. A wave of quiet seemed to follow them as they marched past soldiers seated around campfires, replaced a moment later by hushed conversations.

Cinder's ears perked at the comments raised about Anya. They were rarely about her prowess as a warrior. Instead, they largely focused on her appearance. Some were complimentary and others were not, but in nearly every case, there was an ugly chuckle regarding the pleasure of finding her in their bedroll.

He gritted his teeth, angry at the disrespect.

Anya had noticed the soldiers' comments as well as Cinder's reaction, and she took his hand, giving it a gentle squeeze. "I hear it all the time. And if we had the time, I'd put my boot up their asses."

"How do you put up with it?" Cinder asked.

"Because I have to," Anya replied, giving his hand another squeeze. "Let it go. We have more important things to talk about, like Genka's plan. It's a good one, but there are also places where it can be improved."

Cinder did his best to do as she suggested, which was made easier when they exited Shang Mendi's camp. "It can be improved because he doesn't know us and our capabilities," he said in response to Anya's observation. "Individually, he judges us as being equivalent to one of his Immortals or even a *hashain.*

From the corner of his eye, Cinder caught Benk stiffen in outrage. During the week-long journey here, there had been several sparring sessions, and the *hashain* had finally come to accept that Cinder and Anya were as superior to him and his men as the assassins might be to an untrained farmhand when it came to combat.

"You are the Grimyogi and she is the Lady of Fire," the *hashain* said. "You are both worth far more than any dozen of his Immortals."

Benk's observation was true but unimportant. "I'm concerned about how he plans on using the Ninth," Cinder said.

"I saw the same thing," Anya said. "His plan would destroy the Ninth. I don't trust him."

"Neither do I. Genka has his own motivations, and they aren't the same as ours."

"Which is why we can't let him use the Ninth as he sees fit," Anya said. "We can't let him sacrifice those entrusted to our care."

"And we won't. It's also time to contact Fastness and the Shokans." Cinder patted the *divaspana* in his *null pocket.* "Last I spoke, they've all opened a Chakra and have learned to conduct *Jivatma* and source *lorethasra*, at least to a degree. We'll need them."

Anya smiled. "It'll be good to see them again."

Vel Parnesth viewed their approaching allies through calculating eyes. The elves of Shima Sithe and the dwarves of Aurelian Crèche had arrived last night, and although their numbers were welcome, they wouldn't be enough. It was 'too little, too late,' as the saying went. Even quadruple the numbers, and it wouldn't have been enough, not against the wraiths, much less the rakshasas. And there was only so much preparation that could be done in the four days before they arrived.

The creatures had progressed unerringly toward Cord Valley, a straight shot. And all the traps, deadfalls, and ambushes hadn't done a lick at slowing them down. All the flights of arrows, small mountains of hurled boulders, and cavalry charges had been as worthless at halting their progress as kindling arresting a forest fire. Nothing worked. The wraiths were a force of nature, especially bolstered as they were by the rakshasas, the black-chitinned monsters, horned and red-eyed.

It was a terrifying force that descended on Cord Valley, and Vel knew they were dead men walking. What force could stop the wraiths and rakshasas? What army? As far as he knew, there were none, and although Genka hid it well, he realized it, too. Recognized that nothing would be left of the Sunsets except ruin. Nothing would be left of the world but desolation.

Then why had the elven and dwarven officers been brimming with confidence? No fear had traced their faces. They had chatted in good humor, actually having the audacity to laugh. Was it really because of Cinder and Anya? The ones that the elves and dwarves proclaimed to be Shokan and Sira Reborn, the *Zuthrum lon Varshin* and the Lady of Fire?

Vel might have scoffed at the declaration, except for one fact. With the man and woman were reported to be five sects of *hashains*, clearly loyal to their cause.

Thus, this morning's assembly to which Vel had minimal hopes, a sentiment shared by the two dozen men comprising the army's senior staff. They milled about, whispering their worries, but careful to keep their voices lowered since today's meeting was to be held directly outside Genka's tent, in full view of the army. The *Garnala lon Anarin* wanted his men to see the leadership discussing the situation and taking heart from the arrival of allies.

And here they were: General Spalinkar and five aides; Colonel Rum and two others from his crèche; Mahav Benk to represent the *hashains*; and a human Vel had yet to meet. The stranger had the demeanor of a hard-bitten warrior. Ahead of that column rode Anya Aruyen on a chestnut gelding, a Yavana, and next to her was Cinder Shade.

Vel's mouth dropped in shock.

"He rides a Yavana stallion," one of the aides whispered.

And it wasn't just any Yavana. He was Sunbane, the brother to Genka's Midnight's Silence, the stallion no one could tame, and yet Cinder Shade had managed it… just as rumors had proclaimed.

Cinder dismounted, a signal for the others to do so as well, and he led his group forward. Vel studied him anew. Last night he had been tired, his mind hazy with fatigue, but this morning he was alert. And what Vel saw told him that Cinder Shade and Anya Aruyen were a matched pair. They were warriors and commanders, walking in the smooth, confident manner of those accustomed to leadership.

Vel blinked in further shock when he noticed Sunbane keeping pace behind them. What was this?

"We didn't have much time to talk last night," Cinder said, speaking without preamble.

Genka stirred but controlled himself. He detested being spoken to as an equal. "Then let's see what we can do together. Me—the *Garnala lon Anarin*—and the two of you, the *Zuthrum lon Varshin* and the Lady of Fire."

Vel smiled to himself. The listing of their mythical titles wasn't a coincidence. By calling them out in the manner that he had, Genka had declared himself the first among equals, no matter what the elves and dwarves—or their own men—might believe.

"We reviewed your plans from last night," Anya said, "and we have a few suggestions."

Cinder picked up the explanation. "We agree with how you intend on using the Ninth, as support to plug any holes in your lines, but we have a different notion of who should command. In addition, the dwarven Fortieth shouldn't be a separate force."

Now it was Anya who spoke. "We should intersperse them into the Ninth. Their ability with Earth is superior to your Immortals."

Vel eyed the two. They appeared to have rehearsed their explanation.

"They can slow the wraiths," Anya continued. "Give your men a chance to either retreat or rally."

Cinder spoke without a break between his words and Anya's. "In addition, while ultimate command of the armies will be in your hands, the Ninth and the Fortieth will be led by Bones." He gestured to the man with him. "While your army and ours seek out the wraiths and lock them in place, the *hashains* of Mahav Benk will remain with me and Anya. We'll kill them ourselves."

"How do you plan on this?" Genka asked, evincing the same disbelief Vel was feeling. "Killing them?"

"Special units of your Immortals and *hashains* will risk close contact with the enemy," Cinder answered. "They should be able to draw away small groups of wraiths from the main herd. If we're lucky, it might even be in clusters of fives or tens. Once we have them separated…" He shrugged. "That's the end of it."

Vel stifled a smirk at the man's arrogance, stilling his expression when he noticed Sunbane staring his way. The stallion seemed to be considering him like a wolf eyeing an injured fawn.

"You may think him arrogant, but he is as he claims. You should remember this."

Stunned exclamations rolled out from amongst Genka's generals and leaders, all of them recognizing what had just happened. It was a disbelief Vel shared. A Yavana rarely spoke to its rider, and even less commonly were they known to speak to anyone else *but* its rider.

Vel stared dazedly at Genka, heartened to see his friend maintain a facade of equilibrium. "Sunbane, I presume."

The stallion dipped his head. *"I was known as Sunbane, but I prefer the name Fastness."*

Genka returned his attention to Cinder and Anya. "And for your aid, what do you want in payment?" His question caused a ruffling of feathers amongst the other group, meant as it was to insinuate that Cinder and Anya were only mercenary in their help.

"You know what we want," Cinder said. "Mede's Orb."

Genka shook his head. "Impossible. Mede's Orb is our holiest relic."

"So was the Orb of Eretria in Surent Crèche," Cinder said. "The Orb of Moss of Yaksha Sithe and the Orb of Undying Light for Bharat. And yet all were destroyed so our people can achieve their fullest potential."

"We know how to achieve our fullest potential," Genka declared. "The Orb is the means through which an Immortal is fashioned."

"Can the Immortals do this?" Bones asked, stepping forward. From one footfall to the next, he disappeared.

Astonished exclamations arose again from the senior officers of Shang Mendi. They had seen the Immortals create something akin to what Bones had done, but he wasn't an Immortal, was he?

"Can they?" Bones asked, reappearing then.

Vel had kept silent this entire time, but with Genka appearing too wide-eyed to respond, he had to. "You still cannot have Mede's Orb."

Cinder's lips briefly thinned. "In the end, you will still give it over. That isn't negotiable."

"Either that," Anya said, "or we'll simply take it. Now or when this battle is over."

Genka regained control of himself. "The Orb is far away and hidden. And I find it troubling that our allies would dare threaten us with the theft of our most holy relic."

The clip-clopping of an additional horse, one moving swiftly, captured Vel's attention. Who was this now? He gazed in the direction of the sound, surprised when he saw Midnight's Silence rushing toward them. Vel pitied the groom who had let him escape.

Genka moved to intercept his stallion, but Silence evaded his hands, slamming to a stop before Fastness. The black stallion bent his forelegs, bowing low before the white Yavana. *"Sunbane, my Brother. It is wonderful to see you again."*

Vel briefly closed his eyes at this latest amazement. He had heard Silence's voice, just like everyone else, and the stallion had sounded overjoyed.

"It is good to see you, too, Brother," the white Yavana replied. *"But I am known as Fastness now. And before that, I was known as Sapient Dormant. And prior to that, Keal Sonnet, the holder to Shokan and Sira, to the Blessed Ones standing before you.*

"Keal Sonnet," Silence said as if tasting the word. *"The name fits you.*

How may I serve?"

Vel was wrong. He could be further shocked.

"Mede's Orb is in your tent," Cinder had said only minutes earlier. "Deliver it to us."

Those had been the man's words after Fastness' staggering declaration and Silence's equally staggering confirmation. Genka's senior staff had heard the statements, witnessed everything from the morning's meeting. Their presence and everything spoken had forced Genka's hand. Seeing no other option, he had vowed to deliver Mede's Orb to Cinder and Anya after the wraiths were defeated.

He had grave doubts anyone could actually accomplish the latter, but if the miraculous occurred, by then he'd have a plan in place to keep the Orb.

"What do you think?" Vel asked. The two of them were alone in Genka's tent, meeting to discuss their next step.

"Are you asking if I think they are Shokan and Sira?" Genka asked. Whether they were or not was immaterial. As he'd stated to himself on many an occasion, he would bend the knee before no one. Nor would he give over what was his.

"No," Vel said. "I mean about Fastness. Is he really Sapient?"

Genka stared at his friend in bewilderment. That's what he was asking about? "Of course not. Sapient Dormant was a Mythaspuri, a human. Not a Yavana."

"But if he was reincarnated, couldn't he have returned to life in whatever form suited him?"

Genka's bewilderment increased, transitioned to disappointment. Vel was serious about this. "Only if you believe in reincarnation." Which Genka didn't.

"You are the *Garnala lon Anarin*," Vel reminded him. "Mede Reborn."

Genka scowled, hating to acknowledge Vel's point. Yes, he was Mede

Reborn, but Mede had been human, and so was Genka. He wasn't a horse.

"Silence seems to believe it, too," Vel added.

"Silence may be a Yavana, but he's still just a horse."

"Just one of the greatest Yavana stallions of the past several generations," Vel countered. "And Fastness was prophesied at birth to also serve someone around whom history is written. A *thoraython.*"

Genka was abruptly tired of the conversation. "I don't want to talk about it anymore. What else did you notice?"

Vel heeded him, switching the topic of conversation. "Their men are well trained."

"Cinder's man was well trained," Genka corrected. When Silence had arrived, rather than stare at him, Bones' attention had gone elsewhere, looking for danger concealed amidst the distraction. The *hashain* had done so, too. But not the elves and dwarves. Only belatedly had they cast about for possible harm, well after it would have already occurred. Likely, they hadn't fought in so long that they'd lost a warrior's instincts.

"What about his *hashains*?" Vel asked. "How did he capture their loyalty? And why hasn't Cinder confronted us about sending *hashains* to kill him?"

They were the very questions that troubled Genka's thoughts. One answer might come about when he spoke to his own *hashains*. "I don't know, but if he's convinced them he's the Grimyogi—"

"Which is the same as Shokan."

Genka grimaced. Perhaps Cinder was Shokan and Anya was Sira, but he steadfastly refused to place all his hopes on the so-called Blessed Ones. In his life, the only people Genka had ever been able to count on were himself and Vel. "Whatever the case, that would be the only way for him to earn their loyalty."

"But all five sects? That's what my spies tell me. Cinder has five sects of *hashains* in his camp. Sixty of the assassins shouldn't be so easy to convince."

No, they shouldn't. "What do you think happened?" Genka asked.

Vel could usually parse through the possibilities in ways that he couldn't.

Vel sighed, leaning heavily on a cane as he shuffled over to a chair and collapsed. He closed his eyes, fatigue evident.

Genka viewed him in concern. Vel seemed to age more and more rapidly with every passing day. He arose late in the morning, slept away most of the afternoon, and was awake for only a few hours in the evening. Right now, he was tired, but he was also a warrior, and as a warrior, he would fight—long enough anyway to see this latest threat by the wraiths put down.

Either that or he'd die during the battle so he wouldn't have to witness the destruction of the Sunsets.

Vel opened his eyes after a moment of quiet. "I think they've leashed themselves. The commander alone would suffice. It would leash the rest as well. Make them unable to do anything other than what Cinder would want. It's what I would do."

Genka stared at his friend a few seconds longer. *Leashing.* If true, it was a wise and cunning move on Cinder's part. Genka might not have seen it himself. "You believe Cinder has that level of sharpness?"

"I do. The man doesn't miss much. Neither does Anya. They were studying us even as we were studying them. And they saw deep."

"And if they prove responsible in defeating the herd…" Which still struck Genka as an impossibility. A single pair of warriors able to defeat over four hundred wraiths on their own? Along with fifty rakshasas?

"If they are seen to have been responsible in destroying the wraiths and rakshasas, then you'll have no option but to give them the Orb. The men will demand it."

"I'll bow down before no one," Genka growled.

"It might be the better part of valor to do so. If they defeat the wraiths—

"Which is impossible."

Vel inclined his head in acknowledgment. "I'm only dealing in possibilities. If they defeat the wraiths, no matter how unlikely, you'll lose the army and likely your empire. The people themselves will proclaim

Cinder and Anya as being Shokan and Sira. Better to bend now than break later."

It wasn't what Genka wanted to hear, but he listened anyway. Refusing to countenance troubling possibilities was the mark of a moron. "We'll see what happens," he said at last, unwilling to agree to anything more.

Vel grunted understanding. "What about their idea of separating groups of wraiths from the main body?"

Genka had given this a great deal of thought. Cinder and Anya's plan actually had merit, whether it worked or not. "That's actually our biggest problem in handling the wraiths. They're spread out in every direction, running through forests and rough terrain. We can't bring overwhelming force to bear. We have to bring them together, at a location of our choosing before we can cut them apart."

"You're planning on using the army as bait?"

Genka nodded. "Cord Valley actually makes a great location. We'll pull back into the grasslands. Set traps and ambushes, use them to funnel the wraiths into a wide gorge ten miles south of here." He indicated the map, but Vel never bothered rising, likely already knowing the one he had in mind.

"That valley is a steep-walled bowl on the side opposite the forest."

"Exactly. We'll have the high ground. We can encircle the wraiths and see if Cinder and Anya are all talk."

"And if they are?"

Genka shrugged. "Then we'll have learned something. And it will still be our best chance at turning away the herd."

Brilliance prowled behind the massive lines of two-legs. It was called an army, which wasn't a new term to her, but she had hoped it would be for Kela. Of course, it hadn't been. The dog was simply too smart and too knowledgeable. At least Hima hadn't known the word. The little deer was still new to the world and still required plenty of instruction.

She would also likely need lots of saving in the upcoming battle.

Not for the first time did Brilliance wonder if she had made a mistake in coming here. When she'd learned that all her other two-legs, the ones called the Shokans—named after her personal human—were leaving Shalla Valley for a deadly battle, Brilliance had figured they'd need her wisdom to see them through. Who else could keep them out of harm's way? Especially when the idiots constantly ran headfirst into overwhelming danger?

Then again, had Brilliance known the fight would be against wraiths, she would have never come.

She glanced to where Hima shivered in fear. *"I don't like this,"* Hima said.

Brilliance went to the young *aether*-cursed, nudging her with her nose. *"Stay with us, and we'll keep you safe."* It would have once been a strange vow to make—protection of a creature Brilliance had initially wanted to eat, but somewhere along the way, she had come to think of Hima as her kitten.

"I still don't like it," Hima replied.

Brilliance stared at the doe, waiting for the rest of her words, surprised when none came forth. Usually, once Hima started talking, she never stopped. Brilliance licked the deer's forehead. *"I don't like it, either."*

"We can't do much good here," Kela said. *"Risking ourselves against wraiths. I don't think service to others is supposed to mean suicide on their behalf."*

"I don't want to die," Hima said with a whimper.

"We won't die," Brilliance told her.

"Will your human keep us safe?" Kela asked.

"Of course, he will," Brilliance said, no doubt in her mind. He had to. That was his purpose in life: to see to her needs and care. In fact, he should be nearby right now. She peered about, over the heads of the two-legs. Where was her human and her people? She couldn't see them. They were close, though, that much she could tell—through her bond to Cinder, and by extension, Anya. Somewhere over there.

She made to lead Kela and Hima to where she sensed her two-legs but stopping her was Estin.

"You're not going with Cinder and Anya," he told them. "You're staying with us, the Shokans."

Brilliance crouched low, ears flat, growling softly. She didn't want to stay with the Shokans. She wanted to go to her two-leg and his mate.

Estin frowned, hands on his hips. Brilliance had figured out most of the expressions the two-legs could make with their faces and bodies, and right now, the elf appeared frustrated.

Well, Brilliance was, too. But rather than swipe at Estin like she wanted and he deserved, she held on to her patience. Of course, if she had batted at Estin, it would probably only annoy him further. Worse, he might hit her on the nose. He'd done that once and she didn't like it. So rather than suffer that indignity, Brilliance waited for Estin's explanation.

"Cinder and Anya are going to be in the hardest part of the battle," Estin said. "Our job is to get the wraiths steered to a place where they can kill them."

Brilliance straightened, ears perked and no longer growling. Kill them? Did he mean the wraiths? No one could kill as many of those horrid monsters as she could smell out to the north. There had to be hundreds of them. *Do you really think they can kill that many?*

Estin didn't reply at once. Instead, he stepped closer, reaching up to rub a spot behind one of her ears. Brilliance automatically tilted her head to grant him better access, her mouth opening in pleasure.

Kela, the little whimperer, whined, wanting to be petted also. His tail wagged, and eventually, he finally got the same treatment. Then it was Hima's turn.

"Come on," Estin said, giving Hima a final pat. "Let's go find the others."

Brilliance tagged along after the elf, realizing only after a bit that Estin had never answered her question.

50

Genka gazed down into the valley where, if things worked the way he intended, the wraiths would be gathered and destroyed. Both were mighty large "ifs" though, and truth be told, although he had some confidence his army could do the first, getting the latter done would bleed the Sunsets dry. And that was only after the fucking monsters had desecrated Cord Valley.

He scowled, not liking to even consider such an outcome. Even though Genka had ordered the valley emptied of all Yavanas and people, the land itself might be despoiled, burned to ash and made inhospitable. Then again, what could he do? In all of Seminal, Yavanas only bred true in this place, in Cord Valley.

And this didn't even account for how the rest of a generation of young men might be killed. The Sunset Kingdoms might win this battle and war and still be left in ruins.

Genka did his best to shove down any worries about the tragedy to come and wrest his mind on the present.

The sun steadily marched across a sky decorated with lazy summer clouds, and he inhaled deep when a warm wind, calm and inviting, brought the lush fragrance of grass, growth, and manure. The scents reminded him of something good and worth protecting, and he'd protect this valley, even to the last soldier. A creaking of men in their saddles—the Immortals tasked with protecting him—and the nervous whickering of their horses reminded him of that promise. So did the low growls and high-pitched ululations of the enemy, coming from the forest downslope and across the valley floor.

He glanced to the woods, which on first inspection appeared serene and quiet, at odds with what was soon to occur—a bloody battle that would determine the future of the Sunsets and possibly most of the northwestern nations of the world. Ballistae and polyboloses were staged—maybe they'd get lucky on their shots—and archers were positioned. Heavy cavalry with lances waited to charge. And all of them were aimed at the green bowl of grass down below, several miles wide and half that in length.

Through his spyglass, Genka spied flashing views of light cavalry speeding along trails through the forest. Chasing after them were a number of wraiths in twos and threes along with a sprinkling of black-armored monsters—the rakshasas—who towered, rampaging through the trees, pushing them aside rather than following any kind of path.

The cavalry was doing their best to stay ahead of the monsters, but no doubt, some would be caught and killed, and there was no helping it. Everyone here, from a raw private all the way to Genka himself, could see themselves die in order to save the Sunsets. This was the ground. This was the field. This was the place which would soon be consecrated in the blood of the fallen.

A distant scream, a mix of man and horse, reached Genka. It had already started. He closed his eyes then, praying for one of the few times since he'd last faced the wraiths.

When he opened his eyes, he studied again the array of his troops. It never failed to strike him how odd this battle was. How could it be that so many were needed against so few? Genka's sight fell on the so-called Shokans, the elven Ninth, and the dwarven Fortieth. They had their own arrangement, centered around Cinder and Anya and their grouping of *hashains*.

Another mystery unsolved. The *hashains*, believing Cinder to actually be the Grimyogi, had leashed themselves to him. And with so many involved, sixty assassins, it was a matter that Genka's own *hashains* couldn't disregard.

But was it true? Was Cinder the Grimyogi? Was he Shokan?

And even if he was, so what? Genka refused to believe that anyone was his superior, and the only reason the question of Cinder Shade and Anya Aruyen as the Blessed Ones had any merit was because of how it might affect his men.

Their opinions did matter. If the soldiers believed that Cinder and Anya were the Blessed Ones, and if they were instrumental in defeating the wraiths, Shang Mendi would be ended if Genka still refused them.

He studied Cinder and Anya again, a part of him wishing they and their allies had never come. A part of him wished he could have won this battle on his own, no matter how unlikely the possibility. That way, at least, he'd have forged his own destiny with no concern over anyone stealing his glory.

As he continued to look in Cinder's direction, he caught sight of the man's Yavana stallion, Fastness.

Midnight's Silence shook his head. *"Fastness is the lord of us."*

The Immortals close at hand glanced Genka's way, every one of them in wide-eyed astonishment.

Genka bit back a scowl. They must have heard Silence's words, which Genka wished they hadn't. He wished many things, the most important being—

Ululating screams were his only warning. A pair of gray-skinned terrors streaked out of the forest, down a nearby hill, alone and unsupported, a couple hundred yards away and closing quickly. Clothed in rags, they moved like sharks speeding for the kill. The Immortals shifted to face the attack.

Genka was about to call out orders, but Cinder had spurred Fastness to intercept. Anya rode beside him. Genka waited to see what would happen. Could they do as they promised and kill the wraiths on their own?

In the last battle, it had taken the concerted efforts of large groups of Immortals to bring down just one wraith.

Cinder held his arms in the pose of an archer, holding a golden glow in the shape of a bow. A bright line connected the arms. He seemed to pluck the string, and a bolt of quicksilver shot out. It crashed into the wraiths, punching straight through one and into the other.

The monsters collapsed with their chests blown open.

Excited shouts and conversations filled the air as Genka stared, eyes narrowed in calculation. That had been an easy kill. Was that the extent of Cinder's ability? Or did he have even greater skills?

An instant later, his attention shifted to the far side of the bowl. Another group of wraiths had entered the field, chasing a hundred cavalry. They quickly whittled the distance, likely to catch their stragglers in the next few seconds.

Arrows whistled to cover the retreating cavalry, but it wouldn't be enough. He knew it even before he saw the wraiths dodge the bolts or slap them out of the air.

Genka exhaled heavily.

"*It begins,*" said Silence.

"So, it does," Genka muttered.

A cowling of trees draped the perimeter of a wildflower field warmed beneath a mid-day sun. A scattering of spring clouds lazed in a blue sky as deep as a newborn's eyes. The air held still, humid with summer's moisture and suffused with a lush floral fragrance.

Lieutenant Karak only wished that the peacefulness of the setting in which he and his men found themselves was reflected in the reality of the situation. *Peace.* He smirked at the notion. Ever since Genka

Devesth had arrived on the scene, it seemed like the Sunsets were riven by battle. First, there had been Genka's conquests, then his culling of those involved in civil war against his regime—mostly from Loseth—and then a herd of wraiths, barely turned back. Now, here came another herd, but this time rakshasas were included.

Peace, it seemed, was a desperately rare commodity in Shang Mendi Restored. But maybe if the army defeated this latest foe, that blessed state would finally grace the lands of the Sunset Kingdoms.

Karak snorted. *Unlikely.* After this battle, Genka would probably turn his attention south to Aurelian Crèche and Shima Sithe. Or maybe Shet would attack, sending his zahhacks hurtling north from the southern Hinane Mountains and northern Pischa Hills, where rumor held that they were breeding like cockroaches.

Whatever the case, wars would rage, and Karak and his men—all fifteen of them—would be at the forefront of the fighting. And it might even be like their current situation: staked out in a meadow as bait for the enemy.

Karak shivered, hating the helplessness of waiting. This was the worst part of any battle. Too many gruesome imaginings and grim timbres to his thinkings. He stared into the forest and his fingers found the red feather he'd woven into his helmet. It was a silly affectation, but he liked it. It was pretty and rubbing it helped keep him calm.

He continued to stroke the feather and found himself wishing he could see through the cover of branches and bramble, hear any noises of fear and pain, and scent the stench of a wraith at a distance. Anything but sit here waiting to be killed.

He grimaced in impatience. The scouts should be back soon, and if they were lucky, they'd have a pack of wraiths trailing after them. Then would come the real work. Karak and his men would have to guide the enemy east toward the broad bowl that Genka promised would be a killing field.

But would it work? Genka said it would, but he said much and didn't always deliver. Peace, for one, after uniting the Sunsets. Overwhelming victory, for another, against the first herd. And the end to wars following that last battle against the wraiths.

None of it had come to pass, and yet Karak had hope that this time things might be different. And his hope wasn't based on Genka's promises. Rather, they were based on the presence of the far easterner that some *hashains* called the Grimyogi and the elves and dwarves called Shokan Reborn.

His presence and that of the elf maiden, Anya Aruyen—who might be Sira—were the only reasons Karak had any optimism for this upcoming battle. If they were who others claimed, then the army might actually survive the herd.

His deliberations ended when his second guided his horse over. "We've finished the trenches."

He gestured, and Karak scrutinized the area in question, the far side of the field where a set of stake-lined trenches and pitfalls were hastily being covered with deadfall and debris. And beyond them were a series of hidden traps.

But had they missed anything? Anything that gave the wraiths warning? Because reports indicated that the fuckers always seemed to know where the traps had been laid.

Closely studying the terrain, Karak was eventually satisfied that everything was as it should be. He nodded to his second. "Have the men mount up and hold position. The scouts should be back at any moment."

His second snapped a salute. "Yes, sir."

Moments later, Karak's attention snapped north when a set of shouts rose from the brush in that direction. The men quickly clambered aboard their horses, lined up and facing the direction of the sounds. Bows were strung. Arrows nocked.

Ululating cries and a basso roar echoed across the forest. *Wraiths and at least one rakshasa.* A breaking of branches and limbs heralded the enemy closing on their position.

More shouts. Another set of ululating cries, sounding triumphant this time. No more than fifty yards.

"Warriors! Prepare to receive the enemy."

Bows groaned in response.

The scouts burst from the foliage, mounted and riding hard. Foam flecked at the corners of their horses' mouths. Behind them darted wraiths, ten of them, moving fast. And directly beyond loomed a rakshasa, the height of a barn. It charged straight ahead.

A whistling of arrows sped over the scouts. A few scattered grunts as they impacted the wraiths.

There wasn't time for another flight of arrows.

"Retreat!" Karak shouted. His men followed as he led them into the woods, along a path they'd already cleared so they could run flat out.

The temperature dropped, cool shadows replacing the warm sunshine. The smell of dirt and loam replaced the fresh, floral aroma of the wildflowers. For a moment, the hammering of hooves was the only sound. The woodland animals had gone to shelter. In this, they were wise.

But the high-pitched cries of the monstrous wraiths refused to be overshadowed. Their screams carried, sounding like a crone cackling death. Then came the rakshasa, roaring like a hundred lions. Foliage crashed and cracked as the creatures sped forward.

Karak shouted orders. The path split up ahead but would merge again in another field not too far away. Half of his men would go left while Karak and the rest would go right. They'd be able to travel faster.

The maneuver went off without a hitch. But the wraiths had closed the distance. A high-pitched shriek. A horse had been pulled down. Another scream. Its rider was down. Karak couldn't look to see who it was. A trio of arrows whistled, fired by those farthest back, who sacrificed to buy their brothers more time. Maybe it would only be a few seconds, and Karak prayed it would be enough.

His heart pounded against his ribs, beating every bit as fast and loud as the thudding hooves of his mount.

They burst out of the forest, into sunshine and another meadow. For a brief moment, Karak felt like there was safety in the light even though it was a lie. The members of his squad who had gone left merged with his own. Two horses raced with empty saddles.

Karak dismissed the observation. On the far side of the meadow, the path picked up again. He angled toward it… just as twenty fresh riders—heavy cavalry—erupted from the trail.

Karak wanted to cheer. The heavy cavalry had their lances leveled, but more importantly, five of them were Immortals, recognizable in the way they moved. Even while simply riding, they had a sense of restrained motion. Karak shouted more orders, getting his men turned about. Seconds passed. Just enough time to face off against the wraiths, who yelped and yipped as they entered the small clearing.

The heavy cavalry hammered into them. Several wraiths went down, trampled by steel-shod hooves. But others of their kind evaded the horses, launching themselves at the attacking cavalry. Several soldiers were yanked from their saddles.

"Fire!" Karak ordered.

Arrows hissed, slamming into the wraiths. Several stumbled and fell.

Slashing with shining blades and heavy axes, the Immortals were on them.

A gigantic hammer smashed into the heavy cavalry. The rakshasa had arrived. Horses screamed, pulped to gory ruin. Three Immortals were tossed aside, flung twenty feet in the air like broken dolls. They crashed into a cluster of trees, their bodies crumpling.

And of the trampled wraiths, only one appeared truly injured.

At this rate, they would run out of soldiers and Immortals well before the enemy ran out of wraiths.

Karak's terror heightened. "Ride!" He spun his mount about, tearing toward the path that led away from the field of blood and bone.

Roars and shrieks arose from all around the bowl where Genka planned on battling the wraiths. Where Cinder and Anya had wanted to finish off the creatures as well. Bones trusted that they could. He didn't know how, but they were Shokan and Sira. If they couldn't kill the wraiths, then this battle was already as good as lost.

Shrieks and cries echoed from the forest that rose several hundred yards distant. Bones recognized the noises. Some came from the enemy, shouts of victories. Too many, however, came from human throats, the sounds of pain and dying. Good people were being killed in the woods—green soldiers from what he'd seen. That they were even in the fight was a miracle.

Those brave fools were giving their last, full measure to keep safe their families, and by all that was holy, Bones vowed to take that effort and make it meaningful.

It's what Cinder would do, the best person Bones had ever known, the person on whom he modeled his own behavior. That's the kind of person he wanted to be.

An explosion of leaves and brush drew his attention back to the valley, and through his spyglass, Bones spied a line of cavalry. Their commander, an officer wearing a red-feather plume, led the remnants of his unit out of the forest. And giving chase were ten wraiths and a rakshasa. It was Bones' first view of the monster, and he didn't like what he was seeing.

Clad in black armor, chitinous like a spiderkin, the creature stood on cloven hooves, and was nearly twenty feet tall. Massively muscled, it had a curiously flat face, almost featureless, except for a single horizontal line for its mouth, two slits for a nose, and red eyes that glowed like a furnace. A pair of horns, pitted and dark as sin, swept outward like crescent moons. The monster opened its mouth, roaring, and from its back unfurled bat wings, either for flight or to help it keep its balance.

The rakshasa alone might be more than what Bones' company could face, but then again, that wasn't their role. They weren't supposed to try and kill every wraith or rakshasa they saw, but merely to thin them out. He knew how. "Aim fire at those wraiths!"

A flight of arrows hissed and whistled. Their shadows flashed across the ground, slamming home. The wraiths cried their anger. The rakshasa roared, although any arrow impacting him merely shattered on his chitin.

An expected outcome. The attack hadn't been intended to kill any of the creatures. It was merely to slow them down so the cavalry captain and his men could find safety.

"Fire at will!" His order given, Bones addressed the ballista and polybolos crews. "Line up on those wraiths. Kill them."

"It'll take us a couple shots to get the range and accuracy," the dwarven sergeant in charge told him.

"Riyne!" Bones got ahold of his brother warrior. "Get the range and accuracy. I want a bolt put through that rakshasa inside of ten seconds. That or a couple of the wraiths." He turned away, knowing Riyne would get it done.

"Raise the ballista," Riyne shouted. "Five degrees. To the right. Three degrees."

A creaking of wood, and the ballista was cranked, aimed. A thundercrack as the line snapped. The bolt was away. Bones watched its flight. It crunched into the rakshasa's back, smashing into kindling just like the arrows. The creature spun about, noticing them and grinning.

"Well, damn," Bones muttered. "Arrows. I want those fucking wraiths dead."

This time, their attack provoked a defensive response. The wraiths huddled behind the rakshasa, protected by his crouched bulk.

"Ballista! Bring down that rakshasa."

A sequence of further attacks did nothing. In fact, all they accomplished was infuriating the rakshasa. It rose from a crouch, facing their assaults, swatting aside bolts with its massive hammer or ignoring them. It slowly walked toward them, relentless as the first stones slipping down to create an avalanche.

Bones' mouth went dry. What the hell would stop the creature? He viewed the monstrous rakshasa and the wraiths behind it. They looked like porcupines, but none of them were out of the fight. In fact, the arrows had barely penetrated their thick hides. Even the bolts from the polyboloses seemed like little more than a nuisance. Bones watched as the wraiths began removing the arrows pincushioning their forms. None of them were the slightest bit unsteady on their feet.

But maybe soon they would be.

The captain with the red feather had gotten his men turned about. Somewhere, they'd obtained lances. They were going to run the wraiths down. But only if the damn monsters didn't see it coming.

"Continue fire," Bones called. He called out to the dwarves of the Fortieth. "Trap their legs, focus on the rakshasa." To the Ninth. "Weaves of Fire and Air. Keep their attention."

The dwarves extended their hands, and from the distant ground, tendrils of thorny vines grew from the ground, wrapping around the feet of the wraiths and the rakshasa. The elves sent fiery wisps, red and orange flames, at the wraiths, doing little damage.

Neither attack did much, but it kept the enemy's focus on Bones' unit, and they never noticed until too late when the red-feathered captain and his cavalry rode them down. This time, two wraiths didn't rise to their feet. The others staggered, swiping at the riders, missing. Red-feather waved a jaunty salute toward Bones, who returned it.

Meanwhile, the rakshasa picked up speed. It tore through the desperate braids woven by the dwarves and elves. Walls slowed it some, and collapsed ground briefly hindered its forward progress. But it wouldn't be enough. The damn creature and the wraiths would be on Bones and his squad in no time.

He studied the distance. "Catapult." He only had one of them. "Crack that fucker straight in his damn horns." He addressed the polybolos and ballista crew. "First one to kill a wraith gets all the drinks you want tonight."

A cheer met his offer, and the air was soon darkened by swarming arrows and bolts. Once again, they pincushioned the wraiths, but none went down. And this time, they were even swifter in removing the arrows.

The rakshasa was closing. A hundred yards. The catapult crew were still getting their aim lined up. The wraiths were running pell-mell toward Bones' unit. An instant later, the rakshasa took a boulder straight in the face. It stumbled, blinked, halted, but kept its feet. Seconds later, another boulder crunched it nearly at the same spot as the first. This time, the monster fell straight backward, crushing a wraith.

"Archers!" Bones shouted. "Slow down the wraiths. Ballista, lock on to the enemy. Shokans, sweep down with Fireballs."

Just then, the rakshasa stirred, struggling to rise. With deft effort, it smacked away a stone from the catapult. Struggling for a bit, it slowly swayed to its feet, and picked its way toward them once again.

Bones loosened his sword. "I guess we have to fight them up close and personal."

Estin, Depth, and Wark were riding toward the wraiths, and with them were four Immortals. They bypassed the rakshasa. Orange Fireballs roared into the wraiths. The attacks weren't as hot as what Cinder or Anya could manage, but they were hot enough. Two wraiths went down. The remaining six chased the Shokans and Immortals.

Bones' heart went into his throat when Depth was unhorsed. The Shokan rolled to his feet and was buried under two wraiths. Three Immortals were also down.

And the rakshasa was still coming.

But like a Mythaspuri out of legend, here came Anya, hair glowing golden in the sunshine, riding Barton straight at the monster. She looked so small, but power wafted off her in waves. From her hand extruded a golden bar. It extended, a shape like a spear, and produced a low-pitched drone. It smashed into the rakshasa's chest, drawing black blood and a scream of rage. Again, Anya attacked, and this time, the golden bar cracked the rakshasa's armor, punching through its back.

Its chest a smoking ruin, this time when it fell, it didn't move. Bones saluted Anya before looking to his men and gazing out at where the Shokans were regrouping. His heart fell at seeing who they carried. *Depth.*

51

"We'll be alright. Breathe. We'll be alright. Breathe."

Ishmay looked over at Mirk, who had a pasty expression on his face. He kept on muttering encouragement to himself, which is something he always did. Right before a battle, every single time, Mirk went and got sick. But after he got the hurling out of the way, he'd be fine, even finer once the fighting started. But until then, it was best not to stand too close to the man.

As for the rest of the small squad to which Ishmay had been assigned—himself, Gorant, Mirk, Mohal, and Sash—they were hidden in the forest, Blended and waiting to take some wraiths unaware. Behind them was a roughly cleared area that reached to the valley basin, and through the opening, Ishmay spied a breeze flattening the tall grass and early afternoon sunshine beaming like a blessing.

He wouldn't have minded some of that light and warmth right about now. In the forest shade, it was gloomy and cold. No wind stirred the leaves, and the only smell was the musk of the men mixed with that of loam and dirt. A few dumbass animals—squirrels or some idiotic shits—were making noise, too stupid to know of the monsters in their midst.

Small groups of the bastard wraiths were even now trickling down into that flat bowl of land where the soldiers of Shang Mendi's army were supposed to kill them.

That was a supposition Ishmay didn't believe in. Instead of dying like they should, the fucking wraiths were shitting all over those sent to bait them out of the forest. And by shitting, Ishmay was thinking the soldiers out there were getting right reamed, killed in numbers that would leave the final outcome in no doubt.

At the rate Genka's men were dying, the rest of them would be dead before sunset. The fact of the matter was they weren't equipped to take on this kind of enemy. The Immortals of Mede might have been powerful warriors, but not the ones created by Genka Devesth. They weren't getting it done and neither were the *hashains*.

It was only the redeemers and the Shokans who were seeing off the wraiths to the unholy place. And even then, it wasn't easy.

"Movement a hundred yards in the forest," Mohal stated in a quiet tone. "South of us. They're bypassing our traps. Just like the first group."

Ishmay smiled to himself. This was the second set of wraiths they'd get to kill.

"Eyes sharp," Gorant warned. He was in charge of their squad, and Ishmay didn't resent it. He might have seniority, and the other man might not be fixed to fight one-on-one—he was always worried about hurting the other fellow when it came to sparring—but on the battle-field, he was a right demon of a tactician.

Ishmay wished they all had a little of that demon in them. It might make it easier to kill the wraiths and the four or five dozen rakshasas who'd decided to join this little battle.

"Get your Blends tighter," Gorant warned.

Ishmay did as instructed, reaching through the pain of the blue-and-green lightning, into his *Jivatma* and *lorethasra*, which he couldn't imagine ever letting go. Everything in life was better with them.

Odd scrutinizations occurred then. It always happened in these last few seconds before combat, when the tedium of waiting was about to end. The first observations were how much more alive he felt when using *Jivatma*, and to a lesser extent, *lorethasra*. And how much improved his senses were.

Ishmay cast them out in the direction Mohal had mentioned and quickly noticed that the chattering animals had gone quiet. *Figures. Even the stupidest creatures can get a bit of wisdom.* Next, he heard it: the soft crunching of feet on leaves, of someone trying to be quiet. Finally, filtered out through the woods was the stench of death. There were wraiths out there.

Not that Ishmay had ever doubted Mohal. The last time, he'd also been able to pick out the wraiths sneaking their way through the forest, and because of his warning, they'd managed to ambush and kill the bastards, not losing any of their own.

Ishmay knocked on his helmeted head for luck.

"Twenty yards," Mohal whispered. "They'll bypass us."

Ishmay's wandering mind focused. He could see the wraiths now. Five of them—three men and two women. Red claws, longer than a bear's and seeming to drip blood that disappeared before hitting the ground. Solid white eyes bright as lanterns. Thus far, the wraiths didn't seem to have the weaves and Talents of Ishmay and his brothers, but their bodies and sharp claws were plenty deadly enough.

"We'll take them with Fireballs," Gorant whispered. "Once they're past, we should have a clear line of sight." He called out targets.

Ishmay murmured understanding, reaching past the pain of the blue-and-green lightning, drawing deeper from his *Jivatma*, which wasn't so simple despite how easy Cinder made it seem. Within his right hand, a glowing orb formed, orange whereas Cinder's was white-hot. It didn't matter that his was cooler. It could still injure the wraiths. A couple of Fireballs and his target would be done.

Gorant waited until the wraiths were standing out in the open, which took longer than expected. The fools were taking their time, not charging straight ahead like the other group. Even with the Shokans Blended, maybe they sensed the ambush?

Eventually two of them eased out of the trees.

Gorant whispered orders. "Concentrate fire on those two. Now."

Ishmay hurled his Fireball. All the Shokans let loose. The wraiths spun around, hearing the screaming death headed their way. Five Fireballs impacted them. One wraith lost his head. The other lost a leg and her chest became a smoking hole.

The other three wraiths cried in rage and alarm, charging straight at them.

Shit. In close quarters, the Shokans would lose all their advantages.

Gorant saw it, too. "Ride."

Ishmay heeled his stallion, charged out of the open-sided blind. Right behind Gorant and Mirk. Mohal was behind him with Sash bringing up the rear. The wraiths angled to cut them off.

Fuck. Come on. Ishmay measured the distance, not sure they were going to make it. Fear grew.

"Drop Blends. Get Fireballs ready!" Gorant said, voice calm.

Ishmay took heart from his unruffled demeanor and did as he was ordered.

They burst into the wide valley, the wraiths right on their asses. *Too slow.* The Shokans were through the mess, and Ishmay grinned.

A horse screamed, went down.

"About face," Gorant shouted.

Ishmay got his stallion turned around.

Sash was on the ground, sword out and surrounded. Ishmay didn't wait on Gorant's order. He hurled his Fireball, tossing aside a wraith. Another three impacted a single monster, killing it. The third wraith flung himself at Sash and took a blade through the chest.

But he was still alive. And he ripped his claws through Sash's stomach, nearly bisecting him.

Ishmay stared in horror.

Gorant called out orders. "Fireballs! Kill them!"

The final two wraiths were ended without any further challenge.

It was a victory, but it didn't feel like one. Instead, heartbreak hollowed Ishmay's chest. He stared at Sash's vacant expression, tried not to see all the blood. His brother was gone, and grief argued with pain.

"I know what you're feeling," Gorant said, addressing them all. "I feel it too. Use that grief to fuel your anger. Let it fill you. We will kill whatever wraiths we encounter. We will earn vengeance for our fallen brother."

Ishmay made a choice. He could wallow in the misery of the moment. Or he could do as Gorant said and rage against the wraiths and destroy them.

"We'll kill them all!" Ishmay shouted to the surviving Shokans.

A roar of approval met his words.

The sun shone bright and warm. A few puffy clouds filled the sky, and a gentle breeze blew across the wide valley that Brilliance stood overlooking. But the wind didn't bring scents of the distant forest—life, growth, and cool shadows. Nor did it provide smells of grass, rich soil, and animal musk. Instead, it carried the stink of blood and offal, and Brilliance wanted nothing more than to turn tail and run away.

It was a disaster down below. Brilliance had always known that mayhem ruled wherever two-legs roamed, but never had that fact become more apparent than now, in this battle between wraiths and demons against humans, elves, and dwarves. But in the end, for Brilliance it was still just two-legs fighting two-legs, and she once again wished she'd never agreed to come here.

Many, many people were dying in the forest, chased by wraiths and demons. Their screams echoed in her ears—so much pain—and she wanted to hunch low and cower. Maybe no one would notice her absence amidst all the bedlam. Brilliance was brave, but facing all this death took a different kind of courage. She didn't want any part of this battle. Didn't want to learn what was needed to survive this carnage. She wanted to run home to her snow-covered mountains and clean forests where a river of blood didn't make the ground boggy.

"How are you doing?" Estin said, resting a hand on Brilliance's shoulder.

"*I don't like this,*" she answered.

"*I don't like it either,*" Hima said, resting with her legs folded underneath.

Brilliance glanced over. Hima had grown during the battle, standing nearly as tall as a horse now, and bony antlers—proud enough for any stag—crowned her head. Add in her sharp teeth and cutting hooves, and she'd proved a deadly foe.

"What about you, Kela?" Estin asked.

The dog lay on his stomach, staring at the woods in bright-eyed focused attention. "*I was bred to hunt.*"

A loud sequence of screaming, concussive blasts perked Brilliance's ears. By now, she'd learned to identify the noise. It was Cinder, laying down a line of Fireballs and incinerating the wraiths. A high-pitched whine edging to the painful indicated a Bow. A low drone, like a bell tolling, immediately followed—a Spear.

Brilliance looked down into the valley, to where Cinder and Anya currently fought ten wraiths and a rakshasa. The *hashains* defended their blind spots, too often dying in the process.

Another Spear, and the rakshasa was dead. The wraiths, under withering fire from the human army—a combination of arrows and ballistae—were shortly cut down.

"They make it look so easy," Estin muttered. An instant later, he stiffened. "Look." He pointed and Brilliance followed the line of his fingers. "A trio of wraiths... all by themselves. Let's go kill them."

Bones had shifted his defensive scheme, ordering Estin and the four redeemers to kill any small group of wraiths that had been cut off from the rest of the herd. And the *aether*-cursed were expected to help.

Hima and Kela scrambled upright, and Brilliance reluctantly followed. While she wanted to run away from this battle, she couldn't. Hima needed her, and a mother never abandoned her unready cub.

Estin mounted Byerley, and the four redeemers were already loping down the hill.

"*Same as before?*" Kela asked.

"*Same as before,*" Brilliance replied even as she studied the trio of wraiths. On a one-on-one basis, they were too much for the redeemers to handle. Residar and his kind had lost some of their power when they had turned away from the Hungering Heart. They were still deadly but were also weaker than the wraiths Estin wanted to attack.

This wouldn't be a simple hunt.

"*Which one?*" Kela asked.

Brilliance glanced to Estin and the redeemers, seeing how far ahead they already were. No matter. She, Kela, and Hima could easily catch up. The wraiths had noticed Estin's approach, spreading out to receive him and the redeemers. Their ululating cries caused Brilliance's hair to stand on end. She shivered in fear, suppressing it a moment later.

"*That one,*" she said, nosing out a wraith who had his back to them. "*Mark him.*"

The decision made, Brilliance led the others in charging down the hill. Her unsheathed claws dug into the turf, letting her build up speed. Her ears flattened, and her eyes narrowed. The wind rushed past. Brilliance twisted to the left, nudging Hima, who immediately shifted direction. Kela kept up, right-sided limp and all.

The intensity of the hunt gathered Brilliance's focus. Her heartbeat remained steady. There was no room for fear. Only the prey was important. That big wraith, who wouldn't know what hit him.

Fifty yards… twenty. Brilliance gathered herself. The wraith must have heard something. He began to turn. Not quickly enough. Brilliance crashed into him, carrying him to the ground. She slashed, but her claws merely left grooves in the monster's skin.

The creature tried to backswipe her, but Brilliance was gone. Kela was on the monster, ripping with his teeth at the creature's ankles before pulling away. They'd done no damage so far, and Brilliance had the first trickling of fear. What kind of wraith was this?

The monster crouched, arms outspread, claws red and glowing. "Come get some. I'll eat your hearts."

Hima darted low at the creature's knees. The wraith swung downward. Brilliance launched herself, latching onto the creature's arm, and

Kela grabbed the other one. Brilliance struggled with holding on to the creature's limb. Hima lowered her head, antlers aimed at the wraith's chest.

Right before she connected, the monster freed his arm from Kela's hold. He punched Hima, and she flew through the air, landing in a heap. Kela yipped in pain. He'd been cast aside, deep lines carved across his back, spine exposed. He whimpered, hind legs unmoving. Brilliance released the wraith's arm, moving to defend Kela.

She hazarded a glance at Hima. Her chest looked caved in. Blood foamed at her lips. Brilliance wanted to cry, but a battle needed fighting, and this wraith needed killing. She'd end him and then find Maize. He could heal Kela and Hima. She'd already seen him work miracles today.

Brilliance roared, lips pulled back over her teeth, daring the wraith to come closer. And in that roar, there was also a prayer, Brilliance's first. She would give anything to protect her family, even her life. She wanted what Fastness had promised could be found—a mirror-sheened pool where Brilliance would find a perfect peace. So far, it had always eluded her, but she needed it like nothing else in her long life. She continued to prey even as the wraith sneered.

Please, Devesh.

A shimmering in the near distance filtered into her mind's eye. A perfectly reflective pool glowing under the light of something beautiful that Brilliance couldn't name. It filled her heart with purity and hope, and she dove into the pond, losing herself in its glorious magic. Everything moved slower. All sights, scents, and sounds were of greater clarity. Her mind moved quicker than she had ever known possible, and fresh courage galvanized her heart.

Brilliance roared again, and this time, the grass bent under the power of her bellow. The world seemed to still for a moment, and even the wraith bent low against the blast of her cry. He made to straighten, but Brilliance didn't give him room to recover.

The sweetness of the pond—her *Jivatma*—flowed through her, and she was on the monster, slashing. This time, she carved deep. The wraith tried to counter, but she was gone, circling. He spun to keep her in front of him. Brilliance darted straight at the monster, twisted to her left. Came at him from the side.

She bit his arm. Her teeth ripped through skin, muscle, and bone. The wraith screamed in pain, tugging to free himself. But she wouldn't let go. She wrenched the wraith off balance, dragged him to the ground. He swung ineffectually at her with his good arm. Her teeth closed over his head. With a hard bite, she crunched through his skull, ending him.

She might have roared her victory, but Kela and Hima needed her. She made to go to them, but sudden fatigue weighed her down. She collapsed as the last of her *Jivatma* emptied out of her. Her eyes dipped shut, and the need for sleep weighed her down.

But she couldn't rest. She had to find Maize. She had to save her family.

Brilliance stumbled to her feet, opened her eyes, surprised at the vision greeting her. Maize and his holders had arrived, and the troll cradled Hima. A gentle golden glow spilled from his hands, through his staff, and into the deer.

Brilliance looked to Kela. Jeet and Stren had him in hand. The same gentle glow flowed like golden water, pouring onto Kela, healing him.

The relief at knowing her family would be fine nearly caused Brilliance to collapse again.

She might have, but Maize had reached her, helping her stay upright. "You've done well, young one." He urged her onward. "Come. The middle of a battle is no place to rest."

Brilliance shook off his help. "Will Hima live?"

"She'll be well enough in a day or two."

It was all Brilliance needed to hear. Gratitude poured through her like a blessing.

Genka sat astride Midnight's Silence, calmly observing the battle. The valley below was getting churned into mud, muck, and blood. Pools of red collected, the iron-rich stench rising to where Genka watched. In the distance, a line of clouds had appeared, and by evening, there would likely be rain. Genka could taste its coming. But that was hours ahead since the sun only stood a couple of hours past its zenith.

And none of the blood, piss, and pain would mean a damn thing if the army didn't survive the fury of the wraiths. Hoarse shouts and yells filled the valley. Men, elves, and dwarves were dying down there, fighting desperately. Even as Genka watched, a squad of heavy cavalry aimed themselves like an arrow at a collection of wraiths—only four of them—but the outcome of their attack was unclear. The creatures were that dangerous. A troop of infantry, wearing full plate and supplemented by five Immortals, struggled against the four wraiths.

Up and down the field, it was the same story—chaotic motion and sound. Men rushing about, even around Genka. Shouting, carrying messages, relaying orders. Desperation. Entire companies facing off against tiny numbers of wraiths and barely holding. It was a calculus that couldn't continue because the army was taking heavy losses—excessive ones—and the battle was long from ending.

A battle currently fought in deference to a plan that Genka had developed in conjunction with Cinder and Anya, a plan he was starting to hate. Cinder and Anya—the supposed Blessed Ones—had insisted the army do nothing more than guide the wraiths toward the valley and hem them in place. It was the safest strategy for everyone involved.

Or so they had said, claiming that once the wraiths were locked in, they would turn the valley floor into a killing field.

Genka snorted. It was a killing field alright but not for the wraiths and rakshasas. His men were dying in droves, and where were Cinder and Anya? Sure, there were reports that one or both of them had taken out groups of wraiths and even individual rakshasas, but it wasn't in large enough numbers to make Genka confident of the battle's outcome.

In actuality, he felt the opposite; he was fearful. So far, his forces had lost roughly ten percent of their numbers, which was more than the elves and dwarves, but far less than what they'd suffered in the battle several years ago. Nevertheless, it was still too much, especially with how many wraiths were yet to come against them.

Genka had agreed to this foolish plan, and by now, he was having more second thoughts than a man hesitating on his wedding day. Down on the valley's flat floor, the enemy had all the advantages. The wraiths were nearly as swift as the cavalry but far quicker, nimbler, and sturdier. Some of them were even strong enough to take a horse's charge.

And yet, a stand-up fight was exactly what Cinder had insisted upon. He had wanted the wraiths collected in one place, certain he and Anya could then put them down. *Idiots.* And Genka felt like the greater idiot for agreeing to this plan.

But what were the alternatives? In the woods, the wraiths easily evaded any ambushes and traps laid out for them, and their agility in the dense foliage made them unbeatable. Genka had received too many reports that any unit entering the forest suffered far worse losses than the ones who merely fought to contain the wraiths on the valley floor.

A soaring boulder, whistling as it descended, smashed close to one of the ballistae.

Genka swung his gaze in the direction of the stone's flight. *There.* A rakshasa. Thankfully, only a few dozen of the creatures had arrived thus far, but even one was too much. Standing as tall as a tree, they were deadlier than the wraiths, stronger and far more powerful. Nothing seemed able to penetrate their black-armored hides.

The few times one of them had been killed seemed more a stroke of luck than due to any kind of skill or forethought. The one occasion it hadn't been the case was when Bones, the commander of the Shokans, had killed a rakshasa through concentrated fire from his catapult and ballistae.

That plan had quickly been copied by the rest of the army, but the rakshasas had also learned. They evaded any boulders sent their way and flung them back at their attackers. It was a good strategy. The rakshasas had damn near wrecked half the siege weapons before Genka had ordered them pulled out of range of the black-armored bastards.

Following on from that disaster, Genka had ordered the laying of new snares and the digging of new trenches. The dwarves and elves had been instrumental in creating those ambushes, and although the wraiths never fell for the traps, it didn't matter. That wasn't the point. Rather, the traps were ruses, meant to funnel the creatures into corridors of Genka's choosing. There, heavy cavalry supported by archers and siege weapons could attack them along narrow, preset lines.

It was working at killing a wraith now and then and keeping his men relatively safe, but it also wasn't enough.

"We're not winning," Vel said.

What a brilliant fucking insight. "I know that," Genka snapped, doing his best to rein in his temper. "What would you have me do?"

"You know what's needed," Vel said. "Send in more men. You have to risk it."

Before Genka could reply, a messenger arrived at a sprint, out of breath. "General Halse requests support. Three rakshasas have broken the Tenth and Twentieth."

Genka brought his spyglass to an eye, witnessing the Tenth and Twentieth companies retreating in a disordered mess, harried by a trio of rakshasas and a handful of wraiths. Left behind were half their numbers.

Gazing about, Genka sighted on General Halse's area of control. Several other companies were about to be overrun, if not obliterated. He called orders for reinforcements. "Have the Fifth and Seventh Heavy Cavalry provide cover, and…"

He trailed off. Down below, a man on a white stallion raced toward the retreating Tenth and Twentieth. The speed of the horse—it had to be Fastness and Cinder. He rode hard, his sword unsheathed, angled to the side, reins released, riding with legs alone. From his offhand screamed a rain of Fireballs, billowing white hot. They impacted the wraiths, obliterating them.

But Cinder wasn't done. He launched himself off Fastness, sword aimed like an arrow at one of the rakshasas. A golden bar blazed off his off-hand, sounding a low-pitched drone. It lanced out, carved through the rakshasa's chest. Cinder landed, leapt away from a hammer that would have pulverized him. Rolled behind a rakshasa and cleaved through one of its calves.

He was gone as the creature collapsed to a knee. A series of Fireballs impacted the third rakshasa. This one had a Shield and took the attack. Cinder swung wide, still firing. The rakshasa tried to turn with him. More Fireballs. The Shield brightened, flickered, gave way. Cinder was inside the creature's guard. Five Fireballs hammered the rakshasa. Each one hit the same spot, straight to the face, punching through.

The rakshasa fell over, a fiery hole in its head.

Meanwhile Fastness had plastered the injured rakshasa, hooves rising and falling, crushing its head.

Five wraiths and three rakshasas, killed inside of seconds.

"Devesh," Genka whispered, awestruck in spite of himself. Hope dawned along with a fresh appreciation for the man's plan. He shook off his wonderment. There was a battle to be waged, and for the first time, he felt like they might actually win.

He quickly shut off the hope. Karma had a way of kicking him in the teeth whenever he set his sights on that tricky feeling. Instead, Genka turned to his signalers, shouting out fresh orders. He needed to draw the wraiths and rakshasas out into the valley, no matter how many men it cost him.

And afterward, he'd continue maneuvering the enemy, trick them in the directions he wanted… What about a deep, stake-lined trench where Cinder and Anya could kill the bastards even more easily?

52

The wraiths poured out of the forest in ever-greater numbers. Far more than Immortal Geash Varan, a rare survivor from the original battle against the herd, had ever expected. And the monsters hissed, laughed, and cried out in pleasure as they murdered. Those ululating cries. He'd never get them out of his head.

It didn't matter how sunny and happy was the sky and the day edging toward the middle of the afternoon. Not with the air filled with the screams of those dying and injured. The army was literally being decimated. Hundreds had already lost their lives, thousands injured, and the battle on the valley floor was only several hours old. Blood soaked the ground, leaving it red and boggy.

And what about the so-called Grimyogi and his Bride? Geash had seen neither hide nor hair of them. He'd heard rumors of their exploits—messages passed from Genka himself. But rumors wouldn't save his men. As far as Geash was concerned, the bastard and his bitch might as well have run.

He ground his teeth in anger. He had really hoped the stories about the Grimyogi and Sira had been true. Anything to stem this tide of death.

At least his unit, the Nineteenth Light—a mix of Immortals, *ha-shains*, and regular soldiers—had managed to defeat the four wraiths they'd encountered in their area of control. It hadn't been easy, though. The wraiths were fast, strong, and nearly indestructible. They shrugged off arrows. Swords only left wounds deep as papercuts, and even a dropped boulder wasn't a surefire way of killing the monsters.

And then there were the rakshasas. Geash had seen one of those fucks tear through an entire company before being driven off by a hail of ballista and catapult fire. He was just glad his own unit had yet to encounter one of the black-armored beasts. The wraiths were deadly enough, having already ravaged the Nineteenth. Geash's company had already lost a quarter of its men.

All over the valley, it was the same damn story. Despite ballistae, catapults, and swarms of arrows to support them, the Army of Shang Mendi was being ground down to meat. Men were dying every second, units barely holding, and while Geash thought to support those companies to either side of him, doing so would open a lane for the wraiths to flank the army.

If matters didn't change, he and everyone in his command were dead men walking. The threads of their lives simply hadn't yet been cut.

A cacophony broke the silence and Geash's deliberations, and from the forest emerged seven wraiths and two massive creatures looking like demons of legend. Geash's mouth went dry when they slowly paced in the direction of the Nineteenth.

It seemed fate would snip the threads of their lives within the hour.

"Devesh, save us," his second whispered.

Devesh could save them, but nothing else could. Geash's men couldn't withstand this foe. "Fall back!"

The squad did as instructed, giving way to the marching rakshasas and their wraiths.

A rush of white out of the corner of his eye had Geash snapping his head around. A man on a white horse. He recognized the rider and the mount. The so-called Grimyogi and his Yavana stallion, Fastness. Aimed unerringly at the rakshasas and wraiths. Their presence roused a flicker of hope. Could they…

Geash wouldn't allow the consideration of his wishes. Grimyogi or not, the man would need help. "Arrows!" They wouldn't do any good, but perhaps they could distract the wraiths. "Immortals, Fireball those bastards. *Hashains*, prove your name!"

Before his men could get off their attacks, a droning sound of thunder echoed. A wall of noise that swept across the field. Geash snapped around to see what was happening. A golden bar of light followed by another roar of thunder. Green webbing flickered around a rakshasa as it bent into the blast. Lightning coruscated around the creature's Shield, but it was otherwise undamaged. The other one, though, had taken a hit. It smoked, a hole punched through its armored hide. Black blood leaked.

A series of detonations—Fireballs of unimaginable power and heat—and the wraiths were flung backward. Several of them smashed like kindling when they hit. The remaining four struggled to rise.

The Grimyogi gave them no quarter. He launched upward. At the peak of his leap, a Fireball burned a wraith to charred meat. He landed—blurred and a wraith was cut in two. A blind parry blocked another. A raised blade blocked the fourth wraith, who had gotten behind the Grimyogi.

Did the man have eyes in the back of his head?

Fastness joined. His teeth had elongated to great canines, and from his hooves sprouted claws longer than a lion's. The stallion bore a wraith to the ground, tearing it apart. A second later, Cinder had killed the final wraith.

Five seconds since the two of them had entered the battle.

"Holy Devesh," his second breathed out in awe.

Geash shared his shock, and that flicker of hope became a bonfire.

The rakshasas were on the Grimyogi. He leapt to engage—literally. Spun in the air, leg snapping out, cracking the injured rakshasa in the face. The creature fell back. The Grimyogi rode him to the ground, his blade flickering with lightning. Glowing too bright to look upon. A single stab to the head, and his sword penetrated to the hilt. The rakshasa was down.

The second one roared in outrage, smashed its fists at the Grimyogi. He rolled out of the way, leaving his sword. Behind the rakshasa, Fastness reared, hammering the monster in the back. The noise sounded out like a boulder cracking. The creature tipped forward. The Grimyogi held a shape like a bow. He plucked a golden string, and there emitted a high-pitched whine followed by the sound of rolling thunder. A beam of quicksilver light flew out.

The rakshasa had no chance. The beam blasted past the monster's Shield, smashed it in the chest, and erupted through its back. The rakshasa stood a moment longer before toppling face first.

"The Grimyogi," a *hashain* whispered, sounding reverential while the rest of the men cheered themselves hoarse.

Geash might have joined them, but he had a certain image to maintain. Nonetheless, he frowned at the *hashain*, eyeing him in surprise. The man *was* one of Genka's assassins, not the man called Cinder. But it seemed the *hashain* had changed his opinion.

Then again… Geash mentally shrugged. After the Grimyogi's performance, he'd changed his mind, too. Maybe Shang Mendi's army could actually win this battle. And maybe Cinder Shade truly was Shokan Reborn.

"They're finally gathering," Cinder observed, doing his best to smother the emotions of seeing so many men die. He'd allow himself to feel the pain after the battle.

"So they are," Anya said, seated on Barton, the two of them next to him and Fastness.

"*It's almost time,*" the white said.

"Almost," Cinder agreed, watching as teams of wraiths and thirty or forty rakshasas spilled out of the forest.

The enemy was collected down on the valley floor, under a late afternoon sun that poured golden streams of light through ragged clouds promising rain. But in the end, the precipitation to come and the steadily stirring wind would do nothing to wash away the tragedy of what had occurred on this terrible day.

Men were losing their lives down in the valley, screaming in pain, injured, sacrificed for this moment so he and Anya could at last bring the fight to the enemy and destroy them en masse. Until now, Cinder and Anya had been forced to fight the wraiths and rakshasas in a frustratingly piecemeal fashion, but no longer.

Soon…

Cinder continued to stare as bright sunshine beamed like a spotlight on a large company of rakshasas and wraiths. They moved as furious as a sea in storm, surging and swarming and coming together, fighting ten thousand humans, elves, and dwarves to a standstill. But that standstill wouldn't last. Even though Genka had managed to bring a number of siege engines back into the fight, the rakshasas were already targeting them.

Cinder wouldn't allow them to succeed. He and Anya along with the fifty-four surviving *hashains* gathered behind them would finally have an opportunity to kill the enemy. Until now, the assassins had only occasionally helped in the short, furious fights against the wraiths and rakshasas, an unnecessary hindrance at the time, but that was no longer the case.

"We need to adjust the plan," Anya said. "We're killing the wraiths, but sometimes we're only injuring them. The rakshasas are then finishing them off, stealing *lorethasra* from the wraiths and getting stronger. We can't let that happen. We need to kill the rakshasas first whenever possible."

"They're also distracted when they do that," Cinder said with a nod. "Leave it to me and Fastness. We'll kill them."

"You can't take them on your own. I should be with you, defending your blindside. The *hashains* alone won't do."

"The *hashains* will be defending you, too."

Anya gazed at him, steady and unwilling to back down. "They'll be defending us both. But I'll be the one defending you."

Cinder understood the reason for her disagreement. She worried over what she considered his recklessness. "I'll be careful."

"*No, you won't,*" Fastness disagreed. "*You'll engage the enemy, kill them at great risk to yourself, and do everything to spare Sira.*"

"*Anya,*" Cinder corrected at Fastness' slip of his metaphorical tongue.

Fastness whickered annoyance. "*You know who I mean. And you know I'm right.*"

"Barton and I will fight alongside you and Fastness," Anya said, her tone brooking no dissent. "We can keep up with you better than the *hashains*."

Cinder stared at her, at her unwavering gaze, at the terror lurking in her eyes—fear for him.

He swallowed heavily, hating to see her placed in harm's way. But what other option was there? She'd defend him, whether he agreed to it or not. "We'll do it your way."

She exhaled in relief, flashing a brief, bright smile. "Thank you."

Fastness whuffled a laugh. "*You're thanking him for letting you go into the most dangerous part of the battle.*"

Anya chuckled, reaching across to pat Fastness. "Right next to you, Lord Brat."

"*That's Lord Pest to you. Only Shokan gets to call me Lord Brat.*"

They continued to watch as the wraiths and rakshasas collected, and a vagrant thought occurred to Cinder. "If I had all of Shokan's skills and Talents unlocked, this battle wouldn't even be a challenge. He'd have them all dead inside a half-hour."

"It's too bad we can't take Mede's Orb and destroy it ourselves," Anya noted.

Cinder grunted. He wished the same thing even if it wouldn't do all that much good. He said as much to Anya, explaining further. "The Orbs build on each other, and even if there's only one that's still active, it would still hinder what I can do."

She viewed him in mild curiosity. "By how much?"

He shrugged. "I'm not sure, but it's a lot." He cut off his explanation. The trickling line of wraiths was ending. It was time.

Cinder took a steadying breath. His heartbeat slow and regular. Sweat trickled down his forehead, but no anxiety filled his mind. There was only the Trial to complete. Another steadying breath, and he unsheathed his sword, lofting it like a banner, addressing the *hashains*.

He stared hard at them, jaw squared, visage fierce, intense as he forced them to meet his gaze. "This ride will require every part of your courage and skill. Do not fail yourselves. Do not fail your brothers. We will kill the enemy."

Cheers met his words, and every face was filled with devotion. The *hashains* had seen him at work, and by now, every one of them had no doubt that he was the Grimyogi.

He set aside his distaste for their piety and aimed his sword at the wraiths. "Line up. Three rows. Shields ready. A single flight of arrows on my mark. Cover our flanks. We'll do the rest." A final pause. "Ride!"

Fastness didn't need his instruction. With a rearing whinny, loud as a trumpet, drawing every eye to him, the white raced down the shallow slope toward the enemy. The Army of Shang Mendi opened a line, letting them through.

Impressions impacted Cinder as he hunched low, urging Fastness on, Barton keeping up. Anya's hair, her braid undone, trailed like a golden banner. A flash of sound, of the men cheering, rallying. They were through. Only the wraiths remained ahead, prepared to receive him, Anya, and the *hashains*.

Two hundred yards.

Cinder reached deep for *lorethasra*, sending it through his Chakras. It exited as *prana* through his *nadis*. *Jivatma* was conducted, a deep wellspring. He had plenty for this battle. The world heightened. He sighted the wraiths more easily, their snarling, confident faces. The impassive rakshasas, disregarding him and Anya.

A hundred yards.

Cinder set a reticle on his eye. The wraiths came into greater focus.

Fifty yards.

The rakshasas' disregard ended when Cinder unleashed a barrage of Fireballs. It impacted on the Shields of the black-armored monsters. A distraction. Eyes locked on him. Anya took the diversion, attacked with Fireballs of her own. They screamed, pounding into the wraiths. Dull thunder seemed to roll. The *hashains* launched their attack, whistling arrows pincushioning injured wraiths.

Cinder cast a Spear, blasting a wide swath through the disorganized enemy. Five wraiths went down. Three were wounded, hobbling. He smiled when a rakshasa did as he hoped, going to finish off the injured wraiths. The monster never saw his Bow. It curled around its stomach when his attack landed, folding over dead.

The rest of the rakshasas roared, coming after him.

Swinging around, Fastness avoided their charge. Cinder set a Bow. Fired. The silver light howled, blasted another rakshasa in the back, punched through his Shield and through his torso.

Then it was too close for anything but sword and skill. Cinder began the hard slog of killing every enemy in range.

A small respite allowed Fastness to pull up short and let them both catch their breaths. The white was blowing hard, likely feeling the same fatigue as Cinder. It had been a long day of fighting, and both of them were tired. Riding through the woods, killing wraiths, hounding them out of the trees, and defending any companies threatened with being overrun… it was enough to fatigue anyone.

Cinder's *Jivatma* was drawing down. So was his *lorethasra*, and he wasn't sure he had enough left to see it through to battle's end. He hoped he did, but hope and a prayer during a battle was a sad strategy.

Thankfully, matters weren't entirely dire. By his calculations, he and Anya had killed dozens of wraiths and wounded several score more, and the rakshasas had done what they'd hoped. They'd gone to kill their injured so-called allies, and Cinder had easily killed them in turn.

He distantly noted the Army of Shang Mendi continued to pin the wraiths and rakshasas in position. *Good.* He and Anya needed all the help they could get because this was settling in to be a battle where the two of them would have to face the enemy on their own. The *hashains* were simply of no use. They could help some with the wraiths but not against the rakshasas. Then, the *hashains* just got in the way.

Cinder glanced at Anya. Her mouth gaped, and she sucked breath. She didn't have his reserves, and if he was already feeling the strain, she had to be as well. Barton looked just as tired, his breathing blowing as quick as a rabbit's heart. Foam flecked at his mouth and sweat covered his coat. Cinder wasn't sure how much longer the gelding could go.

The observation had him wishing they'd actually kept the *hashains* closer. If nothing else, Anya could have traded off horses with one of them and stayed in the fight.

No help for it now.

"Sit this one out," he advised her. "I can take this group." They faced a clump of wraiths, six of them, who'd gathered along with a rakshasa.

"I could use a break," Anya agreed. "So could Barton."

"Get yourself a fresh horse. We've got a lot more fighting to do." Cinder flicked his eyes along the line of battle, the groups of wraiths charging the army's lines. They were finally figuring out the traps they'd entered, showing some desperation on breaking out. Watching them, Cinder was forced to acknowledge Genka's skill. The warlord was a fine tactician.

Anya moved Barton closer, and Cinder found her eyeing him with intensity. "You stay alive. Wait for me after this." She continued to stare his way until he nodded agreement. Only then did she swing Barton about, heading toward a cavalry unit that was relatively close.

Her exit had Cinder breathing a bit easier. At least for the moment, she was safe.

Fastness, not needing instruction, surged at the clustered group.

Cinder smiled. For the first time, rather than sneers and smirks, the wraiths had an air of terror, their visages filled with fear. The hunters had become the hunted. As for the rakshasa and his flat, chitin-masked features, Cinder had no idea what the fragging monster was thinking.

Nor did he care.

"You good on your own, old son?" Cinder asked.

"*Go.*"

Cinder patted Fastness' shoulder and leapt off, landing on a wraith. He crunched the creature with a boot to the chest. A spin blocked a slash. Two Fireballs screamed, thudded into a pair of wraiths, roasting them. Cinder backflipped away from the rakshasa who slammed an axe where he'd been standing. He darted farther away, seeking to control the distance.

Fastness, fangs in his mouth and claws on his hooves, savaged a wraith. He back-kicked another, launching it overhead. It landed with a bruising thump before struggling to its feet.

Cinder rejoined the stallion. Together, they faced the two uninjured wraiths and the rakshasa, who appeared ready to retreat.

No chance for that.

"Who are you?" the rakshasa asked.

"Why do you care?" Cinder replied.

"I would know the name of the one who has killed me."

Cinder saw no need to hide the truth. "Most know me as Cinder Shade, but some have known me as Shokan."

The black-armored monster threw his head back and shouted, a rising note that was higher than a rakshasa's normal deep-throated bellows.

Cinder started. *What was that about?* Shaking off the question, he spoke to Fastness. "Keep the wraiths off of me."

Not waiting for acknowledgement, Cinder sheathed his sword and rushed the rakshasa, catching the monster backfooted. An unknowing observer might have thought it silly—a human attacking a foe more than twice his size and thrice his girth. Figured it especially humorous that the rakshasa was the one who sought to flee.

Cinder was on the creature. He leapt high, a Bow ready. He plucked the golden string, and a silver beam roared like a forest fire, cracking the rakshasa in the back. The monster's Shield flared, green webbing visible. He fell, rose to his feet with a snarl, spun around and prepared its weapon. Cinder landed, leaned away from an axe swing. Jumped another one. Rolled until he was only a few feet from the rakshasa and inside its guard.

Another Bow was ready.

The monster tried to gain distance, but the quicksilver beam hammered the rakshasa's Shield—flaring it—punctured through. The rakshasa twisted, taking the blow through the stomach rather than the chest. But it was still dead before hitting the ground.

Cinder looked to Fastness, who was finishing off the last of the wraiths. There were a few who were injured, and Cinder went about the grim task of killing them as well. He stabbed them through the neck, putting them out of their misery. He went to do the same to the one he'd stomped in the chest.

"My name is Wisha Mink," the creature gasped before his blow could strike. She lay on the ground, plain of features, dark-haired and sharing the glowing white eyes of all her kind. She lifted her head, wearing an expression of pain and fear. "Please don't kill me."

Cinder halted, unsure. His heart wanted to do exactly what the wraith asked, but his mind told him it was foolish. Staying out of range of the wraith's claws, he looked to Fastness for advice—to Sapient, who had helped a number of wraiths discover redemption.

The stallion approached. *"Why shouldn't we kill you?"*

"You should," the wraith said, evincing no surprise at hearing the white speak to her. She dropped her head, eyes closed, facing away from them. A tear traced down her face. "Make it quick. I'm so tired of His voice."

"The voice of the Hungering Heart?"

She mutely nodded.

Cinder stepped away from the wraith, gazed about for danger. The battle continued to rage around them. Men were fighting and dying out there. He had to get back to it, but what to do about this wraith? Right now, he couldn't make himself kill her. What if she was like Residar, Brissianna, and Selin and could be saved?

Anya arrived on a fresh horse. A trio of *hashains* were with her, each of them leading a spare mount.

Cinder explained what was going on.

"Can she be saved?" Anya asked, speaking the exact question on Cinder's mind.

He didn't know, but he wanted to give the wraith a chance. Fastness was still talking to her, but that alone wouldn't solve the situation. Nor was there time for it. Cinder Shielded and approached the wraith, his fist filled with strength. He cocked it back and slugged her in the jaw.

She went unconscious, legs locking, arms lifted, and hands making clawing motions. Cinder mentally shrugged. He hadn't meant to hit her quite so hard.

He addressed the *hashains*. "Bind the wraith. Use chains. Wrap her tight but keep her alive."

His words spoken, he vaulted atop Fastness, heading back to the fight.

53

Corvid's eyes widened in horror, unable to make sense of what was going on.

Until now, she had remained in the forest, not venturing into the valley where Genka Devesth's army was making its last stand. As the one holding together the herd, she had figured it better to remain here, safe while her fellow wraiths murdered the humans, elves, and dwarves who dared bring battle against them.

A wise decision, as she calculated matters. All through the day, she had slowly lost contact with an ever-increasing number of wraiths, a few here, a couple there. Nothing unexpected, but dangerous enough since without her, the herd would come apart. Just like it had when Toriaz had been killed.

A few minutes ago, however, that math had changed. Rather than a trickle of deaths, Corvid was losing contact with fives and tens of her wraiths at a time, and she had no notion as to how it was happening. In the last hour, over a hundred wraiths had died, and the losses weren't slowing. If anything, they were swelling, threatening Corvid's ability to complete the tasks set to her by the Hungering Heart.

Until now, it was a duty she had never figured on being unable to achieve. Throughout the journey south—the burning of towns and farms, the violent sorties against Genka's men, and this last battle—she had never doubted her success.

But she did now and shuddered on considering how her Master might punish her ineptitude.

Another five died, leaving Corvid wanting to yank out her hair. How was this happening? What was killing off so many of her wraiths? A natural disaster? Surely, nothing living. Corvid didn't know, and that lack of information was infuriating.

She'd have to leave the forest and find out.

"Our Master did not foresee this," Devik Molten warned, holding her back, his lava-red eyes closed.

Corvid glanced at the towering rakshasa commander. Massive, covered in natural black armor, and helmed in horns shaped like sickles, Devik exuded deadliness. From his dark and dying Realm, he'd come to Seminal, bringing with him fifty of his most fell warriors, and upon their first meeting, Corvid had walked carefully around the creature. She was deadly to anything on Seminal, but the rakshasas—and especially their leader—were to her as she was to one of Genka Devesth's so-called Immortals.

"What didn't He foresee?" Corvid asked, annoyed by Devik's sacrilege. As far as she was concerned, the Hungering Heart saw all. "And how do you know this?"

The rakshasa kept his lava-red eyes closed, frowning like he was communing with someone Corvid couldn't perceive. "My people are sending reports."

The Hungering Heart had granted Corvid direct awareness with the rest of her kind, but she wasn't aware that the rakshasa had a similar link to his own people. She waited on Devik to explain himself.

"Their voices carry," the rakshasa said. "They aren't simply roaring. They are communicating to one another and to me, and what they say gives me pause."

Corvid blinked in consternation. Something was giving Devik pause? "What are they saying?"

"A single phrase: 'The World Killers are here.'"

Corvid frowned. *World Killers?* It was a term to which she was unfamiliar. "Who or what is that?"

"The World Killers," Devik repeated, eyes flashing open. "Shet's daughter first encountered them in a Realm known as Arisa. They killed his child, and it was she who labeled them the World Killers. That was a world that could have fallen to our Master. They then traveled to another Realm known as Earth, and there, the World Killers directly defeated Shet. Another lost opportunity for our Master. Now they have come here. Rukh and Jessira are their true names, but your people know them as Shokan and Sira. However they are called, our task has become monumentally more difficult."

Corvid held still, frozen with trepidation. Shokan and Sira? Was it truly them? The mythical warriors against whom all foes fell like wheat before the scythe? "You said monumentally more difficult," she said. "But not impossible. Can we kill them?"

Devik didn't answer at once, appearing to ponder the matter. It was difficult to tell given the inexpressive nature of his black-chitinned face. His features eventually relaxed. "We can, but it will cost us. If even five of my people survive Shokan and Sira and fifty of your own, it will be a great victory."

Corvid considered the situation. With so few wraiths and rakshasas remaining at battle's end, there would be no chance to kill Genka and secure whatever orb he possessed. But by killing Shokan and Sira... Would the Hungering Heart consider it an acceptable recompense for failing in her primary mission? She had to believe He would. Shokan and Sira had stolen two Realms from Him. In fact, the Hungering Heart would likely be overjoyed with her success.

She shivered in excitement. "Then we must see to their deaths."

Devik gave a grave nod of agreement. "So we will."

Corvid no longer concerned herself with the deaths of her wraiths.

Those who survived the murder of Shokan and Sira would be elevat-ed above all others by the Hungering Heart. Of this, she was certain, which was why she intended on being one of the survivors. She'd lend her aid to the herd, but only when the moment was right, when she could deliver a fatal blow to either one of the World Killers.

That glory would elevate her in the Master's estimation. She reached for the pit of darkness centered within herself, focused inward to where there existed an emptiness, a devoted selfishness, the puissance forged by self-regard to the exclusion of all other kinds of love. It was what made a wraith so powerful and deadly. And there was a way to increase that deadliness, but the Master had yet to teach her.

After killing Shokan and Sira, maybe He would.

"Are you ready?" Devik asked.

Corvid inhaled deep, heaved it out. Another breath, and she filled herself with strength and stamina even as the world seemed to bright-en and all her senses elevated. Her thoughts grew crisp and certain. She nodded. "I'm ready. Let's kill some World Killers."

Devik grinned, his clearest expression—a mouthful of black teeth, jagged like broken stones and the promise of murder. "Indeed."

The fighting seemed endless, but that was only an illusion. The time spent in conflict could be measured. It had been a little more than an hour since Cinder had captured rather than killed the wraith female, and the late afternoon sun descended. Evening would soon grip the land.

But right now, in this pregnant lull in the battle, Anya had time to think, and her mind stirred a difficult recollection. It was of bat-tling through the Webbed Kingdom and how Cinder had done most of the heavy lifting there. He was doing so again, and the awareness had Anya feeling like she was failing him.

She was too weak, and she knew why: it was her elven heritage. Her people lacked the physicality of most humans. Their *lorethasra* wasn't meant for conflicts and war. Even in their *Jivatma*, they were somewhat limited. These were truths that undergirded the creation of elves—something Anya knew better than anyone since she had Sira's memories, the woman who had fashioned elvenkind.

But what could she do about it now?

Nothing. The battle was all that mattered, but afterward, Anya was determined to make a change. If Fastness could grow fangs, then she would also find a way to do more.

For now, though, she hunched over her saddle, trying her best to recover. Her heart thudded against her ribs, faster than she could ever recall. Her arms trembled, her legs shook, and lightheadedness had her vision going in and out of focus. Sweat, dirt, and blood coated her, but the messy way in which she appeared was less important than the tightness in her chest and the struggle she had in taking a deep breath. She panted like a rabbit before the fox.

Abrupt nausea had her leaning aside, dry heaving. Nothing came up, but once the sensation passed, she washed her mouth out with a couple swishes of water, sipping some afterward.

Cinder viewed her in concern. "Maybe you should sit this one out."

She shook her head. She'd sat out enough fights—three in a row—and in that time, Cinder had almost died on four different occasions. He was likely every bit as tired as she, with her *Jivatma* worn down to the ragged edge of drying and *lorethasra* feeling as thin as a blade of grass.

But she'd make it through to the end. She'd fight on, give more. She hadn't yet reached her limits.

"We've almost done enough," Cinder said, breaking into her self-assessment as he indicated the vastly smaller herd. Of their original four hundred or more, they were down to a little less than half. Cut them down by another fifty percent, and the army itself should be able to handle the rest.

Getting there, though…

"What if we back off and collect ourselves for a final push?" Anya suggested.

Cinder viewed the late afternoon sky, and after a moment, he shook his head. "I doubt they'll retreat. Not with hours still left in the day. If we pull back now, they'll probably push us even harder."

"*He's right,*" Fastness declared. "*The wraiths are fresher than we are. If we break away, they'll see it as a weakness to be exploited. We need to stay in the fight until the end.*"

It wasn't what Anya had hoped to hear, although she truly hadn't been expecting anything else. But it was disappointing, nonetheless. She chanced an examination of Fastness. Dirt, blood, and mud coated him in wide splotches, and he breathed hard.

She'd seen him tired like this before, but on those previous occasions, he'd regathered himself, gaining a second wind. But by now, he was probably on his fourth. Whatever the case, Anya had no idea how the white was still going, much less still running faster than any horse could.

"*I'm fine,*" Fastness said, and by the way Cinder didn't react, Anya could tell the stallion's words were directed only to her. "*I won't fail him. I won't fail you. Not now. Not ever.*"

"I know."

"Know what?" Cinder asked.

"Nothing. Just talking to Fastness."

He eyed her with a slight frown, shrugging an instant later. "All of that talk about needing a break leads me to my previous question. Maybe you should sit this one out."

"That isn't a question. It's a suggestion that—"

"Incoming!" Cinder shouted, warning against a rakshasa archer, one of only a handful that they'd thus far encountered. The monster had them in his sights. With him were three of his kind, wielding hammers, and a dozen wraiths.

Anya Shielded. Cinder had already done so, but he and Fastness were also racing directly toward the streaking bolt heading their way. His sword was free of its scabbard, held to the side. A clench of his fist and the blade was sheathed in lightning. It glowed white as he created the Wildness. A simple flick of his wrist and the sword sliced through the bolt. The broken arrow carved a path to either side of him, tumbling as it lost its strength.

Cinder never slowed his charge.

Anya set aside any concern about her health and well-being. She had to get to him. She heeled her mare into motion, her third change of horse since trading out Barton, the others ridden to exhaustion or fallen to the wraiths. The nausea from before rose again, but she ignored it. Her vision threatened to go gray, but by force of will, she kept her sight locked on the archer. She needed to get on his flank—the side opposite Cinder and Fastness.

The rakshasa was already lining up another shot. Anya measured her options. She would have to be efficient in the use of her strength. A Bow might have weakened the rakshasa's Shield and disrupted his aim, but it cost too much. Instead, she chose a chorus of Fireballs. They wouldn't cause any damage, but they would distract.

She sent three of them, and they screamed in a high-pitched wail, exploding against the rakshasa's Shield. Green webbing flared.

A reticle settled over Anya's vision, and she targeted the other two rakshasas. More Fireballs streaked from her hand. Five in less than a second, pounding at the Shields of the other two monsters.

By then, Cinder was there, within the guard of the archer and the closely packed rakshasas. A Spear lanced out. The golden bar cracked through the archer's Shield, blasted through his torso, erupted out his back, and kept going. The Spear impacted on another rakshasa. His Shield went white-hot, failed, but the monster lived.

Not for long. Anya readied a Bow, plucked the golden string, and a silver beam shot forward. It took the defenseless rakshasa through the head, blowing it completely off.

The final rakshasa faced Cinder while the fearful wraiths edged forward. None of them wanted any part of this battle.

Too bad.

Anya attacked. The reticle remained. Another concussive series of Fireballs laid out four wraiths in smoking heaps. Not dead, but out of the fight. Then she was within sword range. Her mare screamed in fear. The world became a mad swirl of reaching claws, ululating cries, and hard blows against her Shield. The mare wanted to run, but Anya prevented her from rearing, kept her close in on the wraiths.

One of the creatures punched through Anya's Shield. She sliced at his arm, severing a few fingers. He howled in pain. The mare kicked backward, creating space, enough for Anya to hurl another set of Fireballs, the blasts sounding like thunder booming. A trio of wraiths were hurled aside, smoking and dead.

An opening for Anya to maneuver, and she and the mare sped away from the wraiths, who only gave half-hearted chase.

A mistake on their part.

Anya spun the mare about, headed back. Three more Fireballs. Two more dead wraiths. Only three of them still stood, and even as Anya readied to take them on, they were blown apart by a single Fireball.

Cinder had finished with the rakshasa. He reined Fastness next to her. "Just another twenty of those, and we might actually survive this mess."

Anya didn't reply. She couldn't, focused as she was inward, staring at the ground, trying to hold down her gorge and stay conscious. Her vision went blurry again, settled, blurred, finally firmed.

She looked up, seeing Cinder viewing her in concern. "I can make it to the end," she assured him.

He eyed her for several long seconds before giving her a grave nod. "Then let's kill the next group of wraiths."

Devik leaned into his body's natural strength. There was no need to focus on his blackened *Jivatma*, which conducted from his own will and desire, or his *lorethasra*. The power of his form was enough, although truthfully, he detested it. Who would ever appreciate existing in such a repellent body? Tall as a tree, wide as a house, and red-eyed and horned like a demon. A final insult was the black chitinous-appearing armor that also served as his skin. It was disgusting, too much like that of the legendary spiderkin of Sheoboth, who was somehow still alive in this Realm of Seminal.

Seminal. Who would have ever believed Devik would actually find his way here? Thousands of years ago, after Indrun had led his followers from the original Realms of the Rakshasas to this place, the rest of their kind had eventually left their dying world behind as well and settled in their new one, a place they had named Salvation. When they'd arrived, it had seemed exactly that: fertile and alive, but over the centuries, the oceans had emptied, the land had become dry as bone, and any green life had faded to gray death. Devik's people dwindled as well, their numbers collapsing.

And he knew why. It was because of their devotion to Zahhack, the one called the Hungering Heart by the wraiths, the Son of Emptiness, the Son of the Empty One. So many titles for a being who demanded obedience, received devotion and prayers, and was the author of his people's tragedy.

But what other choice did the rakshasas have? Closing their Chakras and serving Zahhack was their only means of survival. Devesh had abandoned them, and why wouldn't he? They were a fallen race, wicked and cruel. Those rakshasas acceptable in Devesh's eyes had followed Indrun away from the original Realms, while those in love with their own power had skulked away like rats, dying in the darkness that they ruled.

And on Salvation—was there ever a more misnamed world?—they had passed along that legacy, a single duke ruling over fewer than five hundred of their kind. This compared to when their numbers had been in the tens of thousands—mostly human but plenty in beast form— and life had been far sweeter.

As for Seminal, who knew if they could actually survive this war into which they'd been thrust. It seemed unlikely. The math simply didn't work. Beyond the fifty sent here, another hundred had been drafted into the army of Shet—another legendary being. It left a scant three hundred back on Salvation.

Devik didn't know how those working with Shet were doing, but the ones here were dying in droves. Down to no more than twenty. All because of Shokan. Devik smirked. A third legendary figure. How many more were there in Seminal? Would Devik—if he lived out the day—discover that Jesherol or Heremisth also lived?

He hoped not. The three duchesses were largely responsible for his people's tragedy. The Sisters had fought against Indrun when he and Sachi had already crushed them on the battlefield. But it hadn't mattered to Sheoboth, Heremisth, and Jesherol. They had refused to accept their defeat, kept on fighting like nattering pests, maintaining their stupid theology. It was why the idiots who Devik named his ancestors had maintained their allegiance to Zahhack.

Of course, none of this was of any concern or help for Devik in his present straits. His people would die, either here, or when the last rakshasa faded away into the dry heart of Salvation's desert. But as for him and those who had been forced to Seminal, they would have to accept this black-bodied prison, incarcerated and made biddable to whoever had summoned them, controllable in both words and deeds. In Devik's case, it was to Zahhack Himself.

Bastard.

At least the wraith female had no awareness of how to summon his people. If she had been given that information, Devik had no doubt as to what she'd do with the knowledge. She'd likely be stupid enough to create a black-chitin demonic shell for herself, pour her essence into it, and summon as many rakshasas as she could control. Corvid's mind was as black as her *Jivatma*.

Devik shot her a glance as she raced alongside him, able to keep up, nimbly leaping fallen logs and evading obstructions. She was strong as well. Pretty, too, but whatever attraction Devik might have felt for her was ruined by the woman's unwavering belief in the Hungering Heart.

Corvid held up a hand, calling for Devik to slow down. They were nearing the forest's edge. He crouched low, hugging the ground.

Ahead of them was sunshine—a welcome respite from the forest's clinging darkness—and a confusion of fighting. Dust and dirt filled the air like a brown cloud. The ground had been turned to bloody mud, and an iron-rich tang filled the air along with a different odor that Devik had never before smelled. Corvid had told him it was rain, but she'd probably been lying. Water falling from the sky was a myth.

Screams of pain and shouts of exhortations brought Devik back to the here and now, and he viewed the plain where his people and the wraiths were confronted by an army of men. The human soldiers weren't really trying to kill them, though. Devik scoffed. As if those weaklings actually could. Instead, the men—dying in the process—were succeeding at locking his people south of the forest, leaving them unable to retreat while Shokan whittled them down.

Devik shook his head upon recalling the only direct report he'd received about the man. It had been over an hour ago, and while he had no reason to doubt it, it still defied reason. The man—a mere human—was swifter than a wraith, more powerful than a rakshasa, and wielded Talents that would have left even Indrun hungry with jealousy.

It certainly left Devik feeling that way. If he had just a modicum of Shokan's abilities, he would rule Salvation. No longer a duke's son, but the actual duke. He could have easily killed his father and taken his place.

"Pay attention," Corvid said, giving him a hard stare.

Devik would have scowled at the waspish woman he looked forward to killing, but his ugly, chitin-lined face didn't allow for the expression. He had to settle for a slight snarl, a bare lifting of his upper lip.

"Have you heard anything else from your people?" Corvid demanded.

If Zahhack didn't have command of him, Devik would have bitten off the stupid woman's head—literally—for the tone she took. "I've heard plenty, but nothing new. Shokan and an elf are the ones destroying your people and mine."

"Sira," the woman muttered, appearing momentarily lost in thought. "How many of our people still live?"

Devik listened for his people's communicated shouts. Minutes ago, there had been a little more than thirty. Now it was just under that number. As for the wraiths, they were down to two hundred. Devik revisited the idea of murdering Shokan. If he'd already killed so many rakshasas in their black-armored forms, what chance did any of them have?

Besides which, there was still an army out there, and while Devik feared no man, he certainly feared thousands of them. He was about to suggest they simply watch what happened without interfering, but Corvid had signaled for him to follow.

"There's a gap." She pointed at where she meant. "We can make it through and rejoin our forces. Guide them directly, and we should be able to kill that fucker Shokan and his bitch-bride."

Corvid was gone before Devik could protest. He growled, or at least tried to. In his demonic form, the only noise that came out sounded like kindling crackling.

54

Cinder dismounted, glancing over when Anya reached his side. She looked worn to the nub, face pale, head drooping, breathing deep. He could see her pulse pounding in her neck, tripping faster than what had to be good for her.

He'd asked her to lie low awhile, but she'd steadily refused his entreaties, fighting at his side as if doing otherwise might be a sin.

"I can make it," she said, guessing his thoughts in that way they had. "I'm not out of it yet."

Despite her declaration, Cinder worried over her. He feared that she had nothing left to give, and as far as he was concerned, she had nothing left to prove.

Neither did Fastness have anything to prove or give. The white's head remained proudly erect, but the blowing bellows of his lungs and the pounding of his great heart told a different story. He was exhausted, coming up or exceeding what was safe.

And truth be told, so was Cinder. This latest fight had his *Jivatma* looking like a shallow puddle and his *lorethasra* a thin stream. And there were still so many of the enemy to kill and so much time left in the day. The sun wouldn't set for another hour or so.

"I have more left to give," the white said.

Cinder wasn't sure. Their last run had taken every last bit of Fastness' strength and stamina. It had followed an indecisive battle against a score of wraiths when Cinder, Anya, and Fastness had killed half the enemy before being forced to flee. They'd raced away toward the safety of the army's lines, chased by the wraiths, who only pulled up short when a flight of arrows and bolts taught them caution. If not for that, Cinder didn't think they could have made it.

Still, every minute spent outside the battle—

"You need to rest," Anya said, interrupting his thoughts. "We all do. The army can hold the wraiths. They're rotating. See."

Cinder stared over in the direction she indicated. Close by, members of the army were catching a break. A number were even eating and chugging water while their brother warriors fought. It was the same with the wraiths and rakshasas. They were regrouping as well.

Fine. He'd rest. "Stay here," Cinder told Anya and Fastness. "I'll get us food and water. We break for fifteen minutes, and then we're back in it, but only if I think the two of you can help."

Not waiting on their replies, Cinder stalked through the army until he located food and water. The entire time, he made sure to talk to whichever men he encountered, encouraging them. Mostly it was a similar litany of telling them that one final push would earn them victory today, anything to give them heart.

Afterward, he hustled back to Anya and Fastness.

"You were gone for longer than fifteen minutes," Anya noted.

Cinder studied her. Her cheeks had better color, and she didn't look quite so haggard. There was even some brightness to her eyes.

"How long was I away?" Cinder asked. He set out a bowl of water for Fastness and passed a canteen to Anya.

"A half-hour." Fastness also looked better. His ears didn't droop, and his chest no longer heaved.

A half-hour? Cinder had no idea. He immediately set to studying the situation on the valley floor.

"Nothing's changed," Anya said. "The army's holding. The wraiths are contained. Even the rakshasas. We can rest and recover some more until we're needed."

"We're needed now," Cinder growled, doling out the food: oats for Fastness and jerky and hardtack for him and Anya.

She stepped close, clutching the back of his arm, making him look her in the eyes. "We are needed. You're right, but we can also wait a little longer. We need this rest. *You* need the rest. We're close. We can get this done, but not if you're on your own or Fastness and I are on the bad end of worn out."

Cinder heard her, knew she spoke wisdom, but in spite of all that, he still didn't want to wait. He was standing here, eating, drinking, and resting while good men were fighting and dying. It was wrong. He should be out there protecting them. He should—

Anya rested a hand against his cheek, whispering. "*Priya*, please."

Cinder's circular thinking crashed to a halt, and a chill understanding swept over him, granting him cold clarity. He breathed deep, eyes closed. Anya was right. Save himself now, recover a bit longer, and then fight to the end.

She continued to cup his cheek, smiling when he opened his eyes. "Just remember that now and again, that I'm right."

"How could I forget when you remind me of it all the time?" he said with a faint smile.

She grinned. "If you actually remembered it, then I wouldn't have to remind you, would I?"

Cinder chuckled. "I suppose not."

Anya's humor fled. "Give me ten more minutes, a fresh horse, and I'll be ready. We'll crush the wraiths and end this."

He nodded agreement, still reluctant even as he quietly ate his food, trying to will his *Jivatma* and *lorethasra* to recover.

And while the three of them waited out the ten minutes, a messenger arrived. He was little more than a boy. "Compliments of Lord

Devesth," he said, passing over a folded piece of paper before dashing off.

Cinder stared in sorrow after the boy. *Child soldiers.* Genka had to use them against the wraiths. Tragedy didn't begin to describe such a need, and evil didn't properly name those who forced such a situation.

When this was done…

He broke off his considerations. He'd take care of the future when it arrived, but for now, he unfolded the paper, quickly reading it, sharing it with Anya.

"There's a deep trench to the east lined with stakes," she said, frowning. "Genka has been trying to drive the wraiths in that direction."

Cinder scowled. "It would have been nice if someone told us before now."

Anya sighed. "We're barely able to just keep them in place. How are we supposed to drive them anywhere?"

Cinder shook his head. "I think we better talk to Genka."

He broke off his considerations. He'd take care of the future when it arrived, but for now, he unfolded the paper, quickly reading it, sharing it with Anya.

Aia winged north, as fast as she could. Rukh was in danger. He'd been in danger all day, and she hadn't been there to help. He'd fought alone, except for Jessira and a friend who Aia had thought long dead.

Was Sapient truly a horse now? She shook her head in disbelief. Why was Sapient a horse? And what were those monsters he, Rukh, and Jessira were fighting? Aia had never before encountered them. She'd only received a few brief impressions. Some kind of twisted creatures with white eyes and corrupted souls.

But then there were other enemies who Aia *did* recognize. Rakshasas. Demonic in form. They were nearly as large as she and possessed weapons and abilities that could hurt her. That wouldn't stop her, though. She would reach her human, protect him, and kill anyone who tried to cause him harm.

Her wings swooped harder. She had to make it in time.

The sun hung low. A harsh scent filled the air, incompletely masking the stench of blood, gore, and mud. The promise of rain from earlier in the day seemed ever more likely as lightning crackled in the distance and thunder rumbled. The valley floor was a boggy mess of churned blood and mud, leaving uncertain footing.

Close at hand, the several hundred wraiths and couple dozen rakshasas were making a stand. They formed a hard nugget that the army couldn't defeat, mostly because they couldn't close with the enemy.

Genka's idea of driving the wraiths into a deep, stake-lined trench had been a good one, but he simply couldn't execute it. By now, while the siege weapons were still effective, the army didn't have enough of them, and mere arrows did no good against the wraiths and rakshasas... except for providing the creatures a ranged weapon. Hurled arrowheads cracked hard enough to penetrate plate, and entire companies had been decimated by their own weapons.

Thankfully, whenever the wraiths tried to break through the lines, Cinder, Anya, and Fastness were there to close the breach, sometimes on their own, but generally supported by the Shokans, the *hashains*, or whatever Immortals were available. Other times it was Brilliance, the other *aether*-cursed, and the redeemers who drove back the wraiths.

The battle had become a stalemate, but it was one that wouldn't last or end in their favor. The situation had Cinder worried. The wraiths only had to keep pressing their attacks, and they'd eventually find an opening to exploit. Then they'd be out, able to flank the army and the weary soldiers. If that happened, Cinder wasn't sure he'd have enough left to stop them.

At least the current respite hadn't ended. The soldiers were afforded a chance to further collect their wounded and hustle them to safety. Screams of the injured carried over the battlefield, and they didn't arise only from the front lines but also from the surgical tents set up on the hillside, well back from the fighting.

The steady sucking sound of a horse making its way through the mud and toward them had Cinder glancing to the side. Out of the muck approached Genka Devesth and his aide, Vel Parnesth.

"Look sharp," Cinder said to Anya.

She lifted her head, sighted Genka, and gave a weary sigh. Nonetheless, she straightened. So did Fastness.

The warlord had stayed out of the direct fighting, performing his role of guiding the army. His armor was covered in splashes of mud but was otherwise clean of blood. His eyes locked on Cinder, and he wore a stern expression, that of a ruler viewing a supplicant.

Cinder stiffened, not liking that one bit. While now wasn't the time for pettiness, he couldn't leave it unaddressed. This moment wasn't the only one that mattered. There was also the future and how the army viewed Cinder and Genka's relationship. It couldn't be like this.

Genka didn't bother dismounting. "What word?"

Cinder frowned. "What are you asking? I'm sure you've received reports from the army. And dismount. I don't want to strain my neck staring up at you."

It was a suggestion couched in a command, and the tone Cinder used left no doubt as to that fact. A murmuring from soldiers close enough to hear spread outward.

Genka noticed, and he briefly scowled before dismounting Silence. "I mean what word about you? How are you doing? I need one final push. Drive the enemy into the trenches, and we'll handle the rest."

"I'm doing well enough," Cinder lied. "But I don't like the idea of one final push. We should continue whittling the enemy like we've been doing. Every time they try to break our lines, Anya, Fastness, and I kill a few stragglers who get separated. We'll eventually wear them down."

Genka leaned close, his features severe. "We've already lost over half the Immortals and *hashains*. Your Shokans have taken casualties as well. Your plan leaves too many of my men at risk of dying." By the end of his statement, he was squeezing tight on Cinder's arm.

Vel cleared his throat. "My lord," he cautioned.

Cinder merely glanced at the offending hand, waiting until it was removed. However, whatever he might have said in response to Genka's words was wiped away when a cry arose. The wraiths were attacking. The respite had ended.

Cinder mounted Fastness and stopped worrying about Genka's idea for a hard push. "Can you get us there?" he asked the white.

"I can, but I don't know how much good I can do when I get there."

"Get to that breach and close it," Genka said.

Cinder rolled his eyes. Where did the warlord think they were going?

Anya was astride her latest mount, a sorrel stallion, and she ignored Genka as well. "I'm good to go," she said, infusing her voice with what Cinder could tell was false heartiness.

He wished again he could keep her out of this fight.

"I'll be with you," Anya said, as if in promise to his fears.

Cinder stared at her an instant longer, eventually nodding his head in agreement. He heeled Fastness and they were off.

It was a quarter-mile dash to where roughly fifty wraiths and ten or eleven rakshasas surged against soldiers desperately seeking to hold them back. Bones was already there, along with Shima's Ninth and Aurelian's Fortieth. So were Brilliance and the *aether*-cursed along with the Shokans, although several of them were missing.

Cinder didn't let absence distract him. He could grieve for them once this battle was over. He sighted the wraiths. They clumped around a female, protecting her. The rakshasa did the same with the largest of their kind. Were they the commanders?

Fastness stumbled, recaptured himself, pushed on the final distance. The Ninth opened for them. The white stumbled again. Nearly collapsed.

He'd gone far enough, Cinder launched himself off the stallion, who had nothing left. He soared over the final two rows of elven warriors fighting against the wraiths.

Cinder landed, Shielded and ready. A Fireshower billowed outward, knocking wraiths off their feet. It did no damage but did disorient them. A reticle settled over one of his eyes, and through it he sighted what was needed and swung his arm in a wide arc.

A torrent of screaming Fireballs exploded into the midst of the wraiths. From this close, their Shields quickly failed. Five of them were killed in the initial burst.

The rakshasas arrived, a tougher nugget. Cinder took blows on his Shield before gaining space. He shifted deeper into the midst of the wraiths, where the rakshasas couldn't attack without harming their allies. More blows fell against his Shield. The green webbing flared, brightened to a dull red glow.

Anya relieved the pressure. Fireballs streamed from her hands, only orange in color. Barely damaging the wraiths.

But they did enough.

Cinder recovered, added another wave of his own Fireballs. *Jivatma* strained with his need, and by now, *lorethasra* was only a trickle. But if he could get to the female wraith he'd seen the others protecting… She was the key. Even as Cinder attacked, she dove behind one of her own kind.

He blasted apart the wraith behind which she hid, pressed toward her, sword blocking claws. Punching and kicking to gain room. A Spear rocked a rakshasa off her feet. Her Shield dissolved, and Anya, off her stallion, was there. She sent a single Fireball to the downed rakshasa's face, ending the monster.

Cinder reached Anya, and they fought back-to-back, mostly using their swords. He ducked a slash, returned with a slash of his own. A wraith clutched her ruined neck, blood spurting from between her fingers. He pulled back from a diving wraith. Caught the creature with a punishing knee to the face. Hammered the hilt of his sword into the back of the wraith's head, dropping him.

A Fireball to the chest launched a wraith into two of her fellows, bowling them over. The dropped wraith rose to his knees, shook his head, groggy. A straight thrust to his throat, and he was done.

The quick kill allowed more wraiths to hurl themselves at him. Cinder had to accept attacks on his Shields. Noted Anya doing the same, but hers flared brighter, edging toward yellow. It threatened to give way.

Cinder set aside his fear. A certainty guided his movements. If he killed the female commanding the wraiths, he felt sure the rest of the herd would come apart. She was right there, only twenty yards distant, pointing at them, shrieking, ululating.

But when Cinder drove toward her, she stumbled away behind a line of rakshasas, pausing then to grin at Cinder.

Just then Anya's Shield whined like a tortured animal, ready to fail, and Cinder's fear punctured his warrior's heart.

Corvid grinned at the human she knew was Shokan. He and his mate, the elf who was Sira, would soon die. Their Shields gave away the truth. They struggled to maintain them. All it would take was one last attack from the herd, and those two fiends would finally be gone from this world.

Then she could crush this army, kill them all, eat their brains, and steal their *aether*, especially the foul fuckers who had left the Hungering Heart's service. She'd noticed them, knew their names. They'd once been wraiths, just like her. They'd accepted the power of their great Master and then dared to defy Him. They were the traitors who had departed the service of the Hungering Heart. The change in their eyes, the sense that they were now better than the wraiths, purer, of higher morals…

It grated, and she couldn't wait to kill them, couldn't wait to kill everything on this blood-soaked field. Too many of her own kind had seen the once-wraiths, heard them shout about how they'd returned to Devesh and been welcomed; that they'd purged the blackness from their souls and expunged the influence of the Hungering Heart.

Lies. All lies.

But nevertheless, those lies had landed. Some had listened, and although none had broken like Residar, it might yet happen.

Corvid couldn't allow it. What good was there in killing Shokan and Sira if the herd ended up betraying the one who had given purpose to their broken lives?

She had to silence the traitors, sacrifice them to the Master and become even more powerful, more powerful than any wraith in history. It was her greatest goal.

Cinder stood back-to-back with Anya, enclosing her in his Shield. Her Talents and skills were gone. And while she still battled, it was with an unenhanced sword. She was unable to damage the tough wraiths.

But she was still defending Cinder's back, protecting him like she always had, even at the cost of her own life. He worried this latest battle might exact just that price—for both of them. They were surrounded, both still fighting, but quickly waning in strength. He'd killed at least a dozen wraiths so far. It had to be enough for the Shokans and the rest of the Ninth to reach them.

But where were they?

Cinder buckled as a clang of heavy steel caused his Shield to glow yellow-white.

The rakshasas had entered the fray. They'd thrust aside the wraiths, bringing the fight directly to Cinder and Anya. Meanwhile, the wraith commander smirked at them from a safe distance. Cinder glowered her way, wishing he had been able to kill her.

Then there was time for nothing but the fight.

Cinder swayed away from a falling axe. Nicked the rakshasa's fingers, earning a howl of rage. But he couldn't follow up on it. He had to stay close to Anya. If he moved too far, she'd be defenseless. Thankfully, the rakshasas didn't take advantage of his limited movement. They peered at him, as if studying a fascinating bug.

Just then the clash of steel on hardened wraith flesh and desperate cries reached Cinder. Bones roared orders, sounding yards away. Brilliance and Kela were with him, howling their battle cries.

"We're almost there!" Brilliance shouted. *"Don't die."*

Cinder took heart. He and Anya only had to hold a few more seconds.

He took three heavy blows on his Shield from a rakshasa's war hammer. Two more, and it went white-hot, shrieking. Another four blows landed, and the Shield failed. An immediate cry from behind told him that Anya had taken a wound.

Cinder desperately struggled to reignite his Shield but lacked enough *Jivatma*. He fought, defending and evading blows. Protected Anya when able. A quick glance showed him she'd taken a wound to her left shoulder. It hung limp, and blood poured from her injury. Nevertheless, she fought on. This couldn't be it, not after all they'd been through.

The large rakshasa, likely their commander, pointed at Cinder and shouted, a basso roar.

But his cry was deafened by a deeper, louder bellow arising from the heavens. Lightning flashed below the clouds, and the roar echoed again, a sound of absolute rage and the promise of death. It rang out above the battle's din, suspending all fighting as both sides searched for the source.

Cinder used the distraction to seize Anya, dragging her to Bones and the Shokans, who helped sprint them away to safety.

The bellow repeated, even louder this time.

"What the fuck is that?" Ishmay asked.

Cinder poured everything he had left into a braid of healing for Anya, who nodded acknowledgement, rolling her left arm. Only then did he gaze to the skies where a white dot was swiftly growing larger. It quickly grew in size, coming into focus. Cinder inhaled sharply. Winging toward them was a creature from myth. He blinked, shook his head, wanting to make sure he was seeing right. Another blink, but his sight never changed.

It was the Calico dragon, her back and head covered in fur that was shaded in oranges, browns, and blacks, and a belly as white as snow.

Cries of alarm arose from the wraiths and rakshasas. Apparently, they recognized the Calico as well. They broke off from the battle, streaming away from the rapidly growing dragon.

"*I come,*" a familiar, feminine voice whispered.

An instant later, the Calico dove like a falcon, ending her plummet by snapping open her wings, her tail fanning outward as well. She glided overhead. Her chest expanded, compressed, and a white-hot line of flame blazed forth. It rumbled, a guttural roar like a forest caught in a conflagration, vibrating Cinder's insides. Shapes formed within the fire—shock diamonds were what they were called, a phrase he dredged from Shokan's memory.

The dragon's fire reached the wraiths, swept over them. Battered the rakshasas. Their Shields instantly flared yellow, white, failed. The Calico streaked past, her fire ending.

"*I never thought I'd see her again.*" Fastness had arrived, looking no less fatigued than before, but hope evident in the lift of his head.

"*It is good to see you as well, horse,*" the same feminine voice said. "*Horses are tasty.*"

Fastness snorted, sounding amused.

Cinder briefly glanced from the white to the dragon. They were clearly familiar with one another, friendly, too.

Next, he stared at the results of the Calico's pass. At least twenty wraiths had been incinerated, their ashes already drifting in the wind. Even the rakshasas had been consumed. Six of them were dead, while another three were gravely wounded.

Less than a hundred wraiths had survived the Calico, and they broke north, opposite of Cinder. The army parted for them, knowing better than to get in their way. The creatures were broken and fleeing, their purpose here ended. The dozen or so rakshasas who still lived sought to escape as well.

But the Calico arrived before they could reach the forest. Again, a long line of shock diamond-shaped fire blazed into the wraiths and rakshasas, killing twenty or thirty more. The survivors never slowed, finally getting to the forest. There, the Calico gave up the chase. She bellowed her triumph before swinging about.

"What does this mean?" Genka demanded, having just arrived along with Vel Parnesth.

No one bothered answering his question.

"She's coming this way," Bones said.

"The Calico," Estin breathed. "It's really her."

The dragon arrived, backwinging hard, raising a stiff wind against which everyone hunkered. Then the Calico landed—a gentle thud—and Cinder discovered her directly in front of him. Her head was lowered to his level. She stared at him and Anya, eyes open, ears erect, and she purred of all things. *"Hello, Rukh. Hello, Jessira."* She edged closer. *"My chin is very itchy."*

Cinder glanced to Anya in confusion, but she looked just as uncertain as he. Who were Rukh and Jessira? And why was the Calico acting like a cat?

Fastness sighed. *"We have a lot to explain."*

55

The summer sun shone warm on Titan's Reach, and the smell of grilled meat, baked bread, and sugary desserts mingled with the shouts of laughter and revelry coming from the village square. The buildings were garlanded in festive arrangements of flowers and streamers made of old, worn-out clothing that were dyed in fanciful golds, greens, reds, blues, and purples. Everyone was happy and families walked the streets, smiling and laughing while their children ran around playing during this rest day.

Even the farmers were able to take part. They'd worked hard the past few days, laboring longer than usual during this lovely spell of daily sun and nighttime rain, and their toil had paid off. As a result, last week the entire village had decided to take an afternoon of rest.

Residar only wished he could join in with the people he'd come to know and love. The Council of Forebears just had to make the right decision, and all would be well.

"It will be fine," Willa said, picking up on his agitation, reaching up to hold his hand.

Residar glanced at her, calmed by her words and grateful to have her with him. When the world was hard, Willa made it soft. When life looked like it might become a mess, she helped him figure out how to clean it up. Or when the Hungering Heart tried to talk to him, she muted the Evil One's voice. Best of all, under Willa's influence, the love Residar had for Brissianna became easier to express, especially when he realized she felt the same way for him.

They'd held off on marrying only so Brissianna's brother could attend the ceremony. Residar smiled, thinking of how Bones would react. The two of them had become friends during their time in the Daggers, and he figured the other man would be overjoyed.

And right now, the joy with which Residar faced every day made him appreciate Willa all the more. Anger, fear, hatred... those emotions remained with him—guided him at times—but they didn't control him. He was a better version of himself and living alongside her for all these months had graced Residar with a clarity and peace he'd never expected to experience.

Just as wonderful, Willa, Simla, and Derius had done the same for the people of Titan's Reach. The Shetawarin had largely moved past their beliefs about Shet and broken off their budding alliance with the ugly-hearted dwarves of Surent Crèche.

Which made the outcome of today's meeting a foregone conclusion... at least Residar hoped so. But even if the Council of Forebears chose differently than what he wanted, so what? Whatever would be would be, and he would be fine with it, working harder the next time around.

Brissianna and Selin arrived, and with them were Simla and Derius.

"Are you ready?" Brissianna asked.

Residar stared at her a moment, still surprised at the natural brown color filling her irises. Not even a hint of white anymore. The same with Selin. He smiled her way, shrugging slightly. "It's not in our hands anymore, but I guess so."

Selin, prim and proper as always in his demeanor and garb, scoffed. "It may not be in our hands, but that doesn't mean we can't be more ready than an '*I guess so.*'"

Residar viewed the man in confusion.

"What I mean," Selin explained, "is that you should always be certain in how you answer questions, even if you're not."

Residar had no idea what Selin was talking about. "If I don't know the answer, why would I pretend that I do?"

Selin sighed. "Because you're a leader now. That's how we see you, those of us who were wraiths."

"We're redeemers now," Brissianna corrected.

"That's right," Residar agreed. "We're redeemers."

Selin stared hard from one of them to the other. "Are you even listening to me?" he asked, sounding peeved.

"We heard you," Residar said, staying calm even when Selin wasn't. "But I'm not a leader. I'm a farmer who happened to live through a terrible event."

Selin dipped his head, appearing abashed. "I'm sorry. I shouldn't have yelled." He honestly sounded ashamed, and he lifted his gaze staring Residar in the eyes. "It's just that… you may not think you're a leader, but I do. I came here because of you. Not because of Fastness. You went against Toriaz. You refused the Hungering Heart. I would have never done anything like that. And I'm a better person because of your inspiration."

Residar clapped Selin's shoulder, smiling. "You're who you are because you wanted forgiveness, and Devesh granted it." He shrugged. "Maybe I showed you a way, but you walked that path on your own."

Selin offered a responding smile. "And this is why I'm saying you're a leader. You lit that path with guideposts just as much as Fastness."

"We're here," Brissianna said, indicating the single-room cabin where the Council of Forebears held their meetings. "Maybe table the discussion for later?"

Residar held Selin's gaze, smiling slightly. "I guess so."

His words got the laugh he was hoping for. "I can't believe I'm following a farmer from the back end of nowhere," Selin said.

Residar grinned. "We prefer the term hillbilly." He held them back from entering the cabin just then. "I want to tell all of you how much I've appreciated having you around these past few months"—he faced the dwarves—"especially the three of you. Without you, I don't doubt none of this could have happened." He indicated the village as a whole. "The people here have turned away from Shet. They've stopped hating woven. They're becoming good folk, like Fastness told us humans had been before Shet ruined it all."

Willa, still holding his hand, tugged him down, kissing his cheek. "It's been our pleasure," she said. "Learning how to help in the ways that we can has been a blessing for us as well."

"Yes, it has," Derius said. "Until we came here, we'd learned to achieve internal tranquility, but helping you, Briss, and Selin achieve it, too…" He smiled, appearing amazed. "I'm fulfilled like I never thought I could be. Wait until I tell Sriovey and Hotgate."

Brissianna bent low to the dwarf, hugging him. "We've all been fulfilled by this."

The door opened, and moving outside to confront them was a glowering Mael. Of all the people in Titan's Reach, he was one of the few who had never accepted the dwarves and their Serenity. "The vote went in your favor, so let's not waste any more time pretending you need to present your case. Come on in, and let's get this done."

His words spoken; he stomped back inside.

Residar shared a happy grin with the others. Even with Mael's irritability, the happy sunshine seemed brighter, and the beautiful day even lovelier.

Persistence tried to blow warmth into her gloved hands, but she might as well have tried to blow out the sun. It was freezing here, but here she had to remain—this cliff face that rose above them, gray and obdurate with snow flailing about, obscuring vision in all directions and a blustering wind that whipped brutally cold spikes into every opening in her heavy clothing. Her breath frosted, and it felt like her nose was about to fall off. She touched it, making sure it was still in place.

Guile appeared no better off. Her fellow rishi was hunched over, hands over his woolen-hat-covered ears, trying to keep them warm. Their rakishis were in a similar strait, all of them crouched low, heads wrapped in scarves, hands gloved, and thick coats and clothing to keep them warm.

Not that it did them any good. Bharat was warm all year 'round, blistering hot in many months, and never cold. Which was to say, none of them were built for this kind of climate.

"Are you sure we're in the right location?" Guile asked, having to shout over the howling wind.

"Yes," Persistence said. "This is where our people were told to come if we ever wished to visit Shalla Valley. The yakshins are supposed to come for us and show us the way through."

However, in spite of her words, Persistence found herself glancing about in concern. It had taken most of the afternoon to hike up a steep, icy incline to reach this bare cliff, and the sun would soon set. Following would come the true danger as whatever warmth the day possessed would evaporate with the night's emergence. The temperature would plunge, and they might very well freeze to death on this granite shelf.

Persistence readied to relay the order to set up camp, although even that wouldn't necessarily keep them safe. The battering wind could easily uproot the stakes and send their tents flying off into the distance. Nevertheless, it was either that or die of the cold.

Just then a large face—the color and texture of bark—pressed out of the cliff.

Persistence stepped back in shock while gasps of alarm arose from the rakishis. She refused to give in to her surprise, however, quickly mastering herself and holding her poise. Although she'd never before encountered such a skill—the ability to swim through stone—she knew what it was that was coming through the rock: *a yakshin*. Soon enough, the face emerged farther until a neck, shoulders, arms, torso, and legs became evident.

"You are rishis and rakishis," the yakshin said, standing in front of the cliff. Her moss-like gray hair lay still, defying the wind. "I am called Turquoise. Take my hand and form a chain. I will guide you into Shalla Valley."

Relief flooded Persistence as the tree maiden gave instructions so the horses and pack mules wouldn't be left behind, and the rakishis scrambled to get themselves sorted out.

Giving a satisfied grunt, the yakshin grasped Persistence's hand in her gnarled one. "Come."

By the barest of margins, Persistence held off from flinching when the yakshin pulled her directly into the stone. Instincts warned that she would smack her face into the rock, but that's not what happened. Instead, she merged with the stone—a single step—and her skin tingled like it had been asleep and was coming back to life. Darkness filled her vision, replaced in an instant by the light of a rainbow bridge.

Another step, and she was out, stumbling, regaining her balance before tugging Guile on in. The rest of the rakishis followed with Tobias bringing up the rear. He nodded to her, indicating that they'd left no one behind.

Persistence took a moment then to gather her bearings. First, came the understanding that she was warm which caused her to smile in satisfaction. She unwrapped her scarf, removed the gloves from her hands, and rid herself of her heavy coat. A rakishi darted forward to collect her belongings, and she passed it off to him, not bothering to look his way, intent on what was before her.

This was Shalla Valley.

Persistence stood on the lip of a peak, staring out at an immensely long and broad valley perimetered by the tall fangs of the Dagger Mountains. Directly below her was a forest of conifers, but past a certain point, the evergreen trees transitioned to hardwoods that themselves gave way at the valley's floor to swaying grasses and palm trees that touched the shores of a blue lake of many coves.

"We have a long walk," Turquoise said, ending the interlude.

Only then did Persistence notice the three other yakshins

downslope, camouflaged as they were amongst the trees. There were also fifteen armed and armored men and women in place. Holders, no doubt.

"But first, your rakishis must wait elsewhere," Turquoise added. "I will take them to one of the other entrances, a warmer place."

Persistence hadn't expected this, didn't like it either. "We never go anywhere without our rakishis."

"You will in this case," Turquoise said. "The order comes directly from Mahamatha."

"And if we refuse?"

"Then you will be removed."

Persistence eyed the holders, disliking the situation and how helpless it made her feel. She needed Shalla Valley, needed to talk to Mahamatha, and apparently this was the only way to see it done. In addition, while the holders outnumbered her and Guile's dozen rakishis, it went further than that. On a one-on-one basis, the holders were better. And she didn't like her chances against the yakshins, even with Guile's support.

"As you will," Persistence said in the end. She addressed Tobias. "Do as she says."

There were mutterings of disapproval, but the rakishis did as they were bid.

"This will not take long," Turquoise said, taking hold of Tobias' hand. She stepped through the cliff face once again, and shortly thereafter, the rakishis were gone from the ledge overlooking Shalla Valley. Persistence stared at where they had disappeared, wearing a discontented frown. She and Guile were alone with no one else to support them.

"You need not worry for your warriors," one of the yakshins said. "They will be fine."

Persistence nodded, not bothering to correct the tree maiden's reasoning.

Minutes later, Turquoise returned, and they set off, journeying the rest of the day. Just prior to nightfall, they made camp in a small clearing amidst the hardwoods, and following a quick supper, settled in for the night.

The next morning, they awoke at first light, and after a hearty breakfast, were off again.

It took most of the morning to reach the savanna, where a fecund aroma filled the air and the sun blazed bright and hot. All manner of strange beasts roamed, including lions, elephants, gazelles, cheetahs, leopards, and giraffes. And none of them seemed particularly concerned with the armed party passing through their home.

Hours later, Persistence set aside any observations of the various animals when she caught sight of a stand of large trees. From a distance, they appeared relatively unremarkable, but Persistence knew they were anything but. It was the Shriven Grove she was viewing, and centered within was Mahamatha, the oldest and wisest being in all of Seminal.

Persistence's heart raced, and she did her best to stifle her fluttering nervousness. She had come all this way to meet Mahamatha, and she wouldn't give in to nerves and fears at this late hour.

The afternoon sped along, and the grove grew ever closer. Turquoise was pointing out different sights and animals to Guile, talking nonstop about various aspects of life in Shalla Valley. He listened attentively, but then again, he had always enjoyed new knowledge about plants and animals.

As they continued onward, other yakshins became evident. Some stood soaking in the sun, but most were bent to various unnamed tasks. There were also forty or fifty holders in the midst of training, and they briefly eyed Persistence and Guile before resuming their exercises. But Persistence had a mind only for the Ashoka trees, which soon loomed directly ahead of them.

It was there, at the borders of the Shriven Grove, that an older yakshin confronted them. Arrayed behind her were five holders, hands on the hilts of their swords and a hard look in their eyes.

"I am Sadana," the older yakshin said. "Both of you come with me, and we will see if Mahamatha deems you worthy." Without another word, she turned about and headed for the heart of the Shriven Grove.

Persistence and Guile followed, but she wanted to stop and stare. The Ashoka trees towered hundreds of feet above her, acres of shade beneath their limbs. Each one its own nation, and they made Persistence feel small like she hadn't felt in decades or longer. In addition, from them emanated a sense of peace, especially the tallest of them—*Mahamatha.*

The tree maiden halted near the massive tree. "Place your forehead upon Mother Ashoka's trunk, and if she chooses to speak to you, she shall."

Persistence stared at the yakshin, wondering if there were any other instructions, but apparently not. Shrugging to Guile, she stepped towards the giant Ashoka and hesitantly placed her forehead against the trunk.

A sensation of falling into a vast gulf caused her to gasp. She clawed for a way to halt her progress, but on its own, her flight was arrested—

And she stood in a wildflower field. A woman, pale of face and hair, danced before her. Bells chimed from her elegant anklets.

"The two of you have traveled far," the woman said, her voice lilting. "And you have far to travel."

"Mahamatha?" It was Guile. He stood nearby and bowed before the woman. "It is an honor meeting you."

Mother Ashoka's laughter was like wind chimes. "No need to be so formal, Rishi Guile."

"We have many questions," Persistence said, wanting to bite her tongue an instant later. She was always so blunt. It wouldn't do when speaking to Mahamatha.

"I know of what you seek," Mother Ashoka said, "but I cannot speak every answer you wish to know."

Disappointment crashed through Persistence. During the entirety of her travels, she had never once suspected that Mahamatha wouldn't know the answers to the questions that had blazed within her mind ever since she had been defeated by Cinder Shade and Anya Aruyen.

"I did not say that I did not know the answers," Mahamatha chided.

"I merely said that I cannot speak them. But it is also immaterial for your ultimate wants. You are needed in Apsara Sithe. You must prepare them for what is to come. If they are to survive Shet, they need counsel. They need the acumen of a warlord."

A warlord? Who? An instant later, Persistence had a guess as to the person Mahamatha was referencing. "Genka Devesth? Is that whom you mean?"

"Only if he is willing."

"The Sunset Warlord will defend Apsara?" Guile asked.

"He will defend all the eastern nations. But first, Apsara must pay him heed. If they do not, my parents will have a far more difficult task."

Parents? Persistence shared a wondering look with Guile. Nowhere had she ever heard mention that Mahamatha had parents. And what did that even mean? How could a tree have parents?

Mother Ashoka continued. "I would love to speak to you in greater detail, but our time is limited. You cannot stay in my valley. Rest for the day, but then you must depart. Turquoise will guide you to the exit closest to Apsara. It is where you will find your rakishis."

"But there's still so much more for us to learn," Persistence said, unwilling to leave after such a brief conversation.

"And you'll learn the answers when you next see my parents. They will teach you what it truly means to be a rishi, to be a servant."

A shoving sensation pushed Persistence away from the meadow, back into the darkness, until with a popping sound, her head came free of Mother Ashoka's trunk. She briefly shook her head, clearing her sight, momentarily confused. Another headshake and she grew aware of her surroundings.

"I can't say that was worth all the months of journeying here," Guile said in disgruntlement.

Persistence disregarded Guile's irritation. Instead, she frowned, considering everything said by Mahamatha. Eventually, a delighted and relieved smile spread across her face as awareness took hold. "We didn't receive clear answers, but we did receive answers."

Guile grunted. "If you say so."

Persistence explained. "We learned that Genka Devesth is the key to defending the eastern nations from Shet."

"Assuming Shet is as deadly a threat as legend states," Guile muttered.

"Which he has to be given how easily Cinder defeated the two of us. He could have killed us, and you know it."

Another grunt. "What else did you learn?"

"That Mahamatha has parents and that we've met them before. She said when we next see her parents." Persistence continued to smile. "Whom do you suppose that might be?"

Guile's brow furrowed until after a few seconds, a smile of understanding spread across his face. "So, we did receive an answer." A moment later, his smile trailed away. "Why couldn't she just tell us that?"

Persistence shrugged, not really caring. "No doubt it's because of some secret to which she is bound."

Fifty rakshasas, controlled by Zahhack and ordered into battle against simple humans, had been sent to the Sunsets through the anchor line connected to the new Realms. Clothed as demons, they should have killed anything they encountered with surpassing ease, and yet, something had instead wiped them out.

Forty-one of her kind had died, and Heremisth had felt their deaths. After all, she had been the one to bring them to Seminal. She was the one who had chosen to remain linked to them, learning some of their thoughts and regrets before they were killed.

And it seemed their deaths alone weren't their greatest sorrow. Rather, it was their lives and their failing home. Salvation was what the new Realm was poorly called, originally alive but now dying. Heremisth's people were also dying, and she wasn't sure how she felt about it.

Possibly sorrow, but why? Why care about the struggles of strangers? Their troubles didn't personally impact her.

Curiosity, then?

Heremisth shrugged to herself. That was the most likely answer. She had wanted to know how her kind were faring, learn what they'd made of themselves after Indrun and Sachi had led so many of their people to Seminal and then elsewhere, closer to their slavemaster, Devesh.

Are you not also a slave?

It was a whispered question from within the recesses of Heremisth's mind—a product of a secret treason that had grown steadily stronger as she had gradually awoken to her fate.

Ever since she had let slip the anchor line north of the Savage Kingdoms, Heremisth had found herself able to think with ever greater clarity. She recalled again her illustrious past when she and her sisters—the Duchesses—had conquered a kingdom, and tens of thousands of supplicants had been forced to bend the knee, and the world tamed to their needs.

It had been glorious. Heremisth and her sisters had maintained their rule for decades, crushing all opposition, and destroying any pretenders who dared contest their thrones. But ultimately, they had found themselves bored. Every person, no matter their status, needed a purpose, and at some point, Heremisth and her sisters had lost theirs. Stepping on the figurative and, at times, literal necks of those who couldn't challenge their rule had eventually grown dreary and life an endless repetition of unchanging days.

It had been then that Jesherol had discovered a lost theology. The worship of the Empty One and His Son, Zahhack.

At first, it had simply been a joke, to see if she and her sisters could spread a false faith. Why not? They had long since conquered the bodies of their subjects, but what about their hearts and minds? Could they convince the people to willfully knuckle under their authority and do so in the most absolute way possible? Through a religion that essentially confirmed Heremisth and her sisters' right to rule? In so doing, the people wouldn't just bow before them but worship them, too.

There was also great promise in the Empty One's theology. A restoration of youth was only the beginning. Immortality and power such as Heremisth and her sisters had never imagined. And when Zahhack had actually responded to their worship, it had seemed like destiny itself had forged them for this role.

But they were also careful. While the Son of Emptiness offered much, He was dangerous. Heremisth knew it. So did her sisters, and they ensured that nothing they accepted from Zahhack would ever allow Him to directly touch their world.

For centuries, their plan had worked. The spread of their new faith, the subjugation of their entire world, and a life full of boundless promise and command. And through it all, although Heremisth and her sisters had proclaimed that bringing their Realm closer to the Empty One would make everyone's lives more ordered, organized, and powerful—Jesherol and Sheoboth had actually grown to believe such lunacy—they never really made the attempt.

But all good things were destined to end, and when Indrun and Sachi offered the people a different vision to power—the worship of Devesh—Heremisth and her sisters had found themselves unable to adapt. Killing the enemy in droves, torturing their leaders, sacking entire provinces… none of it had made a difference in the spread of Indrun and Sachi's faith.

Worse, the actions taken by Heremisth and her sisters had ultimately murdered their world, irrevocably polluting and desecrating it. Indrun and Sachi had led their own people—the Mythaspuris—from their fading Realm to Seminal. But for those rakshasas who remained faithful to the Empty One, through Zahhack's help, they managed to make their way to a new world—to Salvation.

But the cost of the Son's aid had been for Heremisth and her sisters to also journey to Seminal, a simple service they could provide Zahhack along with the promise of even greater power. That had been His command and vow, the last a glistening lure that still held Jesherol and Sheoboth enraptured, but one that Heremisth no longer found so shiny.

For her, that simple service had stretched for three long millennia, and her mind split into three parts—each one focused on maintaining an anchor line with two to the new Realms of the Rakshasas and the third one linked directly to Zahhack at Ardevesh. And if Heremisth failed in her concentration, punishment from the Son of Emptiness would have been the least of her concerns. The spontaneous loss of an anchor line would have resulted in her being cast into the Web of Worlds, where she would die, fading away to nothingness.

So, yes, she was a slave, and she didn't know how to free herself.

With these thoughts in mind, Heremisth stared at the grounds of Ardevesh, at the bright sunshine and the birds chirping and flitting amongst the trees: robins and cardinals and a falcon up high. She watched the subtle play of wind rippling across grass, inhaled the fresh-turned dirt as Manifold worked the land. There he was, hoeing a line in his vegetable garden.

It was a pleasant, bucolic scene that Heremisth had seen many times before and to which she could never truly take part. For short periods of time, she could step beyond the bounds of Ardevesh's main temple, but if she was gone too long, the anchor line to Zahhack would falter, and she would be wrenched into the Web of Worlds.

In many ways, it meant that the temple was her jail, which was another form of slavery.

Heremisth grimaced. That word again: slave. It seemed to be on her mind today, and she glanced into the heart of the temple, at the area near the altar, the black gaping wound in the heart of the world that led to her Master and jailer.

Over the millennia, especially the past few years when her mind had cleared, Zahhack had promised to repay her for all that she'd done in maintaining the anchor line. He would teach her how to close her final two Chakras and even mentioned the mythical eighth.

But when her gaze went to the bright sunshine, she questioned what was in her best interest. Would Zahhack do as He vowed and teach her greatness? And even if He did, would He not still expect her service? After all, why free such a formidable slave?

And what about her people? They were strangers, but they were still of the same blood as her. Did they not deserve a better life? Before Indrun and Sachi had ruined it all, she had provided it for them. She could do so again. She suspected the healing of this new Realm of the Rakshasas, the world called Salvation, was within her means.

Heremisth smiled to herself. Why continue to wear another's collar when she could rule? It would mean the betrayal of her Master, but what of it? She was no one's slave.

56

"**W**e have a lot to explain," Fastness said to Cinder and Anya. *"But before that, let me talk to the Calico and let her know what's happening."*

Trotting, tail aloft, and whinnying with joy, he approached Aia, his friend. He'd never expected to see her again and had trouble believing she was still alive. His joy ebbed when he realized he better keep Aia quiet about certain events that were finally reaching their climax. Loose lips could ruin everything.

"It is good to see you again, Sapient," Aia said. *"Or do you really prefer to be called Fastness?"*

"Fastness will do." He leaned forward, pressing his forehead to Aia's, whickering in pleasure. *"It is good to see you again. So much has happened, and there's so little time to tell it all."*

"Why don't you start at the beginning," Aia suggested, her tone gentle. *"You aren't alone in this."*

For a moment, relief and gratitude had Fastness unable to speak. Aia had always been kinder to him than he deserved, especially after all the pain he'd put her through. And here she was, kind to him again.

After a bit, he collected his thoughts and explained all that had happened to him—his awakening within the body of a Yavana stallion; the Three Sisters still alive and serving their master, Zahhack; Manifold trapped as a necrosed in Mahadev, watching and waiting; The Orbs of Peace; Shokan and Sira as Cinder and Anya and the braids that kept their true selves hidden from Shet and how it interfered with their memories. He was about to explain the reason for it, but Aia interrupted him—

"You're saying that in order to hold onto the past, you made my human forget his?" A burr filled her voice. *"You made his mate forget hers, too?"*

Fastness didn't want to argue with Aia, especially when he hadn't seen her in so long. But still, it was irritating having her second-guess the hard choices he and Manifold had been forced to confront. Nonetheless, on behalf of their friendship, he did his best to hold down his annoyance. *"We didn't have many alternatives,"* Fastness said. *"The past must be kept intact. Time itself won't allow for any significant changes, and we might not like what would happen if events don't occur as they already have."*

Aia stared at him a long moment. *"And this is the only way you can see us defeating Shet? For Rukh and Jessira to not know themselves? To not recognize Aranya, their daughter? For Jessira to feel confused in her love for Rukh?"*

Fastness sighed. He wished for a great many things, but the path he and Manifold had chosen was for the best. *"It was the least-worst of our choices. We even explained our reasoning to Shokan and Sira when they exited the Lucid Foe. They agreed with us."*

"What happened afterward? Who formed the weave?"

Fastness grimaced. He didn't want to say. Aia might be gentle now, but her anger was fierce, and he didn't want to experience it.

"Sapient," Aia said, her tone sharp, *"what happened."*

"It was Rabisu."

Aia straightened, literal fire in her eyes. Flames escaped her nostrils.

"*Rabisu? You let that demented fiend touch my human!*"

"*He was the only one with the skill!*" Fastness shouted back. "*And it wasn't as if we were utterly careless.*" But they had been overly confident. "*We took precautions. They largely even worked. Rabisu's weaves were contained, including the duplicity he tried to include.*"

"*Largely worked?*"

Another grimace. "*Rabisu managed to hide himself in Sira for a time. Early on after the weave, she and Shokan were at each other's throats. But Sira found him out, and Aranya had Rabisu removed. There was no long-term harm.*" The reminder of Mahamatha had Fastness latching onto another explanation. "*And when Aranya found out what had happened—about having Rabisu form the weaves—she also agreed with me and Manifold, that Shokan and Sira needed braids to keep their pasts obscured until after the Orbs of Peace are destroyed. She was even the one who re-created them.*"

"*You're lucky she was there to fix your mistakes,*" Aia said with a growl and another snort of fire.

"*They weren't my mistakes,*" Fastness snapped, no longer worried about having an argument with his old friend. "*We did what was necessary. And if there were mistakes made, most of them were made by Shokan and Sira. They were too cocky and sure of themselves. They are more to blame for their situation than anyone.*"

"*You're wrong. They aren't to blame, and they didn't make a mistake. They accepted this burden because that's who they are. They're generous.*"

"*So then it wasn't a mistake?*" Fastness asked, frustrated. "*Make up your mind. I don't like what they're having to endure any more than you. Probably less. And I most assuredly don't like that Sira has to somehow hate Shokan just so her past self can see it and react to it. This is painful for all of us.*"

Aia seemed to deflate. "*I can imagine.*" A deep breath. "*I'm sorry. This isn't how I wanted our first meeting to go.*"

"*It isn't how I wanted it to go, either,*" Fastness muttered with a snort.

They fell quiet a moment, and Fastness was about to suggest they rejoin the others, but Aia spoke before he could make the proposition.

"You're also wrong about something else. Jessira didn't hate Rukh. I don't think she's capable of hating him, not in any incarnation. I was there. So was Shon."

Fastness didn't bother reminding her that he had been there, too, as Sapient Dormant, Overward of the Necrosed. But at the time, his only thought had been on how to survive Shet. The so-called god had been furious at his betrayal.

"Shon and I talked about it," Aia continued. *"He could peer into the elven Jessira's thoughts and know the truth. She didn't hate Rukh."*

Fastness jerked his head back in startlement. *"But she's always been so sure of what she saw."*

"She was certain, and nothing Shon or I ever said changed her mind. She hated that future self with every bit of her passion, but she never hated Rukh."

"I don't understand."

Aia sighed. *"Jessira has always been too hard on herself. She worries for Rukh. She's afraid she won't be there to defend him like she wasn't when Mistress Arisa found a way to kill Jareth and Brinatha—her children. She knows it's illogical and that there was nothing she could have done to save them, but it also doesn't matter to her. Jessira has always felt the guilt, and it's why she's always been so afraid for Rukh."*

Fastness remained confused. *"How does this relate to what happened on that anchor line?"*

"What Jessira saw as hatred in her future self was confusion. Her elven self didn't hate Rukh. She was confused by him. I think her heart told her she should love him, but her mind told her something else. That's what Shon believed, and he also believed that given enough time, her heart would have easily won."

Fastness glanced back in consideration at Cinder and Anya. *"They seem to love each other now. I can't imagine that would ever change in the way you're saying."*

"You said they have another braid that confuses them even more," Aia mentioned. *"The one they apply when they speak to Shet. Have you ever seen them when they wear it?"*

Fastness started. He hadn't seen that other braid. Was that the missing piece for what had happened on the anchor line? Could it be so simple? He shook off his contemplations. *"I haven't seen it, but it also seems as if our time is done. They're waiting."*

He indicated Shokan and Sira, who had been joined by the surviving Shokans as well as Genka Devesth. The Sunset Warlord appeared calm and patient, but Fastness could sense that the man was anything but.

"I still expect Rukh to scratch my chin," Aia said. *"I've waited a long time for this."*

Fastness and the Calico looked like they weren't anywhere close to wrapping up their conversation. They'd been at it for a few minutes now, and it had even seemed to have gotten heated at times. What were they talking about?

"Sash and Depth didn't make it," Bones said to Cinder under his breath.

For a moment the words didn't penetrate Cinder's mind. Sash and Depth hadn't made it? Then awareness swept over him, and he closed his eyes, swallowing heavily. He nodded understanding, blinking back tears. He'd already noticed their absence, but he'd hoped they had only been injured.

He forced his face into an unfeeling mask, aiming for a professional distance from his sorrow. If he gave in to it, he doubted he'd be able to keep from crying out his anguish. Now wasn't the time. Grief could come later. He cleared his throat. "How are the brothers?"

"They're getting through it," Bones answered. "But I think they're too stunned at surviving the battle to feel much of anything."

"Once the shock wears off, they'll feel plenty," Anya said, likely speaking from personal experience. "The Shokans will need you both. Especially Mirk. He was closest to Sash."

After her advice, they fell silent, and Cinder turned his attention back to Fastness and the Calico. As he considered the dragon, his grief was subsumed by the shock and awe of meeting another mythic figure—the Calico, Shet's bane, the dragon who had destroyed so many of the supposed god's armies during the *NusraelShev*. History had said she had died during the great war, but here she was, majestic and powerful. She'd obliterated a herd of wraiths and twenty or more rakshasas in mere moments.

With her aid, the battle against Shet suddenly seemed eminently winnable.

"Here they come," Anya whispered, cutting into his reverie.

Fastness trotted back to their side, while the Calico merely paced forward a few steps and stretched forth her head.

"Who are Rukh and Jessira?" Cinder asked when the white reached his side. The names the Calico had spoken… they had a haunting familiarity.

"My human and his mate," the Calico answered. *"You and Anya remind me of them."*

Brilliance, standing close at hand and next to Kela and Hima, puffed out her chest. She addressed the Calico. *"Just know that this one is already claimed."* She indicated Cinder with her nose. *"He is my human. You cannot have him."*

Cinder wanted to plant his face in his hands. Of all the stupid things Brilliance could have said and done, challenging a dragon was amongst the stupidest. He moved to stand in front of the idiotic snowtiger. "What she means is that—"

He was cut off when Aia laughed, a terrifying mix of a growl like thunder and a harsh barking noise. *"Little kitten,"* she said, speaking to Brilliance, *"your human is yours for only so long as I allow him to be yours."*

Cinder had to give Brilliance credit. She didn't back down. *"He is mine,"* she growled, facing off against the Calico, crouched low, ears flat, teeth bared, and glaring. In many ways, the snowtiger was a coward, but apparently not in this case. And Kela and Hima supported her foolishness.

But the Calico didn't appear the slightest bit impressed, and why should she? She was larger than a rakshasa, massive even compared to Brilliance and especially Kela and Hima.

However, an argument between a dragon and three *aether*-cursed was the last thing Cinder—or anyone—wanted after a battle that had already seen so many die. But still, the Shokans took no chances, remaining alert and wary. They spread out, hands going to the hilts of their swords even as Genka backed away, his guard closing around him.

Cinder looked to Fastness, hoping he knew what to do.

The Calico billowed smoke over Brilliance, causing her to cough. *"Are you truly willing to fight and die for him?"*

"I am."

The Calico smiled. Though she was a dragon, it was what Cinder imagined from the twisting of her features. *"You are lucky I've grown my heart,"* she said to Brilliance. *"You are alive because of it. You can hold your human for now."* She tilted her head, taking in Kela and Hima. *"But it also seems like you've found yourself a family. Is a human really what you want or need?"* Ignoring Brilliance, the Calico bent closer to Kela and Hima. *"Hello. Are you a puppy?"* she asked Kela.

His tail went between his legs when the Calico loomed over him, but a moment later, he must have gathered his courage. The tail came out. *"I'm a dog. The blood of wolves flows through me, so be careful, dragon."*

"I'm a deer," Hima helpfully supplied. *"Or maybe I'm still a fawn. I'm not sure. But what are you? Are you a bird? Like an eagle? Your wings sure are pretty. Is that fur? Wait, I thought birds had feathers."*

Aia rumbled amusement. *"I am a dragon, and you, little fawn, need to go find something to drink. You look thirsty."*

"I'm not thirsty. Why would you think that? Are my lips parched?"

"Yes, they are," Kela said, apparently recognizing the Calico's dismissal. *"Come along before the dragon decides to eat us."* He grabbed the smaller *aether*-cursed by the scruff of her neck and dragged her away.

Brilliance didn't leave just yet, though. She continued to glare at the

Calico. *"Just remember he is my human."* Her words spoken, she finally departed.

The Calico yawned in indifference to the snowtiger's warning, and she glanced around those gathered. *"Who has possession of Mede's Orb?"*

All eyes went to Genka Devesth.

Cinder had to give the man his due. Rather than shrink or cower, he stood resolute and upright.

"I am Genka Devesth, the *Garnala lon Anarin.*" He inclined his head to the Calico. "It is an honor to meet you. Your legend doesn't do you justice."

Thus far, Cinder felt like an outsider to the conversation, like he was merely observing it rather than participating. It was time to change that. "Before we discuss the Orb, we need to clear out anyone who doesn't need to be here. Fastness stays." He addressed Genka. "Vel can remain but not the rest of your guard."

"I do not take orders from you," Genka said hotly. "And I bend the knee to no man."

"What about a dragon?" the Calico asked. *"Have your men depart. Now."*

Genka appeared to balk.

"I would do what she says," Fastness said. *"The Calico isn't the most patient of dragons."*

The Sunset Warlord stared at the Calico for several seconds before turning away. He barked orders, and the small area was quickly cleared, granting their small group a modicum of privacy.

Around them, the Army of Shang Mendi was carrying on, organizing litters and triage tents. Screams abounded from all the injured. The wind, previously full of the promise of rain, was now consumed by the charnel house stench of blood, burnt flesh, and offal.

Cinder wondered how he could have ignored the sensations even momentarily. And he'd have to continue to ignore them. There was still work to be done. He faced Genka Devesth. "We had an agreement. We kill the wraiths and rakshasas, and you give us the Orb."

Genka drew himself up. "In point of fact, the Calico killed the wraiths and rakshasas, but…" He sighed, gesturing to Vel, who held a wooden box. "You did as you promised," Genka said. "And I will do as I promised. I present to you Mede's Orb."

Cinder took the box from the advisor, cracking it open. Inside was a glowing blue globe with a streak of lightning frozen within, and he stared at it, lost in abrupt reflections. Their work here was nearly done, and neither he nor Anya had nearly died. Just thousands of others. *Depth and Sash.*

In addition, he had to hand it to the warlord. He hadn't expected the man to carry through with his promise.

"Thank you," Cinder said, reaching for the Orb, drawing it forth, and tucking it away in his *null pocket*. "We won't forget this. There is also more for us to discuss. This battle is the first of many before we defeat Shet. We'll need your help."

Genka's lips thinned to an angry line. "I am no mercenary."

"Never said you were," Cinder said in as even a tone as he could manage. By Devesh, did Genka see an insult in everything said to him? "But Shet is coming. If we don't stop him in the east, he'll come for you next."

"That sounds like a problem for you and the eastern nations."

"Or maybe Shet will come for you first," Anya stated. "After all, he can create his own anchor lines. Why not attack and overcome the Sunsets when you're already weak?"

Genka sneered. "And let me guess, you won't lift a finger to stop him?"

"Why should we?" Anya asked. "We already fought and bled for your land."

"Besides, like you said, our problems are in the east," Cinder added.

Genka stared at them; his eyes narrowed. "What do you want from me?"

"Your loyalty," Anya said, speaking without hesitation. "Your help in the east. The eastern armies need your kind of leadership while we take on Shet directly."

Cinder forced himself not to glance at Anya. He hadn't expected that sort of answer from her.

"Loyalty?" Genka snorted derision. "That makes me sound like your servant."

"You will be in charge of all the eastern armies," Anya said, "but ultimately, yes, you will answer to us."

Another measuring gaze. "My work here is done," Genka said, inclining his head to Cinder and Anya and lastly to the Calico. He gestured to Vel, and they made ready to depart.

"That's not an answer," Cinder said, halting the two of them.

"It's the only answer you'll get."

"We require a firmer one now," Anya stated.

Genka stiffened. He abruptly marched back to Anya, halting less than a foot away from her, brow furrowed in a glare. Cinder's hand dropped to his sword hilt.

"I will do as you ask," Genka hissed. "I will serve because I see the way of the future. Shet must be defeated. And after him, the two of you. But never think that I will be anyone's servant."

"I wouldn't expect anyone to be our servant," Anya said. "But remember this. A warrior subjugates, an official administers, and a ruler disciplines, but the conquered deceive. We will be watching. And we remember Swift Sword."

Genka snarled at her, but an instant later, he spun on his heel and marched away.

"He's going to be a problem," Cinder said, watching Genka depart.

"He was always going to be a problem," Anya said. "He sent *hashains* to kill you in Swift Sword. I won't forget that. We shouldn't let him forget it, either. And this way, he knows where we stand and we know where he does."

Cinder grunted agreement. "I'm just surprised he actually turned over Mede's Orb."

"My name is Aia."

Cinder glanced back at the Calico, who reared over them. During the discussion with Genka, he'd almost forgotten about her and Fastness.

"Next, she's going to say that her chin itches," the white said.

"It does itch. And I don't mind if you scratch it." She bent low, leaning forward until she was less than a foot from Cinder, her eyes slitted shut. *"Go on."* She shifted, inching her head closer. *"I really don't mind."*

Cinder shared a wondering look with Anya. What a bizarre swing to their discussions; a strange way to end this day of events: the battle, the Calico's destruction of the wraiths and rakshasas, the argument with Genka, and now this utterly odd request.

Anya gestured for him to get on with it, and giving himself an inward shrug, Cinder reached for Aia. He touched the area where she had a number of willowy whiskers, surprised at the softness of her fur. She rumbled slightly, shifting closer, pressing her head against his hand, and he found himself smiling, gently stroking her face.

"I think you like that," he said, moving down to her chin, where the fur was thinner, barely softening the hardness of her jaw. He scratched, soft at first, but harder when Aia breathed out a warm, satisfied exhalation.

She rumbled again, sounding like a purr, and her mouth flattened. She arched her neck, giving Cinder easier access to scratch more of her chin. *"I missed that so much."*

Instinct had him reaching out his other hand, and he rubbed the area above her nostrils, back to her whiskers, amazed again at the softness of her fur. Despite being a dragon, Aia had a feline aspect, and Cinder studied her—the black fur around her right eye like a patch and the strangely soothing quality of her rumbling.

After a few minutes, Aia sighed, opening her eyes and lifting her head out of reach. *"That was nice. Thank you."*

Cinder viewed Aia in concern. There had been a longing note in her voice. "Is something wrong?"

"Nothing is wrong, and nearly everything is right."

"Is that something Rukh used to do?" Anya asked.

"Yes, but his mate, Jessira, did it even more wonderfully."

Those names. Why did they sound so familiar and so right? And the Calico's name: Aia. Cinder frowned. "I thought Aia was a Kesarin. She was Shokan's steed."

"Shokan was her human, not the other way around," Aia said, a waspish tone in her voice. *"And once, she was a Kesarin. No longer."*

This time it was Anya who gave him an appraising look, and he could imagine what she was thinking. This dragon couldn't be the same as Aia the Kesarin, could she? Which would mean that he wasn't only Shokan, but he was also this other person—Rukh. But which one of them came first? And which version was truest?

"We need to talk about what happens next," Fastness said, shifting the conversation.

"We already know what happens next," Anya said.

"We'll travel back to the Flatiron, call for Liline, and go to Naraka where Shet will destroy Mede's Orb."

"And after that, we need to find the Orb of Wings," Anya said with a tired sigh. "Manifold didn't know where it was."

Cinder eyed Anya in concern. Her golden skin was pale, and her forehead was sheened with perspiration. She had given everything she had during the battle, but he also thought she had recovered some after Aia's arrival. Now, though, she looked like she was on her last legs.

She needed rest. They all did, even Fastness, who was struggling to keep his head from drooping.

"I have the Orb of Wings," the Calico said.

Through the cloud of Cinder's worry, it took him a moment to recognize the meaning of Aia's words. "You have the Orb of Wings?"

She gave a brisk nod. *"It's in my home by the sea."*

Cinder stared at her a moment before barking laughter. At least the final Orb would be easy to obtain. He looked to Anya, who offered a soft smile, her eyes shining in spite of her tiredness.

"You can't have it."

Cinder's relief crashed. "What? Why not?"

Aia viewed him a moment before blinking rapidly. Her mouth twisted, and Cinder got the sense that she was laughing in delight. *"I'm just joking. Of course you can have it."*

Cinder chuckled, hoping Aia wasn't about to tell him *no* again.

Fastness snorted. *"Don't mind her. She's always been like this—a prankster. Quite the pest, really."*

"You used to play pranks all the time," Aia said.

"He still does," Cinder said. "I can't count the number of times he tried to step on my toes, flicked his tail in my face, or whined for apples."

"We don't need to talk about that," Fastness hustled to say.

Aia straightened, her attention locked on Fastness. *"Whined for apples? Is that what you do?"* Again came that expression of delight, like she had thrown her head back and was laughing.

This time Fastness' snort was one of long suffering.

Cinder rubbed the white's forelock. "We're just teasing you, old son," he said, taking pity on the white. "You were about to tell us what we have to do."

"Did you have to tell her about the apples? She'll never let me forget it."

"I'm sorry," Cinder said, this time in greater contrition.

"She's so mean about it, too."

"I really am sorry."

"I'm not mean," Aia protested.

"Why does this seem like children arguing?" Anya asked.

Fastness butted his head into Cinder's chest. *"You can make it up to me by fetching me some apples, preferably stewed."*

Cinder laughed. "You and stewed apples."

"They're tasty."

"We'll see," Cinder said, speaking to Aia next. "Where is your home?"

"A cave off the coast of the Coalescent Desert," Aia said. *"I can show you."*

A flash of information coursed into him, like a bolt of lightning striking directly in front of his eyes—no heat or pain, though. Cinder was suddenly aware of exactly where Aia's cave was located. It wouldn't be easy to reach.

"You'll need Shon," Aia said.

"Shon?" Anya fixed Aia with a frown. "Sira's Kesarin?"

"He's a dragon now," Aia explained. *"Shet has him asleep."*

Anya's eyes widened in understanding. "The tawny dragon. He's mine."

"My brother. And you're his person."

Cinder came to a similar realization. "And I'm your human. I'm Rukh, whoever that is."

"One day, you will be, but not yet." Aia straightened to her full height. *"I need to return to my home. I can't leave the Orb unattended for too long. But before you come for it, free Shon. I won't have my brother enslaved."* Her words spoken, Aia launched herself aloft, winging south and quickly disappearing.

Cinder watched her go, still amazed that he'd actually met the Calico. He was also confused. She had been absolutely sure that he was Shokan, and that Anya was Sira. Which meant there was no further questioning that truth. But what about Shet? With their awareness of their true pasts, wouldn't he recognize them? Perhaps not since they had the weaves they used whenever they were in Naraka.

"I'm tired," Fastness proclaimed. *"Wake me if you need me."* With that, the white also departed, headed for the Shokans.

"Getting some rest sounds like a great idea," Anya said as the white clip-clopped away. "You could use some, too."

"There's a few more things to talk about first."

"It can wait until the morning," Anya said, her voice firm.

Cinder considered her words, and a moment later, he blew out a breath. "You're right. It can wait."

Anya grinned. "Say that again."

Cinder chuckled. "I think not. Let's head back to the Shokans." His lips thinned. "They'll need us."

Anya wrapped an arm around his waist as they paced out of the muck and mud. "Sira and Shokan. We really are them."

"Which means we're married." He paused a beat. "Again."

Anya chuckled. "Which also means you'll never get rid of me."

Cinder halted their progress and gazed at Anya, staring into her emerald eyes. "I'd never want to."

Anya smiled. "Good answer."

THE END

A Last Note

You reached the end! Congratulations! And thank you again for getting this far! If there weren't people like you supporting what I write, I'd have no chance of doing what I'm doing.

Also, if you don't mind too much, could you leave a review for the book? Or even just a rating! I'll take ratings! I'm not picky. Honest.

And if you're feeling *super* ambitious, please consider signing up for my newsletter. It includes all of my latest news, and while there's usually not a lot to tell, at least you'll be up to date with what I'm writing.

As for Cinder and Anya and everyone else, their story continues in book 5. I'll get to it.

Glossary

Absin Morewe: Weapons master at the Third Directorate.

Aether: Akin to *lorethasra*, but it is the magic imbued in the world at large. Also known as *lorasra*.

Aia: Mythical steed of Shokan. Thought to be of a species of cat called Kesarins.

Antalagore the Black: Mythical black dragon.

Apsara Sithe: An elven empire known for their agriculture and horses. They are perpetually infuriated that their horses are not a match for the Yavanas.

Anya Aruyen: Younger princess of Yaksha Sithe. She is the first and only elven woman to attend and graduate from the Third Directorate. She is also a ranger.

Avan Aruyen: Consort to Sala Yaksha, empress of Yaksha Sithe. Anya's father.

Bharat: Powerful island nation of the rishis, who claim to be direct descendants of the Mythaspuris.

Bishan: General definition means student, but in *Shevasra* it translates as '*incompetent person who has potential*.

Bones Jorn: Human warrior. Cadet at the Third Directorate and in the same class as Cinder Shade. He was formerly a student of *Steel-Graced Adepts*.

Breech: A holder who protects the troll, Maize Broad.

Brow Cowl: Human warrior. Cadet at the Third Directorate and defeated by Cinder Shade in the Maker's Tournament. A former student of the *Jasmine Water* martial academy.

Braid: Also known as a weave. A practical use of *lorethasra*.

Brilliance: An *aether-cursed* snowtiger.

Brissianna Jorn: A wraith. She trains Residar and later follows him after he betrays the Hungering Heart.

Capshin Sonsing: Lieutenant and master/instructor in History at the Third Directorate.

Cariath Gelindun: Elven cadet at the Third Directorate who is in the same class as Cinder Shade.

Certitude: City in Yaksha Sithe. It is closely aligned with the Third Directorate.

Chakras: Potential loci of power within all beings that allows more instinctual control of weaves and braids.

Cinder Shade: Human. An unusual warrior of superlative skill. He has no recollection of his past.

Crail Valing: Elven cadet at the Third Directorate and in the same class as Cinder Shade. Killed in the Unitary Trial.

Crèche Prani: Holy text of the dwarves.

Depth Knarl: Human warrior. Cadet at the Third Directorate and in the same class as Cinder Shade.

Derius Surent: Dwarven cadet at the Third Directorate and in the same class as Cinder Shade.

Devesth: The capital city and name of one of the Sunset Kingdoms. It is the home of the famed Yavana horses.

Dorcer Surent: Dwarven cadet at the Third Directorate and in the same class as Cinder Shade. Killed during the Unitary Trial.

Dorr Corn: Former student at *Steel-Graced Adepts*.

Drak Renter: One of Shet's Titans.

Duchess of Certitude: Hereditary position and currently held by Duchess Marielle Cervine. Historically, the Duchess of Certitude is also a high-ranking member in the succession for the imperial throne of Yaksha Sithe.

Enma Aruyen: Elder princess and heir to the throne of Yaksha Sithe.

Estin Aruyen: Prince of Yaksha Sithe. He is also an elven cadet at the Third Directorate and in the same class as Cinder Shade.

Fain Kole: Journeyman at *Steel-Graced Adepts*.

Farin Eshanwe: Elven cadet at the Third Directorate and in the same class as Cinder Shade. Killed in the Unitary Trial.

Fastness: A white Yavana stallion.

First Directorate: Yaksha Sithe's shadowy organization of spies.

Forever Triumphant: Elven holy text.

Gandharva Federation: A human nation. It is allied with Yaksha Sithe and Rakesh.

Garad Mull: One of Shet's Titans. Like the other known Titans, he lives in a statue-like state and is currently kept within the Quad at the Third Directorate.

Garlin Fairsent: Warrior of Rakesh. Defeated by Cinder in the Maker's Tournament.

Genka Devesth: Warlord from the Sunset Kingdom of Devesth. He believes himself the heir spoken of in the *Medeian Scryings* and intends on recreating Shang Mendi, Mede's ancient empire.

Gorant Sin Peace: Student at *Steel-Graced Adepts*.

Hashains: Legendary assassins from the Sunset Kingdoms.

Halin Dorund: Cavalry master at the Third Directorate.

Hima: An *aether*-cursed doe.

Holder: A species of woven who are the pre-eminent warriors in all of Seminal. Little is known about them other than they have no known lands of their own and are entirely devoted to the protection of yakshins and trolls.

Hungering Heart, the: The voice that commands the wraith. He is Zahhack.

Indrun Agni: A Mythaspuri.

Isha: Common definition is 'instructor', but in *Shevasra*, it means 'master'.

Ishmay Sensow: Human cadet at the Third Directorate and in the same class as Cinder Shade. Originally from the Gandharva Federation.

Isthrim: A type of *aether*-infused dwarven steel that is able to kill vampires and necrosed.

Jameken Battalion: Veteran battalion of Yaksha's imperial army. Colloquially known as the 'James'.

Jasmine Water: A martial academy in Swift Sword.

Jeet Condune: A former *hashain*, who is now leashed to Cinder Shade.

Jine Kole: Master at *Steel-Graced Adepts*.

Jivatma: Supposedly the soul. Largely thought to be mythical, although some accounts of the Mythaspuris indicate it was the source of their power.

Joria Javsheck: Human cadet at the Third Directorate and in the same class as Cinder Shade. Killed in the Unitary Trial.

Jovick Sonsen: Unarmed combat master at the Third Directorate.

Jozep Surent: Dwarven cadet at the Third Directorate and in the same class as Cinder Shade.

Kela: An *aether*-cursed dog.

Koran Yaksha: Founder and first empress of Yaksha Sithe.

Lamarin Hosh: Secret society in Yaksha Sithe. They seek to discover and aid the reborn Shokan and Sira. Founded by Duchess Sarienne Cervine of Certitude, who was a quelchon.

Lerid File: Owner/master of *Steel-Graced Adepts*.

Liline Salt: Known as Water Death. One of Shet's Titans. Along with Rence Darim, they are the only two female Titans. She is also frozen in a statue-like state and housed in a courtyard in Apsara Sithe.

Lisandre Coushinre: An elven ranger and occasional instructor at the Third Directorate. Brother to Riyne Coushinre.

Loial Company: Small unit decimated during a recent Unitary Trial.

Lor Agni: An ancient holy text centered around the proper means of righteous living and the worship of Devesh. Mostly limited in importance to Gandharva and Rakesh (translated as *the Secret Fire* in *Shevasra*).

Lorasra: Synonym for *aether*, although the term has fallen out of favor and is rarely used any longer.

Lorethasra: A mystical source of power by which woven are able to create weaves and braids that impact the world.

Loriam Stilwen: Elven cadet at the Third Directorate and in the same class as Cinder Shade.

Mahadev: The fallen city of the Mythaspuris.

Maize Broad: A troll who meets Cinder Shade at the Third Directorate and recognizes him.

Manifold Fulsom: Along with Sapient Dormant, one of the leaders of the Mythaspuris.

Marielle Cervine: Current Duchess of Certitude and the leader of the Lamarin Hosh.

Mede: Ancient warlord from Parn, who set out to conquer the world. He was largely successful, and his empire was known as Shang Mendi. However, upon his death, his empire quickly fell apart into strife and civil war.

The Medeian Scryings: Holy text written by Mede and said to be inspired by the voice of Devesh. Much of the book is a biographical account of Mede's life and conquests as well as his philosophical beliefs.

Mirk Bassang: Human student at *Steel-Graced Adepts*.

Mohal Holwarein: Elven cadet at the Third Directorate and in the same class as Cinder Shade.

Molni Cirnovain: Master librarian at the Third Directorate.

Mother Ashoka: Mother to all the Ashoka trees and yakshins on Seminal. Also known as Mahamatha and Aranya.

Mythaspuris: Powerful humans who entered Seminal during the *NusraelShev* and are thought to have turned the tide in the battle against Shet.

Naraka: Shet's ancient empire.

Nathaz Surent: Dwarven cadet at the Third Directorate and in the same class as Cinder Shade. Killed during the Unitary Trial.

Nuhlin Genhin: Master/instructor of Tactics and Strategy at the Third Directorate.

NusraelShev: Translated as *the Disastrous Submission* in *Shevasra*. The ancient war against Shet and his forces.

Pitch Shade: Brother to Cinder Shade.

Quelchon: A rare woven who can 'recite' a person and thereby learn a hint of their future.

Quelchon Ginala: Elderly elf with the power of a quelchon. She is not what she appears.

Rakesh: A human nation. Allied with the Gandharva Federation and essentially a vassal state to Yaksha Sithe.

Redwinth Wheat: Prince of Apsara Sithe and presumed fiancé to Enma Aruyen of Yaksha Sithe.

Rence Darim: Known as the Illwind. One of Shet's Titans. Along with Liline Salt, they are the only two female Titans.

Residar Charvin: Originally a farmer, he is transformed into a wraith upon the murder of his family. He is now a redeemer.

Revelatory Dreams: A set of scrolls written by the trolls and yakshins. Translated from *Shevasra*, and there are conflicting versions.

Rishis: Rulers of Bharat, who claim to be the human descendants of the Mythaspuris.

Riyne Coushinre: Elven cadet at the Third Directorate and in the same class as Cinder Shade. Brother to Lisandre Coushinre.

Rorian Molinking: Human cadet at the Third Directorate and in the same class as Cinder Shade. Killed in the Unitary Trial.

Sadana: The oldest of the yakshins.

Sala Yaksha: Current empress of Yaksha Sithe.

Sapient Dormant: Along with Manifold Fulsom, one of the leaders of the Mythaspuris.

Sash Slice: Human student at *Steel-Graced Adepts*.

Savage Kingdoms: Group of rival human kingdoms that were formed from the remnants of Shand Mendi, Mede's empire, in the far northeast of the world.

Selin Heron: A wraith who is now a redeemer.

Sepia: A yakshin. She saves Cinder during his Secondary Trial.

Serwil Opturund: Archery master at the Third Directorate.

Shadion Carrend: A dwarven spy from Surent Crèche. He often pretends to be a merchant and has a donkey named Pretty.

Shalla Valley: Home of the yakshins.

Shaloce Astreas: Colonel and commander of Jameken Battalion.

Shella Marsh: A wraith who is now a redeemer.

Shet: A self-proclaimed god, who battled much of the world three thousand years ago in the *NusraelShev*. He was supported by seven Titans.

Shokan: A mythical human warrior. Along with his wife, Sira, they are said to be Shet's greatest foes and are collectively known as the Blessed Ones.

Shon: Mythical steed of Sira's. Thought to be of a species of cat called Kesarins.

Simone Trementh: Dowager Duchess and aunt to Marielle Cervine.

Sira: A mythical human warrior. Along with her husband, Shokan, they are said to be Shet's greatest foes and are collectively known as the Blessed Ones.

Sriovey Surent: Leader of the dwarven cadets at the Third Directorate who are in the same class as Cinder Shade.

Stren Coldire: A former *hashain*, who is now leashed to Cinder Shade.

Sture Mael: The greatest of Shet's Titans.

Sunset Kingdoms: Group of rival human kingdoms that were formed from the remnants of Shand Mendi, Mede's empire, in the far northwest of the world.

Surent Crèche: Dwarven crèche and somewhat allied to Rakesh and Yaksha Sithe. By tradition, surnames are taken from the mother's side of the family, but to everyone not of the crèche, the surnames are always told as being 'Surent'.

Swan Yaksha: Second empress of Yaksha Sithe.

Swift Sword: Capital of Rakesh.

Sylve Arwan: General and commandant of the Third Directorate.

Taj Wada: Complex of buildings that comprise the imperial palace of Yaksha Sithe.

Third Directorate: Yaksha Sithe's preeminent military academy.

Tomag Jury: Known as the Shield Render. One of Shet's Titans. Twin brother to Tormak Jury.

Tormak Jury: Known as the Sword Breaker. One of Shet's Titans. Twin brother to Tomag Jury.

Trolls: A species of woven known for their ability to apply Justice, a type of braid/weave by which they allow the truth of a matter to be truly known and never forgotten. They are also the only woven who procreate by parthenogenesis.

Turquoise: A yakshin. She is the one who names Cinder 'Maynalor.'

Vampires: Species of woven who are beholden to Shet. They have a type of flight and gather blood slaves as a means to acquire power.

Wark Nil: Human warrior. Cadet at the Third Directorate and in the same class as Cinder Shade.

Weave: Also known as a braid. A practical use of *lorethasra*.

Woven: General name for all self-aware beings on Seminal other than humans.

Wraiths: Twisted humans, who apparently have the means to source either *lorethasra* or conduct *Jivatma*. They are universally insane and lust for flesh and brains.

Yakshins: Tree maidens. A type of woven known for their deeply held bonds to trees and nature.

Yavanas: Finest breed of horse in the world. They only breed true in the Cord Valley or Devesth, one of the Sunset Kingdoms.

Zahhack: Name given to the woven who are beholden to Shet. It is also the name of a mythical being of whom very few know, who is reputedly the son of the Empty One, Devesh's great foe.

About the Author

Davis Ashura is a bestselling author, a full-time practicing physician, and a one-time wordworker. His motto has generally been, *'Try it. The worst you can do is fail.'* It usually works out—except when jumping out of airplanes. Davis is best known for his *Instrument of Omens* series, which is part of the *Anchored Worlds* universe, a set of linked epic fantasy series.

His books are hopeful in nature. He likes to write about heroes who see themselves as servants first. Heroes who fall in love and become partners and make time for family, friendship, and fellowship. His characters are folk with whom it would be fun to have drinks and dinner, but who could also handle any trouble that might crop up.

Davis is married and shares a house with his wonderful wife who somehow overlooked his eccentricities and married him anyway. Living with them are their two sons, both of whom have at various times helped turn Davis' once lustrous, raven-black hair prematurely white. And of course, there are the obligatory strange, stray cats (all authors have cats—it's required by the union). They are fluffy and black with terribly bad breath. Additionally, there is the rescue dog— gnarly-toothed, beady-eyed, and utterly sweet.

Visit him at www.DavisAshura.com and sign up for his newsletter to learn the latest information on his books or simply follow him on Facebook, Instagram, or Twitter.

Ingram Content Group UK Ltd.
Milton Keynes UK
UKHW041833280323
419329UK00014B/168/J